The Arena of Satire

Oklahoma Series in Classical Culture

Oklahoma Series in Classical Culture

The Arena of Satire

Juvenal's Search for Rome

DAVID H. J. LARMOUR

UNIVERSITY OF OKLAHOMA PRESS : NORMAN

Paragraphs from the introduction were previously published in *The Sites of Rome: Time, Space, Memory*, edited by David H. J. Larmour and Diana Spencer (New York: Oxford, 2007).

Some paragraphs from chapter 1 were previously published in David H. J. Larmour, "The Incurable Wound of Telephus: Noise, Speech and Silence in Juvenal's *Satire 1*," *Intertexts* 8 (2004): 55–76; and David H. J. Larmour, "Tracing Furrows in the Horatian Dust: Echoes of Horace's *Epistles* in Juvenal 1," *Illinois Classical Studies* 35–36 (2010–2011): 155–73.

Library of Congress Cataloging-in-Publication Data

Larmour, David H. J. (David Henry James), 1959– author.
   The arena of satire : Juvenal's search for Rome / David H. J. Larmour.
      pages cm — (Oklahoma series in classical culture ; volume 52)
     ISBN 978-0-8061-5156-4 (hardcover) ISBN 978-0-8061-9417-2 (paper)
 1. Juvenal—Criticism and interpretation.   2. Satire, Latin—History and criticism.
I. Title. II. Series: Oklahoma series in classical culture ; v. 52.
   PA6448.L36 2016
   871'.01—dc23

2015023991

The Arena of Satire: Juvenal's Search for Rome is Volume 52 in the Oklahoma Series in Classical Culture.

The paper in this book meets the guidelines for permanence and durability of the Committee on Production Guidelines for Book Longevity of the Council on Library Resources, Inc. ∞

To Brian Scott, who first taught me the pleasures of reading Juvenal, and to Allen Miller, *interlocutor satiricus praecellens,* who has nourished them for over two decades.

Contents

Illustrations

Acknowledgments

This book has been several years in the making and I am grateful to all of the satirical colleagues, students and friends who have helped me along the way with pertinent advice. I am also grateful for insights received from the colleagues and students I have encountered through my teaching and research in ancient sports and spectacles. I wish to thank the audiences who gave me valuable comments and suggestions after presentations of parts of this book at numerous venues, including the universities of Birmingham, Budapest, Columbia, Geneva, London (UCL), Paris (Sorbonne), Singapore, South Carolina and Western Ontario. I am particularly grateful to Alexandre Grandazzi for his insights on specific passages and his early support of my use of Kristeva and to Diana Spencer for her witty and wise responses to almost every line herein from which resulted many vital improvements. Above all, I owe an enormous debt to Allen Miller who has for many years generously shared with me not only his profound knowledge of Latin satire but also the fruits of his remarkable facility with literary and critical theory. The final contours of this particular project would not have taken shape without his incisive criticism and rigorous refinement of its theoretical underpinnings.

I am grateful to Cait Mongrain for assisting me with the index and Latin texts and to Justin Miller for his assistance with the bibliography. I thank Lavinia Ciuffa for her help in the Photographic Archive at the American Academy in Rome; Ellen Greene for recommending the University of Oklahoma series as a venue for publication; John Drayton who drew up the initial contract; and the staff at the OU Press for all their kind assistance.

The Arena of Satire

Introduction

The Search for Rome

A charioteer charging across the same plain as his great predecessor Lucilius: this is how the satirist styles himself when he hails us at the beginning of Juvenal's collection. Satirist as charioteer certainly emphasizes the combative and competitive aspects of the genre, but also signals that the reader of Juvenal's poems is in for an exhilarating and unpredictable ride. In the company of this particular charioteer, satire becomes an adventure of perpetual movement, of sharp turns and sudden switchbacks, as we career across the literary and ideological landscape of Rome. At times the chariot threatens to veer out of control into incoherence and fragmentation. This satirist-charioteer whom we call Juvenal is, moreover, a figure without a face. He eludes a direct encounter, so that we catch glimpses of him only as a reflection in the faces of others or when he makes fleeting (and not fully authenticated) appearances in three epigrams by his rough contemporary, Martial. The first 6 lines of Martial's *Epigram* 12.18 imagine a certain Juvenal—who is, presumably, his younger satirical companion—traipsing across Rome: in the noisy Subura, on the Aventine or Caelian hills, or at the doors of the powerful. Although it makes him sweaty and tired, Juvenal continues on his way, unable to stop.

> Dum tu forsitan inquietus erras
> clamosa, Iuvenalis, in Subura
> aut collem dominae teris Dianae;
> dum per limina te potentiorum
> sudatrix toga ventilat vagumque
> maior Caelius et minor fatigant . . .

3

> While you perhaps wander restless,
> Juvenal, in the noisy Subura
> or wear down the hill of mistress Diana;
> while round the thresholds of the powerful
> a sweaty toga wafts you and as you roam
> the Greater and the Lesser Caelian tire you out . . .[1]

This description of the restless—and certainly "unquiet"—roamer through the city suggests one way we might approach the *Satires:* it points to the continual "wandering" that underpins Juvenalian satire and to its preference for noisy and noisome urban settings. In contrast to Martial, who speaks from a far-off country retreat, the satirist is always on the move, traversing the cityscape of Rome, both its naturally occurring geographical features and those constructed by its inhabitants. The positioning of the satirist *per limina potentiorum*, round the *thresholds* of the powerful—or those "more powerful [*than you*]"—is telling: this stance is marginal in relation to the putative center of authority. Horace had used the same phrasing in his *beatus ille . . . Epode* 2.7–8, when Alfius touts as one of the joys of country life "avoiding the Forum and the proud thresholds of more powerful citizens" (*forumque vitat et superba civium / potentiorum limina*), with all the activity and anxiety that they entail. Juvenal's speaker also evinces a longing for the simple habits of country living, but remains curiously enthralled by spectacles produced in the urban arena he so despises.

In recognition of the rambling qualities of the Juvenalian text and the network of literary, mythological and historical allusions, rhetorical tropes, and thematic cross-references and verbal echoes that resonate within even a single poem, let alone across several, the approach here will be to trace certain recurring motifs, juxtapositions, and objects of scorn in the collection. It is often said that the number of plots available to storytellers is quite limited and that it is in the telling that the potential for novelty and variation arises; so it is with the satirist, the staples of whose repertoire are relatively few in number but can be combined in many different ways. Juvenal remarks in *Satire* 1.85–86 that *quidquid agunt homines, votum, timor, ira, voluptas, / gaudia, discursus, nostri farrago libelli est* (whatever people do, prayer, fear, anger, pleasure, delights, running about, is the mishmash of my little book). Although this is a large

---

1. Martial contrasts life in his native Bilbilis with Juvenal's in Rome, cf. Merli 2006. L. and P. Watson 2003, 145, believe that the Iuvenalis mentioned is "almost certainly the satirist." Colton 1991, 6–10, discusses this poem and two others (7.24 and 7.91), and although he says Martial "apparently, does not know Juvenal as a satirist," it is striking that all three poems in which he is mentioned contain a suggestive or obscene element of a kind not incapable of being purveyed by Juvenal himself.

helping of the "practice of everyday life," it is quite apparent to anyone who surveys the surviving corpus in its entirety that the repetition of motifs, allusions, and terminology is an important feature of the form. For instance, to speak in only the broadest terms, *Satires* 7 and 8 show clear signs of repeating material from 1, 2, and 3, albeit with numerous subtle variations.[2] In this, Juvenal is not unlike Lucian, who, as Graham Anderson has amply demonstrated, generates a sizable corpus from a more or less finite set of motifs and ideas.[3] There is, one suspects, a certain repetitiousness in most successful satire, if only because it aids reinforcement of its particular slant on the world. In the BBC's *Little Britain*, catchphrases and characters, even situations, reappear regularly in successive episodes, as they did, for instance, in Fox's *In Living Color* in the United States. The repeated appearances of characters such as the garrulously inarticulate chav, Vicky Pollard, reinforce the ridicule of the social types they represent.

The main interest of Juvenalian satire, as far as this study is concerned, lies neither in the search for narrative coherence of the sort readers might expect from a traditional epic or a realist novel or a "well-made" play, nor in intricately designed schemes to separate poet from persona;[4] rather, it is to be found in its repeated and merciless exposure of the fault lines of Roman self-definition and of the cracks it probes in the permanently fractured subjectivity of the *civis Romanus*. This book considers the process of reading Juvenal's satires as a repetition of the search for anchors of stability to which the Roman male subject might affix his identity and of the almost total failure to find such points of security. Put another way, Juvenal's books offer (only) the realization that the master signifiers that promise to guarantee wholeness—*amicitia*, masculinity, Rome, the Emperor, marriage, *nobilitas*, objects of ambition or desire and so on—cannot in fact do so.[5] Book 1, after the programmatic *Satire* 1 in which these anxieties are set out in broad terms, evaluates the current condition of masculinity (*Satire* 2), the city of Rome (*Satire* 3), the Emperor (*Satire* 4), and *amicitia* (*Satire* 5). Masculinity is shown to be a façade, Rome a nightmare of the "non-Roman," the Emperor a mass murderer, and the *cena* a

2. Braund 1988, esp. chaps. 2–3.

3. G. Anderson 1976; Courtney 1980, 624–29; Bozia 2015, 16–51.

4. See esp. Kernan 1959; W. S. Anderson's essays (1982); Winkler 1983; Braund 1988. For a contrary view, esp. on *Sat.* 15, see Tennant (1995). Uden's (2015) approach is grounded in the "invisibility" of Juvenal and his avoidance of a consistent persona. See also Iddeng 2000; Rosen 2007, 220–22, and chap. 3.

5. Habinek 2005a notes that "even as [satire] seeks to prepare the elite Roman male, it substitutes for his performance mimesis of a much more complex and diverse array of alternative selves. Indeed, satire's need, as part of its playful construction of identity, to help stage alterity may help to explain another striking aspect of the history of satire: that it never succeeds" (182).

playground of social humiliation. Running through book 1 is a preoccupation with the perversion of the "proper" patron-client relationship, which is emblematic of broader confusion.

Book 2 contains a single poem, *Satire* 6, devoted to the topic of marriage—another central institution in Roman society holding its fabric together—that is likewise shown to offer no stability to the Juvenalian subject. This parallels *Satire* 2's depiction of the atrophying of Roman masculinity, by making the disappearance of *pudicitia* lead into a detailed account of the resulting expression of unconstrained female desire. In Juvenalian discourse, gender confusion shakes the traditional order of *Romanitas* just as powerfully as the untying of the bonds of *amicitia*, which was primarily a male affair. Book 3 again focuses on power relations in *Satires* 7 and 9—between writers and patrons in 7, a catalog of abused and unrewarded wordsmiths, and between a client sexually servicing his patron in 9, with another hefty dose of "masculinity undone" in the dialogue with the rent-male Naevolus. There is a more extensive undermining of the idea that *nobilitas* offers any guarantee of noble actions in *Satire* 8, whose opening question—*Stemmata quid faciunt?* (What good are pedigrees?)—is ultimately answered by "Not much, and Romans are all descended from asylum-seekers anyway."

In book 4, the subject matter revolves around the goals and aspirations of the typical Roman citizen. *Satire* 10 shows that the things people wish for are destined neither to satisfy nor to save them, since their desires are misplaced and the objects of their striving cannot possibly deliver what they promise. *Satires* 11 and 12 explore greed and its pollution of personal relations, in 11 through the contrast between the speaker's simple dinner of wholesome country fare and the vulgar excesses of other hosts, and in 12 via the startling image of a merchant symbolically "castrating himself" by throwing his goods overboard in a storm so he can live to trade another day, which leads into an exposé of legacy hunters, who are infinitely more life-threatening than the waves. Book 5 proves two disturbing truths: in *Satire* 13, that there is no point trusting in Justice if you are a victim of crime; and in 14, that education is no guarantee of proper behavior, especially when parents set such a bad example. The main conclusion of *Satire* 15, with its vivid account of how the citizens of Ombi in Egypt, when attacked by their neighbors from Tentyra, tore one of them to pieces in a religious frenzy and ate him raw, is that one can forget about feeling superior to foreigners or animals: things every bit as brutish and uncivilized go on right here in Rome. Finally, the fragmentary *Satire* 16 appears to be gearing up for a wide-ranging indictment of the special privileges enjoyed (at everyone else's expense) by the army, the supposed guarantor of both the state's frontiers and the individual citizen's security.

Scholars have often detected differences of "tone" within the Juvenalian corpus, and some have argued for significant shifts in perspective in particular books. Books 1 and 2, for instance, are regularly grouped together in contrast to the rest, with *Satire* 7 marking a new beginning and a "more controlled" or "less angry" stance. Book 4 is often viewed as more introspective or philosophical than the first three.[6]

There may well be something to such claims, but how far they can be pushed is debatable.[7] Although it is certainly useful to consider the five books individually, I tend to see differences in tone and such as manifestations of the text's inherent fluidity, which cannot be separated from its repetitiousness. Barbara Gold speaks of "a continuing thread of themes, tones, and words that evolve and act as an intertextual and intratextual ongoing commentary on their earlier counterparts in previous Satires." She also notes that the technique of "multiple focalization"—via different speakers, voices, interlocutors—allows Juvenal "to modulate and vary his voice, thus achieving a kind of inner dialogue and creating the illusion that there is more than one Juvenal. It is, however, only an illusion."[8] Catherine Keane observes that in book 5 the satirist is not in fact repudiating, but "probing the emotions and topics of his own early satire (anger and its consequences, the family, the city, foreigners, the disenfranchisement of the poor citizen) as if to confirm their centrality to his satiric program."[9] Ken Dowden has spoken appositely of the "symphonic" architecture of Juvenal's books, with the various "movements" playing off each other.

As far as the "philosophical" Juvenal is concerned, one of the purposes of this study will be to point out areas of common ground between Juvenal and Seneca, particularly in the choice of imagery to treat the search for stable categories in a world that is out of joint. In comparison with the Greek satirical tradition, where philosophical concerns are very much to the forefront, and with the avowedly Stoic disposition of Persius, and even with the milder philosophizing of Horace, it has often seemed that Juvenal's poems lack a significant

---

6. See, for example, Braund 1988 on the disappearance of *indignatio* in 7: "The predominant feature is the sustained use of irony coming from a voice which sounds much more rational and intelligent than that of the earlier persona, a voice which allows objections to be raised and counters them calmly and reasonably" (25). Cf. F. M. A. Jones 2007 on the gradual revelation of the inadequacy of *indignatio* as a response (90).

7. Richlin 1992 acknowledges the Horatian features of 11–16 but says that, in terms of the structure of the world, "Juvenal continues to see extravagant behavior from the viewpoint of one who cannot afford it, so that his message is, 'Be good—or else!'—a wistful threat" (200).

8. Gold 2012, 99, 111.

9. Keane 2006, 140; on the last two books as more in the way of "supplements," see F. M. A. Jones 2007, 151–53.

philosophical element.[10] In fact, however, Juvenal's satirical discourse is rooted in the same sources as Seneca's moral discourse, and it can be most instructive to note the conceptions of masculinity, *virtus* and *Romanitas*, the two have in common. The fact that they share a storehouse of vocabulary, imagery, and metaphor suggests that these writers may shed more light upon each other than has generally been assumed. When Juvenal in 10.28–53, for example, compares the attitudes of Heraclitus and Democritus to what they witnessed as soon as they put a foot beyond the threshold (*quotiens a limine moverat unum / protuleratque pedem*, 29–10), and comes down in favor of Democritus, it is very likely that he was inspired by Seneca's contrast between the two in *De Tranquillitate* 15.2–3, where a similar preference for the "laughing" philosopher is expressed.[11] Seneca's own interest in satire, witnessed by the *Apocolocyntosis* and his references to Horace's *Satires* in his *Letters*, should not be forgotten, nor should the capacity for Juvenalian intensity of language visible in his tragedies, with their emphasis on spectacles of the grotesque and their fascination with the infliction of pain and the mutilation of the body.[12]

Seneca often blends the sharply satirical with the philosophical, a formula that is not so far removed from what we see in Horace and Persius. Seneca even sounds like the satirist in places: for example, in *Natural Questions* 7.31.1, he sums up the progress of vices as follows: *Id quod unum toto agimus animo, nondum perfecimus ut pessimi essemus; adhuc in processu vitia sunt. Invenit luxuria aliquid novi, in quod insaniat* (That which we strive for with our whole mind we have not yet achieved—to be as bad as we can; vices are still making progress. Luxury discovers something new, in which it can revel mindlessly). Both Seneca and Juvenal make extensive use of the technique of displaying negative examples, although they do not have the same confidence in the possibility of improvement or on the reliability of the transcendental signifiers of Roman *virtus*. Seneca's advice wavers between the instructive and the corrective, while Juvenal appears to have given up most, if not all, hope of correction. In spite of (presumably) positive endorsements like *victrix fortuna sapientia*

10. On philosophy in Lucian, see Georgiadou and Larmour 1998; satire and philosophy, Mayer 2005 and Bartsch 2012.

11. Courtney 1980, 449–50, and chap. 4 herein. On connections between Seneca and Juvenal, see Schneider 1930; W. S. Anderson 1964 on *De Ira*; Dick 1969; Braund 1988, 82–84, 111–13; Braund 2004, 369; Larmour 2005a on *Satire* 12. Morford 1977 says that Juvenal frames *Satire* 5 in the terminology of philosophy (229). F. M. A. Jones 2007 says that Juvenal generally disavows philosophical professions, unlike Horace and Persius, although he draws upon the "moralising-philosophical tradition" when, for example, talking about friendship in *Satire* 3 or the development of civilization in 15 (124). On book 5, see Keane 2007 and chap. 4 herein.

12. Deroux 1983 suggests Juvenal may have written parts of *Satire* 4 with a passage from *Thyestes* in mind (294–295, 703–705).

(13.20),[13] we cannot say that the satirist is an embodiment of Seneca's *sapiens*; his anger rules that out, for one thing, and he is often more like a parody of it. But as concerns proper comportment, masculinity versus effeminacy, looking around oneself, excess versus simplicity, the mixing of categories, foolish wishes, and so on, their discourses are closely related.[14]

How then to approach these satires? To posit a standard pattern in connection with a genre as freewheeling as satire and a collection as variegated as Juvenal's always runs the risk of being reductive, but we can identify the dominant discursive strategy in the satires as "the rhetoric of exemplarity": the listing and castigating of individuals and types in rapid succession, so as to ram home the point the satirist wishes to make, not only through observational acuity and concomitant linguistic artistry, but also by sheer weight of numbers.[15] This is not to erase the fact that *Satires* 4 and 15 are obvious exceptions to such a pattern, with 9 and 13 also showing significant divergences. In *Satire* 4, for instance, there is a lengthy prelude on Crispinus (an *exemplum* worthy of special elaboration, perhaps) and then the main part of the poem is a mock-epic tale of how the giant turbot makes its way from the Adriatic to Domitian's inner circle (34–154); exemplarity is confined, for the most part, to brief but insightful sketches of the emperor's closest "friends" (75–152), which are embedded within the unfolding narrative. Moreover, informative as lists of *exempla* undoubtedly are about the satirist's aims and ideological moorings, it is in the parts of a poem where the rhetoric of exemplarity is held in check—extended narrative or description, direct speech, or dialogue—that we can find some of the most promising points of entry into a text whose twists and turns pose continual challenges to conventional modes of interpretation.

The discussion of *Satire* 1 in chapter 1 ("Satires from the Edge") outlines the approach to Juvenalian satire adopted in this study. The opening of any poetic collection repays close attention, and this is especially true for a genre

---

13. In a contrast between advice in philosophy's "sacred books" and what is learned from "Life the teacher" (*vita magistra*, 19–22); on irony in *Satire* 13, see Courtney 1980, 533–37.

14. Keane (2007) speaks of satire's "ambivalent parasitic relationship to diatribe and philosophy" and suggests that "perhaps the most inclusive way of looking at the relationship is to regard philosophical discourse—with all its historical and stock figures, terminology, and available modes of address—as a set of tools for which a satirist devises new uses, thereby engaging in a kind of philosophical inquiry that becomes a part of his own genre" (50, 29).

15. *Exemplum* is the first word of *Satire* 13: *exemplo quodcumque malo committitur* ("whenever a bad example is set"); cf. 2.48; 114; 8.184; 10.49; 15.32. See Freudenburg 1993 on exempla as an instructive device in Horace, more in tune with philosophical usage than Juvenal (35–36); Seneca too relies heavily on a rhetoric of exemplarity, especially in his letters. On using examples from history, see Kenney 2012, 130–33; in poetry, Seo 2013. For an analysis of Roman "exemplary discourse" linking actions, audiences, values and memory, through various kinds of monuments, see Roller 2004; for a broad-based study of exemplarity, Gelley 1995.

in which how the satirist positions himself, in relation to his predecessors and his contemporaries in the literary landscape, is always a prominent issue.[16] Moreover, introductory and concluding lines stand outside the series of exempla and are as such especially informative; several scholars have, for instance, scrutinized the framing scenes of Umbricius's speech in *Satire* 3, which portray the satirist's farewell to his friend at the Porta Capena.[17] Consequently, we shall pay particular attention to the first thirty and the closing twenty-five lines of *Satire* 1. Together, these two sections of the poem constitute a diptych loaded with directions for interpreting the fifteen diverse satires that follow. The opening statement of purpose (1–21) is where several tensions are introduced:[18] between speech and silence, between fixity and fluidity, and between objects of desire and the failure to reach them. Juvenal ends with an undertaking to imitate Lucilius by charging onto the plain where he drove his chariot, but we shall trace here echoes not only of Horace's *Satires* but also of his *Epistles*, which turns out to be one of Juvenal's main sources of inspiration.

Next, we shall examine the satirist's first catalog of targets (22–30), for a flavor of his rhetoric of exemplarity, before moving on to three vignettes: the youth who has frittered away his patrimony hurtling along the Flaminian Way in his chariot to impress his girlfriend (58–62); the Egyptian Arabarch's statue polluting the ranks of sculptured luminaries in the Forum Augusti (128–31); and the blowout of the lone diner followed by his death in the bath shortly thereafter (139–46). All these scenes highlight the tension between fixity and fluidity in Juvenal's representation of the world and how this is mapped onto the body—of the satirist, his targets, and the Roman imperial subject—as well as onto the cityscape of Rome, whose monuments and spaces flicker throughout these poems. We shall then consider the central scene of the poem (95–126), the doling out of the daily *sportula* (little basket of sustenance) by the monied man of influence to his hangers-on. The liminal positioning of the speaker as he introduces himself—whether at the crossroads, on the doorstep, or at the city gates—is a self-conscious gesture of marginalization, which facilitates exposure of the vulnerability of the talismans of male citizen identity. In these

16. So, for instance, Juvenal positions himself in relation to Lucilius in lines 19–20 and 165–70, and to Horace in 51. Horace in *Satire* 1.4 and 1.10 expends considerable effort in relating his own poetry to the Lucilian model; on Persius's allusions to Horace, see Hooley 1997. The "anxiety of influence" among Horace, Persius, and Juvenal and their attempts as poets under the empire to come to terms with Lucilius, the voice of Republican *libertas*, is well delineated in Freudenburg 2001. On programmatic devices and openings, see W. S. Anderson 1982, 277–92.

17. Braund 1996a, 173–78, 230–36; Motto and Clarke 1965; Larmour 2007. On openings in Horace, see Gold 1992.

18. Henderson 1995; Freudenburg 2001, 209–13, 238–41; Larmour 2004.

border zones, the categories and hierarchies upon which such ideals as *amicitia*, *libertas*, *pudicitia* and *virtus* depend are revealed to be dangerously unstable. The demands of *genus* for clarity and delimitation, however insistently they are shouted out, cannot be met.

Finally, we shall consider how the satirist, as he wanders through Roman space and time, is confronted by what must be abjected in order to protect his identity. This is a process that tends inevitably toward the abjection of the self, captured most graphically in the image of the speaker's charred body being dragged across the arena, the consequence of opening his mouth too wide (155–57). By this stage, we have reached the concluding segment of the poem (147–71) and the end of a journey the satirist has made not only across the city but, in metapoetic terms, from the battlefield of Lucilius to the arena of Horace. By recalling Horace's representation of himself as a gladiator in the *Epistles* and the deployment of arena imagery in his two books of satires, Juvenal begins to delineate the contours of his own "arena of satire." Conscious of the danger of ending up as a participant in an arena spectacle, he takes for himself the role of producer or *editor*. Juvenal's appropriation of this role is of critical importance for understanding his purposes in writing satire. *Satire* 1 ends with the speaker disavowing the Lucilian *libertas* he had originally claimed to be imitating, with the statement that he will attack only the dead (171).[19] The opening poem thus sets the model for "Ro(a)ming" across time and space, and the Latin genre of *satura*, in the (doomed) search for anchorage; the "journey" from Lucilius to Horace is a pathway that will be recalled later on—for instance, in the transition, however ill-defined, from *indignatio* to the philosophical mode or, more subtly, in the shift of interest from "warlike" Romulus to *placidus* Numa in *Satires* 1–3, but none of these movements supplies a definitive answer to the crisis.

Subsequent chapters explore related issues across the collection as well as in individual poems. Chapter 2 ("Beyond the Pale") considers the traversal of space and boundaries in the *Satires*, ranging from the city of Rome to the edges of the Empire. It demonstrates the close connections between traversing space and the crossing of gender lines by examining how the motifs, devices, and vocabulary used to depict the atrophying of maleness in *Satire* 2 are refashioned for the negative examination of women and marriage in *Satire* 6 and again for the dialogue with Naevolus in *Satire* 9. Seneca's ideas on "walking about" offer helpful insights into how the Juvenalian speaker rejects the role of the *sapiens*

19. Presumably by name ("those whose ashes are covered by the Flaminian and Latin roads"); on different translation possibilities, see Freudenburg 2001, 235; Miller 2005, 7–14.

and instead paints himself into the scenery he describes. Chapter 3 ("The Arena of Satire") expands the discussion of the gladiatorial vignettes so prominent in *Satires* 2 and 6 to consider the arena as the building in the urban landscape which is most closely aligned with the satiric perspective, focusing on how its solidifying and consolidating architecture is undermined by the floating and divided subjectivity that marked the experience of spectatorship. The porosity of this most solid of buildings points to other leaking structures in the cityscape, including gates, sewers, and even the *domus*. A survey of gladiatorial and re-lated imagery in other satirical texts, from Lucilius to Martial, places Juvenal's fascination with the arena and consumption in a larger literary context as a prelude to readings of *Satires* 4 and 5. Chapter 4 ("Melting Down the House") brings together passages from a number of poems to show how statues, orna-ments, furniture, and other solidifying items participate in the undoing of per-manence by the forces of change and transitoriness in the satirical world. Such objects are emblematic of decay and impermanence, as they become alienated from the original context of their creation and are transformed, or melted down, into other forms. Poverty here becomes a synonym for a lost cleanliness and propriety. The interplay of display and destruction recalls not only what hap-pens in the arena but also how satire dissolves other elements into itself. This is also where the later satires of books 4 and 5 come into play, with their more restrained but much more radical destruction of the talismans of *Romanitas*. Satire truly is the "myth of winter" in Northrop Frye's seasonal formulation: amid all the displays of consumption and excretion, it is images of rootlessness and sterility, of death and the Underworld which overwhelm any prospect of rejuvenation or rebirth in Juvenal's Rome. As David Wiesen says, "Juvenal offers us no dreams. . . . The withholding of any alternative to the absurdity of an intolerable world justifies the application of the term nihilism to Juvenal."[20] Such satire is de(con)structive, rather than corrective. And yet, as Allen Miller has argued, the ironic truth of such satire is that there emerges from its rheto-ric of excess and its multivalent aggression toward alterity the possibility—if nothing more—of a responsive and responsible mode of existence.

The devastated landscape left behind by Juvenalian satire is considered fur-ther in this book's conclusion ("The Plague of Satire"), which takes up the ef-fects of a rhetoric of exemplarity characterized by a material excess that at once exceeds, undermines, and inaugurates the possibility of meaning and reflec-tion. This excess occurs amid intimations of decay, disease, destruction, and death as manifestations of the deconstruction of the traditional signifiers of

20. Wiesen 1989, 733.

Romanitas. The satirist takes us to a place where nothing is (any longer) what it seems, or claims, to be; yet, as Plato well knew, it was precisely the disjunction between appearance and reality that was the beginning of reflection and hence the beginning of philosophy. Juvenal, through the rhetoric of exemplarity, through the evocation of the grotesque and leaking body, and through the destabilization of the very cognitive topography that constituted *Romanitas*, demands that we think anew about the nature of both our individual and our collective identities, about their predication on that which they must exclude.

Of course, the genre of Juvenalian satire extends far beyond this corpus of sixteen poems, and the conclusion also offers some suggestions as to how we may recognize Juvenalian discourse in the works of later satirists, especially those prone to similar images of bodily abuse and abjection and those for whom crumbling signifying systems no longer hold weight. Many of these take their lead from Jonathan Swift's *A Tale of a Tub, Gulliver's Travels,* and *A Modest Proposal,* which reinvent the Juvenalian mode for modern times. Evelyn Waugh's *Decline and Fall, Vile Bodies, A Handful of Dust,* and *Black Mischief* offer good examples from the first half of the twentieth century. Among the more striking manifestations of Juvenalian techniques among contemporary writers are Viktor Pelevin's novels of post-Soviet Russia, such as *The Life of Insects* and *Generation П,* and Martin McDonagh's explosive satire on Irish Republican terrorist groups, *The Lieutenant of Inishmore.* In all these cases, we can see an interdependence of the topographic and the somatic, which is quintessentially Juvenalian: Swift plays upon the smallness or hugeness of Gulliver's body and its consuming and excretory functions as he travels from one realm to another. Waugh embodies the decline of the English aristocratic social order, and the Empire that sustained it, in a series of corrupted, enfeebled, and isolated characters. Pelevin assimilates the effects of drugs, alcohol, consumer goods, and physical violence to the individual's traumatic yet exhilarating experience of the transition from the USSR to "new" Russia. And McDonagh's play culminates in a surreal scene of shocking self-mutilation, which mirrors the confused and destructive forces at play in both Irish nationalist circles and politics in general. The distinctive feature these texts have in common is that they are written at the breakdown of an ideological system, heading toward zero-point, or, in Foucauldian terms, in the period of transition between one episteme and the next.[21]

21. Foucault does theorize this transition in detail, but the breakdown of one established belief system and its replacement by another has come to be closely associated with his conception of the epistemological break; the term *rupture épistémologique* was introduced by Gaston Bachelard (see Balibar 1978).

Into the Labyrinth

From the opening lines, there is a distinct chronotopic and referential fluidity about Juvenalian satire: the frequency of synecdoche and metonymy illustrates the extent to which it is preoccupied with fragmentation and deferral. Periphrasis is perhaps its favorite technique, so that, as with the literary and mythological allusions, the reader is obliged to follow a circuitous path to fuller understanding.[22] The repetition inherent in the chains of exempla works powerfully against narrative closure, since the effect is more one of "piling up" rather than of progression toward a conclusion.[23] As Seneca suggests in *Epistle* 65, exempla provide a useful shortcut: *longum iter est per praecepta, breve et efficax per exempla.* The rhetoric of exemplarity is characterized by repetition, not only in the sense that one object of derision follows another, but also because the basic types of targets and the techniques for attacking them are established in the first two books, especially in the first three poems. After that we soon begin to find variations on themes already laid down, verbal echoes, and returns to particular people and places. So, for example, the Porta Capena, where the satirist says farewell to his friend Umbricius in *Satire* 3, is revisited in *Satire* 8 during the portrayal of Lateranus.[24] The linguistic labyrinth into which the reader is thrust gets grafted onto the physical space of the city, so that reading the satires becomes a walk around Rome in which one is confronted by shocking sights amid the familiar landmarks. In *Satire* 3, which gives free rein to the rhetoric of exemplarity, Rome is presented at its most labyrinthine: in the narrow twisting of its streets (*arto / vicorum in flexu*, 3.236–37), it is full of dangers around every corner for the "virtuous" man like Umbricius. Consequently, he leaves for Cumae like the "weary Daedalus" who landed there after fleeing from Crete.[25] As Daedalus constructed the labyrinth to contain the monstrous hybrid that was the Minotaur, so the satirist constructs a textual labyrinth in which he tries to enclose contemporary Roman monstrosities.[26]

22. Cf. the discussion by Uden 2015 of the "open satiric text" (36–42; cf. 144, 176).

23. The pile and the heap in Roman satire, Freudenburg 2001, 186–88, 207–208. Satiric closure, Griffin 1994, 95–114; on Horace's *Satire* 1.5 as having "the most definite yet most open-ended ending in Latin literature," see Gowers 2012, 185–86.

24. Probably Plautius Lateranus, consul designate under Nero in 65 c.e.: see Courtney 1980, 406. On echoes between the two gate scenes, see Larmour 2007; on the themes of 8, see Braund 1988, 69–122; Henderson 1997. For the descriptions of Gracchus's appearances in the arena in *Satire* 2 and 8, see chaps. 2 and 3 herein.

25. For resonances, see Rutledge 1967 and 1971–72; Fitzgerald 1984; Putnam 1987; Catto 1988. Fredericks 1975 says that Daedalus is introduced here "in no offhand way . . . Umbricius, like Daedalus, must save what is left of his life" (48). On Fronto's desire to flee Rome to Marcus at Baiae, Champlin 1980.

26. Rutledge 1971–72 on Daedalus as proto-Aeneas and the labyrinth on his doors at Cumae as "prefiguring of both the labyrinth of the Underworld through which Aeneas must pass and the maze of confusion

The notion of the city as a labyrinth is perhaps the most important motif in Walter Benjamin's studies of the urban experience, especially Naples, which he finds "pre-modern" in its remarkable "porosity." Such concepts, as we shall see, are of considerable value in reading Juvenalian Rome for, like Benjamin's Naples, it is a prime site of disorientation and decay, of spectacle and performance.[27] Latin satire is an urban phenomenon and, beyond that, a form tied specifically to the city of Rome itself to an extent that pastoral, for example, another quintessentially urban genre, is not.[28] When Quintilian wrote that *satura quidem tota nostra est* (Satire at any rate is entirely our own, 10.1.93), he may well have had this in mind. The satires of Lucilius, Horace, and Persius are all to a considerable extent grounded in the topography of Rome, but it is only with Juvenal that satire and the city become inseparably intertwined. Many well-known locations in Rome are mentioned en passant throughout the *Satires*— the Forum, the Capitol, the Campus Martius, the Circus Maximus,[29] and numerous temples[30]—so that, when these are combined with references to the hills, the Tiber, and the three main roads out of the city (Flaminian, Latin, and Appian), the topographical highlights of the imperial *Urbs* are reconstituted in the text.[31] Nonspecific locations, such as gardens and theaters, arenas and gladiator schools, streets and street corners, baths, taverns, and doorways, contribute to the metropolitan mosaic. Then there are the internal private spaces, such as atriums and porticoes, dining rooms and bedrooms, into which the rest of the city continually seeps. As the collection unfolds, a cityscape emerges, made up of an apparently haphazard, yet nonetheless surprisingly comprehensive, collage of the most famous and significant sites of Rome.[32]

Juvenal's *Satires* thus functions as a city-text, as Peter Barta defines it in reference to James Joyce's Dublin or Andrei Bely's St. Petersburg, where a

---

and intrigue in Latium above which Aeneas has to rise and which he must master before the Trojans can settle in Italy" (113); cf. Miller 1995.

27. Gilloch 1996: "Porosity...is interwoven with three different visions of the city, which come to constitute a set of recurring motifs in Benjamin's city writings. The metropolis appears as a place of losing oneself and disorientation (labyrinth), as a site of decay and transience (ruin), and as a place of spontaneity and performance (theatre)." See Larmour and Spencer 2007, introduction.

28. See Braund 1996a, 32 and n66; the two are closely linked, however, and satire exhibits several pastoral "moments." In *Satire* 9.102, Naevolus is addressed as "*o Corydon, Corydon.*"

29. Forum: 1.128–29 2.142, 4.7, 6.58, 7.132, 10.25, 11.50, 16.47; Capitol: 1.116, 6.47–48, 10.65, 14.91; Campus: 2.131–32, 6. 153–54, 524–25, 529; Circus: 3.65, 6.582–83, 588–90, 11.197–98.

30. Temples and altars: Castor, 14.260; Ceres, 9.24, 14.219; Concord, 1.116; Fides, 1.113; Fortuna, 14.90; Hercules, 8.13, 14.90; Isis, 6.528–29, 9.22; Juno, 6.48, 386; Mars, 14.261, 10.83; Pax, 1.115, 9.23; Pudicitia, 6.308; Vesta, 4.11; Victoria, 1.113; Virtus, 1.113.

31. Hills: in general, 8.239; Aventine, 3.85; Esquiline, 3.71, 5.78, 11.51; Quirinal, 2.133; Vatican, 6.344; Viminal, 3.71. Embankment: 6.291, 588, 8.43, 16.26. Tiber: 5.104, 6.523, 8.265, 14.202. Roads: Appian, 3.316, 4.117–18; Flaminian, 1.61, 171; Latin, 1.171, 5.55.

32. See also Larmour 2007, from which some of the following remarks are drawn.

complex interweaving of the particular and the general (similar to what we see with Rome's inhabitants) creates a sense of epic totality: "Collage or montage . . . is achieved by using the perspective of the walker. As he roams the streets, he is exposed to the flotsam and jetsam of urban life—a veritable chaos of phenomena—which, when thrown together, begin to make sense. . . . Readers can rearrange the seemingly unconnected pieces of trivia, as they wander back and forth in the text."[33] We can add Rome to the cities of Dublin, Berlin, St. Petersburg, and similar urban locations that generate compelling literary and artistic expressions of the troubled consciousnesses they embody: these cityscapes have all been witnesses to violent political turmoil, dramatic social change, or sudden shifts in the cultural identity of their inhabitants. War and war crimes, invasion, civil disorder, executions, and repression or enslavement leave their marks not only on the façades of buildings or the heads of statues, but also on the mental apperception of the city by those who encounter its chronotopic complexity. As Benjamin says, "Living means leaving traces," and it is primarily through examining the spaces and structures where these traces inhere that a city's social life can be understood.[34]

As he moves around the city, Juvenal's satirist-narrator undertakes a mapping of Rome in its spatial, temporal, literary, and ideological dimensions, so that the horizontal movement across the city is accompanied by a vertical descent into its past. The monuments and geographical features of Rome are emplotted as sites of significance in the text, where the combination of place and person, or place and action, is particularly revealing.[35] The instantly recognizable visual features of Rome are imbued with such a weighty historical and cultural *gravitas* that we can designate them as *lieux de mémoire*, to use the term coined by Pierre Nora as the title of his multivolume work on the construction of the French past through "traditional national memory." Nora's aim, he explains, is "to search out the principal loci, material or immaterial, in which this memory had become embodied and which, through the actions of men or the work of centuries, remained their most specific representations and most dazzling symbols."[36] In spite of the culturally specific nature of its genesis, the term

---

33. Barta 1996 speaking of Andrei Bely's *Petersburg*, James Joyce's *Ulysses*, and Alexander Döblin's *Berlin Alexanderplatz* (98).

34. Gilloch 1996, 6; cf. Benjamin 1978, 169. On the centrality of criminal and erotic activities, and the demimonde, see Coverley 2010, 13, 15.

35. For more thoughts on the sight-site combination, see Larmour and Spencer 2007, intro.

36. Nora 2001, xviii–xx. The original purpose of the project was "to demonstrate empirically the hidden connection between all true memorials—monuments to the dead, as in the Panthéon—and objects as seemingly different as museums, commemorations, archives, heraldic devices or emblems," but the inquiry soon extended beyond these confines to royal palaces, institutions, legal codes, administrative categories, "natural

lieu de mémoire has been productively appropriated by Roman cultural histo-rians.[37] It is, for instance, used by Alain Gowing in *Empire and Memory*, with reference to places and structures in Rome "associated with Republican events, activities, and individuals" (133) and the memories evoked when they are viewed from an Imperial perspective. The disjunction between the way things are now and the way they used to be is a central preoccupation of the Juvenalian speaker, for whom memory and metropolis are intertwined as they are for Benjamin, so that he projects this inconcinnity onto buildings, statues, and other sites in the cityscape.[38] Such *lieux de mémoire* are both signposts and markers along satire's circuitous paths through Roman history and culture as well as through the satiric genre, mapping the demise of the "idea" of Rome and of the ideals of *Romanitas* as they go.

The absence of much in the way of detailed description of particular sites shows that this is not where the main interest of the poems lies.[39] It is the spatial and verbal meandering of the speaker that takes center stage in the sa-tirical performance, unfolding against a background of fleeting topographical "moments," similar to what happens in Joyce's *Ulysses*. Juvenal makes Hor-ace's *Musa pedestris* of satire into a pedestrian in the streets of Rome, and his are poems of departure rather than arrival.[40] The roaming of the satirist-narrator has its counterpart in the loose structure of the poem, which so disturbs crit-ics who are overinvested in conventions of order.[41] Juvenalian satire *requires* the narrative incoherence it manifests, because it depends for its effects on the cu-mulative weight of verbal lightning strikes far more than it does on a conven-tional storyline. It also relies upon the reappearance of locations, words, and motifs, and the juxtaposing of these, within a given satire, across books, and throughout the collection as a whole. The reader is thus forced to look out for connections just as much on the metaphoric as on the metonymic level of

---

realities like forests and seacoast or artificial ones like national borders" and "even to categories of mental constructs such as painters' landscapes, or to cultural practices, whether popular (as proverbs or songs) or social (as conversation)."

37. Nora 2001 describes it as "an elegant but untranslatable neologism" (xx); rendered *Realms of Memory* in the author's English version. See Nora 1996.

38. See Gilloch 1996, 95; cf. 68 on memory and the city as both labyrinthine; Szondi 1988 observes that "the labyrinth is thus in space what memory . . . is in time" (22).

39. In fact, as I have argued elsewhere (Larmour 2007), only the Porta Capena and Grove of Egeria on the way out of the city on the Appian Way at the beginning of *Satire* 3 receive sufficient attention to qualify as detailed descriptions (191).

40. Hor. *Sat.* 2.6.17: *satiris Musaque pedestri.*; On his *sermones repentes per humum* ("conversations creeping along the ground") in *Epistle* 2.1.251, see Freudenburg 1993, 180–84.

41. Griffin 1994 notes attempts to "domesticate" the transgressive satyr and turn him into a moral citi-zen and to resist satire's farraginous nature and claim thematic unity and formal clarity (6); cf. Edmunds 1972 on whether *Satire* 13 is "confused" or "consistent" in its argument (59–60).

signification. Frederick Jones speaks of the "polygeneric cocktail" and the "anarchic patchwork" of literary borrowings in the Juvenalian text.[42] The traversal of the cityscape occurs on multiple temporal levels, as the narrative time of any given satire—close to the Formalists' notion of the *syuzhet*—moves through the course of a day in the experience of the speaker (as in *Satire* 1) or an evening farewell to his friend (in *Satire* 3) or a dinner party (in *Satire* 5), while other time spans—of human life from birth to death, of Roman history from its beginnings through the Republic and into the Empire, of the growth and expansion of the city, and of the genre of satire from Lucilius through Horace to Juvenal—are encoded within the broader context of the *fabula*.[43]

The fragmented and disjointed structure of each satire—as the thread of metonymic *enchaînement* is subsumed under a torrent of lurid exempla and pointed observations—is matched by the seemingly random and incomplete image of the city that emerges as the poem progresses. In both cases, however, the predilection for fragmentation is controlled by a web of connections that is considerably more complex than it might at first appear to be. In attempting to characterize Juvenal's *Satires*, we can speak of *mosaics* of urban images and incidents, as we would when considering Benjamin's *Denkbilder* of Naples or Moscow.[44] The combination of topographical confusion with linguistic complexity enables us further to describe Juvenalian discourse as labyrinthine in the mode of several of Jorge Luis Borges's short stories: pathways of allusions and chronotopic ambiguity force us into the labyrinth of language, and once inside, our hold on what we assumed was secure knowledge becomes increasingly tenuous. At the same time, this process of trekking through the maze brings us paradoxically closer to the satirical vision.[45] The phenomenon of the startling opening or the unexpected ending, *aprosdoketon*, is quite in keeping with this trekking: it is akin to turning a corner or emerging from a street and being confronted by a scene that temporarily stops the wanderer in his tracks.[46] As

42. F. M. A. Jones 2007, 111, 147. He notes that the contrast between Lucilian satire and "safe" literature at the end of *Satire* 1 also "looks backwards, questioning the validity of Lucilian satire as a cultural icon, part of the Roman self-image" (147).

43. Drawing upon the distinction between the "raw material" of the *fabula* and the "employment of narrative" in the *syuzhet*, as delineated by Propp and Shklovsky.

44. On this, see Gilloch 1996, chap. 1, esp. p. 49. Cicero *Orator* 149, quotes Lucilius 84–85, in which Scaevola pokes fun at the overworked style of Albucius: *quam lepide lexeis compostae ut tesserulae omnes / arte pavimento atque emblemate vermiculato* (cited Freudenburg 1993, 172; cf. 200, 209). Cicero is discoursing on the joining of final syllables with following initial ones, advising against too much exactness, *nam esset cum infinitus tum puerilis labor*. G. Anderson 1976 notes "mosaics of motifs" in Lucian (23).

45. Borges 1964, "The Garden of Forking Paths" and other stories in *Labyrinths*.

46. Gilloch (1996), on the disappearance of Benjamin from the text, notes that the hapless reader, left to his or her own devices, "undergoes what can only be described as 'textual shock'" in the text-as-city, "a

Quid Romae faciam? mentiri nescio (Juv. 3.41). Rome, Museo della Civiltà Romana, plastic model, 1970. Fototeca Unione Collection (FU.13279). Courtesy of the American Academy in Rome, Photographic Archive.

Gilloch observes on the "shocking" as an urban experience: "The text becomes the site of shock and ambiguity, of the heterogeneous and paradoxical. . . . It is inhabited by a range of diverse, eccentric figures . . . One does not know what one will encounter as one innocently turns the next corner or page" (1996, 182). Many of Juvenal's poems come to a halt with a sudden image or observation whose import is however, potentially epiphanic in nature. Richlin notes a similar tendency within individual vignettes: "Juvenal likes to cap his pictures with an unexpected final twist, an abrupt shift of angle or context that forces the reader to turn a mental corner while proceeding with the text (hence his many parentheses)."[47]

In the list of ingredients that go into his *farrago*, the last mentioned by Juvenal was *discursus*, "running about": the satirist certainly makes fun of those

space in which the sense of sight is paramount, where vision dominates" (182). Gowers 2012, 15–18, on provisional endings and false closures in Horace's *Satires*.

47. Richlin 1992, 207, on 6.312–13.

who rush around in pursuit of material goods, wealth, or power, but he also includes among his targets the locations, objects, individuals, and idea(l)s, the various and interconnected signifiers to which Roman identity is so precariously affixed. Those who rush about in quest of satisfaction through *amicitia* or marriage or *virilitas* will also be sorely disappointed. Seneca speaks of getting on to the right path as the goal of the *sapiens* (*De Tranq.* 2.2): *ut fidem tibi habeas et recta ire te via credas, nihil avocatus transversis multorum vestigiis passim discurrentium* (having *fides* to yourself and trusting that you are on the right path, not led astray by the many cross-tracks of those who are running about in every direction). Juvenal uses images of the *iter* (7.172) and *semita vitae* (10.363), yet there is something disconcertingly banal and unconvincing about the advice at the end of Satire 10.363–64: *semita certe / tranquillae per virtutem patet unica vitae* (Certainly the only path to a tranquil life lies through virtue).[48] There is also a strong metapoetic component to all the "running about," for the satirist himself gives every impression of being engaged in the type of *concursatio* that Seneca warns against in *De Tranquillitate Animi* 12.2–5, when he criticizes those who bustle aimlessly through the cityscape:

> Circumcidenda concursatio, qualis est magnae parti hominum domos et theatra et fora pererrantium; alienis se negotiis offerunt, semper aliquid agentibus similes. Horum si aliquem exeuntem e domo interrogaveris: "Quo tu? Quid cogitas?" respondebit tibi: "Non me hercules scio; sed aliquos videbo, aliquid agam." Sine proposito vagantur quaerentes negotia nec quae destinaverunt agunt, sed in quae incucurrerunt. Inconsultus illis vanusque cursus est . . . vitam agunt, quorum non inmerito quis inquietam inertiam dixerit. Quorundam quasi ad incendium currentium misereberis; usque eo inpellunt obvios et se aliosque praecipitant, cum interim cucurrerunt aut salutaturi aliquem non resalutaturum aut funus ignoti hominis prosecuturi . . . postero die erraturi per eadem illa vestigia.

> We must curtail the restlessness that a great many men show in wandering through houses and theaters and forums; they thrust themselves into the affairs of others and always appear to be busily

---

48. Opinion differs, of course; see Lawall 1958 and Dick 1969. Courtney 1980 sees "a real alteration in his outlook on life, though it did not persist unadulterated beyond this book" (446). Braund 2004 notes the "wry tone" of the ending and suspects the seriousness of the advice in the piece (265).

engaged. If you ask one of these as he comes out of the house, "Where are you going? What have you in mind?" he will reply to you: "Upon my word, I really do not know; but I shall see some people, I shall do something." They wander without any plan looking for employment, and they do not what they have determined to do, but whatever they have stumbled upon . . . their way of life, which one may not unjustly call "busy idleness." When you see some of them running as if they were going to a fire, you will be sorry for them; so often do they collide with those they meet and send themselves and others sprawling, though all the while they have been rushing to pay a call to someone who will not return it, or to attend the funeral of a man they do not know . . . and on the next day they will wander over the selfsame track.[49]

The list of activities reads like an index of Juvenal's subject matter, and the way they tumble upon one another is very reminiscent of the apparently chaotic organization of many of the pieces in the collection. If one's literary style and mind are inseparable, as Seneca often suggests, then the speaker's own way of going—in terms of speed and agitation—implies that he too is headstrong and angry, not quite *sanus*.[50] Almost all critics would agree that this applies to the first six satires in the collection, whether or not they believe that the remaining books then demonstrate the limitations of *indignatio* as a response to contemporary conditions.

The Juvenalian satirist is not only a wanderer, but also a loiterer who hangs about on the fringes of public and private space, waiting for someone or some activity to catch his eye. Again, I would suggest that these ancient texts can profitably be related to modern literary works arising from a troubled urban consciousness. In his book *Loiterature*, Ross Chambers speculates on the figure of the loiterer and "loiterly" literature, which he distinguishes by its preference for "beguiling" narrative over closure. Middles are more important in this genre than beginnings and endings. Using *Tristram Shandy* as an example, Chambers observes that "the trick of loiterly narrative is so to question the conventionality of beginnings and endings that the alleged story becomes all middle" (1999, 21) and that "beguiling narrative—or better still: beguiling narration as an alternative to narrative closure—isn't a bad phrase with which to characterize loiterature generally" (25). Nor is it a bad phrase with which to

---

49. Trans. Basore 1928–36.
50. Sen. *De Tranq.* 2.2, 11.1; Sen. *Ep.* 40.2, 114.22; cf. Hor. *Sat.* 1.10.1 of *Lucilius: incomposito . . . pede currere versus.*

characterize Juvenalian satire. The *locus classicus* of loiterature is the *trivium*, the intersection of three roads. As Chambers notes: "Before it came to mean insignificant, the trivial was associated with people, places, and practices of ill repute, particularly as they involved the body and the satisfaction of its needs. . . . Three-way crossings weren't places for triumphal arches and noble monuments; what flourished there were taverns and brothels and gambling-dens" (8–9).

The crossroads gives rise to ambiguity and misleading appearances, for while some people stand around aimlessly, others loiter "with intent." Juvenal's satirist is just such a loiterer, no neutral observer but one with a definite purpose: to identify, expose, and punish. In the programmatic *Satire* 1, the speaker situates himself at the *quadrivium*, in the middle of the crossroads where *four* roads meet (63–64): *nonne licet medio ceras implere capaces / quadrivio, cum . . .* (Surely then I am allowed to fill spacious tablets, in the middle of the cross-roads, when . . .). The word *quadrivium* is rare—the only other occurrence in literary sources is Catullus's *in quadriviis et angiportis*, where Lesbia sucks off various males.[51] It suggests a place of significant confluence, the perfect van-tage point for the satiric loiterer to view the passing parade of disreputables and immerse himself in Rome's quotidian flow.[52] This is the site where the text is generated, as the satirist jots down his notes with exempla coming at him from all directions. By placing himself here, the speaker reminds us that satire is a genre formed by the conglomeration of conspicuous exempla and also by the confluence of different literary forms, conventions, and techniques. Satire tosses into its bubbling, spicy *farrago* all other genres—epic, pastoral, drama—to make the spectacle more vivid and effective, and it consumes various literary forms, including *consolatio*, thanksgiving (*prosphonetikon*), *propemptikon*, diatribe, and dialogue. These poems are sites of continuous intersection and place signifi-cant demands on the listener and reader, who must keep their ears and eyes open, as they become *flâneurs* in the text, following the satirist as he lists and catalogs, pauses, loiters, digresses, changes direction, retraces his steps, and relentlessly keeps going without obviously getting anywhere.[53] Part of the joke

51. Cat. 58.4; cf. Juv. 6.412 (*trivium*), 9.112–13 (*compita*).
52. Gruet 2006, 111. Cf. *Sat.* 9.112–13, where the crossroads is the source of gossip from inebriated slaves telling on their masters. See F. M. A. Jones 2007 on Juvenal's satires as a space in which he acts out the wran-gling and discords of all sorts of genres, and his notion of Juvenalian satire as a "supergenre" presiding over the rest (153–54).
53. For Juvenal, walker and voyeur are the same. In his essay "Walking in the City," de Certeau (1984) cites New York as the place where the division between the walker (at street level) and the voyeur (atop the skyscrapers) is most extreme, but Juvenal's satirical eye has the totalizing gaze of the voyeur, which sees the city as an entity (91–110, esp. 92–93). In his playing the role of *editor*, as we shall see later in this introduction, this is given an arena setting.

is that satire is very much like the environment it describes (and condemns) even as it tries to rise above it as Seneca's *sapiens* strives to do.

Chambers identifies the pleasure or *jouissance* of digression as central to loiterly literature and observes that it is a form of expression that often brings with it criticism of modes of authority that strive to present themselves as orderly and stable:[54]

> To demonstrate, by a shift of perspective, that certain things are
> the case (certain propositions hold true, certain perspectives are valid)
> only within a limited context, and that they're dependent on a certain
> "forgetfulness" with respect to the other-sidedness of a given situation,
> is to show, on the one hand, that the claims of authority are not
> universally valid and, on the other, that the condition of intellectual
> comprehension is a certain failure of comprehensiveness. (1999, 15)

As a loiterer, the Juvenalian satirist has what Chambers calls a "fringe consciousness" whose view from the margins appraises the center from a critical perspective:

> A peripheral subject (one who knows the mainstream as well as
> the periphery, that is) is able to read in two directions. The loiterly
> subject is not only one who reports on life at the margins for the
> benefit of those who inhabit the center, but is also in an excellent
> position to acquire a relativized knowledge of life at the center
> of things (where people are too single-mindedly absorbed in what
> they are doing to be able to read their own existence) and to
> report (to all who read) on the deficiencies of that life, which are
> of course those of self-enclosure, blindness, and the exclusions and
> marginalization—the ignorance of the other—that these give rise
> to. (1999, 61)

By observing the rest of society from a position whence it appears out of joint and, by virtue of his critical stance and the raising of his voice, the satirist is habitually "on (the) edge." Whether or not there is a clear progression in Roman satire from Lucilius to Horace to Persius of increasing marginalization, it is certainly true that by the time we get to Juvenal we can speak of a discourse of deep-seated alienation on the one hand and of radical deconstruction on the other.

The argument made here will be that Juvenal's *Satires* systematically unravel the claims of Roman authority as expressed in its great signifiers—*amicitia, pudicitia, nobilitas*—through digressive techniques and liminal

---

54. Chambers 1999, 8; on the subversiveness of the wanderer, see Coverley 2010, 85, 93.

Substitit ad veteres arcus madidamque Capenam (Juv. 3.11). Looking toward the Circus Maximus from the Porta Capena. Photograph by David Larmour and Corby Kelly.

positioning similar to those found in loiterature. Digression into the past is a means of both escaping and criticizing the present and, beyond that, of undermining the privileged status of linear narratives. To direct the reader away from the contemporary awfulness of Rome into other chronotopes is also to point him unerringly towards it.[55] As Chambers puts it, digression is "as etymology proposes, a stepping away from, but a stepping away from that's sutured to that from which it steps. Digression isn't only travel that doesn't need to leave home; it's also travel that can't quite manage to leave home, ever, step away as it might" (25). This ambiguity underpins Juvenal's *Satire* 3, in which the speaking voice splits into that of Umbricius, who is leaving Rome (but not before delivering a compendious tirade against its corrupt inhabitants), and the satirist-narrator, who will stay in the city, come what may.[56] Benjamin's

55. Griffin 1994, 60: on Juvenal, "to remember the past is not to be guided by it or to hope to bring it back but to rub Roman noses in a dirty imperial present from which they cannot escape." Much the same technique is deployed by Swift in *Gulliver's Travels.*

56. Cf. various interlocutors, like Laronia and others unnamed, the dialogue with Naevolus, even the speaker-addressee relationship. On the "doubling" motif in the city-text, see Coverley 2010, which cites Stevenson's *Jekyll and Hyde* (18); Barta 1996 on the Doppelgänger in Bely's *Petersburg* (39–40).

observation that in the Naples he finds so horribly intriguing "nothing is enjoyable, except the famous drinking water" testifies to a similar ambiguity,
and one that remains similarly unresolved.[57] The satirist's desire to relocate—
evident in repeated references to escaping to far-off places, like Britannia or
the land of the Sarmatians—is really a desire to recover what has been lost at
home, to find the original Rome in Rome.[58] The results are inevitably fraught
with contradictions. To cite one early example, Umbricius's rural idyll of
sartorial (and, by implication, economic) equality in *Satire* 3.171–78 is surprisingly accommodating of Greek terms, especially coming from the mouth of
someone who has just told his fellow citizens (60–61) that he cannot stomach
a "Greek Rome" (*non possum ferre, Quirites, / Graecam Urbem*:[59]

> Pars magna Italiae est, si verum admittemus, in qua
> nemo togam sumit nisi mortuus. Ipsa dierum
> festorum herboso colitur si quando **theatro**
> maiestas tandemque redit ad pulpita notum
> **exodium**, cum personae pallentis hiatum
> in gremio matris formidat rusticus infans,
> aequales habitus illic similesque videbis
> **orchestram** et populum . . .

> There is a large part of Italy, if we tell the truth, where
> no-one wears the toga unless he is dead. Even when the
> grandeur of festival days is celebrated in the grassy **theater**
> and the familiar **farce** has at last returned to the stage,
> when the rustic baby shrinks back in his mother's lap
> terrified by the gaping of the whitened mask,
> there you will see the same clothes, identical for
> **orchestra** and populace alike . . . [60]

57. Gilloch 1996: "The city is the space simultaneously of intoxication and of inhumanity. This incon-
gruity, however, is not one that Benjamin will resolve in his subsequent writings on the city. It is, rather, precisely the paradox that animates and pervades all his cityscapes" (36).

58. Edwards 1996, "Alien City" (125–29); cf. Sen. *Ep.* 86.1, on visiting Scipio Africanus's villa in the
Cumae region, praising him for his departure (*aut Scipio Romae esse debebat aut Roma in libertate*) and 3 (*aut
libertas Scipioni aut Scipio libertati faceret iniuriam*).

59. See Spencer 2010 where she speaks of Greekness as "a kind of palimpsest for Roman use" (31, 61,
65) and on fake landscapes (80–83); Uden 2015, chap. 3: "Romans and Greeks: New Views in the *Graeca Urbs*,"
esp. 104–16 on 3.58–125.

60. For more on this passage, especially its role in the Juvenalian "satriric antithesis," see pp. 118–19
herein. Fredericks 1973 examine it as a prologue. The "grassy" theater contrasts with the absence of *herba*
around the spring in the marbled (and corrupted) Grove of Egeria at 3.20 (see Larmour 2007, 197–98). Although Umbricius is referring to an Italian form with the Greek term (in 6.71, *exodium* is applied to Atellan farce),
the conjunction is at least mildly arresting. Greek words are employed for ridicule in 67–68, where their close
proximity to *rusticus* and *Quirinus* enhances the effect: *rusticus ille tuus sumit trechedipna, Quirine, / et ceromatico*

The unpretentious stability of the rural idyll is contrasted with the *ambitiosa paupertas* that animates Rome (182–83).[61] Greek terms and practices are perhaps to be viewed as less invasive in this setting. There is a difference, we might say, picking up on Benjamin's designation of the city as a place of spontaneity and performance, between the theater of the urban center, where everyone is playing a role and is part of the spectacle, and these locally organized and temporally circumscribed performances in the country: here, the child is frightened by the mask precisely because it is unfamiliar. Yet we do find instances of similar contradictions, for example, in *Satire* 11, where we are treated to the description of a no-frills meal, supposedly typical of rural simplicity, to be served in the middle of Rome, that is defined almost exclusively in opposition to urban dining habits.[62] Like Horace's moneylender Alfius, on the very point of becoming a country dweller (*iam iam futurus rusticus*) in *Epode* 2.68, the Juvenalian satirist is but a rustic manqué.[63] Catharine Edwards, noting that "the contrast between vicious city and virtuous countryside, as well as that between corrupt contemporary Rome and pure early Rome, is subtly compromised" in Juvenal 3, observes that "after all, perhaps, as Ovid implies [in his exilic poems], what is distinctively Roman is rather the city's thoroughgoing cosmopolitanism" (1996, 128).[64]

The Search for Rome

As a prototype of the restless flâneur, the satirist-narrator strays across the physical space of Rome, wandering through an ideological landscape laden with chronotopic significance that might solidify his identity as a subject, but always

---

fert niceteria collo. Hor. *Sat.* 1.10.32–35 says Quirinus appeared to him in a dream and forbade him to write in Greek. See Courtney 1980, and Braund 1996a for discussion of terms. Umbricius's choice of the Greek colony of Cumae as refuge has also occasioned comment (Edwards 1996, 128; F. M .A. Jones 2007, 85–87). It is near Baiae, on which as labyrinth, see Fronto, *Corr.* 6. Marcus to Fronto from Baiae: *apud Baias agimus in hoc diuturno Ulixi labyrintho* and Van den Hout 1999, Sen. *Ep.* 51 on Baiae likened to Canopus (3), and praising Scipio for having gone into exile at Liternum rather than Baiae (11, *honestius . . . ruina eius non est tam molliter conlocanda*).

61. Wearing a toga at the arena, Edmondson 1996, 85–86, 97; Mart. 1.49, citing the benefits of country life, including the absence of the *querulus cliens*, notes *lunata nusquam pellis et nusquam toga / olidaeque vestes murice* (31–33).

62. Rimell 2005: "set up to look like a pure organic experience, turn out to be a yuppie farce held within earshot of the Circus, possibly the epicenter of urban filth" (89).

63. Mart. 12.57 contrasts how rich Sparsus enjoys peace and quiet amid *rus in urbe*, while for him *transeuntis nisus excitat turbae / et ad cubile est Roma*, and he goes to his villa when he's fed up with it and wants to sleep (26–27).

64. Of the kind elaborated by Sen. *Cons. Helv.* 6, wherein he describes Rome as *quae veluti communis potest dici*; also the empire as "looking back to" an exile as its founder: *Romanum imperium nempe auctorem exulem respicit*. Seneca wrote this while in exile himself, under Claudius.

fails to do so.[65] In a manner not unconnected to the way that epics and novels enact the search for home, father, or identity (and often all three), Juvenal's *Satires* are a search for Rome, for those fixed points of *Romanitas* to which the subject can attach his floating subjectivity. The speaker seeks *anchorage* that will "fix the floating chain of signifieds in such a way as to counter the terror of uncertain signs," as Roland Barthes expresses it in regard to the reading of images.[66] Seneca uses similar imagery when he cites the recommendation of Diodorus the Epicurean for "the repose of a life spent at anchor in a safe harbor" (*aetatis in portu et ad ancoram actae quietem, De Vita Beata* 19.1).[67] The monuments and sites of Rome should offer this, but in their Juvenalian projection, if they are not inherently repellent like the Subura or the Circus Maximus, they are important public spaces, freighted with historical and cultural significance, that have become repulsive through their contamination by outside elements or repellent behavior of people who frequent them. This can be observed in the jaundiced description of Egeria's Grove, where Umbricius takes his leave of the speaker in *Satire* 3.10–20, or the burgled Temple of Mars in 14.261–62.[68]

The search for Rome and the pull toward fixed points or anchors is analogous to a longing for the lost Roman *vir*. In place of the impossible return to the Golden Age, in which there is unity, fulfillment of desire, and pervasive harmony, the satirist, as John Zomchick suggests, offers the next best thing, namely the (re)establishment of sexual difference: "In its negation of the negation of sexual difference, the satire attempts to produce a positive alternative to its will to annihilate the social world that has transformed a phantasmatic absolute difference into a confusing continuum. In this regard, the positive

65. Barta 1996 on the *flâneur* and the *badaud* (5–12). For related issues in Propertius, see Janan 2001 and T. S. Welch 2005. On Horace's having *les dehors d'un flaneur*, Breguet 1956, 89. On related questions of the subject in "landscape"—using the term in its broadest possible sense—see the comprehensive study of Roman landscape, and its symbolic and ideological underpinnings, provided by Spencer 2010.

66. Barthes 1977, 39; cf. 38–41: "All images are polysemous; they imply, underlying their signifiers, a 'floating chain' of signifieds. . . . In every society various techniques are developed intended to fix the floating chain of signifieds in such a way as to counter the terror of uncertain signs; the linguistic message is one of these techniques. . . . the caption . . . helps me to choose the correct level of perception, permits me to focus not simply my gaze but also my understanding. . . . Anchorage [*l'ancrage*] is the most frequent function of the linguistic message and is commonly found in press photographs and advertisements . . . [Hence] text and image stand in a complementary relationship."

67. He does so as he voluntarily commits suicide, happy in the knowledge of his own goodness and having run the race that Fortune set him.

68. The flâneur as an already nostalgic figure, Coverley 2010, 20, 57–58. Gowers 2012 observes that "Roman satire, like Roman pastoral, is essentially nostalgic: it mourns the lost conditions for its existence and classifies itself at the moment of potential extinction" (7). The Londons of Defoe and Blake, distorted and defiled by plague and corruption respectively, have much in common with Juvenal's Rome (Coverley 2010, 35–42).

In vallem Egeriae descendimus (Juv. 3.17). Looking toward the Porta Capena and the Grove of Egeria. Photograph by David Larmour and Corby Kelly.

moment of satire acts through a productive absence, upon which rests an absolute sexual difference."[69]

The first two examples in the satirist's catalog of miscreants in 1.22–23 are the eunuch who marries and the woman Mevia who hunts in the arena like an Amazon. These constitute an inversion of the He-hard / She-soft binarism (see chap. 2), and out of this blurring of gender lines all sorts of other exempla grow,

69. Speaking of Charles Churchill's "The Times," an Augustan piece which attacks homosexual practices in English society: "In order to restore sexual difference to an increasingly polymorphous—thus dangerous and disordered—world, the satirist takes it upon himself to negate the negation of that difference through the textual production of his own 'Manhood' and its outrageous service to the other" (Zomchick 1995, 349).

like an infection, to populate the entire corpus. This is precisely the image used in *Satire* 2.78–81, speaking of the "effeminization" of the Roman male:

... Dedit hanc **contagio** labem
et dabit in plures, sicut grex totus in agris
unius **scabie** cadit et **porrigine** porci
uvaque conspecta **livorem** ducit ab uva.

... **Infection** causes this stain
and will cause it in more men, just as a whole herd in the fields
dies from the **scab and mange** of a single pig
and a bunch of grapes takes on **discoloration** from the sight of another
     bunch.

The permeability of the border between appropriately masculine men and disgustingly effeminized ones, and between appropriately feminine women and threateningly masculinized ones, lies at the heart of the Juvenalian abject; this is why it receives immediate attention in *Satire* 2 and such sustained treatment in *Satire* 6. It is here that the satirist's attack is the most frenzied—and the abjection of the body at its most violent—because it involves what is at the core of Roman identity, that is, Roman masculinity and the alarming instability at its core.

Satire 6 begins with a brief and ironic vision of the Saturnian Golden Age and then moves to the departure of Pudicitia (and her sister Astraea) from the world, so that the rest of the poem becomes a vain search, through a labyrinth populated by monstrous exempla, to find her again and, more broadly, a search for security in traditional Roman ideals of femininity and marriage, a lynchpin of male citizen identity. This search is undertaken at the same time as, and even primarily by means of, a journey back and forth across the public landmarks of Rome (in addition, of course, to streets, doorways, bedrooms, and so on). These locations are freighted with significance; for example, the altar of Pudicitia was embroiled in the political and social discord between the patricians and the plebeians, as described by Livy 10.23.6–10.[70] Here it gets pissed upon by the drunken Maura and her friend Tullia (6.306–13):[71]

---

70. See Coarelli 1985; there were two altars of Pudicitia and their story is emblematic of the tensions within Roman social history. Pudicitia Patricia had a shrine in Forum Boarium (Livy 10.23.3). Courtney (1980) says it was not there but on the Vicus Longus, and Livy 10.23.6–10 tells how Virginia, of patrician birth, married a plebeian consul and dedicated part of her house on that street to Pudicitia Plebeia after being excluded from Pudicitia Patricia in the Forum Boarium. See Palmer 1974; Langlands 2006, chap. 1 on Pudicitia, esp. 44–51 on Livy and 55–56 on Juvenal.

71. For the text here, I follow Clausen's (1992) presentation of the lines (with 308 transposed before 307), rather than Braund's without the transposition; Courtney 1980 notes the confusion and suspects 307 is spurious (297); see also Miller 2005, 284–85; L. and P. Watson 2014, 167–70, 283–86.

I nunc et dubita qua sorbeat aera sanna
Maura, Pudicitiae veterem cum praeterit aram,
Tullia quid dicat, notae collactea Maurae.
noctibus hic ponunt lecticas, micturiunt hic
effigiemque deae longis siphonibus implent
inque vices equitant ac Luna teste moventur.
Inde domos abeunt: tu calcas luce reversa
coniugis urinam magnos visurus amicos.

Go now and ask yourself with what grimace Maura gulps the air,
when she passes the ancient Altar of Pudicitia;
what Tullia says to her, sister nursed on the same breast as infamous
   Maura.
Here at night they stop their litters, here they piss
and fill the image of the goddess with their long sprays
and ride one another in turn and writhe about with the Moon as
   witness.
Then they go off home: and, when the daylight returns, you tread
in your wife's urine on your way to see your important friends.

As Richlin observes (207), this is a prime example of the technique of the
Juvenalian "abrupt shift of angle" so that the audience "visualizes clearly how
the wife's misbehavior physically stains her husband . . . the defilement is bad
enough, but the husband is, like the poor men in *Satires* 1 and 3, up early to pay
the duty calls of a humble client; and he cannot know whose urine he has
stepped in." The satirist relies here upon the repulsion generated by the conjunction of bodily outflows and a specific location in the Roman public space,
with Maura and Tullia being the contemporary heirs of Pudicitia and Astraea
who have long since absconded.[72] The name Tullia also evokes a notorious figure from Rome's early history, the daughter of Servius Tullius who ordered her
muleteer to drive over the corpse of her father—it was in the road as she was
hurrying to her lover (and his killer) Tarquin: the name *Vicus Sceleratus* (Wicked

---

72. The pissing over Pudicitia in 6.307–13 is itself preceded by a reference in lines 295–97 to the story
of L. Postumius, the Roman ambassador, and the two scenes are, as Miller 2005 points out, thematically
linked: since the disappearance of poverty and the arrival of luxury, says the satirist, . . . *huc fluxit et Isthmos /
et Sybaris †colles†, huc et Rhodos et Miletos / atque coronatum et petulans madidumque Tarentum* (into here have
poured Corinth and Sybaris and Rhodes and Miletus and Tarentum, garlanded, insolent, and drunk, 285).
According to Dio Cassius 9.7, a drunken man stood over Postumius at a festival of Dionysus in Tarentum in
281 BCE and relieved his bowels over his clothes.

Alley) was then given to the location where this happened.[73] On the one hand, this passage is very much about the consuming, excreting, and copulating body; it is also, on the other, about what makes Rome Roman. Rome proper is the self-contained city that is neither flooded with Greeks and other foreigners nor urinated on by them. As Allen Miller has put it, "*Pudicitia* is unmolested. There is no micturation, in Latin a synonym for ejaculation. Women do not ride, and men do not walk through their fluids. Rome is in its original essence dry, sere. It does not foam. It does not pour."

As we shall see in chapter 4, all sorts of other monuments in the city-text prove to offer transient, rather than fixed, meanings as they fall victim to political and cultural climate change. The fates of Nero's colossus or statues of English monarchs in Dublin after Irish independence, or Soviet-era images of Lenin and Stalin after the collapse of the USSR, furnish salient examples.[74] Statues offer powerful visions of solidity amid the fluidity of time, yet in terms of meaning this is not at all guaranteed. In Benjamin's phraseology, the monument has an "after-life" that negates the original intent of its construction.[75]

At the end of *Satire* 6, after all the wandering through Roman space and time, and after all the encounters with multifarious examples of female degeneration and wickedness in this very long and digressive poem (by far his most expansive production), the reader is finally brought to a halt in an undefined space without borders: a zone of danger and deceit, where women behave like men and men like women; from which *virtus* and *pudicitia* have fled, leaving only simulacra in their stead. Marriage now offers nothing more than deceit, dishonor, and death. As Wiesen puts it (724), the world of this satire is "loveless, hard, cynical, materialistic." A startling image says it all, placing a monstrous female from Greek myth in a Roman street or, more accurately, in *every* Roman street: *Clytaemestram nullus non vicus habebit* (There's no street that won't have its Clytemnestra, 656). The venomous relations between husband and wife that this allusion encapsulates—*Satire* 6 ends with examples of poisoning and murder in the home—parallel those between parents (especially fathers) and children, which are frequently mentioned in Juvenal's poems and

---

73. Livy 1.48, Varro *LL* 5.159; she had just reached the end of the Vicus Cyprius (Good Alley), where the temple of Diana had recently stood, and was turning onto the Clivus Urbius in the direction of the Esquiline.

74. See fig. 11, with a relocated Lenin now pointing east, in the grounds of the fortress in Narva, Estonia; as one Russian tourist quipped to me, it is "telling us to go home."

75. See Gilloch 1996, 72–77, and n35. On statues, see chap. 4 herein.

elaborated at length in *Satire* 14. Fathers who are absent, weak or dissolute, whether in moral or physical terms (thus abdicating their role as *pater* and *vir*), signify the fracturing of another lynchpin of the identity system of the *civis Romanus.*[76]

The satirist-narrator's failure to locate the means of "anchoring" himself is, on one level, yet another manifestation of the Romans-as-exiles theme that becomes so prevalent in imperial literature.[77] Satirists are often drawn to exile as a theme, because it offers the (false) hope of flight to an uncorrupted loca-tion, or at least one far away from where they are; it also enables the satirist to parade as an exile in his own land. Both are taken up by the Juvenalian speaker, who wishes he could escape to the far north (*Ultra Sauromatas fugere hinc libet et glacialem / Oceanum* [I'd like to flee from here beyond the Sarmatians and the icy ocean], 2.1–2) and has Umbricius justify his departure for Cumae with the aphorism "There's no place for a Roman here in Rome" (*non est Romano cuiquam locus hic*, 319).[78] The description of the city as occupied by Greeks plays upon the "Rome as Troy" theme that runs through several satires.[79] Going back in time to the foundation of Rome or to the Trojan past is another form of flight, but it reveals only the same gaping lack of security.[80] In such a setting, *Troiuge-nae*, like *Quirites*, can only have a painfully ironic ring, as at 8.181–82: *at vos, Troiugenae, vobis ignoscitis et quae / turpia cerdoni Volesos Brutumque decebunt* (But you, Trojan-born, excuse yourselves, and behavior that would be disgrace-ful for a laborer will be found fitting for the Volesi or a Brutus). *Fortuna non mutat genus*, Horace remarked of a social upstart in *Epode* 4.6, but at the end of Juvenal's *Satire* 8, having been guided through a picturesque exhibit of degen-eracy among nobles, we arrive at a pessimistic conclusion of just how worth-less aristocratic pedigrees are (8.269–75):[81]

---

76. E.g. *Sat.* 3.43–44, 8.142–44, 12.119–20, 14 *passim*.

77. See, for example, Prop. 4.1 and, more generally, Dench 2005 (esp. chap. 4, "Flesh and Blood," 222–97), and Edwards 1996, chap. 5, "The City of Exiles"; Edwards suggests we might see "the idealised longing for Rome of Ovid's exile poetry as the specific object of savage parody in Juvenal's negative representation of the city" (127).

78. Cf. Mart. 3.38.13, 4.5.1–2; Colton 1991, 96–97.

79. There are numerous references to the *Aeneid* in the first book: Ucalegon and the fire scene in 3.197–214 (cf. Assaracus); a "little Aeneas playing" in 5.138–39; *Troiugenae*: 1.100; 8.56, 181. In 8.220–21 the climax of Nero's immorality is singing the role of Orestes and composing a *Troica*. On Troy as labyrinth, see Heller 1946; Catto 1988; Miller 1995; Habinek 2005b, 254. On the Vergilian subtext to *Sat.* 11, see Winkler 1990, 375–78. Edwards 1996, "Roman Troy—Trojan Rome" (63–66).

80. Cf. Lucan's account of Caesar wandering around the ruins of Troy: *circumuit exustae nomen memo-rabile Troiae / magnaque Phoebei quaerit vestigia muri*; he ends his speech to the *Di cinerum* with: "*restituam populos; grata vice moenia reddent / Ausonidae Phrygibus, Romanaque Pergama surgent*" (9.961–99).

81. Braund 1988, 121–22; Uden 2015, 143–44 and chap. 4, with Henderson 1997, on the themes of *Sat.* 8.

Malo pater tibi sit Thersites, dummodo tu sis
Aeacidae similis Volcaniaque arma capessas,
quam te Thersitae similem producat Achilles.
Et tamen, ut longe repetas longeque revolvas
nomen, ab infami gentem deducis asylo;
maiorum primus, quisquis fuit ille, tuorum
aut pastor fuit aut illud quod dicere nolo.

I prefer that your father were Thersites, as long as you were
like the grandson of Aeacus, and brandishing Vulcan's weapons,
rather than that Achilles fathered you to be like Thersites.
And yet, when you follow your name all the way and unroll it far back,
you trace your family from the notorious asylum;
the first of your ancestors, whoever he was, was
either a shepherd or something that I don't want to mention.

Right at the beginning of the whole Roman story, then, Juvenal tells us, there was an influx of highly dubious people into this place, undermining any notion that it can satisfy the demands of genus. So much for the wholesome Latin shepherds trotted out as exemplars of rustic purity in *Satire* 2.127 and elsewhere.[82] The repetition of *longe* in 272 and the two verbs with the *re-* prefix, and the placement of *nomen* at the end, emphasize the theme of searching and reaching for the anchor-point that, it turns out, undoes the whole justification for the enterprise in the first place. The word *revolvas* suggests the unrolling of a scroll, and *deducis* has significant literary overtones, so that tracing the *nomen* back in time is assimilated to reading one's way through the poem.[83]

The wandering satirist-narrator can also be related to the "Exile who asks, 'Where?'" as described by Julia Kristeva in her book *Powers of Horror: An Essay on Abjection.* She introduces the figure of the "deject," "the one by whom the abject exists," in the following passage:[84]

The one by whom the abject exists is thus a *deject* who places (himself), *separates* (himself), situates (himself), and therefore *strays* instead of getting his bearings, desiring, belonging, or refusing.

82. On rusticity, see Spencer 2010, esp. chap. 3, "Those Happy Fields? DIY Landscaping," and chap. 4, "Landscape: Time and Motion."

83. See Courtney 1980, 423; on *deduco*, cf. 1.157, 13.207, and see the discussion in chap. 1 herein.

84. Kristeva 1982, 8. For speculations on Kristeva and satire, see Dunn 1995, Hinnant 1995, Larmour 2007. Comic (and satirical) abjection is a thread running through Rosen 2007.

Situationist in a sense, and not without laughter—since laughing is a way of placing or displacing abjection. Necessarily dichotomous, somewhat Manichean, he divides, excludes, and without, properly speaking, wishing to know his abjections is not at all unaware of them. Often, moreover, he includes himself among them, thus casting within himself the scalpel that carries out his separations.

Instead of sounding himself as to his "being," he does so concerning his place: "*Where* am I?" instead of "*Who* am I?" For the space that engrosses the deject, the excluded, is never *one*, nor *homogeneous*, nor *totalizable*, but essentially divisible, foldable, and catastrophic. A deviser of territories, languages, works, the *deject* never stops demarcating his universe whose fluid confines—for they are constituted of a non-object, the abject—constantly question his solidity and impel him to start afresh. A tireless builder, the deject is in short a *stray*. He is on a journey, during the night, the end of which keeps receding.

To the reader of Juvenal's *Satires*, this figure will sound oddly familiar. The straying of the satirist is, as we have seen, underpinned by the linguistic devices and rhetorical strategies of Juvenalian discourse. Allusions to figures from myth and history open up further opportunities for deferral, because when Achilles or Romulus are mentioned, for instance, there are usually several ways that they can be concretized in the overall pattern of meaning. The speaker's pervasive tone of disparagement and belittling undercuts, and greatly complicates, the device of allusion itself. So, while Aeacus, the paragon of nobility and justice, torturing the guilty dead (mentioned in the opening lines of the collection, *Satire* 1.9–10), clearly suggests the satirist punishing his own deserving victims, the whole scene is at the same time overlaid with such scorn and ridicule of epic and mythological commonplaces that it is hard to take anything seriously.[85] Such ambiguity will make Umbricius in *Satire* 3 *both* a persuasive critic of Roman corruption *and* an object of derision, or the picture of pre-Roman, Saturnian simplicity at the beginning of *Satire* 6 (lines 1–20) simultaneously alluring as a nostalgic vision of lost innocence and repellent as a fragrant picture of rude cave-dwellers. As Courtney puts it, in reference to the latter instance, Juvenal's "satiric astringency likes to deflate even what he holds up for imitation."[86]

---

85. For more detailed discussion of Aeacus and the introduction to *Sat.* 1, see chap. 1 herein, Henderson 1995, Larmour 2004.

86. Courtney 1980, 262; cf. 6.47–59; F. M. A. Jones 2007, 69.

One might wonder whether anything at all is held up for imitation. Escaping from the labyrinth, leaving the Underworld with a new purpose, acquiring the object of the quest, and escaping to a place of refuge are all images of what Rose Zimbardo, in her book *At Zero Point*, calls the "satiric antithesis." Here is how J. P. Sullivan rosily characterizes Martial's version:

> Almost all of Martial's work is focused by a unified and hierarchical vision of imperial society as it should be, which inspires the eulogist with the ideals against which the satirist judges and condemns the defects and the failings. It is a vision which is coloured by a very personal view of how life should be lived and the Epicurean values it should manifest, a life that is sheltered in the bosom of generous friends with a modest competence secured by a warm acceptance of the status quo.[87]

As we shall see, a "vision" of this kind never comes into focus in Juvenalian satire. As Ronald Paulson puts it (29), what we remember is "the city with a Clytemnestra in every street and houses toppling on unwary pedestrians—in short, the complex and fantastic world that results when evil is dominant and regarded by an isolated, agitated, good man." Rather than showing a way of "killing the monster" that threatens to overwhelm the categories upon which meaning depends, and showing a way out, Juvenalian satire constructs an ideological and literary labyrinth of indeterminacy and of certain failure in the quest to redeem what is pure and beautiful—that is, whole and stable—and then follows the thread to the way out. Zimbardo defines as "deconstructive satire" that variety in which there is no "satiric antithesis" to which the satirist appeals as an alternative—and idealized—way of the world. As Paulson notes of Juvenal, we have "only the sketchiest advice as to a way of conduct: the ideal of the past offers little but a signpost from which the reader can take his bearings in the labyrinth of Juvenal's fictional embodiment of evil."[88] Although she is delineating what she terms "Restoration deconstructive satire," Zimbardo promotes a general category of "zero point satire" which "is not concerned to 'correct' behavior or to hold up models for emulation; it is, indeed, not concerned with external existents at all. . . . This satire signals the collapse of all order; it erases all constructs; it exposes as illusory all that we perceive or

---

87. Sullivan 1991, 115, citing Mart. 4.77.1–3. The target of this paragraph is the misreading of Martial as fragmented and random in his choice of poetic subjects. Cf. Mart. 10.47 on the elements of a happy life.

88. Paulson 1967, 29. He regards the Juvenalian persona as "a point of view and an ideal and little more," and "the good man" as a rhetorical device.

conceive."[89] As Wiesen observes in a similar vein: "The satirist's rejection of the present and his will to better the world are undone by a lack of belief that the energy and ideas are available to effect improvement. . . . At the center of Juvenal's Roman society is a terrifying nothingness. Meaninglessness is the meaning."[90]

The implications of this claim for our conception of the genre are significant. A binary model that "determines that in order to be satire a text must direct its reader to a positive norm, or must at least by implication, uphold a clear alternative to foolish and vicious behavior, a moral 'satiric antithesis'" is, she argues, inappropriate to the deconstructive satire we find in Rochester (John Wilmot), William Wycherley, or Swift in *Tale of a Tub*.[91] And this kind of satire is, according to Zimbardo, first produced nowhere other than in "the self-combative, deconstructive discourse of Juvenalian satire":

> The abundance, the redundancy, the abrupt transitions and
> idiomatic instability, the furious, seemingly irrational pace of a satire
> by Juvenal proclaim satire's self-referential, linguistically self-
> contained nature. A Juvenalian satire is not a "cogent . . . argument
> between rational men"; it is a semiotic battleground. In a Juvenalian
> satire it is language itself that is in violent and always dubious
> turmoil.[92]

Although it is possible to take issue with some of her more sweeping statements, there is no doubt that Zimbardo is alert to some key features of Juvenalian discourse that have largely escaped the attention of classical scholars, with Wiesen being one notable exception:

> The magnificent mine of classical culture is worked out. Where
> to look for authority? The world is truly out of joint, but to set it to
> rights, Juvenal has neither a new doctrine nor even a valid old one
> to transmit, but rather a sophisticated verbal art which conveys the
> message that the denunciation of evil is also an elaborate form of
> literary wit and play calling into question that very denunciation.[93]

---

89. Zimbardo 1998, 16; cf. 17: "Restoration deconstructionist satires are texts that overrun all limits. They are *processes*, dubious systems of signs having relation without positive terms that can never arrive at closure. . . . They recognize no empirical 'reality' but rather simultaneously inscribe and erase conceptual frames, which, because they too are linguistic, are inherently dubious."

90. Wiesen 1989, 714; with respect to Juvenal, Mason 1963.

91. Zimbardo 1998, 17.

92. Zimbardo 1998, 18, 66. The "cogent . . . argument between rational men" is a characterization of Horatian satire offered by Howard Weinbrot 1982 (xiii).

93. Wiesen 1989, 713 and *passim*.

The position taken here will not be that there is no "satiric antithesis" in Juvenal—since there are several passages (including those already cited from *Satires* 3, 6 and 11) which at least hint at its contours—but that it is severely attenuated and on its way to extinction.[94] It is clear that there is no definable "antithesis" in Juvenal's satiric vision, in contrast to what we find in Horace: he opened his first book of *Satires* lamenting how people lack stable points of reference, being always discontented and seeking other paths to fulfillment (1–23), and then proceeded to attempt to define something very close to a "satiric antithesis" in the rest of the book. The philosophical ideals of moderation and self-reflection that underpin Horace's definition, however, survive in Juvenal only as fleeting dreams of an old-fashioned *simplicitas* that is largely defined by its absence rather than in positive terms. We can see this in *Satire* 11, where the description of the satirist's simple rustic dinner soon moves into examples of dissolute extravagance drawn from the "typical" urban dining experience (see chapter 4).

Likewise, rather than speaking in terms of the collapse of *all* order, and the erasing of *all* constructs, it is more accurate to view Juvenalian discourse as a discourse of anxiety about *fading* borderlines, *permeable* boundaries, and *lost* markers. Juvenalian satire, in other words, is not quite at zero point but at crisis point. One may also question whether a definition of the alternative— "Horatian" satire—along the lines of Zimbardo's accurately describes all of Horace's satires; there are clear indications, for example, of a move in the direction of Juvenalian rootlessness in book 2.[95] It is often said that Juvenal's later satires are "more Horatian" but this too is debatable, beyond some intermittent moderation in the tone of expression. One could argue that the deconstructions of talismans of *Romanitas* in these poems are all the more devastating and far-reaching precisely because they are framed in a more "organized" and "restrained" discourse, or couched in a recognizably "philosophical" mode of expression.[96] Although, as I will argue in chapter 1, Juvenal's journey across the city of Rome in *Satire* 1 and through the hours of a day is also an account of his movement away from an unrestricted Lucilian *libertas* toward Horatian circumspection, this does not in any substantial way signal a turn toward Horace's philosophical professions. One suspects that, for Juvenal, such moralizing discourse is just one more literary form that gets thrown into the mix.

94. E.g., 3.168–79, 11.64–182, 14.70–85.

95. See Oliensis 1998, chap. 1.

96. See chap. 4 herein on the endings of later satires: Are they any less bleak than earlier ones? *Satires* 12 and 13 end up with punishments of the guilty (sort of), while 10 and 14 elevate Fortuna to a prominent role in affairs; 15 brings the excesses of far-away Egypt to Rome.

Satiric Nausea

Juvenal's use of epic vocabulary and the hexameter, the meter of the quest, and the references to Theseus, Jason, Hercules, and Aeneas, as well as allusions to content found in *The Odyssey, The Aeneid,* or *The Argonautica,* all signal that his satires are a voyage of similar ilk. Indeed in *Satire* 1.149–50 the speaker declares his intention to set sail on the sea of satire: *utere velis, / totos pande sinus* (Hoist the sails, open all the canvas). It is clear, however, that while his course may be set, in the sense that he knows what he is aiming for, the satirist is also casting himself adrift, with no safe harbor to conclude the voyage. Maritime metaphors may seem an odd way to approach an urban form like satire, but there is a well-established pattern of such imagery, most obviously the ship-of-state tradition.[97] Horace often speaks of Rome in terms of swelling seas and waves, as, for example, in his *Epistle to Florus* (2.2.84–86): *hic ego rerum / fluctibus in mediis et tempestatibus urbis / verba lyrae motura sonum connectere digner?* (Here, amid the waves of affairs and the tempests of the city, am I to deign to weave words which will move the sound of the lyre?).[98] When he laments the lot of impoverished Romans, who can no longer afford to live a decent life in the city, Juvenal's Umbricius says (3.164–66): *haud facile emergunt quorum virtutibus obstat / res angusta domi, sed Romae durior illis / conatus* (It's not easy for those whose tight personal resources block their virtues to climb out [of the water], but at Rome it's even harder to attempt).[99] Nautical imagery is not at all uncommon in Roman satire, and in moralizing discourse in general, especially the idea of the wicked man drowning in a sea of vices; so in Persius *Satires* 3.31–34, the visitor asks the lassitudinous student if he is not ashamed to live like Natta, a man so deadened by vice and "submerged so deep that he sends no bubble up to the surface" (*et alto / demersus summa rursus non bullit in unda,* 33.34). The general association of the sea with loss (through drowning and shipwreck, exile and emigration), evident in both ancient and modern literary works, is often lurking behind maritime allusions.[100] In *Epistles* 19 and 87, Seneca conveys through nautical imagery his advice about the pursuit of *otium*

---

97. Aesch. *Sept.*; Oliensis 1995 traces the imagery in the Maevius-at-sea scene in *Epode* 10, especially the "drowning of the ship of anti-state, along with its Antonian passenger" (91–95).

98. Cf. 200–204: *ego, utrum/nave ferar magna an parva, ferar unus et idem/non agimur tumidis velis Aquilone secundo:/non tamen adversis aetatem ducimus Austris* (I, whether I am carried on a ship large or small, I shall be carried one and the same. We are not borne with swelling sails by a favourable North wind: yet we do not drag out our life in adverse South winds). See Brink 1982, 314.

99. Cf. Lucr. 2.13: *ad summas emergere opes rerumque potiri*; see Konstan 2008 on the metaphor (35–36).

100. See Larmour 2005a; Coverley 2010, 36, 68, 133. John Banville's *The Sea* (2005) offers a fine contemporary instance of the interweaving of maritime and personal themes.

rather than wealth, such as *in freto viximus, moriamur in portu* (We have lived on the sea, let us die in the harbor, 19.2) and *naufragium, antequam navem ascenderem* (I was a castaway, before I got on board the ship, 87.1).

The sea is also associated, naturally enough, with being buffeted by winds and storms, and hence with floundering about amid the vicissitudes of life. In *Satires* 1.4.119–20, Horace recalls how his father molded his moral character by telling him things like *simul ac duraverit aetas / membra animumque tuum, nabis sine cortice* (When time has toughened your limbs and your mind, you will swim without water wings). We find several instances where vacillation and lack of fixed points of reference are spoken of in terms of floating or swimming. In *Satire* 2.7.6–8, Davus the slave's opening words to the poet run as follows: *pars hominum vitiis gaudet constanter et urget/ propositum; pars multa natat, modo recta capessens,/ interdum pravis obnoxia* (Some men persist in enjoying their vices and hold to their course; the greater number floats about, now making for the right, sometimes giving way to depravity).[101] The verb *natare* has the basic meaning of swim, or being tossed about on the sea, and hence metaphorically to waver or fluctuate.[102] This latter usage is popular with Seneca, who writes in *Epistle* 35.4 that "changing one's will indicates that the mind is 'at sea'" (*mutatio voluntatis indicat animum natare*)[103] and in 74.11 that "our plans are all at sea, and no amount of prosperity can satisfy us" (*natat omne consilium nec implere nos ulla felicitas potest*). In 95.45–46, he comments that, as sailors must use a star for navigation (*veluti navigantibus ad aliquod sidus derigendus est cursus*), so life without an ideal to aim for is wandering or erratic (*vita sine proposito vaga est*). Ideals require doctrines (*decreta*), which offer the voyager fixed points to navigate by and provide him with secure anchorage.[104] In the opening of *De Tranquillitate Animi*, Serenus explains how he is torn between the desire to plunge into public service (*in mediam ire rem publicam*, 1.10; *prosilire . . . in forum*, 12) and to return home and live within his own walls (*intra parietes suos vitam coercere*, 11), and asks Seneca for a remedy for his *fluctuatio* (17), expressing his mental turmoil with the maritime metaphor: *non tempestate vexor sed*

---

101. Cf. Verg. *Aen.* 4.346 and 5.703; see Muecke 1993, 215.

102. Extended to the eyes, as, for example, in Quintil. 11.3.76: *lascivi et mobiles et natantes . . . (oculi) numquam esse debunt*. The two ideas are awash or overflowing and floating about, without a fixed position. Statius uses it of poems "overflowing" (*carmina in ipso ore natant, Silv.* 2.1.18). Varro has the verb of linguistic usage in *LL* 8.74; 9.71; 10.16; and, with reference to the mind, "waver," "be unstable," or "be at a loss." Cic. *ND* 3.62 (on deriving *Neptunus* from *nare*): *in quo quidem magis tu mihi natare visus es quam ipse Neptunus*.

103. Cf. Manil. *Astron.* (on Capricorn and the lengthening of daylight hours) 4.257–58: *hinc et mobilitas rerum, mutataque saepe / mens natat* (hence comes a restless quality in their lives and a mind which is often changed and floats this way and that).

104. Later, he writes as follows on the need for doctrines: *Quae res communem sensum facit, eadem perfectum, certa rerum persuasio; sine qua si omnia in animo natant, necessaria sunt decreta, quae dant animis inflexibile iudicium* (62).

nausea. Detrahe ergo quicquid hoc est mali et succurre in conspectu terrarum laboranti (It's not the storm that distresses me, but seasickness. Take from me, then, whatever this trouble is and rush to rescue me as I struggle in full view of land).

In two of his later poems, *Satires* 12 and 14, Juvenal explores at some length the satiric possibilities of the storm at sea, especially in connection with greed, the acquisition of material goods, and the loss of prized objects. In 12, personal fortunes and a tempest are woven together in the narrative of an "existential shipwreck," when Catullus the merchant commits a desperate act of self-preservation, likened to self-castration by beavers when faced with hunters who are after their testicles, and throws his expensive goods overboard (12.33–36):[105]

> . . . decidere iactu
> coepit cum ventis, imitatus castora, qui se
> eunuchum ipse facit cupiens evadere damno
> testiculi: adeo medicatum intellegit inguen.

> . . . he began to make a partial payment to the winds
> by throwing things overboard, imitating the beaver, who makes
> himself a eunuch in his desire to escape through the loss of a
> testicle: so well does he understand his medicinal groin.

The ship limps back to harbor, emptied of the contents of its interior and with its mast snapped off. Inspired by the extremity of Catullus's "seasickness," the satirist proceeds to plumb the nauseating depths of behavior among legacy hunters and family members who treat each other in the most shameful manner for personal gain. *Satire* 12 owes much to recurring nautical images in Seneca's moral discourse, where *nausea* is not only seasickness (e.g., *Epistle* 53.3), but also associated with an insufficiently philosophical mode of living (*Epistle* 108.36–37):

> Exempla enim se ipsos inutilis disciplinae circumferunt nulli
> non vitio, quod insequuntur, obnoxii. Non magis mihi potest
> quisquam talis prodesse praeceptor quam gubernator in tempestate
> nauseabundus. Tenendum rapiente fluctu gubernaculum, luctandum
> cum ipso mari, eripienda sunt vento vela; quid me potest adiuvare
> rector navigii attonitus et vomitans? Quanto maiore putas vitam

---

105. Cf. Prop. 3.7.37: *natura insidians pontum substravit avaris* ("Nature made the sea level to ambush the greedy"). Horace notes in *Sat.* 1.4.29–33 that the seafaring merchant, like others marked by greed and ambition, hates poets. On the Lucretius passage (2.1–13), see Newlands 2002, 170–71, and Konstan 2008, 29–37.

tempestate iactari quam ullam ratem? Non est loquendum, sed
gubernandum.

> For those who are liable to every fault which they castigate advertise
> themselves as patterns of useless training. A teacher like that can
> help me no more than a sea-sick pilot can be efficient in a storm.
> He must hold the tiller when the waves are tossing him; he must
> wrestle, as it were, with the sea; he must furl his sails when the
> storm rages; what good is a frightened and vomiting steersman to
> *me?* And how much greater, think you, is the storm of life than that
> which tosses any ship! One must steer, not talk.[106]

Juvenal's hypocritical moralizers of *Satire* 2 are as useless as a seasick pilot because they are themselves infected by the disease (*morbus*) of effeminacy, that
is, of behaving like women rather than proper Roman males. In *Epistle* 95.19,
Seneca speaks of the inappropriate mixing together of food items as a cause of
indigestion and illness and of overflowing (i.e., vomiting):

> Vide, quantum rerum per unam gulam transiturarum permisceat
> luxuria, terrarum marisque vastatrix. Necesse est itaque inter se
> tam diversa dissideant et hausta male male digerantur aliis alio
> nitentibus. Nec mirum, quod inconstans variusque ex discordi cibo
> morbus est et illa ex contrariis naturae partibus in eundem compulsa
> redundant.

> Mark the number of things—all to pass down a single throat—
> that luxury mixes together, after ravaging land and sea. So many
> different dishes must surely disagree; they are bolted with difficulty
> and are digested with difficulty, each jostling one against the other.
> And no wonder, that diseases which result from ill-assorted food are
> variable and manifold; there must be an overflow when so many
> unnatural combinations are jumbled together.

Such mixing together is immediately connected with examples of women behaving like men (21):

> Adeo perversum commentae genus inpudicitiae viros ineunt . . .
> Beneficium sexus sui vitiis perdiderunt et, quia feminam exuerant,
> damnatae sunt morbis virilibus.

---

106. Trans. Gummere 1917–25. On Seneca's nausea and "existential" experiences, see Lampe 2008; on
the sea and declining moral standards, see Edwards 1993, 147–48.

They devise the most impossible varieties of unchastity, and in the company of men they play the part of men. . . . Because of their vices, women have ceased to deserve the privileges of their sex; they have put off their womanly nature and are therefore condemned to suffer the diseases of men.[107]

Thus, the blending of categories that should be kept separate—whether food items or gender roles—leads to confusion and sickness. Later in the same epistle, Seneca notes that people are ashamed when "separate things" and flavors are mixed into one (*piget esse iam singula; coguntur in unum sapores*, 95.27) and that "no vomited up food could be more jumbled" (*non esset confusior vomentium cibus*, 95.28).[108] In *Satire* 6.98–102, Juvenal sets one of his most extended scenes of category mixing on board ship, as he describes how Eppia the senator's wife sailed to Egypt with a troop of gladiators:

Si iubeat coniunx, durum est conscendere navem,
tunc sentina gravis, tunc summus vertitur aer:
quae moechum sequitur, stomacho valet. Illa maritum
convomit, haec inter nautas et prandet et errat
per puppem et duros gaudet tractare rudentis.

If her husband orders her, it's hard to get on a ship,
then the bilge-water is sickening, then the sky spins:
but the one who accompanies her lover has a strong stomach.
   The other
vomits all over her husband, but this one dines among the sailors
   and wanders
up and down the ship and enjoys handling the rough ropes.

The violation of boundaries in Eppia's actions is vividly paralleled in the image of the "compliant" wife throwing up all over her husband, with the verb *errat* and her dining *inter nautas* reinforcing the point. The double use of *durus* in lines 98 and 102 binds the scene together.[109]

There is a line of connection, then, that runs from being "all at sea" in philosophical and ideological terms, through the nausea caused by modes of life defined by excess, to the revolting confusion that arises from the mixing of

---

107. Trans. Gummere 1917–25.
108. Cf. Vitellius's gluttonous concoction, the "Shield of Minerva," in Suet. *Vit.* 13.2, with Ash 1999, 100–102, and chap. 3 herein.
109. Later in the same poem, the wife's puking after binge drinking on wine makes her husband nauseated (6.430–33); see chap. 2 herein.

naturally separate and distinct categories.[110] This underpins, for example, Tacitus's account in *Annales* 15.37 of the notorious "floating" banquet of Nero and Tigillinus[111] on Agrippa's Lake, in which dining on exotic food is accompanied by equally exotic sexual indulgence, involving participants of all social classes, including slaves and gladiators, and culminating in Nero's marriage to Pythagoras.[112] "Satiric nausea" can be used first and foremost to describe the reaction of disgust by the satirist to what he sees and experiences, not only in raw physical terms (stench, violence, disfigurement, and so on) but also in ideological terms, encapsulating the satirist's social queasiness. But, beyond this, in *De Constantia* 10.2, Seneca describes as "the complainings of a nauseated mind" (*querellas nausiantis animi*) those reproaches made from "the sense of humiliation of a spirit hurt by a dishonoring word or deed" (*humilitas animi contrahentis se ob dictum factumve inhonorificum*)—such as not being received or having been placed on the lowest couch. These are central preoccupations of the Juvenalian speaker (generating, for example, most of *Satire* 5, where the dinner guest is humiliated and degraded by the host, who serves him disgusting food and drink all evening). The satirist also attempts to provoke nausea in his reader, primarily by presenting an array of disgusting types, images, and situations. In this context, it is worth noting how Seneca connects nausea with lack of novelty (*Nihil novi facio, nihil novi video; fit aliquando et huius rei nausia* [I do nothing new, see nothing new; sooner or later one sickens of this too])[113] and with satiety (*Epistle* 47.8):

> Adice obsonatores, quibus dominici palati notitia subtilis est, qui
> sciunt, cuius illum rei sapor excitet, cuius delectet aspectus, cuius
> novitate nauseabundus erigi possit, quid iam ipsa satietate fastidiat,
> quid illo die esuriat.

> Think also of the poor purveyors of food, who note their masters'
> tastes with delicate skill, who know what special flavours will
> sharpen their appetite, what will please their eyes, what new

---

110. Oliensis 1998 regards Horace's inability to end his *Epodes* with poem 10 as symptomatic of his "involvement in a civil war that jeopardizes the very distinctions that underwrite closure" and his *fluentem nauseam* (flowing nausea, 35) as a symptom of "the blurring of clear boundaries, corporeal and moral" (91).

111. Or Tigellinus; I have adopted the spelling Tigillinus throughout.

112. See chap. 3 herein.

113. *Epist.* 24.26: *nullius rei finis est, sed in orbem nexa sunt omnia, fugiunt ac secuntur* (There is an end to nothing, but all things are connected in a circle, they flee and are pursued). Also cf. *Epist.* 16.3: [Philosophy is not pursued] so that the nausea that comes from leisure may be relieved (*ut dematur otio nausea*). . . . It sits at the helm and directs the course of those wavering among uncertainties (*sedet ad gubernaculum et per ancipitia fluctuantium derigit cursum*).

combinations will rouse their cloyed stomachs, what food will excite
their loathing through sheer satiety, and what will stir them to
hunger on that particular day.[114]

One thinks here of the role of the satirist in arousing the palate of his readers.
If, as the speaker says in 1.147–49, posterity will add nothing to our ways and
"all vice stands on the edge of the precipice" (*omne in praecipiti vitium stetit*),
then it is his role not only to hoist all the sails and take the reader on a rough
voyage but also, as *obsonator*, to arouse the interest of the bilious viewer by laying before him some enticing new creations. As Paulson observes in *The Fictions of Satire*, at the center of almost every satire there is an image that a reader
cannot easily forget (such as sawing off a head in Waugh's *Decline and Fall*):
"What we remember from a satire is neither character nor plot per se, but a
fantastic image, or a series of them" (9).

We can also use the term "satiric nausea" to describe the full experience
of Juvenalian satire, because it captures both the "floating" quality of the Juvenalian subject—who cannot find any secure anchors—and the disgusting,
stomach-churning individuals and actions that fill the text to overflowing.
Satire in the Juvenalian mode is designedly nauseating, often in the explicitness
of its description of bodies, body parts, and bodily outflows, but also in its
depiction of the lowest kinds of motivation for acts against another person,
whether a relative, a friend, or a complete stranger. In this Juvenal manages
to rival some of Georges Bataille's livelier passages.[115] Satiric nausea is the
queasiness—physical, ideological, and psychic—that arises from such things
as the dizzying changes in position, narrative voice, and genre; the disjunction
between signifier and signified; the repetition of telling words and images;
and the "stuffed to bursting" form of the text, crammed as it is with visual and
aural stimuli. Dustin Griffin, speaking of satire as provocation—via difficulty,
paradox, and the undermining of ideals—says that the ultimate form of this is
to make us look in the mirror wanting to see one of Gulliver's Houyhnhnms
but instead seeing one of his Yahoos.[116]

The lack of fixity and the nausea of which we speak here can be contex-
tualized by viewing them as part of the experience of abjection. With her
memorable image at the start of *Powers of Horror* of the nausea provoked by

114. Trans. Gummere 1917–25.
115. I have in mind his novels *Histoire de l'oeil* (1928) or *Le Bleu du ciel* (1957); for an incisive discussion
in connection with abjection, see Reader 2006, 59–74.
116. Griffin 1994, 55–64, esp. 62.

encountering the skin on the surface of milk, Julia Kristeva designates "food loathing" as the "most elementary and most archaic form of abjection":

> Loathing an item of food, a piece of filth, waste, or dung. The spasms and vomiting that protect me. The repugnance, the retching that thrusts me to the side and turns me away from defilement, sewage, and muck. The shame of compromise, of being in the middle with treachery. The fascinated start that leads me toward and separates me from them.[117]

In Kristeva's analysis, subjectivity never reaches a state of stability or permanence, and what we think of as the subject is, rather, merely the "inside" that is presumed to exist only because it is encompassed by walls, but these turn out to be permeable. Because the walls that might enclose the subject are never actually finished, or sealed, the experience of subjectivity is marked by intense ambivalence, uncertainty, and even paranoia. "We may call it a border; abjection is above all ambiguity," she writes. "Because, while releasing a hold, it does not radically cut the subject off from what threatens it—on the contrary, abjection acknowledges it to be in perpetual danger."[118]

One defensive tactic deployed in response to this threat is the notion of *le corps propre*, "the clean and proper body," which is what we imagine we are referring to in our fantasies of secure selfhood when we speak of "I" or "I myself." Yet, the sense of security that *le corps propre* promises is constantly undermined by the flows that cross its skin—urine, excrement, vomit, blood, semen—and that cause such anxiety.[119] The preoccupation of Juvenalian discourse with food and consumption and with various forms of expulsion and excretion—not only of fluids, but also of noise, anger, and desire—is evidence of its genesis or inspiration in the defensiveness that defines abjection. These flows are emblematic of the linguistic "spilling out" that floods satiric discourse: the piling up of exempla, rhetorical exaggeration, constant allusiveness, metaphorical expansion, changing personae, and narrative fluidity. The abject is also to be found in the fevered language of the text, especially its repeated ellipses

---

117. Kristeva 1982, 2.

118. Kristeva 1982, 9. On paranoia as a vital part of the urban experience, see Coverley 2010, 120.

119. In her discussion of why corporeal waste represents the objective frailty of the symbolic order, Kristeva posits the following: "Excrement and its equivalents (decay, infection, disease, corpse, etc.) stand for the danger to identity that comes from without: the ego threatened by the non-ego, society threatened by its outside, life by death" (71). See Miller 1998 for a study of the "boldily grotesque" in Roman satire from a Bakhtinian perspective.

and exclamations. Kristeva analyzes in detail Céline's graphic novel about the Second World War, *Rigadoon*, to show how it brings the abject to the surface through violence done to the body and a general breakdown of order.[120]

The focus on the skin or outer coating of the body as the site of the drama of abjection can be extended to an unease about borders, boundaries, and lines of distinction in general. Kristeva explains:

> It is thus not lack of cleanliness or health that causes abjection but what disturbs identity, system, order. What does not respect borders, positions, rules. The in-between, the ambiguous, the composite. The traitor, the liar, the criminal with a good conscience, the shameless rapist, the killer who claims he is a savior. . . . Any crime, because it draws attention to the fragility of the law, is abject, but premeditated crime, cunning murder, hypocritical revenge are even more so because they heighten the display of such fragility. . . . Abjection . . . is immoral, sinister, scheming, and shady: a terror that dissembles, a hatred that smiles, a passion that uses the body for barter instead of inflaming it, a debtor who sells you up, a friend who stabs you. (4)

These are precisely the targets of the satirist's greatest hostility: the *delator* (informer), the *corruptor*, the *captator* (legacy hunter), and prize-winning examples of trimmers, hypocrites, dissemblers, and gigolos.[121] An epigram by Martial is comprehensively informative in this context:

> Et delator es et calumniator,
> et fraudator es et negotiator,
> et fellator es et lanista. Miror
> quare non habeas, Vacerra, nummos.

> You're an informer and a slanderer,
> you're a swindler and an operator,
> you're a sucker and a gladiator trainer.
> I wonder, Vacerra, why you don't have any money. (11.66)

---

120. Céline 1997; see the conclusion herein on Martin McDonagh's satirical play *The Lieutenant of Inishmore*. One of McDonagh's purposes is to portray the various forms of noise—of linguistic and bodily violence and ideological confusion—surrounding Irish terrorists.

121. As Richlin 1992 says of Juvenal's targets in *Satire* 1, "What qualifies these figures to be the butt of satire is that they can be perceived as out of kilter, abnormal, and also as potentially harmful and threatening, since they are not just, for example, thieves and murderers but deceitful thieves and murderers. By pointing out these vices in a derisive way the satirist reassures himself and his audience that they themselves are not abnormal or vicious, and are not deceived by those who are" (199).

With all these skills, he should be a rich man. The conjoining of *fellator* with *lanista* will prove helpful when we come to consider in chapter 2 the condemnation of Gracchus for marrying a man and entering the arena as a *retiarius* in *Satire* 2. At the beginning of that piece (11–21), Peribomius, who is openly a *pathicus*, is said to be preferable (*verius ergo / et magis ingenue . . . horum simplicitas*) to those men who feign manliness while doing exactly what he does. Peribomius's Greek name and the obviousness of his "disease" in his face and walk make him less of a threat than those whose hairy arms "promise" an *atrocem animum* but whose "smooth arse" and "swollen figs" give away the truth.[122]

What is so disturbing, then, is the disjunction between appearance and reality. This is the essence of Juvenalian satire, in which the signifiers that claim to anchor the Roman male to the ideological bastions of *Romanitas* turn out in fact to offer no such security at all. All of the satires deal with different manifestations of this false promise, the failure to provide a stable point of reference in a sea of chaos and flux. This is a world in which appearances— whether of individuals, buildings, or even names—and their real content do not match: *frontis nulla fides* (There's no trusting appearances), as *Satire* 2.8 succinctly has it.[123] Lowell Edmunds observes of the main theme in *Satire* 13, "The decay of *fides* in Juvenal's time would have seemed the surest sign of the general decay of Roman institutions."[124] It is because Rome is awash with embodiments of the "sinister, scheming, and shady" that the satirist is so preoccupied with shoring up boundaries and demarcating difference. As Miller puts it:

> Roman satire, through its deployment of the grotesque, privileges by
> negation the closed, the solid, and the unfinished over the open, the
> fluid, and the boundless. . . . On the one hand, the satirist's pose as the
> scold of decadence and the maintainer of boundaries requires that
> such a partition between same and other, masculine and feminine,
> and good and evil be strictly enforced. This is the essence of the

---

122. *hispida membra quidem et durae per bracchia saetae / promittunt atrocem animum, sed podice levi / caeduntur tumidae medico ridente mariscae.* The resonances of this passage are numerous; see the discussion of *Satire* 2 in chap. 2 herein. Keane 2006 notes that the "smiling doctor" is the satirist himself, discovering the truth and relishing the infliction of pain (64). See also Konstan 1993.

123. The word *frons*, meaning forehead or countenance, also refers to the façade of a building, and in *Sat.* 2.1–10 the speaker condemns the "Curios who live like Bacchanals" not only for displaying a manly appearance while acting as *cinaedi*, but also for filling their houses with busts of Chrysippus and other philosophers to give an impression of respectable seriousness. A similar thought about the deceptive potential of busts in the *atrium* is expressed in 8.19–20. See chaps. 2 and 4 herein.

124. Edmunds 1972, 61.

ideology of the bounded form. On the other, the binary logic of the partition itself creates a kind of structural desire for the excluded, without which the boundary, and hence the satirist, could not exist.[125]

The speaker in this kind of satire tries to "build walls" to enclose the subject and to enable a recovery of the "clean and proper" body, and he does so by mapping his anxieties onto the physical geography of Rome. Consequently, it is the holes and gaps, the fissures and leaks in the urban fabric that are foregrounded in the satirical cityscape.[126] The satirist, text, body, and city are thus locked in a four-angled relationship, so that each one of these four elements always points to the other three. We as readers are in the position of the speaker *in quadrivio*, with a simultaneous view down four lively streets.

Porosity denotes a lack of clear boundaries—between public and private, sacred and profane, old and new—and the concomitant anarchy of social intermingling. Interpenetration and instability are the lynchpins of Juvenalian discourse, which itself spills out all over text, body, and city. Critics have noted the porosity that exists between Benjamin's texts and the urban complex he attempts to represent:

> The metropolitan environment itself comes to offer a model of innovative textual practices, a radical, vital literary architectonics. With its abrupt, often bewildering captions pilfered from the semiological cityscape, its profusion of startling signs and distracting images . . . imbued with that sense of disorientation, transience and shock . . . The text becomes "city-like" just as the city becomes a "linguistic cosmos," a text.[127]

When, for Naples, he establishes porosity as the "inexhaustible law of the life of this city, reappearing everywhere," Benjamin could equally well be speaking of the Rome presented by Juvenal in his satires.[128]

The Rome that is created in Juvenalian satire draws our attention not to its "wholeness" or to its "wholesomeness," but to places of ambiguous status, and

---

125. Miller 1998, 411.

126. There is a general movement from public to private space as the Juvenalian corpus proceeds, and the focus shifts from outside space in *Satires* 1–4 to inside space in 9–14, perhaps paralleling a more "inward-looking" tone that some have detected in the later books; but by 15 and 16, we are back outside in the public realm, so any such divisions within the collection should not be pressed very far.

127. Gilloch 2002, cf. 101. Schlegel 2005, in chap. 3, views Horace's body in *Sat.* 1.5 as "the satiric substitute for Rome, the body politic. As this journey takes its toll on Horace's body, so do too Octavian and Antony wear down Rome."

128. Gilloch 1996, 25; Benjamin 1985, 171.

to what we might term "liminal zones." It is in these zones, in fact—where the fluidity of boundaries is most acutely experienced—that the satiric speaker is to be found on most occasions. Estranged and isolated amid the swirling populace of the city, the satirist shares some features with Poe's "man of the crowd" who is no longer at home in the urban environment, in the way that his predecessor Horace perhaps still was.[129] The central scene of *Satire* 1 (95–126), describing the *sportula* (the daily handout distributed by a wealthy patron to his entourage of hangers-on or, in Roman terms, clients),[130] positions the speaker on the *limen*, where "the Trojan-blooded nobles crowd the doorway" along with the rest (*ipsos Troiugenas, nam vexant limen et ipsi / nobiscum*, 100–101). On the edge, without a share in the distribution: this is a foundational image of self-abjection in Juvenal's Rome.[131]

It is instructive to compare where Horace positions himself: in *Satire* 2.6.16, on what Ellen Oliensis calls "the safe heights (social as well as geographical)" of his mountain citadel—*Ergo ubi me in montes et in arcem ex urbe removi* (So, now that I have taken myself onto the hills and into my citadel away from the city)—or later in the same poem on the Esquiline or at the *limen* of Maecenas (31–58), which *he* will be invited to cross.[132] Oliensis observes that Horatian satire "publishes and promotes the poet's own progress from the obscure margins to the shining center of Roman society";[133] Juvenal moves in the contrary direction. Picture him in the squalid recital room lent by a mean patron, who himself pens verses (7.39–42):

> . . . tu si dulcedine famae
> succensus recites, maculosas commodat aedes.
> Haec longe ferrata domus servire iubetur
> in qua sollicitas imitatur ianua porcas.

> . . . If you, fired by the sweet allure of fame,
> give a recitation, he lends you a squalid house.

---

129. Cf. Coverley 2010, 60, 64.

130. This begins at the middle of the poem proper—about halfway between lines 22 and 171—and functions as its central episode: see Larmour 2004, 65–67. The *sportula* reappears in 3.249, 10.45–46, and 13.31–34.

131. On the solemn aspects of the *limen*, with ref. to *Epode* 2.8, see L. Watson 2003, citing Meister 1924–25, 222.

132. Oliensis 1998; she notes that Horace moves from a "relative nobody" in *Satire* 1 to this position and sees a transition in *Satire* 1.6, which recounts a day of aimless rambling, "free of parasitism" and yet marks the beginning of his bonds of *amicitia* with Maecenas (46–48). It is worth noting that Martial in the epigraph above does not picture Juvenal on the fashionable Esquiline (12.18.1–6).

133. Oliensis 1998, 17; cf. Zetzel 1980; and Gowers 2012 on Maecenas and Horace "united in their splendid isolation from the rest of humanity" (59) in *Sat.* 1.1.

This far-off building, he will order to be put at your disposal,
barricaded with a door that sounds like squealing sows.[134]

As Donka Markus observes, "The rented hall is so remote and so inaccessi-
ble that it resembles a beleaguered city and, instead of inviting its audience,
shuts it out. . . . By assigning a liminal setting to the fictional performance, Juvenal points by means of contrast to the ideal setting of a dignified *recitatio*,
namely a prestigious audience and social visibility."[135] In the same poem (82–
90), Juvenal ridicules Statius for his captivating readings from the *Thebaid* but
having to sell pantomime scripts to the likes of Paris in order not to go hungry
(*quod non dant proceres, dabit histrio*, 90). Statius in the *Silvae*, however, presents himself as performing in rather more dignified and elevated settings,
ranging from contests like the Augustalia in Naples or the Capitoline Festival
in Rome—even one held at Domitian's residence in Alba Longa—to venerable
Greek settings such as Olympia or the *vocales lucos Boeotaque tempe*.[136]

The Arena of Satire

In Juvenalian satire, the Grand Narratives upon which the idea of Roman society is built, such as the foundation myth of the *Aeneid* and the progress of History and Destiny narrated by Livy's *Ab urbe condita*, are subjected to a critical
reading of a kind that Horace would not have wanted to perform. The city of
Rome—the hub of the Empire—and its most centrally located and centrally important monuments are here refracted through a liminal lens. To explore this
refraction, several key passages from the *Satires* of Juvenal will be read here
through one of the central locations of Roman cultural display and self-
validation, which reached its apex in the days of this particular poet: the arena.
There are already numerous references to gladiators and *spectacula* in Lucilius
and Horace, the latter of whom makes some very telling associations between
poetry and the arena. Statius in *Silvae* 5.3.215–27, expatiates on the *munus* of
poetic skill received from his father who is a spectator (*felixque tui spectator
adesses / muneris*, 216–17),[137] as well as an *editor* of the show. Seneca provides ample
evidence for the incorporation of the arena and the gladiator into the moral and

---

134. Reading *porcas* with Jessen 1900; Ferguson 1979; Braund 1988, 215n93; and Braund 2004. Courtney 1980 prefers *portas*.

135. Markus 2000, 152–53. See also Roche 2012.

136. Markus 2000, 163–68, 172–73; *Silv.* 3.5.28–29, 4.2.65, 5.3.215–33; and Gibson 2006, 351–53.

137. An echo of Turnus's words in *Aen.* 10.443 before his combat with Pallas; see Gibson 2006,
348–49.

philosophical discourse with which Juvenal was undoubtedly familiar. Seneca finds it possible to present the gladiator as the embodiment of Roman *virtus* and as a source of inspiration for the young man seeking to set his life upon the right course:[138]

> Eadem honestissimi huius et illius turpissimi auctoramenti verba sunt: "uri, vinciri ferroque necari." Ab illis, qui manus harenae locant et edunt ac bibunt, quae per sanguinem reddant, cavetur, ut ista vel inviti patiantur; a te, ut volens libensque patiaris. Illis licet arma summittere, misericordiam populi temptare; tu neque summittes nec vitam rogabis. Recto tibi invictoque moriendum est. Quid porro prodest paucos dies aut annos lucrificare? Sine missione nascimur.

> The words of this most honorable oath are the same as those of that most disgraceful one, namely: "to be burned, to be chained, and to be killed by the sword."[139] From those men, who hire their hands to the arena, who eat and drink what they will pay for with their blood, security is taken that they will endure such things even though they are unwilling; from you, that you will endure them willingly and gladly. They are permitted to lower their weapons and test the pity of the people; you will neither lower your weapons nor beg for your life. You must die standing straight and unconquered. What profit is it anyway to gain a few days or years? We are born without any possibility of reprieve. (*Epistle* 37.1–2)

Juvenal finds the arena similarly inspiring for his literary project, and I shall suggest that he, faced with new social circumstances and examples of vice to work with, set out to reformulate this old relationship. He could no doubt see its potential to convey the focal points of his vision. The *panem et circenses* aphorism is, after all, his—a succinct summing-up that can only have emerged from a consciousness with a capacious understanding of the phenomenon. He creates his own "arena of satire" by expanding upon the nexus of ideas he found in both his predecessors in the genre and other imperial authors. His imagery of the arena is provocatively multivalent. Following up on Horace's appropriation of arena language, flotsam and jetsam, for literary purposes, Juvenal exploits all the complexities of the now fully developed arena culture. Juvenal knows the arena is a paradoxical space: the epitome of power and solidity, a locus of separation and hierarchy where difference is carved out on the body, it

138. Dunkle 2008, 38.
139. See chap. 3 herein for further discussion.

is simultaneously a locus of ambiguity and collusion. We shall examine the cases of Gracchus the "noble" *retiarius* (*Satires* 2 and 8) and Eppia the respectable *matrona* turned *ludia* (*Satire* 6) in detail, as well as Domitian's multiple arenas in *Satire* 4. Juvenal's arena of satire is also a literary space that, like the Colosseum, strives for three things: entertainment, consolidation, and intimidation, all of which may be subsumed under the heading of "strategies of containment." In both cases, however, the circle of containment is constantly breached: just as a divided and floating subjectivity defined the arena experience for the imperial spectators, so the attempts of Juvenalian discourse to contain ambiguity and disorder are undermined by the linguistic "spilling out" and the holes, fissures, and aporias that it reveals in the process.

Satire 1, as we are about to see, takes us on a journey from the wide-open Lucilian battlefield to the confines of the Horatian arena and thence to Juvenal's own "arena of satire," in which we are invited to be spectators not only of the exotic fauna of Rome and the products of the Empire but of the satirist himself. The greater the degree of fascination with the spectacle, of course, the greater the danger that the categories of difference upon which it relies will disintegrate and, with it, constructions of the self.[140] For the fascinated, all categories dissolve, including those by which he or she defines the self. At the end of his programmatic statement in *Satire* 1, he makes much of the claim that a Lucilian approach, directly attacking contemporaries, now results in becoming a victim burned in the arena on the command of the emperor, the *editor* who gave spectacles and *munera* and had the final say on the outcomes of fights. So Juvenal's solution is to claim this role for himself: he becomes the maker of spectacles, of fights, disputes, encounters that he brings before us for entertainment. His books of satires are in this sense his *munera*.[141] It is quite understandable in such a context why Varro posits a connection between *munus* and *moenia* in his etymological discussion: *moenia* (walls) were so named because they *muniebant* (fortified) the towns through work (*opus*), and a wall (*moerus*) supported what they heaped up (*exaggerabant*); because carrying was done for the sake of fortifying (*muniendi*), the work was a *munus* (duty) and because they enclosed the town by this *moenus*, it was a *moerus* (wall). Fortifying the city by means of walls is a common duty, he says, and *municipes* are so called because they perform this task.[142]

---

140. On fascination, see Barton 1993, 85–106.

141. For the book as *munus*, cf. Hor. *Ode* 1.18.7 (*at ne quis modici transiliat munera liberi*); 2.1.11 (*grande munus*, of Pollio's history of the Civil Wars); Mart. 3.2.1. Conversely, the *libellus gladiatorum* was a "form book" for enthusiastic fans (Fagan 2011, 210–14).

142. Varro *LL* 5.141, 5.179; Collart 1954, 235. On *munus*, see Ville 1981, 72–78; Edmondson 1996, n1.

As will become clear in the chapters hereafter, one of Juvenalian satire's most striking achievements is a novel incorporation of the satirist, the reader, and the text into the arena, by bringing the positions of *auctor, editor, gladiator,* and *spectator* into close and suggestive proximity. In the reading offered here, the arena is the ultimate urban meeting place, the site of confluence of city, body, and text, toward which the satirist-flâneur is always tending. Our satirist *in quadrivio* is also the satirist *ad harenam.*

1

Satires from the Edge

> Poets are not, as officious mythology would have it, sons of Apollo,
> but of Marysas. In his death cry they hear their own name. . . . Thus
> even to the writer, perhaps to him more than others, silence is a
> temptation, a refuge when Apollo is near.
> —George Steiner, "Silence and the Poet," 38–39

Given the parrhesiastic claims of satire in general, and the foundation of
Roman satire in Lucilius's celebrated *libertas* (roughly, "free speech" or "outspokenness") in particular, it is no surprise that the first theme to announce itself
in Juvenal's poetry should be the tension between speech and silence, especially
with regard to the satirist who addresses his reader and compatriots. Roman
satire's central preoccupation is subjectivity, and especially how the male citizen speaks and what restrictions are placed upon his speaking.[1] As Allen Miller
has recently observed, satire "is the most Roman of genres because it is the form
whose subject is *libertas*. . . . The subject of satire is both the form's subject
matter and the speaking subject who is empowered to forge this hash of humorous observations, personal reproof, and grotesque degradation. . . . *Satura*
is wholly Roman, then, because its evolution is inseparable from the intertwined
political, aesthetic, and legal issues that define what it means to be *civis Romanus*

---

1. On *libertas*, see Wirszubski 1950, esp. chaps. 1, 4, and 5; Arena 2012, chap. 1. For a good discussion of
Hor. *Sat.* 1.4, see Gowers 2012, 147–52, 154–55.

[a Roman citizen].[2] As Thomas Habinek puts it, elaborating Quintilian's dictum, "We are the best at satire, but also, there is no 'we' without satire."[3] It is Juvenal, writing furthest into the imperial era, who gives the dilemma between speaking and not speaking its most extended treatment. The series of questions at the beginning of the collection reminds us that satire is concerned not so much with *What is to be done?* as with *Who is to speak?* (1.1–14):[4]

Semper ego auditor tantum? Numquamne reponam
vexatus totiens rauci Theseide Cordi?
Inpune ergo mihi recitaverit ille togatas,
hic elegos? Inpune diem consumpserit ingens
Telephus aut summi plena iam margine libri
scriptus et in tergo necdum finitus Orestes?
Nota magis nulli domus est sua quam mihi lucus
Martis et Aeoliis vicinum rupibus antrum
Vulcani; quid agant venti, quas torqueat umbras
Aeacus, unde alius furtivae devehat aurum
pelliculae, quantas iaculetur Monychus ornos,
Frontonis platani convolsaque marmora clamant
semper et adsiduo ruptae lectore columnae.
Expectes eadem a summo minimoque poeta.

Must I always be only a listener? Am I never to pay back
for being harassed so many times by the *Theseid* of raucous Cordus?
With impunity then shall this one here have declaimed his plays at me,
that one his elegies? With impunity shall that huge *Telephus* have
    taken up
the whole day, or an *Orestes* that fills even the margins of a big book
    and
still isn't finished even when it is written on the back cover?
No man's house is more familiar to him than that Grove of Mars
is to me, or Vulcan's Cave near the Aeolian Rocks;
what the winds are up to, which shades Aeacus torments,
whence that other one carries off the gold of a stolen fleecelet,
how big the ash trees hurled by Monychus are—

2. Miller, 2005: as he has it in his headings, *Satura nos est* and *Satura est nostra libertas* (4, 7, 14). On politics and invective, see Roller 2012.

3. Habinek 2005b, 116.

4. Cf. Horace's opening to *Satire* 1.1: *Qui fit, Maecenas . . . ?*; Gold 1992.

endlessly the plane trees and the quaking marble statues at Fronto's
    house
cry out, and the columns shattered by the unrelenting reader.
You can expect the same things from the best and the worst poet
    alike.[5]

Juvenalian satire provokes confusion in the reader from the very beginning.
Who is this shouting at us, and what does he want? Four questions follow upon
each other in six lines, gradually getting longer and more involved, presaging
how the discourse of this particular speaker seeks to close off the possibility of
response and to silence the listener, in exactly the same way that he complains
of being silenced by Cordus and the other declaimers of epics and tragedies.
So, from the moment he opens his mouth, the satirist is marked by many of
the features he imputes to those he is attacking. This is a very important realization, for it locates the satirist firmly *within* the realm he is describing from
his self-consciously marginalized subject position. His outburst occurs against
a background of noise—the verbal, literary, and ideological noise of Rome—to
which it contributes, even as it struggles to be heard in contradistinction to it.
As we shall see, for all its vehemence in setting up targets to assail, and in striving to reassert difference through such attacks, Juvenalian satire is not simply
lashing out in reactionary panic like England's *Daily Mail* or America's Fox
News; this is a discourse that, in spite of itself, ends up provoking as many questions as it answers.

   Immediately after the first question, the theme of punishment appears
(*numquamne reponam vexatus totiens . . . inpune . . . inpune*) and is then picked
up in the allusion to Orestes (the last word of line 6 and the finale of the quar-
tet of questions), who is the ultimate tragic avenger of wrongdoing.[6] The speaker
is as much concerned with taking vengeance upon poets like Cordus as he is
with breaking free of his own speechlessness; in fact, the two are synonymous.
Giving reciters some of their own medicine was no doubt a topos.[7] Horace, in
Epistle 1.19.35–40, a passage Juvenal may well have had in mind,[8] distances himself from those who take revenge on other poets by reciting themselves:

   5. On echoes of Martial, see Colton 1991, 17–19.
   6. Mentioned in more detail in 8.216–17, see p. 59. Cf. Lucil. 19.594 on another hoarse Orestes.
The only time *impune* reappears is in the summation of Domitian's murders: *inpune et vindice nullo*
(4.152).
   7. On recitation (especially of epic), see Markus 2000; discussing Pers. 1.19–21, she notes the emascu-
lating effects of passively submitting to the allurements of the reciter's voice (157).
   8. With *vexatus*, cf. *Epist.* 2.2.90: *qui minus argutos vexat furor iste poetas?* For other echoes of the
Epistles in *Satire* 1, see pp. 97–99; 1.3–4 echoes *Epist.* 2.2.91 (see Brink 1982, 319); 7.193–94 reworks *Epist.*

Scire velis, mea cur ingratus opuscula lector
laudet ametque domi, premat extra limen iniquus:
non ego ventosae plebis suffragia venor
impensis cenarum et tritae munere vestis;
non ego, nobilium scriptorum auditor et ultor,
grammaticas ambire tribus et pulpita dignor.

You want to know why the ungrateful reader praises and loves
my little pieces at home, but criticizes them unfairly beyond the
    threshold?
I am not one who hunts for the votes of the fickle public
by standing dinners and by donating worn-out clothes;
I am not one who, a listener to noble writers and a requiter,
deigns to go around courting the tribes of professors and their
    platforms.[9]

In this, as in many other areas, Juvenal would appear to have but little respect for his predecessor's reserve, even if he reworks many of his motifs and
themes. In Horace's *Satire* 1.4, which may be regarded as his own programmatic
statement in the genre, he contrasts himself with the long-winded Crispinus
and Fannius and says that he recites only when he has to and then to his
friends, "not just anywhere and in front of no matter whom." He further distinguishes himself from the "empty-headed" who like to recite in the middle
of the Forum or at the baths because the enclosed space produces an echo
(73–76).[10] In *Satire* 1.3, a discussion about the need to differentiate among
crimes and to exercise moderation in punishment is introduced via Tigellius,
a singer who would not sing when his friends asked him to but would not stop
singing if unasked.[11] Martial has an epigram in which he depicts himself as
harassed by the reciting Ligurinus, around whom "there is flight" (*fuga est*, 2)
and who pursues the author as he seeks refuge in various locations, such as
the baths and at the dinner table (3.44). Listening to other poets recite, in

---

1.1.106–108 (see Braund 2004, 314–15). Other echoes have been noted, e.g., between Juv. 15.63 and *Epist.*
2.1.25–51 (Keane 2006, 70); Juv. 5 and *Epist.* 1.17–18 (Morford 1977, 226–28).

9. The translation of *ultor* as "requiter" (of recitations endured) is one option, based on the meaning of
ulciscor, while "avenger" (of the attacks launched against poets in 35–36) is another (see Mayer 1994, 267).

10. Cf. 1.4.22–25 for similar reluctance to recite; also, in 65–67, Sulcius and Caprius, "awfully hoarse
with their little books" (*rauci male cumque libellis*), walk the streets, "each a great terror to robbers"; they may
be satiric poets, who, unlike Horace, are concerned with publicity (see Ullman 1917, Gowers 2012, *ad loc.*).

11. At the end of the *Ars Poetica*, the mad poet becomes the *recitator acerbus*, scattering everyone, like a
bear breaking out of its cage: "If he catches someone, he holds him fast and kills him by reading, a leech that
will not let go of the skin until filled with blood" (475–76).

other words, motivates a poetic journey as an attempt to escape from, as well as to respond to, what the satirist hears.[12]

But the Juvenalian *auditor* fits into a much larger category of the satirist as *ultor*, or punisher.[13] For him, it is a short step from punishing other poets to punishing people in general. Indeed one of the satirist's main roles is to "make an example" of his targets, both literally—by including them in his lists of miscreants—and metaphorically—by chastising them with his rhetorical whippings.[14] In *Epistle* 2.2.124, speaking of the exertion concealed by the player in a pantomime (*ludentis speciem dabit et torquebitur*), Horace speaks of the torture in achieving art that conceals art; here the torturing (of others and of language) *is* the art (of satire).[15] The satirist produces a textual Triumph, a procession of "captured" enemies, whose crimes and punishments are vividly enacted for the pleasure of the reader.[16] Here the image of Aeacus "torturing the shades (*umbras*)" in 10–11 telegraphs exactly what the satirist will set out to do in the last two lines of the poem: "I will attempt what may be permitted against those whose ashes are covered by the Flaminian and Latin roads" (*experiar quod concedatur in illos / quorum Flaminia tegitur cinis atque Latina*, 170–71). Since, as we shall see, he decides that it is too dangerous to attack the living by name, the satirist will judge the "shades"—in this case a parade of deceased Romans—and mete out appropriate punishment.[17] This establishes a link between Rome and the Underworld that is exploited at various points hereafter, especially in the vision of the shocked shades of the Republic meeting dissolute recent arrivals at the end of *Satire* 2 and the departure of the speaker's old friend Umbricius ("the shadowy one") for Cumae, the location of the entrance to Hades in Roman myth, at the beginning of *Satire* 3.[18] Safer as it may be to direct barbs

12. As Gowers 2012 says of Horace's *Satire* 1, "The chief bogeys of the book are not sinners but talkers—long-winded street philosophers, divas, malicious gossips, quacks, litigants and loud-mouthed salesmen" (14).

13. Other uses of *ultor* include 8.216 (of Orestes) and 10.165 (Hannibal's ring containing poison, the "avenger of Cannae"). The vengeance-taking aspects of satire are well known; see Kernan 1959; R. C. Elliott 1960; Paulson 1967; Richlin 1992, 197–200.

14. Cf. Nemesis, goddess of justice and righteous indignation, whose role was to punish violations of Roman order, found in arenas: Hornum 1993; Kyle 1998, 100; chap. 3 herein.

15. Cf. Brink 1982, 345–47.

16. Ostenberg 2009 on the performances of war tableaux: "Crime and punishment were the two main components in the triumphal display of captured enemies. . . . By staging the misdeeds performed by the principal enemies in war, the scenes identified and explained their crimes against Rome that had also brought about their punishment—triumphal presence and death. . . . The scenes compensated for what the triumphal procession lacked due to the absence of the captives themselves: the display of their final subjection and punishment" (260–61).

17. On recovery and uncovering the horrors of the recent past, see Freudenburg's (2001) excursus on "ghost-assault" and the "indignation industry" (215–42).

18. On the name's connections with *umbra*, a word with numerous meanings including shadow, shade, and ghost, see Braund 1996a, 177, 231–32. There is also a suggestion of poetic *umbra*.

at those in the past who cannot answer back, this is, of course, a periphrastic attack on the present, as any reader of Mikhail Bulgakov's *The Master and Margarita* or Russian satire in general will readily appreciate. Juvenal plays with the permeability of the boundary to great effect. As Courtney observes, "In fact he often speaks of the dead as if they were still alive" and, one might add, of the living as if they are already dead (119).[19]

The satirist's role as punisher is subtly expanded by the mention of Orestes in 6 and of Monychus hurling ash trees in 11.[20] These two figures (each placed at the end of their respective lists) also alert us to the satirist's preoccupation with the violation of established gender roles. Orestes killed the dangerously "masculine" Clytemnestra, and when Juvenal mentions him again in *Satire* 8.216–17, he offers a comparatively positive characterization (as a counterexample to Nero, who, by killing his mother, committed the same crime but for a different motive): *quippe ille deis auctoribus ultor / patris erat caesi media inter pocula* (The fact is he was, by the authority of the gods, the avenger of his father, who was murdered among his cups).[21] In Ovid's *Metamorphoses*, Monychus was the centaur who roused his cowed companions to destroy Caenis/ Caeneus—the celebrated transsexual warrior of Greek myth—by wielding suitably phallic tree trunks.[22] A figure rescued from his relative obscurity in myth (the name "One-Hoof" may have been invented by Ovid), Monychus's violent attack on a "hybrid" forms a doublet with Aeacus's torturing the dead to encapsulate the speaker's own program.[23] It is not much of a leap for the reader to imagine the satirist as an Orestes or a Monychus, assailing contemporary incarnations of hybridity (nouveaux riches, foreigners living in Rome, and, above all, "feminine" males and "masculine" females) and, if they cannot

---

19. In *Sat.* 3, Umbricius heads to Cumae—the traditional gateway to the Underworld—in search of a more authentically Roman lifestyle, and the poem plays upon notions of Rome as a doomed or destroyed Troy and as a realm of the dead.

20. See Henderson 1999, 263–64 and 266–67 for detailed analysis and the "Ovid-Lucan-Valerius Flaccus-Juvenal" line of influence; Larmour 2004, 60–61.

21. In 6.655, the culmination of women's murderous behavior is reached when there is "a Clytemnestra in every street" (*Clytemnestram nullus non vicus habebit*). By contrast, in Pers. 3.118, Orestes is cited, in the final line of the satire, as the representative of madness: *nec sanus . . . Orestes*. Aul. Gell. 13.4.1 mentions Varro's *Orestes vel de Insania* (*Orestes, or On Insanity*). Hor. *Sat.* 2.3.133: was he *demens* when he killed his mother, or did he go mad afterward? He did nothing reprehensible from the moment he was considered mad, opines Damasippus, in his speech on the Stoic doctrine that all except the wise man are mad (134–41). See Muecke 1993, 146–47.

22. Monychus: for the story of Caenis/Caeneus, see Gantz 1993, 278, 280–81; Ov. *Met.* 12.498–509; Larmour 2004, 60–61.

23. Henderson 1999, 267 and n46. He observes how Monychus's ash trees "hurtle all the way from Ovid's writing through Lucan to Valerius and into Juvenal's next verse . . . to cruise between the plane-trees and damage the recitation-hall, as once they 'tore' and 'smote' the Lapith foe" (264).

be "speared" or "blooded," attempting to "bury" or "suffocate" them, to take away their voice and breath under the barrage of his rhetorical missiles.[24]

Hurling missiles and vituperative forms of verse are naturally associated: *iambus* was thought to derive from *iapto* (throw), and so in Horace's *Epode* 17.10 the verses he now regrets having aimed at Canidia are analogous to the "sharp weapons" that Telephus hurled at Achilles (*tela acuta torserat*).[25] There is a metapoetic coloring to Juvenal's use of *torqueo* with reference to Aeacus's torturing the shades (in 6.449–50, the female scholar "brandishes her speech and hurls—*torqueat*—a rounded syllogism").[26] By contrast, the words ending lines 7–9 (*lucus, antrum, umbras*) conjure up, amid the noise and the storm, a fleeting image of the rural peace and quiet that poets are often said to seek or need, as in *Epistle* 2.2.77–78: *scriptorum chorus omnis amat nemus et fugit urbem, / rite cliens Bacchi somno gaudentis et umbra* (The whole chorus of poets loves the grove and flees the city, duly clients of Bacchus who enjoys sleep and shade).[27]

What is especially interesting here is the way in which punishing satire is connected with traveling and the quest, and, beyond that, with open-endedness and lack of closure. The first mythological allusion in the poem is to Theseus, recalling his clearing the road to Athens of monsters but also the labyrinth (1.2). In spite of Theseus's success in killing the Minotaur and escaping, the labyrinth retains its power here as a symbol of endless wandering, partly because Cordus's poem has been going on for so long amid other interminable works on mythological subjects. The winds of Aeolus allude to storm scenes in epic, such as in the *Odyssey* or the *Aeneid*, which tend to blow the hero off course and prolong his journey, while Aeacus recalls an Underworld *katabasis*, which usually comes in the middle of a hero's progress. The

24. Cic. *De Orat.* 2.316, throwing a spear and rhetoric. Richlin 1997, 99 on effeminacy and social inferiority as analogous categories in oratorical performance; Markus 2000, 161–62.

25. Thus L. Watson 2003, 547–48; also 125 of satire as iambic's "kindred genre." See also Brink 1982 on *Epist.* 2.2.127 (*torquet ab obscaenis iam nunc sermonibus aurem*), who notes that the verb is applied to speech as early as *Ad Her.* 3.25 (168).

26. 6.449–50: . . . *aut curvum sermone rotato / torqueat enthymema*; see Courtney 1980, 320. Juv. 14.57–58 uses *ventosus* of a cupping-glass (*ventosa cucurbita*) used to relieve madness by drawing blood from the head, in this case from one empty of brains (*vacuumque cerebro*). The winds (*venti*) perhaps recall Horace's dismissal in *Epist.* 1.19.37 of seeking the votes of the *ventosa plebs*, the "fickle" or "changeable" mob; Horace's ideal reader, and one suspects Juvenal's too, is *ingenuus* as opposed to one of the plebs (*Epist.* 1.19.34; cf. *Sat.* 1.10.78–91). *Ventilare* is used of "shadow-boxing" or play fighting by Sen. Eld. *Controv.* 3 Praef. 13: *totum aliud est pugnare, aliud ventilare*, in comparing the rhetoric school to the arena; cf. Juv. 1.28 of Crispinus waving his ring and of the speaker's toga wafting him around Rome (12.18.5).

27. In *Satire* 7, his "second" programmatic piece, Juvenal notes that the "outstanding bard" (*vates egregius*) is the product of a mind "free from worry and all bitterness" that "longs for the woods" (*cupidus silvarum*; 53–58).

belittling characterization of Jason as *alius* undercuts the grand object of his particular quest, now just for "the gold of a stolen fleecelet."[28] The overall effect of these allusions, then, is to create an impression of long, drawn-out, perhaps interminable, wanderings with no attainment of the original aim of the journey. In this regard, the fact that the Orestes story is unfinished "even when it is written on the back cover" is suggestive: it implies that the avenging hero never gets to complete his task or reach the cure for madness or be vindicated for the dispensing of justice.

The mythological caves, winds, and torturings in lines 7–10 reinforce the opening themes of noise (*antrum / Vulcani; quid agant venti*) and violent revenge or punishment (*quas torqueat umbras / Aeacus*). The four indirect questions relating to the content of these well-worn stories in lines 9–12—all vividly relayed to us in the present tense—parallel the four direct questions in 1–6 about the ranting poets who compose them. Meanwhile, the plane trees and statues of Fronto's house continually cry out in pain (*clamant / semper*), as its columns are shattered by the "unrelenting reader" (*adsiduo . . . lectore*).[29] The *semper* of line 13 echoes the first word of the poem, *adsiduo lectore* picks up *rauci Cordi*, and the *vexatus auditor* is paralleled by the *convolsa marmora* and *ruptae columnae*, so that listener and location are fused as victims of poetic noise.[30] Just how unrelenting the barrage is we can appreciate from the single eight-line sentence that extends over lines 7–13. We might expect the *domus*, a place of private retreat, to be at least relatively free from noise, but the image of Fronto's reverberating garden and pulsating peristyle puts paid to that hope of quietude. Here Juvenal again seems to be striking a contrast with Horace's programmatic satire, in which the poet presents himself as quietly (*compressis . . . labris*, lips sealed) reflecting on his and others' behavior, while reclining on his study couch or strolling in his colonnade (*cum lectulus aut me / porticus excepit*, 1.4.133–34). Juvenal's concluding observation that you may expect to hear the same stuff from the greatest and the least of poets is not simply a throwaway line, contrary to the opinion of those who wish to delete it. A similar formulation appears in 6.349—*iamque eadem summis pariter minimisque libido* (Nowadays the greatest and the lowest of women alike have the same lust)—and the purpose is to introduce the theme of the confusion of categories.[31] It represents the oxymoronic

28. The formulation also makes the gold the focal point, which fits in with Juvenal's generally critical remarks about the acquisition of money and wealth.

29. Cf. Uden 2015, 25–29 on Fronto; Spencer 2010, 27–30, 130–33 on plane trees.

30. Courtney 1980, *ad loc.* notes that *convolsa* and *rupta* are "technical medical terms for strained limbs," linked by Plin. Eld. *HN* 20.36, 22.79, 28.140.

31. On the text, see Courtney 1980, Braund 1996a, *ad loc.*

collapse of all hierarchies in the moment of their assertion. From the intermingling of the best and worst poets, thanks to a lapse in standards of judgment and criticism by those who should know better—or in fact do—the speaker expands his scope to the confusion of categories throughout Roman society.[32]

We should consider here the significance of the reference to Telephus, whose story has two basic components: his silence and his wound. This hero's reputation for maintaining silence with unusual dedication creates an ironic contrast with the voluminous daylong play about him in Juvenal's opening lines. If Telephus's lengthy silence was connected with expiation of guilt or punishment for murder, as some sources suggest, then the irony is all the more palpable when the satirist breaks *his* silence, after listening to a long *Telephus*, to attack the criminals he sees around him. We noted above how the speech/silence dichotomy is combined in Juvenal's opening verses with the language of injury and retaliation; this too is echoed in the Telephus allusion, since in the *Cypria* he killed Thersander but was in the process himself incurably wounded by Achilles (grandson of Aeacus, as Juvenal notes in 8.270).[33] Telephus was a very popular figure among the Roman poets Juvenal knew well, who exploited the intriguing detail that the hero could only be cured by the weapon that had wounded him in the first place.[34] As noted above, in his final epode, Horace deploys Telephus as the first allusion in his palinodic recantation of his attacks on Canidia: *movit nepotem Telephus Nereium, / in quem superbus ordinarat agmina / Mysorum et in quem tela acuta torserat* (Telephus moved Nereus's grandson, against whom he had defiantly drawn up the ranks of the Mysians and against whom he had hurled his pointed weapons, 17.8–10).[35]

In many such cases, Telephus occupies a prominent position among a given poet's mythological allusions—as first or final exemplum, in a preface, or deployed to turn the poem in a new direction—and Juvenal may have imitated this by mentioning Telephus in his fifth line.[36] When Propertius, for

---

32. Markus 2000 notes how "the recital of poetry became an integral part of a system of social networking, deeply embedded in the economy of the exchange of favors" (147).

33. See Gantz 1993, 428–31, 576–79. Apollodorus states that he was advised by Apollo that his wound could only be cured by the one who caused it, and, after promising to show the Greeks the way to Troy, he was duly healed by Achilles (*Epit.* 3.20).

34. Even Pliny the Elder discusses how Achilles cured him, either with a plant called *achilleos* or with copper rust "wherefore he is shown in paintings scraping it with his sword from the tip of his spear onto the wound of Telephus" (*HN* 25.19.42).

35. L. Watson 2003 comments that Horace's words "insinuate that Telephus' attack was unwarranted, when in fact he was defending his kingdom" and that "the disparity between Telephus' quondam and subsequent condition was a feature of tragic accounts" (547). For the Euripdean version, see Handley-Rea 1957.

36. Larmour 2004, 68–71, for further details.

example, uses Telephus in a preface, in the opening poem of his second book of elegies, the exemplum has particular point, because the paradoxical connection between wounding and curing in the spear of Achilles can be assimilated to the experience of love. In 2.1.63–64, after stating that "only love does not love the doctor of its disease" (*solus amor morbi non amat artificem*, 57), he cites a number of famous mythological curings, culminating with that of Telephus by Achilles: *Mysus et Haemonia iuvenis qua cuspide vulnus / senserat, hac ipsa cuspide sensit opem* (And the Mysian prince received his cure from the very same spear-tip, the spear-tip from which [he] had received his wound). The spear is a *pharmakon*, with both noxious and curative properties. A similar paradox underpins the project of the satirist in Juvenal's poems: the wounds—the moral and ideological wounds—that the satirist (and his readers) suffer from can only be treated by an application of what has caused it: an encounter—albeit on *his* terms—with all the elements of Roman life that he regards as corrupting. This parallels the speaker's desire to deal with the declaiming poets by shouting out his own compositions. Horace provides a link between rust and the kind of satirical malice he considers excessive when he describes it as *aerugo mera* in *Satire* 1.4.101.[37]

In this variety of satire, however, and in striking contradistinction to the Telephus of myth and the Roman poets, there is to be no restorative cure. If there is any sort of a salve, it is not a matter of purging the city of its undesirable elements but rather of the readers purging themselves of the desire to believe that things can be any different. That is certain to lead to disappointment. There is no Achilles with a healing spear-tip here; or if there is, the cure is simply an awareness of ubiquitous fluidity; of being trapped with no possibility of escape, with no boundaries and no transcendental signifiers to restore order.[38] This is more like the Achilles cited by Seneca (*De Tranquillitate* 2.12) as an exemplum of the body afflicted by the vacillation caused by desires: *modo pronus, modo supinus, in varios habitos se ipse componens, quod proprium aegri est, nihil diu pati et mutationibus ut remediis uti* (lying now on his face, now on his back, placing himself in various positions, just as a sick man does, enduring nothing for very long and using changes as remedies). Hence men undertake *peregrinationes vagae* and wander over *invia litora*, driven by discontent with the present (*semper praesentibus infesta levitas*, 13). Although Juvenal's satire

---

37. Cf. Mart. 10.33.5; Gowers 2012, *ad loc.* writes that "unadulterated copper-rust . . . both corrodes the victim and stains the agent."

38. Keane 2006: "Juvenal's agenda is not to heal society with his attacks" (50). Achilles is himself already "struck down" (*percussus*) in 1.163: so much for the efficacy of that spear. On the *pharmakon* and *pharmakos* in satire, see Gill 1995b on Swift.

is composed in the same meter as Vergil's *Aeneid*, the epic journey that provides the foundation legend and ideological bedrock of *Romanitas*, the opening lines of the collection signal the alienation of the speaker and the reader from any secure anchor-points they might offer the seeking subject. This uncoupling of form and content—of signifier and signified—is what Juvenal's satires are striving to communicate. Rather than restoring the validity of the grounding signifiers of *Romanitas*—*amicitia, imperium*, masculinity, marriage—they demonstrate the impossibility of finding refuge in these false hopes. This is the bleak conclusion that is going to be repeated from satire to satire.

Onto the Field of Satire

> Et nos ergo manum ferulae subduximus, et nos   15
> consilium dedimus Sullae, privatus ut altum
> dormiret. Stulta est clementia, cum tot ubique
> vatibus occurras, periturae parcere chartae.
> Cur tamen hoc potius libeat decurrere campo,
> per quem magnus equos Auruncae flexit alumnus,   20
> si vacat ac placidi rationem admittitis, edam.

> I too have moved my hand from under the teacher's cane, I too
> gave counsel to Sulla, that he should sleep soundly as a
> private citizen. It is a stupid clemency, when you run into so many
> bards all the time, to spare paper that is already doomed.
> Why, however, I prefer to drive onto this plain
> across which the great student of Aurunca turned his horses,
> if you have time, and will listen quietly to reason, I shall now present
>   to you.[39]

The speaker's encirclement by declaimers motivates a momentary scene shift back to his own rhetorical training as a schoolboy, emphasized by the *et nos* repetition. The teacher's rod parallels Achilles' spear, Orestes' sword, and Monychus's ash trees as the association of pain and punishment with language is continued.[40] The wasting of paper echoes the consumption of a whole day (*diem*

---

39. On echoes of Martial, see Colton 1991, 19–23.
40. Hor. *Sat.* 1.3.120 *ferula:* in a discussion of fair penalties for transgressions.

consumpserit, 4) by the "huge *Telephus*" and the amplitude (*plena iam margine*, 5) of the "never-ending *Orestes*" earlier. In this he again reworks Horace, who also "spoils paper" but only when he has the free time to jot down the fruits of his self-reflection (*ubi quid datur oti / illudo chartis, Satire* 1.4.138–39). *Stulta est clementia* is a very bare statement, with something of the motto about *it*: this is how the satirist is going to deal with his targets, both poets and others. The vacillation between staying and escaping to a quieter location (which was immediately voiced in the opening question, *Semper ego auditor tantum?*) is picked up in the schoolroom exercise urging Sulla to retire from public life and have a deep sleep. The *tot* echoes *totiens* in line 2, while *occurras* has overtones of attacking, as well as bumping into, the *vates*.[41] Poets fill the city streets: they have spilled out beyond the confines of Fronto's house, indicative of a porosity that will become ever more apparent. Indeed Fronto's is like Benjamin's Neapolitan house: "far less the refuge into which people retreat than the inexhaustible reservoir from which they flood out."[42] The rapid shifts in time here, and the ease with which the speaker slips from his own *domus* to various mythological locations and back to Fronto's *domus*, contribute further to the sensation of fluidity. So do the changes from singular to plural in the first- and second-person verbs. We move from first-person singular (*ego . . . reponam*, 1; cf. *mihi*, 7) to first-person plural (*et nos . . . subduximus*, 15; *et nos . . . dedimus*, 16) and back again (*edam*, 21), and the addressee is initially singular (*expectes*, 14), then plural (*admittitis*, 21).

The phrase *si vacat*, "if there is time (or space)," implies a break, an opening up of space in "the landscape of noisy life" where one can be heard,[43] while *placidus*, as nominative plural or genitive singular, ambiguously depicts either the satirist or his listeners as "calm." This is, perhaps unsurprisingly, the only time *placidus* appears in the *Satires*.[44] The inspiration for Juvenal's opening appears to have come from Horace's *Epistle* 2.2.87–105, where he describes how rival poets inflict both verses and compliments upon each other, including in 95–98:[45]

Mox etiam, **si forte vacas**, sequere et procul audi,
quid ferat et qua re sibi nectat uterque coronam.

---

41. Cf. *vacuam . . . vatibus*, Hor. *Epist.* 2.2.94 and Brink 1982, 321.

42. Benjamin 1985, 174. On the way that the street migrates into, or invades, interior space and vice versa, Gilloch 1996, 26–27; Burgin 1998, 56, 59.

43. See Gilloch 1996, 7; Benjamin 1974, 5.1056.

44. See below and chap. 4 on Numa as *placidus* and the Romulus-Numa progression.

45. See Larmour 2010–11, from which some of these observations are drawn.

> Caedimur et totidem plagis **consumimus** hostem
> lento Samnites ad lumina prima duello.

> And soon, **if by chance you have time**, follow and close by hear
> what each has to offer and with what each weaves for himself a
>   garland.
> We are cut to pieces and with so many blows **we use up** our foe
> like Samnites in a long drawn-out combat until the first lamps
>   are lit.

And a little later, he adds:

> Multa fero, ut placem **genus irritabile vatum**,
> cum scribo et supplex populi suffragia capto;
> idem finitis studiis et mente recepta
> obturem patulas **impune legentibus** auris.
> Ridentur mala qui componunt carmina; verum
> gaudent scribentes et se venerantur et ultro,
> **si taceas**, laudant quidquid scripsere beati.

> Much do I endure, to placate **the irritable race of bards**,
> when I write and supplicate the people for their votes;
> but now that my studies are finished and my sense recovered
> I would stop up my ears, **with impunity, when they recite**.
> Those who compose bad verses get laughed at; but
> they enjoy writing and revere themselves anyway.
> **If you keep quiet**, they praise whatever they have written, happy souls.
>   (102–108)

The verbal echoes of *si forte vacas* and *impune* with Juvenal's introduction (and of *duellum* with *duelli* in 169 in his conclusion, as we shall see) tie both his opening and closing passages to Horace's poem.[46] Horace presents his poets as gladiators, two Samnites engaged in a long drawn out struggle that goes on all afternoon.[47] This image has numerous resonances: the Samnite was heavily armed, suggesting a poet loaded down with rhetorical and other

---

46. Woodman 1983.

47. See Brink 1982, 315–16, 322–30. In Sen. *De Const.* 1.16.2, the Stoic and the Epicurean are likened to two brave gladiators: *Quaeris quid inter duos intersit? Quod inter gladiatores fortissimos, quorum alter premit vulnus et stat in gradu, alter respiciens ad clamantem populum significat nihil esse et intercedi non patitur.* Cf. Mart. *Spect.* 31, about a fight between Priscus and Verus that drags on (*traheret . . . traheret certamina*, 1) until the emperor awards *missio* to both (*cum duo pugnarent, victor uterque fuit*, 12).

accoutrements.[48] The *lentum duellum* dragging on until the first lamps are lit parallels the long recitations Juvenal complains about, and the notion of using each other up (*consumimus*) echoes themes of consumption surrounding poetic composition.[49] Also, a little later in *Satire* 1, the speaker will ask if the outrageous actions and individuals in his catalog of miscreants "do not deserve the Venusian lamp" (*Venusina digna lucerna*, 1.51). The self-assuredness of even those who compose bad poems (*rident mala qui componunt carmina*) and the silence of Horace the listener (*si taceas, laudent*), not to mention his suffering in the company of the *genus irritabile vatum*, and plugging his ears (*obturem patulas impune legentibus auris*), are all reworked by Juvenal (as the poet as gladiator will be at the end of the poem, 155–71). While Horace's position is that if he doesn't write anything he need not listen, Juvenal's is that he has had enough of listening and now it is his turn to write.

And so at this point, the speaker announces—this time with an indirect question, responding to an imagined query from the reader—his intention to drive his chariot into this space, to "take to the field" (*decurrere campo*) of satire in imitation of the founder of the genre, the "great son of Aurunca" Lucilius (19–21).[50] Ferguson sees in "steered his horses" (*equos . . . flexit*) a metaphor from chariot racing, and it appears that Juvenal is connecting the combative and equestrian associations of satire in his own particular fashion here.[51] Kirk Freudenburg, discussing Horace's first encounter with Maecenas (*Satire* 1.6.56–60), cites his "lack of a noble horse" (*Satureiano . . . caballo*, 59) as one reason why "Horace stays on his mule in the remainder of book 1, keeping to 'who he is,' and writing as if determined not to make a fool of himself by performing above his rank."[52] The circus is certainly another locus of noise for Juvenal, described by the same adjective used of the poet Cordus in line 2

---

48. See Kyle 1988, 45–46; Dunkle 2008, 22–23, 95, 98. Cic. *De Orat.* 2.325: an orator's *prolusio* should not be like those of Samnites who before a fight brandish spears they don't use at all in combat.

49. Cf. Stat. *Silv.* 4.2.4: *aequore qui multo reducem consumpsit Ulixen* (Homer consumes Odysseus); Coleman 1988, *ad loc.* and Newlands 2002, 279.

50. See Braund 1996a, 80–81; Ferguson 1979, 113; Juv. echoes Hor. *Sat.* 2.1.32. Cf. Lucil. 1305 [M]: *sustineas currum ut bonus saepe agitatur equosque.* In *Satire* 2.100, Juvenal quotes *Actoris Aurunci spolium* from Vergil's *Aeneid* 12.94, where it describes Turnus's spear, inherited from the great, and now dead, Actor (9.500, 12.96); as Turnus shakes the weapon, he vows to lay low the body (*sternere corpus*, 97) of the "Phrygian halfmale" (*semiviri Phrygis*, 99), echoing Iarbas's belittling of Aeneas in 4.215 as a second Paris. According to *Schol. Vet.* 1.20.71, there was a satiric poet from Aurunca, called Turnus; he is also known from Mart. (7.97, 11.10) and thirty lines may survive.

51. Ferguson 1979, 113. At the end of his first satire, Horace says that striving to overtake others does not lead to self-contentment and then uses a simile from chariot racing; see pp. 75–76 on 1.1.113–16.

52. Freudenburg 2001, 60–61, cf. Freudenburg 1993, 207; Gowers 2012, *ad loc.*, and on 5.13, 6.105–106; cf. Umbricius and his mule in Juv. 3.317.

above—*raucus*—in 8.59 (*rauco circo*) and as *clamosus* (noisy) in 9.144.[53] But the phrase *decurrere campo* is usually taken as an image drawn from warfare, so that Juvenal's speaker thereby styles himself as an epic hero. When, later in the poem, he pauses in his list of exempla to associate himself with his second predecessor Horace, his words reinforce this:

> Haec ego non credam Venusina digna lucerna?
> Haec ego non agitem? Sed quid magis Heracleas
> aut Diomedeas aut mugitum labyrinthi
> et mare percussum puero fabrumque volantem . . . ?

> Should I not deem these things worthy of the Venusian's [Horace's]
>   lamp?
> Am I not to have my go at them? What would be better, then, stories of
>   Heracles or Diomedes or the mooing in the labyrinth
> and the sea struck by the boy and the flying carpenter . . . ? (51–54)

The stories of Heracles and Diomedes clearly pick up on the epics and plays of the introduction and make the satirist into "a modern-day Hercules or Diomedes or Theseus fighting against crime and vice," as Braund puts it.[54] By the same logic, of course, he is also akin to the inventive Daedalus, who flies across the sea to escape from a nightmarish realm of violated boundaries and chaotic events, and to the impetuous Icarus, who fails in his attempt.[55] This subtly introduces the theme of failure, as well as the notion of escape, which will figure significantly in later satires.[56] There may be an echo here of Horace's likening of himself to a "poet-bird," and his sole mention of Icarus by name, in the last poem of *Odes* Book 2, where he says:

> Iam Daedaleo notior Icaro
> visam gementis litora Bosphori
>   Syrtisque Gaetulas canoras
>   alesque Hyperboreosque campos.

---

53. Cf. *clamant*, 1.12. In 11.197–98 we have *fragor aurem / percutit* ("a roar strikes my ear") of the cheers greeting a winner from the Green chariot-racing team.

54. Braund 1996a, 22, 80; Courtney 1980, 88–89, notes *decurrere* is used of equestrian exercises but subscribes to the characterization of Juvenal as an epic hero.

55. The Daedalus reference is picked up at the opening of *Satire* 3, where Umbricius, about to depart for Cumae, compares himself to him arriving in that town exhausted after his flight from Crete (25). See Fredericks 1975, 148. Chariot racing was, of course, fraught with danger and the real possibility of disastrous failure at every turn.

56. On the notion of failure in Juvenal, see Freudenburg 2001, 209–58.

Now more famed than Daedalian Icarus,
I will visit the shores of the groaning Bosphorus
    and, a tuneful bird, the Gaetulian Syrtes
        and the Hyperborean plains. (20.13–16)[57]

Catherine Connors comments as follows: "Daedalus and Icarus were escaping; their mission could be called a failure. With them, Horace's flight is turning into 'flight': running away. . . . The wish to be more famous than Icarus is puzzling since this is not necessarily to have achieved a great deal; but Horace is plagued by the notion that he will be known for his failure."[58] In this poem which ends the second book of the *Odes*, Horace imagines his own death; we will return to this and a similar piece that concludes the third book when we reach the end of Juvenal's poem (3.30).

The emphatic position of *edam* in Juvenal's proclamation signals the moment that the satiric enterprise begins in earnest with the catalog of targets that follows. The basic meaning of the verb is "emit" or "eject," and this, of course, is what satire does. It bursts out, spews forth, bubbles over. Frequently followed by words having to do with noise and sound, especially loud ones, *edo* also refers to giving birth and the publishing of literary productions.[59] This verb befits the satirist who is so concerned with having his voice heard amid the noise and who at the same time begets his world and creates the figures that inhabit it. The word carries connotations of authority and importance and the right to speak, as well as judgment (and potentially punishment) for crimes. Ovid uses it at the start of his *Amores* 1.1.1–2 in explaining how he originally planned to write epic (*arma gravi numero violentaque bella parabam / edere, materia conveniente modis* [I was preparing to tell in a solemn rhythm of arms and violent wars, with the subject matching the meter]), and it is used by Vergil and Horace of the responses of priests or oracles, suggesting that it was a marker of some solemnity.[60] The oracular, sometimes almost enchanting or magical properties of satiric speech have often been noted.[61] Juvenal employs it again in a

---

57. *Gaetulus:* Juv. 5.53, 59; 10.158; 11.140; 14.278; *Hyperboreus,* 6.470. The "mooing in the labyrinth" recalls the *Theseid* of "hoarse Cordus" at the opening; Horace cites his own *biformis* shape, half-man, half-bird, *Odes* 2.20.2.

58. Cf. Hor. *Odes* 4.2.1–4: whoever strives to rival Pindar relies on wings fastened by Daedalian craft (*ope Daedalea,* 2) and "is doomed to give his name to some sea."

59. Giving birth: Juv. 2.123: *si bos ederet agnam,* and 4.141; sounds: *clamorem;* 7.196, *vagitus;* 10.261, *planctus;* literary publication: Cic. *Brut.* 5.19; Hor. *AP* 390; Mart. 4.33.3.

60. Verg. *Aen* 5.693; Hor. *Sat.* 2.4.10; 2.5.61; cf. *Odes* 1.1.1: *Maecenas atavis edite regibus.*

61. See R. C. Elliott 1960. The repetition and ringing which characterize Juvenalian speech, giving it a chantlike sound, may also owe something to this connection.

proclamatory manner at 14.316–17 near the end of his disquisition on the mal-education of the young: *Mensura tamen quae / sufficiat census, siquis me consulat, edam* (Yet if someone consults me, as to the amount of wealth that is sufficient, I will tell him).

But *edo* has a second range of meaning, of "cause" or "perform," with refer-ence to battles, *caedes, tumultum, ruinas,* or *strages,*[62] which is then extended to cover the producing of theatrical plays, *ludi,* and *spectacula.*[63] Seneca (*De brevitate vitae* 13.6) uses it of Pompey's notorious *venatio* with elephants in the circus (*Pompeium . . . in circo elephantorum . . . pugnam edidisse*). The verb is used of "putting on" or "presenting" gladiators and of a *munus gladiatorum* by Suetoni-us.[64] Juvenal uses it in just this sense in *Satire* 3.36, where Umbricius dis-parages two former small-town arena musicians who now put on gladiatorial shows (*munera nunc edunt*).[65] Evidence from inscriptions also testifies to the com-mon appearance of the related nouns *editio* and *editor,* in such formulations as *editio muneris* or *ludorum* and *editor muneris.*[66] In using this verb, Juvenal ap-pears to be casting himself as an *editor,* who is going to give us a show, a series of *spectacula,* in his own arena of satire. Seneca the Elder adapted the role of the arena *editor* to his literary and oratorical purposes when he likened himself to the producers of spectacles, presenting his fourth book of *Controversiae* to the reader:

> Quod munerarii solent facere, qui ad expectationem populi
> detinendam nova paria per omnes dies dispensant, ut sit quod
> populum et delectet et revocet, hoc ego facio: non semel omnes
> produco; aliquid novi semper habeat libellus, ut non tantum
> sententiarum vos sed etiam auctorum novitate sollicitet. Acrior est
> cupiditas ignota cognoscendi quam nota repetendi. Hoc in
> histrionibus, in gladiatoribus, in oratoribus, de quibus modo aliquid
> fama promisit, in omnibus denique rebus videmus accidere: ad nova
> homines concurrunt, ad nota non veniunt.

> I am doing what gladiator-producers often do, when, in order to
> maintain the suspense of the populace, they distribute new pairs

---

62. Battles: Livy 8.9; *caedes:* 5.13; *strages:* Verg. Aen. 9.527, 785.

63. Plays: Plaut. *Cas.* 13; *ludi:* Tac. *Ann* 1.15; 3.64; Suet. *Caes.* 10; *spectacula:* Tac. *Ann* 14.7; Plin. Eld. *HN* 10.50.

64. Suet. *Caes.* 44 (*naumachiam spectaculum ediderat*); *Aug.* 45 (*gladiatores sine missione edi prohibuit*); *Tib.* 35; *Cal.* 18 (*munera gladiatoria . . . edidit*). See also Livy 28.21.1 (*munusque gladiatorium . . . edendum rediit* [Scipio]); Tac. *Ann.* 4.63.1; Plin. *Pan.* 33.2 (*in edendo liberalitatem*).

65. In 3.74–78, the word appears again, not in connection with gladiators, but still related to perfor-mance, for Umbricius is complaining about the versatility of Greeks who can adapt themselves to any role that you "set out" or "ordain": . . . *ede quid illum / esse putes?*

66. *editio muneris* (*CIL* 2. 6278.18), *ludorum* (8.11345; 9.1156); *editor muneris* (10.539).

over each day of the games, so that there is always something to
please the spectators and bring them back—I am not bringing all my
declaimers on at once; let a book always have something new, to keep
you on your toes by means of the novelty of the speakers as well as of
the epigrams. The desire to get to know the unknown is keener than
the desire to go back to the known. We see this everywhere—in
connection with actors, gladiators, and orators, at least where
reputation has promised something beforehand: men flock to the
new, avoid the old.[67]

Making sure that he pleases the spectators and stirs their interest by novelty is
also a serious concern of the satirist, especially given the repetitious features
of the form.[68] The role of *editor* is also connected with that of *ultor*, since the
arena was a place where, through wounding and mutilation of the body—and
ultimately death—those who have been marked for death as criminals or who
are judged unfit to live are killed. Alison Futrell comments thus on the epigram
that celebrates the presumed producer of the *munus* in the eponymous Magerius
mosaic: "His capacity to command the resources of empire demonstrated
simultaneously his cultural sophistication, his organizational skills and his
understanding how best to use the power of life over death. The members of
the community vigorously recognize his favor and recognize his effort as a
model for past and future interactions of imperial authority. This is why Magerius is the figure being crowned by Mercury, officially hailed as the true victor
of the games."[69]

Hovering on the *Limen*

Cum tener uxorem ducat spado, Mevia Tuscum
figat aprum et nuda teneat venabula mamma,
patricios omnis opibus cum provocet unus
quo tondente gravis iuveni mihi barba sonabat,   25
cum pars Niliacae plebis, cum verna Canopi
Crispinus Tyrias umero revocante lacernas

---

67. Trans. Winterbottom 1974. Mart. 3.2.1 styles his book as a *munus* in the apostrophe *Cuius vis
fieri, libelle, munus?* (Whose present do you wish to be, little book?), as it is sent off to Rome (*Romam vade,
liber*, 3.4.1).
    68. See Coleman 1996 on "how the taste for the known was in constant competition with the taste for
the new" in arena productions (64).
    69. Futrell 2006, 49–51 with illustration.

ventilet aestivum digitis sudantibus aurum,
nec suffere queat maioris pondera gemmae,
difficile est saturam non scribere.

When a soft eunuch takes a wife, when Mevia
spears a Tuscan boar and holds the hunting spears with one breast bare,
when one man who made my beard rasp while shaving me in my youth
single-handedly challenges all the patricians with his wealth,
when part of the Nile mob, when the home-born slave of Canopus,
Crispinus, as his shoulder hitches up a Tyrian cloak,
waves in the air a gold ring on sweaty fingers
and cannot bear the weight of a larger gemstone,
then it is difficult not to write satire.

In the presentation of these first examples from the practice of everyday life we can see what the lightning rods of Juvenalian discourse are: first, the violation of boundaries (of gender by the eunuch and the "Amazon" Mevia, then of social hierarchy by the wealthy barber and impoverished aristocrats), and second, the invasion of space by outsiders (Crispinus the Egyptian *verna* in Rome).[70] As Amy Richlin puts it, "The unifying factor in most of Juvenal's victims is their abnormality. . . . Those he satirizes are abnormal, excessive, and different" (199). On the metapoetic level, this reinforces the violation of literary boundaries that Juvenalian satire enacts as it confounds epic meter and language with "low" themes, deploys the techniques of rhetoric for comic effect, and imports pastoral conventions into an urban setting.[71] The spatial sweep of this carefully crafted sentence, with its parallel *cum* clauses of four lines each, is broad: a marriage ceremony, an arena hunt, a barber's shop, a patrician house, the street or the imperial court, in addition to locations farther afield in Etruria, Egypt, and Phoenicia.[72] The conjunction of person and place in both *Mevia Tuscum* and *Canopi* / *Crispinus Tyrias* makes clear that these individuals and locations acquire meaning through their relation to each other. The epithet *Tuscus* is generally positive in Juvenal—suggesting simplicity of tableware (11.108) and old-fashioned purity in women (6.289). There is a similarly effective conjunction

---

70. On echoes of Mart., and a possible reference to the *tonsor* Cinnamus who rose to become an *eques* (7.64), see Colton 1991, 22–27. In *Epode* 4, Horace imagines his upstarts on the Via Sacra and the Via Appia, as well as in the front row of seats at the arena or theater (7, 14, 115–16).

71. On Juvenal's mixing of genres, see F. M. A. Jones 2007; we might compare Joyce's use of lists and his blending of linguistic styles in *Ulysses*.

72. Depending on where Crispinus is imagined: in the street, perhaps in a litter, or, as in *Sat.* 4, in his palatial colonnades and groves near the forum and at court (5–7, 108–109).

in 6.185–86: *nam quid rancidius quam quod se non putat ulla / formosam nisi quae de Tusca Graecula facta est* (For what is more nauseating than the fact that no woman thinks she's beautiful unless she's made herself from a Tuscan into a Greeklette). Canopus has no such positive resonances—being infamous for its criminality (6.84, 15.46)—while *Tyrius* is the luxurious color assigned to three morally tainted objects: the female athlete's tracksuit (6.246), the cloak of the *causidicus* (7.134), and Messalina's adulterous imperial couch (10.334).[73] Temporal shifting is also evident, as we contemplate Juvenal's barber, both now and when the speaker was young, and Crispinus, who rose to prominence in earlier times under Domitian. The targets are a blend of particular individuals, named or unnamed, and of representative types, like the *spado*. Mevia's unmatronly appearance in the arena with her hunting spears is neatly echoed by the barber's impertinent "calling out" or challenging (*provocet*) of all the patricians.[74]

Like the city itself, Juvenal's text-as-city bombards the viewer with shocking manifestations of hybridity and paradox.[75] Through synecdoche our attention is drawn to eye-catching parts that reveal the state of the whole (*pars Niliacae plebis*, Mevia's bare *mamma*, or Crispinus's sweating *digiti*), just as these individuals stand in a synecdochic relationship with the rest of Rome.[76] "Of course, there's no actual correlation between perspiration and guilt," protests Richard Nixon in Peter Morgan's *Frost/Nixon*, but in Juvenal sweaty fingers are part of a chain of instances that associate sweating with consciousness of crime. Later in this poem, the heart sweats with silent guilt when Lucilius blazes forth (*tacita sudant praecordia culpa*, 1.167), and in 13.220 the guilty man has extraordinary sweats at night when he sees the victim of his crimes (*quod praecipuis mentem sudoribus urguet*).[77] While for Horace sweating is associated with the labor of writing poetry (*Ars Poetica* 241, 413; *Epistles* 2.1.169), Juvenal makes it accompany less noble activities or personages, such as Gracchus, who sweats while running with the Sacred Shields in 2.126 (but marries another

---

73. 6.246: *endromidas Tyrias*; 7.134: *Tyrio stlattaria purpura filo*; the adjective also describes Hannibal in 12.107.

74. The verb is used twice elsewhere, of inappropriate challenges in salacious contexts in 6.321 (Saufeia, probably an aristocrat, challenges the slaves of the brothel keeper) and 376 (a man made a *spado* by his mistress challenges Priapus); it is commonly used of calling out to individual combat or to a military engagement (see *OLD* 3a and c); one kind of gladiator was known as a *provocator* (*OLD* 1b; Cic. *Sest.* 134). Intriguingly, in Hor. *Sat.* 1.4.14, it is a Crispinus (mentioned in 1.1.120 and 3.140) who challenges (*provocat*) Horace to a writing contest; he appears to be a long-winded poet and/or Stoic. See Leigh 1997 on usage in Lucan and Seneca (274n104).

75. On shock and the metropolis, see Gilloch 1996, 182–83.

76. On this technique in city-texts, see Barta 1996 on Bely and Joyce.

77. Morgan 2007; cf. 3.50: the guilty man's mind seethes (*aestuat*) with secrets.

man, 117–24, and enters the arena, 143–48), or the *Graeculus*, who begins sweating as soon as you say "I'm hot" (3.103). It is a phenomenon of slaves (10.48) and women (6.259, 420). Crispinus himself is pictured in 4.108–109 as arriving at Domitian's palace "sweating with morning perfume hardly matched by the reek of two funerals" (*matutino sudans Crispinus amomo / quantum vix redolent duo funera*). Sweat is moisture leaving the body and points to themes of overflowing and porosity, yet it was also applied to the satirist himself by Martial, who wrote that Juvenal's sweaty toga wafted him around the thresholds of the powerful (*dum per limina te potentiorum / sudatrix toga ventilat,* 12.18.4–5). This captures something important about the urban satirist: his "heat," the frenetic and incontinent nature of his speech, and his tireless pacing of the cityscape.

There is, however, rather more heat than light generated in such situations, to use a burned-out metaphor. It is the cumulative weight of examples that gives birth to satire, yet we are given no explanation other than the list itself, in which each item is frequently more excessive, or more expansive, than the last. The rhetoric of exemplarity is also a rhetoric of excess: the meaning generated by it is at least as much a product of its form as it is of the denotative content of the names on it. Indeed, it is precisely this insistent naming action, the very iterative quality of the list as list, that generates a supplemental set of meanings that goes beyond a simple catalog of names and types. Why two or three or four examples, for instance, rather than just one? The supplemental meaning accrued by every additional name or incident consists less in the contribution each new item makes to the larger mosaic than in the way they together resist meaning through deploying the very material excess they are said initially to represent and indict. The status of the example is in itself inherently problematic, for by its very nature it always says more than its rubric allows: it presents an un-abstracted, concrete moment in the service of a more generalized thesis. Likewise, apparently univocal allusions to mythical and historical figures like Theseus and Telephus, Daedalus and Aeneas, for instance, or places like the Porta Capena and Egeria's Grove, the Campus Martius and the Temple of Jupiter Capitolinus, always open up a chain of ambiguity and deferral. The labyrinthine and nauseating effects of Juvenalian discourse evince an awareness of being existentially lost amid the constant, excessive reminders of what has been lost from a putatively pure *Romanitas*, from the Golden Age of the *maiores*.

As *Satire* 1 continues, the specific locations in the city function in a similar fashion to its individual inhabitants like Mevia and Crispinus. For instance, there is the Flaminian Way, along which a young show-off races his chariot to impress his girlfriend:

cum fas esse putet curam sperare cohortis
qui bona donauit praesepibus et caret omni
maiorum censu, dum pervolat axe citato
Flaminiam puer Automedon? Nam lora tenebat
ipse, lacernatae cum se iactaret amicae.

[How can I not write satire . . .] when someone thinks it's right
   to hope
for command of a cohort, who has given his worldly goods to his
   stables,
and has used up an entire family fortune, while he flies along
the Flaminian Way at top speed, a boy Automedon?
For he was holding the reins himself,
while he showed off to his girlfriend in his army cloak. (58–62)[78]

Here a generic youth of dissolute character, distanced by the mythological name and stigmatized by its Hellenic provenance, is set in a specific location, although not at any particular point on this long road, and the scene is given overtones of a race in the circus. The rushing along the road parallels the young man's consumption, or pouring out, of wealth on the maintenance of stables for racing horses. The circus, itself a locus of massive outward flows—of money, noise, and bodily fluids—and a frequent target of Juvenal's scorn, has in this image spilled out beyond the confines of its walls to contaminate the city at large. Like the arena, it is a vortex into which everything gets sucked. In 11.197, we find *totam hodie Romam Circus capit* (Today the Circus holds all Rome). In his first satire, Horace ends with a picture of the man who chases wealth like some chariot racer:

Sic festinanti semper locupletior obstat,
ut, cum carceribus missos rapit ungula currus,
instat equis auriga suos vincentibus, illum
praeteritum temnens extremos inter euntem.

As he hurries like this someone richer always stands in his way,
just as, when the hoof speeds the chariots released from the
   starting-gates,

78. Cf. Horace's reference to the son who is "crazy about his prostitute girlfriend" (*meretrice . . . insanus amica*) and makes his father furious (*ardens*) by leading revels to her door before it is even dark (*Sat.* 1.4.8–52). Cf. Prop. 4.8.17–18, of Cynthia driving along the Appian Way at full speed, making a *spectaculum* of herself *ausa per impuros frena movere iocos* (20–21).

Totam hodie Romam Circus capit (Juv. 11.197). Circus Maximus and Palatine Hill.
Photograph by David Larmour and Corby Kelly.

the charioteer presses upon the horses leading his own, despising
that other man who has been passed and is among those at the rear.
   (1.1.113–16)[79]

Making the Via Flaminia, the formal route through the Campus Martius,
into a racetrack, as opposed to a ceremonial highway, is a piquant demonstration of the "slippage" in satire's urban topography. In literary terms, the "boy
Automedon" can be assimilated to the bombastic, self-glorifying poets the
speaker yearns to get away from in the opening salvo of *Satire* 1, and hence to
a kind of anti-Lucilius, charging not across the battlefield or around the racetrack fired by moral purpose, but merely along the Flaminian Way for the gratification of his excited girlfriend.[80] The verb *pervolo* is used again in *Satire* 6.398
of the woman who goes racing all over the city (*totam pervolet Urbem*), brazenly

79. Gowers 2012, *ad loc.* Earlier in 1.1.90–91, teaching him to retain the love of relatives would be like
training a donkey to gallop on the Campus Martius in obedience the reins (*ut si quis asellum / in campo doceat
parentem currere frenis*).
   80. Townend 1969. In Ov. *Ars Am.* 1.3–8, the speaker twice styles himself the Automedon of Love
(*Automedon dicar Amoris ego*, 8) as he embarks upon his poetic love manual: *Amor* requires the rule of *Ars*, just
as do nimble chariots (*arte leves currus, arte regendus Amor*, 4). Juvenal's reference here to the charioteer of
Achilles anticipates his mention in 1.163 and elsewhere. Automédon is the name of a vintage car show in Paris.

conversing with generals and spreading news of foreign affairs and gossip about local ones to anyone she meets at the crossroads or in the street (*quocumque in trivio, cuicumque est obvia, narrat*, 412). In 2.7, which is the climax of Horace's second book of *Satires*, Davus deploys the figure of the charioteer as he characterizes his master's vain attempts to "cheat" (with wine and sleep) the anxiety caused by his dangerous adventures with married women: *frustra: nam comes atra permit sequiturque fugacem* (114–15).[81] Earlier in the piece, Davus had drawn an extended contrast between his own casual liaisons and Horace's adulterous ones, with all their attendant perils and humiliations (2.46–67), on which Niall Rudd comments as follows: "The frankness of Davus' transaction is symbolized by the bright lamp (*lucerna*) in v.48; the furtive guilt of the adulterer by the concealing cloak (*lacerna*) in v.55. So the all-important difference depends upon a single vowel. The effect may be unintentional, but who can say it was an accident?" (191). We might also wonder whether Juvenal's uses of *Venusina . . . lucerna* (51) and *lacernatae* (62, cf. *lacernas*, 27) have some Horatian resonances.

Immediately after this scene of youthful foolishness, the satirist places himself in the cityscape, but in a liminal location, taking notes at the crossroads: *nonne licet medio ceras implere capaces / quadrivio, cum . . .* (Surely then I am allowed to fill capacious notebooks, in the middle of the crossroads, when . . . , 63–64). A parade of frauds and criminals follows.[82] The "capacious tablets" are the satirist's response to the voluminous works of the poets of the opening. The speaker is positioned literally on the *limen* in central scene of *Satire* 1, waiting on the doorstep of the wealthy patron's house for the distribution of the *sportula* (daily handout):

> Nunc sportula primo
> limine parva sedet turbae rapienda togatae.
> Ille tamen faciem prius inspicit et trepidat ne
> suppositus venias ac falso nomine poscas:
> agnitus accipies. Iubet a praecone vocari
> ipsos Troiugenas, nam vexant limen et ipsi
> nobiscum. "Da praetori, da deinde tribuno."
> Sed libertinus prior est. "Prior" inquit "ego adsum.

---

81. He is trying to escape from himself like a runaway slave: *teque ipsum vitas fugitivus et erro* (113); Rudd 1966 comments that "the picture of lust as a charioteer is in the grand style" (193).

82. One is reminded of Tacitus's account of how Vitellius was surrounded by hordes of the worst sort of people, buffoons, actors, and jockeys: *adgregabantur e plebe flagitiosa per obsequia Vitellio cogniti, scurrae, histriones, aurigae, quibus ille amicitiarum dehonestamentis mire gaudebat* (2.87). See further Ash 2007, *ad loc.*

Cur timeam dubitemve locum defendere? Quamvis
natus ad Euphraten, molles quod in aure fenestrae
arguerint, licet ipse negem? Sed quinque tabernae
quadringenta parant. Quid confert purpura maior
optandum, si Laurenti custodit in agro
conductas Corvinus oves, ego possideo plus
Pallante et Licinis?"

             Now the small dole sits
on the front step waiting to be snatched by the toga-clad crowd;
but that patron first inspects your face and is afraid that you are
    coming
under false pretenses and claiming under someone else's name:
once identified, you'll get it. He calls for the herald to summon
even the ones born of Trojan blood, for they too harass the threshold
along with the rest of us. "Give to the praetor, then the tribune."
But a freedman is in front. "I was here first," he says,
"why should I be afraid or hesitate to defend my place? Although
born by the Euphrates—the effeminate windows in my ears would prove
    this even if I deny it—yet I own five shops that earn me four hundred
    thousand. What thing as desirable does the broader purple stripe
bring, if Corvinus guards a leased flock of sheep in the Laurentian
    field
while I have more than Pallas or people like Licinus?" (95–126)[83]

The patron orders his herald to "give a handout to the praetor and then to the
tribune," but a freedman intervenes ("I was here first," 101–102) and goes on to
claim priority in the line by virtue of his own—no doubt recently acquired—
great wealth. We hear nothing from the speaker in this scene, as he is pushed
aside and silenced. The word *limen* is used twice: the *sportula* is handed out
primo limine (right on the step, i.e., the clients are not even admitted) and the
Trojan-blooded nobles crowd the doorway along with the rest (100–101). The
verb *vexant* harks all the way back to *vexatus* describing the speaker in the second line of the poem. The second part of the scene, with the crowd of a hundred
litters coming by for their coins (*densissima centum / quadrantes lectica petit*,

---

83. This begins at the middle of the poem proper—about halfway between lines 22 and 171—and functions as its central episode: see Larmour 2004, 65–67. The *sportula* reappears in 3.249, 10.45–46, and 13.31–
34. On Martial and the *sportula*, see Colton 1991, 45–56. Cf. Verg. *Geor.* 2.461–62 and Hor. *Epodes* 2.7–8 on
the *sportula* as one of the negative features of city, as opposed to country, life. On the treatment of *clientes*, see
L. Watson 2003, 91.

121–22) combines the *sportula* with the recurring image of the litter (*lectica*) in Juvenal's poems.[84] The litter, which carries its occupant over the heads of the crowd, enabling him to look down his nose at them, is another signifier of the speaker's liminality and exclusion. The word *sportula* has another connotation, as it is mentioned by Suetonius as the term used by Claudius for a brief, impromptu gladiatorial *munus*.[85]

After the *sportula* scene, the diurnal sequence of events rolls on, and we are next given a glimpse of "the Forum and Apollo the legal expert" (*sportula deinde forum iurisque peritus Apollo*, 128).[86] This refers to the Forum Augusti, which according to Pliny the Elder contained an ivory statue of Apollo (*Apollinem eboreum qui est in foro Augusti; Historia naturalis* 7.53.183).[87] The resonances of this location are numerous, including the moment in Horace's *Satire* 1.9.78 when the hapless victim of the Bore finally makes his escape, "rescued by Apollo" (*sic me servavit Apollo*).[88] Juvenal's speaker thus finds his way to the Forum in the footsteps of Horace; indeed the traversal of the cityscape as the hours go by recalls Horace's hectic day in Rome, recollected in the tranquility of the countryside, in *Satire* 2.6.16–60. Some further detail about the Forum Augusti is now supplied: *atque triumphales, inter quas ausus habere / nescio quis titulos Aegyptius atque Arabarches, / cuius ad effigiem non tantum meiere fas est* (and the triumphal statues, among which some Egyptian tax officer has dared to inscribe his titles, at whose image it's certainly right and proper to do more than piss, 129–31). The foreign word *Arabarches* (tax official) intrudes into the midst of the Latin sentence just as the bust intrudes into the ranks of sculptured Romans. The mention of a specific site—the colonnade in which Augustus placed statues of Roman military heroes in triumphal garb—offers the opportunity for a sarcastic comment on the pollution of an important public space by an inappropriate interloper, in this case a nameless foreigner

84. Cf. 3.239–48 for another extended description and 10.35. In 1.65–8, there is a picture of a forger in a litter, lounging like Maecenas (whose presence inevitably recalls the era of Horace and Vergil, as in *Satire* 12). On the litter in Juvenal, see also 4.18–21; 5.97–98, 137–40; R. D. Brown 1983.

85. As Edmondson 1996 notes, the term was carefully chosen "since it maintained the association of patronal gift-giving that was fundamental to the term *munus*" 77n30). Also used of food gifts at arena, Suet. *Dom.* 4.5: *panariis . . . sportellis* (of large and small baskets distributed to senators/equestrians and the plebs).

86. As in Mart. 4.8: *Prima salutantes atque altera conterit hora, / exercet raucos tertia causidicos, / in quintam varios extendit Roma labores* (1–3); see Colton 1991, 57.

87. Mart. 2.64.7–8 has *fora litibus omnia ferent, / ipse potest fieri Marsua causidicus*, referring to the statue of Marsyas in the Forum Romanum (mentioned in Hor. *Sat.* 1.6.120 and at the opening of Juv. *Sat.* 9). Apollo *Tortor* is mentioned in Suet. *Aug.* 72.

88. Braund 1996a, 103. On the Forum Augusti, see Platner and Ashby 1929, 220–23; *LTUR* 2.289–95. The forum and *limina* are linked in *Epode* 2.7–8.

from Egypt. The reference is a clever one. The word *Arabarches* was used derogatively by Cicero of Pompey, so that the statue also signals the disruptive force of civil war (*Letters to Atticus* 2.17.3).[89] That the choice of which famous figures of the Republic to include and which to leave out was determined by political and ideological considerations is obvious; Juvenal's belittling comment on the statue and inscription of the nameless Egyptian Arabarch is thus at the same time a pointed statement about the priorities of the imperial Roman state in his day. It also recalls the attack on the Egyptian Crispinus in the opening lines of *Satire* 1 (26–29).

The fate imagined for the statue also has several resonances.[90] It recalls the words of Horace's wooden Priapus in his *Satire* 1.8.37–39:

Mentior ac si quid, merdis caput inquiner albis
corvorum, atque in me veniat mictum atque cacatum
Iulius et fragilis Pediatia furque Voranus.

If I am lying in any way, may my head be fouled by the white droppings of crows, and may Julius and the weakling Pediatia and the thief Voranus come to piss and shit on me.

And at the end of the *Ars Poetica*, Horace says of the poet:

Nec satis apparet, cur versus factitet, utrum
minxerit in patrios cineres, an triste bidental
moverit incestus . . .

Nor is it sufficiently clear why he keeps making verses, whether he pissed on ancestral ashes, or sacrilegiously disturbed a sinister plot of consecrated ground . . . (470–72)

There is also something of a precedent in Persius from his *Satire* 1, in which the satirist is locked in lively debate with an interlocutor (as he will be at the end of Juvenal's poem). In response to a warning that he should take care that "the thresholds of the powerful do not grow cold toward you" (*ne maiorum tibi forte / limina frigescant*, 108–109), the speaker says:

---

89. We do not know if Pompey was included among the *triumphatores*; see Degrassi 1937, 8; Dudley 1967, 128–29.

90. One is reminded of the fate of the Soviet war memorial in Budapest, which had to be fenced off a few years ago to prevent just such actions. It is close to the American Embassy, and a statue of a striding President Reagan has been erected in the vicinity. Defiling statues and tombs is a common theme: in Petr. 71, Trimalchio fears *ne in monumentum meum populus cacatum currat*. In the tomb of the Olympic Games at Tarquinia, a man is shown apparently in the act of defecating; Maxwell 1996 connects it with scatological humor in mime (276).

Nil moror. Euge omnes, omnes bene, mirae eritis res.
Hoc iuvat? "Hic," inquis, "veto quisquam faxit oletum."
Pinge duos anguis: "Pueri, sacer est locus, extra
meeite." Discedo? Secuit Lucilius Urbem,
te Lupe, te Muci, et genuinum fregit in illis.
Omne vafer vitium ridenti Flaccus amico
tangit et admissus circum praecordia ludit,
callidus excusso populum suspendere naso.
Me muttire nefas? Nec clam? Nec cum scrobe? Nusquam?

Never mind. Bravo everyone, well done all, you're marvelous.
Will that do? "Here," you say, "I forbid anyone to defecate."
Paint two snakes: "Boys, this is a sacred place—piss outside."
I leave? Lucilius tore the city, you Lupus,
you Mucius, and broke his teeth on them.
Horace touches every fault in his laughing friend
and, once inside, plays around his heart,
clever to dangle the people from his unblocked nose.
Am I forbidden to mutter? Not even secretly? Not to a hole? Nowhere?
    (111–19)[91]

This passage looks forward to Juvenal's closing lines in *Satire* 1, where the issue of speech and silence reappears, together with mention of Lucilius and Mucius Scaevola. Acts of expulsion of bodily fluids—whether shit, piss, or nasal mucous—have a metapoetic force for both Horace and Persius, and this is imitated by Juvenal in his pausing at the Arabarch's statue in the forum. Since the Temple of Mars Ultor dominated the Forum Augusti, the speaker's statement *cuius ad effigiem non tantum meiere fas est* can be taken as an instruction for an act of vengeance in keeping with the god's presence and a reminder of the satirist's role as punisher.[92]

The urge to piss—and even better to shit—on the intruder's image is, moreover, fundamental to the experience of abjection. For his impact the satirist relies upon the conjunction of the repulsion generated by bodily outflows with a specific location in the Roman public space. Even if the wall running around the Forum Augusti, for example, was massive enough to create the

91. The text and translation here draw heavily upon both Jenkinson 1980 and Braund 2004.
92. As Platner and Ashby 1929 note, this temple, dedicated by Octavian at Philippi *pro ultione paterna* (Suet. *Aug.* 29.1; Ov. *F.* 5.545–98), "formed the essential element of the forum as the temple of Venus Genetrix did that of the Forum Iulium" (220). They add that it was sometimes called the Forum of Mars because of the temple of Mars Ultor, relying upon the scholia on 14.261 (*in foro Martis*).

Ex quo Mars Ultor galeam quoque perdidit (Juv. 14.261). Rome, Forum of Augustus, Temple of Mars Ultor. Drawing by Augusto Trabacchi (1918–1948). Gatteschi Collection (Gatteschi.66). Courtesy of the American Academy in Rome, Photographic Archive.

impression of a hermetically sealed enclosure, the satiric speaker reveals that the walls surrounding Roman public space are in fact porous and unsealed, as is the skin supposedly containing the "clean and proper body," so that there are constant anxieties about both effluence and influx.[93] Earlier the speaker attacked Crispinus, who is *pars Niliacae plebis* (part of the Nile mob, 26), and an unnamed freedman who pushes his way to the front at the *sportula, quamvis natus ad Euphraten* (although born on the Euphrates, 104). The designation of these two representatives of the foreign Other through the rivers of the regions they come from is not accidental: rivers like the Nile and the Euphrates are powerful, unstoppable flows, and in the psychogeography of the speaker they discharge themselves, and their human detritus, into Rome. In *Satire* 3.61–62, Umbricius asks "Yet how small a portion of our sewage are Achaeans? For a long time now the Syrian Orontes has been emptying into the Tiber" (*Quamvis quota portio faecis Achaei? / Iam pridem Syrus in Tiberim defluxit Orontes*).[94]

---

93. Livy's foundation myth has at its core a belief in the sanctity of walls, according to Ogilvie 1965, 54; Fantham 1998, *ad loc.*, on Ov. *F.* 4.250.

94. Note how the Tiber is enclosed by *Syrus* and *Orontes* in the line. On rivers more generally, Farmer 2013. We might compare the role of the marshes as the breeding ground of subversion and violence

Now we have reached dinnertime in Juvenal's progress through the day, as the "old and tired" clients leave to buy their "cabbages and firewood" (1.132–34). Meanwhile, their *rex* dines alone on the best that wood and sea produce; he and others "eat up their patrimonies at a single table" (*una comedunt patrimonia mensa*, 138) on gourmet items like boar and peacock:

> Quanta est gula quae sibi totos
> ponit apros, animal propter convivia natum.
> Poena tamen praesens, cum tu deponis amictus
> turgidus et crudum pavonem in balnea portas.
> Hinc subitae mortes atque intestata senectus.
> It nova nec tristis per cunctas fabula cenas;
> ducitur iratis plaudendum funus amicis.

> How big the gullet that puts before itself whole
> boars, an animal made for dinner parties.
> Punishment however is immediate, when you take off your cloak
> and, bloated, you cart the undigested peacock into the baths.
> Hence sudden death and intestate old age.
> The latest, un-tragic news goes round all the other dinner parties;
> the funeral is held to the applause of angry friends. (140–46)[95]

With this final scene, his own Mr. Creosote, the satirist returns to the themes of punishment (*poena praesens*) and noise (*plaudendum*), while the boar, a popular animal in satiric texts, makes a second appearance.[96] The diner's unrestrained consumption echoes that of the "boy Automedon" using up his patrimony. Similarly, in 11.38–41 the wallet of Rutilus and his like shrinks in proportion to the growth of the *gula:*

> Quis enim te deficiente crumina
> et crescente gula manet exitus, aere paterno
> ac rebus mersis in ventrem fenoris atque
> argenti gravis et pecorum agrorumque capacem?

> For what end awaits you as your wallet fails,
> and the appetite of your gullet grows, when your paternal inheritance

---

in Bely's *Petersburg* (and the marshes as source of trouble for respectable and law-abiding citizens in Juv. 3.305–308).

95. On echoes of Martial, see Colton 1991, 58–65.

96. In 5.116 a whole boar is put before the host, and in 167 the guests are still hoping for a slice; by contrast in Hor. *Sat.* 2.2.89 the boar is kept aside for guests who may arrive late; in 2.8.6, boar as a "starter" signals a rich meal.

and property have been sunk into your stomach, which swallows
investments and heavy silver and herds and estates?

Two important social spaces are here combined as sites of excessive consumption and expulsion: the dining room and the bath. The connection between dining and bathing is also picked up in *Satire* 11, when Juvenal tells his friend who is coming to a simple, rustic meal that he can go to the baths before noon with a clear conscience.[97]

Juvenal's greedy diner alludes to Horace's "rare case" who departs from life *contentus*, "like a satisfied dinner-guest" (*uti conviva satur*, *Satire* 1.117–19).[98] As critics have noted, the "death in the bath" scene gives every sign of being a homage to Persius, whose own version is a tremendous triumph of satiric nausea.[99] It functions here as a *spectaculum*, a show of textual killing offered by the satirist to his readers. The victim is upbraided directly (*cum tu deponis*) and then comes immediate punishment and sudden death, with the one who selfishly refused entry to the hungry clients at the door being carried out dead across the threshold to the applause of his angry (because excluded) friends. The dining room becomes an internal arena where the peacock and the boar—the animal speared by Mevia in the opening catalog—wreak their gruesome revenge on the glutton. Instead of "cooking" the raw, undigested peacock in his stomach in the hot water of the bath, the diner is himself swallowed up unexpectedly and suddenly by death. The vocabulary is put to effective use elsewhere in the collection: *gula* reappears in *Satire* 5 of the voracious appetite of the host (94) and the rumbling stomach of the abused *cliens* (158), and in 6.203 of dinner guests who are "raw" (or perhaps "bloated") because they have not yet digested all they have eaten. In 15.90 it is used of the first Tentyran maw to taste the body of the fallen Ombite, while the frenzied crowd is described as *contenta cadavere crudo*, satisfied with the raw corpse, which they need not waste time cooking.[100] The adjective *crudus* is elsewhere used of dangerously unripe apples (11.76) and of Nero's tyranny (8. 222–23), described as *saeva crudaque* in connection with the vengeance it merited (*debuit ulcisci*). This word, which carries the force of both "raw"

---

97. Also in 11.156, one sign of the wholesomeness of the slave-boy serving at the meal is that he doesn't yet cart his teenage testicles to the baths. In 7.178–85, the *dominus* by whom the rhetoric teacher is paid a pittance spends lavishly on his baths, a portico (for driving his chariot in the rain), and a dining room.

98. Itself an echo of Lucr. 3.938 (*cur non ut plenus vitae conviva recedis?*), cf. 959–60. See chap. 4, p. 249 herein.

99. Pers. 3.98–106; Braund 1996a, 105; Kenney 2012, 128–29.

100. Finally, we may note that in 11.19–20, there is a transition from a *gulosum fictile* (a gourmet's earthenware dish) to the *miscellanea ludi* (gladiatorial school mash), as we contemplate the gourmandizing spendthrifts who end up having to sell themselves to the arena.

and "crude" in English, not only marks the border between the raw and the cooked but also designates glistening or bleeding flesh whose exposure to view signifies pain.[101] It is, at the same time, all the more powerful for its exposure. When "the populace fresh from victory" (*populus modo victor*) are confronted with the spectacle of the dissolute lawyer Creticus pleading his case in a see-through toga in *Satire* 2, Juvenal adds the detail that the onlookers still have raw wounds (*vulneribus crudis*, 73). *Crudus* also describes satire itself: raw and indigestible at times, yet vigorous because of its "unbaked" state.

Roman City Limits

Personally I have no bone to pick with graveyards, I take the air there willingly, perhaps more willingly than elsewhere, when take the air I must.
—*Samuel Beckett,* First Love

At the end of *Satire* 1, there is a dialogue (recalling Horace's with an unnamed critic in his *Satire* 1.4 or in 2.6) between the satirist and an imaginary interlocutor about the practicalities of the project now set in motion:

> Nil erit ulterius quod nostris moribus addat
> posteritas, eadem facient cupientque minores,
> omne in praecipiti vitium stetit. Utere velis,
> totos pande sinus. Dicas hic forsitan "Unde
> ingenium par materiae? Unde illa priorum
> scribendi quodcumque animo flagrante liberet
> simplicitas?" Cuius non audeo dicere nomen?
> Quid refert dictis ignoscat Mucius an non?

> There will be nothing more that posterity will add to our habits,
> our descendants will do and desire the same things.
> All vice stands on the edge of the precipice. Hoist the sails,
> spread out all the canvas. Here perhaps you might say, "Where
> will you get the talent equal to the topic? Where will you find
> that frankness of your predecessors in writing whatever their
> blazing spirits wanted to?" Whose name do I not dare to mention?
> What does it matter if Mucius excuses me or not? (147–54)

---

101. *OLD* lists examples under uncooked or raw, in a natural state, undigested or having undigested food in the stomach, bleeding or raw of wounds (Ov. *Pont.* 1.3.16; Pers. 5.162; otherwise rare), unripe, fierce or savage; also youthful or vigorous (Verg. *Aen.* 6.304).

The nautical metaphor reinforces the notion of satire as a sea voyage, with all the implications outlined earlier, while the four questions, two from the interlocutor matched by two from the speaker, parallel the four that burst forth in the poem's opening.[102] Courtney comments that "Juvenal makes his interlocutor speak from the mouth of Lucilius," but the dialogue also recalls Horace's with an unnamed critic in his *Satire* 1.4 and other instances, including 2.3, 4, 7, and 8.[103] It is worth remembering how Horace's satires become much more dialogic as we move through his second book and that the device of the interlocutor is a means of distancing the speaker, and the author, from the views expressed in the text.[104] It is presumably the *simplicitas* of Lucilius that the speaker has in mind (he attacked Mucius Scaevola in his verses), but it is striking that he does not use the word we expect, namely *libertas*.[105] This is all the more surprising given the command to open all the sails (*totos pande sinus*), which would suggest a full-throttle approach. The word appears numerous times in the other satires, but usually in an ironic context: for example, the "freedom to speak in a broken voice" (*fracta voce loquendi libertas*) among effeminate men in 2.111–12 or the "freedom in making wills" (*testandi . . . libertas*) that exists only among gladiators and their trainers in 6.216–17.[106] The satirist encapsulates the *popina* where Lateranus, consul designate under Nero, mingles with all sorts of unsavory types by observing: *aequa ibi libertas, communia pocula, lectus / non alius cuiquam, nec mensa remotior ulli* (There is equal "freedom" for all: common drinking cups, no separate couch or table set apart for anyone, 8.177–78).[107] The disjunction in meaning between Lucilius's *libertas* and these occurrences in Juvenal points to that "strong sense of the passing of time" that

---

102. There could be an echo here of the end of Hor. *Epist.* 2.2, with its nautical imagery (199–204), cf. *Sat.* 1.4.120 (*nabis sine cortice*). The phrase *eadem . . . minores* recalls the line *expectes . . . minimoque poeta* discussed on pp. 61–62 above (Juv.1.14). On the passage as a whole, see Miller 2005, *ad loc.*

103. Courtney 1980, *ad loc.*, and 164.

104. Roller 2012 says the interlocutor is "rhetorically positioned as 'metasatiric'" (295). Cf. Pers. 1, esp. 44: *quisquis es, o modo quem ex adverso dicere feci. . . .* For a stimulating exploration of the interlocutor's genesis in oppressive conditions in which free speech is constrained, see Carmen Martín Gaite's novel *El cuarto de atrás* (1991) and collection *La búsqueda de interlocutor* (2000).

105. Ferguson 1979: "We expect *libertas*: indeed Cicero has a similar phrase with the word (*Planc.* 13.33 [*ubi illa antiqua libertas?*])" (123).

106. Other instances are: Creticus, "the fierce and indomitable champion of *libertas*" (*acer et indomitus libertatisque magister*, 2.77), an echo of Lucan 1.146 on Julius Caesar; Umbricius's bitter remark that the "poor man's *libertas*" (*libertatis pauperis haec est*, 3.299) consists of being beaten up then being allowed to plead to be let go; and the "face and *libertas* of a parent" (*frontem libertatemque parentis*, 14.56) worn by a father who in his old age behaves worse than his son. Cf. 6.140; 7.116; 8.263; 14.230.

107. Similar imagery to a very different effect in Stat. *Silv.* 1.6.43–45, celebrating Domitian's Saturnalian banquet: *una vescitur omnis ordo mensa, / parvi, femina, plebs, eques, senatus: / libertas reverentiam remisit.* On the legal import of *aequa libertas*, see Wirzubski 1950, 9–15.

Freudenburg discerns in "the abrupt change of satiric targets from the poet's Mucius to the cautious friend's Tigillinus." There is also a sudden confusion in definitions of high and low: Mucius was highborn and had an illustrious career in the Senate, whereas Tigillinus (praetorian prefect under Nero) rose from the dregs to a position of influence over the emperor. As Freudenburg observes: "The world of Lucilius, the world his would-be imitator understands and intends to work within, has been turned completely upside down by the likes of Tigillinus and Nero. And that is what makes Juvenal's reprise of Lucilius so utterly unthinkable in a first-century, totalitarian context."[108] The term *libertas* has become so debased by now that the satirist chooses to replace it with the less-charged *simplicitas* (cf. 3.192).[109] As for *libertas*, we might consider Seneca's more up-to-date, internalized definition in *Epistle* 51.8–9 more apposite—as freedom from the passions by which he will be torn asunder, pulled apart (*distrahar, immo discerpar*):

> Libertas proposita est; ad hoc praemium laboratur. Quae sit libertas, quaeris? Nulli rei servire, nulli necessitati, nullis casibus, fortunam in aequum deducere. Quo die illa me intellexero plus posse, nil poterit. Ego illam feram, cum in manu mors sit?

> I have set freedom before my eyes; and I am striving for that reward. And what is freedom, you ask? It means not being a slave to any circumstance, to any constraint, to any chance; it means compelling Fortune to enter the lists on equal terms. And on the day when I know that I have the upper hand, her power will be naught. When I have death in my own control, shall I take orders from her?[110]

The close proximity of *libertas* with death is telling in this rather pessimistic vision.[111]

In Juvenal 1, the exchange between the speaker and his interlocutor continues:

---

108. Freudenburg 2001, 243–44; Roller 2012, 292–99.

109. The words are clearly similar, but *simplicitas* lacks the political and literary reverberations of *libertas*. Mart. 10.47.7 has *prudens simplicitas*, which would mean "circumspect frankness" or "frankness tempered by discretion" as with L. and P. Watson 2003, 141.

110. Trans. Gummere 1917–25.

111. See Gallia 2012, chap. 1, on the revival of *libertas* in the year of rebellion, 68 C.E.. Stat. *Silv.* 4.9 offers what Newlands 2002 calls a "transvaluation" of *libertas* (259): "The political liberty of a Brutus may be obsolete, but the poet can explore other means of literary autonomy, even if that in the end means withdrawal from engagement with a poetics of empire. *Libertas* now resides, if at all, in the realms of domesticity and aesthetic, not politics."

Et latum media sulcum deducis harena (Juv. 1.157). Colosseum, exterior. Photograph by David Larmour and Corby Kelly.

"Pone Tigillinum, taeda lucebis in illa
qua stantes ardent qui fixo gutture fumant,
et latum media sulcum deducis harena."[112]
qui dedit ergo tribus patruis aconita, vehatur
pensilibus plumis atque illinc despiciat nos?
"Cum veniet contra, digito compesce labellum: 160
accusator erit qui verbum dixerit 'Hic est.'
Securus licet Aenean Rutulumque ferocem
committas, nulli gravis est percussus Achilles
aut multum quaesitus Hylas urnamque secutus.
Ense velut stricto quotiens Lucilius ardens
infremuit, rubet auditor cui frigida mens est
criminibus, tacita sudant praecordia culpa.
Inde ira et lacrimae. Tecum prius ergo voluta
haec animo ante tubas: galeatum sero duelli
paenitet." Experiar quod concedatur in illos   170
quorum Flaminia tegitur cinis atque Latina.

---

112. On textual problems including a possible lacuna, see Braund 1996a; Miller 2005, *ad loc.*; there is a movement in any case, either abrupt or slightly less so, from the silenced mouth to the dead body.

"Describe Tigillinus, and you'll burn brightly on that torch where men
    stand and burn and smoke with their throat transfixed
and trace a broad furrow through the middle of the arena."
So, is someone who has given aconite to three uncles to be carried
on swaying feather pillows and look down on me from there?
"When he comes near, put your finger to your lip:
whoever says the word 'that's the man' will be treated as an accusor.
You may safely pit Aeneas and the fierce Rutulian together,
Achilles struck down or Hylas much searched for, after he
followed his water jar, will not endanger anyone.
Whenever Lucilius, as if with sword in hand,
roars, the hearer, whose mind is cold with crimes,
grows red, his heart sweats with silent consciousness of guilt.
Hence rage and tears. So, turn these things over in your mind
before the war trumpets sound: once you've put your helmet on,
it's too late to repent of the battle." I will try what may be permitted
against those whose ashes are covered by the Flaminian and Latin
    roads. (155–71)

Tigillinus is exactly the kind of individual the satirist would like to target. In Suetonius's account, he is responsible for arranging entertainments in the arena that were followed by Nero's notorious marriage to another man. This is a juxtaposition Juvenal will shortly use in his criticism of Gracchus in *Satire* 2.[113] The introduction to *Satire* 1 culminated with the speaker charging into battle like Lucilius, but now the conclusion imagines him being dragged across the arena for speaking out too boldly about his contemporaries.[114] Being "transfixed by the throat," referring to the curved hook that was put through the chin in this form of punishment,[115] is the most brutal image linking speech with violence in the entire poem, and it encapsulates both the dangers inherent in

---

113. Suetonius, *Nero* 28.1. On Tigillinus, see Tac. *Hist.* 1.72; in *Ann.* 16.18, one Petronius [presumably author of the *Satyricon*] is said to have incurred his hostility *quasi adversus aemulum et scientia voluptatem potiorem.*

114. Cf. *Satire* 10.118–32 on how Demosthenes' and Cicero's talent for eloquence caused their deaths, and in the latter's case, mutilation of the body: *largus et exundans leto dedit ingenii fons. / ingenio manus est et cervix caesa, nec unquam / sanguine causidici maduerunt rostra pusilli* (119–21).

115. Ferguson 1979, 123; Freudenburg 2001, 245; Keane 2006, 50–52, 63–64. Sen. *Ep.* 14.4–6, discussing the parade of horrors inspired by fear *ex aliena potentia*, includes *uncum et adactum per medium hominem, qui per os emergeret, stipitem* (the hook, and the stake which they drive straight through a man until it protrudes from his throat). Interestingly, when Otho contrived to make Tigillinus commit suicide (see Tac. *Hist.* 1.72; Plut. *Otho* 2; Ash 1999, 86–88), he did so amid orgies with prostitutes and with delaying tactics, "blackening his notorious life with a dishonourable death" as Tacitus puts it, and he did it with a cutthroat razor (*novacula*) more suitable to a street fight (Mart. 7.61.7).

speaking and the painful reality of enforced silence.[116] There is another reworking of Horace's programmatic *Satire* 1.4 here: he had claimed he was afraid to
recite publicly "because there are some who don't enjoy this genre, since most
of them deserve censure" (24–25), and the satirist is regarded as a mad bull (*fae-
num habet in cornu: longe fuge* [He has hay on his horns: move away], 34).[117] In
Juvenal's case, as Keane observes, "Satiric attack comes back to haunt the poet
himself, converting satiric author to victim, exemplum, and spectacle all at
once. . . . The entire process of satiric violence becomes, for Juvenal's reader and
his punisher's audience, the subject of scrutiny. The image is a fitting climax
not just to Juvenal's high-flown program poem, but to the entire tradition of
violent programmatic images presented by his predecessors."[118] The hook was
used to drag the bodies of executed criminals out of the arena—very likely accompanied by abuse and mutilation—and hooks were inserted into the mouths
of convicts at trials to prevent them from uttering abusive language to the
judges.[119]

The Juvenalian speaker's fall from his "high horse" is emphasized in the
numerous contrasts between up and down, high and low, that run through the
final scene. Once again the litter features prominently in the hodgepodge of
images, elevating above the crowd a man who poisoned three uncles and now
"looks down upon" the speaker, who, however, dare not say anything.[120] Turnus and Achilles have both fallen in battle and are now down in the Underworld, Hylas has descended into his pool, the three uncles are in their tombs
while their poisoner rides on high—these images not only capture the topsy-
turvy realm Rome has become but also evoke the experience of the spectator
gazing down at the participant in the arena and of him looking up in turn at
the viewers. This is nicely captured in Pliny's scene of the spectators looking at
the *delatores* paraded in the arena in the brave new world ushered in by Trajan
after the fall of Domitian:

> Nihil tamen gratius, nihil saeculo dignius, quam quod contigit
> desuper intueri delatorum supina ora retortasque cervices.

116. Echoes of Hor. *Sat.* 2.1, Kenney 1962; of Lucil. 30, Griffith 1970.
117. On the bull and iambic poets, see Freudenburg 1993, 78–79, 105; Keane 2006, 47. Freudenburg 2001
comments that we now see "Juvenal himself, the madman satirist . . . the principal spectacle of uncontrolled *ira*"
(254). The concluding image in Horace's defense of his art was *disiecta membra poetae* (the limbs of a dismembered poet, 62), Orpheus's fate (see Gowers 2012, 161). Oliensis 1998 sees the textual dismemberment that occurs
when the word order is disrupted as "a microcosm of civic upheaval and confusion of social orders" (23–24).
118. Keane 2006, 51.
119. Kyle 1998, 156 and n6; Potter 1996, 151, on convict hooks in the eastern empire.
120. Cf. the diner in *Satire* 5.83, 125–27, and chap. 3 herein.

Agnoscebamus et fruebamur, cum velut piaculares publicae
sollicitudinis victimae supra sanguinem noxiorum ad lenta supplicia
gravioresque poenas ducerentur.

Yet nothing was so popular, nothing so fitting for our times as the
opportunity we enjoyed of looking down at the informers at our feet,
their heads forced back and faces upturned to meet our gaze. We
knew them and rejoiced; like victims chosen to atone for the
sufferings of their country, treading in the blood of the criminals
before them, they were led to long-lasting punishment and more
fearful retribution. (*Panegyricus* 34.3–4)[121]

It is safe, assuredly, to "pit" (*committere*, 163) Aeneas against Turnus, like a pair
of gladiators,[122] but going out to battle like Lucilius, with drawn sword and
helmet, brings only "rage and tears."[123] This is the first (but not the last)
mention of Aeneas, pointing to the struggle between him and Turnus in
book 12 of the *Aeneid;* Achilles harks back to Telephus at the beginning of
the poem, and "much searched-for Hylas" (who, of course, drowned in a
pool) recalls Jason's sea voyage from the opening and Heracles in 52.[124] Aeneas serves as a reminder of the promise—and failure—of Rome to offer guarantees of *Romanitas*. The much searched-for Hylas recalls those unfinished
quests at the start of the poem, while the glancing reference through the participle *percussus* back to Icarus in line 54 (*mare percussum*) reinforces the theme
of failure.[125]

    The use of the phrase *deducere sulcum* (trace a furrow) makes the connec-
tion between the satirist's poetic program and his potential fate in the arena
especially clear; the verb has the meaning "spin" or "spin finely" and is used of

---

121. Trans. Radice 1969. Cf. *Pan.* 35.2: as real criminals now nailed to rocks which had been the cross of
many an innocent man; see Uden 2015, "Satirist and Informer: The History of a Relationship" (29–35).

122. The use of *committo* is repeated in 6.436, where the female scholar is being ridiculed for pitting
poets against each other and weighing them in the balance (*committit vates et comparat*). The idiom is recorded
in Mart. 7.24.1 of his rivalry with none other than Juvenal: *cum Iuvenale meo quae me committere temptas*. On
Aeneas and Turnus, cf. Leigh 1997, 248–49.

123. Cf. Hor. *Epist.* 1.19.41: *hinc illae lacrimae*, echoing Ter. *And.* 125 which became proverbial (cf. Cic.
Pro Cael. 25.61).

124. These figures still have multiple resonances, however: see Oliensis 1998, 83. Achilles is an ambiguous figure when it comes to Roman ideology: he is the archetype of the hero, but also represents the
threat to Troy and, if imperial Rome is the new Troy, this creates something of an aporia.

125. Hendry emends to *pertusus* (perforated) accepted by some editors, but not by Courtney 1980 (118).
Percutio (strike, strike through, kill, shock) is a favorite verb of Juvenal's: 3.271, 4.124, 9.30, 10.149, 11.198,
12.20, 14.286, 15.21, 15.66. Cf. *percussor* used as "hitman" in Suet. *Nero* 47.3, in connection with suicide; Plass
1995, 234n5 (sometimes he was a gladiator).

spinning verses first by Horace in his *Satires* (1.10.43–44; 2.1.4).[126] He also uses it in *Odes* 3.30, the *exegi monumentum* poem that ends the volume, when he describes himself as *princeps Aeolium Carmen ad Italos / deduxisse modos* (the first to have introduced Aeolian song to Italian meters, 13–14).[127] The verb is also used of leading captives in triumph back to Rome, a sense that Horace exploits in his self-glorifying poem.[128] Juvenal by contrast deploys it of himself in a most degrading image. While Horace in 3.30.6–7 says that *non omnis moriar multaque pars mei / vitabit Libitinam* (I shall not wholly die, and a major part of me will avoid Libitina),[129] Juvenal twists this around to suggest that certainly if he were to follow the path of Lucilius, and perhaps even the more cautious steps of Horace, he would end up tracing a furrow in the sand of the arena—and we know that corpses were dragged out through the Gate of Libitina, the *Porta Libitinensis*.[130] The verb is used in a similarly degrading manner in 8.273, of the suspect line of descent from the inhabitants of Romulus's originary asylum (*ab infami gentem deducis asylo*).[131] We ought to pay passing attention to the *sulcus* too. In Varro's etymological excursus into the vocabulary of city-founding and the origin of the Pomerium (*post murum/moerium*) he describes how the process began by making a furrow with a plough so that the inhabitants of the city might be fortified with a ditch and a wall (*aratro circumagebant sulcum . . . ut fossa et muro essent muniti*), and the circle (*orbis*, which was *post murum*) was the beginning of the *urbs*.[132] The satirist had set out initially all fired up to restore the original boundaries of *Romanitas*, to demarcate "the clean and proper Rome," but by the end of *Satire* 1, it is a very different kind of *sulcus* which he imagines himself tracing. As we shall see in the opening lines of *Satire* 2, he will not be talking about the same sort of *fossa* (ditch) as Varro either.

That Juvenal is aware of the literary overtones of *deducere* is quite apparent from a passage in *Satire* 7, which, as we have noted, is his "second" programmatic piece opening the third book, as the speaker renews his dedication to his

126. See P. M. Brown 1995 and Muecke 1993, *ad loc.*; also *Epist.* 2.1.225 (*tenui deducta poemata filo*) and *AP* 128–29 (*tuque / rectius Iliacum Carmen deducis in actus*); cf. Verg. *Ecl.*. 6.5 (*deductum dicere Carmen*); 6.71 (*deducere montibus ornos*). *OLD deduco* 4b, Prop. 1.160.41; *OLD duco* 23d, Prop. 4.6.13. See also Spencer 2010 in connection with Evander's tour of the future Rome (53).

127. Connor 1987, 13–14; Nisbet and Rudd 2004, 375–76.

128. Connor 1987, 13; *OLD deduco* 10a; Hor. *Odes* 1.37.31. Cf. *Illic heu miseri traducimur*, Juv. 2.159.

129. Juv. 12.122: *nam si Libitinam evaserit aeger*; Hor. *Sat.* 1.6.19 on avoiding Libitina by retreating to the country in the autumn.

130. Auguet 1972; Kyle 1998, 156, 161–67; Dunkle 2008, 190. Dio 73.21.3 says Commodus's helmet was taken out through this gate.

131. See intro., p. 33 herein.

132. Varro *LL* 5.143.

craft after the first two books of the collection.[133] The theme of the poem is patronage, elaborated through a series of exempla including poets, historians, orators and schoolteachers; the opening line makes the point that only the Emperor (presumably Hadrian or Trajan) offers the hope of proper support. Horace's good fortune in having Maecenas receives an appropriately nostalgic mention (7.94).[134] The phrase *deducere sulcum* is picked up when the satirist laments the difficulty a poet has in securing a decent recitation hall from his parsimonious patron:

> Nos tamen hoc agimus tenuique in pulvere sulcos
> ducimus et litus sterili versamus aratro.
> Nam si discedas, laqueo tenet ambitioso
> consuetudo mali tenet insanabile multos
> scribendi cacoethes et aegro in corde senescit.
> Sed vatem egregium, cui non sit publica vena,
> qui nihil expositum soleat deducere . . .

> Yet we keep doing this and trace furrows in the thin sand
> and turn over the seashore with our sterile plough.
> For if you try to give up, the itch for writing
> —a bad habit, it has an incurable hold on many—
> holds you in its ambitious noose and grows to old age in your sick heart.
> But the outstanding bard, who has no ordinary vein of talent,
> who is accustomed to spin nothing vulgar . . . (48–54)

Such a poet—who desires the woods (*cupidus silvarum*, 58)—can only be imagined these days, one who is free from anxiety and bitterness because he is comfortably off; and it is Horace whom the speaker imagines: *satur est cum dicit Horatius "euhoe"* (Horace was full when he said "Evoe!" 62).[135] Poets who are not so fortunate, among whom the speaker seems to include himself, now "trace furrows in the sand," which is a waste of effort and does not produce anything. In addition to the use of *sulcus* and *(de)duco*, the image of the noose (*laqueum*), implying strangulation and the cutting off of speech from the throat, ensures that this passage in *Satire* 7 harks back to the concluding Tigillinus

---

133. See Larmour 2010–11, from which some of the following remarks are drawn. Courtney 1980, 348–50; Braund 1988, 24–68. Hor. *Sat*.1.1.15: *quo rem deducam*, of poetic "sign-posting." See Gowers 2012, *ad loc.*

134. More flatteringly than in *Sat*. 1.66, where Maecenas is referenced fleetingly when the *signator falsi* (forger) exposing himself in an open litter is likened to him (*multum referens de Maecenate supino*, 66) cf. 12.39: *teneris . . . Maecenatibus.*

135. On Statius's *Silvae* (Woodland") and landscape, see Spencer 2010, 26–30, 104–13.

scene of *Satire* 1.[136] The description of the "squalid" recital hall immediately preceding, with its tiered seating reminiscent of the arena, reinforces the link (7.43–47);[137] similarly, at the very end of *Satire* 7, we are invited to contemplate the humiliating lot of the teacher who has to keep watch *in loco parentis* over naughty boys:

> "Haec" inquit "cura," sed cum se verterit annus,
> accipe, victori populus quod postulat, aurum.

> "That's your job," says the father, but at the turn of the year,
> take the same gold as the crowd demands for their winner. (242–43)

The point is that the *grammaticus* earns in a year what a gladiator gets for a single victory and, thus, to quote Courtney, "Brains are dragged down to the level of brawn."[138]

To return to the Tigillinus passage, the unusual word *duellum*, as we saw above, was used by Horace in his comparison of rival poets to dueling Samnites in *Epistle* 2.2.98,[139] and indeed the phrase *galeatum sero duelli / paenitet* (It's too late to regret going into battle once you're helmeted) could well be a hint at gladiatorial combat;[140] putting on the helmet just before battle suggests the gladiator as much as the soldier, since gladiators wore elaborate helmets, and this was the most striking and distinguishing part of their costume.[141]

---

136. In 6.107, *sulcus* of the furrow in a gladiator's face, made by his helmet. In *Sat.*1.4.65–70, Horace mentions Sulcius [derived presumably from *sulcus*] and Caprius (who may be fellow satirists, see Ullman 1917) as sources of danger to the robbers Caelius and Birrius; the latter name might be derived from a gladiator used by Milo, called Birra: see Rudd 1956 and Gowers 2012, 170.

137. Markus 2000, 151. See intro., pp. 49–50 herein.

138. Courtney 1980, *ad loc.*; cf. 7.113–14 of lawyers and charioteers. See also Clarke 1973.

139. Ferguson 1979 wonders why Juvenal uses the archaism at 1.169: "probably to give his caution a kind of hieratic wisdom and religious validity" (124). Braund 1996a comments on Juvenal's use of *duellum:* "archaic form of *belli*. Horace uses this form (in hexameters at *Epistles* 1.2.7, 2.1.254, 2.2.98), which may point to Lucilius having used it" (110). Or it may simply point to Horace's having used it: Courtney 1980 says it is one of Juvenal's "striking archaisms" and that Horace "evidently tried to popularise it" (118). Brink 1982, on *Epist.* 2.2.98, thinks it is used meaning "duel" for the first time here (324); in *Epist.* 1.2.7 *lento duello* refers to the Trojan War, also of course the proverbial subject of poets.

140. Keane 2006 certainly views it this way: "like an unwilling combatant who has been thrust into the arena and the city's gaze" (51).

141. One of the questions asked near the end of *Satire* 1 is *unde ingenium par materiae?* which could also have a gladiatorial resonance: cf. Hor. *Sat.* 2.6.44, a question asked during his hectic day at Rome: "*Thraex est Gallina Syro par?*" and in *Sat.* 1.7.16 Diomedes and Glaucus are unevenly matched, *disparibus* (150–51). Mart. *Spect.* 31.8, of a contest with no clear winner, says: *pugnavere pares, succubuere pares*. Sen. *De Ben.* 5.3.3, speaking of the giver and the receiver of benefits, says: *penes neutrum erit palma. Solet enim fieri, ut, etiam cum alter multis vulneribus confossus est, alter leviter quidem saucius pares exisse dicantur, quamvis alter videatur inferior* (The palm will belong to neither. For, it is customary that, even when one has been pierced by many wounds, and

While Horace sees himself as having achieved a degree of immortality and raised a *monumentum*, Juvenal's speaker, precisely to avoid a premature and painful death, positions himself by the *monumenta* of the dead along the roads leading out of Rome. Horace sees himself as a victorious athlete, wearing a laurel crown (*Odes* 3.30.15–16); the satirist says that he will "try what he can get away with" against only dead opponents. This has the flavor of a palinode, like Horace's above-mentioned *Epode* 17, in which he regrets his abuse of Canidia because of the deleterious effects her spells have had on him and pleads for release—just as Telephus was healed by Achilles.

At the end of the programmatic *Satire* 1, then, the satirist chooses the arena for one of the most important points he wishes to make: the dangers associated with this combative and outspoken brand of poetic activity. If you say the wrong thing about, or even mention, the wrong person, then your corpse will end up marking a line through the sand. One thinks here of Pliny's recalling that under Domitian, if someone were not careful with his expressions of enthusiasm or preference for a particular gladiator, he could be transformed from spectator into spectacle, dragged off by a hook or to the flames:[142]

> Iam quam libera spectantium studia, quam securus favor! Nemini impietas ut solebat obiecta, quod odisset gladiatorem; nemo e spectatore spectaculum factus miseras voluptates unco et ignibus expiavit. Demens ille verique honoris ignarus, qui crimina maiestatis in harena colligebat.

> Now [under Trajan] how freely the spectators could express their enthusiasms and show their preference without fear. No one risked the old charge of impiety if he disliked a particular gladiator; no spectator found himself the spectacle, dragged off by the hook or to the flames to satisfy grim pleasures. He [Domitian] was a madman, ignorant of the true nature of his position, who used the arena for collecting charges of high treason. (*Panegyricus* 33.3–4)[143]

---

the other only slightly wounded, they are said to have left evenly matched, even though one is seen to be weaker).

142. Suet. *Dom.* 10.1 records an instance of a paterfamilias thrown to the dogs for making a disparaging remark about Thracian gladiators in Domitian's presence. Mart. 10.5 elaborately curses an anonymous lampooner for circulating his poems about the city's nobility, perhaps under Mart.'s name, which could be dangerous: see L. and P. Watson 2003, 99–105, and Suet. *Dom.* 8.3.

143. Trans. Radice 1969.

An even better example is provided by Suetonius's anecdote (*Caligula* 27) of how Caligula had a writer of Atellan farces burned alive in the arena because of a line that had an amusing double entendre.

Through the mention of Tigillinus, Juvenal's punishment recalls in particular Nero's human torches made from Christians.[144] According to Tacitus, it was in order to quench the persistent rumor that the Great Fire had been started deliberately that Nero was prompted to make Christians into scapegoats. They were duly punished by the most extreme measures (*quaesitissimis poenis*) and were fixed to crosses and/or set on fire, so they could be used as torches to light up the night (*Annales* 15.44).[145] Nero offered his gardens for the spectacle (*spectaculo*) and "produced" it (*circense ludicrum edebat*), even mingling with the crowd as a charioteer. The victims were apparently dressed in the *tunica molesta*, which Juvenal specifically mentions in *Satire* 8.235 as the appropriate punishment for criminals—like Cethegus and Catiline—who planned to set homes and temples on fire. The connection between the punishment and the crime has more than minor relevance to the satirist himself: as a speaker who is "on fire" or who "burns" (Lucilius, after all, is *ardens*, and anger burns— *ardeat*—the speaker's liver), he runs the risk of causing a conflagration by his verses and hence could end up being punished as the Christians were.[146] The manner in which Tacitus's Great Fire narrative is bound up with Nero's building plan for Rome, including the Domus Aurea, was probably not lost on Juvenal. Tacitus takes the time to explain that the streets in the city were broader after the fire and that buildings and people had fewer "protecting shadows" from the sun. In his startling arena allusion, then, the satirist manages to combine, in a complex web of association and suggestiveness, various motifs, including fire, speech, punishment, and spectacle with the cityscape of Rome and the generic landscape of satire.

Being dragged through the sand after being burned alive is an effective image of failure and humiliation, as well as of the abjection of his own physical and literary body,[147] but why does the satirist choose to associate himself

---

144. Cf. also Suet. *Dom.* 4 on his innovation of night-time gladiatorial shows lit by torches.

145. †aut crucibus adfixi aut flammandi† *atque ubi defecisset dies, in usum nocturni luminis urerentur.* Mart. 10.25.5–6 recounts the behavior of a criminal who was forced to play the part of Mucius Scaevola by putting his hand in the fire—in order to avoid the worse fate of being burned alive, *tunica praesente molesta*)—and who, according to Mart., would have been more heroic if he had refused the order *"ure manum"*: see Colton 1991, 345–46; also Barton 1993 on his silence (100).

146. See 1.45 and 165; on fire in *Sat.* 1, Bertman 1968. Cic. *Phil.* 4.16: *me auctore et principe ad spem libertatis exarsimus,* cf. the concluding exhortation of *Phil.* 6.19: *de libertate decernitur . . . populi Romani est propria libertas.*

147. Gowers 2012 notes instances of abjection in Hor. *Sat.* 1: 2.127–33, 6.81–82, 6.106 (116, 239, 243).

with the arena in this particular way? One possible source is Horace's famous
recusatio to Maecenas in the opening lines of his first book of epistles:

> Prima dicte mihi, summa dicende Camena,
> spectatum satis et donatum iam rude quaeris,
> Maecenas, iterum antiquo me includere ludo.
> Non eadem est aetas, non mens. Veianius armis
> Herculis ad postem fixis latet abditus agro,
> ne populum extrema totiens exoret harena.
> Est mihi purgatam crebro qui personet aurem:
> "solve senescentem mature sanus equum, ne
> peccet ad extremum ridendus et ilia ducat."

> You of whom my first Muse told, of whom my last shall tell,
> you, Maecenas, seek to shut me up again in my old school,
> although displayed enough and already presented with the foil
>   of retirement.
> I'm not of the same age or mind. Veianus has hung up his arms
> at the doorpost of Hercules and lies hidden in the country,
> so that he does not have to plead with the mob at the edge of the
>   arena.
> There is someone who keeps shouting in my well-cleansed ear:
> "Be sensible in good time and let the aging horse go, so that he doesn't
> stumble at the end and lose his wind for all to laugh at." (1.1–9)

Horace's likening of himself to a gladiator who has been presented with the
wooden sword of retirement (*rudis*) is usually read as frivolous or as a clever
conceit to mark his transition from lyric to the genre of the philosophical
epistle.[148] In her exploration of the "discursive web of associations raised by
this image of laborious showmanship sponsored by another," Bowditch argues
for a more pointed reading and suggests that the gladiatorial metaphor is Horace's "humorous demystification of the ideal of voluntarism and disinterested-
ness in literary patronage as practiced by Augustus and Maecenas."[149] *Specta-
tum* casts Horace as on display in the sand, while Veianius is a gladiator who
has retired to the country (*latet abditus agro*) and no longer has to plead
with the populace at the edge of the arena, whether for his life, rewards, or

---

148. On the *rudis*, cf. 6.113; Mart. 3.36.10, *rudis* as discharge from thirty years of (unrewarding) *amicitia*
with Fabianus.

149. Bowditch 2001, 172, 174; she discusses *Epist.* 1.1 in 1–10 and 170–81. The link between *amicitia* and
the arena is clearly an intriguing one for Roman satirists.

popularity. In Juvenal's *Satire* 7, the speaker offers advice to the teachers of rhetoric, deploying gladiatorial imagery in the Horatian mode:

> **Ergo sibi dabit ipse rudem**, si nostra movebunt
> consilia, et vitae diversum iter ingredietur
> ad pugnam qui rhetorica descendit ab umbra,
> summula ne pereat qua vilis tessera venit
> frumenti; quippe haec merces lautissima.

> So this is the advice I have for anyone who comes down
> from the grove of rhetoric to fight for the tiny fee which
> buys his cheap corn coupon (after all, that's the most lavish
> reward he can expect). If he'll follow my advice, **he'll take
> early retirement** and enter a different path of life. (171–75)[150]

The second telling image, of an aging racehorse, is introduced via someone who repeats loudly in the poet's ear that he should be let go now, so that he doesn't stumble at the end of the race.[151] The repetition of *extremus* (*extrema . . . harena*, *ad extremum*) connects the tired racehorse with the retired gladiator, and thus links the poet with the two roles. It also intimates a liminal positioning of the kind that we have noted in connection with Juvenal's speaker, who speaks "from the edge" when he first addresses us and again from the outskirts of the city when he leaves us by the tombs along the Flaminian and Latin roads. The Horatian *recusatio* has some clear links with Juvenal's opening lines too: the retreat of Veianus to the countryside echoes Sulla's retirement from politics, as well as Umbricius's departure from Rome in *Satire* 3. Horace has been on view and shut up in the *ludus* long enough (*satis*); Juvenal's satirist has been confined to listening and has been "shut up" in another sense long enough. Both these prefatory passages focus on the seeking of approval and popularity, but to different effect. "Letting the old horse go" is similar to urging Sulla to retire, and the equine characterization of Horace is paralleled by the image of Lucilius charging off in his chariot. Horace's statement that he is going to devote himself to what is *verum atque decens* and pursue *vera virtus* actually strikes a similar, if

---

150. Trans. Braund 2004. Cf. Sen. Eld. *Controv.* 9 Praef. 5: *velut ex umbroso et obscuro prodeuntes clarae lucis obcaecat, sic istos e scholis in forum transeuntes*. The metaphor of the *pugna* picks up on the use of *sagittae* (arrows) of arguments launched in rhetorical compositions in 7.156: *Quae veniant diversa parte sagittae*; Courtney 1980 comments that "here the metaphor is probably gladiatorial" (173); Cic. *De Orat.* 2.316–17, 200, 220 (*telum orationis*); Sen. Eld. *Controv.* 3 Praef. 10, 13 (*Hoc ita semper habitum est, scholam quasi ludum esse, forum arenam*); 4 Praef. 1; 9 Praef. 4 on gladiators and orators; cf. Quintil. 2.17.33, cause is set against cause as two gladiators trained under the same master *componuntur*. Other examples, Quintil. 2.12.2; Tac. *Dial.* 26.4.

151. For *pecco* of stumbling in the linguistic or artistic sense, Mart. 2.8.5.

less angry, note to Juvenal's speaker's announcement of his reasons for writing satire. Both speakers appeal to reason (*solve . . . mature sanus / si . . . placidi rationem admittitis*).

Finally, it is worth noting that *Epistle* 1.19, mentioned earlier for its combination *auditor et ultor*, also ends with a series of combat and gladiatorial images as the recital hall becomes an amphitheater:

> ad haec ego naribus uti
> formido et, luctantis acuto ne secer ungui,
> "displicet iste locus," clamo et diludia posco.
> Ludus enim genuit trepidum certamen et iram,
> ira truces inimicitias et funebre bellum.

> At this I am afraid to turn up a scornful nose and,
> lest I be cut by a sharp nail if he struggles with me,
> I cry, "This place you have chosen doesn't suit me" and demand a
>   pause.
> For the combat begets tumultuous strife and anger,
> and anger fierce quarrels and a war to the death. (45–49)

The word *diludium* denotes a pause in the combat, to adjust positions or restore a level playing field and is found only here.[152] It is likely, then, that the interweaving of gladiatorial and equestrian imagery so strikingly deployed in Horace's *Epistles* was reworked by Juvenal to formulate his own poetic stance. The suggestive association of poetry and fighting—whether on the battlefield or the arena—which he found in Horace's *Epistles* and perhaps elsewhere may well have inspired Juvenal to present his own craft in a similar manner.

In book 1 of his *Satires*, Horace has Crispinus, a long-winded poet with Stoic pretensions, and Tigellius, the profligate singer and familiar of Julius Caesar and Octavian, as objects of ridicule in his first four poems; Juvenal has Crispinus and Tigillinus (or Tigellinus), henchmen of Domitian and Nero, respectively, as his stars.[153] Whether or not the use of the same name Crispinus and the close similarity of Tigellius and Tigillinus are deliberate references to Horace's poems on Juvenal's part, the contrast in their use points up

---

152. Cf. Lucil. 3.117, *internecio*. R. Mayer 1994 notes that the collection has come full circle with this reminder of the first image of *Epist*. 1 (268). He explains that 19 is really the last epistle in the collection because 20 is a direct address to Maecenas (269).

153. Described as *ineptus*, *Sat*. 1.3.138; in 2.7, Davus has picked up his Stoic themes by a circuitous route—the eavesdropping *ianitor* of Crispinus.

some critical differences in approach. With examples of the caliber of *his* Crispinus and Tigillinus to deal with, Juvenal cannot possibly maintain that restrained tone so carefully modulated by Horace.[154] His enthusiastic validation of Lucilius's martial zeal in the opening lines of *Satire* 1 was followed by the more oblique incorporation of Horace (he does not name him until his second programmatic piece, 7.62) through the Venusian lamp image. Both Lucilius and Horace are initially presented through their birthplace: Lucilius's in Aurunca and Horace's in Venusia.[155] While Lucilius rides into battle against substantial foes who must be attacked with all the urgency and severity with which Aeneas had to face Turnus, Horace sheds light—a less confrontational mode than the flaming brand—on miscreants. So although the speaker holds up Lucilius as his model, the deployment of the Venusian lamp image marks a deliberate moving away from him. This process reaches its conclusion at the end of the poem, where the consequences of the Lucilian approach—tempting and justifiable as it might be—are vividly portrayed.[156] These are that the speaker becomes a torch, shedding light for sure, but at the cost of his own body and life. There is a danger, in other words, of being consumed by the very fire that drives the satirist to speak in the first place or by the flames of indignation he kindles. Rome burns the body of the poet who takes fire to it.[157] It is better to hold up a lamp than be a torch.[158] The trick for the satirist is to be *auctor mortis*—of others, not his own.[159]

There is indeed a distinction, then, between *pitting together* Aeneas and Turnus (himself connected to Aurunca in a Vergilian allusion in *Satire* 2.100), who are dead or mythical, and *going out oneself* to do battle with living contemporaries. Lucilius, and to a significantly limited extent, Horace may have been

154. Both have entertainment connections. Cf. Juvenal 9's Naevolus and the Naevius of Hor. *Sat.*1.101 (and Gowers, *ad loc.*, on a possible Lucilian provenance) and 2.2.68.

155. Cf. *Sat.* 2.1.35; *Odes* 1.28.26.

156. On the lamp, cf. Hor. *Sat.* 2.7.48: Davus's prostitute receives his "blows" *sub clara nuda lucerna*; Juvenal refers to lamps on several occasions: Messalina goes back to the emperor's couch from the brothel with her cheeks dirty from the smoke of the lamp (6.131–32; cf. 10.339); in 7.225–28, the schoolteacher's copies of Horace and Vergil get blackened by soot from lamps.

157. On the poet's body as a stand-in for Rome in Hor.'s Journey to Brundisium poem, see Schlegel 2005, chap. 3. Cf. Benjamin's (1985) inscriptional introduction to *One Way Street*: "This street is named Asja Lacis Street after she who like an engineer cut it through the author."

158. As Keane 2006 demonstrates in her discussion of the "theatrics of satire" (13–41), Juvenal evinces a keen interest in the "transforming nature of spectatorship" and the slippage between viewer and viewed (35); Freudenburg 2001, 251.

159. The term comes from Sen. Eld. *Controv.* 8.6: *concitatissuma est in morte rabies et desperatione ultima in furorem animus impellitur. quaedam ferae tela ipsa commordent et ad mortis auctorem per vulnera sua ruunt. abscisa missione gladiator quem armatus fugerat nudus insequitur. praecipitati non quod impulit tantum trahunt, sed quod occurrit, et naturali quodam deploratae mentis adfectu morientibus gratissimum est commori.*

able to go into such a battle—even to play the active part of gladiator—but for Juvenal's speaker this role is only momentarily appealing. Keane observes that Horace "dramatizes the satirist figure's movement between the roles of aggressor, victim, and spectator to violence. His experience in these roles highlights their instability, and so the instability of a system of definition and correction that relies on them. This introduces into satire the theme of the satirist's own vulnerability." This vulnerability is substantially magnified in Juvenal, who, in an attempt to avoid the fate of victim in a *spectaculum*, opts to take on the role of *editor* (even though, as we shall see, he inevitably ends up playing both parts).[160] He does not want to be confined, he wants to do the confining; hence the concern with borders and boundaries whose permeability threatens his ability to enclose the targets of his distaste within the walls of his arena of satire. The constraining of *libertas* that *Satire* 1 enacts parallels the enclosing of freeborn *virtus* within the arena, which, as many have argued, replaced the traditional battlegrounds where it could be exercised: military campaigns, political advancement, oratory in the Senate or the law courts.[161] Horace's "solutions" to the problem of freedom of expression—of a *libertas* for a new era—as elaborated in his *Epistles* and *Satires* are in the forefront of Juvenal's consideration of the same issue as he embarks on his own satirical voyage.[162] His audience would have understood very well why the lamp of Horace was the better method.[163]

This transition from Lucilius to Horace, from plain to arena, necessitates a new programmatic stance, and it is that the dead only will be attacked. Juvenal's "journey" in this satire continues the journey made by Horace in his own programmatic piece *Satire* 1.4 (up to which 1–3 lead), complete with imaginary interlocutors and justifications. That poem was followed by the journey to Brundisium, in which the relationship between the poet and Maecenas was negotiated over the course of a journey along the Via Appia (1.5). And so now the Juvenalian speaker embarks on a route out of the city past the burial grounds of the Flaminian and Latin roads, with the Flaminian recalling the earlier

160. Keane 2006, 57. Cf. the end of Hor. *Sat*.1.2.127–33, an adultery mime wherein Horace moves from being a spectator to playing the role of the adulterer in danger of being apprehended by the returning husband; see Hooley 1999; Gowers 2012, *ad loc.*

161. See Hopkins 1983; Barton 1993; Kyle 1998; and chap. 3 herein.

162. On the *Epistles*, see especially Johnson 1993, a study of book 1 from the standpoint of the "dialectic of freedom"; Rudd 1966 discusses considering the *Epistles* as the non-Lucilian part of Horace's satirical corpus; he notes that Persius draws freely on them (155–59). Schlegel 2005 argues that by *Satire* 1.10, Horace cannot continue with silence, and is vulnerable both because he criticizes Lucilius and because his own satires will be criticized (chap. 7).

163. Gowers 2012 observes of *Satire* 1.3 that there is a suspicion that Horace "is expediently making the loss of *libertas* into a virtue" (121).

image of the young Automedon careering along at breakneck speed, show-ing off.[164] If the Automedon figure is indeed analogous to the bombastic poets ridiculed in the opening verses of *Satire* 1, then Juvenal promises a different kind of poetic track: one that moves out of Rome or at least to the city limits, and one that is more involved (it claims) with the dead than the living.[165] The Horatian resonances of the arena imagery at the end of *Satire* 1 are thus critical for understanding the poetic journey taken by the Juvenalian speaker. It is a journey very much akin to Horace's own, with its continual negotiating be-tween high and low status positions, between inclusion and exclusion,[166] and marked by striking images of reversal and inversion, such as in the Saturna-lian dialogue with Davus in *Satire* 2.7.[167]

Around the point where the Via Latina forked off from the Via Appia—the route taken by Umbricius on his way to Cumae—in a southeasterly direction, there were numerous tombs. One of the major sites in this area was the Tomb of the Scipios, emblematic of the idealized Republican past, and Scipio Ae-milianus was a well-known supporter of Lucilius.[168] But while Horace makes his justification of satire on the basis of a less Lucilian, less wounding, and more self-reflective mode, even leading to correction of his own behavior, Juvenal makes no apology for his astringency or his punishing stance.[169] His mode will also be less Lucilian, however, in the sense that he will not attack living indi-viduals *by name*. The names of the dead are fixed in time, as their monuments are fixed in space; those who are attacked under pseudonyms or as generic rep-resentatives are not necessarily part of this group. They become the new mon-uments of Rome, created by the satirist himself. Here he follows a trend already apparent in Horace, whose *libertas* with regard to living personages was itself significantly moderated.[170] Rudd says that 2.1 is actually the last of Horace's

164. The Via Flaminia is mentioned only in these two places by Juvenal.

165. Oliensis 1998 likens Horace's withdrawal to the country to his retreat in book 2 from the role of the satirist as constituted in 1.1–3 (51).

166. See Freudenburg 2001, 63; Keane 2006, 115; opinion differs, of course, on the extent of Horace's adaptability—even he seems uncertain; see Freudenburg's (2001) conclusion to his discussion of *Satire* 2: "In the end I think this poet is not so ready to adapt and he finds all sorts of ways to let us know that" (117).

167. This opens with the satirist encouraging his slave to speak out *libertate Decembri* and ends with his looking for a stone and arrows and threatening to make Davus a labourer on his Sabine farm (4–5, 115–17).

168. Cf. Cic. *Tusc.* 1.7.13: *An tu regressus Porta Capena, cum Calatini, Scipionum, Serviliorum, Metellorum sepulcra vides, miseros putas illos?* (When you leave the Porta Capena, and see the tombs of Calatinus, the Scipios, the Servilii, the Metelli, do you consider those men unhappy?); cf. Livy 38.53; *LTUR* 4.281–85.

169. Hor. *Sat.* 1.3.19–37. Rudd 1966 notes that Horace never denies that his poems may have an "aggres-sive tone" and does not condemn "Lucilius' spirit" (90–91).

170. Coffta 2002, 28. Cf. *Sat.* 2.1.5 *quiescas*, which advises Trebatius in response to Horace's acknow-ledgment that his satires are not popular with everyone. Rudd 1966 discusses the names in Horace and notes that there are fewer in book 2 (132–59).

satires and describes it as "the most brilliant piece of shadow-boxing in Roman literature." It is designed, he says, as "a bridge leading from the cultivated but open ground of Book 1 to the walled garden of Book 2."[171] The move from open to walled that Rudd detects in Horace's first eleven satires is accomplished by Juvenal within the space of a single poem, as we shift from the *campus* on which Lucilius drove to the arena in which the satirist fears to find himself. Juvenal, then, we might say, is "Lucilian" only in a post-Horatian sense.

The short-lived heroism of the satirist at the beginning of the poem recalls the phantasmagorical character of the urban hero for Baudelaire and Benjamin, who both mock the self-deceptive conceit of the bourgeois heroically facing the hazards of city life. They each, however, elevate the urban poet—who simultaneously represents and resists the fluidity of urban experience—to heroic status, along with the flâneur. As Gilloch puts it, "for Benjamin, the distinctive heroism of the *flâneur*, whether poet or not, resides precisely in his refusal to become part of the crowd. The *flâneur* is not merely a pedestrian, he is the heroic pedestrian." At the same time, this figure is the true urban hero only because he is not a hero at all: he is playing the role, acting the part.[172] The fine line between stressing that endurance of the city is in some sense heroic and exposing the illusory nature of this heroism is precisely what is blurred in Juvenal's discourse.

The decision at the end of *Satire* 1 to talk only about the dead is thus much more hard-hitting than its superficial justification suggests. Juvenal presents us with a Roman cityscape that is populated by corpses, almost a Night of the Living Dead.[173] It is, moreover, only among these corpses that satiric *libertas* can find a place to express itself. For all its promises of truth-telling or *libertas* on the Lucilian model, then, Juvenalian satire is a discourse endlessly negotiating between speech and silence. Such backtracking may have been traditional in the genre, but here it undermines the presentation the speaker gave of himself in the earlier part of the satire, precisely because he was so vehement from the start.[174] This in turn begins to shake the sense of security we have about the speaker's moral stance and consistency. Such loosening is, however, quite in keeping with the nature of this project as a whole: the unexpected shifts of subject, the changes in speaker, and the suddenness of both beginning and

171. Rudd 1966, 128, 131; on the effect of Actium in between the two books, see Gowers 2012, 5; Freudenburg 2001, 71–82.

172. Gilloch 1996, 153, 155–57; cf. 175.

173. See Duret and Néraudau 2001 on "La ville des morts" (169–77).

174. Braund 1996a, 117–19.

ending make for a sense that the ground is constantly shifting, and the reader has to struggle to keep on track. The undercutting of the speaker's own points of reference in regard to his predecessors and his genre, enacted within a cityscape whose most illustrious monuments and spaces offer little comfort, let alone stability, signals the loss of faith in all other hopes of security that will follow.

2

Beyond the Pale

With *warbling eunuchs* fill a licensed stage,
And lull to servitude a thoughtless age.
> —Samuel Johnson, "London: A Poem in Imitation
> of the Third Satire of Juvenal," 59–60

In this chapter, we shall consider how the traversal of space—of the city of Rome and the regions of the Empire beyond its walls—is connected in Juvenalian satire with anxieties about masculinity and femininity. In particular, how crossing the boundaries of gender identity—by "unmasculine" men and "unfeminine" women—is mapped onto borders of various kinds, such as those between internal and exterior space (signified by the doorway, or *limen*), the limits of the city of Rome (marked by walls, gates, and towers), and the edges of the Empire (including the Danube and Rhine rivers and such provinces as Armenia and Britannia). There are especially close connections between space and gender in *Satires* 2 and 6, which attack insufficiently "masculine" men and "inappropriately" behaved women, respectively.[1] *Satire* 2 ranges rapidly, even chaotically, over the entirety of Roman space, from private homes into the city streets and beyond, to the outposts of the Empire, as the border-crossing perpetrated by feminized men spreads like a contagion to populate the text

---

1. Richlin 1992, 69–70, and chap. 7, "Sexual Satire"; on Juvenal, 195–209; on 2 and 6, see Braund 1995, 211–13. On 2 and 9, see Bellandi 2009, Gold 2012, 100–105; Uden 2015, 65–85. On boundaries, Worman 2009 and, more broadly, Fögen and Lee 2009.

and the world with noxious *exempla*. Specific locations in the city are few, but redolent with significance: the Campus Martius (132), Valley of Quirinus (133) and the Via Sacra in the Forum (142), all in the vignette of Gracchus, who distinguishes himself first in the role of bride at a wedding and then as *retiarius* in the arena. Like Horace, who goes into the Forum in search of exempla of excess in *Satire* 1.2.25–27 and finds Maltinus *tunicis demissis* and others behaving badly the speaker heads into the public spaces of Rome. In *Satire* 6, amid references to numerous locations scattered across the Empire, the search for security in traditional ideals of femininity and marriage is undertaken through a journey back and forth across the public landmarks of Rome. We move from the rustic caves inhabited by the unkempt specimens of the Golden Age (1–13) to the Aemilian Bridge (32), the Capitoline Temple of Jupiter (47–48), the Campus Martius (153–54, 524–25, 529), the Portico of Agrippa (153–54), the embankment between the Colline and Esquiline gates (291, 588), the Altar of Pudicitia (308), Julius Caesar's house (345), the Temple of Isis (489, 528–29), and the Circus Maximus (582–83, 590).[2] *Satire* 9, with Naevolus the rent-male in dialogue with the satirist, picks up many of the same themes, moving from various rooms inside the *domus* to specific sites in the city—such as the statue of Marsyas and the Forum, the Temple of Isis, the Circus Maximus—and beyond to Cumae, Athens, and the locations around Sicily of Odysseus's encounters with Polyphemus and the Sirens.[3]

In these poems, the satirist takes us on a chronotopic tour not only across the spaces of Roman identity but also through its historical markers. After the poetic journey undertaken across the city (and the genre) in *Satire* 1, the second takes us back in time to the high and low points (mainly the latter) of the Republic, as the decay of traditional ideals of masculinity and *virtus*, which, after all, began then, is scrutinized through some startling contemporary examples of immorality. The destabilizing irruption of the Bacchanalia of 186 BCE is recalled, as are the disgraceful displays of Clodius and Mark Antony, while references to the heroic deeds of Scipio and Curius serve to underline the stark contrast between them and their descendants. Names and places freighted with memory flicker across the text continually. Chronotopic shifts are paralleled by semantic fluidity: *libertas* continues to be redefined, trailing in its wake the other signifiers of *Romanitas*—*concordia, simplicitas, pudicitia, virtus*, and the like. Stripped of their original referents, these terms are redeployed in

---

2. Cf. Ovid's tour of Rome in *Tr.* 3.1.

3. Bellandi 2009 sees 9 more closely linked with the set of issues raised in 3 and 5 (469); Rosen 2007, chap. 6 on 5 and 9, esp. 236–42.

scandalous settings, so that they come to mean close to their exact opposite in many cases.

Two aspects of space traversal are especially important in relation to gender. The first is the tension between centrifugal and centripetal movement: centrifugal movement is away from Rome, the hub of satiric space—from city to country and from the capital of the Empire to regions far away. It also involves going back in time to famous events in Roman history, especially during the Republic, but also to the foundation legend of Aeneas and to the mythical Golden Age. Finally, it includes movement from the world of the living to the realm of the dead. A particularly frequent form of centrifugal motion is the escape fantasy of the satirist, which is related to the motif of the gods abandoning a world become hopelessly corrupted—as in the flight of Pudicitia and Astraea (6.19–20) or the absence of Mars (2.130–32). There is, of course, no "beyond," and the wish for escape proves as futile as all the others unraveled in *Satire* 10, which opens with a view of the Empire from Cadiz to the Ganges, matching the extent of the "fog of error/wandering" (*erroris nebula*) through which men strive to discern what are *vera bona*. For Juvenal, flight of this kind seems to be primarily associated with the masculine positioning of the satirist, as illustrated by Umbricius heading out of Rome.[4] The kind of gender dynamics that constitutes fertile ground for, and the *materia* of, satire is the "right" and "authentic" one when constituted in binary fashion: men go outside and struggle, women stay inside and focus on the home.[5] The sort of women who have quasi-masculine characteristics, however, cannot perform either kind of movement correctly, so they zig-zag in pointless and destructive ways through the city or beyond, as does Eppia the senator's wife, who follows a gladiator on a ship to Egypt, shamelessly abandoning her home and family.[6] They roam about uncontrolled as they "flee" from their proper role, like the one training for the arena in 6.253–54: *Quem praestare potest mulier galeata pudorem, / quae fugit a sexu?* (What sense of modesty can a helmeted woman demonstrate, who flees from her sex?), and by "sex" here, the speaker includes the iconography and corporeality of gender, along with its societally fashioned

4. The general absence of gods as a significant force in the poems, at least in the first three books, leaves space for satirist as a god or would-be god; see chap. 4 herein. This is part of the satirist's role as punisher/avenger: see Larmour 2012. On Umbricius as reenacting the same mythos of withdrawal, Motto and Clark 1965; they regard him as the "shade or umbra representative of the deceased Eternal City . . . of the Golden World who is at long last withdrawing from the broken satiric world of corrupted men" (275–76).

5. Before Mrs. Dalloway, the *flâneuse* is sexually and socially suspect; for Benjamin and Baudelaire, she is basically a prostitute.

6. See intro., p. 42 herein, and Barton 1993, 81.

behavioral aspects.[7] Maura and Tullia are a vagabond nocturnal pair, reincarnations of Canidia and Sagana in Horace's *Satire* 1.9, by whose witchcraft creatures from the realm of the dead penetrate the world of the living: *serpentis atque videres / infernas errare canis* (34–35).[8]

Centripetal movement, by contrast, involves the influx into Rome of foreign elements, especially Greeks and Egyptians with their "feminizing" ways, but also the products of the Empire in general. As such, it is interwoven with themes of consumption, greed, and the acquisition of material goods. These directions of movement are also associated with entry and exit from the body (and the body politic)—things are stuck into it, and materials flow out from it, poison enters the body, and disease spreads through it. Thus, in *Satire* 6, Pudicitia and Astraea leave, and in come Maura and Tullia, voiding their bladders all over Pudicitia's altar. Juvenal's vision is underpinned by the notion that contagion enters from the outside via some site of vulnerability, some wound or point of entry, whence it spreads out to corrupt what was (once) healthy, pure, and good. As writers like Daniel Defoe and Thomas Dekker, or, in the twentieth century, Mikhail Bulgakov and Albert Camus, have demonstrated, satire and plague meet at the intersection of numerous commonalities: societal and cultural disturbance, domestic and urban porosity, corporeal and linguistic fluidity. Plague, like vice, expands along an axis of centripetal and centrifugal force: it penetrates the individual body—Kristeva's "clean and proper" body—and it spreads out, infecting others. Quite apart from lurid accounts of corporeal corruption and disease, a feature every bit as present in Juvenal as in Defoe's *Journal of the Plague Year* (1722), we are presented with the uprooting of secure anchors of meaning as words like *libertas* and *simplicitas* are detached from their ideological moorings.

Sometimes satire includes a literal plague—as in Bulgakov's *The Fatal Eggs* (1925), in which a plague wipes out all the chickens in Russia, and a race of giant snakes emerges in their place—but just as often plague is put to effective metaphorical or metapoetic use. To speak of vice as a plague or a disease comes quite naturally to Juvenal's speaker. The theme of the plague allows the satirist to graft his moralizing and corrective urges onto a recognized "natural" phenomenon, while reminding the reader that corruption and its ultimate form,

---

7. See Barton 2001, "Poise of Shame," 202–43; Kaster 2005, chap. 2, "Fifty Ways to Feel Your *Pudor*."

8. The moon blushes and hides behind tombs to avoid being a witness to them, but is there for the antics of Maura and Tullia (*Luna teste*, 6.311). As Gowers observes of Horace's pair (2012, 279), "It is significant that the witches escape into the city" (*in urbem*). Bulgakov's *Master and Margarita* (1996) plays with similar violations of the boundary between the everyday and the supernatural, the living and the dead, to satirical ends.

death, cannot be shut out or prevented from seeping through the perilously porous borders of Roman subjectivity. As the subject, whether regarded as the integrity of a physical body or as a function of that body's incorporation in the political or natural order of things, is put under special pressure by the crisis of plague, so the deconstruction of secure notions of identity, as one episteme gives way to another, is framed with special piquancy in certain texts—such as those in the tradition of Juvenalian satire—through our engagement with epidemic disease.

The disingenuous question "unde?" is often asked in Juvenalian satire: whence, from what source, does this or that manifestation of corruption come? By asking "unde?" the satirist both pretends not to know and expects the reader to know the answer. The satirist's pose is to gaze around and ask, "Where do these people come from?" The truth, of course, is that they are homegrown. It also hints at an ideal world, a Golden Age, in which they don't exist or are safely tucked away, buried or immobilized elsewhere, but one has to ask, What would such a place look like in an *orbis terrarum* now everywhere susceptible to Roman oversight? It is Rome's very expansion that has brought them in to be paraded before our eyes. As Victoria Rimell observes, "The point is that in Juvenal[,] Rome *is* the world: it has become so saturated with people, influences, vices, that it has both devoured the whole globe and come to represent it in freakish concentrate. . . . In other words, these poems perform imperialism."[9] At the end of *Satire 2*, the phrase *heu miseri traducimur* (Alas, we are paraded in disgrace, 159) marks an inversion of the traditional Triumph, the purpose of which was to display to the citizenry what Ida Ostenberg terms the "pronounced other" so as to (re-)define *Romanitas* and to secure their participation in the humiliation and scorning of the conquered *externus*; here, however, Romans themselves are the object of ridicule.[10]

The second aspect of spatial movement we shall consider is the *limen*, the doorway or threshold, as the dividing line between the inside and outside; we have already seen its significance in the *sportula* scene of *Satire 1* as the locus of economic and social humiliation, as well as of the breakdown of trust in *amicitia*. The *limen* is of particular importance with regard to marriage, since the doorpost plays a special part in wedding ceremonial (6.51–52, 79) and other family celebrations, such as the celebration of the birth of a son in 9.85–86: *foribus suspende coronas: / iam pater es* (Hang garlands on the doors, now you're a father)—but in this case, it is a sordid inversion of the happy ideal, because it

9. Rimell 2005, 83.
10. Ostenberg 2009, 8; cf. 262, 265–66, 274–79.

Certe sanus eras. Uxorem, Postume, ducis? . . . Cum tibi vicinum se praebeat Aemilius pons? (Juv. 6.28, 32). Aemilian Bridge (Ponte Rotto). Photograph by David Larmour and Corby Kelly.

was Naevolus the rent-male who made his wife pregnant (*tota vix hoc ego nocte redemi / te plorante foris* [I spent all night at it and only just managed to save the situation, with you weeping outside the door], 76–77). His penetration of the *limen* and of the wife is the real reason for the celebration. The porosity of *limina* exemplifies the "invasiveness" defining the centripetal motion outlined above: various vices enter the *domus* when the bride or other undesirables, like lovers and gigolos, foreigners and criminals, cross the threshold.[11]

As we might expect, there are numerous correspondences between *Satires* 2 and 6 in terms of motifs for characterizing the violation of idealized gender roles. These are reinforced by verbal echoes and repeated allusions, so it becomes clear that the poem attacking unfeminine women is to be read in close association with its predecessor skewering unmasculine men, and also the later dialogue with Naevolus.[12] Both poems are peppered with famous

---

11. Fredrick 2002 on penetrability in theater, forum, and domus.

12. On Naevolus as the archetypal satirist, see Braund 1988, 170; Rosen 2007 takes up the idea, suggesting that Juvenal deploys Naevolus as "an alter-ego who in some sense reflects the prototypically beleaguered, abject life of the satirist" and whose very unseemliness "in fact aligns him all the more closely with the unstable and morally ambiguous stance of the Juvenalian satirist himself" (228–29). Habinek 2005a discusses the Juvenal/Naevolus exchange and says he also calls to mind "the archetypal Roman the satirist seeks to

names from Roman history, and the traversal of space and the location of actions in particular places contributes to the satirist's apparent overall plan (he knows it is hopeless anyway) of reestablishing the boundaries between male and female. As we saw in the introduction, the body is ground zero in the satirist's attempt to reestablish the lines of *genus* as his primary response to the yearning for a return to the lost Golden Age.[13] Like Livy, who opened his history with a catalog of idealized men and women in heroic and virtuous roles, the satirist draws upon the standards of *mos maiorum*, but as Wiesen observes, "Just as for Juvenal there is nothing to look forward to—and hence no future—so there is no real past, for the past is a wretched congeries of dead traditions, absurd legends, rhetorical exempla, topoi, and lies" (709).

We might pause here to examine the opening of *Satire* 6, wherein flight takes on a temporal as well as a spatial dimension, as the speaker conjures up what Edward Kenney calls an "ironic, but curiously affectionate" vision of family life in the Saturnian Golden Age, when shaggy and big-breasted women nourished their offspring in country caves and *Pudicitia* was a still a presence on the earth:

> Credo Pudicitiam Saturno rege moratam
> in terris visamque diu, cum frigida parvas
> praeberet spelunca domos ignemque laremque
> et pecus et dominos communi clauderet umbra,
> silvestrem montana torum cum sterneret uxor   5
> frondibus et culmo vicinarumque ferarum
> pellibus, haut similis tibi, Cynthia, nec tibi, cuius
> turbavit nitidos extinctus passer ocellos,
> sed potanda ferens infantibus ubera magnis
> et saepe horridior glandem ructante marito.   10
> Quippe aliter tunc orbe novo caeloque recenti
> vivebant homines, qui rupto robore nati
> compositive luto nullos habuere parentes.
> Multa Pudicitiae veteris vestigia forsan
> aut aliqua exstiterint et sub Iove, sed Iove nondum   15
> barbato, nondum Graecis iurare paratis

---

entertain, to constitute, to be" and is "the elite male Roman in a state of flux, even disintegration—a figure of ridicule, but a serious figure as well" (185–87). As a Roman *vir*, he is possessor of the phallus, which he uses on both men and women.

13. Gunderson 2005: "Vile, castrated bodies are the prerequisite for the satirical nostalgia for wholeness"; he connects the marrying eunuch and the Amazonian gladiator Mevia of 1.22–23 with Gracchus's male-male marriage and his appearance as *retiarius* in 2.117–48 (229).

per caput alterius, cum furem nemo timeret
caulibus ac pomis et aperto viveret horto.
Paulatim deinde ad superos Astraea recessit
hac comite, atque duae pariter fugere sorores.   20

I can believe that Chastity lingered on the earth during Saturn's reign and that she was visible for a long time during the era when a chilly cave provided a tiny home, enclosing fire and hearth god and herd and its owners in communal gloom, when a mountain wife made her woodland bed with leaves and straw and the skins of her neighbours, the beasts. She was nothing like *you*, Cynthia, or *you* with your bright eyes marred by the death of your sparrow. Instead she offered her paps for her hefty babies to drain, and she was often more unkempt than her acorn-belching husband. You see, people lived differently then, when the world was new and the sky was young—people who had no parents but were born from split oak or shaped from mud. It's possible that many or at least some traces of ancient Chastity survived under Jupiter too—but that was before Jupiter had got his beard, before the Greeks had taken to swearing by someone else's name, at a time when no one feared that his cabbages or apples would be stolen but people lived with their gardens unwalled. It was afterwards that, little by little, Astraea withdrew to the gods above with Chastity as her companion. The two sisters ran away together. (1–20)[14]

Cynthia and Lesbia mark the link with "modern" Rome, as does the adjective *montanus*—it suggests the Seven Hills of Rome, according to Courtney, and it looks ahead to the satirist's consolatory remark to Naevolus in 9.130–31 that he won't be without a *pathicus amicus* "as long as these hills are standing."[15] The only other use of the word *pudicitia* in the extant poems comes in 10.297–98, *rara est adeo concordia formae / atque pudicitiae*, of a son whose "excellent body" only makes his parents anxious because, no matter how pure and simple his upbringing—*sanctos licet horrida mores / tradiderit domus ac veteres imitata Sabinos* (though his unsophisticated house has a tradition of pure morality,

14. Trans. Braund 2004.

15. See p. 115 herein. Courtney 1980, 134; cf. 8.239; Braund 1996a, 143, cf. Cic. *De Dom.* 74; Tac. *Hist.* 2.12; Rome was originally a place called *Septimontium* according to Varro *LL* 5.41. Richlin 1992 observes that the satirist "imagines the whole city of Rome as pathic" (202). On the unwalled gardens and lack of boundaries, or fear of thieves, cf. Hor. *Sat.*1.3.105–106, 116–17. Adams 1982 notes that *hortus* is not usually sexual, but Priap. 5.4 = *culus* (84); see Callebat 2012, 80–81.

in imitation of the ancient Sabines, 298–99)—he is not permitted "to be the man [in sexual intercourse]" (*non licet esse viro*, 304).[16] Returning to the Golden Age might seem the way to restore boundaries, but the vignette of the cave woman is riddled with paradox: while her big teets express gender difference, the shagginess (*horridior*) of the *montana uxor* militates against it, and the lack of barriers between human and animal makes it hard to take this satiric antithesis seriously.[17] Wiesen describes it as "a frontal attack on some of the very core-elements of inherited Greco-Roman culture: religion, Hesiod, improving nostalgic myths, vacuous moralizing, over-refined love poetry."[18] Neither the primal community of speluncar dwelling nor the political landscape of the Republic offers a satirical antithesis: the former is "singularly unappealing," while the latter "is the era of Clodius himself," as Paul Miller observes, wondering exactly what period the satirist means by *tunc* in 6.342–45:[19]

Et quis tunc hominum contemptor numinis, aut quis
simpuvium ridere Numae nigrumque catinum
et Vaticano fragiles de monte patellas
ausus erat? Sed nunc ad quas non Clodius aras?

And in those old days, what human being ever scorned divine power?
What human being had ever dared to laugh at Numa's earthenware
    ladles
or the black bowls or the brittle dishes from the Vatican hill?
But these days, is there any altar without a Clodius?[20]

It is not surprising then that the first poem after Juvenal's programmatic opening should roundly attack men in Rome who are "unmanly." Noting that invective is "perhaps the most powerful line-drawing, difference-making tool in the satirist's kit," Matthew Roller sees it at its most effective when directed

16. "Unosphisticated" is Ferguson's (1979) rendering of *horrida*. The flight of Pudicitia gets a reprise in 11.55–56, describing fugitive bankrupts: *sanguinis in facie non haeret gutta, morantur / pauci ridiculum et fugientem ex Urbe Pudorem* ("not a drop of blood lingers in their faces, few detain mocked Shame as she rushes out of Rome"). Cf. *pudor paupertatis* 6.357; in 6.137, by contrast, Caesennia's husband is willing to call her *pudica* because she brought him money. Lucil. 30.1046: *quandoque pudor ex pectore cessit*; 1047: *sublatus pudor omnis, licentia fenus refertur.*

17. Cf. Hor.'s version, *Sat.*1.3.99–113, esp. 99–100: *cum prorepserunt primis animalia terris / mutum et turpe pecus* and 109–10: *more ferarum / . . . ut in grege Taurus.*

18. Wiesen 1989, 724; cf. Edmunds 1972, 66–68 on *Sat.* 13.28–70. For the cave-scene as programmatic and generic commentary, see Keane 2002a.

19. Miller 2005, 287; he adds that consistency is not the hallmark of "either *indignatio* or its skillful portrayal" but, for Juvenal, that is perhaps the point. *Tunc* is defined only in opposition to *nunc*, see chap. 4 herein.

20. Trans. Braund 2004.

at "sexual deviance" and especially at the figure of the *cinaedus*.[21] The target is, initially, hypocritical philosophers, the supposed teachers of *virtus*, a theme already exploited by Martial in 1.24:

> Aspicis incomptis illum, Deciane, capillis,
> > cuius et ipse times triste supercilium,
> qui loquitur Curios adsertoresque Camillos?
> > Nolito fronte credere: nupsit heri.

> Do you see that man, Decianus, with unkempt hair
> > of whose stern brow even you are afraid,
> and who keeps talking of the Curii and our champions the Camilli?
> > Put no faith in his appearance: yesterday he got married—to
> a man.

This epigram contains core themes of Juvenal's own poem, and it seems likely that he drew upon it, but as the satire expands far beyond the *domus* and the city to incorporate the whole Empire, and as the "infection" of effeminacy spreads far and wide, the message, in Juvenal's hands, is given a global significance.[22] The signifiers that anchor *Romanitas*—masculinity, the male body, and by extension the Empire that was founded upon its *virtus*—are immediately shown to be fundamentally unreliable. We live in the age of She-hard and He-soft. That Juvenal chooses to launch his second tirade among the philosophers (as he did his first in *Satire* 1 among the poets) indicates that he is both appropriating and undermining the discourse of *virtus* employed by Seneca and others. Horace used the Stoic *sapiens* as a foil for mapping out his own contrasting position, while Persius closely associated himself with such a figure; now Juvenal gets in on this game, by deploying terminology and imagery from the Stoic moralizing tradition for his own purposes, making the *sapiens* into a "searcher" for Roman *virtus*. In the openings of *Satires* 1 and 2, then, he expatiates on the two constitutive elements of Roman satire—poetry and philosophy—but his streets teem with talentless poets and false philosophers. While Horace had to deal with but one pest in his *Satire* 1.9, Juvenal is confronted by hordes of imposters.

Juvenal's first poem after his programmatic introduction also follows in the tradition of Horace's second satire, whose persona Gowers describes as "cynical, swaggering and Priapic" and whose opening line "with its mixture of Aramaic, Latin and Greek words, displays the contaminated aspects of Rome so

---

21. Roller 2012, 299, 300–305.
22. Thus Howell (whose translation I quote) 1980, 158–60; Richlin 1992, 138–39, 201–202.

often suppressed in nobler representations, while hinting at the magical wiles used by women to undermine male power."[23] Richlin sees Juvenal's *Satire* 9 as even more Priapic in its stance than 2 "since it assumes that the whole of Rome is filled with pathics suitable for Naevolus' intentions. The satirist in effect rapes Rome with Naevolus as his agent—an agent at whom he jovially sneers."[24] As with the blurring in *Satire* 1 between the roles of organizer of arena entertainments and participant in them, then, there is in *Satire* 2 (and its companions 6 and 9), an excitingly unstable aspect to the satirist's position, which geographical and chronological dislocation serves to emphasize. This confusion can be read in various ways. Erik Gunderson argues that the satirist's success in seeking out outrageous instances of perverse behavior shows he is an expert in it himself. Roller comments that "satirists who draw lines employing moralizing invective tend to catch themselves, or parts of themselves, on the wrong side," and "the more insistently the satirist inscribes the line that distinguishes himself and his audience from the *cinaedus*, the more permeable that line seems to become."[25] Our speaker seeks to "draw a line in the sand" against moral decay, but the *sulcus* drawn across the arena by the satirist's body becomes a sign of how he is drawn into the spectacles he presents for our pleasure.

Open Wide

Here we shall consider several moments in *Satire* 2 whose details have clear parallels in 6 and 9, in particular: (1) Greek insurgents, reenacting the disruption caused by the Bacchanalia, as recorded by Livy; (2) streetwalking and the confusion between male- and female-sanctioned space; (3) disgraceful displays, with Creticus, Gracchus, and others recalling notorious examples from the late Republic, like Clodius and Mark Antony, especially as detailed in Cicero's second *Philippic;* and (4) the incorporation—or infection—of the realm

---

23. *Ambubaiarum collegia, pharmacopolae. . . .* Gowers 2012, 86–87; cf. *nil medium est* "leads into a spectrum of deviant sexual tastes" and Republican heroes Cato and Sallust are "salty, lecherous men about town" (28, 88–89).

24. Richlin 1992, 202; see further 2009, 307, 315–16; Rosen 2007, 230–31.

25. Gunderson 2005, esp. 227, 232–53; Rosen 2007, 231; Roller 2012, 303–305; and Bartsch 2012, 181, on *Sat.* 2 and Stoic philosophers like Seneca as *cinaedi* ("their passive attitude about the boundaries of their own bodies renders them . . . models par excellence of unmanly penetration"). Rimell 2005, 90–91, on the complex insecurities of *Sat.* 9. Gowers 2012 on Hor. *Sat.* 1.2, as illustrating one of the main paradoxes of the genre, that "moralizing poetry is potentially besmirched by its filthy subject matter" (88). Cf. on 1.9.5 and "the peculiar double identity of Priapus" which we might relate to that of Umbricius.

of the "beyond" or the margins, including the furthest reaches of the empire and the Underworld. *Satire* 2 opens as follows:

> **Ultra Sauromatas fugere hinc libet** et glacialem
> Oceanum, quotiens aliquid de moribus audent
> **qui Curios simulant et Bacchanalia vivunt.**
> Indocti primum, quamquam plena omnia gypso
> Chrysippi invenias; nam perfectissimus horum,
> si quis Aristotelen similem vel Pittacon emit
> et iubet archetypos pluteum servare Cleanthas.
> **Frontis nulla fides; quis enim non vicus abundat**
> **tristibus obscaenis?** Castigas turpia, cum sis
> **inter Socraticos notissima fossa cinaedos?**
> Hispida membra quidem et durae per bracchia saetae
> **promittunt atrocem animum**, sed podice levi
> caeduntur tumidae medico ridente mariscae.
> Rarus sermo illis et magna libido tacendi
> atque supercilio brevior coma.

> **I'd like to flee from here beyond the Sarmatians** and the icy Ocean,
> whenever **those who pretend to be Curii but live like Bacchanals**
> dare to say something about morality.
> First of all, they are ignorant, although you'll find all their houses filled
> with plaster busts of Chrysippus; for, of course, he's the most perfect of
>   them
> who buys a likeness of Aristotle or Pittacus
> and orders his shelf to preserve originals of Cleanthes.
> **There's no trusting appearances: for what street isn't awash**
> **with stern-faced perverts?** Do you castigate disgusting behaviour when
>   you are
> **the most notorious "ditch" among the Socratic** *cinaedi?*
> Hairy limbs and the stiff bristles all over your arms
> **promise a hard spirit**, but it's from a smooth arsehole
> that the laughing doctor slices off your swollen "figs."
> Conversation is rare among them and there's a great desire for silence
> and the hair is cut short above the eyebrows. (1–15)

The escape fantasy of fleeing "from here" to "there"—beyond the Sarmatians and the icy Ocean—positions the satirist (at least wishfully) as far away as he can get from the houses of the Stoic *cinaedi*. The word *ultra* signals a wish to escape "beyond" known places and names—beyond, in other words, the "naming" reach of Rome. The references to the far north and the Sea of Azov will be echoed by the British Isles and Armenia at the satire's end, representing the edges of the Empire, but with a sting in the tail: young men from such faraway places take dissolute Roman habits back with them to their home provinces.[26] *Satire* 2 is remarkable for the variety of spaces traversed as it pursues the targets of its attack, namely men who are "unmanly" in all they do, frequently contrary to appearances. The theme is summed up in line 8: *frontis nulla fides.*[27] The word *fides* is a quilting point in the Roman system of exchange, while the *frons*, the face/forehead, is the part of the body supposed to be the most openly expressive of inner content.[28] The *frons* is the space on which *pudor* (or its absence) is inscribed, analogous to the façade of the *domus.*[29] This *sententia* in the Senecan mode encapsulates the split between signifier and signified upon which Juvenalian discourse is predicated: nothing is what it seems or pretends to be.[30] Henceforth, we should beware all performance, as the conjunction of *tristibus obscaenis* reiterates. According to Varro, the word *obscaenus* originally referred to something that should not be said openly—only on the stage (*De lingua Latina* 7.96).

The opening lines establish the porosity between interior space and the public, outside realm,[31] as we move from *domus* to *vicus*, the latter itself a

26. On the topicality of the Sarmatae, see Mart. *Spect.* 3.4 and Coleman 2006, *ad loc.*

27. Cic. *Phil.* 4.14: *in quo est incredibilis crudelitas, fides nulla*; Walters 1998, 350–52. On *fides* as the theme of *Sat.* 13, see Edmunds 1972, esp. 61. There is a similar moment in Hor. *Sat.* 1.70–71, when the talking penis speaks of a *magno prognatum . . . consule cunnum / velatumque stola* ("a cunt sprung from a great consul and veiled in a matron's robe"), during a discussion of adulterous liaisons; cf. 87–95.

28. Cic. *De Orat.* 2.221: *in ore sunt omnia; animi est enim omnis actio et imago animi vultus.* Cf. *Sat.* 6 on make-up on a woman's face below (6.143, Sertorius fancies Bibula's *facies*, "not the wife") and other uses of *frons* 6.503 ("from the front you will see an Andromache, but from behind she's smaller"; 11.96 on the modest bronze front of a couch in early times. *Frons* as façade of building, see *OLD* 5a (e.g. Vitr. 4.3.3). Henderson 1995 calls Fronto of 1.12 "Mr. Façade" and "Mr. Forehead."

29. See Courtney 1980 on 8.189; 11.204 (*salva fronte = salvo pudore*); 13.242 on "forehead as the seat of shame." In 8.189, *populi frons durior*, the hardened gaze of the populace watching antics of the Fabii; in 13.242, *eiectum semel attrita de fronte ruborem*, cf. Mart. 7.26.5 and Galán Vioque 2002, *ad loc.*, and 8.59.2 on loss of the capacity to blush from rubbing brow so it becomes hard. See *OLD* on the brow as the mirror of feelings, as expressing modesty or lack thereof, as masking true feelings (entries 2–4). For a topographical use of *fides* in Prop. 1.16, see Corbeill 2005.

30. See Walters 1998 on *Satire* 2: "The play of seeming and being, of seeing and being seen, is sited from the start of the invective in the body" (357); cf. Braund and Cloud 1981, 207. On the large role of theater and spectacle in Juvenal, see Keane 2006. See Barton 1993 on the ubiquity of the hypocrite (75).

31. Cf. the contrast between the *vir bonus* in public and in private explored by Hor. *Epist.* 1.16.40–62: public life is not enough, one also needs to know what goes on in private. Horace writes from the country, whence he can better evaluate the incomplete or unreliable morality of the city. In that sense, only "one of us" can be a satirist.

staging post between the private and the civically public.[32] The homes of the uneducated are graced by plaster casts of Chrysippus, portraits of Aristotle, or originals of Cleanthes.[33] One notes the progression toward authenticity in this formulation (*gypso . . . similem . . . archetypos*, cf. *perfectissimus*), but none of these images can disguise the fact that those who feign to be like the Curii actually live "like Bacchanals," with *cinaedos* at the end of line 10 tellingly echoing *Cleanthas* in line 7. This is Juvenal's version of the common reproach against philosophers quoted by Seneca in *De Vita Beata* 18.1: "*aliter loqueris, aliter vivis*" (You say one thing but do another). These busts are reminiscent of the images of ancestors that dignified Roman houses and were most publicly visible in funeral processions. Hence Gracchus in the arena is but a poor "image" of his noble ancestors, and there follows immediately a vision of shades of Republican heroes in the Underworld, looking with dismay at the latest arrivals. The particular case of the *Stoicidae* (descendants of the Stoics), then, stands for the more pervasive lack of *fides* to originals that Juvenal describes, a subject to be taken up at much length in *Satire* 8.

Greek space invaders have conquered the inner reaches of the Roman *domus*, as the close proximity of *Curios* and *Bacchanalia* in line 3 emphasizes. In *Satire* 3, Umbricius will abandon what has become a *Graecam Urbem* (61), complaining about the ability of Greeks in Rome to play any role or assume any mask to suit their circumstances (*ede quid illum / esse velis* [Just say what you want him to be], 3.74–75). In *Satire* 6, there is a long description (184–99) of the "nauseating" ways in which Roman women adopt Greek speech and, along with it, other bad habits:

> Nam quid rancidius[34] quam quod se non putat ulla
> formosam nisi quae de Tusca Graecula facta est,
> de Sulmonensi mera Cecropis? Omnia Graece.

> After all, what is more nauseating than the fact that no woman thinks
> she's beautiful unless she's turned herself from a Tuscan into a
>   Greeklette,

32. *Vicus*=row of homes; cf. Varro *LL* 5.8; 145, 159–60. The *vici* give us the urban texture of "blocks," routes and zones, places that sit beneath the bigger civic framework of Roma Capitale, as it were.

33. One might compare Sen. *De Tranq.* 9.4.7 on books bought for show and decoration, rather than learning or Plin. Eld. *HN* 35.6 on how *imagines* used to be the only decorations in noble homes, but now people buy statues of strangers because they are valuable. Mart. 2.90.5–6, *differat hoc patrios optat qui vincere census / atriaque immodicis artat imaginibus*. The word *archetypus* is used by Juv. only here, but appears in Mart. 7.11.4, 8.34.1; see Colton 1991, 69.

34. Of affectation in bad taste according to Courtney 1980, *ad loc.*; literally, offending good taste; in 11.135 of food—rotten, nauseating. Cf. Pers. 1.33; Hor. *Sat.* 2.2.89; Mart. 7.34.7; and Galán Vioque 2002, *ad loc.*

from a woman of Sulmo into a pure Cecropian woman? Everything is in
Greek. (185–87)[35]

Of course, Greek terms have entered Roman satire as well—one thinks of the
Greek terminology used with such insouciance by Umbricius in his country
idyll in *Satire* 3.[36] If *satura* really is *tota nostra*, then Greek incursions—words,
names, myths, and actual Greeks—provoke a special frisson. While Horace and
Persius seek to make connections with the Greek world, Juvenal, perhaps more
in the Lucilian tradition (although it is hard to know for sure), uses them
almost entirely as a source of ridicule, making claim to a "fully Roman" stance.
The joke, however, is that *tota nostra* is always a hollow claim in the sense
that, as even Romans acknowledge, they are never fully and monolithically
Roman—as the disparaging remarks about Romulus's motley crowd of found-
ers at the end of *Satire* 8 make all too clear.

As the lens of *Satire* 2 pans from inside the *domus* to outside, we have the
image of every street (*vicus*) abounding with "stern-faced perverts"; this has a
corollary near the end of *Satire* 6:

Occurrent multae tibi Belides atque Eriphylae
mane, Clytaemestram nullus non vicus habebit.

Numerous granddaughters of Belus and Eriphyles will run into you
in the mornings. There's no street that won't have its Clytemnestra.
(655–56)[37]

The equivalent of the stern-faced male philosopher who is in reality up to all
sorts of immoral activities is the Roman woman who behaves like Clytemnestra or one of the Danaids at home, having learned much more sophisticated—
and less detectable—ways of disposing of her husband than these ladies of myth
ever practiced. And this is not to forget that the originals were themselves already adept at exploiting the gap between outward appearance and hidden
intentions.

The speaker of *Satire* 2 next moves from the face with its "grim" or "stern"
expression to the part of the body that actually does tell the truth, namely the
anus (*fossa*).[38] There is a slight echo here perhaps of the truth-telling act of

---

35. Trans. Braund 2004; see L. and P. Watson 2014, *ad loc.*

36. See intro., p. 25 herein; Gowers 2012 on Hor. *Sat.*1.10.20–35, 43–44.

37. This also echoes bumping into bards in the streets (*vates occurras*) in *Sat.* 1. Wiesen 1989, 715 on
abundare as suggestive of sewage overflowing in the Roman street.

38. As Wiesen 1989 observes, "the tension between the two parts of the stern profligate's personality is
resolved on this grotesque image: the *cinaedus* is nothing but a walking anus!" (716).

defecation on the Arabarch's statue in *Satire* 1.[39] The word *fossa* (ditch) was applied to both the vagina and the anus in sexual parlance and the addition of *notissima* suggests that this particular ditch was much used.[40] Similar vocabulary will be used in 9.43–46 when Naevolus asks:

> An facile et pronum est agere intra viscera penem
> legitimum atque illic hesternae occurrere cenae?
> Servus erit minus ille miser qui **foderit** agrum
> quam dominum.

> Or is it easy and straightforward to drive a proper-sized penis
> into your guts and there bump into yesterday's dinner?
> The slave who digs the field will be less miserable than the one
> who **digs out** his master.

As Miller notes, "This passage contains images of eating, excrement, and sexuality in a context which is rich with metaphors of the earth and agriculture, yet is completely sterile. Food produces excrement that, far from representing a potential source of renewed fertility, serves only as an obstacle to a sexual activity that brings neither pleasure nor fruit to the speaker" (300). This contrasts with the wholesome sort of digging of furrows performed by the strapping rustic sons of Punic or Pyrrhic war veterans in 14.169–70. Barely two acres is taken as a generous enough token of the *fides patriae* by such men, who dwell in cottages reminiscent of the primeval caves of the opening of *Satire* 6, and contentedly so.

> Saturabat **glebula** talis
> patrem ipsum **turbamque casae**, qua feta iacebat
> uxor et infantes ludebant quattuor, unus
> vernula, tres domini; sed magnis fratribus horum
> **a scrobe vel sulco** redeuntibus altera cena
> amplior et **grandes** fumabant pultibus **ollae**.
> Nunc modus hic agri nostro non sufficit horto.
> **Inde** fere scelerum **causae**.

> **A clod of earth** like that was enough
> for the father himself and **the crowd in his cottage**, where his pregnant

---

39. See chap. 1 herein, esp. pp. 79–81.

40. The only usage in Juvenal; cf. *fodere* Mart. 1.92.2 (cf. Priap. 52.8); 7.71.4 (*nec rigidus fossor sed nec arator eget*) Cf. *OLD s.v. fossor:* 1a, digger of ground in agriculture (Juv. 11.80); 1b, clumsy or uncouth type (Cat. 22.10; Pers. 5.122); Adams 1982, 85–86 (*fossa* = *culus* or *cunnus*), 151–2, *fossor* and digging of sexual acts.

wife lay and four children were playing, one a home-born slave
and three masters; but when their strapping brothers returned
from the ditch or the furrow, a second dinner was waiting for them,
a larger one, and **the huge pots** were steaming with porridge.
Nowadays, this amount of land is not enough even for our garden.
That's the cause of most crimes. (14.166–73)

There are notions here of fullness in an idealized rustic landscape. Like the cave,
the cottage is crammed with all its virtuous inhabitants. The wife is engaged
in childbearing and -rearing—the big pots steaming with porridge echo the
cave woman's milk-laden breasts.[41] The word *scrobis* avoids the sexual overtones
of *fossa*, while once again the *hortus* suggests a small space of sufficiency—we
may compare Umbricius's little plot (*hortulus hic puteusque brevis*) where, in a
momentary dream of the Voltairean jardiniste, he will be master of just one
lizard (3.226–31).[42]

The hairs all over the legs and arms (which are visible) "promise a hard
spirit" (*promittunt atrocem animum*), adapting Horace's *atrocem animum Catonis* (*Odes* 2.1.24), but "the swollen figs on a smooth anus" (which are hidden
from view) "are sliced off by the laughing doctor." The smoothness of the anus
suggests depilation, already a sign of effeminacy,[43] but the swollen figs reveal
the activity that has been going on in this popular ditch.[44] Lots of things are
distended in satire, but here the image is striking because it connotes swollen
fruit, ripe for the plucking, and the "cutting" or "slicing" off by a laughing
doctor parallels the "surgery" of the satirist.[45] Both have, so to speak, sliced open

41. Cf. Keane 2002a on the nursing breasts of the cave woman (14–17). *Glaebula* appears again only in
12.85 in a similar setting and this is the only "cottage" in the corpus. Contrast the pies steaming with maternal poison for fatherless orphans in 6.631: *livida materno fervent adipata veneno*.

42. Adams 1982 describes *virginalem scrobem* in Arnobius *Nat.* 4.7 as "probably an *ad hoc* metaphor"
(86). *Fossa*, however, has altogether more wholesome associations with *murus* and the Etruscan ritual for the
foundation of a town, according to Varro *LL* 5.143; cf. Collart 1954, 236n3, *ad loc.* See also Ov. *F.* 4.821–25 (*fossa
fit ad solidum*, 821; *designat moenia sulco*, 825); 839–40 (*neve quis aut muros aut factam vomere fossam / transeat*),
with ref. to Romulus (cf. Plut. *Rom.* 1.10).

43. Cf. Naevolus of his ungrateful patron in 9.95: *nam res mortifera est inimicus pumice levis*.

44. As piles only in Juv., but cf. Mart.12.33: *Ut pueros emeret Labienus vendidit hortos / nic nisi ficetum
nunc Labienus habet*. The *ficus marisca* is a large and inferior variety of fig: Cato *De Agr.* 8.1; Varro *RR* 1.6.4. For
the sexual ramifications of figs (and digging and ploughing), Mart. 7.71.1–4 (*ficosa est uxor, ficosus et ipse mari-
tus, / filia ficosa est et gener atque nepos,/ nec dispensator nec vilicus ulcere turpi / nec rigidus fossor nec arator
eget*) and Galán Vioque 2002 *ad loc*; also 7.25.7; 11.18.15; 12.96.9–10. Priap. 50.2: *ficosissima . . . puella*; of anus
and female genitalia. Adams 1982, 113–14 on *marisca* as "insipid" or "un-tasty" (*fatua*) in comparison with the
"Chian" *ficus*, when it comes to anal penetration of one's wife rather than of boys. In 11.18.15–16, *non mariscae /
ridere . . . possunt* (in a tiny garden): the "grin" or "split" indicates ripeness (cf. Kay 1985, 108).

45. Paulson 1967: "punishment is also objectified in the satirist's image of himself as a surgeon or
public executioner—with the effect of drawing the reader's attention away from both persuasion and

the secret of the *obscaenus*, whose vice has overripened, and gleefully inflicted a wound that is at the same time a cure.[46] The doctor's knife thus echoes the allusion to Telephus and the spear of Achilles in the first satire. The scene is a vengeful and bloody wounding by the "rough" and "hard" of the smooth and swollen, of the soft and rotten.[47] As Paulson observes, when the satirist engages in nostalgia for the time of order, "the result is less an imitation of exuberance than of overripeness, rottenness, a sinister often horrible quality."[48] The hemorrhoidal figs also anticipate the poem's central image of the discolored bunch of grapes (78–81).[49] As to the face and its taciturnity (*rarus sermo illis et magna libido tacendi*) and hair shorter than the eyebrows (*supercilio brevior coma*): hairy limbs, short hair, and *taciturnitas* are conventional signifiers of Stoic education and masculinity—*Stoici virilem ingressi viam . . .*, as Seneca has it in *De Constantia* 1.1—but underneath, so to speak, a different libido is at work, one that requires depilation and encourages lack of sexual restraint.[50]

The disjunction between appearance and reality takes us back to the original complaint that Curii were in fact Bacchanals, which in turn points back to Republican history and to Manius Curius Dentatus. Dentatus was censor in 272 BCE, and he was responsible, during his time as consul, for the defeat of Pyrrhus. This was a pivotal event in Roman history, for it effectively excluded him (and any other) Greek insurgent from Italy and Sicily.[51] In *Satire* 11.78, Curius is pictured cooking "little vegetables" from his "small garden" on his "modest hearth" making him more than slightly Umbricius-like in his taste for modest living and his distaste for Greeks.[52] This Curius was thus both an enforcer of moral standards and a bulwark against invasion.

---

presentation to the interesting image of the performer and his operations" (14). For a similar scene, Hor. *Sat.* 1.2.45–46: *accidit ut quidam testis caudamque salacem / demeteret ferro*, of an adulterer.

46. Wiesen 1989 says that this scene is "strictly speaking, unnecessary to the point the satirist is making" (716), but see Keane 2006, 64 on the satirist as the laughing medic and the scalpel as power and knowledge; Walters 1998, 358, says *caeduntur* is also suggestive of anal penetration. Cf. 6.42: Ursidius is *moechorum notissimus* but is getting married, and so the speaker calls upon the doctors to "lance the swollen vein" (*o medici, nimiam pertundite venam*, 46).

47. Martial uses similar ideas in his epigrams about the *cinaedus* Pannychus, who is always talking about philosophers (9.47.1–2) and who has hairy legs and chest but a "depilated" mind (2.36.5–6): *nunc sunt crura pilis et sunt tibi pectora saetis / horrida, sed mens est, Pannyche, volsa tibi*.

48. Paulson 1967, 18–19.

49. Cf. Gowers 2012 on Hor. *Sat.* 1.7.30, *vindemiator* (pruner of vines), who "trims evil excrescences in the vineyard" noting that it also suggests *vindex, vindicare*.

50. Cf. Juv. 9.141, 11.145; Mart. 11.11.2–3 (*pocula . . . / trita patrum labris et tonso pura ministro*); Lucil. 30.1048: *inberbi androgyni, barbati moechocinaedi*.

51. Plut. *Pyr.* 25.

52. Juvenal contrasts him with the *squalidus . . . fossor*, in a passage about traditional Roman virtues, albeit not without a hint of condescension. Cf. the "tiny garden" topos in Mart. (8.61; 9.97; 11.18) and possible ties to Cato's cod-nostalgia about farming; Spencer 2010, 141–42.

The mention of Bacchanals recalls the scandalous outbreak of societal disorder associated with the worship of Bacchus in 186 BCE, recorded in Livy 39.8–19. As the historian's account makes clear, it was the violation of boundaries and hierarchies that made the Bacchanalia seem such a threat to the stability of the state.[53]

Livy's narrative is structured upon four motifs, which find clear echoes in Juvenal. First, respectable appearances conceal underlying vice: the consul Postumius tells the citizens that they "do not know what this thing is" (*quae ea res sit, ignorare*, 15.7), with some believing it is a form of worship of the gods, others that it is "an allowable play and enjoyment" (*concessum ludum et lasciviam*). He observes that "nothing is more deceptive in appearance than a depraved religion": *nihil enim in speciem fallacius est quam prava religio* (16.6). The size and nature of the city itself conceals the vice: *primo urbis magnitudo capacior patentior talium malorum ea celavit* (9.1). Similarly, the noise surrounding Bacchic rites covers up the cries of those being raped or killed: *multa dolo, pleraque per vim audebantur. Occultebat vim quod prae ululatibus tympanorumque et cymbalorum strepitu nulla vox quiritantium inter stupra et caedes exuadiri poterat* (8.8).[54] Getting to the truth requires speaking above the din, rather as the satirist must, and Hispala's and Postumius's speeches are delivered in high-pitched rhetoric.[55]

Second, these nefarious activities have a foreign origin (*non patrio sed externo ritu*, 16.9), specifically, a Greek one: Livy attributes them to the arrival in Etruria of a *Graecus ignobilis*, a *sacrificulus et vates* (8.3).[56] He spreads his *error* not by openly proclaiming his creed (*nec . . . aperta religione*) but through secret nocturnal gatherings (8.4).[57] "What sort of gatherings," Postumius asks, "are held at night and with men and women mixing together?" (15.12). "Should young men from this foul shrine be given arms and made soldiers? Are they going to fight to the death *pro pudicitia coniugum ac liberorum vestrorum?*" (15.13–14). It was with good reason, he says, that foreign cults were forbidden

---

53. For full accounts, Pailler 1988, 1998, 2005; Briscoe 2008, 230–90. On Bacchus in Greek and Roman landscape, see Spencer 2010, 19–22.

54. Cf. Hispala's words in 10.7; Postumius's in 15.6: *crepitibus . . . ululatibusque nocturnis, qui personat tota urbe.*

55. Consternation (*perturbata*, 10.2), anger (*accensus ira*, 13.3) and much pleading mark these performances.

56. The same sort of notion appears in 7.2.3–4: how the Romans' only form of spectacle was the circus but then (during a time of plague) drama came in from abroad, via Etruria.

57. There are a dozen references to nighttime meetings in Livy's version; several of Juvenal's most execrable instances of vice occur under cover of darkness. cf. Sen. *Ep.* 122 on darkness as a veil for vice and the *turba lucifugarum* (15).

and *sacrificulos vatesque* were cleared from the Forum, Circus, and City (*foro, circo, urbe*, 16.8).

Third, the vice spreads like a disease or plague, radiating out first to a small number and then to many more, eventually infecting the entire city: *initia errant quae primo paucis tradita sunt deinde vulgari coepta sunt per viros mulieresque*, 8.5 . . . *huius mali labes ex Etruria Romam veluti contagione morbi penetravit*, 9.1. The disease, originating in Etruria, both penetrates and spreads out. Hispala says that there is now a *multitudinem ingentem* effectively constituting an *alterum populum*, among whom are certain men and women of high rank (13.14). Postumius echoes this by observing that the *coniuratio* gains strength daily (*incrementum ingens virium habet quod in dies plures fiunt*, 15.10; cf. *crescit et serpit cotidie malum*, 16.3).[58]

Fourth, the violation of boundaries threatens the loss of difference between male and female, free and slave, high- and lowborn, rich and poor and of any meaningful sense of *pudor*. This is repeatedly emphasized: *et nox et mixti feminis mares, aetatis tenerae maioribus, discrimen omne pudoris exstinxisset* (8.7). The *stupra promiscua ingenuorum feminarumque* lead in turn to a loss of faith in what is said or written or witnessed (*falsi testes, falsa signa testamentaque et indicia*, 8.7) and even to poisonings and murders. As is the view of Juvenal's speaker, considering nothing off-limits (*nihil nefas ducere*) becomes the sign of greatest success or devotion, and the limit of criminality is reached in male homosexual activity: *plura virorum inter sese quam feminarum esse stupra*, declares Hispala, distinguishing between those *minus patientes dedecoris* and those *pigriores ad facinus* (13.10–11).[59] Postumius, feet firmly planted in the ideological landscape of the speaker in *Satires* 2 and 6, says that women are of course the ultimate source of the problem (15.9), but "the men very similar to the women" are also very much to blame (16.1): *primum igitur mulierum magna pars est et is fons mali huiusce fuit; deinde simillimi feminis mares, stuprati et constupratores, fanatici, vigilis, vino, strepitibus clamoribusque nocturnis attoniti*.[60]

Throughout Livy's account, the watchwords *pudor, pudicitia*, and *libido* appear frequently.[61] The foreign-born contagion enters first through individual homes, but then spreads across the city, which, because of its size and capacity for tolerating such evils, initially conceals its true danger. The "conspiracy"

---

58. Briscoe 2008, *ad loc.*, sees medical imagery in this expression.

59. Taken to refer to passive and active partners respectively; cf. 10.8: she urges Aebutius *nec se eo praecipitaret, ubi omnia infanda patienda primum, deinde facienda essent*.

60. The speaking quality of the name Postumius (Varro *LL* 9.60–61) is not dissimilar to that of Umbricius in *Satire* 3.

61. For the Bacchanalia, Livy uses *officina* (10.6), *praecipitare* (10.8), *furor, gurges* (16.5).

is exposed through the machinations within one emblematic household—
the youthful *eques* Publius Aebutius, his aunt, and the former slave and courtesan Hispala Faecennia—as the *probus adulescens* is about to be lured (by his
devious mother) into *obscena sacra* (11.7). Thus it comes to the attention of the
consul who, with Hispala's help, recognizes the threat to the state and convenes
the Senate in emergency session. Matters have been brought "out of secret darkness into the light" (*ex occultis . . . tenebris in lucem*, 16.11) by the gods, he says,
not so that they should remain unpunished (*impunita*) but *ut vindicarentur et
opprimerentur*. In such circumstances, with behavior presenting a threat to the
state itself, the private/public divide is no longer relevant:

> Minus tamen esset si flagitiis tantum effeminati forent—ipsorum id
> magna ex parte dedecus erat—a facinoribus manus, mentem a
> fraudibus abstinuissent: numquam tantum malum in re publica
> fuit, nec ad plures nec ad plura pertinens. Quidquid his annis
> libidine, quidquid fraude, quidquid scelere peccatum est, ex illo uno
> sacrario scitote ortum esse. Necdum omnia in quae coniurarunt
> edita facinora habent . . . iam maius est quam ut capere id privata
> fortuna possit: ad summam rem publicam spectat.

> Yet it would not be less serious if their wrongdoing had merely made
> them effeminate—that was in great measure their personal
> dishonor—and if they had kept their hands from crime and their
> thoughts from evil designs: never has there been so much evil in the
> state nor affecting so many people in so many ways. Whatever
> villainy there has been in recent years due to lust, whatever to fraud,
> whatever to crime, I tell you, has arisen from this one cult. . . . It is
> already too great to be a purely private matter: its objective is the
> control of the state. (16.1–3)[62]

The satirist appropriates a similar duty to himself to bring to light (*haec
ego non credam Venusina digna lucerna?* 1.51) what really goes on—especially
behind closed doors—and, standing in for the gods (who have largely if not
entirely absented themselves from the quagmire), to urge and mete out punishment. The outbreak of the Bacchanalia is, then, no casual reference at the
beginning of *Satire* 2, for it provides a celebrated historical exemplum
against which to read this poem and the subsequent satires. In those days, we
are invited to remember, the threat could be crushed by the legal and military

---

62. Trans. Sage 1936.

apparatus of the state. Livy describes how Postumius galvanizes the Senate into action, and a ruthless suppression of those involved in the Bacchanalia ensues (15–18). Those who are *stupris aut caedibus violati . . . qui falsis testimoniis, signis adulternis, subiectione testamentorum, fraudibus aliis contaminati* are punished by death, others by imprisonment, sites are destroyed, and there are to be no more unlicensed Bacchanalia or similar gatherings anywhere in Italy (18.4). As often in Juvenal, in whose day the mechanisms for a moral clampdown no longer exist, movement in space is accompanied by a movement in time, back to a more appealing, pre-imperial chronotope.[63]

Walking the Streets: Peribomius and Laronia

The second satire continues as follows:

> Verius ergo
> et magis ingenue Peribomius; hunc ego fatis
> imputo, **qui vultu morbum incessuque fatetur.**
> Horum **simplicitas** miserabilis, his furor ipse
> dat veniam; sed peiores, qui talia verbis
> Herculis invadunt et de virtute locuti
> clunem agitant.

> Therefore Peribomius
> behaves more honestly and honourably than they do: I put down
>   to fate
> a man like this **who admits his disease in his look and his walk.**
> The **openness** of these people arouses pity, and their madness itself
> grants them forgiveness. But far worse are those who attack such
>   conduct
> in the words of Hercules and, after talking about virtue,
> wiggle their bottoms about. (15–21)

We have seen how the satirist links the body, lack of *frontis fides*, and wandering about in a condemnatory chain; but then he offers something of an exception, namely Peribomius, a Greek (or a Roman with a Greek name) who is not as bad as others because he is at least open about his behavior: he makes his

---

63. Morford 1977 on *Satire* 5 notes that in it "Roman history is used primarily as the symbol of liberty" (235). Waugh's use of Arthurian names in his description of Hetton Hall in *A Handful of Dust* both exemplifies and parodies this kind of nostalgia: see Waugh 1997, 17–18, 31, 82, and conclusion herein.

"disease" obvious (as does Naevolus's arse-wiggling patron, *cevet* 9.41).[64] Such *simplicitas* (18) receives grudging, backhanded praise. *Simplicitas* was, of course, the quality the speaker was worried about finding in order to exploit the abundant raw material in *Satire* 1.151–53 (*unde illa . . . simplicitas?*); he has found some here, but only in the service of corrupted (and corrupting) desires.[65] In a similar fashion, at the very start of the poem Naevolus's *frons* and *facies* reveal all too clearly his self-induced misery:

> Scire velim quare totiens mihi, Naevole, tristis
> occurras **fronte obducta** ceu Marsya victus.
>
> . . . .
>
> Non erit **hac facie miserabilior** Crepereius
> Pollio, qui triplicem usuram praestare paratus
> circumit et fatuos non invenit. Unde repente
> tot rugae? Certe modico contentus agebas
> vernam equitem, conviva ioco mordente facetus
> et salibus vehemens intra pomeria natis.

> I'd like to know why you so often run into me, Naevolus, looking
>   gloomy
> **with a frowning brow**, as if you were the beaten Marsyas.
>
> . . . .
>
> Crepereius Pollio will not have **a more miserable face,**
> who goes around ready to offer triple the interest rate
> and cannot find anyone foolish enough to take him up on it.
> Whence, all of a sudden, so many wrinkles?
> Certainly, being contented with nothing much, you used to play
> "the homebred knight," the elegant dinner guest with biting humor
> and forthright with your witticisms bred within the city limits.
>   (9.1–2, 6–11)

The reference to the statue of Marsyas in the Forum has some intriguing ramifications, for it was associated with *libertas*. Statues of Marsyas were set up in the forums of free towns under *ius Italicum*.[66] Naevolus has neither

---

64. The Greek name, in combination with the philosophers whose busts adorn the atria and "the Socratic *cinaedi*," all point to Hellenic influx, with its attendant threats to Roman masculinity. In *Sat.* 9, a line of the *Odyssey* is given a parodic twist to make the point that *cinaedi* will always find patrons. Edwards 1993 on effeminacy and Hellenization (92–97).

65. Sen. *De Tranq.* 3.2: *parum tuta simplicitas est.*

66. Small 1982, a place for accusers and bail (77–79); Edwards 1996 on Marsyas as site of Julia's disgrace (61–62). On Marsyas as allusion to Socrates, see Henderson 1989, 65; Habinek 2005a, 185–86; he

freedom nor freedom of speech but is given the appearance of license within the satirical dialogue, where his voice is appropriated by the speaker. The description of Naevolus parading around as a *verna eques* ("home-grown knight")[67] with "witticisms born inside the city limits" carries associations of border violation. Varro derives the word "Pomerium" from *post murum (postmoerium)*.[68] It had religious significance—Augustus excluded Egyptian rites from it, and theaters had to be built outside the boundaries it defined—and it was a marker of full Roman citizenship.[69]

Thus, Naevolus is introduced amid reminders of the literal and cultural foundations of the city whose *mores* he now embodies, disreputable and brazenly perverse as he is in the speaker's eyes. Some of his bodily features, like the hairy, undepilated legs, recall the *Stoicidae* of *Satire 2*, but here they testify openly, albeit in a roundabout way, to his profession, because they are signs of his neglect of his normal working "uniform," which would demand professional smoothness. In his current appearance, there is plenty of *frontis fides* all right:

> Omnia nunc contra: vultus gravis, horrida siccae
> silva comae, nullus tota nitor in cute, qualem
> Bruttia praestabat calidi tibi fascia visci,
> sed fruticante pilo neglecta et squalida crura.
> Quid macies aegri veteris, quem tempore longo
> torret quarta dies olimque domestica febris.

> Now everything's the opposite. Your face is solemn, your untreated hair
>   a bristling forest, none of that sheen on your skin, which strips of hot
>   Bruttian pitch used to produce; instead, your legs are neglected and
>   dirty with hair growing bushy.
> Why this emaciation of a sick old man, whom the quartan fever been
>   burning for ages
> and long since became a member of the household? (12–17)

---

appears in Hor. *Sat.* 1.6.120 and Gowers 2012 sees a possible echo in the name Marsaeus in 1.2.55 (189). Marsyas has Bacchic connections and his statue was *signum liberae civitatis*, according to Serv. *Aen.* 3.20: *in liberis civitatibus simulacrum Marsyae erat, qui in tutela Liberi patris est*; see Wiseman 1988, 4–5.

67. Following Braund 2004; Green 1974 and Ferguson 1979 give "provincial squire"; Miller 2005 notes the oxymoron and that it "conflates two social categories." Cf. *verna Canopi* of Crispinus in 1.26. Rosen 2007 suggests that "in happier times, it seems, Naevolus would have been perceived as a witty Horatian dinner guest; now as a 'flayed Marsyas,' ruined artist, he has sunk to an even lower level of poetic degradation, and his *indignatio* reaches a pitch that Juvenal had claimed for himself in the first *Satire*" (227).

68. Varro *LL* 5.143.

69. For the *Pomerium*, see Livy 1.44 and Ogilvie 1965, *ad loc.*: a line drawn by a plough to mark the boundary between inside (sacred) and outside (profane). Cf. Platner and Ashby 1929, 392–96; Richardson 1992, 293–96; Dio 53.2.4. This is the only time the term is used in Juvenal, and we may connect it with the uses of *sulcus* noted elsewhere: see chap. 1, pp. 91–93 herein.

Apollo flayed Marsyas as a punishment, and in *Satire* 2.1.62–5 Horace describes Lucilius as stripping the skin off Romans parading around; similarly, Juvenal strips Naevolus (who used to strip hair off his legs) bare of his façade. Fever enters a household and takes up (unwelcome) residence, rather like Naevolus himself. Then comes a restatement of how transparent Naevolus is, as is the case with Peribomius:

Deprendas animi tormenta latentis in aegro
corpore, deprendas et gaudia; sumit utrumque
inde habitum facies. Igitur flexisse videris
propositum et vitae contrarius ire priori.

You can detect the torments afflicting the spirit as it lies in the sick body,
and can detect its joys, too; from there the face takes on either
    disposition.
So you seem to have changed from your life course
and to be going in the opposite direction from before. (18–21)

The name Peribomius is curious; there is a suggestion of going about, perhaps to altars or temples, and a scholiast appears to think of a specific *gallus* known for displays of *impudicitia* in public.[70] It is worth pausing on the notion of "going about" and how not only Peribomius's face, but also his way of walking (*incessus*) reveals his *morbus*. Juvenal is tapping into a powerful web of associations linking walking and gait with the *vigor* (or *mollitia*) of the individual's *animus*.[71] A fragment of Lucilius (26.62) has *animo qui aegrotat, videmus corpore hunc signum dare*.[72] Quintilian comments in a section on gesture (*Institutio oratoria* 11.3.66) that "from the face and gait the disposition of minds is perceived" (*ex vultu ingressuque perspicitur habitus animorum*), and Seneca provides numerous examples of this set of associations in the service of philosophical discourse, such as the following:

Non potest alius esse ingenio, alius animo color. Si ille sanus est, si
compositus, gravis, temperans, ingenium quoque siccum ac sobrium
est: illo vitiato hoc quoque adflatur. Non vides, si animus elanguit,
trahi membra et pigra moveri pedes? Si ille effeminatus est, in ipso
incessu apparere mollitiam? Si ille acer est et ferox, concitari

70. See Courtney 1980, who concludes "Juvenal probably did not have a historical person in mind, but chose the name for the associations indicated by the scholiast" (125); Braund 1996a, 124.
71. See Corbeill 2004 and O'Sullivan 2011; Cic. *De Orat.* 222: *est enim actio quasi sermo corporis, quo magis menti congruens esse debet.* Cf. Edwards 1993, chap. 2, on *mollitia*; Corbeill 2002; Fögen 2009 on self-presentation and fear of *mollitia* (brevity and a vigorous style are analogous to the "strong and robust" male body, while signs of effeminacy point to lack of self-control and a tendency toward excess; 33–37).
72. Miller 2005, *ad loc.*, says Juvenal 9.18–20 paraphrases Lucilius's words.

gradum? Si furit, aut quod furori simile est, irascitur, turbatum esse
corpus motum nec ire sed ferri? Quanto hoc magis accidere ingenio
putas, quod totum animo permixtum est, ab illo fingitur, illi paret,
inde legem petit.

A man's ability cannot possibly be of one sort and his soul of another.
If his soul be wholesome, well-ordered, serious, and restrained,
his ability also is sound and sober. Conversely, when the one
degenerates, the other is also contaminated. Do you not see that if a
man's soul has become sluggish, his limbs drag and his feet move
indolently? If it is womanish, that one can detect the effeminacy by
his very gait? That a keen and confident soul quickens the step? That
madness in the soul, or anger (which resembles madness), hastens
our bodily movements from walking to rushing? And how much
more do you think that this affects one's ability, which is entirely
interwoven with the soul—being moulded thereby, obeying its
commands, and deriving there from its laws! (*Epistle* 114.3)[73]

Being enervated, effeminate, passionate, headstrong, insane, or angry are all
manifested in one's way of going, according to Seneca.[74] Very few people, if any,
in Juvenalian satire exhibit the dryness and sobriety that would merit his
praise.[75] Peribomius certainly does not, as his *redende Name* makes clear.

Throughout *Satire 6*, the inappropriate "going about" of Roman women
comes under similarly baleful scrutiny, including Ogulnia's visits to the games
(352–54), or the daughter of the Lamiae who is obsessed with musicians and
music competitions (385–95), and the following extended passage describing
the woman who seeks out and broadcasts the latest news from all over the globe:

> Sed cantet potius quam totam pervolet Urbem
> audax et coetus possit quae ferre virorum
> cumque paludatis ducibus praesente marito
> ipsa loqui recta facie siccisque mamillis.
> Haec eadem novit quid toto fiat in orbe,
> quid Seres, quid Thraces agant, secreta novercae

---

73. Trans. Gummere 1917–25.

74. Cf. Sen. *NQ* 31.2: *tenero et molli ingressu suspendimus gradum (non ambulamus, sed incedamus)* amid
criticism of *luxuria, impudicitia,* wearing cosmetics and jewelry; Cic. *De Off.* 1.131 on extremes of gait, after a
discussion of male *dignitas* (as opposed to female *venustas*) and before one about *cogitatio* (as opposed to
appetitus).

75. Cf. Hor. *Sat.* 1.3, attacking extremes of intolerance, he expatiates on the inconsistency manifested by
singers and in particular Tigellius who "sometimes rushes, sometimes crawls along" (9–11).

et pueri, quis amet, quis diripiatur adulter;
dicet quis viduam praegnantem fecerit et quo
mense, quibus verbis concumbat quaeque, modis quot.
Instantem regi Armenio Parthoque cometen
prima videt, famam rumoresque illa recentis
excipit ad portas, quosdam facit; isse Niphaten
in populos magnoque illic cuncta arva teneri
diluvio, nutare urbes, subsidere terras,
quocumque in trivio, cuicumque est obvia, narrat.

But it's better for her to be musical than to go brazenly racing all over
    Rome,
the sort of woman who can attend men-only meetings and actually
    converse
with the generals in their uniforms in her husband's presence
with her face unflinching and her nipples dry.
This is the woman who knows everything that's happening throughout
    the world—what the Chinese and the Thracians are up to, the secrets
    of the stepmother
and the boy, who's in love and which Casanova they're fighting over.
She'll tell you who got the widow pregnant and in which month. She'll
    tell you the words each woman uses in bed and how many positions
    she knows.
She's the first to see the comet that's bad news for the king of Armenia
    and Parthia. She picks up the latest tales and rumours at the city gates
    and she invents some herself. Niphates is on the move, threatening
    whole populations, and massive flooding has engulfed all the fields,
    cities are teetering, tracts of land are subsiding—that's what she'll say
    to anyone she meets at any street corner. (398–412)[76]

This does much more than make fun of women roaming about in the city when
they should be at home; it also treats the breakdown of gender boundaries accompanying this roaming, what Richlin (1992) terms "the uncomfortable role
reversal" produced in Juvenal's scheme (204). Her nipples are dry (in contrast
to those of the maternal cave woman), but this dryness—unlike the style of
the ideally *compositus* and *temperans* man-about-town in Seneca's passage (*ingenium ... siccum ac sobrium*)—illustrates her brazen (*recta facie*) incursion
into what should be male-only territory. She flies through the whole city (*totam*

76. Trans. Braund 2004; see L. and P. Watson 2014, *ad loc.*

pervolet urbem) and knows what's happening in the whole world (*toto . . . in orbe*).[77] Her knowledge extends from the edges of the Empire and far beyond, even to the Chinese, and back to the sordid goings-on within the household, with which she might be expected to be all too familiar. This woman is pictured at the city gates (like Umbricius), picking up and inventing news, and at the crossroads (where the satirist is, taking notes), telling anyone she meets about floods in Armenia, which devastate fields, cities, and regions. This final detail picks up on the dry nipples earlier and ties it to the destructive potential of a lack of containment.[78] It also enlarges the view from individual outflows to catastrophic floods in the body of the Empire.[79] *Satire* 6 makes much of a connection between outpourings of various kinds of liquids (especially from the female body) and the outpouring of speech from the woman's mouth, as we shall see in a moment.[80]

The centrifugal impetus of *Satire* 2 leads next from a series of contemporary examples back in time to some less than positive figures from the fag-end of Republican history, beginning with the Gracchus brothers and including Verres, Milo, Clodius, Catiline, Cethegus, and "Sulla's three disciples" (Octavian, Lepidus, and Antony)—a real Ciceronian crowd.[81] This culminates in an attack on Domitian for reviving laws against adultery "fit to terrify even Venus and Mars" while having an adulterous and incestuous relationship with his niece Julia. That "union worthy of tragedy" (*tragico . . . / concubitu*, 29–30) takes us back into inner space, but this time of the imperial palace, with a climactic scene of Julia "unsealing her fertile womb with abortion inducers" and "pouring out lumps looking like uncle" (32–33).[82] The vivid character of this moment of bodily abjection brings it into close association with the slicing off of the figlike piles mentioned earlier.[83] Both

77. Only elsewhere in Juv. in 1.60, of a dissolute youth (*puer Automedon*) squandering his inheritance. See chap. 1, pp. 75–76 herein.

78. Cf. the imperious wife who keeps "moving on": *sed mox haec regna relinquit / permutatque domos et flammea conterit: inde / avolat et spreti repetens vestigia lecti. . . .* (6.224–26)

79. Freudenburg 1993, 158–59; Newlands 2002, 140–41.

80. Cf. Worman 2009 on rivers and meandering (45–62). Pers. 1.16–17 on effeminate signs in the epic *recitator: . . . liquido cum plasmate guttur / mobile conlueris, patranti fractus ocello.*

81. Cf. Hor.'s satirical summary of the Republic in *Sat.* 1.6.7–44, in political and social terms, with P. M. Brown 1995 and Gowers 2012, *ad loc.*

82. In 4.65, Domitian is styled *Atrides* and *Sat.* 6 ends with a parade of female murderers and poisoners from tragedy (the victim is also *Atrides*, 6.660); thus the contemporary example in 2 anticipates a major concluding point in 6. On abortion, cf. 6.594–97.

83. Gowers 1993a notes: "Julia's womb becomes an edible pig's stuffed womb disgorged of its contents: the pregnant woman, *satura*, dissolved into misshapen bits" (198).

kinds of lumpy flesh reveal the ugly truth about their owner's sexual activities. In *Satire* 6.114–35, there is a corresponding, although much more extensive, scene of imperial debauchery, namely Messalina in the brothel, while the theme of bodily outflows is taken up in several passages throughout the poem. The opening question of that Messalina passage makes clear the analogy between the ordinary *domus* and the emperor's palace: *quid privata domus, quid fecerit Eppia, curas?* / *respice rivales deorum* (Are you worried about what went on in a private house, what Eppia did? Look at the rivals of the gods, 6.114–15). Miller appositely describes Messalina's bed-bouncing body as "a sort of shock absorber" with "a mind of its own, representing a species of erotic hunger that knows no satisfaction."[84]

After *Satire* 2's uplifting glimpse into the imperial household, we move to a speech by one Laronia, who, smiling ironically (*subridens*) like the doctor earlier, takes on one of the hypocrites noising off (*clamantem*) that the "sleeping" *Lex Julia* on adultery (itself suggestive of the imperial bedroom) needs to wake up:

> Habeat iam Roma pudorem:
> tertius e caelo cecidit Cato. Sed tamen unde
> haec emis, hirsuto spirant opobalsama collo
> quae tibi? Ne pudeat dominum monstrare tabernae.[85]

> Let Rome have a sense of shame:
> a third Cato has fallen from the sky! But, by the way, where
> did you buy this balsam which wafts from your hairy neck?
> Don't be ashamed to point out the owner of the shop. (39–42)

In *Satire* 6, Pudicitia has fled from the earth *ad superos*, here a "new Cato" drops down as the harbinger of *pudor*.[86] The only shame involved, however, is in pointing out who sold him the perfume for his bristly neck. The disjunction between a law's provisions and its (non-)effects is another symptom of the lack of *fides*. The Julian Laws rewarding parenthood are alluded to in 9.87, but in

84. Miller 2005, 280; cf. L. and P. Watson 2014, *ad loc.*; Wiesen 1989 on appearance vs. reality here (718).

85. As a locus of vice, cf. Cat. 37.1, *salax taberna vosque contubernales* and intro., p. 22 herein, on *quadrivium*.

86. Ovid *F.* 5.551–52 has Mars descending to view his new temple in the Forum Augustum: *Ultor ad ipse suos caelo descendit honores* / *templaque in Augusto conspicienda foro*; in Juvenal, such notions are ironically burlesqued in the idea of a "third Cato" falling from the sky (2.110). Mart. 9.7.14 uses *Catoniana lingua* of a hypocritical moralist. Hor. *Sat.* 1.2.31–35 quotes the *sententia dia Catonis* endorsing brothels as better than adultery; in 95, he mentions Catia, a matron notorious for adultery with a *tribunus plebis*. As Gowers says (2012, 111), "In name and actions, she is the antithesis of Cato (like Catius in *Sat.* 2.4)."

the context of Naevolus's criticizing his patron's lack of gratitude for having had his children fathered for him.

Laronia then skewers these "descendants of the Stoics" by comparing them unfavorably with women when it comes to the maintenance of appropriate gender identity. If it's a matter of waking up laws, then it should be the *Lex Scantinia*—look first, she says, at men, before criticizing women. There is *concordia* in Rome (despite her temple being inhabited by storks in *Satire* 1), but (only) among the wrong sort of males:[87]

> Magna inter molles concordia. Non erit ullum
> exemplum in nostro tam detestabile sexu.
> Tedia non lambit Cluviam nec Flora Catullam:
> Hispo subit iuvenes et morbo pallet utroque.
> Numquid nos agimus causas? Civilia iura
> novimus? Aut ullo strepitu fora vestra movemus?
> Luctantur paucae, comedunt colyphia paucae.
> Vos lanam trahitis calathisque peracta refertis
> vellera, vos tenui praegnantem stamine fusum
> Penelope melius, levius torquetis Arachne,
>
> . . .
>
> horrida quale facit residens in codice paelex.

> Great is the Concord among effeminates.
> There won't be any example so disgusting among our sex.
> Tedia doesn't tongue Cluvia, nor Flora Catulla,
> but Hispo goes under young men and is pale from both diseases.
> Do we plead cases in court? Are we experts in civil law?
> Or do we disturb your forums with any uproar?
> Few women wrestle, few eat the meat rations [of athletes].
> You spin the wool and bring the worked fleeces back in baskets,
> you turn the spindle pregnant with fine thread
> better than Penelope, more deftly than Arachne,
>
> . . .
>
> the sort of work a disheveled mistress does as she sits on a log.
> (2.47–57)[88]

87. On Lex Scantinia, see Courtney 1980 and Braund 1996a, with Edwards 1993, 71. On Concordia, see above, pp. 106, 112, and 15.159: *sed iam serpentum maior Concordia*; for the term in marriage discourse, Braund 1995, 209.

88. On the obscurities of lines 55–57, see Courtney 1980; Wiesen 1989, 718–19; Konstan 1993, 12; cf. *codex, non mulier*, Petr. 74.13, of Fortunata.

Here the absence of women from courtrooms or the forum, or, in most cases, from athletic training programs, is contrasted with men's migration to the traditional territory of the woman—either to the spinning wheel or the punishment block of the slave-turned-mistress.[89] The *horrida* recalls the *hispida membra* of the Stoics earlier and anticipates the *horridior* of the shaggy cave women of *Satire* 6.[90] According to Laronia, there has been an incursion of men into space designated as female, without any corresponding violation of gender boundaries by women. She is a stand-in for the satirist here (anticipating Umbricius in *Satire* 3), perhaps fittingly in the topsy-turvy world of gender inversion of *Satire* 2.[91] Such is the truth-telling power of Laronia's speech that the Stoicidae run away in fright, an echo of the speaker's wish in the opening line to flee beyond the Sarmatians from the awful truth of satire:

> Fugerunt trepidi vera ac manifesta canentem
> Stoicidae; quid enim falsi Laronia?
> The descendants of the Stoics fled, terrified at her uttering obvious
>   truths;
> for what did Laronia say that was false? (64–65)

Canentem suggests prophesying and implies that Laronia has access to genuine understanding.[92] Her name includes LAR, perhaps a reference to the sanctity of the household, and her behavior recalls that of Hispala, the high-minded courtesan and freedwoman (*scortum nobile libertina . . . non digna questu cui ancillula adsuerat*, 9.5) who testifies to the true nature of the Bacchic rites to the consul in Livy's narrative. Her denunciation of the corruption in the city was unusually forceful (*cum verba tum perturbationem tantam*, 10.3) and focused heavily on the antics of men initiated into what was originally a female rite. Like Hispala's unsparing dissection of the dangers posed by the Bacchanalia, and her intimate knowledge of how they have spread, Laronia's speech cannot fail to impress, in spite of the notionally unreliable mouth whence it emerges.[93] The ambiguous characterization is perhaps similar to

---

89. On spinning, cf. 6.289–90.

90. Cf. the name Hispo, Courtney 1980, 130 (he compares Hispulla in 6.74, 12.11); Braund 1996a, *ad loc.*

91. For Laronia's possible origin in Martial, see Colton 1991, 73–74; on Laronia, not as prostitute but of "relatively high social status," see Braund 1995, 208.

92. On the possibility of an "inspired" and truth-telling Umbricius, see Hardie 1998, who posits a sacral setting in the tradition established by Plato's *Phaedrus*.

93. Gold 2012 notes that Laronia "may be the only focalizing female voice" in Juvenal and that this "strong and autonomous woman's voice" is heard only briefly (107–108). F. M. A. Jones 2007 thinks there is some reason to doubt the truth of her words, noting that some of her claims appear overstated, while "Juvenal's exaggerated *imprimatur* on the speech must be intended to provoke disbelief" (140–42). Cf. 151–53 on how the question of moral judgment is "implicated in Juvenal's tendency to paradox."

the "Umbricius problem" of an effective speaker flawed by inconsistency; here, perhaps one point is that the Stoicidae are so lacking in vigor, thanks to their "diseased" condition, that Laronia's outburst, imperfectly modulated as it is, is sufficient to send them packing. There is a similar ambiguity about the persuasiveness of Naevolus's attack on his ungrateful *pathicus* patron in *Satire* 9.[94]

More generally, of course, the reliability of rhetoric is itself unstable in a world in which boundaries are failing, and *frontis nulla fides* applies to words as much as it does to faces. Laronia claims women are not much involved, but her speech sets up categories of difference to be exploited in *Satire* 6. Inflows of foreign corruption are matched by outflows of female incontinence—whether of speech, noise, lust, or liquids. These outflows in turn are linked with lack of restraint among males and the loss of trust in respectable outward appearances.[95] Satire itself becomes part of the scenery, as it bursts and overflows literary and linguistic, temporal and spatial boundaries.

And yet, there is something uniquely arresting about Laronia's tirade, precisely because it breaks out from the background noise of rampant misogyny, just as there is about the condemnation of the Bacchanalia from the lips of a former slave and courtesan. It is Aebutius's mother who sets out to corrupt him (*via una corruptelae Bacchanalia erant*, 9.3–4), but the plot is also revealed by a woman.[96] Scafuro, delineating the comic frame of Livy's patriotic narrative, suggests that Hispala is "a perfect witness for the State . . . precisely because of the marginality and fluidity of her status" (129) as a figure who crosses the boundaries between "daytime and nighttime society" (137). As Livy uses the comic frame "to depict a situation in which status and character are out of alignment" and Hispala to "unite private household and State" (135), so Juvenal deploys a similarly paradoxical figure—a member of the generally despised category of females who nonetheless sees and speaks the truth about the breakdown of structuring boundaries. The fear that makes the Stoicidae flee from Laronia *vera ac manifesta canentem* (2.63) is the satirist's wishful echo of the panic in Rome and beyond that ensued after the Senate's decree (*terror magnus urbe tota fuit, nec moenibus se tantum urbis aut finibus Romanis continuit, sed passim per totam Italiam . . . trepidari coeptum est*, 17.4).[97] There

94. See Courtney 1980, Braund 1996a, Miller 2005, *ad loc.*

95. Edwards 1993 on fluidity and prodigal pleasures (173–75).

96. In league with his stepfather, who has been misappropriating his ward's property. They wish to kill him or make him dependent in some way, cf. 11.1–2. On Juvenal's numerous examples of familial corruption: 1.77–78, 158, and chap. 4 herein.

97. Cf. 18.1: *tanta fuga ex urbe facta erat.*

were not supposed to be Bacchanalia in Rome again, but they have, so to speak, reappeared. What the senatorial forces did with arms and executions, he can achieve only through verbal punishment, a "literary form of *flagitatio*," as Jonathan Walters has it.[98]

Meanwhile, in *Satire* 6, the possibilities of women making incursions into the wrong places—male territory, whether spatial or intellectual—are exploited to the limit: *luctantur paucae* claims Laronia, but for women athletes we need look no further than the vicious *matrona* who lashes out at her neighbors or a barking dog and goes off to the baths for a strenuous workout (413–33).[99] This character is sandwiched between the "news hound" (398–412) discussed above and the chatty critic-cum-grammarian (434–47), both examples of excessive outflows of speech and forays into male territory, spatial and intellectual. Cavorting at the baths while her dinner guests are left hungry and sleepy, she orders her army of servants around like a general moving camp (the newshound enjoys chatting with generals in their uniforms, *paludatis ducibus*, 400), sweating amid the noise, and having a massage before bathing, just like a male athlete. Then she lets out a shriek when brought to climax by the expert fingerer of her *crista* (419–23).[100] This ejaculatory moment is followed by another when she comes home, overheated and thirsty for the flagon of wine:

> Tandem illa venit rubicundula, totum
> oenophorum sitiens, plena quod tenditur urna
> admotum pedibus, de quo sextarius alter
> ducitur ante cibum rabidam facturus orexim,
> dum redit et loto terram ferit intestino.
> Marmoribus rivi properant, aurata Falernum
> pelvis olet; nam sic, tamquam alta in dolia longus
> deciderit serpens, bibit et vomit. Ergo maritus
> nauseat atque oculis bilem substringit opertis.

> At long last, she arrives, face flushed and thirsty for the whole
> flagon of wine which is set at her feet brimming
> with a full three gallons; from this two pints

---

98. Walters 1998, 360–62.

99. The wording of 6.242–45 would appear to contradict what Laronia claims, but of course the speaker is different.

100. With this meaning only in Juv., an *ad hoc* sexual metaphor, says Adams 1982, 98; cf. 6.256 with the wife auctioning off sword and crests and greaves; the emperor's crest goes up at the fisherman's flattery in 4.70. Also how Tullia wets herself and Apula yelps as they watch Bathyllus the dancer in 6.63–64.

are downed before dinner, to create a raging appetite,
until they come back up and strike the ground along with her washed-out
    insides.
Streams rush over the marble floors, the golden basin
reeks of Falernian; for like a long snake that fell into a deep vat,
she drinks and vomits. And so her husband
feels nauseous and keeps down his bile by closing his eyes. (425–33)[101]

Again, liquid flows into the house: the wife returns home from the baths and
makes rivers (rivi) in a graphic display of consumption and expulsion. Satiric
nausea manifests itself not only in the vomit streaming across the floor but in
the blurring of gender distinctions that accompanies it.[102] The episode recalls
Cicero's description of Mark Antony's public display of vomiting after drinking too much at a wedding the night before:

> Tu istis faucibus, istis lateribus, ista gladiatoria totius corporis
> firmitate tantum vini in Hippiae nuptiis exhauseras ut tibi necesse
> esset in populi Romani conspectu vomere postridie.

> With that gullet of yours, that chest, that robust physique befitting a
> gladiator, you engulfed such a quantity of wine at Hippias' wedding
> that the following day you found it necessary to vomit in full view of
> the Roman people. (Philippic 2.63)[103]

Burping would have been bad enough in a Magister Equitum, never mind the
fragments of food stinking of wine that he threw up all over his lap and the
whole of the tribunal (vomens frustis esculentis vinum redolentibus gremium
suum et totum tribunal inplevit).[104]

Peribomius and Laronia are then truth-telling in different ways. The former shamelessly shows what he is (as does Naevolus), while the latter uncovers
the reality behind the facade (like the satirist). Hidden acts at home seep out
into the streets and public spaces, here and in Satire 9. Indeed, when the speaker
responds to Naevolus's request that he keep his confidences secret, he offers a
description of the permeability of the domus that sums up Naevolus's own
"openness" on all levels:

---

101. Colton 1991 finds a model in Martial 7.67, on the athletic Philaenis, but notes that the floor, basin,
and nauseated husband are Juvenal's own touches.

102. The snake image, cf. 6.641: saevissima vipera (of a stepmother's poisoning two sons).

103. Trans. Shackleton Bailey, 2009.

104. Edwards 1993 on incontinentia as subset of mollitia (81–84); cf. 191–92.

O Corydon, Corydon, secretum divitis ullum
esse putas? Servi ut taceant, iumenta loquentur
et canis et postes et marmora. Claude fenestras,
vela tegant rimas, iunge ostia, tolle lucernam,
e medio fac eant omnes, prope nemo recumbat;
quod tamen ad cantum galli facit ille secundi,
proximus ante diem caupo sciet, audiet et quae
finxerunt pariter libarius, archimagiri,
carptores.

O Corydon, Corydon, do you think a rich man can have any secret?
Even if his slaves keep silent, his asses will talk,
and the dog and his doorposts and his marble floors. Close the shutters,
cover the chinks with curtains, fasten the doors, put out the light,
make everyone go away, see that nobody sleeps nearby;
still, what the master does at the second cock-crow
the nearest shopkeeper will know before dawn, and likewise he'll hear
whatever the pastry cook, the head chefs, and the carvers have made up.
(102–10)

See-through Men: Creticus and Contagion

The satire now moves into a more public and spectacular mode, continuing with
Creticus, a lawyer with a Greek name who wraps up his prosecution of two adul-
teresses clad in a gauze toga, using the heat of July as an excuse for his see-
through attire:

. . . nudus agas. Minus est insania turpis.
En habitum quo te leges ac iura ferentem
vulneribus crudis populus modo victor et illud
montanum positis audiret vulgus aratris.

You should plead stark naked. Insanity is less base.
Look what you wear when citing laws and statutes, as the populace,
flushed with victory with their wounds still raw, along with that
mountain mob, who have put down their ploughs, listen to you. (2.71–74)

Infamous examples of the corruption of the late Republic, and especially Mark
Antony, seem to be in the speaker's mind in this part of the poem. One is reminded of Cicero's castigation of him in *Philippic* 2.44.20 to the effect that

he put on the toga of manhood and "immediately turned it into a woman's" (*sumpsisti virilem, quam statim muliebrem togam reddidisti*), suggesting his role as a passive partner in homosexual relationships. It is worth remembering that in 10.125–26, Juvenal refers to *Philippic* 2 in glowing terms (*conspicuae divina Philippica famae*).[105] In *Philippic* 2.85–86, describing Antony's approach to Caesar as a Lupercus (*ita eras Lupercus ut te consulem esse meminisse deberes*), Cicero condemns him for being naked: *O praeclaram illam eloquentiam tuam cum es nudus contionatus! Quid hoc turpius, quid foedius, quid suppliciis omnibus dignius?* In a similar but much pettier vein, Creticus makes a spectacle in silk for an amazed populace (*populo mirante*, 67).[106] As witnesses of the scene, Juvenal summons what Braund terms "the archetypal uncorrupted Roman populus, made up of courageous soldiers and hard-working rustics, groups which evoke the idealised past, before luxury and peace-time decadence corrupted Rome." Anyone who has heard political candidates ranting against the "Washington urban elite" or the "London metropolitan class" will relate to the device of the "country flashback" to invoke the idealized past, but such "rural moments," as we have already noted, are never free of ambiguity reminding us that there is no real possibility of escape.[107] As Wiesen observes, "This picture is pure nostalgic myth. . . . Indeed the piling up of the details drawn from the standard romantic myth of the early republic calls attention more to the insubstantiality of that ideal as a counterpoise to the outrageousness of Creticus than it does to Creticus' crime" (719). A similar rural moment appears in *Satire* 9, as Naevolus asks for a few acres from the patron's estates in Apulia or the Bay of Naples (54–60); as we just saw, the satirist also addresses him "O Corydon, Corydon" (103) in a playful allusion to Vergil's *Eclogue* 2.69. In *Satire* 6.58–59, just dwelling in the countryside is not enough to guarantee probity:

> Quis tamen adfirmat nil actum in montibus aut in
> speluncis? Adeo senuerunt Iuppiter et Mars?

> But who claims that nothing happened on the hills
> or in the caves? Have Jupiter and Mars become so senile?

---

105. There he recalls how Cicero's rhetorical eloquence cost him his life—if only it had been as risible as his poetry, he would have survived (120–26). We see here echoes of the anxieties about too free speech at the end of *Satire* 1.

106. Cf. *miratrix turba*, 4.62. In 8.38, among those "noble" in name only, Creticus is clearly a descendant of the famous one; here he may be an eminent lawyer.

107. Braund 1996a, 142; on Roman self-fashioning via the farmer-citizen, see Spencer 2010, 13–14, 33–41, and her chap. 3 in general. One thinks too of the *silva*, the scenery in the arena which simulated the natural habitat of the animals in the *venationes* or executions *ad bestias*, see Mart. *Spect.* 24.7; Auguet 1972, 99–100; Coleman 1990, 52; Edmondson 1996, 94; Dunkle 2008, 230–31.

Although the interpretation is somewhat uncertain, the import of the observation is that a woman who lives in a country town like Gabii *may* retain her good character, but even hills and caves are potentially places of seduction, far different from those primeval ones at the beginning of the poem.[108] "Playing the rustic" in such a setting is more akin to the behavior of Marie Antoinette or Rupert Birkin than to that of Cato. Answering another *Unde?* the speaker replies that it is only by going back in time that a different kind of woman can be found:

> Unde haec monstra tamen vel quo de fonte requiris?
> Praestabat castas humilis fortuna Latinas
> quondam, nec vitiis contingi parva sinebant
> tecta labor somnique breves et vellere Tusco
> vexatae duraeque manus ac proximus Urbi
> Hannibal et stantes Collina turre mariti.

> But where do these monstrosities come from, you're asking, what's their
>   source?
> In the old days it was their lowly position that kept Latin women pure.
> What kept the contamination of vice from their tiny homes was
> hard work, short sleep, hands chafed and hardened from handling
>   Tuscan fleeces, Hannibal close to Rome, and their husbands manning
>   the Colline tower. (6.286–91)[109]

This is a picture of a time when boundaries and fortifications were secure, stiffened by an obvious outside threat. Unlike the *Tusca* who happily and shamefully changes herself into a *Graecula*, these women worked diligently indoors with Tuscan wool and did not roam about, keeping vices from tainting their tiny homes, while their husbands stood on the suitably phallic Colline tower primed to repulse the invader.[110]

The country flashback in the Creticus vignette also motivates the central imagery of *Satire* 2, which now makes its appearance, with a nod to the figs and *fossa* earlier:

> Acer et indomitus libertatisque magister,
> Cretice, perluces.[111] Dedit hanc contagio labem
> et dabit in plures, sicut grex totus in agris

---

108. On caves in Bacchic rites, see Livy 39.14.13 and Briscoe 2008, *ad loc.*
109. Trans. Braund 2004.
110. Edwards 1993 on good women spinning (79–80).
111. Cf. 11.13 *perlucente ruina* (cracks in façade let in light already); 3.190, 196; 10.107.

unius scabie cadit et porrigine porci
uvaque conspecta livorem ducit ab uva.

You fierce, indomitable champion of liberty,
Creticus—you are transparent! Infection causes this stain
and will cause it in more men, just as a whole herd in the fields
dies from the scab and mange of a single pig
and a bunch of grapes takes on discoloration from the sight of another
   bunch. (2.77–81)[112]

The first line could well describe the heroic Lucilius of *Satire* 1, or Cicero in his *Philippics*,[113] but then we see that it is being used ironically—the first of several occasions when the word *libertas* is deployed in settings that make the loss of its original signified all too clear, as was the case with Peribomius' *simplicitas*.[114] Teaching *libertas* to Romans ought to be like bringing coals to Newcastle but isn't. The stirring words of *Philippic* 6.19 have no resonance in Juvenal's Rome:

Populum Romanum servire fas non est, quem di immortales
omnibus gentibus imperare voluerunt. Res in extremum est adducta
discrimen; de libertate decernitur. Aut vincatis oportet, Quirites,
quod profecto et pietate vestra et tanta concordia consequemini, aut
quidvis potius quam serviatis. Aliae nationes servitutem pati
possunt, **populi Romani est propria libertas.**

It is against divine law for the Roman people to be enslaved, since
the immortal gods willed that they rule over all nations. The
ultimate crisis is upon us: freedom is at stake. Either you must
be victorious, Men of Rome, as you surely will be thanks to your
patriotism and your strong united will, or—anything but slavery.
Other nations can endure servitude, but **the birthright of the Roman
people is freedom.**[115]

Juvenal's description of the contagion emphasizes two elements: how one diseased creature infects the entire herd and how others take on the hue of the

---

112. Martyn 1970a on echoes of Vergil's plague in *Georg.* 3.440–566.

113. It is actually from Lucan, 1.146 of Caesar; see Courtney 1980, *ad loc.*, and also on the proverbial nature (and possible spuriousness) of Juv. 2.81.

114. Cf. 6.140; 206; 216–17; 327.

115. Trans. Shackleton Bailey 2009.

discolored grape just by looking at it.[116] In 6.161, *grex* is used of women and in 533 of the priests of Anubis.[117] We may recall Livy's wording in 9.1, *huius mali labes ex Etruria Romam veluti contagione morbi penetravit*. All being infected by one is a powerful centrifugal image, and it comes to be applied to Rome itself at the end of the poem, where the city's dissolute ways are taken back to the far-flung provinces of the Empire by young men.[118] As Seneca advises in *De Tranquillitate* 7.4, just as in times of plague one doesn't sit near anyone infected, for fear even of their breath, so in choosing friends one must seek out those with fewest stains: *initium morbi est aegris sana miscere* (To mix sick with healthy is the cause of disease). In 14.59–69, the satirist condemns parents who take the trouble to clean the dog shit out of the house when a guest comes but not to ensure that the son sees a home *sine labe vitioque carentem* (without taint and free from vice, 69).

In the proverb of the discolored grapes the idea of ripeness—far from being positive, as Courtney suggests—ties in with the swollen figs lanced by the doctor. Vice explodes from Rome, just as hemorrhoids explode from the arsehole. The passage that follows, detailing Creticus's initiation into the rites of the Bona Dea, clarifies the insidious nature of the progression of vice and its furtherance by what one sees and hears, a version of the centripetal penetration motif:

Foedius hoc aliquid quandoque audebis amictu;
nemo repente fuit turpissimus. Accipient te
paulatim qui longa domi redimicula sumunt
frontibus et toto posuere monilia collo
atque Bonam tenerae placant abdomine porcae
et magno cratere Deam. Sed more sinistro
exagitata procul non intrat femina limen:
solis ara deae maribus patet. "Ite, profanae,"
clamatur, "nullo gemit hic tibicina cornu."

---

116. Cf. *lividulus* in 11.110; Mart. 11.20.1 and Kay 1985, 112: originally meant just the blue color of a bruise but then came to be used of "unpleasant things" like poisons and "uncongenial emotions" like jealousy.

117. Niobe ("more fecund than the *scrofa alba*") has *greges natorum* (6.175–77); used of astrologers 10.94 and slaves 12.116. Dunkle 2008 notes that a group of gladiatorial fighters (inferior to duelists) were called *gregarii*, also used of a company of actors (62–63); cf. *CIL* 2.6278, lines 35–37 in Futrell 2006, 49. In Mart. 5.60.11, *scabies* has the metaphorical sense of "itch to do something" and in Sen. *De Tranq.* 2.11–12, is used along with *ulcera* of desires that drive the mind to toil and vexation. In Juv. 6.631, the children's pies are *livida* with maternal poison. Hor. *Sat.*1.4.93, on the satirist viewed as *lividus et mordax*.

118. Cf. how in Bely's *Petersburg*, the time bomb to assassinate the senator is concealed in a sardine tin; from this small and ordinary item, revolutionary disorder is supposed to spread across the entire country. See Barta 1996, 20–28.

Some day you will dare something more disgusting than this clothing.
No one ever became utterly abominable overnight. Little by little you'll be
welcomed by men who in the privacy of their homes wear long bands
on their foreheads
and have their necks entirely covered with jewellery and who placate
the Good Goddess with the udder of a young sow and with a large bowl
of wine.
But by inversion of the normal custom, women do not cross their
threshold and are sent packing: the altar of the goddess is open to
males alone. "Get away, you impure women!" is their cry. "No music
girl with her horn pipes here." (2.82–90)[119]

For the notion that no one becomes *turpissimus* overnight, we may compare Livy's observations on how the excesses of the Bacchanalia fostered gradual corruption (8.6, 10.78). Juvenal's tableau of religious impropriety takes us
across the *limen* and back into interior space. This particular *limen*, however, is
not crossed by women, only by men, in a startling reversal of normal gender
movement.[120] The inclusion of men into previously female-only rites was the
trigger of the Bacchanalian scandal, but the satirist's version is more extreme:
the men now exclude women and have taken over the ceremony completely,
leading to rampant effeminacy (13.8–9). In *Satire* 9, Naevolus unsurprisingly
pursues his business opportunities at the shrines of Isis and Ganymede and
the palace of the "imported mother" (22–24).[121] Lamenting his patron's unwill-
ingness to give him even a few acres of country land (45–58), he asks:

Melius, dic, rusticus infans
cum matre et casulis et conlusore catello
cymbala pulsantis legatum fiet amici?

Tell me, is it better that your rustic child,
with his mother and toy houses and puppy playmate,
should be bequeathed to your cymbal-clanging friend? (60–62)

---

119. Trans. Braund 2004.

120. *frontibus* echoes *frontis nulla fides* earlier. The stomach of the *porca* (female) recalls the infection of
the *porcus* (male) in the description of the contagion earlier; on *porcus*, which is colloquial, and similar terms,
see Brink 1982, 189–90. He notes that Juvenal's female scholar sacrifices a pig to Silvanus in 6.447; cf. Mars
Silvanus in Cato *De Agr.* 83. Courtney 1980 notes women were excluded from the cult of Silvanus (*ad loc.*). In
6.158–60, we find a triad of foreigners, incest and pigs in the mention of Agrippa II of Judaea and Berenice.

121. On the Temple of Isis and associated rituals of female fanaticism, 6.528–41; in 529, the temple
"towers next to the ancient sheepfold" (*antiquo quae proxima surgit ovili*), referring to the polling booths in the
Campus Martius; see Courtney 1980, "What a disgraceful neighbor for the Ovile with its roots in Roman tradition!" (330).

The question is all the more potent, since Naevolus was the one who serviced his patron's wife so that he could have a son in the first place (70–89).[122] Miller summarizes the matter: "Why should Virro leave his property to a priest lacking the very instrument whereby Naevolus earns his keep, and which would be necessary to enjoy the boy properly?"

The Bona Dea rites feature prominently in *Satire* 6 as well (314–45), where amid the squeals and drips of lust, we see how:

attonitae crinemque rotant ululantque Priapi
maenades. O quantus tunc illis mentibus ardor
concubitus, quae vox saltante libidine, quantus
ille meri Veneris per crura madentia torrens!

The maenads of Priapus are carried away, whirling their hair and
    howling.
How their minds are all on fire to get laid then,
how they squeal to the dance of their desire, how abundant a torrent
of undiluted lust runs over their dripping thighs! (316–19)[123]

The climax is reached when the participants have been aroused to fever pitch:

Tunc **prurigo** morae impatiens, tum **femina simplex**,
ac pariter toto repetitus clamor ab antro
"Iam fas est, admitte viros."

That's **the itch** of impatience, that's the moment of **pure Woman.**
The shout's repeated in unison from the entire grotto:
"Now's the time! Send in the men!" (327–29)[124]

The *prurigo* echoes the *scabies* and *porrigo* of *Satire* 2; *simplex* suggests another manifestation of *simplicitas* but again it is the wrong sort, not positive at all, but shamelessly revelatory, like that of Peribomius or Creticus.[125] The cave recalls the opening of *Satire* 6 and suggests that the Bona Dea has effectively

---

122. Miller 2005 suggests that the priest "must serve as an image of the kind of depravity that would ensue if the already depraved patron did not make a bequest to his equally depraved client" (301). The *rusticus infans / cum matre* recalls 3.176: *in gremio matris formidat rusticus infans.*

123. Richlin 1992, 205–206; Gold 2012, 108–109, says the passage in 6 fleshes out the one in 2: "Now we know what 'really' went on."

124. Trans. Braund 2004.

125. Gunderson 2005: "The 'true speech' of the depraved body is the ideal interlocutor for the philosophy of satire. And much like the most passive of the Socratic interlocutors, the body here can either only assent to the force of the satirical arguments made against it or else provide the satirist with yet more grist for his mill" (227–28).

replaced Pudicitia. The speaker then reminds us of the initial profanation of the rites by Clodius, who hauled in "a penis bigger than both of the *Anti-Cato* speeches written by Julius Caesar" (in whose home the ceremony took place), and he concludes with the question, "*sed nunc ad quas non Clodius aras?*" (336–45).[126] *Satire* 2 would appear to confirm this, depicting a setting amid the worshipers of Cybele where there is no *pudor* or *reverentia* and only the wrong sort of *libertas*:

> Hic nullus verbis pudor aut reverentia mensae,
> hic †turpis† Cybeles et fracta voce loquendi
> libertas . . .

> Here there is no sense of shame in words, no table manners,
> here is Cybele's disgusting (?) . . . and the freedom to speak in a broken
>   voice . . . (2.110–12)[127]

Cicero reminds his listeners that all of Clodius's "conflagrations" were ignited by Antony (*eius omnium incendiorum fax*) and that he was already "up to something" in his house (*Phil.* 2.48). Much is made of Antony's riotously inappropriate occupation of Pompey's house (*cum omnis impuritates pudica in domo cotidie susciperes vino lustrisque confectus*, 7) and profanation of his *limen*:

> tu etiam ingredi illam domum ausus es, tu illud sanctissimum
> limen intrare, tu illarum aedium dis penatibus os impurissimum
> ostendere? . . . Me quidem miseret parietum ipsorum atque
> tectorum. Quid enim umquam domus illa viderat nisi pudicum,
> quid nisi ex optimo more et sanctissima disciplina? . . . Huius in
> sedibus pro cubiculis stabula, pro conclavibus popinae sunt.

> Did you actually dare to enter that house, to cross that hallowed
> threshold, to show your debauched face to the household gods of that
> dwelling? . . . For my part, I pity the very walls and ceilings. What
> had that house ever seen that was not decorous, what that was not in
> accord with the highest and strictest moral code? . . . Now in this
> man's dwelling there are brothels in place of bedrooms, cheap
> eateries in place of dining rooms. (68–69)

Similar motifs appear in regard to Antony's occupation of M. Varro's villa in 104–105: *At quam multos dies in ea villa* **turpissime es perbacchatus.** *Ab hora tertia*

---

126. Richlin 1992, 97–99.
127. Cf. Apul. *Met.* 8.26; see Beard 1994 and J. Latham 2012 for detailed surveys and bibliography on Cybele.

bibebatur, ludebatur, vomebatur. O tecta ipsa misera (But how many days did you spend **disgracefully carousing** in that villa! From eight o'clock in the morning there was drinking, gambling, vomiting. I pity the very building). Varro, Cicero fumes, intended it to be a retreat for his studies (*iura populi Romani, monumenta maiorum, omnis sapientiae ratio omnisque doctrinae*), but when Antony was its tenant *personabant omnia vocibus ebriorum, natabant pavimenta vino, madebant parietes, ingenui pueri cum meritoriis, scorta inter matres familias versabantur* (Every room echoed with the shouts of drunkards, the pavements swam with wine, the walls were wet with it, boys of free birth mingled with child prostitutes, harlots with married ladies).[128]

To return to Creticus, on display inside the house (where long headbands now cover *frontes*, 84–85) are various types of pseudo-males, including one who holds a mirror (*speculum*), described (99–100) as the *pathici gestamen Othonis, / actoris Aurunci spolium*: spear has been replaced by looking-glass.[129] The last three words are an allusion to Turnus, but the adjective Auruncus also brings Lucilius back to mind.[130] Otho used to admire himself in the glass, we are told, clad in armor and giving battle orders. He killed Galba while pampering his skin, aspired to the Palatine throne while plastering dough on his face. This mirror scene brings together the ordinary *domus* and the super-*domus*, the imperial palace, while suggesting that the pursuit of *virtus* has been replaced by concern for cosmetics, something which not even Semiramis or Cleopatra managed to do (echoing Laronia's point that women's vice pales in comparison with men's).[131] Geographically, the scenery ranges from the heart of the Empire, the Palatine, outward to the battlefield of Bebriacum and then beyond to Assyria and Egypt. This momentary cut to the palace of the emperor thus draws the Empire as a whole into this single house of ill repute. Palace, bawdy house, and military camp merge.[132]

Makeup features in *Satire 6*, where the woman who applies face packs for her lover is unrecognizable until she peels off the *tectoria prima* (467), but even then, it's not easy to tell, *facies dicitur an ulcus?* (Is it a face or an ulcer? 473).

128. Trans. Shackleton Bailey 2009.

129. See Ash 1999 on Otho as a Nero-clone (86); Suet. *Otho* 2.2; Tac. *Hist.* 1.12.2. He did, ironically enough, force Tigillinus to commit suicide (*Hist.* 1.72). See chap. 1, p. 89n115 herein. On the mirror and masculinity, see Taylor 2008, 19–23; and debauchery, Sen. *NQ* 1.16 on Hostius Quadra.

130. Cf. *Satire* 1 and pp. 64, 67 herein.

131. Konstan 1993, explaining the integration of 102–109 into the concerns of *Sat.* 2, "a conquering Roman general, who should be the embodiment of dominant manliness, behaves in a way more effeminate than a defeated barbarian queen" (13).

132. Cf. Miller 2005 on the assonance of *lupanaris* and *pulvinar* in 6.132, which "identifies the imperial bed with the bordello" (280).

Another daubs her face while beating her slaves (*verberat atque obiter faciem linit*, 480) or whips her hairdresser for a curl out of place (490–96). There is in both cases an intriguing connection between makeup and violence; in the case of the woman, she has her own "council" in which opinions are sought (497–98) "as if it were a matter of reputation or of life itself" (*tamquam famae discrimen agatur / aut animae*, 500–501). She "builds" her head (*aedificat caput*) high with so many stories that you see an Andromache from the front (*a fronte*) but from behind she's so much smaller that you would think it's someone else (502–504). This scene is followed by an account of the worshipers of Bellona and the Mater Deorum (511–41), complete with big eunuch (*ingens / semivir*). In the house of the Bona Dea in *Satire* 2, the account ends, (un)naturally enough, with a scene of castration, Phrygian-style:

> Quid tamen expectant, Phrygio quos tempus erat iam
> more supervacuam cultris abrumpere carnem?

> What then are they waiting for? For whom it is already time
> to cut off their superfluous flesh with knives in the Phrygian manner.
> (115–16)

The adjective *supervacuus* suggests that the male genitals have become completely superfluous and useless, like Julia's aborted lumps.[133] Rhetorically, this is another climax scene, a sort of "and now the moment has come when . . ." motif, marking the ultimate in feminization.[134]

Gracchus: *Transitur Ad Galeam*

Juvenal now transitions into his final spectacle, Gracchus, who not only married another man but also fought in the arena. This move from castration to the arena is motivated by a connection through disgrace and *infamia*.[135] Seneca, in *Natural Questions* 7.31.3, writes:

> Cotidie comminiscimur per quae virilitati fiat iniuria, ut **traducatur**,
> quia non potest exui; alius genitalia excidit, alius **in obscaenam ludi**

---

133. Echoing the doctor slicing off the "swollen figs" of the *pathicus* in the opening passage. Cf. 10.54: *ergo supervacuae aut quae perniciosa petuntur?*; *supervacuus* in 13.137 [=16.41] of worthless document; the adjective is used by Seneca frequently.

134. Sen. Eld. *Controv.* 10.4.17 on rich men who have *castrorum greges*, so they can use them longer and because *ipsos pudet viros esse*, they make sure that as few exist as possible; cf. Sen. *Ep.* 122.7.

135. Barton 1993 on castration (72–73); Walters 1998: "For a man's body to be sexually penetrated, used 'like a woman' by another man, and for his body to appear as spectacle in the arena were both conceptualized as paradigms of the state of being in the power of another" (364).

partem fugit et, locatus ad mortem, infame armaturae genus in quo **morbum** suum exerceat legit.

Daily we invent ways by which harm may be done to manliness, so that **it may be ridiculed**, because it cannot be cast off; one man cuts off his genitals, another flees to play **an indecent role in a gladiatorial school** and, set out for death, chooses a disgraceful kind of armament in which to practice his **disease**.

Seneca speaks of "practicing" one's disease, in language reminiscent of Juvenal. Slightly later, he laments the fact that nobody is concerned with philosophy unless the games are called off and that schools of philosophy are dying out because no teachers can be found, although there are plenty for the [theatrical] arts of Pylades and Bathyllus:

Privatum urbe tota sonat pulpitum; in hoc viri, in hoc feminae tripudiant; mares inter se uxoresque contendunt uter det latus mollius. Deinde, sub persona cum diu trita frons est, **transitur ad galeam**.

The home acting-stage resounds throughout the entire city. On it both men and women dance. Husbands and wives contend with each other over which of the two may bare their flank more salaciously. And then, when the brow has long been worn smooth under the mask, **it's time for the gladiator's helmet**. (7.32.3)

The reprise of Gracchus's arena appearance comes in *Satire* 8.200–10. It is set up by having him face the ignominious choice between the sword and the mime stage: *finge tamen gladios inde atque hinc pulpita poni* (105). From there, only the gladiatorial school remains (*haec ultra quid erit nisi ludus?* 199), so that again the arena constitutes the nadir.

Juvenal's arena scene in *Satire* 2 is prefaced by an account of Gracchus's wedding ceremony, which is a continuation of the castration motif, as a man "becomes" a woman in the bridal role (117–36). This too has an Antonian precedent, for Cicero skewers him in similar fashion for his relationship with Curio: *sed cito Curio intervenit, qui te a meretricio quaestu abduxit et, tamquam stolam dedisset, in matrimonio stabili et certo collocavit* (But quite soon, along came Curio, who took you out of the prostitute's trade, gave you a married lady's robe as it were, and settled you down in steady wedlock, 44).[136] For the satirist, an event like Gracchus's marriage is akin to monstrous births (*monstra*), expressed in the *adynaton* of a woman giving birth to a calf or a cow to

136. Cf. 50: *ut . . . viri tui similis esses.*

Sic veniunt ad miscellanea ludi (Juv. 11.20). Remains of practice arena in Ludus Magnus, near the Colosseum. Photograph by David Larmour and Corby Kelly.

a lamb (122–23). Once again the rural setting, with its supporting cast of Latian shepherds, provides a contrast to the corrupted urban space, elaborated in the succeeding lines:

> Segmenta et longos habitus et flammea sumit
> arcano qui sacra ferens nutantia loro
> **sudavit** clipeis ancilibus. O pater Urbis,
> unde nefas[137] tantum Latiis pastoribus? Unde
> haec tetigit, Gradive, tuos **urtica** nepotes?
> Traditur ecce viro clarus genere atque opibus vir,
> nec galeam quassas nec terram cuspide pulsas
> nec quereris patri? Vade ergo et cede severi
> iugeribus campi, quem **neglegis.**[138] "Officium cras
> primo sole mihi peragendum in valle Quirini."
> "Quae causa officii?" "Quid quaeris? Nubit amicus,

137. Cf. *fas est* in 1.131; the speaker takes on role of deciding what is *fas/nefas* in the absence of the gods. See Larmour 2012.

138. Cf. 5.16 of *cliens*; 9.15 of legs (*neglecta et squalida*) and 92 *neglegit* is the first word of Naevolus's reply, complaining about lack of attention from his patron.

nec multos adhibet." Liceat modo vivere, fient,
fient ista palam, cupient et in acta referri.

He's wearing the bride's flounces, long dress, and veil—the man
who carried the sacred objects swaying from the mystic thong
and who **sweated** under the weight of sacred shields. O father of Rome,
where has it come from, **this itch** that taints your descendants,
     Gradivus?
Look: a man illustrious in family and fortune is handed over in marriage
     to another man—and you're not shaking your helmet, or striking the
     ground with your spear, or complaining to your father? Off with you,
     then—withdraw from the acres of the stern Campus which **you
     neglect.** "Tomorrow at sunrise I have a ceremony to attend in the valley
     of Quirinus." "What's the occasion?" "Oh, just a friend of mine
     marrying a man, and he's invited a few guests." If we are allowed to
     live
just a little longer, those marriages will take place,
they'll take place openly, they'll even want to be reported in the news.
     (2.124–36)[139]

The flouncing clothes recall Creticus's see-through toga, contrasted with im-
penetrable shields. The setting of the marriage in the valley of Quirinus creates a startling juxtaposition; this is one of very few specific locations mentioned
in the poem.[140] Gracchus is one of the Salii, priests of Mars (closely associated
with Quirinus), whose colleges were on the Palatine and Colline. Later on, there
is an allusion to the Lupercalia when young men ran along the Via Sacra in the
Forum (and the scene of Antony's disgrace).[141] Mars is addressed as *pater Urbis*
and *Gradivus*, but in spite of all that goes on, he is not shaking his helmet or
striking the ground with his spear.[142]

Helmets figure quite prominently in Juvenal: in 6.253–54, for example, the
woman without *pudor* who trains as a gladiator and "flees from her sex" is *galeata*, while the satirist himself is imagined as *galeatum* at the end of the first
satire. In a similar vein, hairnets seem to have replaced helmets, at least in

---

139. Trans. Braund 2004, slightly adapted.
140. Courtney 1980 notes the degeneracy from Quirinus and compares 126, 8.14 (145); Ovid may mention this site (*F.* 4.375), although MSS tend to favor *colle* rather than *valle*; Braund 1996a, 157. On the marriage
of Callistratus and Afer in Mart. 12.42, see Colton 1991, 79–82.
141. As noted in chap. 1, herein, sweating is not generally positive in Juvenal: 1.167; 3.103; 4.108; 6.259;
13.220.
142. Cf. 6.393–94: *antiquissime divom / respondes his, Iane pater?*

Otho's case.[143] The image of the god departing from the "stern" Campus Martius will be picked up by the departure of *Pudicitia* in *Satire* 6, and there will be echoes of Mars's humiliation here in the pissing over the altar of Pudicitia by Maura and Tullia, "directing their urine in streams as if they were men" to quote Richlin.[144] The *urtica* (itch) which has touched Mars's descendants recalls the *scabies* and *porrigo* in the contagion image earlier.[145] Just as the male marriage is akin to castration, so the betrothed "die sterile," at least one thing the speaker can celebrate, which he does at some length in 137–42.

After the wedding, Gracchus commits the ultimate act of boundary violation by heading into the arena and putting himself on display:

> Vicit et hoc **monstrum**[146] tunicati fuscina Gracchi,
> **lustravit**que fuga mediam gladiator harenam
> et Capitolinis generosior et Marcellis
> et Catuli Paulique minoribus et Fabiis et
> omnibus ad podium spectantibus, his licet ipsum
> admoveas cuius tunc munere retia misit.

> Yet even this was outdone by the **monstrosity** of tunic-clad Gracchus with
>   his trident,
> when as a gladiator **he traversed** the middle of the arena in flight,
> a man of nobler birth than the Capitolini and Marcelli
> and the descendants of Catulus and Paulus and the Fabii
> and all those watching in the podium, and you add to them
> the man himself, in whose *munus* he threw the net on that occasion.
>   (2.143–48)[147]

Gracchus is disgraced not only by entering the arena, but by doing so as a *retiarius;* the spectacle of a descendant of a venerable line in such an ignominious role is striking enough to get a lengthy second take in *Satire* 8.200–10,

---

143. See chap. 1, p. 88 herein: *galeatum sero duelli / paenitet.* Cf. 11.104–107, the soldier's helmet depicting the twin Quirini or Mars naked without his shield and spear on his way to Rhea Silvia. Hairnets: Otho's in 2.96; cf. 6.0.22.

144. Richlin 1992, 206. In 7.7, *migraret Clio;* on Gradivus, Ov. *F.* 5.556. Mars is hardly worthy of the designation *Ultor:* his temple has been robbed in 4.261–62. See Larmour 2012.

145. Cf. 11.168, used in account of arousal to ejaculation point of spectators of Spanish dancers. On itches and desires, cf. Sen. *De Tranq.* 2.11–12: *ut ulcera quaedam nocituras manus adpetunt et tactu gaudent, et foedam corporum scabiem delectat quidquid exasperat, non aliter dixerim his mentibus, in quas cupiditates velut mala ulcera eruperunt, voluptati esse laborem vexationemque.*

146. Sen. *NQ* 1.16.6 on Hostius Quadra: *illud monstrum obscenitatem suam spectaculum fecerat;* Moussy 1977 on *monstrum.*

147. See the discussion of Rutilus, who does the same, in 11.6–8, below, pp. 281–82. On the relevance of this scene to the issues of *Sat.* 2, Konstan 1993, 14.

complete with Salian priestly clothing. Appropriate objects of the gaze do not include citizens of noble lineage in gladiatorial garb, especially this one: the *retiarius* was naked except for a loincloth and, uniquely, wore no helmet. He was lightly armed, and with his net and trident he was associated with the sea rather than with soldiering on land. The pairing of *secutor* and *retiarius*, the standard contest by the second century, pitted the type of a well-armed Roman soldier against this barely armed fighter.[148] The *retiarius* also features in the description of the house of a "professor of obscenity" in the Oxford fragment (O.1–34), which is compared—unfavorably—with the gladiatorial *ludus*:

> In quacumque domo vivit luditque professus
> obscenum et tremula promittens omnia dextra,
> invenies omnis turpes similesque cinaedis.
>
> . . .
>
> Purior ergo tuis laribus meliorque lanista,
> in cuius numero longe migrare iubetur
> psillus ab euhoplo. Quid quod nec retia turpi
> iunguntur tunicae, nec cella ponit eadem
> munimenta umeri †pulsatorisque† tridentem
> qui nudus pugnare solet? Pars ultima ludi
> accipit has animas aliusque in carcere nervos.

> In any house where a professor of obscenity lives and sports,
> His fidgety right hand suggesting he stops at nothing,
> You'll find that everyone is disgusting—no better than *cinaedi*.
>
> . . .
>
> That makes the gladiator trainer's establishment purer and better than
>   your holy hearth. In his troop Skin is told to keep well away
> from Loaded. Then there's the fact that the nets aren't kept
> alongside the tunic of disgrace, and that the shoulder guards
> and the trident of the gladiator who fights naked
> are not stored in the same locker. Such lost souls
> are relegated to the lowest section of the school
> and in their prison they have different chains. (1–3, 7–14)

The text is problematic, but the main point seems to be that the "light-armed [and/or depilated, hence effeminate] gladiator" is ordered to keep well away from

---

148. Reeve 1973 on nudity and *retiarius*; Cerutti and Richardson 1989; Dunkle 2008 sees the *retiarius* as a "sexually charged figure" because of the exposure of the body (49). In art, *noxii* are usually naked or almost, cf. Kyle 1998, 92.

the "heavily armed" one, with the Greek terms naturally adding a layer of contempt.[149] The equipment of different kinds of gladiators is likewise stored in different locations, although, again, with the corruption of the text, it is difficult to discern the hierarchy implied here. The (professional) net-man may be ranked above the amateur in the *turpis tunica*, perhaps with sexual overtones in the *pulsator* wielding the trident.[150] It is thanks to the *dominus'* wife that he is forced to mingle with such creatures, who act as her instructor, including on getting married and divorced. The vocabulary recalls that used in *Satire* 2, including *fides*:[151]

> Haud tamen illi
> semper habenda fides: oculos fuligine pascit
> discinctus croceis et reticulatus adulter.
> suspectus tibi sit, quanto vox mollior et quo
> saepius in teneris haerebit dextera lumbis.
>
> But he's not always to be trusted.
> He'll enhance his eyes with soot,
> his saffron outfit unfastened, a hair-netted adulterer!
> The more sensuous his voice, the more often his right hand lingers
> in his smooth crotch, the more suspicious you should be.
>   (6.0.20–24)[152]

The Gracchus arena-and-marriage conjunction deftly picks up on the reference to Tigillinus at the end of *Satire* 1, because after his sanguinary work in the arena was done, he arranged Nero's marriage to a man. The spouse was the philosophically named (if not minded) Pythagoras, and in Dio's account the event was preceded by a full program of spectacles—*venatio, naumachia,* and gladiatorial *munus*.[153] The verb *lustravit* has a double meaning: traverse and purify (its sense in 157, coming up); Varro connects it etymologically with

---

149. See Courtney 1980; and L. and P. Watson 2014, *ad loc.*; Braund's 2004 translation, which I reproduce here with minor alterations, ably captures the contrast in weaponry and sexual position with "Skin" and "Loaded" (265).

150. See Courtney 1980 who finds Leo's (1910) *pulsatoremque* best, with *pulsator* as a variety of gladiator; Colin 1952–53; Ferguson 1979 ("as the *retiarius* is referred to by his weapon, the homosexual is also referred to by his dress. Others take the *retiarius tunicatus* as a condemned criminal. To admit a *cinaedus* to your household is like admitting a condemned criminal to your troops").

151. The two references to the right hand emphasize that it is being put to use not for wielding the *gladius* in the army, but for sexual fingering.

152. Trans. Braund 2004.

153. See further discussion in chap. 3. Suet. *Nero* 28; Tac. *Ann.* 15.37.4; Dio Cass. 62.28.2–3, 63.13.1–2; Courtney 1980 compares Mart. 12.42 and 1.24.

ludus.[154] There is much emphasis here on the spectacle produced *for the view-ers*, including those in the front row and the *editor*, the emperor himself, in this case perhaps Nero.[155] The *editor* is also Juvenal, of course, as he "puts on" this spectacle for the reader, in a sort of mise en abime taking us into the op-erations of satire. It is worth noting here that Artemidorus links dreaming of a gladiator as signifying marriage: if a man fights a Thracian, he will have a wife who is rich, crafty, and ambitious, and if he fights a *retiarius*, he will have a poor and wanton wife who consorts with anyone who wants her (2.32; cf. 1.5).[156]

We recall that in the opening catalog in *Satire* 1 the first two exempla are the "soft eunuch" who takes a wife and Mevia who spears a Tuscan boar, with one breast bare like an Amazon (21–22).[157] In *Satire* 6, we find aristocratic women in love with gladiators: Lentulus's wife and the more extended story of Eppia, wife of a senator. In 78–81, the speaker addresses Lentulus, who is get-ting married:

Longa per angustos figamus pulpita vicos,
ornentur postes et grandi ianua lauro,
ut testudineo tibi, Lentule, conopeo
nobilis Euryalum murmillonem exprimat infans.

Let's put up the long platforms along the narrow streets,
let the doorposts and the doors be decorated with lots of laurel,
so that in his tortoiseshell cradle, Lentulus,
your noble child can remind you of Euryalus the *murmillo!*

The standard wedding preparations lead into a scandalous moment of recog-nition of familiar features in the little baby's face, and the juxtaposition of *nobilis* with *Euryalum murmillonem* neatly mirrors the entrance of vice into the household. This is followed by the much longer embedded narrative of Eppia, who accompanies a whole school of gladiators on a ship, as (with painful irony) Egyptian Canopus condemns Rome for its monstrous morality (82–114). She abandons her *domus*, husband, and sister, *patria*, her crying children (*natos*), and—even more amazingly—the games and her actor friend, Paris, and

154. Move over/through; pass through (dangers); circle around repeatedly; spread light; survey/scan. Also with shields, according to Varro, discussing *armilustrum*, ceremony of purifying arms *LL* 6.22 cf. Livy 27.37.4.

155. See Courtney 1980 and scholiast. He is not named, reminiscent of how Domitian is named indi-rectly in *Sat.* 4 and never seen, so that it is the names of murdered nobles and others that stand out. In 6.61–62, the speaker despairs of finding a suitable woman in the seats: *cuneis an habent spectacula totis / quod securus ames quoque inde excerpere possis?*

156. Antipater cites the example of man who dreamt of intercourse with a piece of iron but the outcome was not a gladiatorial contest, rather his penis was cut off (4.65). Cf. Toner 1995, 36.

157. On the possibility of female *bestiariae*, see Coleman 2006 in connection with Mart. *Spect.* 7 (70–75).

braves the sea (85–87). Like Gracchus, she has long since despised her reputation: *contempsit pelagus, famam contempserat olim* (90). On board the ship, she wanders around on deck and dines with the sailors (*et prandet et errat*, 101) and enjoys pulling the rough ropes (*duros gaudet tractare rudentis*, 102). The speaker then asks why Eppia wanted to be Sergius's *ludia* (104)—what on earth did she see in his disfigured face with a furrow (*sulcus*) dug by the helmet and a weeping eye (107–109)?[158] Comes the answer, "But he was a gladiator" (110), and so:

> hoc pueris patriaeque, hoc praetulit illa sorori
> atque viro. Ferrum est quod amant. Hic Sergius idem
> accepta rude coepisset Veiiento videri.

> this she preferred to her sons and her fatherland, this to her sister
> and her husband. The iron is what they love. This same Sergius,
> once he'd been retired, would have begun to be regarded as a Veiiento.
>   (111–13)

Thus the story of a gladiator effectively gaining entrance to the house of Lentulus, via his supposed child, is paralleled by Eppia's abandoning her home and her children for a gladiator.[159] The scandalous journey to Egypt vaguely recalls the antics of Antony, for whom one of Cicero's favorite insults was "gladiator" (*gladiator nequissimus*, 2.7).[160] The cataclysmic civil war that finally brought down the Republic is thereby assimilated to the breakdown of a senatorial household.

Then in 6.246–67 we have a lengthy account of a woman training to be a gladiator, sandwiched between examples of disputatious activity in the courts (242–45; *nulla fere causa est in qua non femina litem /moverit*, 242–43) and argumentative behavior in the bedroom (268–85: *semper habet lites alternaque iurgia lectus / in quo nupta iacet; minimum dormitur in illo*, 268–69).[161] While athletic training and courtroom activity contradict Laronia's statement in *Satire* 2 that women don't engage in this sort of thing, the arena is in a sense the logical next step from both wrestling practice (*endromidas Tyrias et femineum ceroma*,

---

158. Juvenal calls Eppia a *ludia* (104, cf. 266) a term he may have procured from Mart. (5.24.10), who praises the gladiator Hermes as *cura laborque ludiarum* (the darling and passion of the gladiators' molls): see Colton 1991, 215–16 and n26, and chap. 3 herein.

159. Gunderson 2005 on Eppia as a "misreader" who "has mis-libidinized power" (236).

160. In contrast to Crassus, with whom he also had many disputes, cf. 2.63, 74. Also *Phil.* 4.15: *Est igitur, Quirites, populo Romano, victori omnium gentium, omne certamen cum percussore, cum latrone, cum Spartaco; Phil.* 3.31 on Antony's brother, Lucius, *ex myrmillone dux* (cf. 5.20 and chap. 3 herein). Miller 2005 sees in Eppia's flight a parody of Helen's leaving Menelaus for Paris in Sappho 16.7–11 (278).

161. For a linking of *munus* with the duty to procreate, see George 1988 on Metellus's "marital *munus*" in Lucilius.

246) and the verbal battles in court or the bedroom. Juvenal starts out with a description of her training with the *palus*, bashed by her sword and shield, suggesting that far from planning to participate in the mock fights at the Floralia (which had, thanks to tradition, at least a veneer of respectability to them), she is preparing for the "real arena" (247–51).[162] Fleeing from her sex (and her *pudor*), she dons a helmet because she likes the violence (*vires amat*, 252–53). We then get a catalog of her gladiatorial accoutrements, belonging to the *Thraex* and *secutor/murmillo* varieties (256–58). Her training is further described:

> Aspice quo fremitu monstratos perferat ictus
> et quanto galeae curvetur pondere, quanta
> poplitibus sedeat quam denso fascia libro,
> et ride positis scaphium cum sumitur armis.

> Hark at her roaring while she drives home the thrusts she's been taught.
> Hark at the weight of the helmet that has her wilting, at the size
> and the thickness of the bandages that surround her knees—and then
>   have a laugh
> when she takes off her armour to pick up the chamber pot. (261–64)

The expulsion of sounds is matched by the expulsion of urine into the chamber pot, a bathetic detail that shifts the focus back to the homely confines of the *domus*. The speaker concludes by asking the descendants of the Metelli and Fabii:[163]

> quae ludia sumpserit umquam
> hos habitus? Quando ad palum gemat uxor Asyli?

> what gladiator's woman ever put on gear like this?
> When does Asylus' wife grunt at the training post? (266–67)[164]

This lady, then, has outdone even the gladiators' wives and, by implication, Eppia our nautical *ludia* from earlier.

The Outer Limits

From the arena and its disgrace, it is but a short step to the realm of the dead— the gladiator is after all, in Seneca's phrase, *locatus ad mortem*. The satire closes

---

162. Used of Priapus's phallus by Hor. *Sat*.1.8.5 cf. Varro, *Men*. 179: *Quid? Tu non vides in vineis, quod tria pala habent, tripales dici?*

163. Cf. 8.191, 11.90. As Courtney 1980 points out, the Metelli and Fabii were now extinct.

164. Trans. Braund 2004.

by imagining the stunned reaction of Curius and others in the Underworld to recent arrivals from Rome like Gracchus:

> Sed tu vera puta: **Curius** quid sentit et ambo
> Scipiadae, quid Fabricius manesque Camilli?
> Quid Cremerae legio et Cannis **consumpta iuventus**,
> tot bellorum animae, quotiens hinc talis ad illos
> umbra venit? Cuperent **lustrari**, si qua darentur
> sulpura cum **taedis** et si foret umida **laurus**.[165]
> Illic heu miseri **traducimur**. Arma quidem **ultra**
> **litora Iuvernae** promovimus et modo captas
> **Orcadas** ac minima contentos nocte **Britannos**,
> sed quae nunc populi fiunt victoris in Urbe
> non faciunt illi quos vicimus.

> But suppose this were true: what would **Curius** feel,
> and the Scipios, Fabricius, and Camillus' shades?
> The legion of Cremera and **the young men consumed at Cannae**,
> the dead of so many wars, what would they feel whenever a shade from
>   here
> like this came down to them? They would want **to be purified**, if
> sulfur were available to them, and **torches** and moistened **laurel**.
> Down there—the shame!—we are paraded in disgrace.
> It's true that we have advanced our troops **beyond the shores of**
>   **Juverna**
> and the recently captured **Orkneys** and the **Britons** who are
>   contented
> with the shortest of nights, but those whom we defeated do not do the
>   things
> which now are done in this city of the victors. (2.153–63)[166]

The mention of Curius takes us all the way back to line 3; Seneca *De Tranquil-litate* 5.5 preserves his aphorism that he'd "rather be a dead man than a live one dead" (*malle se esse mortuum quam vivere*), which would be an appropriate comment in this context.[167] Like him, M. Furius Fabricius fought against Pyrrhus. At Cannae, the young men were "consumed" in performance of their military

---

165. To do with purification, but cf. the trick perpetrated by the Bacchants in Livy 39.13.12: running to the Tiber and plunging torches into water and bringing them out still lit (using sulfur with calcium supposedly).

166. Wiesen 1989: "Thus historical tradition joins religion and philosophy in the trash heap of useless cultural artifacts" (722).

167. And some of this group reappear in *Sat.* 11: Curius (78–79); Fabii, Cato, Scauri, Fabricius (90–91); cf. the opening of 8: Aemiliani and Curii (3–4); Fabius (14).

service, but in Juvenal's time in dissolute activities.[168] *Umbra* recalls the focus on the dead at the end of *Satire* 1 and looks forward to the imminent arrival of Umbricius in *Satire* 3; the *taedis* recall the burning human torches of the Tigillinus passage. The verb *traduco(r)*, used by Seneca of *virilitas*, is advisedly chosen for its connections with spectacles and parades (especially triumphs): Livy uses it of captives in a triumph.[169] This image is analogous to the display of the satirist in his arena. Also, the hint of a parade alludes to the parade of *exempla* to which we have been exposed in the course of the satire itself. In a Triumph, the procession of peoples, cities, rivers, and landscapes enabled "Rome to show Rome to Rome," as Ostenberg puts it. In Juvenal's reworking, the mockery and humiliation of the conquered are inflicted upon the Romans themselves.[170] The satirist raises the possibility that the military victories of Rome have been undermined by what goes on in the city, rather as Otho's were by his gazing into the mirror. Victory is no victory. There appears to be a conscious echo of 143–44, **vicit** *et hoc monstrum tunicati fuscina Gracchi,* / **lustravitque** *fuga mediam gladiator harenam*—*that* is the real moment of triumph in the poem.

The poem ends remotely (and yet, close to home) in the east, with the story of Zalaces, an Armenian "more effeminate than the other youths" who yielded to a lustful (*ardenti*) tribune—as bad as the philosophers—and the following observation:

> Aspice quid faciunt commercia; venerat obses,
> hic fiunt homines. Nam si mora longior Urbem
> induerit pueris, non umquam derit amator,
> mittentur bracae, cultelli, frena, flagellum.
> Sic praetextatos referunt Artaxata mores.

> Look at what our interactions achieve: he had come as a hostage,
> here men are made. For if a longer stay puts the City onto boys,[171]

---

168. Cf. Hor. *Epist.* 2.2.97: *caedimur et . . . consumimus* with reference to rival poets duelling like Samnites (see chap. 1 herein); the theme of consumption which was announced early in *Satire* 1 and will feature heavily throughout the collection. Kyle 1998 notes that Cannae provided a strong impetus to the growth of gladiatorial combat by offering reassurance to Romans via demonstrations of brutal violence (47–49); cf. Dunkle 2008, 154.

169. Livy 2.38.3. cf. Mart. 1.53.3 (*quae tua traducit manifesto carmina furto*); 6.77.5; Prop. 2.24.7; Sen. *Ep.* 108.14; Juv. 7.16, 8.17, 11.31; to cross, carry in parade, expose to scorn, paraded in front of a crowd and exposed to mockery. Nadeau 1983 sees no reference to a triumph, but to the march past the censor and lustrum (15); Braund and Cloud 1981, however, compare 8.17 and see an "ironic evocation of triumphal ceremonies" without any explicit connection with the censor.

170. Ostenberg 2009: "The very existence of a triumphal procession forced Rome to consider how she (consciously or unconsciously) perceived the world and how she was to present it" (9); see also 199–215 on representations of cities; 215–45 of peoples and rivers.

171. Presumably, "clothes them in it"; on *induerit* (from Nisbet) or *indulsit* (cf. 2.140), see Courtney 1980, 149. The verb *indulsit* does appear in the penultimate line of *Sat.*14 (330) and in the last line of *Sat.* 15 (174), cf. chap.4, p. 248 herein. On clothing in Hor. *Sat.* 1.2, see Gowers 2012, 87.

they will never lack a lover and their trousers, knives, bridles, and whips will be thrown away. Thus they carry Roman teenage morality back to Artaxata. (166–70)

Satire 2 is framed by geographical limits and the word *mores* (*ultra Sauromatas . . . glacialem / Oceanum . . . de moribus*, 1–2; *ultra / litora Iuvernae*, 159–60, *Artaxata mores*, 170), bringing together the Roman Empire and Roman morality, in particular the habits of its aristocratic elite. For them, limits and *mores* no longer have any force. Artaxata is a liminal zone, for Armenia was a battleground between powers, including Rome and Parthia, as Juvenal notes in 6.408 (*regi Armenio Parthoque*).[172] There may be a suggestion here of men taking on female roles and perhaps putting on women's clothes, picking up on the attire of Creticus and Gracchus earlier.[173] Eastern boys who were brought to Rome as hostages become "men of the world" (*hic fiunt homines*), but not *viri;* they take bad habits with them back to the East—whence, of course, the Bacchic rites emerged.[174] The implication that the locals would be appalled by what they bring back is the same motif as Canopus condemning Rome in the Eppia story—censure from afar, even from the East with all its traditionally suspect aspects. Like the Armenian Zalaces, Eppia trails her immorality to the East, following very distantly in the footsteps of Helen, but much less distantly in those of Mark Antony. We may note once again the emphasis placed on *young* men being corrupted, as it was in Livy's narrative: for Juvenal, this ties in with the theme of sterility and with the notion of a limitless spreading of contagion. The agricultural images of contagion in the center of *Satire 2*—among pigs and grapes—only serve to emphasize the point, placed as they are amid settings more conventionally associated with production and fertility. Alba Longa, after all, was founded after an encounter with a famously fecund sow.

Now, coming to Rome results in infection for the hitherto unharmed.[175] Ostenberg speaks of the Triumph "staging the world" (*Orbs*) in the City (*Urbs*), and observes that "the *Urbs-orbis* theme implied Roman mastery of the world, but could also be taken to mean that the whole world might be seen in Rome. . . . In addition, the world was not only put on stage but also invited to watch its

172. Cf. Suet. *Nero* 13, on the "welcome" given to King Tiridates of Armenia, which included a public act of supplication and being displayed in the theater, where he sat on Nero's right.

173. Richlin 1992 quotes 1.30–31 "*quis . . . tam patiens Urbis?*" and argues that Juvenal (or his sympathetic listener) will not submit to the city passively—he "will not be a pathic for the city's vices" (197).

174. Thus Courtney 1980, 149. Cf. *non licet esse viro* (10.304), mentioned on p. 113 herein.

175. Cf. Mart. *Spect.* 21.6, on paradox that the tigress is more savage for having come to Rome: *postquam inter nos est, plus feritatis habet*; Coleman 2006, *ad loc.*, on the common nature of the sentiment rather than social criticism of the Tacitean type.

display as part of the performance. . . . In the triumph, Rome and the world were one."[176] In the lens of Juvenalian satire, these notions still hold true, but, after the "parade" of exempla which have been duly subjected to appropriate ridicule by the satirist's crowd of spectators, the viewer is confronted with the realization that Rome and the world are indeed the same, because the *Urbs* has reduced the *Orbs* to the same state of corruption as itself.

Recent scholarship has opened up the possibility of new metapoetic readings of the Juvenalian text, such as Erin Moodie's study of the street thug at the end of *Satire* 1. As the Juvenalian scourge spreads across the boundaries of Roman time and space in *Satire* 2 to incorporate the whole Empire and narratives of self-definition, we might also think of it in these terms. The process of bringing the reader to comprehend the moral devastation requires a repetitive and incremental style, a "plague of satire" in other words, matching the diseased state of the city and the plague of Julio-Claudians who have ruled it.[177] At the same time, this form of satire effectively wipes itself out as well, leaving no obvious heirs to the tradition. As Allen Miller has argued, Juvenalian satire is much more concerned with sterility than fertility, and in Juvenal we see "the end of the line" not only in terms of the Roman elite male but also in terms of the genre of satire itself. One is reminded of what Matz has to say of "terminal satire" and his case study, Hardy's *Jude the Obscure*: "By its final chapter, *Jude the Obscure* seems rendered hoarse from its own howls. And so it reaches an end that appears to be a true terminus, as if to say: *melius fuerat non scribere*."[178]

At the end of *Satire* 6, the companion piece to *Satire* 2, we have the *exemplum* of Mithridates, in which poison figures as the main motif: poison is the influx of the outside par excellence, signifying the noxious penetration of the "clean and proper" Roman by the diseased non-Roman, and hence is a suitable ending for that poem.[179] The precautionary self-inoculation of Mithridates (ironically a long-time enemy of Rome) is now advisable—it took the Romans a long time to do him in, and today one needs to inoculate oneself against the East and women *and* Romans. Yet the Roman household has by the end of *Satire* 6 been transformed into a Greek mythological one, fit for the tragic stage, with the husband now an Atrides and the wife now a Clytemnestra, or an Eriphyle or a Danaid. In making this charge, the satirist denies that he is

176. Ostenberg 2009, 292.

177. In the epitome of Dio 73.13–15.1, the sequence is: famine, races, murder of prominent men, and plague, capped by the observation that "Commodus was worse for the Romans than any pestilence [*nosema*] or crime" (15.1).

178. Matz 2006, esp. 545.

179. Naevolus comments in 9.100 that poison is always cheap.

making things up, raving like a Bacchanal (*fingimus*, 634; *bacchamur*, 636).[180] Richlin comments that it is as if "he perceives satire as the tragedy of a people, rather than of heroes and heroines—with himself, the poet, telling true things, committing to verse what has really happened."[181] Women do away with husbands and children, so that even the self-immunization of Mithridates will not ensure survival:

> Hoc tantum refert, quod Tyndaris illa bipennem
> insulsam et fatuam dextra laevaque tenebat;
> at nunc res agitur tenui pulmone rubetae,
> sed tamen et ferro, si praegustarit Atrides
> Pontica ter victi cautus medicamina regis.

> The only difference is this. The daughter of Tyndareus wielded
> a stupid and clumsy double-headed axe with both her hands,
> but these days the matter is accomplished with the tiny lung of a toad.
> Yet she'll use steel too, if her Atrides has taken the cautionary measure of
> dosing himself with the Pontic antidotes of the three times conquered
>   king. (657–61)[182]

In the three poems we have examined here, the satirist dramatizes how expansion ensures destruction, as the distinction between Roman and non-Roman proves unsustainable. Consideration of these two aspects of movement will lead us eventually to the space of the arena, where centripetal and centrifugal flows converge in a site of continual consumption and expulsion, in chapter 3. The importance of this location in Juvenalian satire is given new emphasis by the eye-catching examples of boundary crossing performed in the company of gladiators by men like Gracchus and women like Eppia.

---

180. Livy 1.46.3, of Tullia: *tulit enim et Romana regia sceleris tragici exemplum.*
181. 1992, 208. Juv. 15.29–32 on the contemporary exemplum of savagery provided by Egyptians, described as the crime of an entire *populus* (*volgi scelus et cunctis graviora coturnis*, 29).
182. Trans. Braund 2004.

3

The Arena of Satire

reddita Roma sibi est et sunt te praeside, Caesar,
deliciae populi, quae fuerant domini.

Rome has been restored to herself, and under your rule, Caesar,
the pleasances that belonged to a master now belong to the people.
—Martial, *De Spectaculis* 2.5–6, 11–12,
trans. Shackleton Bailey 1993

Thus Martial gushes over the sight of the massive new amphitheater (*conspicui venerabilis amphitheatri moles*) constructed where Nero's lake used to be (5–6). This chapter explores the connections between the *Satires* of Juvenal and one of the central locations of Roman cultural display and self-validation, which reached its apex in the days of this particular poet.[1] The monumental presence of the Colosseum in the center of Rome and the increasing frequency of its operation during the year would have drawn the eye of the satirical observer to the arena and its fauna ever more compulsively.[2] The fact that our understanding of the arena is far from complete presents certain difficulties, but several informative interpretations of its dynamic and paradoxical aspects have been

---

1. Edwards and Woolf 2003 open their book *Rome the Cosmopolis* as follows (quoting Mart. *Spect.* 3.1): "This book begins in the Colosseum—that site of so many deaths, human and animal—which is perhaps the most potent emblem of the all-encompassing, all-consuming city of Rome."

2. On the elaborate supply chain and sustaining it, Kyle 1998, chap. 3. For a catalog, Ville 1981.

published in the past two decades.[3] Situated as we are in the West in the post-modern spectacle of desire and deferral, of screens and shopping malls, we are newly attuned to the visual machinery of the Roman arena and its presentation of ideologically laden signs to a mass audience.[4] Its cultural significance in the imperial era can hardly be overemphasized. Alison Futrell describes the arena as "the embodiment of the empire":

> From the center in Rome came the permission to build the amphitheater, quintessentially Roman in style and mass. The seating arrangements replicated an idealization of the Roman polity. The arena itself was a stage for political performance and the demonstration of power within the existing power structure: the immediate favor of the *editor* set off and depended upon the ultimate authority of the emperor. . . . Gladiatorial combat was the imperial process in microcosm, embodying the militarism at the core of Rome's justification of Empire. (1997, 209–10)

Although it was, as Carlin Barton puts it, "merely one ring of the imperial circus," the arena served as a particularly effective means of inculcating the structuring ideals of *Romanitas*, on the model of an Althusserian Ideological State Apparatus, thanks to its manipulation of the gaze of large crowds of spectators.[5] In the city of Rome, of course, the construction of the Colosseum, making a permanent venue for displays which had hitherto been produced in structures intended as temporary, marks a concomitant increase in political control of the populace, as what had originally been small-scale and primarily family-run events (at least until Julius Caesar got hold of them) grew into major public occasions in which the emperor, his entourage, and his triumphs took center-stage. As with much else, the blueprint was created by Augustus and the Colosseum was a natural consequence of his codification of gladiatorial and

3. Hopkins 1983, Veyne 1990, Wiedemann 1992, Barton 1993, Plass 1995, Edmondson 1996, Gunderson 1996, Futrell 1997 and 2006, Kyle 1998, Bomgardner 2000, Köhne and Ewigleben 2000, Shadrake 2005, K. E. Welch 2007, Dunkle 2008, Junkelmann 2008, Fagan 2011.

4. Wiedemann 1992, 19. Contemporary interest—ranging from renewed scholarly attention to the popular success of the Hollywood film *Gladiator* or the TV series *Spartacus*—is doubtless connected with the dominance of consumer capitalism, especially in the English-speaking world, and the development of the cultural phenomenon that we conveniently, if somewhat reductively, term postmodernism. While that nexus of interrelationships is a topic beyond the scope of this book, the spectacle as phenomenon and metaphor in a period of "conspicuous consumption," in a *société du spectacle* in Debord's formulation (1994), is a useful tool for delineating Roman imperial ideology.

5. Gunderson, 1996, 116–20, 146–49; cf. Veyne 1990 on imperial "euergetism" (320–419); Barton 1993, 64; Edmondson 1996, 71; Futrell 1997, 209–10.

other spectacles. Within its impressively solid and solidifying walls, the *munera* presented to the viewers sought to contain violence through violence, and to (re)establish order through disorder.[6]

The Demands of *Genus*

The success of the spectacle depended on the universalizing media of the body and the violence enacted by and upon it. Although recently the body has become a prime location of spectacle, especially in the West but also elsewhere—advertisements, diets, bodybuilding, tattoos, piercings, cosmetic surgeries—bodies have always mattered. Foucault, in his later works such as *Discipline and Punish*, *Power/Knowledge*, and *The History of Sexuality*, gradually moved the human body to the center of the struggle between different power formations: "The body is . . . directly involved in a political field; power relations have an immediate hold upon it; they invest it, mark it, train it, torture it, force it to carry out tasks, to perform ceremonies, to emit signs."[7] Even when such categories as identity, subjectivity, and history are felt to be disintegrating, the body remains notably "real" in relation to the effects of ideology. Pleasure, pain, deprivation, rape, torture, hunger, poisoning, exploitation, discrimination, and disease are all inscribed upon and within the body. Elaine Scarry, in *The Body in Pain*, observes that the body lends its uniquely powerful aura of reality and certainty to ideological constructs, *especially* at moments when they are in crisis:

> The felt-characteristics of pain—one of which is its compelling
> vibrancy or its incontestable reality or simply its "certainty"—can be
> appropriated away from the body and presented as the attributes of
> something else, something which by itself lacks those attributes,
> something which does not in itself appear vibrant, real, or certain. . . .
> At particular moments when there is within society a crisis of
> belief—that is when some central idea or ideology or cultural
> construct has ceased to elicit a population's belief either because it is
> manifestly fictitious or because it has for some reason been divested

---

6. Plass 1995, 25; cf. Cannadine and Price 1987 on how spectacles and ceremonies, promising tradition and order, become increasingly necessary as the stability of the state becomes more uncertain (8). On the Colosseum, see Dunkle 2008, chap. 6.

7. Foucault 1977, 25.

of ordinary forms of substantiation—the sheer material factualness
of the human body will be borrowed to lend that cultural construct
the aura of "realness" and "certainty."[8]

So, in spite of Terry Eagleton's suspicions of what, in *The Illusions of Post-modernism*, he rather pejoratively describes as the "new somatics," there remains, in Scarry's formulation, "the incontestable reality of the body—the body in pain, the body maimed, the body dead and hard to dispose of."[9] It is precisely *this* body that we can scrutinize as the site of ideological inscription and contestation both in the arena spectacle and in satire, that most combative and corporeal of literary genres.[10] The satirical body, like the spectacular body, presents itself as truth-telling through its in-yer-face experience of physicality.[11]

While the arena incorporates and encloses the world within its elliptical walls, we have plenty of evidence that much of the world outside also came to be apprehended in terms of spectacles, gladiatorial combat, and theatrical display, and that the arena, with all its associated phenomena, carried considerable metaphorical force in literary and philosophical discourse.[12] Erik Gunderson (1996) comments on its pervasiveness as follows:

> In practice, there was no "outside" of the arena. Its logic was of one
> piece with the other ideological structures of the Roman
> experience. . . . The arena is a complementary apparatus relative to
> the Roman social order, not a detached or radically originary one. . . .
> The arena is a wholly central and necessary Roman institution and
> not one lying on the cultural periphery. (119–20)

Already Cicero moves with ease from something like his attack on Mark Antony's brother Lucius as a *gladiator Asiaticus* (*Philippics* 5.20; he had fought as a *murmillo* in Mylasa) and as *ex murmillone dux* (*Phil.* 3.31)[13] to various conceptual links between the rhetorician and the gladiator in *De Oratore* 2.317:

---

8. Scarry 1985, 13–14.
9. Eagleton 1996, 71; Scarry 1985, 62.
10. E.g., Braund and Gold 1998; Barchiesi and Cucchiarelli 2005.
11. Gunderson 2005: "You can believe satire because the body does not lie" (228). In-yer-face theater is typified by Sarah Kane's *Blasted* (1995) or Mark Ravenhill's satirical *Shopping and Fucking* (1996).
12. See Barton 1993 for a wide-ranging discussion; Leigh 1997 on *amphitheatrum mundi* and his concluding segment, "The poetics and politics of the amphitheatre" (267, 282–91); Newlands 2002, chap. 7.
13. He was proquaestor in Asia in 50/49 B.C.E.; Lucius was with Antony when he entered the Temple of Concord with his bodyguard: *sanguinem nostrum sitiebat, suum in illa gladiatoria pugna multum profuderat* (He was thirsting for our blood, he had poured out a great deal of his own in that gladiatorial combat).

Nec est dubium quin exordium dicendi vehemens et pugnax non saepe esse debeat, sed si in ipso gladiatorio vitae certamine quo ferro decernitur tamen ante congressum multa fiunt quae non ad vulnus sed ad speciem valere videantur, quanto hoc magis in oratio est spectandum, in qua non vis potius quam delectatio postulatur.

The opening of a speech ought not usually to be of a forceful, fighting character; but if in an actual gladiatorial contest, where the decision is made by the sword, but nevertheless before closing many strikes are made that seem not to be intended to inflict a wound but to be done for the sake of appearance, how much more is this to be observed in making a speech, where what is demanded is not so much force as entertainment.[14]

It is, then, quite possible to view the arena space, with its coordinated display of bodies and the central role of violence, as a meticulously plotted map of *Romanitas*. Responding to the impulses of *genus* toward the clarification of difference and supplying the visual presentation of distinguishable categories, the arena functions as a site wherein the structuring hierarchies and divisions of Roman identity can be viewed, reinforced, and absorbed.[15]

Jonathan Edmondson, in "Dynamic Arenas," cautions that by placing too much emphasis on "the static nature of the amphitheater as an institution that simply mirrored social organization," we run the risk of underestimating its "dynamic force" (74–75). Certainly, the spectacle depended upon several degrees of separation—the gladiators and even those slated for execution were carefully distinguished by categories. At the same time, however, the shifting, contentious, and unpredictable elements of the arena—seating rules, crowd behavior, partisan rivalries, decisions on the life or death of gladiators, imperial appearances and interventions, gambling and lotteries—all highlight the tensions and contradictions that exist within this, as any, ideological matrix:[16]

The social stratifications given form at gladiatorial presentations were not necessarily rigid and inflexible. They cannot, therefore, be

---

14. Cf. 3.86, 200; 220; Cic. *De Opt. Gen.* 17 on Isocrates: *non enim in acie versatur nec ferro, sed quasi rudibus eius eludit oratio* ("his oratory is not performed in battle or with the sword, but plays with wooden weapons, so to speak"); similarly in his philosophical texts, e.g., *Tusc.* 4.47–48, with a quotation from Lucilius on the famous gladiator Pacideianus (see pp. 190–91).

15. Tert. *De spect.* 3: *vias enim et cardines vocant balteorum per ambitum et discrimina popularium per proclivum.*

16. Scobie 1988; Edmondson 1996 (93n107 on *spectacula* used of rows of seats); Barton 1993, 113–14, and Gunderson 1996, 123–26, on seating; Coleman 1996, 55–56 on lotteries.

> seen as reflections of a fixed hierarchical social order. Rather, each
> presentation provided an opportunity for the contestation of social
> boundaries. Even though such challenges did not lead to major
> modifications in social structure, that does not diminish either the
> social tensions that were a constant undercurrent of these perfor-
> mances or the dynamic contribution that they made to the active
> construction of the Roman social order. (74)

We might think, then, in terms of a perpetual dialogue between spectators and participants, including the *editor*, and of a multivocal exchange among the various groups and categories in the matrix, against the background of a structure whose initial orientation and façade were monologic. As Garrett Fagan puts it, "Gladiator and spectator were thus partners in the arena's dance of violence, and each played a key role in its lethal choreography."[17]

In a similar vein, Carlin Barton, in *Sorrows of the Ancient Romans*, offers an associative, psychological reading, presented in an appropriately fragmented format, which seeks to address what she terms "some of the darkest riddles of the Roman psyche." She frames her investigation around the Roman "emotional paradoxes," whose nature it is "both to emphasize distinctions and simultaneously to blur them." In Barton's study, the arena and its gladiators embody that fluctuation of sameness and difference, of boundaries and transparency, which is the basis of the Roman sense of identity. She argues that the metaphorical significance of the arena increases with the experience of civil war, the transition from Republic to imperial monarchy, and social changes that meant "the traditional testimonials of power, freedom, and pride began to signal *as well* powerlessness, enslavement, humiliation" (27).[18] A pivotal moment in this process of change is captured in Juvenal's one-line description of Julius Caesar as the man "who led the tamed citizens of Rome under his lash" (*ad sua qui domitos deduxit flagra Quirites*, 10.109).[19] If Futrell's characterization of the arena, focusing on the solidity and order it promised, essentially echoes the dominant claims of imperial ideology, Edmondson and Barton peer into the fissures and gaps, viewing the arena as a site of liminality and paradox.

While recognizing that the "meaning" of the Roman arena—its purposes, practices, and effects—is much debated and often elusive, we can say that one

---

17. Kyle 1998, 9; Fagan 2011, chap. 7, esp. 273. Gunderson 1996 notes that the arena had different significances for the various groups of spectators (114).

18. On the effect of the transition on *munera*, see Dunkle 2008, 173–85. Cf. Millar 1988, chap. 7.

19. In the context of a wider discussion of how seeking the *summus locus* leads to a downfall, but he does distinguish Caesar with this phrase from the Crassuses and Pompeys and seems to align him with *reges* and *tyranni* (10.108–13); see chap. 4 herein. On *deducere*, see chap. 1 herein.

Nunc se / continet atque duas tantum res anxius optat / panem et circenses (Juv. 10.79–81). Colosseum, exterior. Photograph by David Larmour and Corby Kelly.

of the things it sought to display was a secure division between the combatants in the sand and the spectators in the seats. This much is clear from the architecture, with its "drop" from the front row of senatorial seats to the arena floor. Calpurnius Siculus, in his eulogy of a large amphitheater, presumably the Colosseum,[20] mentions one highly visible and practical aspect of this division:

balteus en gemmis, en illita porticus auro
certatim radiant; nec non, ubi finis harenae
proxima marmoreo praebet spectacula muro,
sternitur adiunctis ebur admirabile truncis
et coit in rotulum, tereti qui lubricus axe
impositos subita vertigine falleret ungues
excuteretque feras. Auro quoque torta refulgent
retia, quae totis in harenam dentibus exstant,
dentibus aequatis . . .

Look at the partition-belt with its gems and the portico in gold
gleam in rivalry; and also, where the end of the arena

20. See p. 177 herein; Dunkle 2008,163–64, 170–73.

presents the seats closest to the marble wall,

magnificent ivory is inlaid on connected beams

and joins into a cylinder which, rolling smoothly on a well-rounded axle,

can by a sudden turn fool any claws set upon it

and shake off the beasts. Also gleaming brightlty are the nets of gold
    wire

which project into the arena hung on whole tusks,

tusks of equal size . . . (*Eclogue* 7.47–55)

The *balteus* had an obvious role in guaranteeing the "health and safety" of the spectators,[21] but, as Edmondson says, the podium wall was "a very real social barrier" separating those who were part of the Roman social order from those who were "socially dead." Gunderson likewise observes that those dying in the sand "have been exiled into the non-Roman space" within the comforting confines of "a stabilized, orderly ring of Romanness girding them."[22]

The security of the separation, however, was subject to continual variation depending upon the type of spectacle presented,[23] and it is interesting that the program of a typical day in Juvenal's time suggests a movement from less permeable to more permeable borders. In the morning, there were *venationes*, wild beast hunts, a spectacle of the domination of nature by civilization, of the *Orbis* by the *Urbs*. Exotic animals displayed in living form the extent of the Empire, as well as the wealth and efficiency of the *editor* who brought them to Rome.[24] At midday came the executions of criminals, to the flames or to the beasts—an abandonment to the devouring forces of nature and to the chaos that obtains beyond society, a violent expulsion from the social body, which the violators' crimes have earned them. As Donald Kyle points out, there was always a surplus of *noxii* in Rome, they were a by-product of empire.[25] Some criminals, however, emerge from within the charmed circle of Roman society, and so their appearance in the arena must have provoked more complex, even

---

21. Dunkle 2008, 254–55; it is also the word for a gladiator's belt (99).

22. Edmondson 1996, 83; Gunderson 1996, 133–34; Fagan 2011, 140–47, and also chap. 4 on "crowd dynamics" and chap. 5 on "arenas of prejudice."

23. Ville 1981, 129–73; Edmondson 1996, 74 and 76, on the full-scale *munus iustum atque legitimum* (Suet. *Claud.* 21.4); Dunkle 2008, 182, 187, 189; Wiedemann 1992, 55–67; Gunderson 1996, 133; Kyle 1998, 41–43 and nn.

24. On the history of these displays in Rome from the late Republic on, see Coleman 1996, 60–64; Wiedemann 1992, 55–67; Dunkle 2008, chap. 5. Note Plin. *Pan.* 51.3 on the Circus Maximus, with its huge façade, as *digna populo victore gentium sedes* (a site worthy of the people which is conqueror of the world), worth seeing on its own account, as well as for the spectacles presented therein. Plass 1995 speaks of a "political zoo" (42).

25. Kyle 1998, 92; he, following Tert. *Apol.* 15.4, uses the term for "hated and doomed victims (slaves, criminals, captives, and deserters) as distinct from trained (and somewhat rehabilitated) gladiators" (31n66).

contradictory, emotions among the spectators as they munched their lunches, consuming the chastisement of the condemned.[26]

In the afternoon came the gladiators. These were marginalized, despised outcasts, certainly—yet some were objects of intense admiration and desire on the part of members of all the groups in Roman society, including emperors themselves.[27] One of the fascinating paradoxes of the gladiator was that, after being rigorously trained in a Roman *ludus* and fitted out in his armor and weaponry—especially perhaps when as a *secutor* or *murmillo* (i.e., heavily armed and not so far removed, in looks at least, from a legionary soldier)— he could potentially embody *Romanitas*, exhibiting, at least temporarily, the *virtus* of the idealized citizen soldier.[28] Thus Cicero in *Philippic* 3.35 urges the senators to meet death bravely and willingly like gladiators, rather than live as slaves:

> Fatum extremum rei publicae venit, quod gladiatores nobiles faciunt, ut honeste decumbant, faciamus nos, principes orbis terrarum gentiumque omnium, ut cum dignitate potius cadamus quam cum ignominia serviamus. Nihil est detestabilius dedecore, nihil foedius servitute. Ad decus et ad libertatem nati sumus: aut haec teneamus aut cum dignitate moriamur.

> The final episode in the history of the Republic has arrived, let us behave like champion gladiators: they meet death honorably; let us, who stand foremost in the world and all its nations, see to it that we fall with dignity rather than serve with ignominy. Nothing is more abominable than disgrace, nothing is uglier than servitude.

---

26. Wiedemann 1992, 68–92; on this aspect of permeability, see Barton 1993, esp. 62–66. On midday meals, Sen. *Ep.* 7 and below. On the different "mood" after noon, see Dunkle 2008, 128–29, and his discussion of [Quint.] *Decl. mai.* 9.6.1–14.

27. On desire, Barton 1993, 65–66; Tert. *De spect.* 22: *arenarios illos amantissimos . . . amant quos multant, depretiant quos probant*; Sen. Eld. *Controv.* 10.4.8 preserves criticism of those who lure good-looking youths into the gladiatorial school: *iuvenum miserorum simplicitatem circumeunt et speciosissimum quemque ac maxime idoneum castris in ludum coniciunt*. On the spectacle of the emperor, and how the arena produces him as a "legible social subject," see Gunderson 1996, 126–33; also Edmondson 1996, 102–107; Coleman 2006, lxx–lxxv. Commodus in arena, see Dunkle 2008, 188–90; as *secutor* (Dio Cass. 73.19.2).

28. Wiedemann 1992, 26–39, 92; Barton 1993, esp. 15–36; Fagan 2011 is not so keen on the "representational model" (200–202), and Maurin 1984 sees the gladiator as making a contrast with the ideal soldier. Toner 1995, noting [Quint.] *Decl. min.* 302, *Auctoratus ob sepeliendum patrem*, which attempts to draw a distinction between *honesta* and *inhonesta pugna*, in connection with the law banning those who hired themselves as gladiators from the seats reserved for *Equites* in the theater (39–48). The *secutor* and *murmillo* seem to develop out of the Samnite type, which fades after the Republic, but bear more superficial resemblances to the Roman legionary soldier than, say, the *retiarius* (not that he was without his own opportunities for valor): see on types, Köhne and Ewigleben 2000, 37–63; Dunkle 2008, 98–113.

We were born for honour and freedom: let us either retain them or die with dignity.[29]

Just about all the watchwords of Roman self-construction appear in this passage—*dignitas, ignominia, (de)decus, libertas*—and the juxtaposition of *gladiatores nobiles*, followed immediately by *honeste*, is a striking one.

The gladiator who fought in an appropriately "Roman" manner could win a reprieve, and could, so to speak, triumph over death.[30] The arena thus functions as a stage for the contemporary reenactment of long-lost, cherished virtues. As Edmondson notes, "Imperial triumphalism was joined with moral and civic instruction—a powerful cocktail," and Barton observes that for some "the arena was a real test of valor that the consulate, the praetorship, the imperial throne was not."[31] The gladiator may also have been a significant source of emotional consolation for the viewers, either because they saw him suffer the fate they feared for themselves or because he managed to escape it and live to fight another day. Tertullian, a hostile but not unobservant source, seems to hit at least one nail on the head when he declares that "they found comfort for death in murders" (*ita mortem homicidiis consolabantur, De Spectaculis* 12).[32] If the gladiator is, as some would argue, a kind of *pharmakos*, he is at the same time sub- and superhuman.[33] He was both a despised Other and a figure inviting potentially dangerous and therefore intensely thrilling self-identification. Perhaps this helps explain why some "respectable" Roman citizens willingly gave themselves to the arena and why even some emperors seem to have made appearances that took them beyond the confines of the royal box.[34] Spectators would have been in for a gamut of paradoxical thrills at any given show, and violations of expectations, deviations from the set script, would have

---

29. Trans. Shackleton Bailey 2009.

30. Dunkle 2008 suggests plausibly enough that bouts lasted ten to fifteen minutes (129; cf. 12–13).

31. Barton 1993, 33; Edmondson 1996, 73.

32. Wiedemann 1992, 35; Barton 1993, 35–36; Plass 1995, 33. Tert. is, however, quite happy to speak of the "second coming" in terms of a *spectaculum* outdoing all others, a recognition of the arena's continuing metaphorical force, *De Spect.* 30.

33. Plass 1995, 58–59, 208n11, 226–27.

34. There were certainly mechanisms for these events to occur (Sen. *Ep.* 99.13: *Aspice illos iuvenes, quos ex nobilissimis domibus in harenam luxuria proiecit*), and Dio 56.25.8 says they were eagerly anticipated. See Wiedemann 1992, 107–11; Barton 1993, 26–36; Edmondson 1996, 106–108; Gunderson 1996, 136–42; Kyle 1998, 87–90. Commodus in entering the arena fulfilled a dream only half-realized by Nero, who used private arenas for such activities, according to Tac. *Ann.* 14.14 (*clausum valle Vaticana spatium, in quo equos regeret, haud promisco spectaculo*; Dio 73.17–22). One recalls the enthusiasm for watching wrestling among members of the British royal family in the 1960s and '70s and the persistent rumor that the "masked man" Kendo Nagasaki was Prince Phillip: see Simon Garfield's piece "Who is that masked man?" in the *Guardian*, 7 October 2001. Recent enthusiasm for "white-collar" MMA offers analogous opportunities for violent slumming.

intensified the experience—it is, after all, the *extra*ordinary that is memorable in such events. Tertullian follows his own agenda in discussing the spectacles but raises a related point about what he sees as the emotional disjunction in the spectator who, at one moment, shudders with horror at the body of someone who has died a natural death yet, at another in the amphitheater, will gaze down "with the most tolerant eyes" upon bodies "gnawed away and ripped to pieces" (*derosa et dissipata et in suo sanguine squalentia corpora patientissimis oculis desuper incumbat*). Likewise, the same man who comes to the amphitheater to show his approval of the punishment of a murderer will also have the gladiator who is reluctant to fight goaded with whips and rods to commit murder, or will call for the *rudis* and the *pilleus* as a reward for a suitably *atrox* gladiator.[35]

It is significant that Gunderson begins and ends his article on the ideological apparatus of the arena with Juvenal, and his concluding comments on the satirist's critical standpoint are well taken: "Juvenal's vision, like Seneca's, is profoundly informed by the optics of the arena, which reveal the sand as a site of the play between the Roman and the non-Roman where the excluded margin is used to constitute the legitimate order even as the abjected object bears the trace of the order which refuses it" (149). As a structure whose architecture was designed to both contain and differentiate, and at the same time a phenomenon that evinces a deep-seated anxiety about borders, the arena offers a productive analogue to the operations of Juvenalian discourse. The collaborative bond that the text seeks to establish between the speaker and his implied reader in the *Satires*, based on a presumed homonymity of perspective, sets up a mental barrier between them and their shared objects of derision, a barrier that is the counterpart of the *balteus* described by Calpurnius Siculus above. The slippage between voyeur and exhibitionist is, as we have seen, an inherent thrill of satire, and especially when it is so visually based. The satirist as punisher is always eventually faced with the uncomfortable realization that he may not be so different from his targets, that they fascinate him for some vital reason, and that he, like them, is just a part of the same great spectacle and could end up as a victim in it himself.[36] If in the imperial age, as Barton argues, the price for advancement was indeed self-abasement, then perhaps it was not such a great leap of the imagination for a citizen (or a poet) to

---

35. Tert. *De Spect.* 21; on the *pilleus*, see below, pp. 212–13, on the *Satyricon*.

36. On fascination, see Barton 1993, 85–106; cf. Gunderson 1996, 115–16, on the "specular effect" noting parallels with Foucault's Panopticon (1977).

see himself in a predicament akin to the gladiator's or as a nameless member of the mob looking on. The same power over life and death demonstrated upon the helpless arena victims was, after all, effectively exercised by the emperor over everyone in the crowd.[37]

It is these contradictory aspects of the arena that seem of special interest to Juvenal. Indeed, he is one of our main sources for an important piece of Colosseum lore, namely the participation in combat events by freeborn Romans, including aristocratic volunteers. Startling examples of this variety of boundary crossing, such as that of Gracchus making his appearance as a *retiarius*, constitute some of the more colorful vignettes of Juvenal's corpus, as we have seen (2.143–48). Here is the reprise of Gracchus' self-display in 8.200–10:

> Dedecus Urbis habes, nec murmillonis in armis
> nec clipeo Gracchum pugnantem aut falce supina;
> damnat enim talis habitus sed damnat et odit,
> nec galea faciem abscondit: movet ecce tridentem.
> Postquam vibrata pendentia retia dextra
> nequiquam effudit, nudum ad spectacula voltum
> erigit et tota fugit agnoscendus harena.
> Credamus tunicae, de faucibus aurea cum se
> porrigat et longo iactetur spira galero.
> Ergo ignominiam graviorem pertulit omni
> volnere cum Graccho iussus pugnare secutor.

> There [in the gladiatorial school] you have the disgrace of Rome: a Gracchus
> fighting not in the kit of a *murmillo*, not with shield or curved sickle;
> for he rejects that sort of gear, rejects it and despises it,
> and doesn't hide his face with a helmet: look, he's wielding a trident.
> After he has with poised right hand cast the trailing net
> without success, he raises his bare face to the spectators
> and flees, all too recognizable, across the whole arena.
> We cannot mistake the golden tunic, when it is stretched out from his
>   throat
> and the ribbon dangling from his tall cap.
> And so the *secutor* ordered to fight against Gracchus
> suffered an indignity more grievous than any wound.

---

37. Plass 1995 connects the arena to enforced suicide, suggesting that "elite Romans must have seen that what was expected of gladiators was expected of them too" (107); cf. Mart. *Spect.* 12.5–6 on the emperor's total power over all animals and humans.

Of course, members of the Roman elite were traditionally on constant display, but this is a degenerated version: there is much emphasis here on what the spectators (are forced to) see and the *ignominia* inflicted *on his opponent* by Gracchus's appearance.[38] There is a clear distinction between the heavily armed *murmillo* and *secutor*, and the Thraex with his shield and slightly curved dagger, on the one hand, and the lightly clad *retiarius* on the other.[39] The despised type is not even named: *movet ecce tridentem* is enough to make the point (203).[40] Gracchus's costume may indicate that he is one of the Salii (as we know he was from the parallel passage in 2.125–26), especially if we read *galero* as referring to the tall hat or *pilleus* (*galerus* is also the term used for the shoulder guard worn by the *retiarius*, the only protecting armor he had).[41] Thus a quintessential representative of the authentically Roman is now on display in what was—notionally, at least—the quintessentially non-Roman space of the arena.[42] Hence the designation *dedecus Urbis* and the emphasis on the absence of a helmet (normal for a *retiarius*, who uniquely did not wear one) and the bare face, which guarantees that he is recognizable (*agnoscendus*).[43] It is also made abundantly clear that Gracchus does all this by choice (*damnat . . . damnat et odit . . . nec abscondit*) and deliberately raises his bare face (*erigit*) as he flees across the whole arena (*tota . . . arena*).[44] The entire passage is framed by the vocabulary of shame: *dedecus Urbis . . . ignominiam . . . secutor*. Edmondson distinguishes between those who fought to show their martial skills unpaid and those who bound themselves to a *lanista* under oath. The former, he thinks, were continuing a venerable Roman tradition, whereas the latter threatened the *dignitas* or the order they came from.[45] Interestingly, it was G. Gracchus who in 122 BCE passed a law excluding equestrian *auctorati* from the

---

38. Cf. Sen. *De Prov.* 3.4: *ignominiam iudicat gladiator cum inferiore componi et scit eum sine gloria vinci qui sine periculo vincitur. Idem facit Fortuna: fortissimos sibi pares quaerit*; he imagines Fortune drawing back from a cowardly adversary as if saying *"levi comminatione pelletur, non potest sustinere vultum meum."*

39. The wording *clipeo . . . aut falce supina* probably refers to the small round shield, the *parma* and *sica* (or *falx*) of the Thracian; see Köhne and Ewigleben 2000, 51–52; Dunkle 2008, who describes him as the only survivor of the "ethnic-based gladiators of the Republic" (101–104).

40. Köhne and Ewigleben 2000, 59–61; Dunkle 2008 says that Gracchus's performance is "unprofessional in its ineptitude" since he throws his net but misses badly (107–11).

41. Dunkle 2008, 47, 106–108.

42. See Courtney 1980, *ad loc.*, for discussion.

43. *Agnoscendus*: recognizable by sight, identifiable (as one's own). Cf. Mart. 11.61 on Nanneius, whose bare face is the most shameful aspect; Kay 1985, 205.

44. The comprehensive nature of the display is also emphasized; cf. Mart. *Spect.* 11.1 of rhinoceros (*exhibitus tota tibi, Caesar, harena*) and 22.1 of bull goaded by flames *per totam . . . harenam.*

45. Edmondson 1996, 107–108. In [Quint.] *Decl. min.* 302, the issue turns on whether the *auctoratus* actually fought or was only exhibited *spectaculi gratia*; families like the Torquati or the Opimii got their names because of *honesta pugna* as opposed to the *inhonesta* variety in the arena, practiced by someone who hired himself as a gladiator out of "self-contempt" (*vilitas*) or "gluttony" (*gula*).

courts. Barton notes how Juvenal's Gracchus despises the armor, weapons, and the helmet, which might have "softened his ignominy . . . or . . . have hidden his shame" and links him with the phenomenon of aristocrats or equestrians who purposefully "despised their degradation" as a paradoxical signifier of empowerment. Jerry Toner points out that the fighter's manner of combat, not his ultimate fate, was the primary concern: "The communal gaze meant that if the gladiator failed then it dishonoured both him and the whole community. . . . The appropriate state for a true man was ritually dramatized, and the losers were, in effect, emasculated."[46] It is clear that Gracchus, having lurched over one fault line of Roman self-definition by marrying a man in *Satire 2*, stands here right upon the cusp of another.[47]

Gunderson makes the intriguing suggestion that for Cicero and Seneca, "the gladiator plays Remus to the normative aristocrat's Romulus," who killed his brother for jumping over the boundary separating Rome from the non-Roman. Thus the murder of Remus "permanently establishes the validity of this boundary and secures the name of Rome for the city: so does the gladiator's death help to found the nobility of the *nobilis*" (139). In *Satire* 10.73–79, Juvenal speaks of the *turba Remi* (not *Romuli*) and its obsessive interest in (only) *panem et circenses*.[48] For Juvenal, there is an ironic interchangeability of roles between gladiator and respectable citizen, as there is between gladiator and poet. In *Satire* 6.206–30, for example, when he warns the husband who feels a "straightforward fondness" for his wife (*simplicitas uxoria*, 206) that his whole life will be dictated by her, as she buries eight husbands in six autumns (an impressive record of dispatch in itself, 229–30), the crux of his commentary is that, unlike him, pimps and *lanistae* have *libertas* in making wills, *as do even gladiators* (*et iuris idem contingat harenae*). Even if the final detail about gladiators is not necessarily accurate, as Courtney argues, the formulation shows how far the satirist is prepared to go in characterizing the degradation of the married male citizen, who has lost his *libertas* and whose *simplicitas* is completely misplaced.

46. Toner 1995, 47; Barton 1993, 27–28 (following Dio 56.25.7) and 25–36 for full discussion. Cf. Sen. Eld. *Controv.* 9.6.2, on madness at the point of death: *abscisa missione gladiator quem armatus fugerat nudus insequitur.*

47. Taking up the question of the *retiarius tunicatus*, Dunkle 2008 thinks the tunic has nothing to do with sexual preference but suggests that Gracchus's husband comes from the lowest level of society ("a horn player, probably a slave or at best a freedman"; 111 and nn). See also chap. 2 herein.

48. Referring to the plebeians; see Courtney 1980, *ad loc.*, on other instances.

The Arena of Inspiration

Literary interest in the arena is not, of course, confined to Juvenal, even if he is one of our most vivid witnesses. Imperial writers in general seem to have found it richly inspirational, and this we may connect with numerous and elaborate representations in mosaics that adorned private dwelling spaces across the Empire.[49] The multifarious ways in which writers and artists used the arena and the gladiator as themes in their works, or how they related their texts and themselves to these ubiquitous elements of Roman life, may be substantially lost to us, but various sources offer intriguing glimpses into what was clearly a rich cross-fertilization, with scope for continual variation.[50] It is worth noting also, amid all the examples of literary appropriation, that, conversely, at least some spectacles in the arena appear to have become increasingly "poetic" over time. We hear of numerous deaths by narrative reenactment, such as when an Orpheus was attacked by bears, or the famous display of courage by Mucius Scaevola was re-presented.[51] There was clearly a complex interaction between art(istry) in the arena and the arena in art.

We may begin with poetry and the rest of Calpurnius Siculus's *Eclogue* 7, which provides the longest surviving account of an amphitheater in action, presumably the Colosseum, in a positive portrayal designed to praise Nero.[52] It is framed as a news report from the pastoral cipher Corydon who has just returned from a visit to Rome. There he saw:

> in caelum trabibus spectacula textis
> surgere, Tarpeium prope despectantia culmen.

> an amphitheatre that rises to the sky on interwoven beams
> almost looking down on Tarepian summit. (23–24)

Urbs and *rus* are melded into a seamless whole, as the speaker likens the arena to a valley surrounded by hills:

> Qualiter haec patulum concedit vallis in orbem
> et sinuata latus resupinis undique silvis
> inter continuos curvatur concava montes:

49. Kondoleon 1991; Barton 1993 on gladiatorial bouts at private dinners (61–62); Plass 1995, 188n7.

50. See Mart. *Spect.* 6, 9–10, 17, 19, 24 and Coleman 2006, *ad loc.*; cf. Coleman 1990; 1996, 53; 67–68; Kyle 1998, 53–55. Kondoleon 1991 says attending a performance involves "picture seeing" (110).

51. Coleman 1990; Coleman 2006 on Orpheus (174–75) and on Scaevola (82, 98).

52. Townend 1980 suggests this is the wooden theater of Nero in 57 c.e. (Tac. *Ann.* 13.31); Hubbard 1998, citing Armstrong 1986 (who concludes Calp. Sic. was not Neronian), thinks it is the Colosseum (176n55). See also Fagan 2011, 119–20.

sic ibi planitiem curvae sinus ambit harenae
et geminis medium se molibus alligat ovum.

Just as this valley here spreads out into a wide circuit,
and its sides slanting, with the sloping forest all around,
stretches its concave curve between the unbroken hills,
so there the sweep of the curved arena encircles the level ground,
and bounds the oval in the middle with twin masses of building. (30–34)

As Hubbard aptly observes, the Colosseum "is figured as a mimetic version of the familiar pastoral landscape . . . not just an imitation but a superior construction" and conversely "serves to frame the bucolic landscape of the Calpurnian eclogues as itself a spectacle on view by a large Roman audience, something exotic and entertaining, but separated from everyday urban reality by the walls of the arena" (176–77).

We have a description of the spectators in 26–29:

venimus ad sedes, ubi pulla sordida veste
inter femineas spectabat turba cathedras.
Nam quaecumque patent sub aperto libera caelo,
aut eques aut nivei loca densavere tribuni.

We come to the seats, where in shabby garments the base crowd
was watching the show among the women's benches.
for the parts which lie exposed beneath the open sky,
were packed with knights or white-robed tribunes.

Whereas Umbricius in Juvenal 3 longs for the sartorial simplicity of rustic Italians in contrast to the *ambitiosa paupertas* of Rome (177–83), Corydon finds his yokel's attire a source of embarrassment:[53]

o utinam nobis non rustica vestis inesset:
vidissem propius mea numina! Sed mihi sordes
pullaque paupertas et adunco fibula morsu
obfuerunt . . .

O if only I had not been clad in rustic garb:
I would have had a closer view of my deity! But my dirty clothes
and shabby poverty and brooch with a crooked clasp
blocked my way . . . (79–82)

---

53. See intro., pp. 25–26 herein.

Contemplation of himself in the context of the crowd as a whole, as a dirty blot on the shining tapestry of the spectacle, produces a moment of self-abjection worthy of Umbricius even if devoid of any satirical bite. The point is emphasized by the elderly man who asks him: *"quid te stupefactum, rustice, . . . / qui nescius auri / sordida tecta, casas et sola mapalia nosti?"* (Why wonder, bumpkin, that you are stunned with amazement . . . who are unfamiliar with gold and know only your humble homes, cottages, and huts, 40–42). *Mapalia* is used elsewhere of the huts in which nomadic Africans lived.

A substantial part of the center of poem is devoted to what Corydon witnessed from the stands (35–72), including *genus omne ferarum* (57), as he stood in amazement trying to take in all the various elements:

> Quid tibi nunc referam, quae vix suffecimus ipsi
> per partes spectare suas? Sic undique fulgor
> percussit. Stabam defixus et ore patenti
> cunctaque mirabar necdum bona singula noram.

> Why should I now relate to you things which I myself could scarcely take in
> with their multiple details? So striking was the splendor on every side.
> I stood, rooted to the spot, with mouth agape and marveled at it all,
> and I had not yet grasped every single attraction. (35–38)

It is the nature of any spectacle to strive to be more "striking" than its predecessors, to rival the effects of nature, like lightning. By comparison, says his informed (and very old) urban interlocutor, everything that was seen in the past was cheap and shabby (*vilia . . . et sordet quicquid spectavimus olim*, 45–46). Corydon is "thunderstruck" by the show, and the phrasing *defixus et ore patenti* makes for an amusing contrast with the ending of Juvenal's *Satire* 1 (*stantes . . . fixo gutture*, 1.156), where of course the device of the interlocutor is also deployed. Both poets present the arena as a place of multiple foci, where anything might happen at any moment.

In a similarly obsequious context, this time flattery of Domitian, we have already noted in Statius's *Silvae* the poet's self-presentation as a performer in a *munus* of poetic skill (given by his father, 5.3.215–17), and managing to impress even senators:

> Qualis eras, Latinos quotiens ego carmine patres
> mulcerem felixque tui spectator adesses
> muneris . . .

How you seemed, whenever I soothed the Latin fathers in song
and you were present, a happy spectator of your own
gift . . . (215–17)[54]

Lines 220–24 continue the suggestion of gladiatorial combat:

Talis Olympiaca iuvenem cum spectat harena
qui genuit, plus ipse ferit, plus corde sub alto
caeditur; attendunt cunei, spectatur Achaeis
ille magis, crebro dum lumina pulveris haustu
obruit et prensa vovet exspirare corona.

Such is the man who has fathered a son when he sees the young man on
   the Olympic sand; he himself is hitting harder,
deep in his heart he himself is struck all the more;
the rows of seats notice him, and it is he who is watched more by the
   Achaeans,
while he covers his eyes with frequent handfuls of dust,
and vows to die if the garland is captured.[55]

As Markus (2000) observes, "Thus he blends the atmosphere and dignity of
the Greek poetic performance with cultural terms that carried weight in the
Roman social context" (167). A more substantial deployment of the arena occurs in *Silvae* 1.6, which treats Domitian's *spectacula* during the Saturnalian
Games.[56] The focus of the piece is on the entertainment and largesse provided (perhaps in the Colosseum) by the Emperor Domitian, who is likened to
Jupiter—appropriately enough, one supposes, as god of this particular arena.
Similarly, Father Mars and bloody *Virtus* are said to laugh at fighting dwarves
(57–64).[57] In addition to the banquet, there are fights with women:

Hos inter fremitus novosque luxus
spectandi levis effugit voluptas.
Stat sexus rudis insciusque ferri:
et pugnas capit improbus viriles.

Amid such hubbub, such novel luxuries,
the pleasure of the spectacle flits lightly by.

54. Trans. Gibson 2006.
55. Gibson 2006, noting that what purports to be a reference only to Greek athletic competition, is also
suggestive of Roman gladiatorial combat (349–51).
56. See the detailed discussion in Newlands 2002, 227–59, chap. 7, "The Emperor's Saturnalia."
57. Cf. Juv. 13.168–73; on such contests, see Dunkle 2008, 120–21 and n259 (noting *pumilos* is emendation of *pugiles*, Shackleton Bailey 2003, 92–93, n2); on women gladiators, 118–23.

The sex untrained and ignorant of weaponry takes stand
and dares to engage in manly combat. (51–54)[58]

As we shall see later with regard to Juvenal's *Satire 4*, which feasts upon the darker aspects of Domitian's behavior, he was an emperor who assiduously used the apparatus of spectacle to underpin his rule. Statius represents himself this time as a spectator. As Carole Newlands puts it: "Domitian, not Statius, is master of ceremonies here; the new culturally coercive power of the amphitheatre absorbs the poet's voice into the crowd. . . . The poet represents himself as a spectator, not a performer; he is both part of the crowd and yet he is also separate from it in his attempt to commit to published form the day's events."[59] She also delineates how the poem plays upon the paradoxical presence of *libertas*, implied by the festivities of the Saturnalia as backdrop. This piece is, she suggests, an exercise in mediation between imperial control and popular freedom, as well as between the poet's commitments to praise of the emperor and to his own literary worth, concluding that freedom "consists not in openness of speech but in its withdrawal from a public occasion."[60]

In the realm of epic, Lucan (whom Juvenal praises in contradistinction to Statius in *Satire* 7.79–87)[61] exploits the possibilities offered by the arena for depicting civil war. The struggle between Pompey and Caesar becomes an extended gladiatorial combat between successive pairs of fighters, an image deployed from the very outset (*nec coiere pares*, 1.129; cf. *parque suum videre dei*, 6.3).[62] The extent of the representation of his narrative as spectacle is revealed in Matthew Leigh's book, *Lucan: Spectacle and Engagement*. Leigh argues that the Scaeva scene in book 6 stands as Lucan's gladiatorial *munus*, noting, for example, how Caesar's walls at Dyrrachium create "a ring in which the gladiators of civil war can compete" (244).[63] Likewise, the sea battle off Massilia in book 3 is his *naumachia*, and the episode of the snakes in book 9 his *venatio*, where we watch the "transformation of Cato the gladiator into Cato

---

58. Trans. Shackleton Bailey 2003.

59. Newlands 2002, 227.

60. Newlands 2002, 256; cf. "A cultural practice based upon freedom is shown in *Silv.* 1.6 to have been resignified as willing compliance with the persuasive fictions of power" (249); and 238–52, on how the troubling associations of the Jovian comparison subtly interrogate these fictions, e.g., "The metamorphic world of the amphitheatre with its fleeting pleasures and sounds produces a disjunction between the fluidity of pleasure and the purported stability of imperial rule associated with Golden Age bounty" (251).

61. To the effect that he "may recline in his marbled gardens, happy with his fame," while Statius supports himself by pantomime libretti, not his *Thebaid*.

62. Ahl 1976, 86–88.

63. See chap. 5, "Scaeva: Lucan's Exemplary Hero," and chap. 7, "A View to a Kill: Lucan's Amphitheatrical Audience."

the spectator" in "Lucan's Stoic amphitheatre."[64] A pivotal moment occurs in 881–87:

> cogit tantos tolerare labores
> summa ducis virtus, qui nuda fusus harena
> excubat atque omni fortunam provocat hora.
> Omnibus unus adest fatis; quocumque vocatus
> advolat atque ingens meritum maiusque salute
> contulit, in letum vires; puduitque gementem
> illo teste mori.

> The outstanding *virtus* of their leader compels them to endure
> such great hardships, as, lying on the bare sand,
> he keeps watch and challenges fortune every hour.
> Although just one man, he is present at every fateful moment; wherever
>   they call him,
> he hastens over and bestows a mighty benefit, even greater than life,
> namely the strength to die; and the soldier was ashamed to die
>   groaning,
> with Cato as a witness.

As Leigh observes, "While at 9.881–83 he was described as directly challenging fortune [in the language of single combat], the Stoic gladiator has now become a witness and a spectator." Leigh also examines Scaeva as an *exemplum virtutis* and argues that Lucan's treatment offers a vivid example of "the corruption of *virtus* in a civil-war situation" and of "how the truths of *virtus* collapse in a hostile context."[65] Leigh emphasizes the spectacular nature of the exemplum and the vital role of visibility in communicating its message, asserting that the exemplum and the gladiatorial *munus* "are not at all separate entities and must be studied together."[66]

In historiography, Suetonius and Dio frequently cite emperors' attitudes to, and engagement with, the arena as a means of delineating character.[67] Tacitus does so too, but he also finds the arena a useful conceptual model when

---

64. Leigh 1997, 265–82, "Cato in the *Harena*," esp. 275. Cf. Ahl 1976, 82–115; Barton 1993, 36–39 (cf. 103–105) on the arena and civil war, with n95 on Lucan: "the whole of the civil war . . . a type of bloody gladiatorial *munus* in which a series of pairs were matched before the eyes of history," citing 6.3, 191–92; 7.695–96, along with precedents such as Livy 7.10.6.

65. Leigh 1997, 160–72, esp. 171–72. Note the gladiatorial resonances of *provocat* and *advolat* (cf. *Advolans*, Mart. 5.24.6, pp. 196–97 herein).

66. Leigh 1997, 181–84; 240, citing Cic. *Tusc.* 2.41 and Sen. *Ep.* 30.8.

67. Newbold 1975; Bradley 1981; Kyle 1998, 32nn74–75. Suet. *Aug.*, *Cal.*, *Claud.* and *Dom.* offer good examples.

describing the street fighting that took place in Rome during the civil war between Vespasian and Vitellius around the period of the Saturnalia in 69 CE:[68]

> Aderat pugnantibus spectator populus, utque in ludicro certamine, hos, rursus illos clamore et plausu fovebat. Quotiens pars altera inclinasset, abditos in tabernis aut si quam in domum perfugerant, erui iugularique expostulantes parte maiore praedae potiebantur . . . Saeva ac deformis urbe tota facies: alibi proelia et vulnera, alibi balineae popinaeque; simul cruor et strues corporum . . . quidquid in acerbissima captivitate scelerum, prorsus ut eandem civitatem et fudere crederes et lascivere . . . nunc inhumana securitas et ne minimo quidem temporis voluptates intermissae: velut festis diebus id quoque gaudium accederet, exultabant, fruebantur, nulla partium cura, malis publicis laeti.

> The populace stood by watching the combatants, as if they were at games in the circus; by their shouts and applause they encouraged first one party and then the other. If one side gave way and the soldiers hid in shops or sought refuge in some private house, the onlookers demanded that they be dragged out and killed; for so they gained a larger share of booty. . . . Horrible and hideous sights were to be seen everywhere in the city: here battles and wounds, there open baths and drinking shops; blood and piles of corpses. . . . Every crime that can be committed in the most savage conquest, so that men might well have believed that the city was at once mad with rage and drunk with pleasure. . . . There was no less cruelty then than now; but now men showed inhuman indifference, and never relaxed their pleasures for a single moment. As if there were a new delight added to their holidays, they gave way to exultation and joy, wholly indifferent to either side, finding pleasure in public misfortune.
> (*Histories* 3.83)[69]

The presentation of civil war as an arena spectacle reflects very poorly on both those fighting and those watching. This has been set up well in advance by the characterization of the followers of Vitellius as akin to animals or performers

---

68. Keitel 1992; Barton 1993, 104–105: Ash 1999, esp. chap. 5, also 45–46. When the main part of the army appeared in Rome, they presented a *saevum spectaculum*, Tac. *Hist.* 2.88. Vitellius is said to have attended a gladiatorial performance in Cremona, as if the dead in battle were not enough (Dio 65.1.3); he sold a favorite to a *lanista* (Suet. *Vit.* 12).

69. Trans. Moore 1925.

in such events. In 2.88, we are told that the soldiers often fought among themselves (*multae et atroces inter se militum caedes*) and that Vitellius distributed rations to them "as if he was portioning out the *sagina* for gladiators" (*singulis ibi militibus Vitellius paratos cibos ut gladiatoriam saginam dividebat*), followed by the comment that *et effusa plebes totis se castris miscuerat*). The mixing of various social categories, like the content of the *sagina*, is designed to provoke a certain disgust.[70]

Other events served up enticing opportunities for spectacular imagery. Dio's account of the water banquet of Tigillinus, Nero's Praetorian commander mentioned at the end of *Satire* 1, begins with an animal hunt, after which the theater was flooded for a naval battle, drained for gladiatorial combat, then reflooded to carry a platform with a central dining area—for Nero and his fellow banqueters—surrounded by taverns and brothels. The crowd of participants was a real mix: women—free and slave; wives, virgins, and prostitutes; plebeian and noble—and men, including slaves and gladiators. "Now a slave would debauch his mistress in the presence of his master, now a gladiator would debauch a girl of noble family before the eyes of her father," we read (62.15.5–6). Tacitus supplies other details, including that birds and animals and sea creatures were brought in from all over the world (*Annals* 15.37.2).[71] The festivities degenerated into brawling and uproar "both among those going in and those standing around outside," says Dio. In the *Epitome* of book 62, the next event cited is Nero's accomplishment of his long-standing desire "to make an end of the whole city and its realm," namely the Great Fire of Rome (16.1). Tacitus's version adds an intervening detail, echoing Gracchus' marriage in Juvenal's *Satire* 2: a few days later, Nero, having defiled himself with all lawful and unlawful acts except one, then married "one of that herd of perverts" (*uni ex illo contaminatorum grege*), whose name was Pythagoras (37.4). Amid all the accoutrements of marriage, "everything was put on show (*spectata*) which night usually covers, even when the bride is a woman," concludes Tacitus. Then *sequitur clades* immediately opens the account of the Great Fire (38.1). Both historians depict the spilling out of violence and spectacle from the arena and the corruption that arises from the collapsing of boundaries and the mixing of categories. In the hands of Nero and Tigillinus, this takes the most dangerous form imaginable, leading to the burning of the city. In Tacitus, this whole segment is constructed to draw parallels between the disorder in the court (and

---

70. 2.87; see below on the satirical *sagina* and Vitellius' gourmet dish, the "Shield of Minerva" (Suet. *Vit.* 13).

71. Tac. places the event on Agrippa's Lake; he adds the detail that the oarsmen were grouped according to age and sexual expertise.

the mind) of Nero and the civil disorder that spread out beyond the confines of the arena into the town of Pompeii, so that the Great Fire emerges as the culmination of a broader pattern of disruption. From the *crematio* of criminals, we follow a trail that leads to the *incendium* of the *Urbs*, and back again, with the burning of the Christians as punishment for their having started the fire. In fact, as Tacitus makes clear, it was the emperor's flouting of all laws and customs that kindled the conflagration.

In philosophy, the moral connection with the arena is best illustrated by Seneca, who finds it a productive source of metaphors and similes for his philosophical arguments. The gladiator is deployed as a figure embodying such virtues as endurance, fortitude, and ambition for glory.[72] This we might term the "positive" appropriation of the arena, one in which mental toughening and philosophical rigor, of the lack of it, are routinely conceptualized through reference to the training of the gladiator and to the trials of combat. For example, in *Epistle* 22.1, he uses gladiators to explain how Lucilius is to withdraw himself from showy and depraved pursuits (*ex istis occupationibus speciosis et malis*) and develop his philosophical skills:

Vetus proverbium est gladiatorem in harena capere consilium;
aliquid adversarii vultus, aliquid manus mota, aliquid ipsa inclinatio
corporis intuentem monet.

There is an old proverb that the gladiator plans his fight in the arena;
as he watches, something in his opponent's expression, some
movement of his hand, the very inclination of his body, gives a
warning.

In other words, for both gladiator and *sapiens*, general skills are acquired in training, but the actual situation always demands specific moves.[73] In recommending that one become accustomed to poverty in advance so as not to be caught off-guard when Fortune turns nasty, Seneca recommends practicing on

---

72. For a detailed survey, see Wistrand 1990 and 1992. See also Barton 1993, 16–19; Gunderson 1996, 137–39; Cagniart 2000. Cic. *Tusc.* 4.41 says that gladiators *aut perditi aut barbari* are praised for their bravery and for facing blows and death, quoting Lucilius's *Samnis, spurcus homo, vita illa dignus locoque*; while it is, he says, very likely that a gladiatorial spectacle *ut nunc fit* is cruel and inhuman, in the days when criminals fought there could be no better *contra dolorem et mortem disciplina*, at least for the eyes (though for the ears there might be many).

73. As Toner 1995 points out, "a myriad shadows of character were thought to be revealed in the conduct of the combatants, conduct which to our untrained eyes would have seemed like no more than an endless repetition of savagery" (39); perhaps an MMA addict might claim the same? Cf. 42 citing Foucault 1963: "a highly selective gaze that 'could and should grasp colours, variations, tiny anomalies'" (89).

the gladiator's "dummy" (*exerceamur ad palum, Epistle* 18.8).[74] The gladiator is put to a related use in his essay *De Ira* 1.11.2, one that, given Juvenal's speaker's initial grounding in *indignatio*, might well be of some relevance to readings of the satires. In the case of gladiators, Seneca says, "skill protects, anger exposes" (*gladiatores quoque ars tuetur, ira denudat*).[75] On a different tack, in 2.8.2, arguing that nothing is more unworthy of the *sapiens* than that his indignation should depend upon the wickedness of others (2.7)—which on one level describes the situation of the Juvenalian speaker perfectly—he says there are always plenty of examples in the Forum or the Circus who "live just as if they were in a gladiatorial school—they eat and fight with the same people" (*non alia quam in ludo gladiatorio vita est cum isdem bibentium pugnantiumque*) and are "a community of wild beasts"—except that, unlike the animals, they do not refrain from eating their own kind and "stuff themselves with mutual laceration" (*mutua laceratione satiantur*, 2.8.2–3).[76]

Speaking of Lucilius's solemn promise to undertake philosophical training in *Epistle* 37.1–2, as we noted earlier, he observes that *Eadem honestissimi huius et illius turpissimi auctoramenti verba sunt: "uri, vinciri ferroque necari"* (The words of this most honorable oath are the same as those of that most disgraceful one, namely: "to be burned, to be chained, and to be killed by the sword").[77] But gladiators are permitted to lower their weapons and test the pity of the people, whereas Lucilius "must die standing tall and unconquered" (*recto tibi invictoque moriendum est*), because "we are born without any possibility of a reprieve" (*sine missione nascimur*). We may note here the conjunction of *honestissimi* and *turpissimi* in the first line: this typifies the ambiguity that defines the gladiator and, indeed, the whole arena experience.[78] The phrase *sine missione* means "without being spared or let off [to fight another day]"[79] and the *sapiens*, then, is to take a significant step beyond the gladiator in refusing to ask for a repieve. In his essay *De*

---

74. *Palus* also refers to the stake to which those condemned to execution were affixed: Cic. *Verr.* 5.72; Livy 8.7.19. For Fortune as *editor*, see Barton 1993, 23, and Sen. *De Tranq.* 11.5: *Fortuna illa, quae ludos sibi facit, "Quo," inquit, "te reservem, malum et trepidum animal?"*

75. Cf. Cic. *Tusc.* 4.48–9. See W.S. Anderson 1964 and chap. 4 herein for more on the "philosophical" Juvenal.

76. On this topos in Juvenal 15, see chap. 4 herein.

77. Dunkle 2008, 38.

78. On the *auctoramentum*, cf. *Ep.* 71.23: *Quid miraris, si uri, vulnerari, occidi, alligari iuvat, aliquando etiam libet?* (Why do you marvel if it helps a man, and sometimes even pleases him, to be burned, wounded, killed, or bound?). See also Petr. 117. Distinguished from *sacramentum* (ritual sacralisation), Kyle 1998: all *auctorati* made a *sacramentum* but not all who took the *sacramentum* were *auctorati* (87).

79. Dunkle 2008, 131–32, 136–37; Livy 41.20.12; Petr. 52.5: *exoratus a nobis missionem dedit puero*, with Trimalchio as *editor*.

Tranquillitate 11.4–6, citing Cicero's comment in *Pro Milone* 92 to the effect that gladiators who appear too eager to save their lives only end up provoking hostility, Seneca says that it is the same for the *sapiens*, who "will be hacked and pierced with more wounds" if he does not know how to "offer his throat" (*praebere iugulum*, 11.5) properly.[80] That the search for philosophical enlightenment, even tranquility, should be presented in terms of violent physical combat tells us a great deal about the Romans, even if the primary basis of the comparison is the ability to face death without flinching.[81] For Seneca and others, it is a question of one's attitude toward the inevitability of death, and here the arena offered an exemplum ready for easy assimilation.[82]

As far as the beast fights and executions are concerned, here too Seneca varies his applications. In *De Ira* 3.43.2, for instance, he draws a link between fate in the arena and in life:

Videre solemus inter matutina harenae spectacula tauri et ursi pugnam inter se colligatorum, quos, cum alter alterum vexarunt, suus confector expectat. Idem facimus, aliquem nobiscum adligatum lacessimus, cum victo victorique finis et quidem maturus immineat.

At the morning performances in the arena we often see a battle between a bull and a bear tied together, and when they have harried each other, an appointed slayer awaits them. Their fate is ours; we harass someone bound closely to us while the end, all too soon, threatens both the victor and the vanquished.[83]

Thus what we see in the arena is a depiction of our own condition of existence. He is not always so neutral, however, and, most famously, in *Epistle* 7 he explains his objections to some aspects of the arena experience. This letter has been trawled with great frequency and hope by those looking for signs of his

80. This is to live according to the contract into which one is born: *hoc sibi cum conciperetur statim condictum . . . formulam* (11.6). It is not something you "sign up" for, it is what you arrive here under.

81. See Barton 1993, 18–24; Sen. *De Tranq.* 9.3 on the circus: *non in cursu tantum circique certamine, sed in iis spatiis vitae interius flectendum est*; *De Const.* 16, on the Epicurean view that the *sapiens* tolerates injuries vs. the Stoic view that he simply doesn't experience them, he likens the difference to that between two gladiators: *quod inter duos gladiatores fortissimos, quorum alter premit vulnus et stat in gradu, alter respiciens ad clamantem populum significat nihil esse et intercedi non patitur.*

82. Cf. Plin. Eld. *HN* 11.114: in Caligula's *ludus*, the two out of 20,000 who didn't blink were invincible because they neither missed any of their opponents' moves nor gave anything away themselves. Such notions appear widespread: Plin. *Pan.* 33: *spectaculum . . . non enerve nec fluxum . . . sed quod pulchra vulnera contemptumque mortis accenderet, cum in servorum etiam noxiorumque corporibus amor laudis et cupido victoriae cerneretur.*

83. Trans. Basore 1928–35.

disapproval of the institutionalized cruelty of the arena, but the catch is rather paltry.[84] Seneca explains very specifically what it is that he finds objectionable. First, there is the danger of mixing with the mob (*multorum conversatio*): *Quid tibi vitandum praecipue existimem, quaeris: turbam* (7.1–2). Second, it is the spectators who are the focus of his criticism, apparently because they gain so much pleasure from executions that lack the "enjoyment, wit and relaxation" he was expecting when he turned up accidentally at a midday show (*lusus expectans et sales et aliquid laxamenti*, 7.3).[85] Instead he was treated to the "undiluted murder" (*mera homicidia*) of those thrown to the crowd without any defensive armor or show of skill, where the outcome of every fight is death: Where's the fun in that? Moreover, when the games stop for the lunchtime intermission, it is announced that "in the meantime some men will have their throats slit, so that there's something happening" (*intermissum est spectaculum: "interim iugulentur homines, ne nihil agatur,"* 7.5).[86]

In *De Tranquillitate* 2.13–14 Seneca again turns his jaundiced gaze upon the viewers, as he criticizes those Romans who are always roaming about, driven by a *semper praesentibus infesta levitas* (fickleness always discontented with the present):

> Nimis diu a plausu et fragore aures vacaverunt, iuvat iam et
> humano sanguine frui: "Iam flectamus cursum ad urbem." Aliud
> ex alio iter suscipitur et spectacula spectaculis mutantur. Ut ait
> Lucretius: "Hoc se quisque modo semper fugit."[87] Sed quid prodest,
> si non effugit? Sequitur se ipse et urget gravissimus comes.

---

84. Gunderson 1996 accurately observes that Seneca "has built his objections entirely within the discourse structured by the apparatus of the arena" which he accepts as a punitive device, but "in playing with the spatial/ontological taxonomies of the arena, he reinscribes the institution on a broader level, seating himself and his readers in a new set of stands ringing the arena" (135–36). A contrary view in Richardson-Hay 2006, 256–60.

85. That the arena could be a site of pleasant relaxation and of forgetting sadness is suggested by Sen. *Cons. Helv.* 17.1: *Ludis interim aut gladiatoribus animum occupamus; at illum inter ipsa, quibus avocatur, spectacula levis aliqua desiderii nota subruit* ("Sometimes we occupy the mind with games or gladiators; but amid the very spectacles by which it is diverted, some slight reminder of its loss undermines it"). Veyne 1990 suggests that Seneca here describes a pleasure that left the spectators with "a dull anxiety" (*une ombre légère de mélancholie*) for the future. Wistrand 1992 disagrees, pointing out that the translation of *levis aliqua desiderii nota* ought to take account of the fact that *desiderium* "in its context means grief and longing for a lost friend or relative. . . . It cannot possibly mean melancholy or sadness in quite general terms here" (45). But the conjunction of watching the spectacles to forget one's grief and then being called back to it by something viewed (presumably some form or moment of death) is telling. Tert., after all, claims that the spectacles of the arena offered a form of consolation to the viewers (see p. 172 herein).

86. Worst of all is that many actually prefer this to "the usual pairs and fights by request" (*ordinariis paribus et postulaticiis*). Cf. *Ep.* 95.33; Suet. *Claud.* 34.

87. Lucretius 3.1068, with added *semper*; cf. Barton 1993, 52–53.

Too long have their ears been without the applause and the din; now
it delights them to enjoy human blood: "Let us now turn our course
toward the city." They undertake one journey after another and
exchange spectacle for spectacle. As Lucretius says, "Thus ever
does each man flee from himself"—but what does he gain if he does
not escape from himself? He ever follows himself and weighs upon
himself as his most burdensome companion.[88]

This we may connect with Horace's comments in his first satire about people
wandering around and vacillating between one thing and another, and with
the phenomenon of "satiric nausea" outlined above.[89] In *Epistle* 2.1, Seneca
praises Lucilius for not engaging in *peregrinatio: non discurris nec locorum mutationibus inquietaris—aegri animo ista iactatio est.* Barton speaks of "the
spectre of satiation" and suggests that "paradoxically, once within the whirl-
wind of lust, the thing that the Roman feared most was not the vortex of
desire but the death of that desire—the nauseous *taedium vitae*, the end of
wanting."[90]

Finally, although we have not discussed Seneca's *Tragedies* here, there is
running through them a deep fascination with the infliction of pain and the
mutilation of the body. Throughout his corpus, then, we might say, the presence of the arena is strongly felt, whether it is used to provide paradigms for
philosophical instruction, ready exempla of vice and degeneracy, or scenes of
bodily abuse and dismemberment.

Satirists

While imperial writers such as Tacitus, Lucan, and Seneca incorporated the
arena into their works with considerable ingenuity, it is among those of the
satirical bent—Petronius, Martial, and Juvenal—that it looms largest as a conceptual framework and as a source of colorful imagery. The notion that satirical discourse can be interrogated through gladiatorial and other performances
operates, of course, within a broader context, namely the close connection between satire and physical violence.[91] Various critics have sought an explanation

88. Trans. Basore 1928–35.
89. See the introduction, pp. 38–39 herein.
90. Barton 1993, and the connection to French *aboulie* "the negative state of being without desire. It is
not contentment; it is despair" (51–53).
91. On satire as *ludus*, non-literary play, including gladiatorial combat, see Habinek 2005a, esp. 177–78;
Habinek 2005b, 110–16.

for the verbal aggression in satire in its "contained release" and its "truth telling" or "corrective" function.[92] There are other good reasons for linking the arena and satire. First, there is the Roman fascination with *ludus* ("play"), an activity which, as Thomas Habinek explains, is intimately connected to the body and to the realities of social interaction, as is gladiatorial play.[93] He views satire as "constructed in part to extend the possibilities of *ludus* beyond the limits of adolescence" and as "the ludic counterpart that makes possible the 'real' performances of oratory" so that "just as Roman social structure writ large requires the ludic performances of the arena, so the elite Roman male requires the *ludus* of satire." Second, both arena and satire are considered autochthonous in their origin, as opposed to practices that appear to be conscious imitations of Greek predecessors; as Habinek puts it, satire is "always already there in the Roman world"—and both can plausibly be traced back to native Italian or Etruscan activities. They were also both the source of some cultural discomfort.[94] Attempts to obscure the origins of gladiatorial combat, for instance, or to distance these activities from the respectable core of Romanness, find a parallel in Horace's anxiety over his relationship to the mouthy founder of the satirical genre, Lucilius.[95] The tempering turn in the form of satire so laboriously achieved by Horace—making it more urbane and less chaotic, more restrained and less violent in its expression, and giving it a cloak of philosophical respectability—is something that inevitably altered it for his successors. In all of them, however, as well as in Horace himself, we can see unmistakable impulses toward the more combative original version.

We may begin our survey of arena borrowings with Lucilius, whose satire included a gladiatorial contest (4.172–85) given by the Flacci between a Samnite named Aeserninus and a certain Pacideianus:

> Aeserninus fuit Flaccorum munere quidam
>> Samnis, spurcus homo, vita illa dignus locoque,
> cum Pacideiano componitur, optimus multo
>> post homines natos gladiator qui fuit unus.

> In the public show given by the Flacci was a certain Aeserninus,
>> a Samnite, a nasty fellow, worthy of that life and station.

92. See Test 1991, esp. chap. 5, 100–25.

93. Habinek 2005b, 110, 113–14; "As with school, so with the arena, play constructs reality" (114).

94. Many were on the edge of the city: Wiedemann 1992, 46–47; on origins, see Kyle 1998, who inclines to the view that Campanian or Samnite origins are more likely than Etruscan ones (44–46).

95. Wiedemann 1992, 30–33; for Tac.'s distancing, see *Ann.* 13.31.

He was matched with Pacideianus, who was by far the best
    of all the gladiators since the creation of man. (172–75)[96]

In 176–81, Pacideianus addresses the crowd or the *editor* using violent and ag-
gressive language:

"Occidam illum equidem et vincam, si id quaeritis," inquit.
"Verum illud credo fore: in os prius accipiam ipse,
quam gladium in stomachi surdi ac pulmonibus sisto.
Odi hominem, iratus pugno, nec longius quicquam
nobis, quam dextrae gladium dum accommodet alter;
usque adeo studio atque odio illius ecferor ira."

"I'll simply kill him and win, if that's what you want," said he.
"But I think it will come about thus—first I'll take his blows on my face;
after that I'll stick my sword in that dunderhead's gullet and lungs.
Curse the fellow, I'll fight in a temper, and not a minute longer
will we delay than it takes either of us to fit his sword to his right hand.
So much am I transported with anger, fed by my passion and hatred of
    him."[97]

In book 3, 109–17, Lucilius describes another combat between two gladiators.
This time the setting is at Capua, and the fighters hurl as many insults as they
do blows:

["Bronci" sunt producto ore et dentibus promentibus . . .]
"Broncus Bovillanus dente adverso eminulo hic est
rinoceros.
Non peperit, verum postica parte profudit.
uno oculo, pedibus duobus, dimidiatus, ut porcus.
Conturbare animam potis est quicumque adoritur.
Ille alter abundans cum septem incolumis pinnis redit et receipt se.
Illud ad incita cum redit atque internecionem"

[" 'Bronci' are men who have a jutting jaw and prominent teeth . . ."]
"This jut-mouth of a Bovillae, with his one little projecting tooth,
    is a very

---

96. Cited freely by Cic. *De Opt. Gen.* 17 in a discussion of the relative merits of Aeschines (like Aeserninus) and Demosthenes (like Pacideianus).

97. Cited by Cic. *Tusc.* 4.48 in a discussion of whether gladiatorial *iracundia* is appropriate in philosophical disputes. Trans. Warmington 1979.

Rhinoceros.

She didn't *bring* him forth but from the hinder part she *sprawled* him forth.

Having one eye and two feet, halved like a pig.

Whoever is the attacker can knock his senses out of him.

Look, one of the two, billowing over with seven feathers lunges again and withdraws unscathed.

When yonder fight comes to a standstill, to slaughter."[98]

The display at Capua appears to have been imitated by Horace in his own journey poem, *Satire* 1.5, with the battle of insults (*pugnam*, 51; *ad pugnam venere*, 56), akin to a legal dispute (*litis*, 53), between Sarmentus the *scurra* and Messius Cicirrus, whose name means "game cock" (50–70).[99] Through their numerous jibes and ripostes, says Horace, the dinner party was thus pleasantly prolonged (*prorsus iucunde cenam producimus illam*, 70). Gowers regards this exchange as the centerpiece of Horace's poem, noting, "It can be no coincidence that the duel is staged in Campania, where traces of satire's native Italian ancestors, Atellan farce and Oscan obscenity, were thick on the ground."[100]

In *Satire* 1.7.16–21, we have perhaps the closest imitation of one-on-one combat, as two litigants, Rupilius Rex and Persius, clash like a pair of well-matched gladiators:

aut si disparibus bellum incidat, ut Diomedi
cum Lycio Glauco, discedat pigrior ultro
muneribus missis—Bruto praetore tenente
ditem Asiam, Rupili et Persi par pugnat, uti non
compositum melius cum Bitho Bacchius. In ius
acres procurrunt, magnum spectaculum uterque.

. . . or ill-matched opponents caught up in war, as with Diomedes
and the Lycian Glaucus, the fainter-hearted would leave the field,
voluntarily dispatching gifts. While Brutus, as governor,
commanded the rich province of Asia, Rupilius and Persius came to blows,
a pair just as well matched as Bacchius and Bithus. They sally forth
keenly into court, each a great sight to behold. (16–21)[101]

---

98. Warmington 1979 (whose translation I use here) assembles the fragments in this way, a little differently from Marx.

99. On this poem, see Gowers 2012. For the *scurra* as close counterpart of the satirist, see Habinek 2005a, 182–85; on Horace and Lucilius, see Fiske 1920 and 306–16 on *Sat.* 1.5.

100. Gowers 2012, 185, cf. 199–204, including on reading the scene as "another potted history of satire."

101. Trans. P. M. Brown 1995.

The terminology of *par* and *componere*, together with the reference to the well-known pair Bithus and Bacchius, figures the court case as gladiatorial combat.[102] The poem ends with a joke of sorts, when Persius asks Brutus, the governor of Asia, why he doesn't slit the throat of Rex (*cur non / hunc Regem iugulas?* 33–34), a perfect job for a regicide. This makes him the equivalent of the *editor* deciding a fighter's fate in the arena.[103] Freudenburg comments: "The satirist is himself a lowlife, relating in the opening lines that he picked up the story from the gossipmongers and barbers with whom he apparently has regular contact. The entire scene he stages as a gladiator fight, which again reflects negatively on his status."[104]

In *Satire* 2.7, the truth-telling dialogue between Davus and his master, licensed by the Saturnalia (*libertate Decembri*, 4), is a back-and-forth exchange around the idea that Horace is no better than his slave.[105] The badinage is combative throughout with numerous images of punishment, and in the course of his argument to prove that Horace is a slave (46–71, which is prefaced by the verb *edo*, 45), Davus includes an insulting image of his master, caught in the act of adultery with a married woman, as an *auctoratus* (i.e., one who has sold himself to a gladiatorial school):

> . . . metuens induceris atque
> altercante libidinibus tremis ossa pavore.
> Quid refert, uri virgis ferroque necari
> auctoratus eas an turpi clausus in arca.

> Full of fear, you're brought inside,
> and you quake to your very bones as panic disputes against lust.
> What does it matter whether you sell yourself as a gladiator to be
>   branded,
> and slain with rods and the sword, or shut up in a foul chest. (56–59)[106]

---

102. See Gowers 2012, 257–58, citing Cic.'s similar conception of his with Clodius in *Att.*1.16; she sees echoes of the Homeric *promachus* in 20–21 and notes that the phrase *muneribus missis* might also evoke the arena, citing *mitto* as the opposite of *iugulare* in *ILS* 5134 "*Missos, missos, iugula, iugula*" and contrasting here with *iugulas* in 35. Sen. Eld. *Controv.* 7.10: *componis in domo par*; cf. 3 Praef. 10.

103. Gowers 2012 on Ciceronian echoes of the word (262).

104. He also notes that in this poem Horace reduces the second book of Lucilius to a single page (208); Fiske 1920, 325–30.

105. As is *Sat.* 2.3 the dialogue with Damasippus, who visits Horace at his Sabine farm during the Saturnalia around 17–19 December. Dunkle 2008 notes that the annual *munus* given by the quaestors was still in December under Domitian, interrupted on December 17 for the Saturnalia (183); cf. Ville 1981, 159–60; Barton 1993, 123–25, 147–47; Wiedemann 1992, 151. See also Freudenburg 1993, 173, 188–95, also 211–23 on the "low-life satirist and Saturnalian exposure"; Miller 2012, esp. 318–20 on Hor. *Sat.* 2.3 and 7.

106. Trans. Muecke 1993.

Later, Davus asks:

> "Vel cum Pausiaca torpes, insane, tabella,
> qui peccas minus atque ego, cum Fulvi Rutubaeque
> aut Pacideiani contento poplite miror
> proelia rubrica picta aut carbone, velut si
> re vera pugnent, feriant vitentque moventes
> arma viri? Nequam et cessator Davus, at ipse
> subtilis veterum iudex et callidus audis."

> "Or when you swoon over a painting by Pausias, you lunatic,
> how is it that you're less guilty than I, when, with straining knees,
> I admire the red-ochre or charcoal-painted battles of Fulvius and Rutuba
> or Pacideianus, just as if they were really fighting,
> striking and parrying as they brandish their weapons,
> real heroes? Davus is a rogue and a dawdler, but you yourself
> are called a connoisseur, and a fine judge of old masters." (95–101)

The Pacideianus mentioned here may be the same person as in Lucilius's fragment or a later namesake. As Muecke notes, the main point is that gazing at paintings (or, perhaps, in the case of Davus here, an advertisement of some sort) is a sign of decadence and compares Horace's *Epistle* 1.6 and Seneca's *Epistle* 8.5 for their Stoic theme of *nil admirandum*.[107] The passivity, tending toward servility, involved in gazing with such intensity is also a negative feature of arena spectatorship, as Seneca pointed out.

Another related example of exploitation of the arena is provided by Martial, who composed a collection of poems to mark the grand opening of the Colosseum, *De Spectaculis*.[108] We need not elaborate on them here, save to note that, although divorced in most modern editions from the books of epigrams that follow them, these "Spectacle Poems" are a prefatory reminder of how the satirical epigram manipulates the curious gaze of the spectator, very often through display of the strange, deformed Other.[109] In the rest of the

---

107. Muecke 1979, 224–25; Sen. *Ep.* 8.5: *Contemnite omnia, quae supervacuus labor velut ornamentum ac decus ponit. Cogitate nihil praeter animum esse mirabile.* On the reputation of Pausias for careful and slow technique and also for licentiousness, see McGann 1956.

108. Comprehensive ed. by Coleman 2006; she notes that only twenty-six other poems deal with spectacles (lxxix).

109. See Plass 1995, 216–17, n13. Sullivan 1991 makes a good case for the inclusion of Martial in discussions of Roman satire (104). On Juvenal's use of Martial, see Colton 1991, 11–16, followed by a voluminous survey of examples in all the satires, and W. S. Anderson 1982, who concludes there is little doubt that "Juvenal used topics and themes which had earlier won wide favor in the epigrams published by Martial" (367).

collection, moreover, references to the arena, gladiators, and animal events pop up quite frequently. The poet, for example, refers to his book as a *munus* (*Cui vis fieri, libelle, munus?* 3.2.1). In 1.5, the Emperor Domitian is imagined as saying:

Do tibi naumachiam, tu das epigrammata nobis:
  vis, puto, cum libro, Marce, natare tuo.

I give you a sea fight, you give me epigrams.
  You want, I think, to swim with your book, Marcus.

In 1.14 we picture him at the *venationes*:

Delicias, Caesar, lususque iocosque leonum
  vidimus—hoc etiam praestat harena tibi—

The entertainments, Caesar, the playful sportings of the lions,
  we have seen—this too the arena offers you—(1–2)

in a poem about a hare with lucky escapes, whose point is summed up with:

Unde potest avidus captae leo parcere praedae?
  Sed tamen esse tuus dicitur: ergo potest.

How is it possible that a greedy lion can spare his captive prey?
  But he is said to be yours: so he can. (5–6)[110]

Elsewhere in Martial's collection, we find, for instance, 3.99.3–4 addressed to a shoemaker who exhibited gladiators:

. . . cur ludere nobis
non liceat, licuit si iugulare tibi?

. . . why should I not be allowed to write playful verses,
if you've been allowed to have throats cut?

The conjunction of cobbler and gladiators is found in Tacitus's account of how Nero on his way to Greece stopped at Beneventum where he attended a show given by the deformed *delator* and scurrilous wit Vatinius (whose misshapen appearance is mocked in Juvenal 5.46).[111] On other occasions, glancing allusions are made through imagery or metaphor: in 5.62, for instance, Martial

110. Cf. 1.6, 22, 48, and Howell 1980, *ad loc.*
111. Tac. *Ann.* 15.34; Dio 63.15.1. See the "Vatinian" cups in Juv. 5.46 discussed in chap. 4 herein.

suggests that a guest at his villa should bring his own furniture, *nam mea iam digitum sustulit hospitibus* (for my own has already raised its finger to [beg for mercy from] the guests, 4).

Two poems are worthy of our particular attention in connection with the arena of satire. First, in 1.43.9–14, Martial describes a dinner for sixty at which a single boar—and a small one too—was served without any trimmings:

> nudus aper, sed et hic minimus qualisque necari
> > a non armato pumilione potest.
> Et nihil inde datum est; tantum spectavimus omnes:
> > ponere aprum nobis sic et harena solet.
> Ponatur tibi nullus aper post talia facta,
> > sed tu ponaris cui Charidemus apro.

> No, naked boar, and a tiny one at that, such as
> > an unarmed midget might lay low.
> And nothing of it came our way, we all just watched.
> > The arena is apt to serve us boar in that fashion.
> After such behavior, I hope that boar will never be again be served you,
> > but that *you* will be served to the same boar as Charidemus.[112]

Charidemus was presumably a criminal executed by being thrown *ad bestias*. The cena and the arena are linked here through the boar (and getting fed and not getting fed), echoing elements of Juvenal's *sportula* scene in *Satire* 1 and the encounter with the abusive host in *Satire* 5.

Second, *Epigram* 5.24 is a piece in mocking praise of a gladiator called Hermes:[113]

> Hermes Martia saeculi voluptas,
> Hermes omnibus eruditus armis,
> Hermes et gladiator et magister,
> Hermes turbo sui tremorque ludi,
> Hermes, quem timet Helius, sed unum,
> Hermes, cui cadet Advolans, sed uni,
> Hermes vincere nec ferire doctus,
> Hermes suppositicius sibi ipse,
> Hermes divitiae locariorum,
> Hermes cura laborque ludiarum,   10

112. Trans. Shackleton Bailey 1993.
113. Dunkle 2008, 126–28.

Hermes belligera superbus hasta,
Hermes aequoreo minax tridente,
Hermes casside languida timendus,
Hermes gloria Martis universi,
Hermes omnia solus et ter unus.

Hermes, favorite fighter of the age,
Hermes, skilled in all weaponry,
Hermes, gladiator and trainer both,
Hermes, tempest and tremor of his school,
Hermes, who (but none other) makes Helius afraid,
Hermes, before whom (but none other) Advolans [the Flying Gladiator]
    falls,
Hermes, taught to win without wounding,
Hermes, himself his own substitute,
Hermes, gold-mine of seat-mongers,
Hermes, darling and distress of gladiators' women,
Hermes, proud with battling spear,
Hermes, menacing with marine trident,
Hermes, formidable in drooping (?) helmet,
Hermes, glory of Mars universal,
Hermes, all things in one and thrice unique.[114]

The use of *ludia* (gladiator's woman or "moll") in line 10 anticipates Juvenal's deployment of the term (to Eppia in 6.104 and the would-be *gladiatrix* in 6.266), as does his use of *tridens* to refer to the *retiarius'* weapon (12), which Juvenal includes in his reprise of Gracchus (8.203).[115] For all its mock-seriousness, this poem does offer a glimpse into the "celebrity" status of the popular gladiator who lived to fight another day, and another after that. The repetition of the name evokes the shouting or chants of his admirers, as well as the repetitive nature of gladiatorial combat, even though this one stands out as a notable performer. Hermes is certainly versatile, fighting as a *veles*, *retiarius* and, perhaps, a *secutor* or *murmillo*, and we have here the embodiment of more than a dozen exempla in a single individual. He is also, however, *eruditus* and *doctus*, terms of praise that would befit a poet. As Howell notes, Hermes was a suitable name for gladiators, probably because of the god's association with speed, but there

---

114. Trans. Shackelton Bailey 1993.
115. In both cases, Colton 1991 says Mart. used the term first and was followed by Juv. (215–16; 345); Dunkle 2008, 44.

may also be an allusion to his role as *psychopompos*, conductor of souls to the Underworld.[116] Hermes is framed by the terms *Martia voluptas* and *gloria Martis*, encapsulating the two sides of the gladiator's appeal.

Juvenal's Arena of Satire

By the time we come to Juvenal, then, the arena is an established source of literary and especially satirical inspiration, and it is safe to assume that he draws upon a storehouse of motifs, vocabulary, expressions, combinations, juxtapositions and ideas to which his acknowledged predecessors in the genre, Lucilius and Horace, and his rough contemporary Martial also had access and had themselves contributed to.[117] Juvenalian satire goes further than any of them, I would argue, and creates its own arena, which is linked to the everyday arena of spectacle and gladiatorial combat through three principal themes:

1. Display and Punishment of the Body
2. Containment and Borders
3. Consumption and Excretion.

This kind of satire proceeds by highlighting anomalies, fissures, aporias, as it strives to reestablish the boundaries demanded by *genus* but ends up showing ever more clearly the pressures they are under. In its discourse of cutting and slicing, mauling and eating, Juvenalian satire magnifies and probes painful points of ideological instability in the Roman imperial body, in a manner whose closest analogy is the spectacle of violence in the amphitheater.[118]

Display and Punish

Jonathan Walters sees the Juvenalian text as a form of spectacle, to be linked with public executions of criminals in the arena.[119] We know that Nemesis was part of the mythical and ideological apparatus of such spectacles: the Magerius mosaic from Smirat in Tunisia of a *venatio* foregrounds the generosity of the

---

116. Howell 1995, 106; Dunkle 2008, 93–94, cf. 149–50 on *defixio*; Dio 73.19.4 on Comodus as *munerarius*, dressed as Mercury.

117. On the complexities of influence and borrowings, see, e.g., Hooley 1997, Freudenburg 2001.

118. Verbal abuse in gladiatorial combat, Ville 1981, 408.

119. 1998, 360–62. Reading a mosaic of gladiatorial combat Plass 1995 notes that power centers on the editor, who transfers power from himself (I kill) to the crowd (we kill) in a "moment of social solidarity" (137). The underpinnings of Fagan's (2011, chap. 5) "arena of prejudice" have many counterparts in the ideological matrix of Juvenal's satire.

editor, Magerius, but includes a winged female figure in hunting boots who could be Nemesis or Fortuna.[120] In fact, the declaiming of the satirist parallels *both* the displaying by the *editor* of his cast of participants (criminals, animals, combatants) *and* the fighting of the gladiator or *venator* against his opponents, for the satirist must always set up targets that he then tries to "punish" or "kill" with his rhetorical weaponry. As Richlin observes: "anger and indignation are misleading terms to use in connection with Juvenal; his attitude is actively hostile and threatening. His satire is not only a vehicle for the particularized listing of the things that make him angry but in itself constitutes a vengeance upon those things by holding them up to ridicule—embodied by the notebooks at the crossroads" (1.63–64).[121]

Just as the arena spectacle calls attention to its theatrical function and to the abilities of the *editor*, who has procured all of its constituent parts, so satire calls attention to its own poetic function and to the skill of the poet. For the *editor*, striking performers and novel combinations of victims show his ingenuity as well as his generosity.[122] Juvenal's rhetoric of exemplarity is very much part of this picture, as he jumps from scene to scene, bringing before our eyes a parade of miscreants and deviants, very often engaged in, or victims of, acts of graphic violence. Barton speaks of a "theater of surprise" at the arena and this is what Juvenal offers with his tumbling series of exempla in his arena of satire.[123] The narrative fluidity and apparent lack of organizational containment ensure that the reader experiences the thrill of the unexpected throughout the text. As Toner points out, excitement in the arena came especially from the way it was done: "The killing of the gladiator was unimportant in itself . . . the climax of the games became only really enjoyable as the fulfilment of a sufficiently long period of fore-pleasure" (42).[124]

Joseph Bentley argues that acts of corrective violence are only rationalized justifications of "the atavistic pleasure of inflicting pain," that is, manifestations of sadism.[125] He believes that satire uses fundamentally the same devices as

120. On Nemesis and the arena, see Hornum 1993; Plass 1995, 150; Kyle 1998, 9, 100; Dunkle 2008, 94–95. Magerius mosaic: long discussions in Futrell 2006, 49–51, and Fagan 2011, 128–32.

121. Richlin 1992, 195.

122. Coleman 2006 notes "the 'record-breaking' instinct" as an important motivation for *editores* (236).

123. Barton 1993, citing Plin. Eld. *HN* 36.24.117–20 on Curio's revolving amphitheater, whose danger only magnified the crowd's enthusiasm and pleasure (62); see also *HN* 15.117–20; Futrell 2006, 57–58; Dunkle 2008, 249–50.

124. Contra, Ville 1981, 320, 417, 423–24. Cf. Juv. 13.244–49, where the speaker tells Calvinus that he may have to wait a long time for the gods to get around to it, but eventually *poena gaudebis amara / nominis invisi*.

125. Bentley 1967, 389. That the Roman spectacles were sadistic seems self-evident; Wiedemann 1992 however argues that since pain was not inflicted randomly or enjoyed for its own sake in the arena it would be wrong to see it as sadistic (70). Satirists might well make similar claims, or not care what we think. Sen. *De Ira* 2.5.1–3 on cruelty and pleasure: *nec . . . verbera lacerationesque in ultionem petuntur sed in voluptatem.*

sadism: in both, the victim's humanity is effaced and reduced to mere body, a commodity. On the "formula of sadism," he says: "Preoccupation with vile flesh in all of its malodorous animality is thus the sadistic constant upon which an intricate structure of violence is based. Reduction to flesh is the rhetoric of sadism." Satire, he says, "employs the same rhetorical maneuver" but with a twist: "Wit, rather than moral purpose, is the primary difference between satiric and sadistic acts."[126] Satire punishes the wicked by putting them on display, in all their "inglorious animality" and by inflicting symbolic pain upon them. The spectacle of gladiators shedding blood provides a sensation of pleasure akin to that generated by the satirist's castigation of his scapegoats. "The victim of the satirist," Bentley writes, "is in a very real sense a scapegoat—the individual whose degradation is intended to have a purifying or cathartic result. . . . But then, having served society by purging it of its awareness of personal inadequacy, satire frequently performs a psychological double reverse by suddenly expanding its field of fire to include all of humanity and thus negates its socialized function."[127] This seems to apply particularly well to the Juvenalian— as opposed to the Horatian—variety of satire.

To approach the matter from a different angle, in the familiar formulation of Lacan, the aim of the sadist is *faire exister l'Autre*, to bring the Other into existence. The victim's pain proves that the Other exists in the real, beyond symbolic fiction, in the fullness of his or her being. The relationship to the unfathomable "object cause of desire" is thereby structured through the enumeration of "objectionable" features and through fantasies about the Other's strange powers in the political, sexual, economic and social realms. Bentley notes that "laughter clearly distinguishes satire from sadism" but adds that laughter depends upon superiority and "is frequently a manifestation of the will to power."[128] This creates the illusion of superiority in the audience, or the spectators, obscuring the more complex coexistence of feelings of both repulsion and attraction, which is the inevitable result of the encounter with the despised Other.[129] So, for instance, *Satire* 3 re-creates the city as arena, with the reader as spectator and the narrator, Umbricius, as both spectator and victim. In the street, he is physically abused on all sides:

126. Bentley 1967, 394, 402. "Since the satirist reduces the victim by excluding mind [all uniquely human attributes], and since the sadistic manipulation follows the same formula, we must conclude that, on the unrationalized level, both in action and in method, satire is sadistic" (404). See S. I. Stein 2000.

127. Bentley 1967, 403.

128. Ibid., 399–401.

129. See Stallybrass and White 1986 on displaced abjection ("the process whereby 'low' social groups turn their figurative and actual power, not against those in authority, but against those who are even 'lower,'" 53); also Newlands 2002, 244; Gowers 2012 on such elements in Hor. *Sat.* 1.6.81–82 (106).

. . . ferit hic cubito, ferit assere duro
alter, at hic tignum capiti incutit, ille metretram.
Pinguia crura luto, planta mox undique magna
calcor, et in digito clavus mihi militis haeret.

. . . one hits me with his elbow, another hits me with a hard pole,
and this one bashes my head with a beam, that one with a wine barrel.
My legs are caked with mud; soon, I'm trampled by huge feet
on all sides, and a soldier's hobnail sticks into my toe. (245–48)

Similar scenes appear in the fragmentary *Satire* 16, where much is made of the
soldier's boots (*Bardaicus iudex datur haec punire volenti / calceus,* 12–13; *tot ca-
ligas, tot / milia clavorum,* 24–25) and the physical violence visited upon the ordinary citizen—teeth knocked out, a bruised face, one eye missing and the
other in an uncertain condition (9–12). Described as "cruel" or "savage," with
its fires and multiple dangers (*incendia, lapsus/tectorum adsiduos ac mille peri-
cula saevae Urbis,* 3.7–9), street thugs and robbers, the city is for Umbricius a
place of sudden, often violent, death, where *grassatores* (gangsters) rush from
their lairs in the marshes into the city, as if into their "game-reserves" (*vivaria*):
sic inde huc omnes tamquam ad vivaria currunt (308).[130]

The city is also awash with foreign elements, and the crux of Umbricius's
desire to escape Rome is summarized in the words *non possum ferre, Quirites/
Graecam urbem,* he cannot stomach a Greek Rome (60–61).[131] The sardonic
view of city life motivates the echoes in Umbricius's speech of the fall of Troy
described in the second book of Vergil's epic.[132] For the Roman in Rome, we
should read the Trojan in Troy, during and after the sacking by the Greeks.
In 119, Umbricius says there is no place for the Roman in Rome: *non est
Romano cuiquam locus hic.* The numerous Greek words scattered throughout this section collectively suggest that Rome has been captured by the enemy. Umbricius duly enumerates the skills of the annoying Greeks who have
flooded into Rome: they are excellent at flattery (3.86–93), unsurpassed at
acting (93–100), imitators of any behavior or emotion (100–103), and hence
highly dangerous—they infiltrate households to seduce or rape members of
their patron's family and to betray and ultimately kill the patron himself,

130. Cf. 4.51 and p. 217, herein, on the whole world as Domitian's *vivarium.* Ferguson 1979: "'like foxes
into a chicken run.' Umbricius and his like are the victims." Also Dunkle 2008, 85–86.

131. In Lucilius 26.636–37, there is reference to avoiding Rome during the *munus* of the Metelli (*rediisse
ac repedasse, ut Romam vitet, gladiatoribus,* 636).

132. E.g., Lelièvre 1972; Estevez 1996 on the dynamic between Umbricius and Aeneas as the last
Roman and the first.

202 THE ARENA OF SATIRE

witness the case of a professor of Stoic philosophy from Tarsus, P. Egnatius Celer, who informed on his patron and pupil Barea Soranus under Nero (109–18).[133] In confronting such characters, Umbricius remarks *non sumus ergo pares*, adopting the language of gladiatorial match-ups (104). It is as if the criminals in the arena are not killed as they should be, but break out and kill Romans themselves.[134]

The distancing of all such figures of Otherness—women, Greeks, east-erners, "effeminate" males, nouveaux riches, aristocratic "slummers"—is, how-ever, undermined by the fascination they clearly exert for the narrator, the *editor* and the *spectator*, all of whom risk becoming a spectacle themselves. It is the fulminating and "cutting" narrator himself who too often holds our gaze—hence no doubt one reason for the popularity of the "persona theory" among critics. One is reminded of Horace's observation in *Epistle* 2.1.194–98 that their stupefied gazing at strange animals already made the Roman people themselves much more of a spectacle in his own day:

> si foret in terris, rideret Democritus, seu
> diversum confusa genus panthera camelo
> sive elephans albus volgi converteret ora;
> spectaret populum ludis attentius ipsis
> ut sibi praebentem nimio spectacula plura.

> If he were still on earth, Democritus would laugh, whether
> it were some hybrid form—a panther confused with a camel—
> or a white elephant which drew the eyes of the mob,
> he would gaze more intently at the people than the performances
>   themselves,
> as offering him greater spectacles by far.

We see here the quintessentially Juvenalian theme of confusion and hybridity (*diversum confusa genus*), which leads us seamlessly into the crowd itself.[135] As Paul Plass puts it: "If the amphitheater was, sociologically, a great public eye, the arena was its object, further kept in focus if awnings shading the seats could

---

133. A backward reference to the Stoics of *Sat.* 2; Juv. may be adapting details to his purpose, as Celer is more likely to have been a mere witness rather than the actual *delator* (on details, see Courtney 1980 and Braund 1996a, *ad loc.*).

134. Cf. the endings of *Satires* 6 and 15: both conclude with a shattering of the illusion of a comforting distance between the Roman and the poisonous/violent Other.

135. The first giraffe was exhibited in Rome by Caesar in 46 B.C.E. Cf. Plin. Eld. *HN* 8.69; in 55, Pompey brought lynx and rhinoceroses (8.70–71) and, in 58, M. Aemilius Scaurus crocodiles and a hippopotamus (Coleman 1996, 61–62); *RE* s.v. Aemilius (Klebs). On this passage and the proliferation of monsters, Barton 1993, 85–91.

be adjusted to spotlight the sun at the center. Rolling the protection back then meant flooding the game into the stands by making the public itself both target of violence and center of action" (76). Barton sets the fascination of Romans and authors like Juvenal within the context of those who lived in a world wherein "everything outside the arena was a loathsome and bitter burlesque" and sees it as "not simply a matter of an idiosyncratic inclination to sadomasochism but a response to an intense and excruciating feeling of humiliation and an attempt to find compensation, even exaltation, within this feeling of inescapable degradation" (46). In this setting, we might view Umbricius's action as a *devotio* entirely appropriate to, and motivated by, the daily battle of living in the imperial city.[136]

Leaky Containers

Colosseum entertainments are displays of literal and symbolic containment: the sunken arena floor, with labyrinthine passages and cells underneath, and the sand soaking up the blood and other fluids;[137] the enclosure of exotic wildlife and the neutralization of dangerous animals and humans; the mock naval battles in which the arena was flooded with water that must have intensified the effect.[138] The outpouring of blood in the Colosseum is paralleled by ideological hailings of spectators, that promise to contain their anxieties and desires—which were being literally "shouted out"—by tying them into *Romanitas* or *Virtus* or *the* subject, the Emperor. This alluring promise to suture the tears that rend the subject relies heavily on intimidation, not only of the representatives of Otherness, but also of the spectators themselves. Borders require policing. In the arena, degradation of the criminal and, more broadly, of the non-Roman Other, was a necessary element in the (at least temporary) restoration of order and proper hierarchy, and the triumph over the destructive forces of barbarism, which the spectacles displayed.[139] Contemporary anxieties are contained within the imposing and comforting circles of Roman History and Destiny. Exotic animals and types of gladiators—Samnite,

---

136. On *devotio*, Versnel 1976; Barton 1993, 40–46; Livy 5.41.3; 8.9.4–12; 10.28.12–18. See also Plass 1995 on how their connections with *devotio* and suicide make gladiators into sacrificial figures (226–27); Dunkle 2008, 20, 184 (on deaths of gladiators satisfying Nemesis in exchange for survival of citizens in battle); Suet. *Cal.* 14.2 tells how people vowed to fight in the arena if Caligula recovered from a bout of illness.

137. Coleman 2006 on *hypogeum* (lxviii–lxx); Mart. *Spect.* 13.1, *sanguinea . . . harena.*

138. Mart. *Spect.* 27–30, 34; Coleman 1993; Kyle 1998, 51; Dunkle 2008,192–201; Cariou 2009.

139. Edmondson 1996, 82, speaks of criminals and animals as "physical specimens of disorder." Cf. Calp. Sic. *deformis scapulis torus eminet* (7.61, of bulls); *silvestria . . . monstra* (64); *deforme pecus* (67, of hippos).

Thracian, Essedarius—recall the successful campaigns of military expansion, and the extension of governmental organization, while famous victories from the past could be recalled in reenactments of battles on land and sea.[140]

The Colosseum is not only a giant eye, a *camera obscura* or *panopticon*, through which can be viewed both the *Urbs* and the *Orbis Romana*;[141] it is also the giant mouth, down which the produce of the Empire is consumed and through which are shouted the fears and desires of the Roman subject. In yet another sense, the Colosseum is the *anus mundi Romani*, out of which are excreted the remnants of the consumed others upon which Rome depends for its survival and sense of self.[142] A body in stone and masonry, it swells with spectators and victims who are consumed as the cycle of life and death is enacted in a single day and place. The entertainment offered by the satirist—verbal wit, parody, allegory, humorous vignettes, the delight of the unexpected—is an analogous attempt to contain the chaos of contemporary existence, to reestablish fading borderlines, to stop change by an appeal to the past. It can also be seen as an effort to contain (in rhetoric, meter, and poetic form) the violence and rage that accompanies these urges to satisfy the demands of *genus*.[143] The satirist tries to intimidate both the objects of his derision and his audience, relying on his *saeva indignatio* and "fiery" anger, which have their parallels in the two favorite methods of execution in the arena, being thrown to the beasts or the flames.

In each arena, of course, the circle of containment is constantly breached. As we have seen, a floating and divided subjectivity was part of the arena experience, where all ranks of spectators (and participants) were engaged in a complex dynamic of mutual self-definition. The constant tension between centripetal and centrifugal movement discussed in chapter 2 is assimilated to the arena as the most striking instance of the porosity that affects the city as a whole. In Juvenal's cityscape, the arena constantly breaks out into the streets and spaces of Rome and sucks the rest of the city into its all-consuming vortex.[144] So, for example, in *Satire* 16, when the speaker complains about the special privileges of the military when it comes to court cases, we read:

> . . . sed tum quoque mille ferenda
> taedia, mille morae; totiens subsellia tantum

---

140. Suet. *Claud.* 21.6; Dio 51.22.6; Edmondson 1996, 72 and n72.
141. Barton 1993, 91–98; Plass 1995, 76; Gunderson 1996, 115–16.
142. See below and n181 on sewers under the arena.
143. On the problem of anger, see e.g. Sen. *De Ira* and W. S. Anderson 1964; Harris 2001.
144. Cf. Plass 1995, 75–77; this happens frequently in Tac.'s account of Nero, see pp. 184–85 herein.

sternuntur, iam facundo ponente lacernas
Caedicio et Fusco iam micturiente parati
digredimur, lentaque fori pugnamus harena.
Ast illis quos arma tegunt et balteus ambit
quod placitum est ipsis praestatur tempus agendi . . .

. . . but then a thousand frustrations and a thousand delays
have to be endured; often the benches are just being set out
and now eloquent Caedicius is taking off his cloak
and now Fuscus is having a piss, and, although ready,
we disperse, and we fight in the sticky sand of the forum.
But those whom weapons protect and the sword-belt girds
have the times of cases set to suit them . . . (43–49)

The forum has become the arena, echoing Lucilius's comment on the verbal
and other interactions of the forum—among plebeians and senators alike—in
terms of fighting:

uni se atque eidem studio omnes dedere et arti:
verba dare ut caute possint, pugnare dolose,
blanditia certare, bonum simulare virum se,
insidias facere ut si hostes sint omnibus omnes.

All give themselves over to one and the same interest and artifices:
namely to be able to swindle with impunity, to fight cunningly,
to strive, using soft words as weapons, to act the "fine fellow,"
to lie in wait, as if all of them were enemies of all men. (1148–51W)[145]

Satire, as we have already seen, is awash with signs of bodily *lack* of
containment—deformities and hybrids, shouting and noise, and especially
fluids: blood, semen, vomit, faeces, and urine. These are all emblematic of
the linguistic "spilling out" that overflows satiric discourse: the piling up of
exempla, rhetorical exaggeration, constant allusiveness, metaphorical expansion, changing personae, and narrative fluidity. Here and there, *tunc et nunc*,
metamorphose into each other, as the boundaries of time and space give way
under the flood of images and exempla, each following rapidly and relentlessly
upon the other, much in the manner of arena spectacles.

---

145. Trans. Warmington 1979. *Balteus* is also used of a gladiator's belt and the safety-barrier in the
arena (see above). Cf. Sen. Eld. *Controv.* 3 Praef. 13: *scholam quasi ludum esse, forum arenam*. On urinating and
the arena, cf. Juv. 3.29–40 (Artorius and Catulus); 6.264 (*gladiatrix* on her potty).

Floating Subjects

Atop all of this floats the subject, whose identity is impossible to pin down. We seek in vain for a clear view of Juvenal or "the satirist" among the crowd. He is constantly moving around, reflected only fleetingly in the faces of his targets. As Paulson observes (28), Juvenal keeps himself rigorously separate from what he portrays: "He purposely reduces the character of his persona to an abstractness far beyond Horace's: he is merely a bundle of old Roman virtues." Wit and epigram, after all, however much they attest to an individual author's brilliance (*sententiae* are pinned to it), ultimately make him more elusive, not less, for they are devices of evasion. While the Juvenalian satirist makes a lot of noise about his targets and the reasons for writing satire, he remains strangely silent about himself and his own position. Like the flâneur, he is a continually shifting presence. There is considerable fluctuation in speakers and the addressees. In the opening of *Satire* 2, for example, the first verb is impersonal (*libet*), and while there are several in the second and third persons (*audent, siumulant, vivunt, invenias*, etc.), it is not until the sixteenth line that we get a first-person statement (*hunc ego fatis / inputo*). In the remainder of the poem, this practice continues, and first-person statements come only from the mouths of characters within the narrative, most notably in the speech of Laronia. Another impersonal form (*liceat*) appears in 135, and the first-person plural is used by the narrator only at the end: *illic heu miseri traducimur . . . promovimus . . . vicimus* (159–63). This effacement of the first person marks a definite change from the programmatic *Satire* 1, in which such forms are frequent, and establishes a pattern that is then sustained through the rest of the corpus. The satirist does not speak from a stable position, and the reader too is constantly seeking a place to occupy, a place defined by reference to both the satirist and the satirized. The members of Juvenal's audience as they follow the satirist about the cityscape attempt themselves to constitute, in the Hegelian sense, both the speaker and the author.

In trying to stabilize the satiric "I," many critics have had recourse to the device of the persona, but even the persona remains intractably difficult to fix, as it is presumed to change—from angry to ironic, for example—as the corpus unfolds. Martin Winkler shows that the persona was a traditional element in Roman satire, which becomes more complicated in Juvenal: his great achievement, he says, matched only by Swift, is to produce a persona who "is not entirely wrong in his attacks, but is open to the same attacks as he unleashes on *his* victims."[146]

---

146. Winkler 1983, 223; cf. 225; on the tradition of the persona, see 59–89; see also Kernan 1959, 64–80; Roche 2012 on self-representation and performativity.

Rose Zimbardo would argue that the notion of a central, unified persona is an attempt to construct unity and coherence where in fact very little is to be found.[147] Ralph Rosen reminds us that persona is a metaphor appropriated from the theater that breaks down at one crucial point: "We are not watching real actors on a stage when we read or listen to one of Juvenal's satires, so when the poet speaks in the first person, there are no physical cues (in the form of a costumed actor, for example) to indicate that we are supposed to conceptualize the poet's 'I' as such."[148] Here we shall not take up this well-worn topic, but bring into brief consideration the figure sometimes thought to lie behind the persona, namely the Etruscan figure Phersu. This masked man who appears on tomb paintings seems to have played different roles at funeral performances and other games, perhaps including that of executioner.[149] Scholars have speculated on whether Phersu was a death demon or god of the Under-world, but the current consensus is that he was, as J. H. Croon says, "a sort of manager of funeral performances" whose mask "must be representative of the spirits of the dead and a reenactment of their appearance."[150] In one painting, Phersu holds a rope that is tied around the legs and arms of another man with a sack over his head and armed with a cudgel; he is also being attacked by a dog, possibly one held on a leash by Phersu. This encounter could presumably end either with the man with the cudgel battering the dog or with the dog tearing him to pieces. The scene could represent a combat between Phersu and the hooded man or a combat between the hooded man and the dog, with Phersu controlling the latter like a puppeteer.[151]

It would seem, from the way the encounter is set up, that the man with the cudgel has few chances to escape his fate (he has already been bitten by the animal) and that, as Jean Paul Thuillier concludes, the principal role of Phersu was as executioner, regulating details of the spectacle according to his own, or the onlookers', wishes. It was effectively in his power to manipulate the

147. Zimbardo 1998, 18–19; cf. chap. 3 "No 'I' and No 'Eye.'"
148. Rosen 2007, 219–22.
149. See e.g., Steingräber 1986, 120; Szemerényi 1975, 309: Phersu appears as a hangman on the Tomb of the Augurs and the Tomb of the Olympic Games, as a racer on the Tomb of the Augurs (left-hand side) and as a dancer on the Tomb of the Pulcinella. Heurgon 1964 interprets the "racer" as Phersu running away from his opponent, and sees him standing at the end of a chariot-race track on the Tomb of the Olympic Games (213). Kyle 1998 notes that it is uncertain whether the "game of Phersu" was execution, sacrifice, contest or performance and that "at best" was a precursor to *venationes* (44 and nn.).
150. Croon 1955, 16. Szemerényi 1975 thinks he is not a death-demon, "although as a hangman he comes close" (310). J. Elliott 1995 speculates on whether the dog is a wolf-like creature from the Underworld.
151. Detailed descriptions in Heurgon 1964, 210–15; Thuillier 1985, 586–93; Maxwell 1996 connects him with mime (275–76; cf. the Laureolus mime mentioned in Juv. 8.187–9), cf. Mart. *Spect.* 7. The painting is on the right-hand side of the Tomb of the Augurs, and there is a similar one on the Tomb of the Olympic Games.

Munera nunc edunt et, verso pollice vulgus / cum iubet, occidunt populariter (Juv. 3.36–7).
Phersu and victim. Corneto, Tarquinia, Auguri Tomb, ca. 1900. Moscioni Collection
(Mos.Corneto.TAugT24132). Courtesy of the American Academy in Rome, Photographic
Archive.

combat so as to give the condemned man more or fewer chances.[152] Jacques
Heurgon describes the victim as a "ludicrous Hercules" locked in some sort of
mythological reenactment. In his interpretation, Phersu is a "nonchalant organizer of tortures" who sometimes has to take to his heels. The scene encapsulates the primal connection between the nervous release of laughter and
the dread of death as well as the role of "frighteners"—such as Manducus—
in early Roman rituals. Heurgon describes the frighteners' role as follows:

> The popular spectacles of early Rome in which Etruscan influence
> was not unknown were full of hallucinating and grotesquely
> scarifying creatures, *formidines*, ogres and bogies, worthy imps, not
> of Satan, but of someone almost as bad, Phersu, and brought out to
> affright and delight children of all ages. At the end of the procession
> which annually paraded around the Circus Maximus on the occasion
> of the ludi maximi, the crowd awaited the entrance of laughable and
> terrifying figures . . . but the one they applauded most was
> Manducus (from *mandere*, "to chew") who would open up his
> terrifying chops, making a sound of horribly grinding teeth.[153]

Although the etymological data is sketchy and the matter is by no means
settled, some scholars believe that the Latin word *persona*, whose primary
meaning is mask, was derived from, or at least cognate with, the Etruscan

---

152. Thuillier 1985, 589.
153. Heurgon 1964, 214; cf. Varro *LL* 7.95; Plaut. *Rud.* 535–36: *ad ludos me pro manduco locem . . . quia pol clare crepito dentibus.*

phersu.[154] Croon says *phersu* does not mean "mask" but "wearer of mask" or "masked person in funeral performance" and connects him, through Perseus, to the Gorgon's head.[155]

This has some intriguing connections with a detail in *Satire* 3 that has long proved perplexing: when Umbricius is describing the theatrical performances in rural Italy, which are marked by what he regards as an admirable uniformity of simple dress (3.171–79), he lingers for a moment on the scaring of the *rusticus infans* by one of the performers' masks:

> . . . cum personae pallentis hiatum
> in gremio matris formidat rusticus infans

> . . . when the rustic baby shrinks back in his mother's lap
> in terror at the gaping hole of the white mask (175–76)

Courtney, for instance, notes that this is a "picturesque detail not required by the train of thought," and Braund offers parallels for the reaction along with the suggestion that Manducus, a stock figure in Atellan farce, might be meant.[156] The scene could also recall the memorable moment in the *Iliad* when young Astyanax, held in his mother's arms, is frightened by the nodding crest on the helmet of his father, Hector. Both these scenes in a way depend upon the notion of an ideal unity for their effect: the tightly bonded trio of mother, father, and son in Troy is echoed by the baby in his mother's lap and the unity that exists among the populace in their white tunics, and between the people and the countryside. At the same time, the presence of death is emphasized: Hector is going off to battle and will not see his family again; in much of Italy, we are told, "no one wears the toga unless he is dead." Umbricius, of course, is heading off to Cumae, and the Gorgons were said to dwell near the entrance to the Underworld.[157]

---

154. Maxwell 1996, 269 and n12. According to this theory, *Phersu, Persephone, Perseus* and *persona* are all related. See Rheinfelder 1928, Altheim 1929. Szemerényi 1975, by contrast, concludes that "Latin *persona* has nothing to do with Etruscan *phersu*" (312). See also Rix 1995, 75; Watmough 1997, 66–67; Wallace 2008, 129–30. Thuillier 2013 sees the Phersu-persona link but says "some would wrongly see in this the prefiguring of the Roman gladiatorial combats that seem to find their source not in Etruria but actually in Campania/Lucania, as shown in many tomb paintings of Paestum" and cites Pontrandolfo and Rouveret 1992 (835). Cf. Kyle 1998, 45–46.

155. Croon 1955, 16. He believes Perseus is the bearer or the wearer of the mask of the Underworld demon, of which Phersu is another manifestation. See also Vernant 1991, 121–22. On Perseus as gladiator's name, Dunkle 2008, 125; cf. Mart. *Spect.* 17.

156. Courtney 1980, 179; Braund 1996a citing Sen. *De Ira* 2.11.12: anger is *deformis*, and thus not to be feared, although it is in practice just like the *deformis persona ab infantibus* (204).

157. Juvenal's only mention of the Gorgons also occurs in *Satire* 3, in a glancing reference to how the Stoic professor P. Egnatius Celer killed his pupil Barea by informing on him: *Stoicus occidit Baream delator*

The scene of performance that Umbricius delineates here perhaps contains some metapoetic comments on the nature of the art of the satirist: rooted in Roman tradition and landscape, and deriving from festival celebrations, it is designed to fascinate and frighten as well as to entertain. In Fritz Graf's succinct formulation: "satire is about blame and about masks."[158] Richlin contends that Juvenal "makes the mask of Priapus his own persona" and that his stance is "part of the perception of the world as divided into strong and less strong, dominator and dominated, the domination being motivated by a fear of being dominated."[159] In Phersu's manipulation of torture as entertainment in public space, then, we can discern some basic components not only of Roman spectacles of combat and execution, which culminated in the elaborately managed shows in the arena, but also of the quintessentially Roman form of satire, in which the satirist puts his victims on display and then punishes them in his text.[160] In Juvenal's *Satires*, we find precisely "la bouffonnerie mais aussi la cruauté," to quote Thuillier's words on Phersu,[161] in a spectacle of laughter and punishment that includes the satirist himself. Rather than worry excessively about distinguishing the putative persona(e) in the text, we should rather acknowledge in Juvenal's satirist the significance of a probable remnant of this masked organizer of tortures.[162]

Consumer Reports

We noted above that displaying the Other creates the illusion of superiority in the audience or spectators. Consuming with the eyes is not unrelated to other

---

amicum / discipulumque senex ripa nutritus in illa / ad quam Gorgonei delapsa est pinna caballi (116–18). The very next line is non est Romano cuiquam locus hic (There is no place for any Roman here, 119).

158. Graf 2005, opening a survey of satire in a ritual context, covering curses, abuse, and lampoons, a society in which public shaming was long used as a means of social control, out of which Lucilius invented satire as a literary genre (192).

159. Richlin 1992, 195–97.

160. Etruscan links have been mooted before: Heurgon 1964 argues that "through all later manifestations of the Italian comic spirit there runs a tenuous but solid thread linking them with Phersu" (214). See also Szilágy 1981 on how Livy's impletae modis saturae links satyric dances in Etruscan vase-painting with the later tradition of Roman satire; Maxwell 1996 on the Etruscan connections with mime and with their violent arena versions, such as the crucifixion of Laureolus (mentioned in Mart. Spect. 7 and Juv. 8.187–89). See also Habinek 2005a on satire as ludus and Graf 2005 on the ritual contexts of satire.

161. Cèbe 1966, 29–30; Thuillier 1985, 587; Plass 1995, 57–58.

162. Habinek 2005a cites a Pyrrhic dancer and figure parodying him (cf. Szilágy 1981, Wiseman 1988): "This image perfectly encapsulates the complex relationship between reality and imitation, elite and professional, ridicule and respect that is at the heart of the Roman concept of play, and, we might suggest by extension, of satire as well. . . . Indeed, far from diminishing its object, this kind of playful imitation calls attention to and enhances its object's importance" (189). See Bentley 1967 on satire and sadism.

types of consumption—of food and other "produce" of the Empire. Gladiators were frequently depicted on cups, lamps, and other articles of consumption.[163] In Petronius' *Satyricon* 52, Trimalchio proudly boasts "*Nam Hermerotis pugnas et Petraitis in poculis habeo, omnia ponderosa; meum enim intelligere nulla pecunia vendo*" ("And I have got the fights between Hermeros and Petraites on my cups, and every cup is a heavy one; for I do not sell my connoisseurship for any money"). The link between food and imperial ideology is, of course, an especially close one, encapsulated in Juvenal's "bread and circuses" aphorism. Empires are engines of production and consumption—whatever the rhetoric of beneficence that seeks to justify them to those who have been forcibly incorporated—and the spectators in their "home" arenas must always be well fed, literally and metaphorically.[164] The British empire brought low-priced food to England for decades, and it was the disappearance of cheap comestibles from the "Commonwealth" in the 1960s that brought home to the population at large the fact that the empire was finally gone. The Soviet empire collapsed at least partly because of its inability to put food on the tables of Russians in Moscow, symbolized by long lines outside half-empty shops. The new empire of American consumer capitalism is everywhere marked by food and its effects—widespread obesity, obsessive dieting, "bulking up" of muscle with protein-laden regimens and supplements, the proliferation of novelty restaurants and innovative cuisines, all against the background of millions undernourished or starving. In *The Loaded Table*, Emily Gowers demonstrates how the human body is the meeting place between individual consumption, the Roman state, and the literary text. The state is an engorged body and the iconography of the banquet is a miniature version of larger celebrations like the Triumph. That this can be extended to the arena seems self-evident: the procession of courses and the gourmandizing search for the exotic dish have clear analogues in the elaborate menu of fights and innovative displays of cruelty that we find in the Colosseum.[165] The connoisseurs of the refinements of violence and cruelty are like connoisseurs of fine food.[166] There are also cannibalistic implications. As Barton notes, "the uninhibited gaze did more than violate, it cannibalized," citing Tacitus's description of Vitellius "having feasted

163. E.g., Gladiator cup found at Montagnole, southern France, in the Metropolitan Museum of Art (81.10.245); Köhne and Ewigleben 2000 for numerous lamps, flasks, and other containers; Hopkins and Beard 2005 for baby's bottle from Pompeii (80). Cf. Coleman 2006 on Mart. *Spect.* 31.6: *lances* and awards to gladiators (229–32).

164. On the amphitheatre as a paradigm of empire, see Newlands 2002, 244–45. On arena and eating, see Kyle 1998, chap. 6.

165. See above intro., pp. 70–71, on Sen. Eld. *Controv.* 4, Praef.; Barton 1993, 53 and n28.

166. On spectators as connoisseurs, see Fagan 2011, 215–19.

his eyes" (se . . . pavisse oculos) on the sight of his dead enemies. The cannibalistic aspects of the arena—metaphorically speaking, at least—hardly need
elaboration.[167]

In this connection, the dinner of Trimalchio in Petronius's Satyricon offers an example of the complex interweaving of food and violence, gladiators
and death. In this colorful performance, food and eating—as things that are
necessary for life, but also as reminders of mortality and associated with decay
and waste—are closely intertwined with arena spectacles.[168] As Charles Saylor
points out, the association is not made explicitly but "through scattered epiph-
anies" much as we find in Juvenal. For instance, when the huge fish dish (which
has four figures of Marsyas at its corners) is served, Trimalchio summons Carpus: processit statim scissor et ad symphoniam gesticulans ita laceravit obsoniam,
ut putares essedarium hydraule cantante pugnare (At once the carver came forward and, gesticulating in time with the music, cut up the meat in such a way
that you would have thought he was a chariot-fighter battling to the music of a
water-organist, 36).[169] The arrival of the boar is depicted in terms of an elaborate and spectacular venatio in an arena:

> . . . donec advenerunt ministri ac toralia praeposuerunt toris, in
> quibus retia erant picta subsessoresque cum venabulis et totus
> venationis apparatus, Necdum sciebamus, quo mitteremus
> suspiciones nostras, cum extra triclinium clamor sublatus est
> ingens, et ecce canes Laconici etiam circa mensam discurrere
> coeperunt. Secutum est hos repositorium, in quo positus erat
> primae magnitudinis aper, et quidem pilleatus, e cuius dentibus
> sportellae dependebant duae palmulis textae, altera caryotis altera
> thebaicis repleta. Circa autem minores porcelli ex coptoplacentis
> facti, quasi uberibus imminerent, scrofam esse positam
> significabant. Et hi quidem apophoreti fuerunt. Ceterum ad

167. Barton 2002, 225; Tac. Hist.3.39; on the Roman gaze, see Bartsch 2006, chap. 3 "Scopic Paradigms
at Rome," esp. 15–52; cf. Kyle 1998, in literal terms on "indirect cannibalism" via distribution of meat of arena
animals, albeit probably for political purposes, to the populace (184, 190–94). Ausonius Ecl. 23.37, admittedly
a late source, is the only one to make the closest thing to an explicit reference, when he says that gladiatorial
shows honored Saturn (falcigerum placant sanguine Caeligenam).

168. Ably cataloged by Saylor 1987: e.g., the serving of the boar as venatio (Petr. 40–41), sawdust on the
floor (Petr. 34), echoes of the prolusio and pompa throughout, and the "agonistic quality" of the diners and
their devotion to the arena (597). Griffin 1994: "Violent acts, threatened or performed, recur with such frequency . . . that any diner might well sit nervously on the edge of his couch" (195).

169. On the scissor, see Fagan 2011, 217–19; for the possibility that he "sliced" through the retiarius's net,
see Robert 1940, 235–36 (no. 299). Juv. 11.136–41, notes that he will not be using the services of a structor revered by a whole school of carvers.

scindendum aprum non ille Carpus accessit, qui altilia laceraverat, sed
barbatus ingens, fasciis cruralibus alligatus et alicula subornatus
polymita, strictoque venatorio cultro latus apri vehementer percussit,
ex cuius plaga turdi evolaverunt. Parati aucupes cum harundinibus
fuerunt et eos circa triclinium volitantes momento exceperunt. Inde
cum suum cuique iussisset referri Trimalchio, adiecit: "Etiam videte,
quam porcus ille silvaticus lotam comederit glandem." Statim pueri
ad sportellas accesserunt, quae pendebant e dentibus, thebaicasque
et caryotas ad numerum divisere cenantibus.

. . . until the servants came and spread over the couches coverlets
painted with nets, and men lying in wait with hunting spears, and
all the instruments of the chase. We were still wondering where to
turn our expectations, when a great shout was raised outside the
dining-room, and in came some Spartan hounds too, and began
running round the table. A tray was brought in after them with a
wild boar of the largest size upon it, wearing a cap of freedom, with
two little baskets woven of palm-twigs hanging from his tusks, one
full of dry dates and the other of fresh. Round it lay sucking-pigs
made of simnel cake with their mouths to the teats, thereby showing
that we had a sow before us. These sucking-pigs were for the guests
to take away. Carver, who had mangled the fowls, did not come to
divide the boar, but a big bearded man with bands wound round his
legs, and a spangled hunting-coat of damasked silk, who drew a
hunting-knife and plunged it hard into the boar's side. A number of
thrushes flew out at the blow. As they fluttered round the dining-room
there were fowlers ready with limed twigs who caught them in a
moment. Trimalchio ordered everybody to be given his own portion,
and added: "Now you see what fine acorns the woodland boar has been
eating." Then boys came and took the baskets which hung from her
jaws and distributed fresh and dry dates to the guests. (49)[170]

The diners are captive and captivated spectators, while the relationship between
the satirical *auctor* and the reader is framed in terms of the gladiatorial *editor*
who "feeds" his spectators.[171] There is an unsettling sense of unpredictability
and danger running thoughout the narrative. Saylor speaks of a "thin line for

170. Text and trans. Heseltine 1913.
171. Paulson 1967: "The satiric image lacks the complete abstraction of the comic: a certain disgust, a
certain physical involvement of the reader is always necessary. . . . The balance is a delicate one between contemplation and arousal" (16).

the freedmen of the dinner between watching a combat and being in one" and sees *munus* and *cena* as basically interchangeable.[172] We know that fighters were fed lavishly the night before they met their fate on the sand of the arena, and Saylor sees this *libera cena* as a recurring motif in Trimalchio's dinner.[173] Trimalchio himself is a grotesquely reduced version of the Aeneas who gives funeral games for Anchises in *Aeneid* 5, declaring that on his tomb the fights of the gladiator Petraites will be depicted: *Valde te rogo, ut secundum pedes statuae meae catellam ponas et coronas et unguenta et Petraitis omnes pugnas, ut mihi contingat tuo beneficio post mortem vivere* (I beg you earnestly to put up round the feet of my statue my little dog, and some wreaths, and bottles of perfume, and all the fights of Petraites, so that your kindness may bring me a life after death, 71.6).[174] The diners' opportunity for escape from Trimalchio's symposiastic arena comes by means of a (false) fire alarm, caused by trumpeters playing loud music for the host's imaginary funeral (78).

If the sacrifice of blood in the arena was indeed a mechanism for staving off death, the audience of Juvenal's satires may also be viewed as a body seeking to stay alive through the nourishment provided by the poet as *auctor*.[175] This nourishment, however, is the symbolic death of those individuals and groups the satirist, as *editor*, has marked for slaughter. When, he asks, was the supply of vices richer? (1.86–87). This miscellany of noxious exempla constitutes the "stew" (*farrago*) that sustains Juvenal's book.[176] The fodder is not in the least meant to be appetizing. In *Satire* 5.120, there is mention of the fish fattened from the flowing sewers of the Subura, the place mentioned by the satirist-narrator at the very beginning of *Satire* 3 as to be fled from (5). With its shops, eating places, and brothels, it was busy and noisy; Gowers styles it the "stomach of Rome," and the satirist finds plenty of ingredients there to lay before his readers.[177] If, as Gowers contends, the kind of food prominent in satire blurs the distinctions between the edible and inedible, between food and rotten or excremental substances, we have some indication as to why satirical discourse is so permeated by images of vomiting, urinating, and

---

172. Saylor 1987, citing Petr. 45. See Plass 1995, 199 and 220n22 on sympotic and arena space (598).

173. On this, see Plut. *Mor.* 1099B and Dunkle 2008, 223–24; cf. Plass 1995, 52; Kyle 1998, 82. Saylor 1987, referring primarily to Trimalchio's contemplation of his own death in 70–71 and note the phrase used in the opening sentence in 26.7 (598–99).

174. "Where we find in epic that games function as art to refine and render death remote (as in the Troy Town exercise), there is no such refinement in the Cena. . . . For game, which is already a model of human action, is made by Trimalchio into a second model, into food and serving of food" (602).

175. Cf. the distribution of gifts (*munscula*) and tokens (*missilia*) to spectators; Dio (66.25.5) mentions cashing in tokens for comestibles or livestock. Coleman 1996, 55–56; Kyle 1998, 191–92; Dunkle 2008, 145–46.

176. Edwards 1993 speaks of the satirist's "insatiable appetite" for vice (204).

177. Gowers 1995 on the Cloaca Maxima and the metaphorical use of sewers as the excretory channels of the body of Rome.

defecating.[178] Martial 12.48 describes the swift passage from a "fine meal" to something "for a luckless sponge on a doomed stick [excrement] or some dog [vomit] or a pot by the roadside [urine]" (*quod sciat infelix damnatae spongea virgae / vel quicumque canis iunctaque testa viae*).[179] Indeed, the physiological pleasures of satire have long attracted attention: the easing, venting, and purging effects to be derived from doing violence to enemies suggest that the punishment of vice in others is accompanied not only by gratification but by the expulsion of the vice from the self. As Rochester put it, "I'd fart just as I write, for my own ease."[180]

Again, the gladiatorial connection is illuminating. The arena is the site of satiation of the hunger for difference and death, and for the temporary sense of renewal that the nourishment provides. Yet the spectacles are served up from the inedibles: dregs, the leftovers, the excreted Others of the Empire.[181] One exemplum from this dark history is explicitly excremental (but none the less worthy of admiration) in Seneca's anecdote of a victim who committed preemptive suicide in the toilet by plunging down his throat one of the sponges on a stick with which Romans used to wipe themselves after defecating (*Epistle* 70). Juvenal juxtaposes the arena and the sewer as sites of influx and effluent to play on the inversion of hierarchy,[182] as we can see from lines 29–41 near the opening of Umbricius's speech in *Satire* 3. Let people like Artorius and Catulus stay in Rome, he says. Once they were horn players for traveling provincial shows (gladiators fought to musical accompaniment); now they give *munera* themselves in Rome, at which they "kill to please" the mob (*occidunt populariter*).[183] Then they return immediately to their jobs, charging for admission to the public toilets (*inde reversi conducunt foricas*, 37–38).[184] Fortune, playing the role of *editor*, so to speak, raises such men when she feels like having a joke, while Umbricius has none of the shameless skills essential for success at Rome (*quid Romae faciam?* 41) and must leave the city.[185] A similar point is made when he

178. Gowers 1993a, 121.

179. See L. and P. Watson 2003, 213–19.

180. *An Epistolary Essay from M. G. to O. B. upon Their Mutual Poems*; Griffin 1994, 170–71.

181. Plass 1995, arena as "disposal area" of social outsiders (26, 36); on "ultimate disposal" see Kyle 1998, chap. 5, and on sewers under amphitheaters, 223–24.

182. Cf. Plass 1995 on Tacitus's account of the small-town "sewage" (*conluvies*) in Nero's theatrical productions, which is followed by the account of a riot at a gladiatorial show in Pompeii (77; *Ann.* 14.15); Fagan 2011, 93–96.

183. Cf. the rise of Vatinius the cobbler and his *munera* in Tac. *Ann.* 15.34 and chap. 4 herein.

184. According to Scobie 1988, there were no toilets in the arena and one had to walk to those in the Forum (225).

185. In Hor. *Sat.* 2.8.61–63, Nomentanus attempts to cheer up the host of a disastrous dinner as follows: "*heu, Fortuna, quis est crudelior in nos / te deus? Ut semper gaudes illudere rebus / humanis.*" Gowers 2012 on *Sat.* 1.4.139 connects with *illudere chartis* and suggests Fortune as satirist. Cf. 3.40 (*voluit iocare*); 6.606 (*adridens*), with (*sub)ridens* of the satirical surgeon and Laronia in 2.13 and 38.

complains that the first fourteen rows in the theater used to be restricted to a property qualification of 400,000 sesterces but nowadays are reserved for "the sons of pimps born in whatever brothel" (155–56).[186] Here the sons of the auctioneer, the "crest-snatcher" (*pinnirapus*) of the arena, and the trainer (*lanista*) enjoy the show, belonging together in the same despicable group as far as Umbricius is concerned (157–58).

The Fish Course

The building stands behind the high red-brick wall known to the entire world. There are many windows in the building, but one was distinguished from all the others because it was lit twenty-four hours a day. Those who gathered in the evening on the broad square in front of the red-brick wall would crane their necks, strain their eyes to the point of tears, and say excitedly to one another: "Look, over there, the window's lit. He's not sleeping. He's working. He's thinking about us."
—Vladimir Voinovich, "A Circle of Friends," trans. Richard Lourie

As a demonstration of the cultural propinquity of satire and arena, and especially of how consuming and expelling are linked with violence and death, as well as with the emperor, let us consider *Satire* 4, which opens with an attack on Crispinus and moves on to Domitian himself, through the tale of the prodigiously huge turbot's progress to the imperial kitchens.[187]

Domitian, the "bald Nero," is introduced as tearing apart the "half-dead world," like a wild animal (*semianimum laceraret Flavius orbem*, 37). This is a strange inversion of the arena: the conjunction of *Flavius* and *orbem* glancingly alludes to the Colosseum, the Flavian amphitheater built on the site of Nero's palace,[188] and Domitian, instead of providing spectacles of bestial laceration for the populace as an *editor* is, as an emperor, lacerating them and the whole world like a wild animal.[189] The world, and Rome, are moribund, or a land of the dead (this is already established with the cemetery visit at the end of *Satire* 1, the Underworld scene at the end of *Satire* 2, and Umbricius's "shady" Rome in *Satire* 3),[190] "half-alive" as David Sweet says "because so many lives had been

---

186. On L. Roscius Otho's law, revived by Domitian, see Courtney 1980, *ad loc.*

187. For a contrasting take on related themes, Stat. *Silv.* 1.6 and 4.2 and Newlands 2002 on these (chap. 7, "The Emperor's Saturnalia" and chap. 8, "Dining with the Emperor"). On Juvenal's parody of Stat. in *Sat.* 4, see McNelis 2012, 258–60; on *Sat.* 4 as an examination of speech and rhetoric, Van den Berg 2012, 279–81.

188. Mart. *Spect.* 2: Colosseum in place of Nero's single house and lake; Coleman 2006, notes on 1.7 that the term "Flavian amphitheatre" is not used by Mart. (lxvi, 11).

189. On Domitian's expert sense of how to manage spectacles, see Newlands 2002, 230–35 and p. 220 herein.

190. Winkler 1995 on allusions to Vergil (229–32).

taken from it by Domitian."[191] As the poem develops, the word *orbis* comes to refer also to the giant fish, which needs to be enclosed in the "wall" of a giant cooking pot (132).[192] The prodigious character of the fish (*monstrum*, 42) and the notion of its having "strayed" from the *vivaria Caesaris* (51) and actually wanting to be caught (69) are suggestive of the flourishing trade in wild animals for arena fights.[193] The whole world is the emperor's *vivarium*, and the *monstrum* is inevitably destined for Domitian[194]—how could it not be when even the seashore is full of his spies? (45–48).[195] We might compare Vitellius's gathering of ludicrously exotic ingredients from across the Empire (pike livers, peacock brains, and other refinements all the way from Parthia to the Spanish Straits, *a Parthia usque fretoque Hispanico per nauarchos ac triremes petitarum commiscuit*) for his "Shield of Minerva"—a concoction that also included a fish. As Rhiannon Ash comments, it was "an abuse of the emperor's privileged position as ruler of the world, *orbis terrarum*. Elsewhere, such centripetal consumption was almost always an indication of a tyrannical personality."[196] The theme of the spectacle is elaborated with the "wondering crowd" outside Domitian's Alban palace and the spectacle of the fish being admitted into the imperial presence as the senators look on from outside:

Utque lacus suberant, ubi quamquam diruta servat
ignem Troianum et Vestam colit Alba minorem,
obstitit intranti miratrix turba parumper.

191. Sweet 1979, 284.

192. Winkler 1995 notes that *orbis* (Plin. Eld. *HN* 32.14) may be a term for *rhombus* and in his thorough discussion draws out the nexus of links among emperor, world, and fish (242–45; see also his 2009, 469–77). Cf. Mart. 4.30, warning a fisherman away from the lake of Baiae, where swim fish *qui norunt dominum manumque lambunt / illam qua nihil est in orbe maius* (who know their master and lick his hand, the hand than which there is nothing greater in the world).

193. *Ipse capi voluit*; cf. Mart. 8.53.12 of lion in arena: *quantaque de magna gaudia morte tulit*. Deroux 1983 on the fish as *prodigium* and the spectacle of Domitian and his court as "a prodigy in itself" (289). Garland 1995 notes how emperors and monsters "gravitate towards each other" via their uniqueness and deformity (49).

194. Sweet 1979, 288. In Tac. *Ann.* 11.24, Claudius says it is traditional to bring conspicuous merit to Rome from anywhere; Edmondson 1996 cites a passage from Modestinus, *De Poenis* (dig. 48.19.31) to the effect that if a provincial governor had any criminals who showed *robor* or *artificium*, of the kind which might make them worthy of being exhibited before the Roman people, he should consult the emperor (82). Cf. Plin. *Pan.* 50.2 praising Trajan for *not* considering all he sees as his own personal property (*est quod Caesar non suum videat*).

195. Dio 67.11.6, on murder via informers, notes that it happened not only in Rome but over almost the whole world; cf. Mart. *Spect.* 4–5. On the parading of informers before they sent into exile: even the vast arena could not hold the guilty (4.3), see Coleman 2006, 54–59. Plin. *Pan.* 34.5 cites with approval the *pulchrum spectaculum* and the vision of the *delatores* shipwrecked on the bare crags of a hostile shore, see Roche 2011, 34. On the parallels drawn by Pliny between the fate of *delatores* and of their victims, see Coleman 2006, 59.

196. Suet. *Vit.* 13.2; in 13.3 he describes Vitellius as *homo non profundae modo sed intempestivae quoque ac sordidae gulae*. See Barton 1993, 53; and Ash 1999, in a good discussion of conspicuous consumption (96–105).

Ut cessit, facili patuerunt cardine valvae;
exclusi spectant admissa obsonia patres.
Itur ad Atriden.

And when the lakes lay below him, where, although in ruins,
Alba still tends the Trojan flame and the lesser Vesta,
a staring crowd blocked his way for a while.
As it moved aside, the doors swung open on easy hinges;
the senators, kept out, watch as the food is allowed in.
The way is made to Atrides. (60–65)

The echoes of the Trojan Horse are unmistakable, with the fisherman acting as a Sinon figure, while Atrides draws in the murderous and cannibalistic history of that notorious house.[197]

The fisherman urges Domitian to make the day a holiday and expand his stomach by stuffing it with the turbot, *propera stomachum laxare sagina / et tua servatum consume in saecula rhombum*: "Hurry up and expand your stomach by cramming / and eat up this turbot preserved for your epoch" (66–68).[198] The somewhat strange mode of expression is significant for several reasons. Gladiatorial events were held on holidays, especially just before the Saturnalia in December, and the tale is set as "death-bringing autumn" (*letifero autumno*) gives way to frosts and the chilling winter wind.[199] *Laxare* means to distend the stomach, but also to relieve it, suggestive of the food/excrement equation.[200] *Sagina* was used of small fry, or bait, for larger fish (suggesting here that the turbot is bait to hook Domitian), and also of a kind of fattening sausage fed to gladiators.[201] Propertius describes it as *immunda* (unclean), speaking as much in moral as nutritional terms, when he urges a freeborn youth not to commit the

197. See Deroux 1983 on prodigy. He suggests that Juvenal may have written *Satire* 4 with a passage from Seneca's *Thyestes* in mind (703–705) and that Domitian is styled as both Atreus's son and Atreus himself (294–95).

198. Ash 1999 notes that potbellies were often associated with tyrants; Nero and Domitian each had one (102). Gowers 2012 on Hor. *Sat.* 1.5.6–7 speaks of "the most 'satirical' part of the body, the full stomach."

199. Annual *munus* moved to December in the early empire, perhaps by Caligula: Ville 1981, 167–68; under Domitian was certainly so and lasted for ten days (see n105 above); Wiedemann 1992, 47; Kyle 1998, 57, and chap. 8.

200. Cf. Sen. *Ep.* 7.3 at the arena expecting *et sales et aliquid laxamenti*, and above. Hor. *Sat.* 1.5.6–7 *ventri / indico bellum* suggests he has dysentery or is starving himself to avoid it.

201. See above Tac. *Hist.* 2.88 on Vitellius distributing food to his troops as if a *gladiatoriam saginam*); in 1.62 he is described as *medio diei temulentus et sagina gravis*. Damon 2003 translates "feed" and notes it is used only of Vitellius by Tac. (ad loc.); cf. 2.71, *luxu et sagina mancipatus emptusque*. Suet. *Cal.*. 27.1 records that criminals were fed to beasts because other meat to feed them for arena (*ad saginam ferarum*) was too expensive. Cf. Kyle 1998, 186; Livy 6.17.3: *saginare plebem populares suos, ut iugulentur*; Apul. *Met.* 4.13, *bestiarum saginas*.

shameful act of selling his life to a gladiatorial trainer (*qui dabit immundae venalia fata saginae*, 4.8.25). This sausage had clearly acquired metaphorical filling of its own: Seneca uses it to symbolize disorder and chaos, as well as lassitude and laziness, while Quintilian has the term *sagina dicendi*:

> Sed quem ad modum forensibus certaminibus exercitatos et quasi militantis reficit ac reparat haec velut **sagina dicendi**, sic adulescentes non debent nimium in falsa rerum imagine detineri et inanibus simulacris usque adeo ut difficilis ab his digressus sit adsuefacere, ne ab illa in qua prope consenuerunt umbra vera discrimina velut quendam solem reformident.

> But although those who find their practice in the contests of forensic warfare derive fresh strength and repair their forces by means of this **rich fare of eloquence**, the young should not be kept too long at these false semblances of reality, nor should they be allowed to become so familiar with these empty shadows that it is difficult for them to leave them: otherwise there is the danger that, owing to the seclusion in which they have almost grown old, they will shrink in terror from the real perils of public life, like men dazzled by the unfamiliar sunlight. (*Institutio oratoria* 10.5.17)

The term is connected in Quintilian's mind, it seems, with a certain suggestion of torpidity and deceitfulness, as well as with nourishment.[202] Winkler says that here "Juvenal presents us with an example of the *sagina dicendi*, the nourishing food of oratory, which sustains the speaker and enables him to triumph over his adversary."[203]

The fisherman, an unnamed man from Picenum, who takes on a mysterious air reminiscent of Dionysus's engagement with Pentheus, hooks the emperor by telling him that the turbot has been preserved for his reign and "wanted to be captured"—a conceit similar to the obedience of beasts before their emperor found in Martial.[204] When he hears this, the emperor's crest rises

---

202. Cf. 2.15.25, citing Plato on slave-dealers who make useless fat out to be real strength: *verum robur inani sagina mentiantur*; 12.6.6: the young man begins with an easy case in the forum as the young of wild animals *molliore praeda saginantur*.

203. Winkler 1995, 236–38. He also notes the moral overtones, e.g., in Cic.'s use of the verb in *Pro Sest.* 78 (*eos qui ab illo pestifero ac perdito civi iam pridem rei publicae sanguine saginantur*), as "climax to his description of mutual bloodshed" and illustrating "the general breakdown of morals and of social and legal stability."

204. *Spect.* 20; 33. Winkler 1995 suggests in wanting to be hooked, Domitian becomes a fool (like the *rhombus* which was thought to be a notably unintelligent fish; 243). The *Picens* is also a stand-in for the satirist. The legacy hunter Pacuvius catches a will in his fishtrap (*nassa*) at 12.123; cf. Hor. *Sat.* 2.5.44; Mart. 4.30.1–2: *Baiano procul a lacu, monemus, / piscator, fuge, ne nocens recedas*.

(*surgebant cristae*, 70), and we may have an allusion here to the plumed helmet many gladiators wore, and perhaps to the variety Domitian was particularly fond of, the *murmillo*.[205] The *murmillo* was apparently named after a Greek word *mormylos* for a fish, and his helmet had an angular crest.[206] The Thracian is another possibility: he wore a brimmed helmet with a griffin's head adorned with a *crista* of feathers. In the first century, the *murmillo* and the Thracian were usually paired against each other, with the former armed like a Roman legionary fighting his emphatically non-Roman opponent. The *murmillo* is, however, often confused with the *secutor* who fought the *retiarius*, although the *secutor's* helmet was low and rounded.[207] Casting Domitian as *murmillo*, *secutor*, or Thracian all open up different possibilities for irony and grim humor. If Domitian is a *murmillo* or *secutor*, potentially the embodiment of *Romanitas*, then his murderous actions against noble Romans are a perversion of that role; if a Thracian, then he embodies non-Roman barbarism. We know from Suetonius that Domitian showed a personal dislike of Thracian gladiators, which adds another layer of complexity to the allusion (10.1). The fisherman may indeed be imagined as a *retiarius:* apart from the obvious idea of "netting" Domitian, we know that as a victor he sometimes snatched the crest of his opponent away (the hapax *pinnirapus* or "crest snatcher" appears in Juvenal's preceding satire, 3.158).[208]

The verbal links between Domitian and the fish, the way both are "netted," and the gladiatorial connections of the *sagina* all serve to suggest that the emperor is destined for the arena himself. This is nicely ironic, given his recorded fondness for the games: among his building projects were four gladiatorial schools, and he added a fourth tier to the Colosseum; he may also have finished the seating and built passages and rooms under the arena. Under Domitian, shows were frequent, elaborate, and expensive, according to Suetonius and Dio, and he was an "interventionist" *editor:* he introduced new regulations to make some combats more difficult—refining the menu, so to speak (Martial, 8.80.1–4).[209] His notorious hostility to the Thracian brand of fighter led him to throw a *paterfamilias* to dogs in the arena for saying that the emperor's

---

205. Juv. 6.256 uses *crista* in this way; Winkler 1995 on *cristae* as revealing of Domitian's "animal nature" (243).

206. Köhne and Ewigleben 2000, 48–51.

207. See Köhne and Ewigleben 2000: in 2/3 cents (48–57). *secutor* vs. *retiarius* became the most popular pairing; see Dunkle 2008, including on fish-connections (104–107). The *murmillo* is often confused with the *scecutor* or *contraretiarius:* see above n28 for various types and match-ups.

208. Appears to be alluded to in Lucil. 3.115, during the contest of gladiators at Capua. Dunkle 2008 cites *ILS* 6635 *pinnirapus iuvenum* (gladiatorial trainer of youths; 123).

209. Suet. *Dom.* 4.1: *spectacula assidue magnifica et sumptuosa edidit;* cf. B. W. Jones 1992, 85–86, 93, 104–105, 124.

partiality to *murmillones* made it difficult for Thracians to compete on fair terms, and to make the point clear, he sent him down wearing a label that read *"impie locutus parmularius"* ("a *parmularius* who spoke impiously").[210] Immediately afterward, Suetonius details Domitian's murders among the senatorial class (*complures senatores, in iis aliquot consulares*) and mentions Acilius Glabrio and Aelius Lamia. Pliny's comment in *Panegyricus* 33.4 throws intriguing light on this aspect of Domitian's personality, again drawing a close connection between the arena and his various murders:

> Demens ille verique honoris ignarus, qui crimina maiestatis in
> harena colligebat, ac se despici et contemni, nisi etiam gladiatores
> eius veneraremur, sibi male dici in illis, suam divinitatem suum
> numen violari interpretabatur, cumque se idem quod deos, idem
> gladiatores quod se putabat.

> He was a madman, blind to the true meaning of his position, who
> used the arena for collecting charges of high treason, who felt
> himself slighted and scorned if we failed to pay homage to his
> gladiators, taking any criticism of them to himself and seeing insults
> to his own godhead and divinity; who deemed himself the equal of
> the gods yet raised his gladiators to be his equal.[211]

Next, the satirist shows us the emperor's "friends" being called in for consultation on the giant fish[212] and again in this procession of *proceres* ("whom he hated," *quos oderat ille*, 73) there are echoes of the amphitheater, with mention of the emperor's *saevitia* (85) and the advisors' fate hanging in the balance (*fatum pendebat*, 88)—as did the fighter's in the arena.[213] Acilius Glabrio is mentioned here: he fought in the arena at the Juvenalia Games while consul and killed a lion; he was later executed, perhaps because Domitian was jealous of his fighting skills, although the suggestion here is that he fought animals to

---

210. Suet. *Dom.* 10.1; Dunkle 2008, 106–107; Edmondson 1996, 83, 106–107, notes hostile anecdotes about Caligula and Domitian in this context: to force Romans to cross the barrier into the arena was reprehensible not only in moral terms but because it threatened the social order of the amphitheater and hence of Rome itself. Suet. *Vit.* 10.3: he encouraged his soldiers with the abominable saying *optime olere occisum hostem et melius civem* (Only one thing smells better than a dead enemy, and that's a dead citizen).

211. Trans. Radice 1969.

212. Echoes of Stat. *Silv.* 4.2; see Newlands 2002, chap. 8. Minucius Felix compares those raised to high places to victims being fattened for sacrifice and garlanded for execution (*Octavius* 37.7); see Barton 1993, 26–29.

213. Cf. Ash 1999, 97–98, and Plin. *Pan.* 49.6, when praising Trajan for not gorging alone, describes his predecessor as "menacingly watching" his guests and "noting what they do" (*spectator adnotatorque convivis tuis immines*); Barton 1993 on the price of being Caesar's friend (28–29). Cf. Stat. *Silv.* 4.2, where only the poet does the watching (*spectare*, 40); Newlands 2002, 272–73.

win the emperor's favor.[214] In any case, the inclusion of Acilius strengthens the connection with the arena and gladiatorial combat:

> Profuit ergo nihil misero quod comminus ursos
> figebat Numidas Albana nudus harena
> venator.

> So it didn't help the unfortunate young man one bit that he speared Numidian bears close up, as a naked hunter in the Alban amphitheatre.
>   (99–101)[215]

The nakedness adds to the disgrace of a noble in such a performance (as we saw in Gracchus's bare-faced appearance as *retiarius* in the arena in *Satires* 2 and 8).

Then Catullus, blind but evincing amazement at the turbot, describes it as if he were praising the fighting of a Cilician gladiator or the skill of boy acrobats in the theater: *sic pugnas Cilicis laudabat et ictus / et pegma et pueros inde ad velaria raptos* (121–22).[216] His rival Veiento, however, tries to outdo him by prophesying a great victory for Domitian. These two are like a pair of gladiators fighting before the emperor, a spectacle in themselves, rather like Horace's two buffoons. Catullus resembles the man with the bag over his head being manipulated by Phersu. In 130, the question is raised as to whether the fish is to be cut up (*conciditur?*)—its fate is in the balance, although it is already dead—but when Montanus the gourmand objects, it is decided that a dish will have to be made which is large enough to hold the "ample circumference" (*spatiosum orbem*) within its "delicate wall" (*tenui muro*).[217] By now, the dish and the arena are virtually synonymous, as are the fish and the emperor.[218] One recalls the *cena libera* but also the strange story in Dio of Domitian's "black banquet" held at night for leading senators and equestrians, at which he served the traditional meal for spirits of the dead (67.9). As Dio says (9.3–4), there was total silence as

214. Courtney 1980 says Acilius is introduced here anachronistically to denigrate Domitian (*ad loc.*). Suet. *Dom.* 19.1 records that Domitian loved archery, and that many watched him (*spectavere*) more than once shoot one hundred animals of different species on his Alban estate. See also Deroux 1983, 297.

215. Cf. story of Domitian's jealousy of Glabrio the consul in the arena, Dio 67.14.3. Acilius's appearance forms an odd doublet with Statius's participation in the Alban poetic contest, where the emperor presided, recalled in *Silv.* 3.5.28–29 and 5.3.227–29; see Gibson 2006, 352.

216. The nature of the Cilician type is unknown, but Fagan 2011 sees it as of same ilk as the *scissor* and as evidence of the developed connoisseurship of the watchers of gladiatorial combat (215). On *pegma*, see Dunkle 2008, 209, 229.

217. Plin. Eld. *HN* 35.163–64 records that Domitian's "Shield of Minerva" plate had to be forged in a special furnace.

218. Connors 2005: "Consumption of this satiric seafood is centralized, just as power is centralized in the imperial household. . . . Juvenal makes Rome itself the meal gobbled by the insatiable emperor" (143).

if they were already in the realm of the dead, "and Domitian himself conversed only about topics relating to death and slaughter." Expecting to be executed, the diners were eventually sent home with presents—as well as a newly heightened sense of fear and of the emperor's position at the very top of the food chain.[219]

The satire ends with a reflection on how the council members, Domitian's bloodstained nodders, had come rushing to the Alban fortress as if dispatches of bad news had been flying to Rome from distant parts of the world (144–49). The effect is one of centripetal movement, like the populace flocking to the arena to see animals and gladiators brought in from all over the Empire.[220] The final impression is that Domitian, "dripping with blood" (*caede madenti*), robbed the city of its noblest men in an arena-style slaughtering of the senatorial elite (Dio says it is impossible to find out the total number executed by Domitian, 67.11.3), with overtones of cannibalism.[221] He did this *inpune et vindice nullo*, with no one to inflict punishment or avenge the dead.[222] This expresses the helplessness of the spectators, including the satirist, as well as the loss of *libertas*:

Atque utinam his potius nugis tota illa dedisset
tempora saevitiae, claras quibus abstulit urbi
inlustresque animas inpune et vindice nullo.

And indeed, if only he'd devoted all of those
savage times to these frivolities, when he took from the city
its famous and glorious souls, with impunity, and no one to avenge
   them. (150–52)[223]

---

219. Dio 67.9.1–6; Winkler 2009, 478–80. This passage comes in the epitome of book 67 after an account of the spectacles and combats he organized to celebrate his "victory" over Decebalus of the Dacians (7–8).

220. F. M. A. Jones 1990 on the *dramatis personae*, as if in a race or competition (55); Mart. *Spect.* 3.7: *festinavit Arabs, festinavere Sabaei*. Coleman 2006 notes that the first three poems introduce the Flavian amphitheater in its international and metropolitan contexts and in terms of its cosmopolitan audience attracted to Rome from all over the world (1–3; cf. 19–20). Cf. also Stat. *Silv.* 5.2.168–71, on the messenger, "swifter than Rumour" from Alba, unbarring the door to high office for Crispinus.

221. To consume fish was always problematic because it involved potential cannibalism, consuming that which might itself have consumed other human beings, as animals in the arena might have; see Kyle 1998, chap. 6. On *Sat.* 4, see Gowers 1993a, 202–11.

222. Deroux 1983 on the pleonasm and the implication that the punishment counts for little because it only occurred after he lost the favor of the common herd (285).

223. Sweet 1979, 293–94; also "for Juvenal's earlier satirist, and especially as he appears in *Satire* 4, there is no remote, satiric sanctuary. The tyrant is shown to have infected them all, and hence the satirist himself becomes the final comment on the times" (300). The poem ends, he says, in "the satirist's confession of his complete helplessness and cynicism" (299). Cf. Newlands 2002 on *libertas* and Stat. *Silv.* 1.6 (249–59).

The narrator adds, however, a two-line Parthian shot: once Domitian began to be feared by the masses—that is, the spectators—he was done for:

Sed periit postquam cerdonibus esse timendus
coeperat: hoc nocuit Lamiarum caede madenti.

But he perished once he began to be feared by the workers:
this did him in, dripping as he was with the blood of the Lamiae. (153–54)

Periit is the language of the gladiatorial record sheet. One of the assassins, we know from Suetonius 17, was an unnamed gladiator, and Domitian was stabbed eight times. According to the late and not entirely reliable Procopius, the body was later cut into pieces.[224] The emperor ended up a victim in his own arena—and now in the arena of satire—recalling perhaps the fate of Caligula or Vitellius, who likewise died during the winter.[225] As Winkler says, "Part of the *laceratus orbis* turns against its *lacerator* and administers the appropriate punishment. . . . The world, the fish and the emperor all share the same fate; they end up *lacerati*." Rimell observes that the Lamiae personify the senatorial class whose revenge is magnified if we remember that they are also "bloodsucking bogeys of Greek myth, victims turned avengers."[226]

It is only with his death that Domitian is brought out of the shadows into view, so to speak. Sweet comments on Domitian's fortifying himself against the outside world in his *arx*, his "menacing invisibility" and how the tale imitates his obscurity.[227] Pliny (*Panegyricus* 51.3–4) waxes lyrical on the contrasting accessibility and visibility of his successor, Trajan, using the spacious Circus Maximus as the setting:

. . . nec minus ipsa videnda, quam quae ex illa spectabuntur . . . nec magis proprius spectanti Caesari suggestus quam propria quae spectet. Licebit ergo te civibus tuis invicem contueri; dabitur non cubiculum principis sed ipsum principem cernere in publico, in populo sedentem.

224. Suet. *Dom.* 17.2 mentions a Satur, Decurion of the chamberlains (Dio 15.1, Sigerus), and a gladiator from the imperial *ludus*.

225. See Suet. *Cal.* 56–58; Wiedemann 1992, 84; Gunderson 1996, 130. Death of Vitellius, 20 December 69 c.e., cf. Suet. *Vit.* 17.1–2. Joseph. *BJ* 4.651–52 says Vitellius emerged from the palace drunk and stuffed with the most luxurious banquet food, then was dragged through the mob and butchered in the center of Rome. Dunkle 2008 observes that the execution of Vitellius, although not in the arena "has much in common with practices there" (92).

226. Winkler 1995, 244–45; Rimell 2005, 88.

227. Sweet 1979, 285–86. By contrast, Stat. *Silv.* 4.2 focuses on Domitian's face; Newlands 2002, 273; Calp. Sic. 7.84 ends with a description of Nero's face as "a combination of Mars and Apollo in one."

... a sight to be seen on its own account as well as for the spectacles
there displayed ... and Caesar as a spectator shares the public seats
as he does the spectacle. Thus your subjects will be able to look on
you in their turn; they will be permitted to see not just the Emperor's
box, but their Emperor himself, seated among his people.[228]

In 49.1, he had described how Domitian tried to protect himself behind walls
from outside threats, but to no avail:

Ille tamen, quibus sibi parietibus et muris salutem suam tueri
videbatur, dolum secum et insidias et ultorem scelerum deum
inclusit. Dimovit perfregitque custodias Poena, angustosque per
aditus et obstructos non secus ac per apertas fores et invitantia
limina irrupit.

Yet although he thought to protect his life behind walls and
masonry, he locked in with himself treachery, conspiracy and the
god who avenges crimes. Nemesis pushed aside his guards and
broke through, and burst in through the narrow and barred
passages, as if through open doors and thresholds inviting her in.[229]

In the context of the *syuzhet* of the satire, it is the arrival of the fish that pres-
ages the long-awaited appearance of Nemesis and Domitian's downfall. The
journey of the giant fish is a passage from the world of nature to the human
realm (*mare in urbe*), from outside to the inside, from freedom to containment,
from life to death. The fish symbolizes the unpredictability of fortune and the
sudden swing of the pendulum from good luck to bad. In his later satires, Juvenal
would perhaps be inclined to speak more in terms of Fortuna than punishment
or Nemesis with regard to Domitian's fate—*Fortuna* appears twice as many times
in the last two books as it does in the first three—but the apparently "random"
nature of the prodigious catch does make the fisherman an agent of both.[230]

Dinner with Friends

After this "fly on the wall" visit to the imperial court, with *Satire* 5 we move
back into the private sphere for part 2 of the gastronomic diptych that ends book

---

228. Trans. Radice 1969; see Roche 2011, 54–59.

229. On Nemesis, see n120 above. Contrast the picture in Stat. *Silv.* 4.2, with an encomiastic description of the palace—occupied by its divine and beneficent host.

230. Cf. Sen. *De Tranq.* 4 that it's no good dropping your weapons and looking for a place to hide, *quasi
ullus locus sit quo non possit Fortuna persequi.*

1: here we are invited to watch the systematic degradation of Trebius at the table of his patron, Virro—styled as *rex*—who treats him as a *scurra* and humiliates him for his own pleasure (14, 130).[231] There is effective force-feeding of the reader by the satirist (*farrago*), not only with piles of exempla, but here, marking the end of the book, with a surfeit of food items, many of them disgusting.[232] The *miratrix turba* outside Domitian's palace is replaced by the *salutatrix turba*, which Trebius always fears has already completed its daily round (*peregerit orbem*, 21), leaving him out of the running for a dinner invitation. But this time, he has been lucky and could not wish for more (*votorum summa. Quid ultra quaeris?* 18). The *cena*, however, is depicted in terms of a brawl, as the diners (like the philosopher Bacchanals of *Satire* 2.2–3) rapidly turn into Corybantes:

> ... de conviva Corybanta videbis.
> Iurgia **proludunt**, sed mox et pocula **torques**
> **saucius** et rubra deterges **vulnera** mappa,
> inter vos quotiens libertorumque **cohortem**
> **pugna** Saguntina fervet **commissa** lagona.

> ... you'll see dinner guests turn into Corybants.
> Insults form the **prelude**, but, once **injured**, you'll soon be **hurling** cups too,
> and dabbing your **wounds** with a reddened napkin.
> whenever **battle is joined** with Saguntine crockery and
> rages between you and the **cohort** of freedmen. (25–29)

Proludunt evokes the *prolusio* (warm-up acts) in the arena,[233] and this vocabulary of fighting leads naturally into the main business of the dueling menus—a mouth-watering one for Virro and a stomach-turning one for Trebius—which are the means of humiliating and abusing the guest.[234] There is a relentless focus on hierarchy and who looks down upon whom; even the lobster sneers down its tail at the diners:

> Aspice quam longo distinguat pectore lancem
> quae fertur domino squilla, et quibus undique saepta

231. Cf. Mart. 12.48.16; *rex magnus* probably positively of Domitian in Stat. *Silv.* 4.1.46; Coleman 1988, 81–82.

232. On force-feeding of the reader by the satirist, esp. Swift, see Griffin 1994, 193–95; and chap. 4 herein.

233. Cic. *De Orat.* 2.325, to the effect that the beginning of a speech should not be like the *prolusio* of Samnite gladiators (cf. above, p. 48); Fagan 2011, 221.

234. Morford 1977 sets out the double menu (245). On *Sat.* 5, see Gowers 1993a, 211–19.

asparagis, qua despiciat convivia cauda,
dum venit excelsi manibus sublata ministri.

Look at the lobster that's brought to the master:
how its long breast makes the dish distinctive, how it's walled on all sides
by fine asparagus, how with its tail it looks down upon the company
as it enters, carried on high by the hands of the tall attendant. (80–83)[235]

While Virro dines upon a lamprey from the waters of Charbydis off Sicily,
Trebius is given an eel, or something worse, something from Rome itself:

vos anguilla manet longae cognata colubrae
aut glaucis sparsus maculis Tiberinus et ipse
vernula riparum, pinguis torrente cloaca
et solitus mediae cryptam penetrare Suburae.

What's waiting for you is an eel, cousin of the long snake,
or a Tiber fish spattered with grey blotches,
like a slave bred on the banks, bloated from the gushing sewer,
who knows his way right into the drain under the middle of the Subura.
(103–106)[236]

Both the Tiber fish and Trebius are slaves, bottom-feeders fed on shit.[237] With
glaucis . . . maculis, we may compare *maculosas . . . aedes* (of the squalid recital
hall lent to the poet by his mean patron in 7.40) and *maculam haesuram* (the
lasting stain on shining lives passed on to sons by parents in 14.2). Trebius is a
mere spectator of the performances of the expert carver (120–22) and will be
yanked out the door if he says anything:

Duceris planta velut ictus ab Hercule Cacus
et ponere foris, si quid temptaveris umquam
hiscere tamquam habeas tria nomina. Quando propinat
Virro tibi sumitve tuis contacta labellis
pocula? Quis vestrum temerarius usque adeo, quis
perditus, ut dicat regi "bibe"? Plurima sunt quae
non audent homines pertusa dicere laena.

You'll be dragged by the foot and tossed outside like Cacus by Hercules
if you ever attempt to open your mouth,

235. Trans. Braund 2004.
236. Trans. Braund 2004.
237. On the Tiberinus, see Courtney 1980, 242–43. In 1.26, Crispinus is described as *verna Canopi*.

as if you had three names [like a free man]. When will Virro toast
you or take up a cup touched by your lips? Who of you is so reckless
or so shameless as to say "Cheers!" to your king? There are many things
people don't dare to say when their coats have holes. (125–31)[238]

Being dragged and struck, abused and holed, and forced to keep silent recall
the warning to the speaker to keep his mouth shut at the end of *Satire* 1, the
original moment of self-abjection in the book and the collection.[239]

The *cena* ends with the image of the client as an unnamed animal—
presumably a monkey—performing on the Embankment:

Tu scabie frueris mali, quod in aggere rodit
qui tegitur **parma et galea** metuensque flagelli
discit ab hirsuta **iaculum torquere** capella.

You get to enjoy a mangy apple—like the one gnawed by the creature
equipped with a **shield and helmet** on the Embankment, who learns,
in terror of the whip, **to hurl a javelin** from the back of a shaggy she-goat.
  (153–55)[240]

Once again, the language recalls the gladiator in the arena. The *parma* was carried by the Thracian.[241] Moreover, *scabies* recalls the original scab of the ef-
feminizing infection of 2.80, while the *galea* echoes *galeatum* in 1.169. We have
come by the end of book 1 to an even more abject image than the corpse in the
arena at the end of *Satire* 1: a trained creature, fearing its master's whip, sitting
upon a she-goat, learning to hurl its toy javelin. Trebius waits, in silence, *stricto
pane* (169, an echo of *ense . . . stricto* like Lucilius in 1.165), for scraps of half-
eaten food. Degraded and voiceless client meets silenced satirist in the shape
of a performing monkey, a hybrid assemblage in a grotesque arena where
Roman abusing Roman is the show. Trebius's ultimate fate is, appropriately,
to offer himself as a *scurra* to be slapped about and as a slave to be beaten:

Ille sapit, qui te sic utitur. Omnia ferre
si potes, et debes. Pulsandum vertice raso
praebebis quandoque caput nec dura timebis
flagra pati, his epulis et tali dignus amico.

---

238. Morford 1977: "The most active participant is the professional carver, a foreigner and symbol of
the luxury and corruption of Rome" (241). Mart. 1.20.1: *turba spectante* as the Virro-esque Caecilianus devours
all the *boletus* mushrooms on his own. See Howell 1980, 152.

239. Cf. *pertusus Achilles*, 1.163; followed by *multum quaesitus Hylas* (by Hercules, of course) in 164.

240. Courtney 1980, *ad loc.*, and schol.

241. Dunkle 2008, 102–107.

The man who treats you like this has good taste. If there is nothing you
  can't
put up with, then you deserve it all. Sooner or later, you'll be offering
to have your head shaved and slapped and you won't flinch from a harsh
  whipping.
That's the kind of banquet you deserve, and that's the kind of friend.
  (170–73)[242]

Amid all the consumption of produce hauled in from the sea (*iam defecit nostrum mare, dum gula saevit*, 94) and the provinces (*instruit ergo focum provin-
cia*, 97), there rages degradation and violence, as there did in *Satire 4*. Juvenal
exploits a widespread Roman experience of social degradation for literary and
satirical effect, as he brings the *cena* and the arena into a close association. As
Barton observes: "The proud and preeminently powerful Romans of the last
century of the Republic and the first century of the Empire, were in a kind of
collective state of shock. They were enthralled by deformity, disgrace, dishonor
(the *dehonestamentum*), particularly their own; tirelessly rehearsing their own
debasement and degradation. The Romans were enthralled because they were
thralls. They were enthralled in order to set themselves free" (1995, 106).

In his second dinner party, in *Satire 11*, the food and arena connection provides the opportunity for a different twist on these themes of social humiliation and abjection. Rutilus is the talk of the town:

> . . . Nam dum valida ac iuvenalia membra
> sufficiunt galeae dumque ardent sanguine, fertur
> non cogente quidem sed nec prohibente tribuno
> scripturus leges et regia verba lanistae.

> . . . for, while his limbs are young and strong enough
> for the soldier's helmet and are hot with blood,
> they say that, with no compulsion from the tribune, but no prohibition,
> he is about to sign up to the rules and regal decrees of the gladiator
>   trainer. (5–8)

The reason is that like other profligate gourmands, he has run out of money
and valuables to pawn and, no longer able feed his habit, is reduced *ad miscellanea ludi*, gladiator-school stew, probably referring to a dish of dubious leftovers
eaten by trainees.[243] The degeneration of the Roman male, accompanied by the

242. Trans. Braund 2004.
243. Cf. Suet. *Cal.* 20: *miscellos ludos* (including oratory contests).

eating up of his patrimony, leads to the ultimate humiliation of the *auctoratus*. He ought to be serving in the army, wearing a soldier's helmet, not submitting to the orders of his *rex*, the *lanista*, and donning a gladiator's helmet. The *miscellanea ludi* recalls the fattening sausage, the *sagina*, and the satirist's *farrago*, as it conjures up the mixing of elements that constitutes satiric nausea, while Rutilus and his like are in turn the scrag-ends that remain of Roman masculinity and *dignitas*. By watching such figures as Rutilus perform in the arena, the spectators are consuming the leftovers of themselves.

4

Melting Down the House

Tomorrow, and tomorrow, and tomorrow,
Creeps in this petty pace from day to day,
To the last syllable of recorded time;
And all our yesterdays have lighted fools
The way to dusty death. Out, out, brief candle!
                    —*Macbeth* (act 5, scene 5, lines 19–21)

This chapter charts the continuation in books 4 and 5 of the search across Roman space and time for anchors of stability. In the later poems, often viewed
as more controlled or philosophical—that is, less driven by (apparently) haphazard blasts of *indignatio*—the satirist's undermining of the promises of *Romanitas* and the demands of genus is even more comprehensive, and his vision
is even bleaker, by virtue of the more orderly presentation of his exempla and
more frequent, but no more convincing, intimations of a satiric antithesis,
couched in the rhetoric of the *mos maiorum* and of philosophical truisms.[1] In
books 4 and 5, the focus is placed on the individual and the family, and especially the malignant interaction between parents and children. The speaker migrates back and forth between internal and external space as he seeks the
quilting points of *Romanitas*, as he did in book 1. There the street was the location for most of the action in *Satires* 1–3, while 4 moved into interior space (the
imperial court), as did 5 (the dinner party), but both of those at the same time

---

1. Keane 2007 sees "the individual poems of book 5 as plots spun from philosophical *topoi* and texts" (31).

ranged allusively across the territory of the empire, via the journey of the turbot to Domitian and the meandering provenance of far-flung comestibles for
Virro's table. In books 4 and 5, the geography of the satirist's movement is similarly wide, as is his Ro(a)ming through history and mythology.

Book 4 opens with *Satire* 10, in which the objects of human desire throughout the inhabited world (*omnibus in terris*, 1)—manifested in the vain and damaging wishes of contemporaries and historical celebrities—are systematically
deconstructed. In the center of the poem, we watch how the body comes apart
in pieces, like Prince Myskin's, as the numerous *faiblesses* of old age overwhelm
the vibrant desires and sensual satisfactions of youth. There are constant reminders of death in a poem about the wishes people make in life and in which,
as Rimell comments, "Juvenal is constantly force-feeding readers the experience of empire itself . . . where every talent and success . . . is ultimately twinned
with failure and deterioration, just as imperial power is doomed to self-
destruct."[2] The mooted alternative to all such prayers—the wish for *mens sana
in corpore sano* and associated virtues, like an *animus fortis*—is crowned by the
observation that it is we humans who make Fortune into a deity (356–66). In
Satire 11, we are again in the realm of food and the arena, as the inherited wealth
of the gourmandizing Rutilus is "melted down" literally and metaphorically
through overspending and excessive consumption, and as a result he marches
off to enroll in the gladiatorial school. The failing individual in such straits is
like a house riven by cracks, with the light showing through and in danger of
collapse (*et cito casurus iam perlucente ruina*, 13). There are attempts to conjure
the satiric antithesis into existence via a *cena* inspired by the nostalgia-bound
clichés of rustic simplicity, but we are drawn back to the corrupt city at every
turn, on a day when "the Circus holds all of Rome" in its thrall. *Satire* 12, which
ends book 4, begins with a mock Thanksgiving for the speaker's friend Catullus, a greedy merchant who survived a potential shipwreck by divesting himself of his goods in a storm at sea, in an act likened to the "self-castration" of a
beaver in a trap, willing to sacrifice his highly prized testicle to escape with his
life. Catullus has survived, however, only to fall potential victim to a much
greater danger, legacy hunters, in his home.

Book 5 opens with *Satire* 13, in which a well-off acquaintance who has been
defrauded of a small sum of money is "consoled" by the prospect of the thief's
eventual punishment by the gods, in a mock version of a formal *Consolatio* to
someone recently bereaved. With this as the rationale, we are treated to a spectacle of rampant criminality in a world where losing even a small amount of

2. Rimell 2005, 82.

money is equated to the pain of bereavement or exile and is mourned with real tears (*ploratur lacrimis amissa pecunia veris*, 134). *Satire* 14 is a long disquisition on how parents mal-educate their children and set them bad examples for life, especially in terms of inculcating avarice and acquisitiveness. In *Satire* 15, we are back in the arena of consumption, as eating and violence are combined in the graphic account of a fight between two towns in Egypt that ended in a frenzied act of cannibalism. Any temptation to seek solace from the exotic Egyptian location of this incident will be thwarted: its "far-off" barbarity has patent parallels closer to home. The focus then shifts to all of humankind, what Seneca terms *res publica generis humani*, where there exists less Concordia than there does among snakes, and where metalworkers produce more swords than ploughshares.[3]

In books 4–5, then, we have further exploration of the topics of greed, consumption, and violence, all pushed to an extreme in the cannibalism motif, which leads to a broad condemnation of all humankind, not just Egyptians or even Romans. The hopelessness on a universal scale as book 5 ends ties in with the global focus of the opening of *Satire* 10. Likewise, the various promises of consolation, whether through a more "philosophical" outlook incorporating moderation and restraint or through a trust in the (eventual) intervention of the gods—gods whose presence is definitely more marked after the first two books, and especially in these later poems—are revealed to be both banal and unsatisfactory.[4]

Footsteps in the Fog

The first poem of book 4, *Satire* 10, opens with a broad geographical flourish from Cadiz to the Ganges, and then takes examples in an eastward track from Rome—Carthage, Greece, and Persia—ending with Assyria, as the speaker prepares his systematic demolition of traditional objects of desire and sources of anxiety:

> Omnibus in terris, quae sunt a Gadibus usque
> Auroram et Gangen, pauci dinoscere possunt
> vera bona atque illis multum diversa, remota
> erroris nebula. Quid enim ratione timemus
> aut cupimus? Quid tam dextro pede concipis ut te   5

3. *De Const.* 19; *De Ot.* 4.
4. On the presence/absence of gods at different points in the corpus, see Larmour 2012.

conatus non paeniteat votique peracti?
Evertere domos totas optantibus ipsis
di faciles. Nocitura toga, nocitura petuntur
militia . . .

In all the lands which stretch from Cadiz as far as
the Dawn and the Ganges, few people are able to distinguish
real benefits from their opposites, having removed the fog of error.
After all, which of our fears and desires are driven by reason?
What project do you undertake with such good omens
that you don't regret the attempt or the accomplishment of your
     wish?
Compliant gods have brought down entire households by granting
their occupants' own prayers. In civilian and military life,
we ask for things that will do us damage. (1–9)[5]

The familiar themes are here: traversal of space right across the Empire; the difficulty of discerning clearly and of telling false from true; wandering around, unable to find the right way out; setting out on a path, but not being happy at its end; roaming about at home and abroad on a quest for destructive objects of desire. The "fog of error" (and/or "wandering") is an effective image, with the metaphorical use of *nebula* being quite rare in Latin; we can, however, connect it with the common term *nebulo*, meaning "fog-man" or "nobody" which is used by Horace among others.[6] The phrasing of *quid enim ratione . . . quid tam . . . ?* recalls the barrage of questions at the opening of *Satire* 1 and the speaker's offer to explain there why he is venturing onto the plain of satire in the first place, *si vacat at placidi rationem admittitis.*[7] There is perhaps an allusion to the rhetorical talents of the satirist himself, recalling his self-abjection as arena victim in *Satire* 1's Tigillinus passage, in the first exemplum of the opening triad:

     . . . torrens dicendi copia multis
     et sua mortifera est facundia; viribus ille

---

5. In addition to the standard commentaries, see Campana 2004; Uden 2015, chap. 5. *Satire* 2 began and concluded with a similarly broad sweep, ending up in Armenia.

6. Courtney 1980 finds it "natural" and cites Dio 38.19.1 as an example, along with Val. Max. 7.2. ext.1 and various Platonic passages as direct sources of inspiration (*ad loc.*); on *nebula*, cf. Pers. 5.7 (*grande locuturi nebulas Helicone legunto*); [Quint.] *Decl.* 36.7 (*confusionis nebulam*); Aul. Gell. 8.10, 20.3; on *nebulo*, Hor. *Sat.* 1.1.104; 1.2.12; Lucil. has *lucifugus nebulo* of a dishonest *quaestor* (499–500), and Nonus 18.24 explains *nebulo* and *tenebrio* as *qui mendaciis et astutiis suis nebulam quandam et tenebras obiciant.*

7. When used of the speaker's, *ratio* is positive (only again at 14.39, if genuine), but otherwise is frequently associated with specious or immoral rationalizing (4.20; 6.95, 223).

confisus periit admirandisque lacertis;
sed pluris nimia congesta pecunia cura
strangulat et cuncta exuperans patrimonia census
quanto delphinis ballaena Britannica maior.

To many, a torrential abundance of speech
and their own eloquence is fatal: one man died from relying on his
    strength
and amazing muscles, but money accumulated with too much care
strangles many others, and wealth outdoing all patrimonies—
by as much as the British whale exceeds dolphins. (9–14)

Elaboration of the dangers of the *torrens dicendi* and of *facundia* follows later in the poem, with reference to Cicero and Demosthenes both dying from their "overflowing font of talent" (*largus et exundans leto dedit ingenii fons*, 119), and Cicero in a particularly unpleasant way (114–32).[8] The man who relies on his muscles and the one who is suffocated by money are generally thought to refer to Milo of Croton and Midas, respectively,[9] but *periit*, as we have seen, is also a term from the "results card" of the arena (cf. *sed uterque perit orator*, 118, of Cicero and Demosthenes).[10] Likewise, *strangulare*, although extended to metaphorical usage, has the basic meaning of "throttle," as with a prisoner or criminal.[11] In 7.50, "the itch to write" was said to hold the poet "in its ambitious noose" (*laqueo . . . ambitioso*) and elsewhere in Juvenal there is always a suggestion of apposite and deserved punishment.[12] The participle *confisus* (with *fides* in its makeup) appears only one other time, in *Satire* 12.58–59, *confisus ligno . . . / . . . taedae*, of the merchant who abandons his possessions to his sinking ship and clings for dear life to a plank of floating pinewood.[13] Several

---

8. The bloodstained rostra need no explanation; Demosthenes "twisting and controlling the reins" of the Athenian assembly (*torquentem et pleni moderantem frena theatri*; 121, 128) is perhaps an echo of the speaker driving onto the plain where Lucilius *equos . . . flexit* (1.20); and see chap. 1 herein on *torqueo* of the satirist.

9. See Courtney 1980; Ferguson 1979, *ad loc.*

10. See chap. 3, p. 224 herein.

11. Tac. *Ann.* 6.25; Ov. *Tr.* 5.1.63 uses it of the tortures of grief, while Sen. *Ep.* 51.13 of *voluptas*: it is the last word in his harangue against Baiae, as he urges Lucilius to drive away all pleasures because they are like the bandits whom Egyptians call "lovers" in that "they embrace us only to throttle us" (*nos amplectuntur, ut strangulent*). Stat. *Silv.* 2.2.151 uses the verb when praising Polla because her money chest does not "suffocate" her wealth.

12. Cf. 10.53 discussed on pp. 237–38. In 13.244, the traitor (*perfidus*) is imagined as putting his feet *in laqueum* (like a hunted animal, says Courtney 1980, *ad loc.*), cf. 10.314 of Hephaestus's nets. Cf. Sen. *De Tranq.* 10.1: *At in aliquod genus vitae difficile incidisti et tibi ignoranti vel publica fortuna vel privata laqueum impegit, quem nec solvere possis nec rumpere.* On the *laquearius* as a type of gladiator or arena performer, see Dunkle 2008, 114.

13. See n41 below.

words are suggestive of excess (*copia, pluris nimia congesta, exuperans*), while the massive whale is a symbol of accumulation and consumption, an expansion of the big fish of *Satire* 4. We might say, then, that *Satire* 10 is a reprise of many themes and ideas that have gone before, setting the stage for a second foray onto the plain of satire. This poem marks a new intake of breath, a regurgitation of previous themes and images, a reassembling of *exempla* and components, for the second "movement" of a satire that is endlessly consuming and excreting, even cannibalizing, itself.

This time, however, the satirist affects to drop the Lucilian mode and invites us to choose between the reactions of Democritus and Heraclitus whenever they set foot beyond the threshold and went out into the world (*quotiens a limine moverat unum / protuleratque pedem*, 29–30, echoing *quid tam dextro pede concipis* in 5): Should we laugh with the former or cry with the latter? There are unmistakable echoes here of Seneca, *De Tranquillitate* 15.1:[14]

> Cum cogitaveris, quam sit rara simplicitas et quam ignota innocentia et vix umquam, nisi cum expedit, fides, et occurrit tot scelerum felicium turba et libidinis lucra damnaque pariter invisa et ambitio usque eo iam se suis non continens terminis, ut per turpitudinem splendeat: agitur animus in noctem et velut eversis virtutibus, quas nec sperare licet nec habere prodest, tenebrae oboriuntur. In hoc itaque flectendi sumus, ut omnia vulgi vitia non invisa nobis sed ridicula videantur et Democritum potius imitemur quam Heraclitum.

> When you reflect how rare is simplicity, how unknown is innocence, and how good faith hardly exists, except when it is profitable, and when you think of all the throng of successful crimes and of the gains and losses of lust, both equally hateful, and of ambition that, so far from restraining itself within its own bounds, now gets glory from baseness—when we remember these things, the mind is plunged into night, and as though the virtues, which it is now neither possible to expect nor profitable to possess, had been overthrown, there comes overwhelming gloom. We ought, therefore, to bring ourselves to believe that all the vices of the crowd are not hateful, but ridiculous, and to imitate Democritus rather than Heraclitus.[15]

14. On Seneca as a source of inspiration, see Courtney 1980, 449–52.
15. Trans. Basore 1928–35.

This is preferable to being seized by *odium generis humani*. Juvenal likewise recommends the example of the cachinnating Abderan, to whom the Roman trappings of *praetextae, trabeae, fasces, lectica, tribunal* were of course unknown (34–35), but who would nevertheless have shaken with laughter at the sight of the gloriously attired praetor in his procession through the Circus at the Ludi Romani (33–46) or upon encountering all the activities and anxieties, joys and sorrows, of men (48–52). He would, moreover, have responded to the threats of Fortune by telling her "to go and hang herself":

> quid si vidisset praetorem curribus altis
> extantem et medii sublimem pulvere circi
> in tunica Iovis et pictae Sarrana ferentem
> ex umeris aulaea togae magnaeque coronae
> tantum orbem, quanto cervix non sufficit ulla?   40
> Quippe tenet sudans hanc publicus et, sibi †consul†
> ne placeat, curru servus portatur eodem.
> Da nunc et volucrem, sceptro quae surgit eburno,
> illinc cornicines, hinc praecedentia longi
> agminis officia et niveos ad frena Quirites,   45
> defossa in loculos quos sportula fecit amicos.
> Tum quoque materiam risus invenit ad omnis
> occursus hominum, cuius prudentia monstrat
> summos posse viros et magna exempla daturos
> vervecum in patria crassoque sub aere nasci.   50
> Ridebat curas nec non et gaudia volgi,
> interdum et lacrimas, cum Fortunae ipse minaci
> mandaret laqueum mediumque ostenderet unguem.

> What if he'd seen our praetor standing conspicuously
> up there in his tall chariot, in the thick of the Circus dust,
> wearing the tunic of Jupiter, with the Tyrian hangings of an embroidered
>   toga
> falling from his shoulders and a huge crown so big around
> that no neck is strong enough for it?
> In fact, a public slave holds it, sweating profusely, and—so the president
>   doesn't get too pleased with himself—he rides in the same vehicle.
> Throw in the bird that soars from his ivory scepter,
> the horn-players there, here the escort in long lines walking ahead of him
> and the snowy white citizens at his bridle,
> transformed into friends by the handouts buried inside their purses.
> Democritus in his time, too, found things to laugh at in every

encounter with people. His shrewdness demonstrates that men of
excellence,
who will make great role models, can be born
in a dense climate in a country of morons.
He would laugh at the anxieties of the mob and at their delights, too,
and sometimes at their tears, while to Fortune's threats he himself would
say,
"Go throttle yourself!" and show his middle finger at her. (36–53)[16]

This "opening spectacle" displays the themes of the satires to come: how wrong-
headed choices, misdirected desires, and bad examples make people anxious or
miserable, and the resulting dominance of Fortune in human affairs. Living is a
coincidence of, or negotiation between, the actions of Fortuna and the choices
made by mortals. The preceding *Satire* 9 had ended with Naevolus complaining
that his *votum miserabile* for a modest home and income—or even just to be
poor—was unlikely to be met by an unresponsive Fortune:

... nam cum pro me Fortuna vocatur,
adfixit ceras illa de nave petitas
quae Siculos cantus effugit remige surdo.

For when Fortune is summoned on my behalf,
she has her ears plugged with wax fetched from that ship
which escaped the Sicilian songs with its deaf crew. (148–50)

The satirist, who assumes a role not so far removed from that of Fortuna in
relation to his own victims, is similarly unresponsive; however, the evocation of
Odysseus, struggling to reach his home of Ithaca, reminds us of the satirist's
own search for the secure anchorage of *Romanitas*.[17] But Naevolus's wishes were,
of course, misplaced and inappropriate, issuing from the mouth of a dissolute
purveyor of sexual favors, thus offering a lead into the theme of *Satire* 10, the
import of whose concluding lines is to throw the onus onto the individual—
who should by now be well informed by the speaker's flood of *exempla*:

Monstro quod ipse tibi possis dare; semita certe
tranquillae per virtutem patet unica vitae.
Nullum numen habes, si sit prudentia: nos te,
nos facimus, Fortuna, deam caeloque locamus.

16. Trans. Braund 2004.
17. See above, chap. 2n112 on Naevolus as satirist; chap. 3, p. 215, and n185, on Fortune as satirist and
editor.

I'm showing you something which you can give yourself; it is obvious
  that
the only path to a peaceful life lies through *virtus*.
You would have no power, Fortune, if people were sensible:
we are the ones who make you a goddess and place you in the sky.
  (363–66)

The rhetoric of exemplarity continues unabated in books 4 and 5; indeed
the term *exemplum* itself is used rather more prominently in the later poems:
in 10.47–50, the satirist counts Democritus among those excellent men
"who will provide great examples" (*magna exempla daturos*, 49), setting the
word in its original context of virtuous lives to imitate, while *Satire* 13 opens
with *exemplo quodcumque malo committitur, ipsi / displicet auctori* (Whatever
is done by way of setting a bad example is disadvantageous to the perpetrator, 1–2), and 14.31–32 observes that *velocius et citius nos / corrumpunt vitio-
rum exempla domestica* (examples of vice in the home corrupt us more speed-
ily and quickly). *Satire* 15.32 promises an exemplum produced by *dira feritas*
"in our time" in the shape of a horrifying instance of cannibalism among
the Egyptians.[18]

This new "philosophical" position of speaker (and reader)—even one mit-
igated by Democritean levity—does not, however, negate the prevailing conditions, the umbral scenery and dark encounters of the world of Juvenalian
satire, merely how we might respond to them. The opening passage of the
Praetor-in-his-Grandeur contains what look like conscious echoes of *Satire* 1 and
of some memorable moments from *Satire* 3. For instance, the train of Quirites
"at the praetor's bridle" (*ad frena*), made into his friends by the *sportula*, recalls
the handout scene in 1.95–126, as well as the theme of the corruption of *amicitia*, while the "snowy white" togas (and the mention of the *praetexta* and *trabea*)
pick up Umbricius's comments on pricy clothing and toga wearing in 3.172,
178–81 (10.33–53).[19] In the use of *defossa*, it is hard not to recall the *fossa* of 2.10
(*inter Socraticos notissima fossa cinaedos*); the Quirites have been "made into
friends" and "tamed" by the "treasure" of the *sportula* "buried" or "inserted" in
their purses, making them likewise into passive receptacles (45).[20] All the
various *occursus hominum* as fertile subject matter echo the satirist's original
farrago of ingredients in 1.85–86 (which included *discursus*), while *materiam
risus* recalls the question "*unde ingenium par materiae?*" of 1.150–52 and the

18. Cf. 10.247; 14.120, 322.
19. 3.180: *hic ultra vires habitus nitor*; cf. 10.99 and below, p. 245.
20. See chap. 2, pp. 119–21.

materiam . . . causasque iocorum provided by the poor man's dirty and torn cloak in 3.147–48 (47–48).[21] The horn players remind us of Artorius and Catulus, the *quondam cornicines* who, Umbricius observes, now produce *munera* and are the type of men whom Fortuna raises from low to high "whenever she wants to have a laugh" (3.34–44). The designation of Democritus's home city of Abdera as *vervecum . . . patria* (50) echoes one of the insults hurled at Umbricius by the street thug: *quis tecum . . . / . . . elixi vervecis labra comedit?* (293–94). The picture of the praetor with his "Tyrian hangings of an embroidered toga and a crown so big around that no neck is strong enough so that it has to be held by a sweating slave" loosely recalls Crispinus wafting his summer ring on sweaty fingers, unable to bear the weight of a heavier gem, *Tyrias umero revocante lucernas* (1.27–29).[22]

In these later books we are still very much enclosed in Juvenal's arena of satire, but, to make an analogy with the sequence of delights presented to the crowd in the developed amphitheater program of imperial times, we have moved from the morning's lurid and unpredictable bloodletting of *venationes* and the midday executions (and combinations thereof) to a series of postprandial managed encounters (like those of matched gladiators) between, on the one hand, the desire for wholeness, differentiation, and the securities of the Golden Age and, on the other, the disparate, confusing, and discordant realities of contemporary Roman existence.[23] We are also treated to match-ups between the reader and the speaker, and tests of his exempla or supposedly philosophical propositions. The text moves along with the schedule of events in the arena: with the morning *venationes* and midday executions of *noxii*, we have Juvenal on *indignatio* and *vitium*, while in the gladiatorial combats of the afternoon, we have Juvenal on *virtus*. The Praetor-in-the-Circus scene, heralding the Ludi Romani, is a spectacle of fundamentally the same order as the arena, with echoes of a triumphal parade thrown in.[24] It is indeed in this first poem of book 4 that what is perhaps Juvenal's most celebrated aphorism appears, when the speaker interjects his characterization of the fickle Roman mob into the middle of his account of the fall of Sejanus: that it cares only—and obsessively so, at that—for *panem et circenses* (72–81).

---

21. Cf. 6.418 (*gravis occursu*); 572 (*occursus . . . vitare*). As mentioned above, one of the devices of satire is that one is constantly "bumping into" or "being confronted" by such glaring examples. Cf. *materia* of poetic production in 7.21.

22. The phrase *magnaeque coronae / tantum orbem* might recall the frequent playing on *orbis* in *Sat.* 4 (39–40).

23. Cf. Sen. *De Ira* 1.11.2, on anger as the undoing of gladiators (*gladiatores quoque ars tuetur, ira denudat. Deinde quid opus est ira, cum idem proficiat ratio?*) and chap. 3, p. 186 herein.

24. Dunkle 2008, 155–56, 163.

Looking ahead, we note that in *Satire* 14, the speaker, continuing in his role as *editor*, says that he is offering an exceptional entertainment (*monstro volup-tatem egregiam*), unmatched by anything to be seen on the stage or produced by the praetor, "if you look at" (*si spectes*) how people risk their lives to increase their wealth (*quanto capitis discrimine constent / incrementa domus*; 256–59).[25] Never mind what you can see at the Floralia, Ludi Cereales, or Megalesia,[26] human activities are much more entertaining: *tanto maiores humana negotia ludi* (264).[27] In *Satire* 15, the escalating savagery of the Egyptian incident, with its arena-style bloodshed progressing from still harmless *prolusio* to full-blown *pugna*, points toward the opening poem of book 6, the truncated *Satire* 16, where we find the speaker in the arena that is the forum (*lentaque fori pugnamus harena*, 47), displaced from his rightful recourse to the law courts for the redress of grievances and injuries by the hobnailed boots of the soldiery and the threat of violence they represent.[28]

Virtuous Vacuity

In the first lengthy section of *Satire* 10, we read how, on Nero's orders, a whole cohort surrounded and besieged (*claudit . . . obsidet*) the homes of Longinus and Lateranus, and the gardens of Seneca, providing immediate proof of the theme of *evertere domos* (7), but are reminded that a "soldier rarely enters garrets" (*rarus venit in cenacula miles*; 15–18).[29] The focus then narrows down to cups and goblets:

> Pauca licet portes argenti vascula puri
> nocte iter ingressus, gladium contumque timebis   20
> et mota ad lunam trepidabis harundinis umbra:
> cantabit vacuus coram latrone viator.
> Prima fere vota et cunctis notissima templis
> divitiae, crescant ut opes, ut maxima toto
> nostra sit arca foro. Sed nulla aconita bibuntur   25

---

25. Cf. Hor. *Sat.* 2.8.79–80: "*nullos his mallem ludos spectasse; sed illa / redde, age, quae deinceps risisti*," to Fundanius describing Nasidienus's dinner.

26. On the Megalesia, see Dunkle 2008, 158, 163.

27. The speaker adds that the displays of the acrobat and funambulist are no more entertaining than "you yourself lingering and living on your Corycian boat" (265–75).

28. On the *prolusio*, see Dunkle 2008, 95–96; Cic. *De Orat.* 2.325; Prop. 4.4.19; Sen. *Ep.* 102.23.

29. Von Stackelberg 2009 on prestigious *horti* as "contested spaces between imperial and aristocratic interests" (600) and Spencer 2010 on the small kitchen garden (141–42).

fictilibus; tunc illa time cum pocula sumes
gemmata et lato Setinum ardebit in auro.

Although you carry only a few cups of plain silver
when you set out on a journey at night, you'll be afraid of swords and
    cudgels,
and you'll be terrified by a reed's shadow moving in the moonlight. A
traveler who is empty-handed will sing in the robber's face.
The first among prayers, and very familiar in all the temples,
is for wealth: let my money grow so that my treasure-chest
is the biggest in the whole forum!" But no aconite is drunk
from earthenware; you should be afraid when you are handed a goblet
studded with jewels, and the Setian wine glows in a golden bowl.
    (19–27)

The traveler carrying only plain silver cups, but who nonetheless fears the night-time footpad, even the twitching of the shadow of a reed in the moonlight, recalls the incident of the street thug who accosts the shadowy Umbricius on his way home or, worse, the *grassator* with his knife (3.285–308).[30] But the *vacuus viator* can even sing, drawing attention to himself. After the popular prayer for more money, which takes us into the forum and temples, the satirical lens enters internal space, for a pointed contrast between dining safely off earthenware and precariously from golden bowls or bejeweled goblets.[31] Plain silver, then, is dangerous enough, but goblets studded with jewels are positively life threatening. It is through them that poison may enter the body, potentially much more devastating than the robber facing the man in the street, for not only the value of the items themselves is involved, but the wealth to be gained by inheritance if their owner is murdered.[32]

Going back to *Satire* 5.29, we remember that *Saguntina lagona* was used of the cheap crockery Virro dispenses to humiliate his guests, and earthenware is elsewhere associated with simple living—no longer popular at Rome—although it is imagined as surviving out in the country, as Umbricius had earlier observed: *fictilibus cenare pudet, quod turpe negabis / translatus subito ad Marsos mensamque Sabellam* (168–69). In 6.342–45, simple black pottery connotes—via Numa and his ladle (*simpuvium*)—long-lost reverence

---

30. Cf. *nocturnus grassator*, Petr. 82.2; the twitching reed perhaps recalls the *Pomptina palus* from where the *grassatores* flood into the "feeding grounds" or "holding pens" (*vivaria*) of the city (3.308).

31. This is neatly sandwiched between its damaging effects, especially when the one who makes the prayer in the safety of common space finds himself alone and vulnerable to attack.

32. One is reminded here of the intrafamilial poisonings that marked the climax of *Sat.* 6.

for the gods, the time when nobody was a *contemptor numinis*.[33] In a similar fashion in *Satire* 11, which contains the satirist's vision of a simple meal fit for a Numa, "ordinary, cheap cups" (*plebeios calices et paucis assibus emptos*) are handed around by a simply attired (*incultus*), Latin-speaking, and thoroughly decent slave-boy from the country (145–60).[34] He can be contrasted with the *nigri manus ossea Mauri* (bony-handed dark Moor) who hands Trebius his cup at Virro's dinner, *cui per mediam nolis occurrere noctem / clivosae veheris dum per monumenta Latinae* (someone whom you'd not want to bump into in the middle of the night while being conveyed past the tombs on the hilly Latin Way, 5.53–55), as well as to the sneering and inattentive "Gaetulian Ganymede" (52–53, 59–65). This objectionable footman is styled as the "bloom of Asia" and was purchased for more than "the assets of Tullius and Ancius" or in fact "all the knick-knacks of the kings of Rome" (*Romanorum omnia regum / frivola*, 56–59).

Thus, what had been, earlier on in the collection, a signifier of poverty and shame, of the *res angusta domi* in Umbricius's words, namely simple pottery, has in *Satire* 10 become a means of staying alive.[35] The suggestion of containment in *angustus* has moral overtones, as we can see from the barbed comment in 6.357–58 on women who spend lavishly on their pleasures (*multis res angusta domi, sed nulla pudorem / paupertatis habet*). We can compare Seneca's comment in *De Constantia* 15.5 to the effect that Fortune does not enter a house characterized by the absence of things that furnish ample opportunities for mischief:

> domus haec sapientis angusta, sine cultu, sine strepitu, sine
> apparatu . . . sed per hoc limen vacuum et ab ostiariis liberum
> Fortuna non transit: scit non esse illic sibi locum, ubi sui nihil est.

> This house of the wise man is cramped, without adornment, without
> bustle, without pomp . . . but over this threshold, empty and free
> from door-keepers, Fortune does not cross. She knows there's is no
> place for her there, where nothing belongs to her.[36]

Such a house is *angusta* because the *sapiens* has kept his desires and appetites within narrow confines by exercising self-containment. In the image of Nero's soldiers "surrounding" and "besieging" the property of Longinus and company,

---

33. See Courtney 1980, *ad loc.*, on the use of earthenware vessels in religious rites.

34. In 11.61–62, the speaker styles himself as Evander, and his guest as Hercules or Aeneas.

35. Cf. 3.164–68: *haud facile emergunt quorum virtutibus obstat / res angusta domi, sed Romae durior illis / conatus*, and the introduction, p. 38 herein.

36. Cf. *De Tranq.* 9.3: *cogendae in artum res sunt ut tela [Fortunae] in vanum cadant.* Hor. *Odes* 3.2.1–3: *Angustam amice pauperiem pati / robustus acri militia puer / condiscat . . .*

we have a different sort of containment, that is, confinement with the threat of violence for the possessors of wealth designated for appropriation by the Emperor.

We may return also to Umbricius's account of the destruction by fire of two contrasting homes (3.198–222), Persicus's *magna domus* and Cordus's miserable attic hovel (*tabulata tertia*):

> Lectus erat Cordo Procula minor, urceoli sex
> ornamentum abaci, nec non et parvulus infra
> centaurus recubans ab eodem marmore Chiron
> iamque vetus Graecos servabat cista libellos.

> Cordus had a bed too small for Procula, six small jugs
> as decoration for his tabletop, and, underneath, a little centaur,
> Chiron, lying on its back, made from the same "marble,"
> and an old box kept his little Greek books safe. (203–206)

The statuette of Chiron was made of earthenware, the same "marble" as the little jugs, if we follow Markland's interpretation.[37] Cordus loses even his "entire nothing" (*totum nihil*) in the fire and is left without food or shelter (*nemo cibo, nemo hospitio tectoque iuvabit*); Persicus, however, with the embers of his pile still smouldering, and even though he is suspected of self-serving arson, gets to replace his lost possessions with generous gifts from his friends (*ardet adhuc, et iam accurrit qui marmora donet*), including statues by Euphranor and bronzes by Polyclitus, books and bookcases, a Minerva centerpiece, and, to top it off, a heap of silver (3.209–222). But from the new perspective of *Satire* 10, Cordus's top-floor garret, which leads to the loss of all belongings—if not of life itself—in the case of a fire, is a place which is not in danger of being raided and whose owner is at least safe from being murdered for his money. Emptiness amid excess has become positively valuable, even desirable. Umbricius heads for *vacuae Cumae* in 3.2, echoed by another deserted town, *vacuae Ulubrae*, in 10.102. This kind of out-of-the-way location comes up in the context of the downfall of Sejanus—"you might well desire all of Sejanus's powers, but what if all that success is accompanied by an equal measure of misfortune?" (*sed quae praeclara et prospera tanti, / ut rebus laetis par sit mensura malorum?* 90–98). Then indeed, instead of wearing the

---

37. Braund 2004; cf. Manzella 2011, 310–11. On the details and textual problems, see Courtney 1980 and Braund 1996a, *ad loc.*; a similar scene occurs in 7.28–29, where the poet Telesinus is pictured writing "elevated" poetry in his tiny garret: *Qui facis in parva sublimia carmina cella / ut dignus venias hederis et imagine macra*—a scrawny bust for a skinny poet.

toga of the man whose corpse is being dragged along (*huius qui trahitur praetex-tam sumere*), it might well be preferable to be the *potestas* in Fidenae or Gabii or *de mensura ius dicere, vasa minora / frangere pannosus vacuis aedilis Vlubris* (99–102). Better to be breaking little vases in the backwater of Ulubrae than be hacked to bits in Rome like Sejanus. The "attenuated" living which is envisaged here as the foil to Sejanus's perilous arc of achievement has obvious echoes with Umbricius's vision (3. 223–31) of the quiet country life in a little garden with a well:

> Vive bidentis amans et culti vilicus horti
> unde epulum possis dare centum Pythagoreis.
> Est aliquid, quocumque loco, quocumque recessu,
> unius sese dominum fecisse lacertae.

> Live, loving your hoe, as the overseer of your vegetable garden,
> from which you will to give a banquest to a hundred Pythagoreans.
> It's something, wherever you are, however remote,
> to have made yourself the master of a single lizard. (228–31)

"So, what are the pointless and damaging things that people wish for?" the speaker of *Satire* 10 asks in 54 as he begins his survey proper (*ergo supervacua aut quae perniciosa petuntur?*). Ironically, "supervacuity" is exactly what they should be aiming at.[38] Poverty here becomes a synonym for a lost cleanliness and propriety. Material used mainly for ridicule of social status in earlier poems now serves as the stuff of a possible satiric antithesis, although, as with the vision of the Golden Age in *Satire* 6, the inherent ambiguities have always already undermined any attempt to establish a clear or convincing alternative to the way things are. Let us consider, for example, a dramatic moment in *Satire* 12, when the merchant Catullus is forced into desperate measures by a storm at sea:

> . . . imitatus castora, qui se
> eunuchum ipse facit cupiens evadere damno
> testiculi: adeo medicatum intellegit inguen.
> "fundite quae mea sunt" dicebat "cuncta" Catullus,
> praecipitare volens etiam pulcherrima, vestem
> purpuream teneris quoque Maecenatibus aptam.

---

38. On the use of the adjective *supervacuus* (empty, pointless, superfluous) in philosophical discourse, see *De Tranq.* 12.1: *ne aut in supervacuis aut ex supervacuo laboremus,* . . . *vanitatem cupiditatum nostrarum* and Courtney 1980, 449. Also *Ep.* 88.36: *qui supervacua usibus comparat et pretiosarum rerum pompam in domo explicat . . . qui occupatus est in supervacua litterarum supellectile.*

> ... imitating the beaver who makes himself
> a eunuch in his desire to escape by losing
> a testicle: so well does he understand his medicinal groin.
> "Throw my things overboard," Catullus kept saying, "all of them!"
> willing to ditch even his finest possessions:
> purple clothes fit even for delicate Maecenases. (34–39)

We have once again the idea that being bereft of possessions brings with it the preservation of life, albeit here at a cost likened to the beaver castrating itself.[39] Back in 2.116, the male genitalia were described as *supervacuam carnem*, ripe for removal "in the Phrygian manner" as the logical conclusion of the effeminate activities described in 83–116.[40] Catullus indeed is unusual in his "self-sacrifice"—who would "have the balls" to do the same nowadays? (*Sed quis nunc alius, qua mundi parte quis audit / argento praeferre caput rebusque salutem? 48–49*). The reprieve for the merchant of *Satire* 12 is, however, only temporary—the man who cheats death, who "esapes Libitina," may all too easily fall victim to a much more common danger, a legacy hunter like Pacuvius:

> Laudo meum civem, nec comparo testamento
> mille rates; nam si Libitinam evaserit aeger,
> delebit tabulas inclusus carcere nassae
> post meritum sane mirandum atque omnia soli
> forsan Pacuvio breviter dabit.

> I congratulate my fellow citizen and do not compare a thousand ships
> with a will; for if the invalid escapes Libitina,
> he will destroy his will, ensnared by the fisherman's trap
> after some obviously astounding service by Pacuvius,
> and with a word or two he will perhaps leave everything to him alone.
> (121–25)[41]

If we pursue the storm and shipwreck a little further, we find that similar scenery is deployed in 14.267–302 (thus forging a link between the two poems, and between books 4 and 5), this time to mock the "desperate and cheapskate

---

39. Cf. 5.163–65: *quis enim tam nudus, ut illum / bis ferat...?* (Who could be so naked [i.e., destitute] to put up with Virro more than once?) Castration: see 34–36 and Larmour 2005a; Uden 2015, 183–94.

40. See chap. 2 herein.

41. He entrusts himself to a plank of pine log (*confisus ligno, digitis a morte remotus / quattuor aut septem, si sit latissima, taedae,* 12.58–59), and in 3.254–56 a long fir log and a whole pine tree nod threateningly above the crowds in the street (*nutant alte populoque minantur*). *Taeda* picks up 1.155, *taeda lucebis in illa* ... from the Tigillinus scene with the body in the arena, so that something formerly a source of danger has again become a hope of salvation. On Libitina, see chap. 1, p. 92 herein.

trader in stinking sacks" (*perditus ac vilis sacci mercator olentis*, 269) and the greedy merchant who who puts himself in danger merely for "bits of chopped up silver and inscriptions with tiny portraits" (*concisum argentum in titulos faciesque minutas*, 291). He can lose everything, being left in rags with only scraps of food to eat—like Cordus left *nudum et frusta rogantem* by the fire (3.210). This line of thought is continued in 14.303–308:

> Tantis parta malis cura maiore metuque
> servantur: misera est magni custodia census.
> Dispositis praedives amis vigilare cohortem
> servorum noctu Licinus iubet, attonitus pro
> electro signisque suis Phrygiaque columna
> atque ebore et lata testudine . . .

> Objects acquired through such great hardships are kept safe
> with even greater anxiety and fear. Guarding great wealth is miserable.
> Superrich Licinus with his fire buckets orders his cohort
> of slaves to keep watch through the night, terrified for his
> amber and statues and columns of Phrygian marble
> and ivory and plaques of tortoiseshell . . .

By contrast, the vat of the naked Cynic doesn't burn and can easily be replaced or repaired if broken; this is the large, lived-in version of the small and simple vases mentioned earlier (14.308–314).[42] The lines that follow these offer some concluding advice as to exactly how much wealth is enough:

> Nullum numen habes, si sit prudentia: nos te,
> nos facimus, Fortuna, deam.[43] Mensura tamen quae
> sufficiat census, si quis me consulat, edam:

> You would have no power, Fortune, if people were sensible:
> we are the ones, who make you a goddess. But, as to what amount
> of wealth is enough, if anyone asks my advice, I shall explain: (315–17)

The phrasing and the use of *edo* recall 1.19–21, suggesting that we have here a second weighty pronouncement, the distillation of all the knowledge picked up hitherto in the arena of satire, since we encountered *edam* the first time (1.21). Any such expectations are likely to be disappointed, however. Epicurus's

---

42. And the antithesis of the big vat of wine in 6.431 in the vignette of the hard-drinking woman athlete; on Diogenes, cf. Sen. *De Tranq.* 8.

43. Echoing *Sat.* 10.365–66; on the text, see Courtney 1980, *ad loc.*

garden and Socrates' house might seem to provide worthy exempla to imitate (*quantum, Epicuri, tibi parvis suffecit in hortis, / quantum Socratici ceperunt ante penates*, 319–20),[44] but the statement *numquam aliud natura, aliud sapientia dicit* (321) is hardly novel, enlightening, or satisfying as a guide to life.[45]

And immediately, the speaker imagines an interlocutor complaining that he is being hemmed in, constricted, by "too severe examples" (*acribus exemplis*, 322). The moment of containment and restraint is fleeting—and exclusively Hellenic—as the speaker turns to Roman ways (*nostris de moribus*, 323): "Take then the amount of money required to sit in the first fourteen rows in the theater, according to the law of Roscius Otho [the Equestrian census of 400,000 sesterces]." Imagining the addressee as insatiable, he continues:

> Haec quoque si rugam trahit extenditque labellum,
> sume duos equites, fac tertia quadringenta.
> Si nondum implevi gremium, si panditur ultra,
> nec Croesi fortuna umquam nec Persica regna
> sufficient animo nec divitiae Narcissi,
> indulsit Caesar cui Claudius omnia, cuius
> paruit imperiis uxorem occidere iussus.

> If this too makes you frown and pout,
> then take two knights, make it a triple 400,000.
> If I have not yet filled your lap, if it stretches even wider,
> then neither the wealth of Croesus nor the kingdoms of Persia
> will ever satisfy you, nor the riches of Narcissus,
> on whom Claudius Caesar bestowed everything,
> and whose commands he obeyed when ordered to kill his wife.
>
>   (14.325–31)

Thus we travel from the small Epicurean garden and modest Socratic house to the Roman theater, to the eastern kingdoms of Lydia and Persia, then back to the intimate yet public space of the imperial household, where Narcissus, the ludicrously wealthy freedman—with a Greek name—who managed Claudius's correspondence, orders a Caesar to kill his wife. With that blunt act, the action of this satire ceases. As the imagined interlocutor cannot be

---

44. This reference to Socrates is certainly more positive than the only other one, in 2.10: *inter Socraticos notissima fossa cinaedos.*

45. Cic. *De Fin.* 59–61, speaking of "extravagant and imaginary desires" which are never attained (*animi autem morbi sunt cupiditates immensae et inanes . . . numquam in sententia permanentes . . . Igitur neque stultorum quisquam beatus neque sapientium non beatus*).

satisfied, the speaker simply stops, rather than ends. There is no *iam satis est* like Horace's following his depiction of the man who departs from life *contentus*, like a satisfied dinner guest (*Satire* 1.1.117–20).[46] The satirical gaze rests first on the body of the addressee—thirst, hunger, cold; forehead frowning (like Naevolus's) and lip pouting; and an ever expanding lap—then it moves to Narcissus with his reputed worth of more than 400 million sesterces—that is, 100 times the qualification for an Equestrian—and thence to Messalina, whose own "insatiability" was graphically described in the brothel scene of *Satire* 6, *lassata viris necdum satiata recessit* (115–32).

The *brevitas* of Messalina's demise in the last line of *Satire* 14 ([*Claudius*] *paruit imperiis uxorem occidere iussus* (331) captures something of the relative swiftness of her actual elimination, to be sure, but, more important in the context of the poem, brings a sudden halt to what has been a lengthy discussion (it is the third longest after *Satires* 6 and 10) of corruption—of children by parents and of everyone by the crimes of *avaritia*—with a sordid execution plot in the imperial family.[47] At the same time, it is a humiliating portrait of the impotent emperor, the *pater patriae*, following orders from a jumped-up Greek. As Courtney says, "Narcissus is the imperator now."[48] Ferguson describes the last line as "a bitter despondent climax," and it is significant that a poem whose subject is the education of children, or rather their mal-education, ends with murder in the highest family of the Empire. The tricking of wife by husband— or husband's agent—parallels the murderous machinations against husbands by wives at the end of *Satire* 6. As there and in *Satire* 2, the chronotopic range is very wide in the service of showing the sterile and moribund condition of the Roman family. Amid all the acquisition of wealth and material goods, the pivotal relationship between parent and child, especially father and son, is on the edge of destruction. In this poem, Juvenal narrows the focus down to one all-encompassing vice, namely acquisitiveness or greed (*avaritia*). This is unfettered desire for consumption, whose end result is cannibalism, a world in which eating people is *not* wrong. Just before it ends, *Satire* 14 repeats the last two lines of *Satire* 10—how "we" make Fortune a goddess—but the concluding lines of the later poem plumb new depths of bleakness and desolation.

---

46. *Inde fit ut raro, qui se vixisse beatum / dicat et exacto contentus tempore vita / cedat ut conviva satur, reperire queamus. / iam satis est.* See chap. 1 herein.

47. For details, see Tac. *Ann.* 11.30–38; she died with her mother in the role of spectator; see O'Gorman 2000 on spectacle and display in Tac.'s account (115–21). On *indulsit*, cf. 15.174 (p. 288 below), and chap. 2n171 above.

48. Tac. *Ann.* 11.37–38 says Narcissus acted without Claudius's authority and informed him only afterward. O'Gorman 2000 nonetheless notes Claudius's "exceptionally passive role" in Tac.'s narrative (116), cf. 121 on how the reader is rendered as passive as Claudius.

Fine Furnishings

We can explore further the description of objects—especially those made of metal—whose very solidity might seem to promise an anchor of stability, like gold in a financial crisis. We shall consider household furnishings first and statues of ancestors and famous public figures second. In the satirist's vision of the world, there is only an appearance of solidity, as these objects are prone to being "melted down" or transformed into other things and are emblematic of the broader deterioration of the body, the *domus*, the state, and indeed of *Romanitas* itself.

Juvenal naturally taps into well-worn Roman discourses about luxury and corruption when he refers to jewel-encrusted goblets or elaborately decorated furniture, but the details he chooses to embellish bring his own fixations into high relief.[49] Take for example, this first appearance of the topos in *Satire* 1.75–76:

> Criminibus debent hortos, praetoria, mensas
> argentum vetus et stantem extra pocula caprum.

> It is to crimes that people owe their gardens, mansions, dining tables,
> antique silver and goblets with embossed goats.

From crimes as their source, we move in gradually from the gardens to the dining room, with its antique silver and the embossed goat on goblets.[50] The table is picked up in 137–38:

> Nam de tot pulchris et latis orbibus et tam
> antiquis una comedunt patrimonia mensa.

> For, from so many splendid, large, round tables, and of such antiquity,
> they consume entire patrimonies at a single sitting.

Again, we zero in centripetally from multiple tables across time and space to just one, as the produce of forest and sea, purchased from amassed fortunes, is brought together before the lone diner, designedly styled as *rex*. In *Satire* 5, we have a similarly regal diner in the shape of the abusive patron Virro,[51] whose dishes are drawn from far and wide. There is a telling contrast between Virro's bejeweled goblets and Trebius's "Vatinian" cup:

---

49. See Edwards 1993, chap. 5; Sen. *De Tranq.* 1.5–9 on modest furnishings, food, and slaves.
50. As Ferguson 1979 notes, bribery is here linked to sexual corruption via the figure of the he-goat (*ad loc.*).
51. See 5.14, 130, 137, 161.

              ipse capaces
Heliadum crustas et inaequales berullo
Virro tenet phialas: tibi non committitur aurum,
vel, si quando datur, custos adfixus ibidem,   40
qui numeret gemmas, ungues observet acutos.
Da veniam: praeclara illi laudatur iaspis.
Nam Virro, ut multi, gemmas ad pocula transfert
a digitis, quas in vaginae fronte solebat
ponere zelotypo iuvenis praelatus Iarbae.   45
Tu Beneventani sutoris nomen habentem
siccabis calicem nasorum quattuor ac iam
quassatum et rupto poscentem sulpura vitro.

Virro himself holds capacious goblets encrusted with amber
and rough with beryl. His gold isn't entrusted to you,
or if it is, a guard is stationed on the spot
to count the jewels and keep a watch on your sharp fingernails.
Don't blame him: his splendid jasper is much admired.
The fact is that Virro, like many people, shifts his jewels from his fingers
to his cups—jewels that might have been set on the scabbard front
of the young man who was preferred to jealous Iarbas.
But you'll drain a vessel named after the shoemaker in Beneventum
with its four nozzles. It's already cracked and looking for
sulphur matches in exchange for its broken glass. (5.37–48)[52]

There are several items of interest here, including the derivation of the nozzles
of the cup from the long nose or facial deformities of the ex-cobbler Vatinius
and the fact that it's already cracked—befitting the sorry state (and status) of
Trebius.[53] This Vatinius is given a succinct but scathing characterization by Tacitus, as he records how Nero on his way to Greece stopped off at Beneventum
to watch a gladiatorial *munus* he was giving:

> Vatinius inter foedissima eius aulae ostenta fuit, sutrinae tabernae
> alumnus, corpore detorto, facetiis scurrilibus; primo in contumelias
> adsumptus, dehinc optimi cuiusque criminatione eo usque valuit ut
> gratia pecunia vi nocendi etiam malos praemineret.

---

52. Trans. Braund 2004.

53. See Ferguson 1979; Courtney 1980; Braund 1996a, *ad loc.*; and Mart. 14.96 *vilia sutoris calicem monumenta Vatini / accipe; sed nasus longior ille fuit.* On the broken glass, cf. the gaping crack (*veteris rimae . . . hiatum,*
3.195) in the impoverished housing of people like Cordus.

This outstanding monstrosity of the court had originated from a
shoe shop. Deformed in body and scurrilous in wit, he had first been
taken up as a butt for abuse. But then he gained power enough to
eclipse any scoundrel in influence, wealth and capacity for damage.
He rose by attacking decent people. (*Annals* 15.34)[54]

Thus the mention of Beneventum and the cups brings with it the exemplum
of the unsavory career of Vatinius and his trajectory under Nero from lowlife
target of abuse to a wealthy member of the imperial court with the power to
hurt others. Returning to Virro's glassware, we may note especially the goblets
Heliadum crustas et inaequales berullo: the triple spondee ending is rare, and
Courtney suggests it "matches the rare objects." It also gives emphasis to the
term *inaequalis*, whose primary meaning is "embossed" but, as Braund says,
also carries suggestions of unfairness.[55] There is a link between the un-
evenness of the goblet and the inequality of not only the meal but the entire
relationship of Virro and Trebius. Horace had used the word in a positive
context, recounting a dinner at which each guest could decide for himself how
much water he wished to add to his wine, and as a result the guests drained
"unequal cups" (*siccat inaequalis calices conviva,* Satire 2.6.68)—a sign of the
freedom of choice and respectful treatment that are completely absent for
Trebius. More generally, *inaequalis* suggests inconsistency and a lack of harmony; goblets with embossed goats and jewels are hybrid creations, carrying
connotations similar to those of other "mixed" elements in Juvenalian discourse. They are inherently suspect—in social, moral, and sexual terms—and
are signifiers of degeneration from a putative, now long-lost simplicity of a
time when men were men, women were women, and cups were cups.

In 12.43–47, when describing how the greedy but panic-stricken merchant
throws his goods overboard in a storm, the speaker takes time to give an in-
ventory of his valuable objects:

Ille nec argentum dubitabat mittere, lances
Parthenio factas, urnae cratera capacem
et dignum sitiente Pholo vel coniuge Fusci;
adde et bascaudas et mille escaria, multum
caelati, biberat quo callidus emptor Olynthi.

He did not hestitate to jettison silver, dishes
made by Parthenius, a three-gallon mixing bowl

---

54. Trans. Grant 1977.
55. Braund 1996a, 284, citing Mart. 4.85; cf. Juv. 14.62: *leve argentum, vasa aspera.*

fit for thirsty Pholus or even for Fuscus' wife,

plus baskets and a thousand plates and many engraved goblets,

from which the wily buyer of Olynthus had drunk.

The Parthenius by (or for) whom the dishes were made is unknown: he could be a *caelator* as the scholiast suggests, or, if the recipient, perhaps a member of Domitian's household.[56] Pholus the centaur (with whom we may contrast the wise Chiron in Cordus's penurious attic, 3.205) used a huge crater as a weapon against the Lapiths and entertained Hercules with an equally capacious one.[57] The "wily buyer" is Philip of Macedon, who used bribery as a means of acquiring cities like Olynthus; he was also a big boozer.

The jewels on Virro's goblet might well have been seen on Aeneas's scabbard (*in vaginae fronte*, 5.44), but that makes their use here all the more inappropriate.[58] Ferguson sees "a neat ambiguity: 'on the front of his scabbard' but also 'in front of his mistress,' with some contrast to the homosexual Virro." The observation that Virro, like many people of his ilk, "transfers jewels from fingers to cups" is a criticism of nouveau-riche vulgarity, like Crispinus's "summer-ring" in the catalog at the opening of *Satire* 1.[59] Juvenal reinforces the link between body and vessel and this proves useful elsewhere for sexual innuendo, such as in 2.95, where the man wearing women's clothes drinks from a phallus-shaped cup made of glass, thus performing *fellatio* as he imbibes.[60] Similarly in 6.0.4–6, in the description of what goes on chez the *professus obscenum*, we have mention of two practitioners of oral sex[61] drinking from shared vessels

56. See Ferguson 1979; Courtney 1980, *ad loc.* Previous owners added luster to valuable items, cf. Mart. 8.6.3 (*argenti stemmata*); Juv. 6.155–60, where Bibula buys, among other precious items, a diamond once worn in a ring by Berenice, who was reputed to have had an incestuous relationship with her brother, Herod Agrippa.

57. Stesich. Fr. 4 [Page]; Stat. *Theb.* 2.563; see Courtney 1980, *ad loc.* who notes that the effect here "is to reduce everything to the mercantile level and link luxuries with corruption." With Fuscus's wife, cf. the one who binges after her exercises, also from a full *urna* (6.426 and chap. 2, p. 137 herein).

58. Courtney 1980 observes that the jasper in *Aen.* 4.261–62 is on the sword, not the scabbard (*ad loc.*); Braund 1996a, "transferral of jewels from military to luxurious context marks the breakdown of Roman morality portrayed in the dysfunctional patron-client relationship in *Satire* 5." Cf. the warning against having a "little Aeneas" running around in your hallway, if you want to become a worthy target of the legacy hunter (5.137–40).

59. 1.28–29, cf. 4.1–34; 7.143–44.

60. See Courtney 1980 and Braund 1996a, *ad loc.*; Plin. Eld. *HN* 33.4.

61. As Courtney 1980 explains, following Housman, the "Gourd" (*Colocyntha*) could mean the mouth of a *cunnilingus* while the "bearded Swallow-tail" (*barbata Chelidon*) might suggest the mouth of a *fellator* "which like the vulva is a receptacle for the penis"; cf. L. and P. Watson 2014, *ad loc.* In 6.300–305, the inebriated "Venus" knows no distinction between head and crotch, as she "chomps giant oysters at midnight" and drinks from a *concha* (perfume-bowl), with the ceiling and table moving about and double lamps; this leads straight into the scene with Tullia and Maura pissing on the Altar of Pudicitia (see chap. 2 herein). Maura is the name of a *fellatrix* in 10.223–24.

that should be broken (*frangenda*, 5) rather than just rinsed out—as a result they are a disgusting prospect by the time they get passed around to the lips of the respectable citizen by his wife, no matter how good the wine might be (14–16).

In *Satire* 11, which contains the lengthiest attempt at depicting a satiric antithesis, through a simple, no-frills meal, the host's simple and wholesome courses (*fercula . . . nullis ornata macellis*, 64) are associated with Curius and other exemplars of Republican morality in a bill of fare that serves as a counterbalance to the dueling menus of *Satire* 5.64–89.[62] Here, where *tunc* is consistently opposed to *nunc*, and the host is cast as a throwback, an Evander welcoming Hercules or Aeneas (60–63), Juvenal takes up the topic of hybrid objects in a far more extended fashion:

> Cum tremerent autem Fabios durumque Catonem   90
> et Scauros et Fabricium, rigidique severos
> censoris mores etiam collega timeret,
> nemo inter curas et seria duxit habendum
> qualis in Oceani fluctu testudo nataret,
> clarum Troiugenis factura et nobile fulcrum;   95
> sed nudo latere et parvis frons aerea lectis
> vite coronati caput ostendebat aselli,
> ad quod lascivi ludebant ruris alumni.
> [tales ergo cibi qualis domus atque supellex.]
> Tunc rudis et Graias mirari nescius artes   100
> urbibus eversis praedarum in parte reperta
> magnorum artificum frangebat pocula miles,
> ut phaleris gauderet equus caelataque cassis
> Romuleae simulacra ferae mansuescere iussae
> imperii fato, geminos sub rupe Quirinos   105
> ac nudam effigiem clipeo venientis et hasta
> pendentisque dei perituro ostenderet hosti.
> Ponebant igitur Tusco farrata catino:
> argenti quod erat solis fulgebat in armis.
> omnia tunc quibus invideas, si lividulus sis.   110

> Back when people quaked at the Fabii and at stern Cato
> and at the Scauri and Fabricius, and when the strict censor's
> rigid morality scared even his colleague,
> and no one thought it a matter of serious concern

---

62. See chap. 3 herein.

what kind of tortoise swimming in Ocean's waves
would make a splendid and illustrious headrest for our Trojan-born
  elite.
Instead, their couches were modest with undecorated sides,
the bronze front displaying a donkey's head garlanded with a vine—
and around this the naughty country children would play.
[Their food matched their homes and furniture]
In those days a soldier was a simple man with no appreciation of Greek
  art.
If there were goblets made by great craftsmen in his share
of the booty from a sacked city, he would break them up,
just so his horse could delight in trappings and his helmet be embossed
  with images
for his enemy to see at the moment of death: Romulus' beast
  commanded
by the order of fate to grow tame, or the twin Quirini under the rock,
or the image of the god swooping down stripped of shield and spear.
No surprise, then, that they would serve their porridge in Tuscan bowls.
What silver they had, they kept to make their armour gleam.
All this you might envy them—if you are of an envious disposition!
  (11.90–110)[63]

Modest couches with undecorated sides—a simple *frons aerea* (it is hard not to
think of *frontis nulla fides* here)—contrast with the elaborately worked furniture
elsewhere, while the little ass-heads are as fitting to the setting as the naughty
country children are.[64] Line 99 is thought by some editors to be spurious, but
it does neatly connect home, food, and furnishing.[65] A Roman soldier of earlier days would break up goblets fashioned by Greek craftsmen, and they would
be used to make medallions for his horses and embossed images on his helmet. These are primal tableaux of the Roman identity narrative with the
original cast—Romulus, Remus, Rhea Silvia, and Mars. The god, whose absence was lamented and lambasted in earlier poems, is now present, but only
as a sign on imagined armor of the distant past. Courtney detects "a tinge of
epic parody" here, and the scene is somewhat reminiscent of the cave dwellers
at the opening of *Satire* 6, even if *rudis* here is a term of approbation, or of
the rustic home of the farming brothers in *Satire* 14, where "big pots steam

---

63. Trans. Braund 2004.
64. In Hor. *Sat.*1.3.134, *lascivi pueri* are representatives of the satirist; Gowers 2012, *ad loc.*
65. Ferguson 1979; Courtney 1980, *ad loc.*

with porridge" (*grandes fumabant pultibus ollae*, 171).[66] When the uncorrupted soldier breaks up the finely fashioned Greek cups and reworks them into traditional accoutrements of Roman masculinity, his action is emblematic of the "breaking down" performed by the satirist, whose aim is to fragment and obliterate the Rome he sees as he attempts to refashion the demarcations of its original form. The last line appears to be ironic in tone; the only other use of *lividus* is in 6.631, of the pastries steaming "darkly" with stepmother's poison.[67]

The speaker continues with a religious interjection, recalling the content of the Grove of Egeria episode at the opening of *Satire* 3, commenting that in those days *templorum quoque maiestas praesentior* (111) and Jupiter—of clay, not violated by gold (*fictilis et nullo violatus Iuppiter auro*, 116)—saved the city from the Gauls.[68] In those days, tables were "homegrown" (117–18): *illa domi natas nostraque ex arbore mensas / tempora viderunt*. The next passage pulls together a number of already enunciated themes and images:

> At nunc divitibus cenandi nulla voluptas,   120
> nil rhombus, nil damma sapit, putere videntur
> unguenta atque rosae, latos nisi sustinet orbis
> grande ebur et magno sublimis pardus hiatu
> dentibus ex illis quos mittit porta Syenes
> et Mauri celeres et Mauro obscurior Indus,   125
> et quos deposuit Nabataeo belua saltu
> iam nimios capitique graves. Hinc surgit orexis,
> hinc stomacho vires; nam pes argenteus illis,
> anulus in digito quod ferreus. Ergo superbum
> convivam caveo, qui me sibi comparat et res   130
> despicit exiguas. Adeo nulla uncia nobis
> est eboris, nec tessellae nec calculus ex hac
> materia, quin ipsa manubria cultellorum
> ossea. Non tamen his ulla umquam obsonia fiunt
> rancidula aut ideo peior gallina secatur.   135

> But nowadays, for the rich there's no pleasure in dining,
> the turbot, the venison has no taste, the perfumes
> and roses seem to stink, unless the broad round tabletops are supported

---

66. As it is of the rustic and *incultus* slave-boy: *tirunculus ac rudis omni / tempore* (143–46).

67. Courtney 1980 says, "The line seems generally odd" (*ad loc.*); but cf. *livor* of the immoral discoloration of grapes in 2.81 and of the abused citizen's facial bruises in 16.11.

68. Cf. 3.18–20: *. . . quanto praesentius esset / numen aquis, viridi si margine cluderet undas / herba nec ingenuum violarent marmora tofum.* See Larmour 2007, 196–99.

by a huge piece of ivory, a rampant leopard with its big gaping mouth,
made from tusks which the gate of Syene sends in
and the speedy Moors and from the Indian who is darker than the
    Moor,
the tusks which the beast shed in the Nabatean grove
when too large and heavy for its head. From this the appetite rises,
from this the stomach gains strength; for to these people, a silver
    table-leg
is like an iron ring on their finger. For this reason, I avoid the haughty
    guest
who compares me with himself and looks down upon my meagre
    resources.
Indeed I am so bereft of ivory, I have no dice or counters made from it,
and even the handles of my knives are of bone. But none of my food is
    rotten
because of them, nor is the chicken carved any the worse for that reason.
    (11.120–35)

The *rhombus* and *latos orbes* glance back to the fish of *Satire* 4, while the ivory leopard "rampant" or "in relief" recalls other embossed items cited earlier. Mention of the *porta Syene* and *Mauri* picks up on disparaging references to Egyptians and North Africans elsewhere.[69] Expensive furniture counteracts the nausea of the rich, whose palates are jaded by extravagance, and brings on the *orexis* (appetite)—a word last used in 6.428, where the athletic woman returning from exercise downs a *sextarius* of wine for the same purpose: *ante cibum rabidam facturus orexim*.[70] The jump from table leg to ring on the finger chimes with previous scenes involving rings and dining or some combination of the two. With *rancidulus* ("rotten" or "a bit off"), we may compare the observation in 6.185–86: "what is more nauseating" (*quid rancidius quam*) than the way no woman thinks she is beautiful unless "she changes from a Tuscan to a Greeklette" (*de Tusca Graecula facta est*)?

The remainder of *Satire* 11 describes the dinner planned by the speaker, in which ideals of rustic simplicity jostle with images of corrupt urban dining (136–82). It is the latter that come to dominate the scene, however, with roughly twenty-seven lines as opposed to twenty, including the "Spanish floor show" with its suggestive dancing leading to ejaculations among the audience (162–70). When Democritus was introduced at the beginning of *Satire* 10, he was

69. Cf. 5.53; 59; 8.160–62: *porta Idymaea* and *Cyane*.
70. See Courtney 1980, "Even the appetite is foreign" (*ad loc.*)

pictured laughing at the spectacle of the praetor in the dust of the circus at the Ludi Romani (36–46); here, the Megalesia festival is being held in the same location:

> interea Megalesiacae spectacula mappae
> Idaeum sollemne colunt, similisque triumpho
> praeda caballorum praetor sedet ac, mihi pace
> inmensae nimiaeque licet si dicere plebis,
> totam hodie Romam circus capit, et fragor aurem
> percutit, eventum viridis quo colligo panni.

> Meanwhile, the spectators are celebrating the Idaean rite
> of the Megalesian napkin, and the praetor sits there as if in a triumph,
> the booty of the nags, and, if I may say so with the permission of the vast
>   mob too huge to count, today the Circus holds all of Rome, and the din
>   strikes my ears
> from which I gather that the Green tunic has won. (11.193–98)

That's fine for young men (*spectent iuvenes*, 201), but the speaker would rather "escape the toga" (204). Using the Circus as a foil to recommend a more modest way of living was already tried by Umbricius (*si potes avelli circensibus*, 3.223), and the idea appears in Seneca's *De Tranquillitate* 9.3:

> Adsuescamus ergo cenare posse sine populo et servis paucioribus
> servire et vestes parare in quod inventae sunt et habitare contractius.
> Non in cursu tantum circique certamine, sed in his spatiis vitae
> interius flectendum est.

> Let us then get accustomed to being able to dine without the
> multitude, to being the slave of fewer slaves, to getting clothes for
> the purpose for which they were devised, and to living in narrower
> quarters. Not only in the race and contests of the circus, but also in
> these circuits of life, we must keep to the inner circle.[71]

The static rural idyll that makes brief appearances in Juvenal's poems is, in one sense, the antithesis to all this noise and movement.[72] But the fragility and vulnerability of the satiric alternative is encapsulated when the speaker tells his guest: *protinus ante meum quidquid dolet exue limen* (Strip off right away

---

71. Trans. Basore 1928–35.
72. Newlands 2002, speaking of Stat. *Silv.* 1.6: "Unlike the stable, quiet world of the villa landscape, the amphitheater offers fleeting impressions and lots of noise" (251).

anything that distresses you in front of my doorstep) and then adds: *pone do-mum et servos et quidquid frangitur illis / aut perit, ingratos ante omnia pone sodalis* (Leave behind your household and your slaves and whatever they have broken or lost, above all, leave behind your ungrateful friends, 190–91). And just before he had said that there will be no mention of "interest due" and no intensification of the "silent rage" caused by his wife's habit of returning suspiciously disheveled, with her dress damp, after a long day away from the house (185–89).

The *praeteritio* exposes the impossibility of anything more than a brief respite from the realities of quotidian squalor. As in *Satire* 14, the good, "philosophical" advice is always already undermined by its surroundings at the moment it is dispensed. "Fleeing the toga" and going to the baths a whole hour before noon "with a clear conscience" (*salva fronte*, 204–205) is certainly a pleasure, but soon becomes *taedia vitae / magna* (207–208) if done for five days in a row. The recipient of the invitation, moreover, is Persicus, whose name is quite possibly suggestive of a taste for extravagance of the very kind the speaker seeks to discourage.[73] The relaxing break (*gratam requiem*) is thus temporary and out of the ordinary, while the annoying and unpleasant aspects of the guest's life are enduring. This defines the relationship between the Juvenalian cityscape and its antithesis: the alternative makes only fleeting and ambiguous appearances, and its contours can never be meaningfully delineated, because it is predicated upon the world of the satires and has no independent existence. It is itself just a part of the discourse.

Statues of Limitations

The later poems pick up the topic of statues, which, like the *imagines* of ancestors, are weighty bearers of memory and *mos maiorum*, but they too inevitably fall victim to the Juvenalian satirist's corrosive view of life. Statues, it is said, have become embodiments of the "insatiable desire for acquisition" (*adquirendi . . . insatiabile votum*, 14.125). We saw in *Satire* 3 that when the burned down home of Persicus is reconstituted, statues play a vital role in the process. Without them (*nuda et candida signa, / . . . aliquid praeclarum Euphranoris et*

---

73. Although the idea has not found favor with most critics, it is at least possible that Persicus is the same man as "the wealthy, childless fraudulent arsonist of 3.221," as Ferguson puts it; at any rate, the echo can hardly be accidental. On various rationalizations, see Ferguson 1979, 280–81; 287; Courtney 1980, 491–92; cf. Hor. *Odes* 1.38.1 (*Persicos . . . apparatus*).

Polycliti / aera, 3.216–18), the restoration would be incomplete.[74] As far as busts and statues inside the home are concerned, that topic was introduced in *Satire* 2, with the likenesses of Greek philosophers adorning the *atria* of the *Stoicidae*, who preach one way of living and practice a completely different one. In connection with the theme of *frontis nulla fides*, we may note Pliny's criticism (*HN* 35.4–14) of the decline in painting portraits with a high degree of verisimilitude or resemblance. Nowadays, he says, heads on statues are exchanged, and interest centers on the material used and the price of works of art.[75] It was different before: in the ancestors' *atria*, there were no statues in bronze or marble by foreign artists, and portraits were there to be looked at (*qua spectarentur*, 6). Houses "celebrated a perpetual triumph" even as their masters changed: *triumphabantque etiam dominis mutatis aeternae domus* (7).

In *Satire* 8, unsurprisingly given the topic of *stemmata*, portraits of ancestors and statues feature on several occasions, such as when the speaker asks Ponticus, "What is the point of displaying the painted portraits of your ancestors?" and:

> ... et stantis in curribus Aemilianos
> et Curios iam dimidios umeroque minorem
> Corvinum et Galbam auriculis nasoque carentem

> ... Aemiliani standing upright in their chariots,
> Curii now in halves, a Corvinus smaller by a shoulder,
> and a Galba missing his ears and nose? (3–5)

Similarly, what is to be gained from being able to trace your lineage all the way back to a Censor or a Dictator or a Magister Equitum:

> ... si coram Lepidis male vivitur? Effigies quo
> tot bellatorum, si luditur alea pernox
> ante Numantinos, si dormire incipis ortu
> Luciferi, quo signa duces et castra movebant?

> ... if, in front of Lepidi, you live a bad life?
> What is the point of so many statues of warriors, if you roll dice all
>   night
> in front of Numantini, if you go to sleep as Lucifer rises,

---

74. In 8.98–112, the plundering of statues and other riches from the provinces by Verres and others is recalled and contrasted with what is left today—*ipsi deinde Lares, si quod spectabile signum* (110). In the age of Dolabella, Antony, and Verres, every house was brimming with such acquistions (*plena domus tunc omnis*, 100).

75. Sen. *Ep.* 86.7, criticizing overdecorated baths, especially of freedmen, comments: *quantum statuarum, quantum columnarum est nihil sustinentium, sed in ornamentum positarum impensae causa.*

which is when those generals began to move forward their standards and
camps? (9–12)

This obviously recalls the opening of *Satire* 2, and the theme of hypocrisy
and bad behavior is taken up at length, but the notion of decay and degeneration predominates. Images and statues of the *gens Aemilia* are treated to
the spectacle of their descendants gambling the night away and other displays of "bad living."[76] Picking up on the damaged statue of a certain Aemilius in *Satire* 7, mutilations and missing body parts of figures from illustrious Republican families symbolize the ruin of their lines (just as their
shades are imagined watching new arrivals in the Underworld at the end of
Satire 2).

This is continued in 8.13–23:

> Cur Allobrogicis et magna gaudeat ara
> natus in Herculeo Fabius lare, si cupidus, si
> vanus et Euganea quantum vis mollior agna,   15
> si tenerum attritus Catinensi pumice lumbum
> squalentis **traducit** avos emptorque veneni
> **frangenda** miseram funestat **imagine** gentem?
> Tota licet veteres exornent undique cerae
> atria, nobilitas sola est atque unica virtus.   20
> Paulus vel Cossus vel Drusus moribus esto,
> hos ante effigies maiorum pone tuorum,
> praecedant ipsas illi te consule virgas.

> Why should a Fabius born in Hercules' house take delight
> in Allobrogici and the Great Altar if he's greedy
> and silly and even soppier than a Euganean lamb,
> if he **disgraces** his unkempt ancestors by having his groin rubbed smooth
> by Catanian pumice, and if his dealing in poison pollutes
> his wretched clan with his **statue that ought to be shattered?**
> Though you adorn your entire atrium with ancient wax portraits in every
>   direction,
> the one and only nobility is personal excellence.
> So, be a Paulus or a Cossus or a Drusus—in morality.
> Rate that ahead of your ancestors' statues,
> let that go ahead of the rods of office when you're consul.[77]

---

76. The use of *signa* in 12 for "standards" is very much a propos, given its other meaning of "statues."
77. Trans. Braund 2004.

In the manner of the descendants of the Stoics and their ilk in *Satire 2*, Fabius "traduces" his ancestors with his depilated softness—as Courtney says "the 'triumph' of this Fabius is over his ancestors, unlike that of Allobrogicus"—while, as a buyer of poison, he "pollutes" them (by murdering), so that his statue deserves to be shattered.[78] The decline and deformation of the *generosus* who is *indignus genere* and distinguished only by a glorious name is conveyed by analogy with calling a dwarf "Atlas" or a bent and deformed girl "Europa"—another obvious instance of how signifier has been irrevocably sundered from signified (30–34).[79] Addressing Rubellius Blandus, the speaker says that he is *nil nisi Cecropides truncoque simillimus Hermae* (nothing but descended from Cecrops and the spitting image of a mutilated Herm, 53).[80] Since it is the phallus that has presumably been mutilated, this adds the implication that Rubellius has lost his virility. With the decline of the house and the line, symbolized by damaged statues, comes failure to reproduce properly. If he is to be impressed, the speaker says, by the person and not the lineage, then he should be given something "which he can inscribe, apart from the titles that we gave, and still give, to those men to whom you owe everything" (*quod possim titulis incidere praeter honores / quos illis damus ac dedimus, quibus omnia debes*, 69–70).

A related topic is the statue made for an unworthy individual—who, of course, much to the speaker's irritation, has the money and power to achieve this—with the first example being the Egyptian Arabarch's among the Roman *triumphales* in 1.129–31), on which he recommended not only urinating. The word used there was *effigies* which appears next in 6.310, of the image of Pudicitia over which Tullia and Maura urinate, thus linking the two by sprays of piss, the first appropriately Roman over a foreign interloper, the second its mirror image.[81] In 7.124–28, the satirist describes an equestrian statue belonging to a patrician lawyer, Aemilius:

> "Aemilio dabitur quantum licet, at melius nos
> egimus." Huius enim stat currus aeneus, alti
> quadriiuges in vestibulis, atque ipse feroci

---

78. Cf. 2.159: *illic heu miseri traducimur* (and chap. 2, pp. 158–59); also 8.142–44: *Quo mihi te solitum falsas signare tabellas / in templis quae fecit avus statuamque parentis / ante triumphalem?*

79. Cf. 3.84–91; on the Roman penchant for ironic, even witty, names for gladiators and animals in the arena, see Dunkle 2008, 124–28.

80. See Ferguson 1979; Courtney 1980, *ad loc.*; the only advantage he has, says Juv., is that the statue's head is made of marble, but his image is alive (54–55). Courtney has: "'you are a living statue' (or more precisely he is his own death-mask)" (394).

81. It is used in a similarly disparaging Egyptian context in 15.4 (*effigies sacri nitet aurea cercopitheci*) and of Nero's ancestors in 8.227.

bellatore sedens curvatum hastile minatur
eminus et statua meditatur proelia lusca.

"Aemilius will charge whatever he likes, even though we did a better job."
That's because there stands a chariot made of bronze
with four tall horses in his entrance hall, and he himself
sitting on a fierce charger, threatens from above with his drooping spear,
a statue with one eye practicing for battle.

The main point may be that the contemporary statue is in poor repair. As Courtney says, "The sculptor has provided no support for the heavy spear-head,
which has dragged down the shaft into a curve, and one of the coloured stones
regularly used to represent eye-balls has fallen out."[82] The chariot of bronze
would be an antique, apparently recalled in the *stantis in curribus Aemilianos* of
8.3. Three other lawyers are mentioned as being ruined financially by attempting to show off on a similar scale, yet the display is successful in terms of
self-promotion (129–38). Coins have been transformed into statues, which are
embodiments of the lawyers' skills at manipulation, signs not of true worthi-
ness in the military or political realm but of the triumph of sophistry. Thus
statues point to the unreliability of a discourse of ideologically loaded terms deployed for self-justifying and self-aggrandizing aims, rather like those paintings and photographs inscribed with "corporate speak" proliferating in company hallways and boardrooms today.[83]

As unworthy individuals and degenerated scions of noble lines gain statues, so the sacred images of the gods suffer damage to theirs; this is a version
of the abandonment motif noted above, with Mars and other divinities leaving
Rome, but it also contributes to the pervasive sense of decay and fragmentation. In *Satire* 13, which aims to convince its addressee, if not us, of the (eventual) dispensing of divine retribution, we see the defrauded victim raising his
voice at Jupiter:

. . . tu miser exclamas, ut Stentora vincere possis,
vel potius quantum Gradivus Homericus, "audis,
Iuppiter, haec nec labra moves, cum mittere vocem
debueris vel marmoreus vel aeneus? Aut cur
in carbone tuo charta pia tura soluta

82. See also Ferguson 1979, who thinks it an "otherwise curious description" (*ad loc.*); Griffith 1969
argues for a mounted archer, with one eye closed to aim (382–83); Killeen 1969 suggests the figure is curved;
cf. Braund 1988, 218 and n116. On lawyers' fondness for such statues, Mart. 9.68.6.

83. Cf. references to *causidici* elsewhere: 1.32; 6.439; 7.106, 113, 136, 148; 10.121; 15.111.

ponimus et sectum vituli iecur albaque porci
omenta? Ut video, nullum discrimen habendum est
effigies inter vestras statuamque Vagelli."

... while you, wretched fellow, yell so as to outdo Stentor,
or, rather, as loud as Homer's Gradivus [Mars], "Do you hear this,
Jupiter, yet don't move your lips, when you really should have spoken out,
whether you're made of marble or of bronze? Otherwise why do we
unwrap our packet of pious incense and put in on your charcoal,
or our slice of calf's liver, or the white fat of a pig? As I see it,
there's no difference between your images and the statue of Vagellius."
    (112–19)

The precise point of Vagellius's statue is obscure, but he may be the "mulish"
declaimer (declamatoris mulino corde) of 16.23, who has perhaps been presented
with a statue by a grateful client.[84] This is followed up by a passage detailing
thefts of parts of the gods' statues in 13.147–53:

Confer et hos, veteris qui tollunt grandia templi
pocula adorandae robiginis et populorum
dona vel antiquo positas a rege coronas;
haec ibi si non sunt, minor exstat sacrilegus qui
radat inaurati femur Herculis et faciem ipsam
Neptuni, qui bratteolam de Castore ducat;
[an dubitet solitus totum conflare Tonantem?][85]

Compare too those who carry off from an ancient temple
large chalices of venerable rust, the gifts of nations,
or crowns dedicated by a king from long ago.
If these things are not there, a small-time desecrator will turn up
to scrape the thigh of gilded Hercules or even the face
of Neptune or to strip the gold leaf from Castor.
[Or would he hesitate to melt down a whole Thunderer?]

The last line is suspected by some editors, on the basis that the melting down
of whole statues of Jupiter can hardly be a minor, or a common, crime. But

84. Courtney 1980, ad loc.; see Ferguson 1979 for other options: "Possibly he was a nonstop talker; it
was a miracle that his statue didn't talk."
85. On the last line and Munro's emendation, an dubitet? solitumst totum conflare Tonantem, see Courtney 1980, ad loc.; he notes that the idea, while "an exaggeration is not without its grain of truth" and compares
Suet. Nero 32.4 and others.

Shackleton Bailey's reading of *solidum* makes some sense if, as he suggests, 153 "answers a possible objection, that so far as the value went, the thefts of 150–52 were no great matter. That, says Juvenal, is only because there is nothing better to steal. The man who scrapes the gilt from a lesser god's thigh would not hesitate to melt down Jupiter himself in solid gold entire—if he had the chance."[86] We may compare 14.259–62, where the satirist is describing the "entertainment" to be derived from looking at how people risk their lives for financial gain:

> incrementa domus, aerata multus in arca
> fiscus et ad vigilem ponendi Castora nummi,
> ex quo Mars Vltor galeam quoque perdidit et res
> non potuit servare suas.

> (for) growth of their fortunes, for the huge purse in the bronze
>   savings-box
> and the cash which has to be deposited under Castor's watchful guard,
> ever since even Mars the Avenger lost his helmet
> and could not hold on to his own property.

While Castor has security guards, Mars—"the Avenger" no less—has had his helmet stolen and has lost the power to safeguard his own possessions.[87] Like other manifestations of the satiric antithesis, the gods are more present in the text of the later poems, but no comfort is to be drawn from that.

The Bronze Henchman

Statues in public places convey a sense of greater permanence than that of mere mortal experience, along with a solidifying sense of having "been there" in the past. Thus they are endowed with powerful symbolism and embody meanings they have accrued over time. Graeme Gilloch observes that for Benjamin, the city in memory and memory in the city coalesce in the monument, which is "a manisfestation of, and focus for, the celebration of those who have triumphed in the past." He alludes here to remarks by Benjamin in *Theses on the Philosophy of History:* "Whoever has emerged victorious participates to this day in the triumphal procession in which the present rulers step over those who are lying prostrate. . . . There is no document of civilisation that is not at the same time

---

86. Shackleton Bailey 1959, 202.
87. Edwards 1993, 160–63, "Building Ruins" and 161n61.

a document of barbarism."[88] The monument is just such a document, "a petrified myth," and is to be revealed as a transient rather than enduring structure; not fixed and final but subject to political changes and transformation and ruination. The Egyptian obelisk in the Place de a Concorde offers a good example (in "One Way Street"). Gilloch observes:

> The meaning of the monument changes in the course of its own history. Monuments to victory are inevitably transformed in time into those of defeat. As an object falls into a state of ruination, the pretensions which accompanied its construction crumble, and its truth is unfolded. The monument has an "afterlife" which negates the original intention. While the city's proud monuments most clearly articulate the glorification of history, in their "afterlife," these same structures come to unmask the modern metropolis as the locus of mythic delusion. (73)

Falconet's equestrian statue of Peter the Great in St. Petersburg is another instance, symbolizing Russia's "opening" to the West (it looks westward) and dynamic movement (its rearing motion is supported by the horse's tail), but the foundational myth that the Bronze Horseman articulates is an ambiguous and controversial one: Who opens what for whom? For readers other than the Tzarist establishment, it potentially connotes the victimization of Russia (not least because thousands of serfs died in building the city). In Pushkin's eponymous poem, the statue moves around the city and torments the "little man" who dwells in a state that does not care about him, and this becomes a recurring topos in the "Petersburg myth."[89] Victimization–like Westernization is itself double-coded: Who is Westernized, who is victimized? The ambiguous statue of Marsyas at the opening of Satire 9 is an analogous example. He was of course flayed alive after an ill-judged contest with Apollo but is also connected with Liber Pater and *libertas*, the Romans' Statue of Liberty, as Gowers puts it. Wiseman notes that he was not a licentious hedonist but sagacity and

---

88. Gilloch 1996, 72 with Benjamin 1973, 258. Benjamin's passage runs: "Whoever has emerged victorious participates to this day in the triumphal procession in which the present rulers step over those who are lying prostrate. According to traditional practice, the spoils are carried along in the procession. They are called cultural treasures, and a historical materialist views them with cautious detachment. For without exception the cultural treasures he surveys have an origin that he cannot contemplate without horror. They owe their existence not only to the efforts of the great minds and talents who have created them, but also to the anonymous toil of their contemporaries. There is no document of civilization that is not at the same time a document of barbarism. And just as such a document is not free of barbarism, barbarism taints also the manner in which it was transmitted from one owner to another. A historical materialist therefore dissociates himself from it as far as possible. He regards it as his task to brush history against the grain."

89. Similarly, in Bely's *Petersburg*, the Bronze Horseman pursues the radical Dudkin. See Barta 1996, 28–29, 41–42.

self-control were attributed to him. We may note Horace's exploitation of the ambiguities in *Satire* 1.6.119–20, where he functions as a symbol of (satirical) *libertas*, whose upraised hand is interpreted as a protest against the oppressive, enslaving nature of legal duties, which, however, Horace, as a public-spirited Roman, must perform.[90]

Public statues of famous individuals are emblematic of the link that binds city-building and the creation of art with the hegemonic forces of money and power, for those who erect them have to have the means to bring about their production and placement. These statues are therefore especially vulnerable to currents of change because they are allowed to stand only as long as anger and frustration among the mass of the population are not allowed to be articulated. Consequently, in social and political convulsions, or in revolutionary actions, the anger of the crowd is often responsible for violence against the symbolic embodiments of hegemonic power. In the context of Imperial Rome, it is associated with *damnatio memoriae*: Tacitus mentions that M. Scribonius Libo's *imago* was not to be paraded by his family, as part of that process (*Annals* 2.32.2). In 8.18, the satirist says Fabius's statue should have been broken up because he disgraced his ancestors, and in 11.38.3, the historian describes how Messalina's memory was expunged *censendo nomen et effigies privatis ac publicis locis demovendas*.[91]

The fate of Domitian's statues is given considerable attention by Pliny in *Panegyricus* 52, as he contrasts him with Trajan, thereby offering a view of both sides of the coin—the despised and the revered:

> Itaque tuam statuam in vestibulo Iovis optimi maximi unam
> alteramve et hanc aeream cernimus. At paulo ante aditus omnes
> gradus totaque area hinc auro hinc argento relucebat, omnes seu
> potius polluebatur, cum incesti principis statuis permixta deorum
> simulacra sorderent. Ergo istae quidem aereae et paucae manent
> manebuntque quam diu templum ipsum, illae autem aureae et
> innumerabiles strage ac ruina publico gaudio litaverunt. Iuvabat illidere
> solo superbissimos vultus, instare ferro, saevire securibus, ut si
> singulos ictus sanguis dolorque sequeretur. Nemo tam temperans
> gaudii seraeque laetitiae, quin instar ultionis videretur cernere laceros
> artus truncata membra, postremo truces horrendasque imagines
> obiectas excoctasque flammis, ut ex illo terrore et minis in usum
> hominum ac voluptates ignibus mutarentur.

---

90. Rawson, 1987, 11–12; Wiseman 1988, 5; Gowers 2012, 89 and on 6.119–21.

91. Cf. Goodyear 1981, *ad loc.*; Vittinghoff 1936, 13–18. Messalina: O'Gorman 2000, "Damnatio Memoriae and Memory Loss," discusses the passage (115–21).

Descendunt statuae restemque secuntur (Juv. 10.58). Lenin Relocated; Narva
Castle (Hermanni Linnus), Narva, Estonia. Photograph by David Larmour.

Of your statues, only one or two are to be seen in the vestibule of
the temple of Jupiter Best and Highest, and these are made of bronze;
whereas only recently every approach and step, every inch of the
precinct was gleaming with silver and gold, or rather, was casting
pollution, since the figures of the gods were defiled by having statues
of an incestuous emperor in their midst. And so your few statues of

bronze stand and will stand as long as the temple itself, whereas
those innumerable golden images, as a sacrifice to public rejoicing,
lie broken and destroyed. It was our delight to dash those proud faces
to the ground, to smite them with the sword and savage them with
the axe, as if blood and agony could follow from every blow. Our
transports of joy—so long deferred—were unrestrained; all sought a
form of vengeance in beholding those bodies mutilated, limbs hacked
in pieces, and finally that baleful, fearsome visage cast into fire, to be
melted down, so that from such menacing terror something for man's
use and enjoyment should rise out of the flames.[92]

Domitian's statues were polluting and defiling the images of the gods, not least
because of his marriage to his niece Julia, alluded to in Juvenal's *Satire* 2.29–
33.[93] Paul Roche considers the contested spaces of monuments with strong Flavian connotations, noting that the smaller ones could be, and were, destroyed,
but in the case of larger ones "it was imperative that their meanings be
reinvented."[94] Pliny's strategy of depicting monuments as "casting off the specious semblance of themselves and assuming their true nature as a result of
sound Trajanic policy" speaks to a mutability in meaning echoed in Juvenal.
In *Satire* 8.227–30, for instance, having made fun of Nero's musical and poetic
performances, the speaker apostrophizes him:

> Maiorum effigies habeant insignia vocis,
> ante pedes Domiti longum tu pone Thyestae
> syrma vel Antigones aut personam Melanippes,
> et de marmoreo citharam suspende colosso.

> Let your ancestors' statues display the trophies of your voice,
> place at Domitius' feet your long gown of Thyestes,
> or your mask of Antigone or Melanippe,
> and hang your lyre on your marble colossus.

The "colossus" may well allude to Nero's giant statue (although it was made of
bronze), which by Juvenal's time had been given a new face and identity, as the
Sun.[95]

92. Trans. Radice 1969. Roche 2011 on "the metaphorical monument" of Trajan's personal virtues and
the devotion of subjects (e.g. *Pan.* 55.9; 50–53).

93. The *Lex Claudia* had permitted such a marriage, however: Suet. *Claud.* 26.3.

94. Roche 2011, "The Panegyricus and the Monuments of Rome" (46, 50).

95. Suet. *Nero,* 31; *Vesp.* 18; Mart. *Spect.* 2.1. Courtney 1980 thinks Juvenal is not referring to the statue
directly, as it was made of bronze, "but he was doubtless indirectly influenced by it in his choice of the word"

By far the most striking statue scene in the *Satires*, however, is the downfall of Sejanus, an archetypal instance of how an individual's spectacular "triumph" leads inexorably to his equally spectacular destruction. This is a substantial scene in the corpus and is the first exemplum of misplaced wishes in
Satire 10, extending more than fifty lines (56–113). The satirist begins with the
toppling of the statue and the smelting of Sejanus's head:

> Quosdam praecipitat subiecta potentia magnae
> invidiae, mergit longa atque insignis honorum
> pagina. Descendunt statuae restemque secuntur,
> ipsas deinde rotas bigarum inpacta securis
> caedit et inmeritis franguntur crura caballis.   60
> Iam strident ignes, iam follibus atque caminis
> ardet adoratum populo caput et crepat ingens
> Seianus, deinde ex facie toto orbe secunda
> fiunt urceoli, pelves, sartago, matellae.
> Pone domi laurus, duc in Capitolia magnum   65
> cretatumque bovem: Seianus ducitur unco
> spectandus, gaudent omnes.

> Some people are toppled by their power, object of great envy,
> some are sunk by their long and glorious roll of honours.
> Down their statues come, dragged by a rope,
> then even the chariot's wheels are smashed and slashed by the axe,
> and the legs of innocent nags are shattered.
> Now the flames are hissing, now that head idolized by the people is glowing
> from the bellows and furnace: huge Sejanus is crackling.
> Then the face that was number two in the whole world is turned into
> little jugs, basins, frying pans, and chamber pots.
> Hang your homes with laurel, drag a huge bull, whitened with chalk,
> up to the Capitol! Sejanus is being dragged by a hook—
> a sight worth seeing. Everyone's celebrating. (56–67)[96]

We are taken into the excitement of the moment with snippets of conversation
among the crowd (67–72), including comments on Sejanus's features:

(*ad loc.*). The fate of Nero's Domus Aurea, which was unfinished at his death and whose parts were gradually
used up in building projects by his successors, including Vespasian, Trajan, and Hadrian, offers a related example, Suet. *Vesp.* 9.1. Gowers 2009 explores the metaphor of decoction in Suetonius and Persius.

   96. Trans. Braund 2004.

> . . . "quae labra, quis illi
> vultus erat! numquam, si quid mihi credis, amavi
> hunc hominem."

> "What lips! What a face that man had!
> I never—believe me—liked the man." (67–69)

The *honorum pagina* (57–58) echoes the *tituli* of the Egyptian Arabarch (1.30), while *mergit* has connotations of being shipwrecked, anticipating the maritime scenes in *Satires* 12 and 14.[97] The objects made from Sejanus's face are everyday items of food preparation, excretion, or urination.[98] Thus we go from one massive image of a tyrannical figure in public space to numerous little items distributed among many ordinary households. Pliny similarly in his account of Domitian's statues says his face was melted down into objects that could be "used and enjoyed." The satirist's vision of decorating the house with laurel takes us into the private space of individuals and other such celebrations in the poems, while leading a whitened animal as sacrifice to Jupiter marks the recovery of public space (65–66). In his account, Pliny goes on to recall (52) the large herds of animal victims going along the Capitoline Way to be sacrificed at the equestrian statue of Domitian set up on the western side of the Forum, linking them with his human victims:

> Ante quidem ingentes hostiarum greges per Capitolinum iter magna
> sui parte velut intercepti devertere via cogebantur, cum saevissimi
> domini atrocissima effigies tanto victimarum cruore coleretur,
> quantum ipse humani sanguinis profundebat.

> Yet previously the vast herds of victims were often stopped on the
> Capitoline Way and large numbers forced to turn aside, for in honour
> of that grim statue of a brutal tyrant the blood of victims had to flow
> as freely as the human blood he shed.[99]

As Courtney observes of the *duc . . . ducitur* repetition in Juvenal's passage, "Sejanus is like a victim felled at the altar," neatly picking up on the designation of him as *adoratus* ("worshiped") in 62 (65–66). He is himself also a spectacle

---

97. 11.39–40: *aere paterno / ac rebus mersis in ventrem fenoris*; 13.7–8: *ut mediocris / iacturae te mergat onus*; cf. 3.164: *haut facile emergunt*. See also on satiric nausea, p. 38 herein.

98. Cf. 3.203 (*urceoli*); 3.277 and 6.441 (*pelves*); 6.264 (*scaphium*).

99. Trans. Radice 1969. See Newlands 2002, chap. 2, "Embodying the Statue," on Domitian's equestrian one.

(*spectandus*, just as Gracchus in the arena was *agnoscendus*), which in his case delights everyone.

The mutilation of the statue and other such actions—like trampling on the bodily remains by the riverbank in 10.86—are "surrogate corpse abuse" in imitation of the treatment of other despised dead. Donald Kyle rightly observes that "death was not the last act in the arena" and points out the difference between dead gladiators, who were carried out (one assumes with at least some dignity) through the *Porta Libitinaria*, and the victims in the executions of the morning: "Their bodies were apparently abused, mutilated, and dragged off by hooks. Both symbolic and efficient, hooks added insult and provided a way to avoid personal contact with an obscene body."[100] Juvenal's wording (62) *caput et crepat ingens [Seianus]* cleverly conveys the crackling of the head in the flames, and Kyle notes that fire was "a legal and spectacular means of torture, abuse, and aggravated execution" and was used along with hot irons to goad men and animals to fight and to check that a victim was dead.[101] He cites the "fatal charade" of Scaevola and the *tunica molesta*. *Crematio* meant execution by fire, usually reserved for the lower orders, but even then there were remains to dispose of. This is perhaps behind Seneca's remarks in *De Tranquillitate* 11.11 that the people chopped Sejanus into "bite-size pieces": *quo die illum senatus deduxerat, populus in frusta divisit*[102] and that "of the man onto whom the gods and men had heaped all there was to bestow, nothing was left for the executioner to drag to the river" (*in quem quicquid congeri poterat di hominesque contulerant, ex eo nihil superfuit quod carnifex traheret*).

There are clear anticipations here of *Satire* 15 in Juvenal's account of Sejanus. As he is melted down into kitchenware and chamber pots, the Tentyran victim is chopped *in plurima . . . frusta et particulas* and nothing is left except bones (which themselves get gnawed, 80) and blood on the ground (which is licked from clawing fingers, 92). In the first case, fire effects the transformation; in the second, they don't even bother to light one. There is also an echo of the street scene in 3.251–67, with the slave rushing along with his big pots, fanning the flames as he goes, and the unfortunate man obliterated under a wagon load of Ligurian marble:

---

100. Kyle 1998, citing Sejanus as an example (155–56 and n106).

101. Kyle 1998, 170. Ferguson 1979, *ad loc.*, notes that *ardet* is "doubly ironic" since Sejanus had been voted a statue for his role in stopping a serious fire (62; Tac. *Ann.* 3.22); see chap. 1 herein on Tigillinus and the Great Fire.

102. Cf. above chap. 1, pp. 91–93, on *deducere*.

Quid superest de corporibus? Quis membra, quis ossa
invenit? Obtritum vulgo perit omne cadaver
more animae. Domus interea secura patellas
iam lavat et bucca foculum excitat et sonat unctis
strigilibus et pleno componit lintea guto.

What is left of the bodies? Who finds any limbs or bones?
Every corpse, crushed indiscriminately, will perish
like its soul. Meanwhile at home, oblivious, they are now washing the
    dishes
and puffing at the hearth with full cheeks, clattering about with
the oily strigils, filling the oil flasks, and laying out the towels. (259–63)

Again, we move instantaneously, effortlessly, from corpse to household kitchen.

The total obliteration of the body (or the statue) of the hated individual offers the comforting thought that there is no chance of his coming back; it also
serves, perhaps, as a warning to others who might try to imitate him. The bi-
zarre description in Procopius of a statue modeled on the dismembered corpse
of Domitian testifies to the anxieties surrounding the finality of corporeal
destruction:

Even after they had chopped his whole body into pieces they felt that
they had not satisfied their rage against him, but through a decree
of the Senate determined that not even the name of this Emperor
would appear on documents nor any likeness of him whatsoever
be preserved. . . . And not a single statue of him is to be seen
anywhere throughout the Roman Empire, with the exception of one
bronze statue, accounted for as follows. Domitian had a wife of noble
character and discreet . . . and she begged only this, that she might
take the body of Domitian and bury it and that she might set up
one bronze statue to him wherever she wished. And the Senate
conceded this. And the woman, wishing to leave to future ages
a memorial of the inhumanity of those who had butchered her
husband, contrived the following. Collecting the flesh of Domitian,
and putting the pieces accurately together and fitting them one to
the other, she sewed up the whole body; then, displaying to the
sculptors, she bade them represent in a bronze statue the fate which
had befallen her husband. So the artists straightway made the statue.
The woman then took it and set it up on the street leading up to the
Capitol, on the right as one ascends thither from the Forum, and it

shews both the features and the fate of Domitian, even to the present day. (*Anecdota* 8.13–20)[103]

According to the historians, Domitian was not hacked to pieces but stabbed repeatedly, and the body was burned by his nurse, Phyllis. Nonetheless, the idea of a Frankensteinian reassembling of the whole from parts of various statues speaks to a fear of the monster's return or reincarnation. The breaking of the legs of the "nags" in Sejanus's equestrian statue (60) is a symbolic prevention of movement, while the resting place of the corpse on the riverbank (*dum iacet in ripa*, 86) points to time-honored disposal by the Tiber flowing out to sea. As Kyle concludes in his study of what happened to corpses from the arena at Rome, "for centuries refuse and bodies, notably of those perceived to be contaminating or threatening the state, were dumped in the Tiber. Traditional and convenient, this added the insult of denial of burial; the water removed the pollution, and it offered protection against hostile spirits."[104] Appropriately enough, then, as Suetonius records, the slogan on news of the death of Tiberius was "*Tiberium in Tiberim*" (*Tiberius* 47).

It is difficult not to recall the Tigillinus episode of *Satire* 1 in Juvenal's account of the downfall of Sejanus, with the image of a body being dragged by a hook, and also in the cautious exchange between someone asking how Sejanus came to fall and his interlocutor (71–72): "An enormous wordy letter came from Capri." "All right, I have no more questions" (*"verbosa et grandis epistula venit / a Capreis." "bene habet, nil plus interrogo"*). Even if his murderous henchman has been removed, Tiberius remains as a powerful reason for discreet silence of the kind recommended by the timorous interlocutor in *Satire* 1.160: *digito compesce labellum*. The downfall of Sejanus, while undoubtedly satisfying on its own terms, does not herald a fundamental change in the conditions of life in the satirical city. As the satirical lens pans out, the speaker interjects his opinion of the "mob of Remus":

> . . . sed quid
> turba Remi? Sequitur fortunam, ut semper, et odit
> damnatos. Idem populus, si Nortia Tusco
> favisset, si oppressa foret secura senectus   75
> principis, hac ipsa Seianum diceret hora
> Augustum. Iam pridem, ex quo suffragia nulli
> vendimus, effudit curas; nam qui dabat olim

---

103. Trans. Dewing 1935.
104. Kyle 1988, 223, and chap. 7, "Rituals, Spectacles, and the River Tiber."

imperium, fasces, legiones, omnia, nunc se
continet atque duas tantum res anxius optat,   80
panem et circenses.

But what about Remus' mob? It follows Fortune, as always, and hates
the condemned. The same crowd, if Nortia had favoured her Etruscan,
if the aged emperor had been caught off guard,
this very hour would be hailing Sejanus as Augustus.
They long since discarded their responsibilities—
since we stopped selling our votes to anyone. For the people that once
    upon a time
used to bestow military commands, consulships, legions, everything,
now constrains itself and longs obsessively for only two things—
bread and circuses. (10.72–81)

The consumption of bread and circuses is paralleled by the transformation of
Sejanus into household pots and pans. The crowd "hates the condemned"—
who were, of course, regularly slaughtered or executed in the arena—but
they are consumers, spectators rather than actors in the destruction of
Sejanus, watching the execution staged for their pleasure by Tiberius. The
crowd contains itself (*se continet*, 79–80) as it is contained by the power of the
emperor, architecturally rendered in Juvenal's day by the encircling mass of
the Colosseum. By calling them the *turba Remi*, the satirist designates contemporary Romans as the inheritors of the dead loser—the twin who lost out
in the fratricidal combat for power in the city.

    Finally, we return to the *secreta murmura volgi*:

       "Perituros audio multos."
"Nil dubium, magna est fornacula." "Pallidulus mi
Bruttidius meus ad Martis fuit obvius aram;
quam timeo, victus ne poenas exigat Aiax
ut male defensus. Curramus praecipites et,
dum iacet in ripa, calcemus Caesaris hostem.
Sed videant servi, ne quis neget et pavidum in ius
cervice obstricta dominum trahat."

       "I hear many are going to die."
"There's no doubt; the furnace is huge." "My friend Bruttidius
was rather pale when I met him at the altar of Mars.
I'm very much afraid that the 'defeated Ajax' will take vengeance
for having been so badly defended. Let's rush in a hurry and,
while he lies on the riverbank, trample on Caesar's enemy.

> But make sure our slaves see us, so they can't deny it and drag their
>   terrified
> master into court with a noose around his neck." (81–88)

Here we have confirmation that the removal of Sejanus does not bring anything more than momentary relief; many will die in the "big furnace"—and not only those who had been too closely connected with him. The historians record that Tiberius was indeed harsher after Sejanus's death and, as Ajax, he is all too likely to slaughter the wrong victims.[105] The closing image of the slave dragging his terrified master to court with a noose around his neck again recalls the constricted speaker in the Tigillinus episode. Trampling on the corpse echoes what happens to Umbricius in the street-arena of Rome (*calcor*, 3.248) and looks forward to *Satire* 15.59–60 where the Egyptians think their brawl is just a game (*ludere se credunt*) because there are no corpses to trample upon (*quod nulla cadavera calcent*).

After this long account of the destruction of Sejanus and his statue, the satirist turns back to his main theme (90–96) and asks, "Would you like to be greeted like Sejanus" (*visne salutari sicut Seianus*) and to have all his powers? And why not? Even those who have no desire to kill like to have the power to do so" (*et qui nolunt occidere quemquam / posse volunt*, 96–97)—rather like Artorius and Catulus who started out managing toilets but now give *munera* and *occidunt populariter* (3.36–37). The speaker then explains what Sejanus's problem was:

> . . . Nam qui nimios optabat honores
> et nimias poscebat opes, numerosa parabat   105
> excelsae turris tabulata, unde altior esset
> casus et inpulsae praeceps inmane ruinae.
> Quid Crassos, quid Pompeios evertit et illum,
> ad sua qui domitos deduxit flagra Quirites?
> Summus nempe locus nulla non arte petitus   110
> magnaque numinibus vota exaudita malignis.
> Ad generum Cereris sine caede ac vulnere pauci
> descendunt reges et sicca morte tyranni.

> By keeping on asking for too many honors
> and demanding too much money, he was building many stories
> in a high-rise tower, from where the fall would be greater

---

105. Suet. *Tib.* 61–62; see Ferguson 1979 and Courtney 1980, *ad loc.* on the Ajax allusion.

and the headlong crash of the toppled ruin disastrous.
What was it that overturned the Crassi, the Pompeys, and that man
who brought under his lash the tamed citizens of Rome?
Simply the top position, sought by every possible means,
and ambitious prayers granted by malicious gods.
Few kings go down to Ceres' son-in-law without slaughter and mutilation,
few tyrants with a bloodless death. (104–13)

The collapse of the tower parallels the pulling down of the statue at the opening of the Sejanus episode and looks ahead to the collapse of other buildings
(*evertere domos*, 10.7; *ruina* 11.13). *Di faciles* have become *numina maligna*. In this
vignette, falling and collapsing are accompanied by transformation into other
items. It is the Emperor who brings down Sejanus, but the broader perspective
of the closing lines incorporates all kings and tyrants into the picture. The
pattern has long been set, going all the way back to the proto-tyrants of the late
Republic. The image of the *Quirites* being tamed and brought under the lash of
(the unnamed, Julius) Caesar strikes a powerful note of subjection and powerlessness taking us right back to the origins of imperial control: their later
manifestation are the *niveos ad frena Quirites*, mentioned earlier in 10.45. *Deduxit*
glances toward the satirist and his constriction at the end of *Satire* 1, perhaps;
the lesson of the dangers of seeking the *summus locus nulla non arte* chimes
one last time with the dangers of outspokenness that were flagged up at the
very beginning of the satirical enterprise (1.9–10). Such disturbing echoes
are not fully banished by the banal observations about kings and tyrants and
the implication that even the mighty may (eventually) fall, with Crassus, Pompey, and Caesar providing proof.

Melting Down the House

Juvenal, as we have seen, plays elaborately with the possibilities offered by statues, drawing on a long tradition, which includes the observation of Lucretius
3.59–64, that sees avarice, blind lust for statues, violation of limits, and crimes
by day and night as all nourished by fear of death:

> Denique avarities et honorum caeca cupido,
> quae miseros homines cogunt transcendere fines
> iuris et interdum socios scelerum atque ministros
> noctes atque dies niti praestante labore
> ad summas emergere opes, haec vulnera vitae
> non minimam partem mortis formidine aluntur.

> Consider too the greed and blind lust of power
> that drive unhappy men to overstep the bounds
> of right and may even turn them into accomplices or instruments of
>   crime,
> struggling night and day with unstinted effort
> to scale the pinnacles of wealth. These running sores of life
> are fed in no small measure by the fear of death.[106]

A little later, in 3.78, when he makes fear of death responsible for unlimited desire, we find: *intereunt partim statuarum et nominis ergo* (Some perish for the sake of statues and a title).[107] In Juvenal's *Satire* 10, the results of this same impulse to cheat death are visible first in the fate of statues and then in the breaking down of the body, which is no longer able to satisfy its desires. Mutilation and decay remain central to his vision when, after the Sejanus episode, the speaker considers the trophies of war:

> Bellorum exuviae, truncis adfixa tropaeis
> lorica et fracta de casside buccula pendens
> et curtum temone iugum victaeque triremis
> aplustre et summa tristis captivos in arce
> humanis maiora bonis creduntur.

> The spoils of war—the breastplate fastened to a tree-trunk trophy,
> and a cheekpiece hanging from a broken helmet,
> and a yoke separated from its pole, and an ornamental stern
> from a defeated trireme, and a miserable prisoner on the triumphal
>   arch—
> these are considered more than human blessings. (133–36)

Courtney observes how Juvenal "emphasizes that most of the trophies are broken, which has obvious symbolic value," and we may recall the earlier use of *truncus* in 8.53 (*trunco simillimus Hermae*), as well as later instances (12.79, *trunca puppe*, of the crippled ship on which the merchant Catullus almost came to grief; 13.178, *corpore trunco*, of an executed robber). In each case, being *truncus* is emblematic of a moral fault.[108] Shortly afterward, the speaker comments on the misplaced desire for fame and the inscriptions on tombs designed

---

106. Trans. R. Latham 1951.
107. Konstan 2008, chap. 2, esp. 39–45, 47–58.
108. Cf. Umbricius 3.48 (*mancus et extinctae corpus non utile dextrae*), who is in a similar position precisely because he refuses to subscribe to contemporary Roman (im)morality; Hor. *Sat.* 1.9.1: *olim truncus eram.*

to ensure it, which will, however, be "split apart" by the invasive growth of a "barren fig tree" (*discutienda valent sterilis mala robora fici*, 144–46).[109]

In the long central part of *Satire* 10, which deals with the wish for a long life, we witness the gradual breaking down of the body, as all the ills of old age take their toll on it and its capacity to experience pleasure (188–288). This sorry catalog of infirmities concludes with Pompey, who survived fevers in Campania to his own eventual detriment:

> . . . igitur Fortuna ipsius et Urbis
> servatum victo caput abstulit. Hoc cruciatu
> Lentulus, hac poena caruit ceciditque Cethegus
> integer et iacuit Catilina cadavere toto.

> And so when he was defeated, his own—and Rome's—Fortune
> cut off the head which she had saved. This was a mutilation,
> this was a punishment which Lentulus escaped; Cethegus died
> with his body whole, and Catiline lay with his corpse intact. (285–88)

Ferguson regards this as "an odd ending to the section," but it does take on some vital resonances if we read it in conjunction with the Sejanus decapitation scene.[110] It implies a randomness in outcome that, like the record of Fortune, is hardly comforting. Combined with the detailed account of the decay of the body, in which virtually no faculty or feature is left untouched (face, teeth, taste, hearing, sight, sexual arousal, memory, bones), it is a bleak prescription for the reader. The final segment of the poem deals with the catastrophic results of wishing for "good looks" especially in young women and men. For a girl, Lucretia's rape and suicide and Verginia's death at the hands of her father are on offer; while for a boy, prevention from taking on the man's role (*non licet esse viro*). The boy's case leads into a reprise of themes from *Satires* 2 and 6, with several examples of adulterers and, worse, the vengeance wrought on the "pure" (*castus*) man by women he has rejected: *mulier saevissima tunc est / cum stimulos odio pudor admovet* (328–29). We are reminded yet again that *Pudicitia* has been exiled from the Roman sexual landscape.

The final scene in the speaker's catalog of exempla involves Messalina, alluding to the case of C. Silius, a handsome patrician, who "is carried off to a wretched death" by her eyes (*rapitur miser extinguendus / Messalinae oculis*, 332–33). The dilemma he faced was to agree to be married to her or to die before evening (*pereundum erit ante lucernas*, 339), but even in the event of his

---

109. Cf. Hor. *Sat.*1.6.17: [*populus*] *qui stupet in titulis et imaginibus*; 1.9.47: *diffisa nate ficus*.

110. Ferguson 1979, *ad loc.*; cf. the example of Cicero in 10.120: *manus et cervix excisa*.

agreeing, he would have only a few days left to live before the news reached the Emperor. Whichever he chose, "his beautiful, white neck was to be offered to the sword" (*quidquid levius meliusque putaris, / praebenda est gladio pulchra haec et candida cervix*, 344–45). This reintroduces Messalina, who made an energetic appearance in the brothel in *Satire* 6, and sets up the reference to her own execution at the end of *Satire* 14. The death of Silius parallels the deaths of Lucretia and Verginia at the beginning of the survey of the benefits of good looks, while offering the neck to the sword has clear overtones of death in the arena.[111] In all such cases, it is the offspring of noble houses who are destroyed (as it was by Domitian's *caedes* in *Satire* 4), and this is magnified in the turmoil within the imperial family, a household in which the idea of marriage has lost its meaning.[112]

Houses themselves participate in the satirical action. As Edwards explains, houses were "especially good to think with" in relation to social status, noting their symbolic importance as metaphors for both their owners and the state in connection with complaints about luxurious building in Roman moral discourse.[113] So, in *Epistle* 86, Seneca contrasts the "basic" bath in Scipio Africanus's villa at Liternum (*in hoc angulo ille Carthaginis horror, cui Roma debet*, 5) with contemporary tastes for luxury in bathing facilities (*pauper sibi videtur ac sordidus, nisi parietes magnis et pretiosis orbibus refulserunt*, 6). We saw earlier how Antony occupied Pompey's house and consumed Varro's resources.[114] For the satirinst, houses are subject to the same vulnerabilities as those who occupy them and hence are often places of premeditated and violent death. Likewise, for example, in 8.76–77, the satirist warns Ponticus not to rely on the *fama* of others, as Rubellius did, *ne conlapsa ruant subductis tecta columnis* (lest the roof falls in when the columns are removed).

In *Satire* 3, the satirist refers to a dread of fires and falling buildings (*horrere incendia, lapsus / tectorum adsiduos*, 7–8) as reasons for leaving Rome, and the action is driven by the metaphorical collapsing of Umbricius's house, which has been reduced to one cart (*tota domus raeda componitur*, 10) for Cumae. Later in the poem, the tears in the poor man's dirty clothes and shoe are analogous to the cracks in his *hospitium miserabile* (166), which is on the verge of falling down (*pendente . . . ruina*, 196). Only poor people's dwellings are in danger of collapse here, but the next two uses of *ruina* will refer to Sejanus (10.107) and

---

111. See chap. 3, p. 187 herein.
112. See chap. 2, p. 133 herein.
113. Edwards 1993, chap. 4, esp. 138–40, 150–59; Newlands 2002, chap. 3 on "Engendering the House."
114. *Philippics* 2.66–67. See also chap. 2, pp. 146–47 herein.

Rutilus (11.13), signaling the transfer of the architectural metaphor to the overly ambitious praetorian and the spendthrift inheritor of a noble patrimony.

In *Satire* 11, Rutilus is about to enter the gladiatorial school: *scripturus leges et regia verba lanistae* (8). The cause is dining (*quibus in solo vivendi causa palato est*, 11) which has drained away his paternal inheritance. Such a man is the most doomed (*miserrimus*), "with the cracks already letting in the light" (*iam perlucente ruina*, 12–13).[115] That, however, does not stop him from seeking out gourmet items from every realm (*elementa per omnia*, 14), with no regard for price:

> Ergo haut difficile est perituram arcessere summam
> lancibus oppositis vel matris imagine fracta,
> et quadringentis nummis condire gulosum
> fictile; sic veniunt ad miscellanea ludi.

> Therefore it is not difficult to raise money that will be squandered
> by pawning plates or by breaking up mother's statue,
> and to flavour their gluttonous earthenware at a cost of 400,000;[116]
> and thus they come to the mash of the gladiatorial school. (17–20)

Creating elaborate dishes, squandering money, melting objects down, and failing to behave as a son should as steward of his patrimony all lead to the confused mash which is the fodder of gladiators.[117] The vortex of the arena becomes the natural finishing point of degeneration and dissolution.

After a brief exposition of the necessity of "knowing thyself" (27) and your own measure, which is to be "kept in view" (*noscenda est mensura sui spectandaque*, 35), both too well worn to carry much weight, the speaker continues:

> . . . Quis enim te deficiente crumina
> et crescente gula manet exitus, aere paterno
> ac rebus mersis in ventrem fenoris atque
> argenti gravis et pecorum agrorumque capacem?

> For what end awaits you as your wallet grows empty
> and your appetite grows, once you have sunk your

115. Cf. Juv. 2.78: *Cretice, perluces*; Sen. *Ep.* 51.11, of Scipio's self-exile from Rome and his villa at Liternum, rather than Baiae: *Literni honestius Scipio quam Bais exulabat: ruina eius non est tam molliter conlocanda.*

116. See above, pp. 248–49, on *Sat.* 14.326.

117. Cf. 12.50–51: *non propter vitam faciunt patrimonia quidam, / sed vitio caeci propter patrimonia vivunt*; on the genuineness of these lines, see Courtney; Ferguson says they seem useful to Juvenal's theme. Sen. *De Tranq.* 8 describes *patrimonia* as the "greatest source of human troubles" (*maximam humanarum aerumnarum materiam*).

paternal inheritance and property in your stomach,
which holds dividends and heavy silver and flocks and fields? (38–41)

The self-abjection into the gladiatorial school is analogous to the "self-castration" in *Satire* 12, where the merchant survives only to be done in by legacy hunters, thus bringing about the end of his family line anyway.

Satire 14 opens with the son and heir learning early on from his father a love of gambling and gluttony, in which case he is already doomed by the age of seven:

> Si damnosa senem iuvat alea, ludit et heres
> bullatus **parvo**que eadem **movet arma fritillo.**
> Nec melius de se cuiquam sperare propinquo
> concedet iuvenis, qui radere tubera terrae,
> boletum condire et eodem iure natantis
> mergere ficedulas **didicit nebulone parente**
> et cana monstrante gula. Cum septimus annus
> transierit puerum, nondum omni dente renato,
> barbatos licet admoveas mille inde magistros,
> hinc totidem, cupiet lauto cenare paratu
> semper et a **magna** non **degenerare culina.**

> If it's ruinous gambling that is the old man's pleasure, his heir is a
>   player, too,
> while still a boy, rattling the very same **weapons in his tiny dice-shaker.**
> And if a young man has learned how to peel truffles, to marinate
>   mushrooms,
> and to douse floating fig-peckers in mushroom sauce
> under **instruction from his waster of a father's** white-haired gluttony,
> none of his relatives can entertain better hopes for him. Such a boy, when
>   his seventh year has just passed by and before his teeth have grown again,
> will always want to dine in lavish style without **falling short**
> **of the high standard of his grand cuisine**, though you bring in
> thousands of bearded tutors on his left and his right. (4–14)[118]

The phrase *movet arma* (as perhaps does *eodem iure natantis*) glances toward the education and training the young man is *not* receiving, enclosed as it is in the line by *parvo* and *fritillo;* likewise, *degenerare* speaks the truth about what is happening, sandwiched between *magna* and *culina.* The designation

---

118. Trans. Braund 2004.

of the father as a *nebulo* picks up *erroris nebula* of 10.4, and is here tellingly placed right after *didicit*. Then we have the example of Caetronius the builder, who frittered away his wealth, and then his son (naturally enough) squandered what was left:

> Aedificator erat Caetronius et modo curvo
> litore Caietae, summa nunc Tiburis arce,
> nunc Praenestinis in montibus alta parabat
> culmina villarum **Graecis longeque petitis**
> **marmoribus** vincens Fortunae atque Herculis aedem,
> ut **spado** vincebat **Capitolia nostra** Posides.
> Dum sic ergo habitat Caetronius, **imminuit rem,**
> **fregit opes**, nec parva tamen mensura relictae
> partis erat. Totam hanc **turbavit filius amens,**
> dum meliore novas attollit marmore villas.

> Caetronius was obsessed with building. He constructed the high roofs
> of his villas at one time on the curving shoreline of Caieta,
> then again on the heights of Tibur, and again in the halls of Praeneste.
> With his **marble brought from Greece and from far away**
> he outdid the temples of Fortune and Hercules,
> just as Posides the eunuch tried to outdo **the Roman Capitol**.
> The result was that, in this kind of accommodation, Caetronius
> **reduced his property and frittered away his wealth**. Yet what was left
> was not a negligible amount. All of that **his crazy son squandered**
> by putting up new villas of even finer marble. (86–95)

The erection of the buildings is paralleled by the shrinking and breaking of the family property.[119] The word *filius* is located between *turbare* and *amens*, which not only describe the behavior of the son and his father, from whom he learned it, but also signify broader social disorder and moral confusion.[120] This is confirmed by the seeking out of Greek marble from far afield and the notion of trying to outdo, or conquer, [the temple of] Fortuna. The analogy is the castrated male, the *spado* Posides, another disreputable freedman of Claudius with a Greek name, who tried to outdo *our* Capitol.[121]

119. Plin. *Pan.* 51.1 praises Trajan for being *parcus in aedificando*; Roche 2011, 48–49.
120. Cf. *furor* and *manifesta phrenesis* of heaping up money, even if it means living like a down-and-out, driven by the *adquirendi . . . insatiabile votum* learned from one's father (136, 125). The miser is viewed as *adquirendi / artificem* (115–16).
121. See chap. 1, pp. 71–73, and chap. 2, p. 148 herein.

In this very long poem of 331 lines, the blame for the corruption of children is laid squarely at the feet of parents or, rather, the father: *mentis causa malae tamen est et origo penes te* (226). Because of his failings as a parent, the father loses control of the reins of his son:

> dat libertatem et totas effundit habenas
> curriculo; quem si revoces, subsistere nescit
> et te contempto rapitur metisque relictis.
> Nemo satis credit tantum delinquere quantum
> permittas: adeo indulgent sibi latius ipsi.

> he gives him *libertas* and lets go of the chariot's reins completely;
> and if you try to call him back, he doesn't know how to stop
> and is swept along, toatally ignoring you and leaving behind the turning
>   posts.
> No one thinks it enough to do wrong only as much as you
> Permit; they give themselves much more license. (230–34)[122]

As well as pointing out once more the contested nature of *libertas*, this puts us in mind yet again of the excesses of the circus. The fire the father kindled breaks out and devours everything (*Ergo ignem, cuius scintillas ipse dedisti, / flagrantem late et rapientem cuncta videbis*, 244–45)—reminding us of other conflagrations we have seen—and, similarly, like a lion, the student will destroy his master (*trepidumque magistrum / in cavea magno fremitu leo tollet alumnus*, 246–67). This glances to the arena, not only because of the lion, but the word *cavea* (here, probably "cage") is also used of seating areas in the theater or at the games.[123] The son waits impatiently for the death of his father who stands in his way (*iam nunc obstas et vota moraris*, 250) and whose long old age "tortures" him (*torquet*, 250). Hence, advises the satirist:

> Ocius Archigenen quaere atque eme quod Mithridates
> composuit, si vis aliam decerpere ficum
> atque alias tractare rosas. Medicamen habendum est,
> sorbere ante cibum quod debeat et pater et rex.

> Seek out Archigenes at once and buy a mixture which Mithridates
> put together,if you want to pluck one more fig,

---

122. Cf. Sen. *De Tranq.* 9.2: *spes effrenatas et animum in futura imminentem velut sub vinculis habere, id agere, ut divitias a nobis potius quam a fortuna petamus.*

123. In 14.241–43, suspected by some editors, the *sulcis* from which the murderous legions of the dragon's teeth sprang—and the trumpeter (*tibicen*) imagined as accompanying them—might also suggest the arena via its use in the Tigillinus scene of *Sat.* 1.

and pick roses one more time. You must have a medicine
which a father, as well as a king, should swallow before food.(252–55)

Archigenes was mentioned as a doctor in 6.236 and 13.98 (and we may recall
how the *medicus ridens* sliced off the "swollen figs" in 2.13) , while Mithridates
and his self-innoculation against poisoning ended *Satire* 6. It is right after this
episode (*monstro voluptatem egregiam . . .* , 256) that the satirist explains that he
is offering an "exceptional entertainment" to his audience.

Thus, in *Satire* 14, with the "melting down" of the house, via the consumption of patrimony and the sundering of the bonds between parents and
children, especially those of father and son, we are invited to contemplate the
wreckage of *Romanitas*. The image of the charioteer losing control of the reins
picks up on the early *exemplum* of the dissolute "boy Automedon" charging
along the Appian Way—he went through his entire patrimony on horse-racing
(*caret omni / maiorum censu*, 1.59–60)—but also on the evocations of the circus
in various other poems. The world is out of joint and out of control, which
might remind readers of Vergil's imagery at the end of *Georgics* 1, 512–14:

ut cum carceribus sese effudere quadrigae
addunt in spatia, et frustra retinacula tendens
fertur equis auriga neque audit currus habenas.

Just as when the chariots have poured forth from the starting gates,
they go faster on each lap, and the charioteer, pulling in vain on the
    bridles,
is carried on by the horses, and the chariot does not heed the reins.[124]

In Vergil, of course, this comes in the context of a prayer for the success of
Augustus's endeavors; in Juvenal there is no such savior on the horizon. There
is certainly a suggestion of a quickening of the pace of the deconstruction of
Romanitas as we progress through Juvenal's later books. Somewhat incongru-
ously with the more restrained and philosophical tone of the speaker, we seem
to be hurtling even more rapidly toward a comprehensive destruction. The
wholesale melting down culminates in this book with *Satire* 15, with its universalized pessimism spreading out from a gory, arena-esque account of Egyptian
cannibalism. The fight between the Tentyrans and Ombites is described in
terms of a *prolusio* that gradually gets out of control:[125]

124. Cf. Gogol's image of the sleigh at the end of part 1 (chap. 10) of *Dead Souls* (2004).

125. Cf. chap. 3, p. 226 herein on *Sat.* 5.26–29; Tac. *Hist.* 2.88: *ad iurgium, mox ad manus et ferrum
transirent*, on the chaotic spectacle unleashed in Rome by Vitellius.

Sed iurgia prima sonare
incipiunt: animis ardentibus haec tuba rixae.
Dein **clamore pari concurritur**, et vice teli
saevit nuda manus. Paucae sine volnere malae,
vix cuiquam aut nulli toto certamine nasus   55
integer. Aspiceres iam cuncta per agmina voltus
dimidios, alias facies et hiantia ruptis
ossa genis, plenos oculorum sanguine pugnos.
Ludere se credunt ipsi tamen et puerilis
exercere acies, quod nulla **cadavera calcent**.   60
Et sane quo tot rixantis milia turbae,
si vivunt omnes? Ergo acrior impetus et iam
saxa inclinatis per humum quaesita lacertis
incipiunt torquere, **domestica seditioni**
tela, nec hunc lapidem, qualis et Turnus et Aiax,   65
vel quo Tydides **percussit** pondere coxam
Aeneae, sed quem valeant emittere dextrae
illis dissimiles et nostro tempore natae.

So first of all, insults start to sound:
when tempers are blazing, these are the bugle call of the brawl.
Then **both sides shout and charge, attacking**
with their bare hands instead of weapons. Few jaws are unwounded,
hardly anyone, or no one, in the whole fight has an uninjured nose.
Through all the ranks you could already see mutilated faces,
features unrecognizable, bones gaping
through torn cheeks, fists full of blood from the eyes.
Yet they think this is a game, a childish
practice fight, because **there are no bodies to trample.**
And after all, what's the point of a brawling mob thousands strong
if no one is killed? So the attack gets fiercer. Now
they look for stones on the ground and
start hurling them with arms bent back. These are the **homegrown**
    weapons of rioters—
not the kind of stone that Turnus and Ajax wielded,
and not as heavy as the one the son of Tydeus **used to strike**
Aeneas' hip, but the kind that modern-day hands,
unlike theirs, can manage to launch. (51–68)[126]

---

126. Trans. Braund 2004.

The account has clear overtones of gladiatorial combat and beast hunts and we know that Tentyrans were reputed to be hostile to crocodiles and came to Rome as keepers when the animals were exhibited.[127] Significantly, the preliminary skirmish leads on, not to a one-on-one combat, on the model of gladiators or the heroic figures of myth, but to a rout in which one side chases the other en masse. This is mob violence translated to the Egyptian desert. It reaches its climax when a fleeing Tentyran slips and is set upon by the frenzied Ombites:

Terga fugae celeri praestant instantibus Ombis
qui vicina colunt umbrosae Tentura palmae.
Labitur hinc quidam nimia formidine cursum
praecipitans capiturque. **Ast illum in plurima sectum frusta et particulas**, ut multis mortuus unus
sufficeret, totum corrosis ossibus edit
victrix turba, nec ardenti decoxit aeno
aut veribus, longum usque adeo tardumque putavit
expectare focos, **contenta cadavere crudo.**

As the people of Ombi chase them, the inhabitants of neighbouring
    Tentyra
with its shady palms turn their backs in rapid retreat.
One of them slips while speeding his departure
in mad panic—and gets caught. **He's immediately chopped into
    hundreds of
hunks and morsels**—to get enough portions from one dead man—
and completely devoured by **the victorious mob**, even gnawing his bones.
They didn't cook him in a blazing pot or barbecue him.
They thought it was far too long and tedious
to wait for the hearth: they were **content with the raw corpse.** (75–83)[128]

The same sort of frenzy was visible in the maltreatment of Sejanus's body and his statue.

In the second half of the poem, what we might call its "more philosophical" part, we have a brief evocation of the early days of communal life among humans, who, unlike the animals, were given a soul; this was a time when people built homes next to each other so as to feel more secure (*tutos vicino limine somnos / ut conlata daret fiducia*), protected a fallen or wounded fellow

127. Strabo 17.1.44; crocodiles were first on display at *ludi* of M. Aemilius Scaurus in 58 B.C.E., see Dunkle 2008, 208–209.

128. Trans. Braund 2004.

citizen (*lapsum aut ingenti nutantem volnere civem*), and were defended by the same towers (*defendier isdem turribus;* 149–58).[129] But, the speaker goes on, now there is more Concord among snakes (*iam serpentum maior Concordia*), and even animals spare their relatives, *saevis inter se convenit ursis* (159–64).[130] He adds in his concluding lines:

> Ast homini ferrum letale incude nefanda
> produxisse parum est, cum rastra et sarcula tantum
> adsueti coquere et marris ac vomere lassi
> nescierint primi gladios extendere fabri.
> Aspicimus populos quorum non sufficit irae
> occidisse aliquem, sed pectora, bracchia, voltum
> crediderint genus esse cibi. Quid diceret ergo
> vel quo non fugeret, si nunc haec monstra videret
> Pythagoras, cunctis animalibus abstinuit qui
> tamquam homine et ventri indulsit non omne legumen?

> But for man it is not enough to have produced a lethal blade
> on an impious anvil, although the first blacksmiths
> were accustomed to tire themselves out forging only
> rakes and hoes and mattocks and ploughshares,
> and didn't know how to beat out swords.
> We behold peoples whose anger is not satisfied
> by killing someone but who think his breast, arms, and face
> are a kind of food. What, then, would Pythagoras say,
> or where wouldn't flee, if he now saw these monstrosities,
> he who abstained from all living things as if they were human
> and who didn't indulge his belly with every kind of vegetable? (165–74)

Horace in his own satirical vision of prehistoric life tells how the first animalistic humans used to fight with fists and nails, then sticks, over acorns and lairs (*unguibus et pugnis, dein fustibus, atque ita porro / pugnabant armis quae post fabricaverat usus,* 101–102)—echoed in how Juvenal's Egyptians "make do" with what is available in terms of weapons—but he does so in the context of a narrative of progress from primitive existence to the development of language, peace, towns, and laws (*Satire* 1.3.99–112).[131] For Juvenal, the farm tools are convenient signifiers of the old days and old ways, even of the Golden Age, and their mutation into other objects, whose purpose is to kill, is nicely

---

129. See chap. 2 herein.
130. See chap. 1 herein.
131. See Gowers 2012, 138–43, on the metapoetic aspects of Horace's scenery.

emblematic of the decline that has taken place. The idea of farm tools meta-morphosing to weapons was, of course, a cliché by his day, as we can see from Ovid, *Fasti* 1.697–700:[132]

> Bella diu tenuere viros: erat aptior ensis
> vomere, cedebat taurus arator equo;
> sarcula cessabant, versique in pila ligones
> factaque de rastri pondere cassis erat.

> For a long time war gripped men: swords are more useful
> than ploughs, horses surpassed the tilling ox.
> The hoe stood still, mattocks were turned into spears
> and helmets crafted from the massy rake.[133]

Pythagoras is an intriguing figure for Juvenal to choose to deploy in his conclusion to *Satire* 15; he evokes a process of continual change, much as he does at the end of Ovid's *Metamorphoses*. We have gone from agriculture and eating food to a different kind of consumption, enacted through war and mur-der; hence perhaps the appearance of Pythagoras, who famously feared that he might accidentally eat people.[134] In Juvenal's narrative, body parts become food items, the ultimate violation of taboos and the ultimate in satirical aggres-sion.[135] It is important that there is no sex in *Satire* 15. We have moved beyond that hitherto central topic to the destruction of the body itself, to *mera homi-cida*, to use Seneca's words about lunch-break executions in the arena.[136] There is a strong metapoetic element too: satire is "cannibalistic" in many ways and often, in its more extreme versions, makes use of the theme.[137]

Pythagoras was also connected with Numa, through a well-established chain of ideas, which points us back to *Satire* 3 and Umbricius. He too speaks of ploughshares and other farm implements being supplanted—this time by chains—in 3.309–14:

> Qua fornace graves, qua non incude catenae?
> Maximus in vinclis ferri modus, ut timeas ne

---

132. Ovid celebrates Pax brought about by the imperial family, 704: *Pax Cererem nutrit, Ceres alumna Pacis.* Bella is captive and in chains (701–702). Other instances include Lucr. 5.1293–96, Verg. *Geor.* 1.508.

133. Trans. Boyle and Woodard 2000. As Green 2004 notes, "The transformation from hoe to helmet is a novel and contrived image, representing a radical change which effectively demonstrates the sheer lengths to which man went to promote war over agriculture" (318).

134. Cf. 2.155–56: *Cannis consumpta iuventus, / tot bellorum animae.*

135. See the discussion of Swift's *A Modest Proposal* (1729) and Waugh's *Black Mischief* (2002) in the conclusion, pp. 308, 313.

136. See chap. 3, p. 188 herein.

137. Likewise, perhaps, hammering out a written work: Cic. *Att.* 15.27.2, Plin. *Ep.* 1.3.4; Tac. *Dial.* 9.3: *magna noctium parte unum librum excudit et elucubravit.*

vomer deficiat, ne marra et sarcula desint.
Felices proavorum atavos, felicia dicas
saecula quae quondam sub regibus atque tribunis
viderunt uno contentam carcere Romam.

What furnace, what anvil isn't weighed down by forging chains?
The greatest part of our iron is turned into fetters, so that you should fear
a shortage of ploughshares and a lack of mattocks and hoes.
Fortunate were the ancestors of our great-grandfathers, and fortunate,
     you'd say,
those epochs that once under the kings and tribunes
saw a Rome satisfied with a single prison.[138]

This comes at the very end of Umbricius's speech; it is the point where he leaves off and heads to Cumae. Thus the question *vel quo non fugeret?* of Pythagoras echoes Umbricius's desire to flee from Rome and ties the endings of these two poems together. At the same time, it adds a philosophical veneer to the discontented and disillusioned figure of the satirist in his earlier incarnation. The fleeing Umbricius is reimagined as the fleeing Pythagoras, but, notably, he still flees. Keane rightly observes: "In *Satire* 15, far from serving as a refuge for troubled souls, philosophy fails to comfort even one of its most famous spokesmen. This is not simple irreverence. Juvenal illustrates the failure of philosophy itself by leaving us with the image of Pythagoras's shocked, directionless flight. This satiric experiment in philosophy defeats the very heroes of its model text: the *sapientes*."[139] One thinks of what Seneca says in *De Tranquillitate* 4.2, 8, speaking in terms of the struggle with Fortune: if it gets the better of someone and deprives him of the means of action, then:

non statim aversus inermisque fugiat latebras quaerens, quasi ullus
locus sit quo non possit fortuna persequi, sed parcius se inferat
officiis. . . . Longe itaque optimum est miscere otium rebus, quotiens
actuosa vita impedimentis fortuitis aut civitatis condicione
prohibebitur; numquam enim usque eo interclusa sunt omnia ut
nulli actioni locus honestae sit.

Let a man not straightway turn his back and flee, throwing away his
arms and seeking some hiding-place, as if there were anywhere a

---

138. For Numa as priestly counterpart to Romulus, see Ogilvie 1965, 88–89: the Numa and Pythagoras link was cemented over time, and by the time the Romans wrote their own history, a "detailed reign of Numa together with his alleged discipleship under Pythagoras was common currency" (89). Cf. Cic. *De Orat.* 3.197: *Numa rege doctissimo.*

139. Keane 2007, 48.

place where Fortune could not reach him, but let him devote himself
to his duties more sparingly. . . . Accordingly the best course by far is
to combine leisure with business, whenever chance obstacles or the
condition of the state shall prevent one's living a really active life; for
a man is never so completely shut off from all pursuits that no
opportunity is left for any honourable activity.[140]

For the Juvenalian, this would hardly be convincing; indeed, it would seem
as trite and pointless as the refrain of Maria von Trapp's "When the Lord
closes a door, somewhere he opens a window" when extracted from its context of a comforting narrative closure.[141] Changing places, in other words,
does not help: the message of the *Satires* seems to be more closely aligned with
Seneca's position in *De Tranquillitate* 2.15, criticizing wandering and traveling
about: *itaque scire debemus non locorum vitium esse quo laboramus, sed nostrum*
(and so we ought to understand that what we struggle with is the fault, not of
the places, but of ourselves).[142]

We might also frame this discussion in terms of a Romulus-Numa shift,
from a warrior-satirist, inspired by Lucilius, to a philosopher-satirist, inspired
by Horace and perhaps Persius, grafting it onto the long tradition of Romulus
as warlike and unlearned and Numa as peace-loving (*placidus*) and sophisticated. Such a shift had been fashioned for metapoetic purposes by Ovid, who,
in his *Fasti* 1.27–44, used it to mark a move away from epic.[143] In the context of
Juvenalian satire (which is, of course, composed in the epic meter), after the
warlike and angry Romulan of the opening salvos, the Numan option—the defining of measure and boundaries, the establishment of religion, the voice and
manner of the *placidus* as opposed to the *indignans*—is duly tried out, only to
be rejected. This change of tack runs in parallel with the Lucilius-Horace shift
that takes place in *Satire* 1, but it will not satisfy the Juvenalian speaker (or reader)
here either. Thus the metamorphic and fluid conclusion of the violent and pessimistic *Satire* 15, with the flight of Numa's associate, Pythagoras, is also, at the
end of the day, a rejection of this less combative direction in writing satire.

As we have seen, one of the basic techniques of satire is to suggest that
walls, borders, and other lines of containment have been breached by all sorts

---

140. Trans. Basore 1928–35.

141. As played by Julie Andrews in the film *The Sound of Music*.

142. On contradictory aspects of Sen.'s view of travel, see Montiglio 2006. Cf. *Cons. Helv.* 6: *mobilis enim et inquieta homini mens data est, nusquam se tenet, spargitur, et cogitationes suas in omnia nota atque ignota dimittit, vaga et quietis impatiens et novitate rerum laetissima.*

143. Cf. Ov. *F.* 3.1–392; Livy 1.19.4; Littlewood 2002, 181. Green 2004 says that in *F.* 1.27–44, Ovid shows the "differing yet complementary characters" of Romulus and Numa and makes Romulus the representative of *arma* and epic Ovid purports to reject and Numa as "both thematically and generically, consistent with the priorities of the poem and the poet himself" (46).

of miscreants. The question is, in blunt terms, can they be reerected? This is perhaps the main impulse of Horatian satire with its continual exhortations to live and behave *intra naturae fines*, as *Satire* 1.1.49–50 has it, or 105–106: *est modus in rebus, sunt certi denique fines, / quos ultra citraque nequit consistere rerum*. In Horatian satire, the speaker at least struggles to recover or retain limits, borders, territories, while in Juvenalian satire, he shows them as irredeemably broken, washed away, obliterated.[144] As we have seen, the confining walls of the arena set out to contain the Other physically, and attempt to do so ideologically and psychologically; in Juvenalian discourse, however, efforts at containment are futile. "Happy those times," says Umbricius, "which saw Rome content with a single prison." In those days, that was the only contained space needed in which to dump violators of the Roman order of things. *Satire* 13 is very telling in this regard, for it is characterized by numerous images and suggestions of containment and restraint, even arguing that the victim of the rather petty crime which sets it all into motion should recognize that his own "ordinary" (*modicam*) experience calls only for "middling" rage (*mediocri bile*, 143). At the end of that poem, we move from the unconstrained criminality of the thief to his eventual confinement when the gods punish him; he may then indeed experience a guilty conscience accompanied by a *perpetua anxietas* (210–39). But, the speaker goes on, as he does in *Satire* 14, with an unsettling coda:

> . . . Tamen ad mores natura recurrit
> damnatos fixa et mutari nescia. Nam quis   240
> **peccandi finem** posuit sibi? Quando recepit
> **eiectum semel attrita de fronte ruborem?**
> Quisnam hominum est quem tu contentum videris uno
> flagitio? Dabit in laqueum vestigia noster
> **perfidus** et nigri patietur **carceris uncum**   245
> aut maris Aegaei rupem scopulosque frequentes
> exulibus magnis. Poena gaudebis amara
> nominis invisi tandemque fatebere laetus
> nec surdum nec Teresian quemquam esse deorum.

> Yet [their] nature, which is fixed and incapable of changing,
> reverts to the ways it has condemned. For who
> ever placed **a limit on his own wrongdoing?** When has
> **the blush of shame** been recovered **once banished from a hardened
>   forehead?**

---

144. See, e.g., the discussion in Uden 2015, 206–18 titled "The Sameness and Difference of Rome."

What man is there anywhere whom you have witnessed content with a
    single
act of criminality? Our **traitor** will put his feet into the snare,
and he will face **the hook in a dingy prison**
or some rock in the Aegean Sea and the crags crowded
with noble exiles. You will rejoice at the bitter punishment
of the man whose name you hate, and, in the end, you'll happily
    admit
that none of the gods is deaf [a Drusus][145] or a Tiresias. (13.239–49)

There is, in fact, no limit to crime, no bringing back shame to the face once it
has been ejected, no satisfaction with just one misdeed. But then we have three
images of the criminal's confinement: in a snare, on a prison hook, or on a rocky
Aegean island full of exiles. This appears to offer Calvinus a guarantee of eventual confinement at the hands of the gods, who, he will then happily admit, are
neither deaf nor blind.[146] If the Drusus reading is correct, then the reference
to Claudius makes an interesting parallel with the end of *Satire* 14.[147] But even
if not, the implication seems to be that the longed-for confinement, and the
punishment of the hated one (*invisi*) which brings joy (*gaudebis*) is not at all
guaranteed.

This speaks to the satirist's project more broadly too: while at the end of
Satire 1, the question is whether to open one's mouth, to castigate the hated
criminal, by *Satire* 13 it has become whether punishment will ever come if one
does so, even in Stentorian tones. The opening lines state that the *prima ultio*
against the perpetrator of a bad example (*exemplo malo*), of trust betrayed (*fidei
violatae*) is that it "is to the disadvantage of" or "disturbs" the doer (*ipsi displicet
auctori*). This is the simplest, and most abject, response to crime, transferring
responsibility for restitution elsewhere—not just to the courts, but to the gods, to
nature, and even to philosophy (19–22).[148] The poem is, according to Ferguson,
"an excuse for castigating the criminality of the age," although, as in *Satire* 14,
there is a momentary glimpse of the satirical antithesis in the (admittedly
pleasing) vision of nature taking its course, which ends in the demise of the

---

145. Thus Courtney 1980 and Braund 2004.

146. Courtney 1980 sees "a proof that after all there is justice in the world and therefore a cause for rejoicing" (560, cf. 533–37 on how the poem "turns serious" at 174). Ferguson 1979 and others interpret the
conclusion as ironic; see Pryor 1962, Fredericks 1971, Edmunds 1972, Morford 1973.

147. Cf. 3.238: *somnum Druso vitulisque marinis.*

148. F. M. A. Jones 2007 argues that in 10 Juvenal has a conventional message and so does not under-
cut the "moralising-philosophical tradition" there, but in 13 rejects philosophical knowledge as "unnecessary
and unhelpful" (123–24).

criminal.[149] There is grim satisfaction from such a result, but one cannot rely on this as the only means of securing justice.[150]

To return to *Satire* 10, with which this chapter opened, Juvenal has by the end of Book 5 ridiculed not only all human desires, but all human actions, and has shown them to be futile in terms of results. In response to the problem of *frontis nulla fides*, the satirist has exhibited a relentless and uncompromising *fides* to the world around him. Things are firmly set for posterity (as he said at the outset in 1.147–48: *nil erit ulterius quod nostris moribus addat / posteritas, eadem facient cupientque minores*), in a sorry sequence of endless repetition— tomorrow and tomorrow and tomorrow—with death the vanishing point whither all reflection tends. Yet, this must raise the question as to whether the satirist's *fides* is not itself futile, since what it demonstrates perhaps most force- fully of all is the meaninglessness, the emptiness, of its own honesty. If the philosophical turn presented in these later books also fails, then what, if any- thing, remains for the reader in the devastated and depopulated landscape to which the satirist has, in the best Roman tradition, laid waste so effectively and comprehensively?

149. Ferguson 1979: "The successful criminal is always uneasy, yet always thinks that he will get away with it again, and sooner or later overreaches himself. This is set as a final consolation to Calvinus. It is not really so. It is the nearest J comes to asserting a moral order in this poem, pessimistically but positively" (295).

150. Keane 2007 observes: "The ending also problematizes the traditional view that the persona of Book 5 rejects the anger and *indignatio* of the early books (Anderson 1982, 281–84). This speaker seems fasci- nated by anger, its dangers, and its pleasures, fascinated enough to make them the subject of the book's first poem and to revisit them in *Satire* 15 where they are embodied in the violent Egyptians. Simply put, these vivid critical portrayals of anger have the effect of reviving the topic and putting it to use" (34–35).

Conclusion

The Plague of Satire

And now was acknowledged the presence of the Red Death. He had
come like a thief in the night. And one by one dropped the revelers
in the blood-bedewed halls of their revel, and each died in the
despairing posture of his fall. And the life of the ebony clock went
out with that of the last of the gay. And the Flames of the tripods
expired. And Darkness and Decay and the Red Death held illimitable
dominion over all.

—Edgar Allan Poe, *The Masque of the Red Death*

An nihil in melius tot rerum proficis usu? the sixty-year-old Calvinus is asked by
the speaker in *Satire* 13.18, who recommends life as a teacher whose lessons can
also lead to happiness, just as much as the sacred books of philosophy, styled
the *Victrix Fortunae*, can. As we have seen, by his foregrounding figures such
as Socrates and Pythagoras, Democritus and Heraclitus, Epicurus and Seneca,
the satirist is clearly moving onto philosophical territory, as is also suggested
by the broadening of perspective to include all of humanity in the opening of
Satire 10 or the universalized ending of *Satire* 15. The aphoristic "conclusions"
of *Satires* 10–15 give every impression of pointing the reader in the direction of
philosophical contemplation, but the unsatisfying nature of the advice on offer
suggests that they cannot be taken seriously or that deeper, more fundamental
reflection and self-examination are necessary. If the latter, then an analogous
entity might be the *synkrisis* (formal comparison) at the end of a pair of Plutarch's *Parallel Lives* (*Demosthenes and Cicero, Solon and Numa*), which is often
banal and simplistic in its analysis of the two subjects' respective virtues and

vices and seems designed to serve as a stimulus to further debate and more searching moral evaluation of the two figures under examination, as well as to consideration of how this exercise might be used to good effect in the reader's self-formation.[1]

Before we consider the nature of the philosophical speculation encouraged by these later poems in more depth, let us review what we have seen as we accompanied the Juvenalian satirist across the cityscape on his search for Rome, a quest that parallels and parodies the Stoic, and especially Senecan, figure of the *proficiens*, the "seeker" or "the man on the path to virtue" (*qui ad virtutem tendit*).[2] We have read the satires here through the labyrinthine experience of urban space and the liminal zone of the arena, with particular attention to the accumulation of colorful, grotesque, and nauseating *exempla* that populate the speaker's rhetoric of repetition and excess. The topographic and the somatic are inextricably bound up with each other, as we are confronted by the porosity of city and body alike.

We have also focused on intimations of disease, decay, destruction, and death as manifestations of Juvenalian satire's deconstruction of the traditional signifiers of *Romanitas* and the anchors of Roman constructions of identity, especially that of the free male citizen. We might expect the cityscape, as the hub of the Roman world with all its originary landmarks of place and architecture, and other embodiments and memories of *Romanitas*, to offer secure anchorage to the wanderer, but of course in Juvenal's re-imagining of Rome instability reigns supreme. What Benjamin recommends for the historical materialist, that is, "dissociating himself as far as possible" from "the document of civilization" and seeing as his task as "to brush history against the grain," is not so dissimilar to the perspective and practice of the Juvenalian satirist. As Gilloch says, Benjamin offers up his own monuments, "personal counter monuments," in order to capture an alternative version of history within the city, "dwelling on the fragile, sorrowful, ephemeral." This gives us a history "which proclaims the sufferings of the past and the persistence of barbarism in the present."[3] Similarly, Juvenal's new *lieux de mémoire* are the homes of Cordus and Persicus (before and after they have burned down), Virro's uncongenial dining room, or the vomit-covered parquet in the home of the binge-drinking *matrona*. His new *triumphales* adorning these places are Crispinus, Virro, Laronia, Eppia, Naevolus, Rutilus, and Gracchus the *retiarius*. In the satirical

---

1. See Larmour 2005b.

2. Sen. *De Vit. Beat.* 16.3.

3. See Gilloch 1996, 75–76; cf. "In the urban setting a particular, persuasive version of the past is constructed and elaborated. . . . In the metropolis, the past is to be eradicated, catalogued, or glorified" (75).

cityscape one is as likely—or, rather, more likely—to encounter a Clytemnestra in every street as one is to run up against a hero of the Republic in any of
them.

Thus we are brought to see that the true nature of Rome's venerable *lieux
de mémoire*, its sites of national memory and hence of identity, is that every one
of them is, in spite of claims to the contrary, a site of Rome's openness to penetration, to being flooded by the Other—typified by the urine-soaked Altar of
Pudicitia, where we loiter with the satirist in the moonlight and then revisit in
the cold light of morning. From Rhea Silvia's violation by Mars to the Rape of the
Sabine women, from Romulus's killing of Remus to the Social Wars, from the
conquest of Greece to the concomitant conquest by Greek culture, Juvenal
shows us that to be Roman is to be penetrated by the Other in the guise of domination. This is the point of the conclusion to *Satire* 8, where all the magnificent Roman *gentes* are traced back to Romulus's always already contaminated
and disreputable asylum and its motley crowd of refugees. As the body in its
fluidity both annihilates stable personal identity and becomes the ground for
all such new constructions, so the monumental landscape of Rome repeats the
same gesture on the political and cultural level.

The speaker himself is a motley conglomeration of malicious and salacious
comments, a disembodied voice that emanates loudly and effusively from no
definable place. He traverses the city in a haphazard fashion, loitering at the
crossroads, peering into bedrooms and brothels, eavesdropping on the imperial cabinet, waiting for an overfed patron to drop dead in the bath. He floats far
beyond the boundaries of the capital, migrating through the territories of the
Empire and ranging across centuries of Roman history, with frequent forays
into the realm of archaic mythology. Even within one poem, he does not speak
from a single position, but produces a hash (*farrago*) in which the body, the
city, social status, family lineage, and above all, gender and ethnicity—all
the potential quilting points of Roman identity, the master signifiers that should
be the anchors of who and what we are—become porous and unstable. In the
face of such discontinuity, it is ultimately neither possible nor desirable to domesticate Juvenal's text—to manufacture a hidden coherence by positing separations of person and persona, controlling philosophical frames, or preexisting
rhetorical schemata, although all of these undoubtedly exist to a limited extent
within the text. If we instead refuse to be seduced by a factitious classicism, by
a too carefully manufactured closure and coherence, we are brought to a text
whose full transgressive nature remains very much on display.

The instability of the speaker is echoed in the satirical space par excellence,
the Colosseum, whose comforting exterior of solidity, of permanence and im-
mutability, is undermined by the liminal experience of the crowd watching

spectacles while simultaneously being part of an even bigger one themselves. In the Juvenalian text—the poet's own arena of satire—viewers and victims, spectacle and spectator, speaker and reader, are locked in a complex dynamic of (mis-)recognition and (non-)identification. Like its physical counterpart, the arena of satire puts its victims on display and punishes them, in ever more striking and colorful ways, as it strives to contain the chaos of daily existence through a rhetoric of violence. But in each case the circle of containment is constantly breached, so that stands and sand, victim and punisher, bleed into each other. Satire nourishes or, more accurately, force-feeds its readers with the innumerable and multiform products of Empire, whose consumption and excretion drive the Roman body through a process of continual transformation. Juvenal's *farrago* coalesces with the *miscellanea* of gladiators, in satire's swollen, bulging and bilious *sagina* of imperial excess.

And so, what does this seeker, this *proficiens* and putative *sapiens*, find? *Frontis nulla fides.* As we have observed throughout, what is so disturbing for the speaker as he moves around the city is the disjunction between appearance and reality. This is the very essence of Juvenalian satire, where signifiers that claim to anchor the Roman male citizen to bastions of *Romanitas* turn out to offer no such security at all. Yet, as Plato well knew, it was precisely the disjunction between appearance and reality that was the beginning of reflection and hence the beginning of philosophy. Juvenal destabilizes the very cognitive topography that constitutes *Romanitas* to such an extent that he demands that we think anew about the ways in which our individual and collective identities are predicated on that which they must exclude.[4]

But we have to be brought to zero point before any such reflection can even be imagined, let alone begun. Juvenal operates with a relentlessly violent discourse of cutting, wounding, and perforating in his arena of satire, an enclosure from which all possibilities of escape are walled off. "*Conciditur?*" "Is it to be cut up?" asks one of Domitian's council of the giant fish in *Satire* 4.130. This passive-voice question where the agent is unnamed, and in a poem where the dangerous presence of the Emperor is all-controlling but never described directly, encapsulates an essential element of Juvenalian satire, namely violent dismemberment. Wiesen observes at several points (with particular reference to *Satires* 2 and 6) how Juvenalian satire dehumanizes the body by dividing it into its (repellent) parts and how the self is detached from its external parts,

---

4. Gilloch 1996, speaking of Benjamin's essays on Berlin, notes that the city is seen as "composed of nothing more than the ceaselessly piled up ruins of the past" but that "this destructive moment of critical, physiognomical reading is balanced by a constructive impulse" (75).

paralleling a lack of organic unity.[5] But Juvenalian satire also engages in the reassembling of disparate elements, as we have seen, and this can be related to long-standing notions of creation through dismemberment, often thought to underpin traditions of sacrifice, which, according to Kyle, offer at least one way of understanding the spectacles of the Roman arena, with particular attention to human sacrifice as a means of enlisting divine aid to resolve a crisis like famine or plague.[6]

Such notions have remained an important part of the theatrical tradition. Here is how Bettina Knapp, in her study of Artaud, describes the performances of his "spiritual ancestor," Alfred Jarry, known as "the pantophile," who wrote about everything that came to his attention, thereby generating a "panoramic vision of the world and its problems":

> All of his works are different, yet they share a common stamp: a corrosive way of looking at life that is somewhat mitigated by a powerful sense of humor. Monstrous beings emerge alive and grotesque from his pages as witnessed by his character Ubu ("King Ubu"), vengeful, gluttonous, brutal, avaricious, and egotistical. Sentimentality is banished and rational coherence totally disregarded. Jarry willfully shocks his audience and readers alike with his provocative language, his use of strange word associations, harsh alliterations, neologisms, unusual rhythmic patterns, bizarre analogies, and seemingly unrelated series of events.[7]

While some of his material is more extreme than most of what we find in the *Satires*, it is a style of performance that is fundamentally a product of the same mode of Juvenalian discourse.[8] As Knapp continues:

> Jarry indicates his disdain for appearances by dislocating or dissociating what seems rational in the character or object at hand. Once the façade has been shattered he recomposes the remaining disparate elements into a new and startling picture to express the true nature of each thing as he sees it.

If violent dismemberment is one route to zero point as the necessary condition for new ways of speculation, another is through the continual and unequivocal rejection of viable alternatives, through the closing off of all avenues

---

5. Wiesen 1989, 716, 720, 727.
6. Kyle 1998, 34–40; Lincoln 1985 and 1986.
7. Kanpp 1969, 48.
8. Ibid. On Ubu, see LaBelle 1980, chap. 3.

of escape. Thus Wiesen argues that, for all their incoherence, the "language" of the *Satires* does in fact convey a coherent vision and that the "consistency" of Juvenal "can be located in his oft-repeated technique of suggesting an alternative to present evil and then showing that that alternative ideal is itself foolish or deceptive." He views this as essentially a "nihilistic" train of thought, and such nihilism we might view as another logical development of Juvenalian discourse.[9] It is striking to note how Juvenal's name crops up in nihilistic contexts. Bulent Diken comments in *Nihilism* that the writings of Michel Houellebecq, the contemporary French novelist and "personage," are "literary rather than literal or reliable statements of a world-view" with their ultimate origins in the likes of Juvenal and that all his characters "adopt the discourse of the abject hero, of the slave in carnival" (106). In these texts, he adds, "it is always 'December' and thus there is no longer any belief or desire to return to 'normalcy'; what is presented is rather a social world subject to permanent transgression and inversion of all values" (108). The titles of some of these novels evince a Juvenalian impulse: toward dismemberment (*The Elementary Particles*) and toward escape (*The Possibility of an Island*). Both present the reader with a riot of unbridled consumption in a desperate search for satisfaction, with an overload of explicit stereotyping and obscene description of sexual encounters. Both conclude with a transition to the neo- or nonhuman realm. In that sense, Houellebecq is perhaps the ultimate Juvenalian, for he invites us to the greatest spectacle of all, the death of the human race.[10]

At the end of chapter 4, we noted that the obsession with death and decay is perhaps the only outward signal of (potentially) reflexive activity in Juvenal's *Satires* and it too may be seen as directing us to zero point. Death is omnipresent because, in the face of the closing off of all other options, it is the only apparent way out.[11] Seneca argues that "some are driven to death because they are always brought back to the same things":

> Hoc quosdam egit ad mortem, quod proposita saepe mutando in eadem revolvebantur et non reliquerant novitati locum. Fastidio esse illis coepit vita et ipse mundus, et subit illud tabidarum deliciarum: "Quousque eadem?"

---

9. Wiesen 1989, 709; although this nihilistic thought does not deserve the term "philosophy," he argues that "the withholding of any alternative to the absurdity of an intolerable world justifies the application of the term nihilism to Juvenal" (709, 733).

10. Diken 2009, 90–111, "Houellebecq's Spiteful Carnival."

11. A notion embodied most strikingly in the validation of suicide as a viable alternative to continuation of a dishonorable, pointless, or painful existence, especially in the imperial era.

This has driven some men to death, because by frequently altering their purpose they were always brought back to the same things, and had left themselves no space for anything new. They began to be sick of life and of the world itself, and from those wasting indulgences arises the question: "How long are we to go on doing the same things?" (*De Tranq.* 2.15)

Death is also paradoxically the only way to get to "Rome proper"—the self-contained city that is neither flooded with Greeks nor awash with foreign filth. But this place which, in Miller's words is "dry, sere, . . . does not foam . . . does not pour," cannot be Rome. It is death. We remember that when Umbricius leaves to find such a world, he goes to Cumae, the entrance to the Underworld:

laudo tamen, vacuis quod sedem figere Cumis
destinet, atque unum civem donare Sibyllae. (3.2–3)

nevertheless I praise him for going to establish his home in empty Cumae
and to donate a single fellow-citizen to the Sibyl.

And in the closing lines, he pictures himself tramping across frozen fields:

. . . saturarum ego, ni pudet illas,
auditor gelidos veniam caligatus in agros.

I'll come to your frozen fields in my boots
to listen to your satires, if they're not ashamed. (321–22)

This frigid destination is a self-enclosed and static world that has no place for the wandering satirist—that has no place, in effect, for the city of Rome. To appropriate Northrop Frye's designation of satire as "the mythos of winter," we might say that the Juvenalian variety operates within a hiemal landscape.[12] The Saturnalian aspects of the form, which were exploited by Horace in, for example, *Satire* 2.7, have been reworked in a manner that precludes any revivifying aspect, making sterility, not fertility, the dominant thrust, as Miller has shown.[13] The Saturnalia is also a pivotal link with arena spectacles, for these were also concentrated at the end of the year, perhaps reflecting an original role in coming to terms with individual death and the cycle of the seasons, as Wiedemann suggests. We know that the annual *munus* was still held in

12. Cf. Winkler 1995 on wintry elements in Juv. 4; in *Sat.* 9.126–29, there is a definite suggestion of heading toward decline and winter in Naevolus's lament for his *velox flosculus* and the creeping up of old age.
13. Miller 1998.

December under Domitian (over ten days) and continued to be long after him.[14] In the imperial era, the calendar became increasingly extended, both for games and Saturnalia. Seneca, in *Epistle* 18.1, cites with approval someone's quip that "once December was a month, now it is a year."[15]

Finally, we have noted at various stages the productive interaction between Juvenalian satire and plague, both of which de-*vast*-ate and create a wasteland. Plague inevitably has an effect on the power to speak, and in such times the satirist's defense against contagion/cacophony is often more contagion/cacophony, as language itself is infected by and reproduces the effects of plague in the text. Like Poe's *Masque of the Red Death*, in Juvenalian satire the message is that the plague which heralds death (not only physical, but also moral, cultural, social, and philosophical) is always already inside: the satirist is none other than its hooded messenger. Juvenalian satire is that form of the genre that depicts a world and language at zero point, and the process of bringing the reader to comprehend the moral devastation requires a repetitive and incremental style—a plague of satire, in other words.

As we discussed at the outset, and as many of our passages have shown, Juvenalian satire works on the reader or listener through an accretion of arresting and provocative examples. There is often a suggestion of progression as each image is frequently more excessive or more expansive than the last. For Juvenal, of course, the exemplum is not merely the momentary illustration that threatens to exceed its logical frame, but is the very principle of his art. This is, to pick up on Varro's etymological musings in *De Lingua Latina* 5.141, his *munus*: by "heaping up" (*exaggere*) through his work (*opus*), he strives to "fortify" the city with walls (*moenia*).[16] But these exempla do not add up to an ordered, rational argument, even when the satirist attempts to adopt a more restrained and coherent approach, as he gives the impression of doing in books 4 and 5. He lays before us not premises in a syllogism, not pieces of evidence fully subordinated to an overarching single thesis, but moments of surplus and enjoyment whose sensuous materiality is exemplified by the rhetoric that deploys them. Their very excess instantiates that which they pretend to indict.

---

14. On the Saturnalia, see D'Arms 1984 and Barton 1993, 109–12; cf. on the arena, Wiedemann 1992, 12, 47; Kyle 1998, 57; Dunkle 2008, 183. The arena spectacles were, originally at least, interrupted for the Saturnalia on December 17. Ausonius says gladiatorial shows honored Saturn: *et gladiatores funebria proelia notum / decertasse foro: nunc sibi harena suos / vindicat extremo qui iam fine Decembris / falcigerum placant sanguine Caeligenam* (*Ecl.* 23.33–37).

15. Plass 1995. Eight out of every ten gladiatorial games were concentrated in December as part of the imperial cult (199n25); cf. Barton 1993 on the "extended" Saturnalia (147–75).

16. See the introduction, page 52 herein.

Consider this sequence of examples offered by the speaker as he discusses the debilitating effects of old age:

> . . . circumsilit agmine facto
> morborum omne genus, quorum si nomina quaeras,
> promptius expediam quot amaverit Oppia moechos,   220
> quot Themison aegros autumno occiderit uno,
> quot Basilus socios, quot circumscripserit Hirrus
> pupillos, quot larga viros exorbeat uno
> Maura die, quot discipulos inclinet Hamillus;
> percurram citius quot villas possideat nunc   225
> quo tondente gravis iuveni mihi barba sonabat.

> . . . all types of disease dance around him in military formation
> and if you ask their names, I could more readily state how many lovers
>   Oppia had,
> how many patients Themison killed off in a single autumn,
> how many partners Basilus swindled and how many wards Hirrus
>   cheated,
> how many men the accommodating Maura sucked off by in a single
>   day,
> how many pupils Hamillus bent over; I could more rapidly run
>   through
> how many villas are now owned by the man who, when he shaved me
> as a young man, made my thick beard grate. (10.218–26)

Here the exempla are obviously linked by the common theme of the impossibility of counting how many lovers, villas, and victims there are, but it is their insistently repetitive nature that foregrounds their resistance to a controlling singular sense. We do not, in fact, advance beyond the list as list, in spite of the individual names that feature in all cases except for the last, the nameless barber (with line 226 being a repetition of 1.25 in the satirist's opening catalog of exempla discussed in chapter 1).[17] In fact, what follows upon this set is another list, this time of the body parts that fail in the elderly invalid: shoulder, groin, hip, eyes, hands, and finally, worst of all, the mind (227–33).

In this arena, ultimately, all is middle, all is circularity. Exempla do not mean what they say, because what they say is by definition radically unstable: they are always both signifiers of excess and excessive in their signification. As

---

17. Although noting concerns about possible interpolation, Courtney 1980 is disinclined to delete 225–26 (*ad loc.*); Braund 2004 retains them without comment, and Ferguson 1979 notes the repetition of 1.25.

such, they simultaneously undermine one set of meanings, even as they produce and disseminate a further set, precisely through their material resistance to meaning, which produces their constitutive moment of nonmeaning. Images like these provoke our enjoyment (*jouissance*) and our own bodily awareness, along with a profound and disturbing sense of our own leakiness and penetrability—whether in regard to fluids and speech, or, as here, money, household, medicine, and marriage. The moment of laughter, the moment when we loiter—in the barber's shop, in the room where the doctor's patient is dying, in Oppia's bedroom, in the school where the teacher helps himself to one of his pupils, or wherever we witness some shady transaction—before turning away in disgust, is also the moment when we return to the Kristevan abject as the foundation of identity, to the unbounded world before the imposition of limits, from which limit itself must spring in the moment of division that constitutes the self.

The rhetoric of excess at play in these texts, then, itself represents the deconstruction of traditional Roman subjectivity—and indeed of any form of identity that situates itself in a closed and hierarchical relationship to a given social and topographical space. At the same time, this rhetoric represents the moment in which self-reflection is born from the recognition of alterity, from encountering the absurd as Camus would argue in a different, yet fundamentally related, context. Hence, from Juvenalian satire, as from the annoying bite of the excessive Socratic gadfly, the *possibility* (if nothing more) of a responsive and responsible existence first emerges. This multivalent aggression is, as Miller has argued, the ironic truth of deconstructive satire. Its multiplicity of meanings, its self-generating excess, is fused in a moment of transgression, a point of nonmeaning, and gives rise not to a new (or newly restored) stability, but to a moment of consciousness that transcends the immediacy of the given. Although here he speaks mainly of Persius, the point is equally valid, if not even more so, for Juvenal:

> Yet where I would argue that truth, for Horace, lies in the self-conscious manipulation and negotiation of these different traditions through the search for aesthetic mastery as a guarantor of personal *libertas* in a changing world, for Persius, it is precisely the mobilization of these same forces as **a violent gesture of transcendence that maintains the possibility of truth.** Persius seeks not to master the intertextual to form a higher synthesis that would give him a position of power from which he can negotiate the treacherous currents of aristocratic life under Nero, but rather **an iconoclastic deconstructive gesture** in which those very forces are

mobilized against themselves **to produce a dramatic and purgative encounter with a truth beyond.**[18]

It is not the role of the satirist, at least for one of the Juvenalian variety, to explain what that "truth" may be. He merely unleashes the plague of satire and takes us on a tour of its devastated landscape. And yet, it is amid the ideological, linguistic, and philosophical emptiness wrought by the astringency of Juvenalian satire that space is opened for new ways of speaking, as it was for Daniel Defoe (most obviously in his *Journal of the Plague Year* but also in his satirical pieces) or for Thomas Dekker in his pamphlet "The Wonderful Year" (1603). Such pamphlets began to circulate in London during the Great Plague when theaters closed and "Villanies were discovered by candlelight." Dekker's readers were treated amid the rampages of the disease to a Juvenalian urban satire of the new century, in which plague serves as a catalyst to reveal what is wrong with the England they inhabit and and where a palpable sense of abandonment prevails, with London becoming "a vast charnel house," "an infernal prison."[19]

And here I would like to end by offering some suggestions as to how we may recognize remnants or reworkings of Juvenalian discourse in the works of later satirists, especially those prone to similar images of physical abuse and bodily abjection, and those for whom crumbling signifying systems no longer hold weight. Charles Martindale says that "Juvenal has resisted successful naturalization in English," but if we look in novels and plays, especially twentieth- and twenty-first century, we find several examples.[20] The tribe of these "modern Juvenalians" is a large and variegated one and is growing all the time; they remain to be treated in a separate study, so a brief survey of three of the most salient examples will have to suffice here: Evelyn Waugh, Martin McDonagh, and Viktor Pelevin. Modern Juvenalism, like its ancient forebear, articulates the anxieties surrounding the decay of established structures of identity, threatened with displacement by alternatives not yet fully defined but nonetheless clearly disturbing, even threatening. Juvenalian satirists react with rhetorical violence to the irruption of the Other, the shock of the new, and the triumph of the unfamiliar. The distinctive feature these texts have in common is that they are written close to the tipping point in breakdown of an

18. Miller 2010, 254–55.

19. "What an unmatchable torment were it for a man to be barred up every night in a vast silent charnel-house; hung (to make it more hideous) with lamps dimly and slowly burning in hollow and glimmering corners?" "The Wonderful Year" vol. 8., p. 38 [Bodley]; in Wilson's 1925 edition of the pamphlets, p. 27; see further Byrne 2006, 224–25.

20. Martindale 2005.

ideological system or, in Foucauldian terms, in the period of extremity in the transition between one episteme and the next.[21]

As with Juvenal, who writes after a "plague" of Julio-Claudians, in *Generation Π* [also known as *Homo Zapiens* or *Babylon*], by the post–Soviet Russian satirist Viktor Pelevin, a wave of advertising companies, slogans, and practices from the capitalist West sweeps like a plague across Moscow and through the bodies of the protagonist and his friends, bringing in its wake a breakdown of existing boundaries and norms. Uncle Sam Sacker ("sucker"), the alternately human and mosquito protagonist of *The Life of Insects*, is a symbolic embodiment of this plague.

In *A Handful of Dust* by Evelyn Waugh, the canvas of an unremittingly corrupt society unfolds primarily through the activities of one decaying marriage—of Tony and Brenda Last—and the death of their only child, John Andrew, but also via descriptions of the London social whirl in which Brenda and her lover, Beaver, play out their affair. The novel is rounded off by an exotically placed scene of the most depressing hopelessness, as Tony Last, the heir to a declining English aristocratic line, survives a near-fatal tropical disease only to face the prospect of reading Dickens aloud for the rest of his days as the captive of a cunning lunatic, Mr. Todd, in the Amazon jungle.

The devastated landscape—moral, linguistic, ideological, and philosophical—of Juvenalian satire finds another corollary in the barren, body-strewn scenery of Martin McDonagh's dramas. In the remote rural locales of *The Cripple of Inishmaan* or *The Lieutenant of Inishmore*—the same locales bathed in the romanticism of *The Quiet Man* and other productions of the same ilk—we are brought face-to-face with the everyday cruelties and utter abandonment (on all levels, geographic, political, and moral) of their inhabitants. In McDonagh's vision, all the Grand Narratives of the Irish identity generated by nationalist discourse are systematically and brutally fractured. The binarisms of *Hibernitas*—and of the Self precariously balanced upon them—are "blown apart" not only metaphorically, through the plays' high-octane language and imagery, but literally through acts of physical violence on the stage.

Before we examine our modern Juvenalians in more detail, we should acknowledge their debt to Jonathan Swift, who is, perhaps, Juvenal's most direct inheritor, and the one who reinvented him for a new era. *A Tale of a Tub*, *Gulliver's Travels*, and *A Modest Proposal* all offer striking instances of Juvenalian discourse at work. For example, *A Tale of a Tub* begins with several preliminary or

---

21. See Oksala 2009, esp. 21–30, and introduction, p. 13n21 herein.

prefatory pieces—*An Apology for the [Tale of a Tub]*, *Dedication to Somers*, *The Bookseller [publisher] to the Reader*, *The Epistle Dedicatory to Prince Posterity*, *The Preface* and *Section I*, *The Introduction*, all of which call attention to its own inability to begin as well as to the undecidability of where precisely its authorship lies. Its margins or "Digressions" are central, while its center, or allegorical tale, is marginal. As Zimbardo puts it, "By satiric mockery and inverted, convoluted self mockery, *A Tale* deconstructs the institution and the 'official' language upon which it rests. . . . [It] is not an eighteenth-century, mimetic, binary satire, designed to correct our manners and morality; it is a deconstructive, Restoration, Juvenalian satire that points toward zero."[22] What is revealed is the emptiness that all institutions attempt to cover, the lack of *fides* in all *frontes*, including writing itself.

In much of Swift's work, we can see that interdependence of the topographic and the somatic, which is quintessentially Juvenalian. So, for example, he plays upon the alternating—and alienating—smallness or hugeness of Gulliver's body and its consuming and excretory functions as he travels from one realm to another:

> "This magnificent Palace would have been burnt down to the
> Ground, if, by a Presence of Mind, I had not suddenly thought of
> an Expedient. I had the Evening before drank plentifully of a most
> delicious wine, called Glimigrim (the Blefuscadians call it Flunec,
> but ours is esteemed the better Sort) which is very diuretick. By the
> luckiest Chance in the World, I had not discharged myself of any
> Part of it. The Heat I had contracted by coming very near the Flames,
> and by my labouring to quench them, made the Wine begin to
> operate by Urine; which I voided in such a Quantity, and applied so
> well to the proper Places, that in three Minutes the Fire was wholly
> extinguished; and the rest of that Noble Pile, which had cost so many
> Ages in erecting, preserved from Destruction." (Chap. 5)

Swift's facility with Juvenalian levels of obscenity and deployment of bodily functions for satirical purposes is well known, and it produces the same kind of nausea in the reader. As Ronald Paulson notes, tying the two together, this kind of satire "rubs the reader's nose in the dirt of which it is trying to make

---

22. Zimbardo 1998, 97; she adds that it is a text "that puts the process of semiotization on show to the end of invalidating it" and that Swift "attacks the house of *words*, fully acknowledging that it is the only house we have" (99).

him aware. It forces him by intimate sensuous contact to suffer such revulsion that he will see a truth he has overlooked. In Gulliver's fourth voyage there are the filthy Yahoos, and in Juvenal's famous portrait of Messalina . . . we smell and feel the sheets, see her feverish body and its gestures."[23] As the *Travels* unfold, we are brought to the unedifying, yet undeniable, realization that human beings are the most disgusting creatures of all, much as Juvenal makes us conclude that Rome is the most corrupt place of all. The thoroughgoing misanthropy of *Gulliver's Travels* has often been noted. Joseph Bentley, speaking of the end of the book, observes that we are made to conclude that "the only trouble with human society, in short, is that it consists of human beings."[24]

Elaboration of the "inhuman" nature of human beings is most effectively accomplished perhaps in *A Modest Proposal* of 1729, with its reasoned argument for the Irish cannibalizing their own children in order to solve the problem of starvation. One human being becomes another's commodity to be consumed, a reduction to bare matter. As Bentley says, the text implies that the "average, sincere, rational Englishman is at the same time a howling savage"—narrowing or erasing the same comfortable gap between civilized and uncivilized as Juvenal does in *Satire* 15.[25] Like the Juvenalian speaker, Swift takes upon himself the role of punisher and even of Nemesis; Frank Boyle argues that his attacks on Modernity are carried out "from the perspective of a theory of satire that identifies vengeful destructiveness as an ethical end of a satirical undertaking."[26] In the epitaph he composed for himself he addresses the traveler as follows: *Abi viator / Et imitare, si poteris, / Strenuum pro virili / Libertatis vindicatorem* (Depart, wayfarer, and imitate, if you can, a man who to his utmost was a strenuous avenger of liberty).[27]

It was not until the twentieth century that this challenge was seriously taken up. One of the best examples of this renewed Juvenalian strain can be seen in the novels of Evelyn Waugh. In his early novels in particular, Waugh presents us with the decline of the English aristocratic social order, and the *Imperium Britannicum* that sustained it, through a parade of corrupted, enfeebled, and isolated characters. These creations populate *Vile Bodies* ("All that succession and repetition of massed humanity. . . . Those vile bodies . . ."), whose

23. Paulson 1967, 15.

24. Bentley 1967, 398

25. Ibid., 397. Paulson 1967 notes that satire uses cannibalism as metaphor for aggression (9).

26. See Boyle 2000, xiii; chap. 1, "Nemesistic Satire"; and chap. 7, "Critical Nemesis." The difference between this piece and, say, Defoe's *The Perfect Englishman*, points out the divergence between the Juvenalian and Horatian methods of satire.

27. On *vindicator* as "avenger" rather than "defender" in late Latin, and Swift's use of the term for Nemesis, see Boyle 2000, 5.

action roams in a fragmentary and disjointed narrative across London (even into the Prime Minister's house) and beyond, ending in the numbing desolation of a European battlefield.[28] They also populate *Decline and Fall*, whose cast is described by one critic, Douglas Patey, as "guardians who don't guard, teachers who don't teach, servants who don't serve, and parents who don't parent . . . priests without faith, unjust judges, a physician who kills, mannish women and womanish men, childlike adults and children such as Peter Pastmaster (at the age of fifteen an expert mixer of cocktails) prematurely catapulted into adult knowingness."[29] With its mocking of various nationalities and races (Sebastian "Chokey" Cholmondley, a black American jazz musician, is a notorious example), its scorn for metropolitan aristocrats (Lord and Lady Circumference), and rural bumpkins (the Welsh) alike, its unreliable speakers, and its numerous topical references, literary allusions, and lively vocabulary including a great deal of contemporary argot, the text is, as David Bradshaw notes, an "all-enveloping satire" that is very much in the Juvenalian mode.[30]

Perhaps most Juvenalian of all in its bleak and unforgiving outlook, however, is *A Handful of Dust*, which focuses on the breakdown of the marriage of Tony and Brenda Last, set in motion by the arrival of the social-climbing parvenu John Beaver. The text charts the breakdown through an adulterous affair carried out behind Tony's back but in the full glare of London social circles. It depicts the atrophying in all areas of the traditional aristocratic order, typified by the impoverished—and, of course, aptly named—Lasts. For Brenda and others like her, the cafard of the irredeemably dull and boring countryside is unbearable, unlike the metropolis where all sorts of stimulating new delights are on offer. Just like Juvenal, Waugh has few, if any, illusions about the supposed virtues of country life. Religion, in the form of Christianity, is not entirely absent in this landscape, but even in the shires it is only vestigial, like Juvenal's Mars and his other fading deities. A representative example is the bland vicar, Mr. Tendril, preaching his "usual Christmas sermon . . . one to which his parishioners were greatly attached . . . through the pages of faded manuscript" (61).

Above all, there is the pervasive theme of parental failure with the sorry story of the raising of the son and heir, John Andrew. This culminates in the boy's untimely and unnecessary death—brought about by Tony's irresponsible

---

28. Waugh's texts contain numerous corpses and corpse-like individuals symbolizing decay (cf. *The Loved One*).

29. Patey 1998, 62.

30. Bradshaw 2001, xxi; he adds that this "allows the reader to succumb to its humour without feeling complicit in the opinions of its characters, its narrator, or its author" (xxi).

management of his horse-riding lessons—and by the exquisite report of Brenda's reaction to the news:

> "What is it, Jock? Tell me quickly, I'm scared. It's nothing awful, is it?"
> "I'm afraid it is. There's been a very serious accident."
> "John?"
> "Yes."
> "Dead?"
> He nodded.
> She sat down on a hard little Empire chair against the wall, perfectly still with her hands folded in her lap, like a small well-brought-up child introduced into a room full of grown-ups. She said, "Tell me what happened. Why do you know about it first?"
> "I've been down at Hetton since the weekend."
> "Hetton?"
> "Don't you remember? John was going hunting today."
> She frowned, not at once taking in what he was saying. "John . . . John Andrew . . . I . . . Oh thank God . . ." Then she burst into tears.

This is an epiphany entirely worthy of Juvenal and his scathing commentary on parental failure and malice in *Satire* 14, as, for one brief moment, Brenda thinks it is her lover, John Beaver, who is dead. Other Juvenalian features include nostalgic allusions to Arthurian figures as glances to a lost Golden Age; metropolitan characters like Lady Cockpurse who have little taste and no morals, merely an eye for fashion; frequent references to food (the quality of meals, cheapskates, debts) and to property and furniture (doing up rooms at Hetton Hall and Brenda's flat in London), and a continual sense of the right things being in the wrong places. Throughout the text, we see the deleterious effects of the irruption of lower-class vulgarity, proletarians, and other outsiders, paralleled by the widespread use of unfamiliar terminology and contemporary slang.

The novel ends, memorably, with Tony in an isolated Brazilian village where he is held captive by a mad recluse, Mr. Todd, who first saves him from death after he is infected with a tropical disease and then forces him to stay forever and read Dickens (whom Waugh generally despised) aloud to him. Tony's wildly centrifugal departure from England to Brazil has echoes of Umbricius's for Cumae. He goes "In Search of a City" (the title of chapter 5) that is not London or anything like it. In his quest to find this lost and mythical place, Tony finds the end point to his sterility and his own personal Underworld. Meanwhile back in England, Brenda, believing that Tony is dead, marries Jock, who is now a successful politician, and Hetton House passes to a cousin.

The Juvenalian impulse explains the Brazilian ending, which has not always found favor with critics,[31] with its sudden move into a radically Other space. For all the criticism it has received, this ending—every bit as disruptive to the demands of narrative as are Juvenal's sudden turns—offers a striking conjunction of centrifugal and centripetal movement, and confusion of here and there, as London and civilization are mapped onto the jungle and barbarism to produce a nightmarish space wherein the barbarity of the jungle is matched by the barbarity at the center of supposed civilization. It turns out that all sorts of savages dwell at home—"Right here where we live. Right here in St. Louis." Thus flight is not really possible, however dramatic and substantial the traversal of geographic space. The banalities of saccharine Dickensian moralizing, endlessly repeated, are emblematic of a moral and philosophical labyrinth, from which it is impossible to escape. This is also the realm of the unchanging, which is death.

In *Black Mischief*, we find the type of the Westernized or "enlightened" ruler, a modernizer named Seth, striving to bring the benefits of his English education to his uncivilized Africans.[32] Although the novel is set primarily in a mythical colony called Azania, which is obviously African, offering plenty of scope for the narrator's prejudices, it throws an unflattering spotlight at the same time on the behavior of the English colonizers—Basil Seal, Prudence, General Connolly, and their ilk. The empty-headed Lady Metroland and Sir Joseph Mannering (a "self-assured old booby," 105) are hardly impressive representatives of the imperial center, either. The journey out to Africa echoes Horace's to Brundisium, with the "surly steward," a "shrivelled, blotchy desert," "Djibouti; port holes closed to keep out the dust," and "four dancing girls huddled together in the corner like chimpanzees" (116–19). The rhetoric of exemplarity appears in the Umbrician list of complaints from "Mahmud el Khali bin Sai'ud, frail descendant of the oldest family in Matodi" and his kinsmen:

> There was no room for a gentleman in Matodi these days, they
> remarked. . . . You were jostled against the wall by black men or
> Indians, dirty fellows with foreskins, unbelievers, descendants of
> slaves; judges from up country, upstarts, jacks-in-office giving

---

31. It had to be changed for the U.S. edition and remains a point of dispute among critics and scholars of Waugh.

32. The resonances of the Egyptian god Seth include that he killed and dismembered Osiris (the civilizer); fought against Horus; and became associated with foreign oppressors and with chaos. In the Hebrew tradition, he is the third son of Adam, a replacement for Abel; and father of Noah (hence of humankind).

decisions against you in the courts. . . . Jews foreclosing on
mortgages . . . taxation . . . vulgar display . . . no respect of leisure,
hanging up wretched little flags everywhere, clearing up the streets,
moving derelict motor cars while their owners were not in a position
to defend them. (123–24)

The posters in the birth control campaign draw on some similar humor, asking, "Which home do you choose?"—the one with or without contraception?
This is the one without:

On one side a native hut of hideous squalor, overrun with children
of every age, suffering from every physical incapacity—crippled,
deformed, blind, spotted and insane; the father prematurely aged
with paternity squatted by an empty cook-pot; through the door
could be seen his wife, withered and bowed with child bearing
desperately hoeing at their inadequate crop. (192)

There is plenty of racist and misogynist commentary here. For example, General Connolly, elevated to Duke after quelling civil disturbances, introduces his
wife, the Duchess of Ukaka, as "Black Bitch" (139). Later, there is a scene where
she gets overexcited before a banquet:

As the time approached Black Bitch's excitement became almost
alarming and her questions on etiquette so searching that the
General was obliged to thump her soundly on the head and lock her
in a cupboard before she could be reduced to a condition sufficiently
subdued for diplomatic society. (177)

The English are much concerned with food (tinned or fresh asparagus?), and
there is a vile dinner party, anticipating a much worse kind of dinner soon to
come (219–26).

Cannibalism is a major motif in the novel, with the fate of Basil's fiancée,
Prudence, after her plane crash-lands in the jungle, kept in suspense until
Basil, who happens to be present of an evening at a wildly Dionysian feast,
sees one of the revelers wearing her distinctive red beret on his head:

Basil shook him violently. "Speak, you old fool. Where is the white
woman?"
The headman grunted and stirred; then a flicker of consciousness
revived in him. He raised his head. "The white woman? Why here,"
he patted his distended paunch. "You and I and the big chiefs—we
have just eaten her."
Then he fell forward into a sound sleep. (302)

After this cannibalistic climax, the ending of the novel is marked by another of Waugh's temporal and topographic shifts: we learn that Azania is now run as a Franco-British protectorate, while Basil is back in London, where his horrible experience cuts no ice with socialites like the flighty Sonia:

> "And went to a cannibal banquet. Darling, I just don't want to hear about it, d'you mind? I'm sure it's all very fine and grand but it doesn't make much sense to a stay-at-home like me."

Basil says that he has "no plans": "I think I've had enough of barbarism for a bit. I might stay in London or Berlin for a bit" (305). With hindsight, it is amusing to note that *Black Mischief* was published in 1932. Paulson contends that Basil's eating of his fiancée is "an evil act" whose purpose is to reveal the truth about Basil, that he is indeed a cannibal and not so different from the Irish landowners in Swift's *A Modest Proposal*. This erasure of boundaries is again reminiscent of Juvenal's *Satire* 15, with its initial narrative of an instance of Egyptian cannibalism leading to a broader reflection upon the rest of humanity, including the Romans who might try to take (false) comfort from the remote and faraway location of the barbarous Egyptians.[33]

The theatrical aspects of Juvenlian satire have been discussed at various points throughout this study, and one good (post)modern example is supplied by the plays of Martin McDonagh, which engage satirically with the foundational talismans of Irish identity, of *Hibernitas*, and especially its construction and expression through nationalism.[34] The nostalgia-bound clichés of Irishness are exposed to withering and merciless scrutiny, through extremes of language and action that have mesmerized, affronted, and attracted audiences and critics alike. McDonagh muddies all sorts of boundaries as he destabilizes traditional gender roles and familial relationships and subjects long-cherished ideals relating to politics, religion, and landscape to extreme stress.

In *The Lieutenant of Inishmore*, the plot turns around the murder of Wee Thomas, a cat belonging to an Irish National Liberation Army (INLA) lieutenant called Padraic, who was thereby punished for his "dissident" stance. As

---

33. Paulson 1967, 19. Cf. Houellebecq, *The Possibility of An Island*, on the remnants of humanity: "With lifted daggers, the males and females of the tribe threw themselves screaming onto the wounded man, who was trying to crawl out of sight; at the same time, the drums started to beat again. At first they cut off bits of flesh that they roasted in the embers, but as the frenzy increased they began to devour the body of the victim directly, to lap his blood, the smell of which seemed to intoxicate them. A few minutes later, the fat savage was reduced to bloody residue, scattered over a few meters in the prairie. The head lay at the side, intact except for the gouged eye" (320–21).

34. On gender, see Kurdi 2007; on morality and mythology, Rees 2007.

Taggart says, "One of McDonagh's main tricks is to off-set an adherence to the brutal abstractions of terrorism with a maudlin attachment to a particular pet" (170). It offers numerous instances of the Juvenalian mode: in scene 2, for example, the curtain rises on a nauseating act of torture:

> A desolate Northern Ireland warehouse or some such. James, a
> bare-chested, bloody and bruised man, hangs upside down from the
> ceiling, his feet bare and bloody. Padraic idles near him, wielding
> a cut-throat razor; his hands bloody. Around Padraic's chest are
> strapped empty holsters and there are two handguns on a table stage
> left. James is crying.[35]

As he wields the razor, Padraic gets a phone call from his father and gives vent to a confused tirade in which confused nationalist outpourings are blended with personal details, so that the dysfunction of the family is immediately seen to parallel the political chaos:

> I've been thinking of forming a splinter group. (*Pause.*) I know we're
> already a splinter group, but there's no law says you can't splinter
> from a splinter group. A splinter group is always the best kind of
> group to splinter from anyways. It shows you know your own mind,
> (*whispering*) but there's someone in the room, Dad, I can't be talking
> about splinter groups. (*To James, politely*) I'll be with you in a minute
> now, James. (*James shudders slightly.*) What was it you were ringing
> about anyways, Dad? (*Pause. Padraic's face suddenly becomes very
> serious, eyes filling with tears.*) Eh? What about Wee Thomas? (*Pause*)
> Poorly? How poorly, have you brought him to the doctor? (*Pause*)

One of McDonagh's purposes here is to portray the various forms of noise—of linguistic and bodily violence and ideological confusion—surrounding the numerous Irish Republican splinter groups, who have been left behind by history, symbolized by the remote setting in the Aran Islands, an archetypically "romantic" location in the far west of Ireland.[36] Gender-bending humor is deployed at various points, as between Padraic and Mairead, who argue over whether she can become a full-fledged member of the organization. He says no, in spite of her ability to "put a cow's eye out from sixty yards." The following snippets of dialogue from scene 6 are typical:

---

35. Taggart 2007, 29; see her further for a fascinating account of audience reactions. She comments that the performance became "a stress-test to near destruction of the fundamental contract between dramatist and audience . . . an intriguing metatheatrical moment" (163).

36. Chambers and Jordan 2007, intro., 6–9, on such locations in his plays.

P: I remember you chasing me begging me to bring you when I left to free the North, and that when you were ten.

M: Eleven. I'm sixteen now. If you get me meaning. Haven't I grown up since?

P: You have. Upwards if not outwards. From a distance I thought, "What's a boy doing sitting there with lipstick on?" then as I got closer I realized it was a lass, just with shocking hair.

. . .

M: Do you prefer Inishmore girls, so?

P: I don't.

M: You don't prefer boys?

P: I do not prefer boys! There's no boy-preferers involved in Irish terrorism, I'll tell you that! They stipulate when you join.

. . .

(Scene 9)

P: Would you let your hair be growing out a tadeen, Mairead? Just to about here, now? Like Evie off The House of Elliot?

M: Would you like me to?

P: Aye.

M: Well, me hair's staying the way it is and feck Evie off The House of Elliot.

P: Ah, Mairead . . .

M: Could Evie blind three fellas from sixty yards?

P: No. But she probably wouldn't want to.

M: Just be content with what you've fecking got, so.

The Juvenalian impulse motivates an arena-style orgy of violence accompanied by a deeply entrenched pessimism, with no hint of an antithesis.[37] The play culminates in a surreal scene of shocking murder and self-mutilation in the house, which mirrors the confused and destructive forces at play in the political sphere in the country at large. Here is the stage direction for scene 9, which opens in the aftermath:

Donny's house, night. As the scene begins the blood-soaked living room is strewn with the body parts of Brendan and Joey, which Donny and Davy, blood-soaked also, hack away at to sizeable chunks. Padraic's two guns are lying on the table. In the adjacent bare room, Padraic is sitting on Christy's corpse, stroking Wee

37. For a good summary, see Burke 2007, 157–58.

Thomas' headless, dirt-soiled body. Through Christy's mouth, with the pointed end sticking out of the back of his neck, has been shoved the cross with "Wee Thomas" on it. Padraic has a sad, faraway look about him.

As Patrick Burke observes, if the audience expects a happy ending in line with traditionally comforting narratives, with Padraic and Mairead getting married, they will be sorely disappointed: "When, however, Mairead learns that the substitute cat, shot earlier by Padraic, was in fact her cat, Sir Roger (named after Sir Roger Casement), she shoots Padraic! Finally, in a kind of *coup de theatre*, a cat bounds onto the set, which we are quickly made to understand is the very alive, sexually predatory, Wee Thomas; in other words, all of the bloodshed had been for the wrong cat!"[38] In the *Irish Times*, Fintan O'Toole observed that the critical question with regard to McDonagh is, "When does the laughing stop and the thinking begin?"[39] One critic complains that, aside from making the point that the "political aims" of violence "have long been subsumed by a desire to terrorize for its own sake," McDonagh's insistence on the "pig ignorance of every character . . . makes any serious debate impossible."[40] Another discerns that this *is* the point, locating it within the tradition of in-yer-face drama that forces the audience "to interrogate the causes of Padraic's dislocation and isolation in a world which no longer remembers the history it is fighting for."[41]

In almost all cases, says Burke, McDonagh's plays "resolutely resist the intervention of conventionally humanizing affectivity, love or softness, or of love familial or sexual: everything is hard-edged or brutal." This is a world in which "sons threaten to kill fathers who in turn dismember their sons' corpses, where girls deliberately try to shoot their brothers' eyes out, where sons trample on their own mothers, where daughters torture mothers, where lovers shoot lovers.[42] In *Lieutenant*, this is taken to unprecedented extremes, with graphic violence depicted on stage through special effects. In the words of one critic, the playwright "tears very large holes in the ideals of religion, family, community and nation dear to popular conceptions of Ireland."[43] In the case of this modern

---

38. Burke 2007, 158.

39. "Murderous Laughter," 24 June 1997.

40. Luckhurst 2007, 119.

41. Rees 2007, 137.

42. Burke 2007, 161. Paulson 1967: "The distinction between Horatian and Juvenalian satire is largely one of focus on fool or knave: Horace focuses on the fathers who are hated, while Juvenal focuses on the sons who kill their fathers" (21).

43. Eldred 2007: "He always presents this decay as a zombie vaudeville show—decomposing representatives of the Irish family, community, and religion stagger across the stage, dropping body parts along the way" (210).

Juvenalian, then, *Hibernitatis nulla fides*. The West of Ireland is the topographic antithesis, akin to Juvenal's "anti-Rome"—a pastoral, exilic, nostalgia-soaked idyll—but for McDonagh it is a place marked by disconnection, deception, rivalry, and petty vindictiveness. The violence in Irish society is every bit as virulent amid the bogs of the West as it is in the streets of Belfast or other towns.

Temporal and other displacements add to the effect, including the destabilizing of gender roles (visible in the presentation of "masculine" women like Mairead). McDonagh himself is displaced, the man from nowhere, while some even say he has a London metropolitan consciousness.[44] Food features prominently in his plays; for example, in *The Cripple of Inishmaan*, eggs are repeatedly broken over the head of the disabled boy, Cripple Billy, by his sister, Helen, while in *The Beauty Queen of Leenane*, the precise role of the omnipresent chip-pan on the stove (itself a pointed comment on nostalgia for "traditional" cooking) becomes apparent only at the end of the play, when the daughter, Maureen, slowly heats up the fat to boiling point—a scene of excruciating discomfort for the audience—and plunges her mother's hand into it.[45] As Eldred observes, "The Ireland of Leenane, Inishmore, and Inishmaan in these plays is a bankrupt state; family, religion, culture and law are powerless to provide coherence. Empty and bored people turn to violence because they have nothing else to do."[46] What better summation of the world of the Juvenalian "arena of satire"?

The painful passage from Republic to Empire that underpins much of the anxiety, anger, and pessimism in Juvenal's view of the world is recapitulated in some of the novels of the post–Soviet Russian novelist Viktor Pelevin. In *Generation Π*, he assimilates the effects of drugs, alcohol, and physical violence to the individual's traumatic yet exhilarating experience of the chaotic transition from USSR to the "new" Russia. To respond both to Russia and the wider post-modern world, which are, in his view, almost beyond satire, he deploys the fantastic as a suitable analogue, drawing upon a tradition already well established in the literary tradition, thanks to such archetypal works as Gogol's "The Nose" or "The Overcoat."[47] In *Generation Π*, all human life is determined by the simple transmission of three impulses through the media: the oral, anal, and "displacing wow-factors." The oral induces a powerful yearning for money to bring happiness; the anal induces the subject to excrete money to attain

44. See Chambers and Jordan 2007, intro., 10; Luckhurst 2007; and Fintan O'Toole, "Nowhere Man," in the *Irish Times*, 26 April 1997.

45. Kurdi 2007, 101–104; 110–13. The kitchen smells not of bacon and sausages but of urine.

46. Eldred 2007, in the context of similarities with the "nihilism and gore" of modern horror films (208).

47. Cf. Begley 2004 on satire and Martin Amis's *Money*.

happiness; and the displacing wow-factor causes the subject to dismiss as irrelevant to the pursuit of happiness anything that does not concern money. We see this through the eyes of the dissolute Babylen Tatarsky, who once dabbled in poetry but now retools Western advertisements so as to appeal to the Russian imagination. His masterpieces include the following for the GAP chain of shops in Moscow:

> RUSSIA WAS ALWAYS NOTORIOUS FOR THE GAP BETWEEN CULTURE
> AND CIVILIZATION. NOW THERE IS NO MORE CULTURE. NO MORE
> CIVILIZATION. THE ONLY THING THAT REMAINS IS THE GAP. THE WAY
> THEY SEE YOU. (63)

The new Russia in which Tatarsky operates is characterized by loss of meaning, detachment of signifieds, and false promises, all in the service of making money.[48] He and his boss Khanin drink to their future in the office:

> "OK, let's have a toast," said Khanin, and he hiccupped again. "Only, you know, one that's not only significant, but epoch-making as well. Komsomol member to party member, you follow?"
>
> Tatarsky held on to the table as he rose to his feet. He looked at the poster and thought for a second before raising his glass and speaking: "Comrades! Let us drown the Russian bourgeoisie in a flood of images!" (107)

As Mark Lipovetsky demonstrates, Pelevin's text fits into a group of works which not only deconstruct "cultural signifiers and entire cultural languages," but also strive to "re-mythologize cultural ruins and fragments" (107).[49]

Sometimes criticized for being repetitive, making the same basic points about Russia over and over again, Pelevin in fact deploys, very effectively, a Juvenalian rhetoric of exemplarity, relying upon colorful language and clever verbal effects. In *The Life of Insects*, which is set in a crumbling hotel at a resort on the Black Sea, we follow the adventures of a visiting American Sam Sacker ("sucker"), who, like his two Russian acquaintances, Arnold and Arthur, is both a human being and a mosquito. This opens up numerous possibilities for satirizing Russia and contemporary society in general, as, for example, in this exchange between Sam and a waitress—also a fly, a greenbottle—called Natasha, as they pass by a pit with the ruins of an unfinished building:[50]

---

48. Livers 2002: "If, in a metaphorical sense, reality has become secondary to the ideological signifiers that represent and ultimately supplant it, Pelevin's *The Life of Insects* recreates this scenario through the proliferation of signs that no longer point to anything in this world (assuming they ever did!)" (3).

49. Lipovetsky 2001, 41.

50. Livers 2002, 9–11, 22.

"Yes," said Sam, when the pit was behind them. "That's really fascinating. One odd thing I've noticed here. They say Moscow's the Third Rome, right?"

"Yes, that's right, the third. And the second Israel. Ivan the Terrible said that. I read it in the newspaper."

"Well, if we write Third Rome in Russian, *Trety Rim*, and then turn the word for 'Rome' backward, we get *Trety Mir*, Third World."

"In Yalta, about three hours from here by launch, there are cable cars. You get in on the ground level and go up to the top of the mountain. They were building a palace of culture or a Lenin museum or something up there, and then they abandoned it, and there's nothing left but the columns and part of the roof. It's huge, just standing there with nothing else near it, like a shrine or something. That's the Third Rome for you. Tell me, Sam, have you been to the first one?"

Sam nodded, and Natasha sighed. (59–60)

The Russian conceit of Moscow as the Third Rome may be a well-worn, and by now much ridiculed topos, but by visiting it yet again, for yet one more joke, Pelevin reminds us of the bankruptcy of all such illusions.

We have noted that a fundamental element of Juvenalian satire is that, unlike the Horatian variety, it imagines no future change—hence the precipice image early on, near the end of *Satire* 1. Things are basically set for posterity. The scene is one of devastation, like the arena at the end of the day or Donny's blood-soaked living room. "And tomorrow and tomorrow and tomorrow . . ." Yet we have argued that it is also amid this devastation that the possibility of genuine reflection takes root. In our modern examples, we can discern different manifestations of this trend. Thus Waugh in his later works, like *Brideshead Revisited* or *Helena*, recommends Roman Catholicism with gradually greater explicitness, and Pelevin shows increasing interest in Buddhism. In the case of Waugh, of course, what we have is really a return to the already existing, that quintessentially Juvenalian nostalgia for the long-lost Land of Virtue, tied to an overarching religious faith. In his early novels, which we can call Juvenalian, such authorial direction is almost entirely unarticulated. With Pelevin, there appears to be more emphasis on self-reflection and self-formation, albeit within a similarly long-established structure of "seeking" the way to truth via religious mysticism. Lipovetsky argues that in Pelevin's texts, the way to freedom lies in "isolation from all forms of power and all intentions to power, in other words, in blessed emptiness."[51] Keith Livers says that, "Conjuring up

---

51. Lipovetsky 2001, 46. Brintlinger 2004 speaks of "Emptiness—Pelevin style" (52–57).

fictional worlds that resemble nothing if not an ash-heap of cultural, ideological, indeed even physiological fragments and ruins, Pelevin's prose nevertheless holds forth the possibility of a partial restoration of reality" and finds this to be especially true for *The Life of Insects*.[52] He adds: "Rather than mirror the thoughts and ideas of others, the author suggests in starkly traditional fashion that we reflect (on) ourselves. This entails moving from a posture of un-reflecting darkness into the enlightened stance of self- knowing—and it is no accident that the passage from darkness to light represents the frame-metaphor of *The Life of Insects*."[53] With McDonagh, there appears to be very little suggestion of any route to improvement, other than realizing amid the devastation wrought by the old ways that they can lead nowhere; but, some critics have, as we saw, picked up on intimations of the need for self-interrogation, and such readings seem increasingly common.[54]

In conclusion, we can make the case that Juvenalian satire, in all its various manifestations, is not merely, or even primarily, corrective, but speculative and philosophical in the most fundamental sense. After pummeling us with examples and rhetorical flourishes of all kinds, and placing us in a devastated landscape of non-meaning, in a body-strewn arena with all escape routes closed off, it hurls the question ". . . and?" in our faces.

52. Livers 2002, 2.

53. Livers 2002, 3; cf. "In this regard, two such important literary and philosophical greats as Chekhov and Marcus Aurelius represent significant allies. For Pelevin both figures signal the path of self-analysis and reflexivity that offers the sole possibility for genuine (self-transformation in a fictional world that abounds in Ovid-like insect metamorphoses" (3).

54. It is interesting to note, additionally, that in the last two decades—more or less contemporaneously with his arrival on the scene—some major, even seismic, changes have occurred in Irish society and politics, changes of an order that would have been barely imaginable before.

Bibliography

Adams, James N. 1981. *"Culus, Clunes* and Their Synonyms in Latin." *Glotta* 59: 231–64.

———. 1982. *The Latin Sexual Vocabulary.* London: Johns Hopkins University Press.

Ahl, Frederick. 1976. *Lucan: An Introduction.* Ithaca, N.Y.: Cornell University Press.

Altheim, Franz. 1929. "Persona." *Archiv für Religionswissenschaft* 27: 35–52.

Althusser, Louis. 1984. "Ideology and the State." In *Essays on Ideology,* 1–60. London: Verso.

Anderson, Graham. 1976. *Lucian: Theme and Variation in the Second Sophistic.* Leiden: Brill.

Anderson, William S. 1964. "Anger in Juvenal and Seneca." *University of California Publications in Classical Philology* 19: 127–96.

———. 1982. *Essays on Roman Satire.* Princeton, N.J.: Princeton University Press.

Arena, Valentina. 2012. *Libertas and the Practice of Politics in the Late Roman Republic.* Cambridge: Cambridge University Press, 2012.

Armstrong, David. 1986. "Stylistics and the Date of Calpurnius Siculus." *Philologus* 130: 113–36.

Ash, Rhiannon. 1999. *Ordering Anarchy: Armies and Leaders in Tacitus' Histories.* London: Duckworth.

———. 2007. *Tacitus Histories Book II.* Cambridge: Cambridge University Press.

Auguet, Roland. 1972. *Cruelty and Civilization: The Roman Games* (Eng. trans., London: George Allen and Unwin; original French ed., Paris: Flammarion, 1970; reprint ed., London: Routledge, 1994).

Aurigemma, Salvatore. 1926. *I Mosaici di Zliten.* Africa Italiana II, Collezione de Monografie a Cura del Ministero delle Colonie. Rome: Società editrice d'arte illustrata.

Balibar, Etienne. 1978. "From Bachelard to Althusser: The Concept of 'Epistemologi-
    cal Break.'" *Economy and Society* 7: 207–37.

Banville, John. 2005. *The Sea*. London: Picador.

Barchiesi, Alessandro, and Andrea Cucchiarelli. 2005. "Satire and the Poet: The Body
    as Self-Referential Symbol." In *Cambridge Companion to Roman Satire*, ed. Kirk
    Freudenburg, 207–23. Cambridge: Cambridge University Press.

Barta, Peter I. 1996. *Bely, Joyce and Döblin: Peripatetics in the City Novel*. Gainesville:
    University Press of Florida.

Barthes, Roland. 1977. "Rhetoric of the Image." In *Image, Music, Text*. Trans. Stephen
    Heath, 32–51. New York: Hill and Wang.

Barton, Carlin A. 1993. *Sorrows of the Ancient Romans: The Gladiator and the Monster*.
    Princeton, N.J.: Princeton University Press.

———. 2001. *Roman Honor: The Fire in the Bones*. Berkeley: University of California
    Press.

———. 2002. "Being in the Eyes: Shame and Sight in Ancient Rome." In *The Roman
    Gaze*, ed. David Fredrick, 216–35.

Bartsch, Shadi. 1994. *Actors in the Audience: Theatricality and Doublespeak from Nero
    to Hadrian*. Cambridge, Mass.: Harvard University Press.

———. 2006. *The Mirror of the Self: Sexuality, Self-Knowledge, and the Gaze in the
    Early Roman Empire*. Chicago: University of Chicago Press.

———. 2012. "Persius, Juvenal and Stoicism." In *A Companion to Persius and Juvenal*,
    ed. Susanna Morton Braund and Josiah Osgood, 217–38.

Basore, John William. 1928–35. Trans. *Seneca: Moral Essays*. 3 vols. Cambridge, Mass.:
    Harvard University Press.

Bataille, Georges. 1928. *Histoire de l'oeil*. Publ. privately [=1979. *Story of the Eye*.
    Trans. Hans Joachim Neugroschal. London: Marion Boyars].

———. 1957. *Le bleu du ciel*. Paris: Pauvert [= 2006. *Blue of Noon*. Trans. Harry
    Mathews. London: Marion Boyars].

Beard. Mary. 1994. "The Roman and the Foreign: The Cult of the 'Great Mother' in
    Imperial Rome." In *Shamanism, History and the State*, ed. Nicholas Thomas and
    Caroline Humphrey, 164–82. Ann Arbor: University of Michigan Press.

Begley, Jon. 2004. "Satirizing the Carnival of Postmodern Capitalism: The Transat-
    lantic and Dialogic Structure of Martin Amis's *Money*." *Contemporary Literature*
    45: 79–105

Bellandi, Filippo. 2009. "Naevolus cliens." In *Oxford Readings in Classical Studies*, ed.
    Maria Plaza, 469–505.

Benjamin, Walter. 1973. *Illuminations*. Trans. Harry Zohn. London: Fontana.

———. 1974. *Gesammelte Schriften*, vols. 1–7. Ed. Rolf Tiedemann and Hermann
    Schweppenhäuser. Frankfurt: Suhrkamp.

———. 1978. *Charles Baudelaire: A Lyric Poet in the Era of High Capitalism*. London:
    Verso.

———. 1985. *One-Way Street and Other Writings*. London: Verso.

Bentley, Joseph. 1967. "Satire and the Rhetoric of Sadism." *Centennial Review* 11:
    387–404.

Bernstein, Michael André. 1983. "When the Carnival Turns Bitter: Preliminary Reflections upon the Abject Hero." *Critical Inquiry* 10: 283–305.

———. 1987. "'*O Totiens Servus*': Saturnalia and Servitude in Augustan Rome." *Critical Inquiry* 13: 450–74.

———. 1991. "'These Children That Come at You with Knives': 'Ressentiment,' Mass Culture, and the Saturnalia." *Critical Inquiry* 17: 358–85.

———. 1992. *Bitter Carnival: Ressentiment and the Abject Hero*. Princeton, N.J.: Princeton University Press.

Bertman, S. S. 1968. "Fire Symbolism in Juvenal's First Satire." *Classical Journal* 63: 265–66.

Bomgardner, David. 2000. *The Story of the Roman Amphitheatre*. London: Routledge.

Borges, Jorge Luis. 1964. *Labyrinths. Selected Stories and Other Writings*. New York: New Directions.

Botting, Fred, and Scott Wilson, eds. 1997. *The Bataille Reader*. Oxford: Blackwell.

Bowditch, Phebe Lowell. 2001. *Horace and the Gift Economy of Patronage*. Berkeley: University of California Press.

Bower, Edward W. 1958. "Notes on Juvenal and Statius" *Classical Review* 8: 9–11.

Boyle, Anthony J., and Roger D. Woodard, ed. and trans. 2000. *Ovid: Fasti*. London: Penguin.

Boyle, Frank. 2000. *Swift as Nemesis: Modernity and Its Satirist*. Stanford, Calif.: Stanford University Press.

Bozia, Eleni. 2015. *Lucian and his Roman Voices: Cultural Exchanges and Conflicts in the Late Roman Empire*. London: Routledge.

Bradley, Keith R. 1981. "The Significance of the *Spectacula* in Suetonius' *Caesares*." *Rivista storica dell'Antichità* 11: 129–37.

Bradshaw, David. 2001. Introduction to Waugh's *Decline and Fall*, ix–xxxiv.

Bramble, John C. 1974. *Persius and the Programmatic Satire*. Cambridge: Cambridge University Press.

Braund, Susanna Morton. 1988. *Beyond Anger: A Study of Juvenal's Third Book of Satires*. Cambridge: Cambridge University Press.

———, ed. 1989. *Satire and Society in Ancient Rome*. (Exeter Studies in History series.) Liverpool: Liverpool University Press.

———. 1990. "Umbricus and the Frogs." *Classical Quarterly* 40: 502–506.

———. 1992. "Juvenal—Misogynist or Misogamist?" *Journal of Roman Studies* 82: 71–76.

———. 1993. "Paradigms of Power: Roman Emperors in Roman Satire" In *Humour and History*, ed. K. Cameron. Oxford: Intellect Books. 59–69.

———. 1995. "A Woman's Voice?—Laronia's Role in Juvenal Satire 2." In *Women in Antiquity*, ed. R. Hawley and B. Levick, 207–19. London: Routledge.

———. 1996a. *Juvenal Satires Book I*. Cambridge: Cambridge University Press.

———. 1996b. "The Solitary Feast: A Contradiction in Terms?" *Bulletin of the Institute of Classical Studies* 41: 37–52.

———. 1996c. *The Roman Satirists and Their Masks*. London: Bristol Classical Press.

———. 2004. *Juvenal and Persius*. Cambridge, Mass.: Harvard University Press.

———. 1983. "Juvenal's Traducement Again (2.153–163)." *Liverpool Classical Monthly* 8: 50–51.

Braund, Susanna Morton, and J. D. Cloud. 1981. "Juvenal: A Diptych" *Liverpool Classical Monthly* 6: 195–208.

Braund, Susanna Morton, and Barbara Gold, eds. 1998. *Vile Bodies: Roman Satire and Corporeal Discourse.* Special issue of *Arethusa* 31.3. Baltimore: Johns Hopkins University Press.

Braund, Susanna Morton, and Josiah Osgood. 2012. *A Companion to Persius and Juvenal.* Oxford: Blackwell 2012.

Breguet, Esther. 1956. "Horace, un homme libre." In *Hommages à M. Niedermann,* ed. Marcel Renard and Georges Redard, 82–89. Brussels: Collection Latomus.

Brink, Charles Oscar. 1963. *Horace on Poetry,* Vol. I: *Prolegomena to the Literary Epistles.* Cambridge: Cambridge University Press.

———. 1971. *Horace on Poetry,* Vol. II: *The Ars Poetica.* Cambridge: Cambridge University Press.

———. 1982. *Horace on Poetry,* Vol. III: *Epistles Book II: The Letters to Augustus and Florus.* Cambridge: Cambridge University Press.

Brintlinger, Angela. 2004. "The Hero in the Madhouse: The Post-Soviet Novel Confronts the Soviet Past." *Slavic Review* 63: 43–65.

Briscoe, John. 2008. *A Commentary on Livy Books 38–40.* Oxford: Oxford University Press.

Brown, P. M., ed. 1995. *Horace Satires I.* Rev. ed. Warminster: Aris and Phillips.

Brown, R. D. 1983. "The Litter: A Satirical Symbol in Juvenal and Others." In *Studies in Latin Literature and Roman History,* ed. C. Deroux, 266–82. Brussels: Collection Latomus.

Bulgakov, Miklail. 1996. *The Master and Margarita.* Trans. Diana Burgin and Katherine T. O'Connor. New York: Vintage.

———. 2010. *The Fatal Eggs.* Trans. Michael Karpelson. Thornhill, Ont.: Translit.

Burgin, Victor. 1998. "The City in Pieces." In *The Actuality of Walter Benjamin,* ed. Larua Marcus and Lynda Nead, 55–71. London: Lawrence and Wishart.

Burke, Patrick. 2007. " 'Like the Cat-astrophe of the Old Comedy': The Animal in The Lieutenant of Inishmore." In *The Theatre of Martin McDonagh,* ed. Lilian Chambers and Eamonn Jordan, 155–61.

Byrne, Joseph Patrick. 2006. *Daily Life in the Black Death.* Westport, Conn.: Greenwood.

Cagniart, Pierre. 2000. "The Philosopher and the Gladiator." *Classical World* 93: 607–18.

Callebat, Louis. 2012. *Priapées.* Paris: Budé.

Campana, Pierpaolo. 2004. *D. Iunii Iuvenalis Satura X.* Florence: F. Le Monnier.

Camus, Albert. 1971. *The Plague.* Trans. Stuart Gilbert. New York: Knopf.

Cannadine, David, and Simon Price, eds. 1987. *Rituals of Royalty: Power and Ceremonial in Traditional Societies.* Cambridge: Cambridge University Press.

Cariou, Gerald. 2009. *La Naumachie.* Paris: Presses de l'université Paris–Sorbonne.

Catto, Bonnie. 1988. "The Labyrinth on the Cumaean Gates and Aeneas' Escape from Troy." *Vergilius* 34: 71–76.

Cèbe, Jean Pierre. 1966. *La caricature et la parodie dans le monde romain antique des origines à Juvenal.* Paris: de Boccard.

Céline, Louis-Ferdinand. 1997. *Rigadoon.* Trans. Ralph Manheim. Normal, Ill.: Dalkey.

Certeau, Michel de. 1984. *The Practice of Everyday Life.* Berkeley: University of California Press.

Cerutti Stephen M., and Lawrence Richardson. 1989. "The *Retiarius Tunicatus* of Suetonius, Juvenal, and Petronius." *American Journal of Philology* 110: 584–94.

Chahoud, Anna. 2004. "The Roman Satirist Speaks Greek." *Classics Ireland* 11: 1–46.

Chambers, Lilian, and Eamon Jordan. 2007. *The Theatre of Martin McDonagh: A World of Savage Stories.* Dublin: Carysfort.

Chambers, Ross. 1999. *Loiterature.* Lincoln: University of Nebraska Press.

Champlin, Edward. 1980. *Fronto and Antonine Rome.* Cambridge, Mass.: Harvard University Press.

Clarke, Martin L. 1973. "Juvenal 7, 242–3." *Classical Review* 23: 12.

Classen, Carl J. 1998. "Satire—The Elusive Genre." *Symbolae Osloenses* 63: 95–121.

Clausen, Wendell V. 1992. *A. Persi Flacci et D. Iuni Iuvenalis Saturae.* Rev. ed. Oxford: Oxford University Press.

Cloud, John D. 1989. "The Client-Patron Relationship: Emblem and Reality in Juvenal's First Book." In *Patronage in Ancient Society,* ed. A. Wallace-Hadrill, 205–18. London: Routledge.

Coarelli, Filippo. 1985. *Roma.* Rome: Laterza.

Coffey, Michael. 1989. *Roman Satire.* 2nd ed. London: Bristol Classical Press.

Coffta, David J. 2002. *The Influence of Callimachean Aesthetics on the Satires and Odes of Horace.* Lewiston: Mellen.

Coleman, Kathleen M. 1988. *Statius Silvae IV.* Oxford: Oxford University Press.

———. 1990. "Fatal Charades: Roman Executions Staged as Mythological Enactments." *Journal of Roman Studies* 80: 48–74.

———. 1993. "Launching into History: Aquatic Displays in the Early Empire." *Journal of Roman Studies* 83: 48–74.

———. 1996. "Ptolemy Philadelphus and the Roman Amphitheater." In *Roman Theater and Society,* ed. William J. Slater, 49–68.

———. 2006. *M. Valerii Martialis: Liber Spectaculorum.* Oxford: Oxford University Press.

Colin, Jean. 1952–53. "Juvénal, les baladins et les rétiares d'après le manuscrit d'Oxford." *Atti della Accademia delle Scienze di Torino* 87: 315–86.

Collart, Jean. 1954. *Varron, De lingua Latina, livre v.* Paris: Belles Lettres.

Colton, Robert. 1991. *Juvenal's Use of Martial's Epigrams: A Study of Literary Influence.* Amsterdam: Hakkert.

Connor, Peter J. 1987. *Horace's Lyric Poetry: The Force of Humour.* Berwick, Victoria: Aureal.

Connors, Catherine. 2005. "Epic Allusion in Roman Satire." In *The Cambridge Companion to Roman Satire,* ed. Kirk Freudenburg, 123–45.

Corbeill, Anthony. 2002. "Political Movement: Walking and Ideology in Republican Rome." In *The Roman Gaze*, ed. David Fredrick, 182–215.

———. 2004. *Nature Embodied. Gesture in Ancient Rome*. Princeton, N.J.: Princeton University Press.

———. 2005. "The Topography of Fides in Propertius 1.16." In *Defining Genre and Gender in Latin Literature*, ed. William Batstone and Garth Tissol, 79–95. New York: Lang.

Corbett, Phillip. 1986. *The Scurra*. Edinburgh: Scottish Academic Press.

Courtney, Edward. 1980. *Commentary on the Satires of Juvenal*. London: Athlone Press.

Coverley, Merlin. 2010. *Psychogeography*. 2nd rev. ed. Harpenden, Herts.: Pocket Essentials.

Croon, J. H. 1955. "The Mask of the Underworld Daemon. Some Remarks on the Perseus-Gorgon Story." *Journal of Hellenistic Studies* 75: 9–16.

Cucchiarelli, Andrea. 2002. "*Iter Satiricum*. Le voyage à Brindes et la Satire d'Horace." *Latomus* 61: 842–51.

———. 2005. "Speaking from Silence: The Stoic Paradoxes of Persius." In *The Cambridge Companion to Roman Satire*, ed. Kirk Freudenburg, 62–80.

Damon, Cynthia, ed. 2003. *Tacitus Histories Book I*. Cambridge: Cambridge University Press.

D'Arms, John H. 1984. "Control, Companionship, and Clientela: Some Social Functions of the Roman Communal Meal." *Echos du Monde Classique* 28: 327–48.

———. 1990. "The Roman *Convivium* and the Idea of Equality." In *Sympotica*, ed. Oswyn Murray, 308–20. New York: Oxford University Press.

Debord, Guy. 1994. *The Society of the Spectacle*. Trans. Donald Nicholson-Smith. New York: Zone.

Defoe, Daniel. 2010. *A Journal of the Plague Year*, ed. Louis Landa and David Roberts. Oxford World's Classics. Oxford: Oxford University Press.

Degrassi, Atillius, ed. 1937. *Inscriptiones Italiae. 13.3: Elogia*. Rome: Istituto Poligrafico dello Stato.

Dekker, Thomas. 1925. *The Plague Pamphlets of Thomas Dekker*, ed. Frank Percy Wilson. Oxford: Clarendon.

Dench, Emma. 2005. *Romulus' Asylum: Roman Identities from the Age of Alexander to the Age of Hadrian*. New York: Oxford University Press.

Deroux, Carl. 1983. "Domitian, the Kingfish and the Prodigies" In *Studies in Latin Literature and Roman History*, ed. Carl Deroux, 283–98. Brussels: Collection Latomus.

Dessen, Cynthia W. 1968. "The Sexual and Financial Mean in Horace's *Serm.*, 1.2." *American Journal of Philology* 89: 200–208.

Dewar, Michael. 2014. *Leisured Resistance: Villas, Literature and Politics in the Roman World*. London: Bloomsbury.

Dewing, Henry Bronson. 1935. *Procopius: Secret History*. Loeb Classical Library. Cambridge, Mass.: Harvard University Press.

Dick, B. F. 1969. "Seneca and Juvenal 10." *Harvard Studies in Classical Philology* 73: 237–46.

Diken, Bulent. 2009. *Nihilism*. New York: Routledge.

Dudley, Donald. 1967. *Urbs Roma. A Source Book of Classical Texts on the City of Rome and Its Monuments*. Aberdeen: Phaidon.

Dunbadin, Katherine M. D. 1978. *The Mosaics of Roman North Africa*. Oxford: Clarendon.

Dunkle, Roger. 2008. *Gladiators. Violence and Spectacle in Ancient Rome*. London: Person.

Dunn, Allen. 1995. "The Mechanics of Transport: Sublimity and the Imagery of Abjection in Rochester, Swift, and Burke." In *Cutting Edges*, ed. James E. Gill, 43–58.

Dupont, Florence. 1997. "*Recitatio* and the Reorganization of the Space of Public Discourse." In *The Roman Cultural Revolution*. ed. Thomas Habinek and Alessandro Schiesaro, 44–59. Cambridge: Cambridge University Press.

Duret, Luc, and Jean-Pierre Néraudau. 2001. *Urbanisme et métamorphoses de la Rome antique*. 2nd ed. Paris: Belles Lettres.

Eagleton, Terry. 1996. *The Illusions of Postmodernism*. Oxford: Blackwell.

Edmondson, Jonathon C. 1996. "Dynamic Arenas: Gladiatorial Presentations in the City of Rome and the Construction of Roman Society during the Early Empire." In *Roman Theater and Society*, ed. William J. Slater, 69–112. Ann Arbor: University of Michigan Press.

Edmunds, Lowell. 1972. "Juvenal's Thirteenth Satire." *Rheinisches Museum für Philologie* 115: 59–73.

Edwards, Catharine. 1993. *The Politics of Immorality in Ancient Rome*. Cambridge: Cambridge University Press.

———. 1996. *Writing Rome: Textual Approaches to the City*. Cambridge: Cambridge University Press.

Edwards, Catharine, and Greg Woolf. 2003. *Rome the Cosmopolis*. Cambridge: Cambridge University Press.

Eldred, Laura. 2007. "Martin McDonagh's Blend of Tradition and Horrific Innovation." In *The Theatre of Martin McDonagh*, ed. Lilian Chambers and Eamonn Jordan, 198–213.

Elliott, John. 1995. "The Etruscan Wolfman in Myth and Ritual." *Etruscan Studies* 2: 17–33

Elliott, Robert C. 1960. *The Power of Satire: Magic, Ritual, Art*. Princeton, N.J.: Princeton University Press.

Estevez, Victor. 1996. "Umbricius and Aeneas: a Reading of Juvenal III." *Maia* 48: 281–300

Evans, Harry B. 1978. "Horace *Satires* 2.7: Saturnalia and Satire." *Classical Journal* 73: 307–12.

Fagan, Garrett. 2011. *The Lure of the Arena: Social Psychology and the Crowd at the Roman Games*. Cambridge: Cambridge University Press.

Fantham, Elaine, ed. 1998. *Ovid: Fasti Book IV*. Cambridge: Cambridge University Press.

Farmer, Matthew. 2013. "Rivers and Rivalry in Petronius, Horace, Callimachus, and Aristophanes." *American Journal of Philology* 134: 481–50.

Farrell, Joseph. 2007. "Horace's Body, Horace's Books." In *Classical Construction*, ed. S. J. Heyworth et al., 174–93. Oxford: Oxford University Press.

Ferguson, John. 1979. *Juvenal: The Satires*. New York: St. Martin's.

Fiske, George C. 1920. *Lucilius and Horace: A Study in the Classical Theory of Imitation*. Madison: University of Wisconsin Press.

Fitzgerald, William. 1984. "Aeneas, Daedalus and the Labyrinth." *Arethusa* 17: 51–65.

———. 1988. "Power and Impotence in Horace's *Epodes*." *Ramus* 17: 176–91.

Fitzpatrick, R. S. 1979. "Juvenal's Patchwork Satires: 4 and 7." *Yale Classical Studies* 23: 229–41.

Fögen, Thorsten. 2009. "*Sermo corporis:* Ancient Reflections on *gestus, vultus* and *vox.*" In *Bodies and Boundaries in Graeco-Roman Antiquity*, ed. Thorsten Fögen and Mireille M. Lee, 15–43.

Fögen, Thorsten, and Mireille M. Lee, ed. 2009. *Bodies and Boundaries in Graeco-Roman Antiquity*. Berlin: De Gruyter.

Foucault, Michel. 1963. *The Birth of the Clinic: An Archaeology of Medical Perception*. Trans. Alan Mark Sheridan Smith. New York: Vintage.

———. 1977. *Discipline and Punish: The Birth of the Prison*. Trans. Alan Mark Sheridan Smith. New York: Pantheon.

———. 1978. *The History of Sexuality*. Vol. 1. An Introduction. Trans. Robert Hurley. New York: Pantheon.

———. 1980. *Power/Knowledge: Selected Interviews and Other Writings, 1972–1977*. New York: Pantheon.

Fredrick, David, ed. 2002. *The Roman Gaze: Vision, Power and the Body*. Baltimore: Johns Hopkins University Press.

Fredericks, Sigmund C. 1971. "Calvinus in Juvenal's Thirteenth Satire." *Arethusa* 4: 219–31.

———. 1973. "The Function of the Prologue (1–20) in the Organization of Juvenal's Third Satire." *Phoenix* 27: 62–67.

———. 1975. "Juvenal: A Return to Invective." In *Roman Satirists and Their Satire*, ed. E. S. Ramage et al., 136–79. Park Ridge, N.J.: Noyes Press.

Freudenburg, Kirk. 1993. *The Walking Muse. Horace on the Theory of Satire*. Princeton, N.J.: Princeton University Press.

———. 2001. *Satires of Rome. Threatening Poses from Lucilius to Juvenal*. Cambridge: Cambridge University Press.

———, ed. 2005. *The Cambridge Companion to Roman Satire*. Cambridge: Cambridge University Press.

Fruelund Jensen, Børge. 1986. "Martyred and Beleaguered Virtue: Juvenal's Portrait of Umbricius." *Classica et Mediaevalia* 37: 185–97.

Frye, Northrop. 1957. *Anatomy of Criticism: Four Essays*. Princeton: Princeton University Press.

Futrell, Alison. 1997. *Blood in the Arena: The Spectacle of Roman Power*. Austin: University of Texas Press.

———. 2006. *The Roman Games.* Oxford: Blackwell.

Galán Vioque, Guillermo. 2002. *Martial, Book VII, A Commentary.* Leiden: Brill.

Gallia, Andrew B. 2012. *Remembering the Roman Republic: Culture, Politics and History under the Principate.* Cambridge: Cambridge University Press.

Gantz, Timothy. 1993. *Early Greek Myth.* Baltimore: Johns Hopkins University Press.

Garland, Robert. 1995. *The Eye of the Beholder: Deformity and Disability in the Graeco-Roman World.* London: Bristol Classical Press.

Gelley, Alexander. 1995. *Unruly Examples: On the Rhetoric of Exemplarity.* Stanford, Calif.: Stanford University Press.

George, David B. 1988. "Lucilius 676M, Metellus, and his *munus.*" *Classical Journal* 83: 298–300.

Georgiadou, Aristoula, and David H. J. Larmour, 1998. *Lucian's Science Fiction Novel "True Histories": Interpretation and Commentary.* Leiden: Brill.

Gibson, Bruce J. 2006, ed. *Statius, Silvae 5.* Oxford: Oxford University Press.

Gill, James E., ed. 1995a. *Cutting Edges: Postmodern Critical Essays on Eighteenth-Century Satire.* Knoxville: University of Tennessee Press.

———. 1995b. "*Pharmakon, Pharmakos,* and Aporetic Structure in Gulliver's 'Voyage to the Houyhnhnms.'" In *Cutting Edges,* ed. James Gill, 181–205.

Gilloch, Graeme. 1996. *Myth and Metropolis. Walter Benjamin and the City.* Oxford: Polity.

———. 2002. *Walter Benjamin. Critical Constellations.* Oxford: Polity.

Glazewski, Johanna. 1971. "*Plenis vitae conviva:* A Lucretian Concept in Horace's *Satires.*" *Classical Bulletin* 47: 85–88.

Gogol, Nikolai. 2004. *Dead Souls.* Trans. Robert A. Maguire. New York: Penguin.

Gold, Barbara. 1992. "Openings in Horace's *Satires* and *Odes:* Poet, Patron, and Audience." *Yale Classical Studies* 29: 161–89.

———. 1998. "'The House I Live In Is Not My Own': Women's Bodies in Juvenal's *Satires.*" In *Vile Bodies,* special issue *Arethusa* 31: 369–86.

———. 2012. "Juvenal: The Idea of the Book." In *A Companion to Persius and Juvenal,* ed. Susanna Morton Braund and Josiah Osgood, 97–112.

Goldberg, Christiane. 1992. *Carmina Priapea: Einleitung, Übersetzung, Interpretation und Kommentar.* Heidelberg: Winter.

Goodyear, Francis R. D. 1981. *The Annals of Tacitus.* Vol. 2. Cambridge: Cambridge University Press.

Gowers, Emily. 1993a. *The Loaded Table: Representations of Food in Roman Literature.* Oxford: Oxford University Press.

———. 1993b. "An Inconsequential Journey: Horace, *Satire* 1.5." *Proceedings of the Cambridge Philological Society* 39: 48–66; repr. in *Horace: Satires and Epistles,* ed. Kirk Freudenburg (New York: Oxford University Press, 2009), 156–80.

———. 1995. "The Anatomy of Rome from Capitol to Cloaca." *Journal of Roman Studies* 85: 23–32.

———. 2002. "Blind Eyes and Cut Throats: Amnesia and Silence in Horace, *Satires* 1.7." *Classical Philology* 97: 145–61.

———. 2009. "Persius and the Decoction of Nero." In *Oxford Readings in Classical Studies,* ed. Maria Plaza 2009, 173–98.

————. 2012. *Horace Satires Book I*. Cambridge: Cambridge University Press.

Gowing, Alain M. 2005. *Empire and Memory: The Representation of the Roman Republic in Imperial Culture*. Cambridge: Cambridge University Press.

Graf, Fritz. 2005. "Satire in a Ritual Context." In *The Cambridge Companion to Roman Satire*, ed. Kirk Freudenburg, 192–206.

Grandazzi, Alexandre. 1997. *The Foundation of Rome: Myth and History*. Trans. Jane M. Todd. Ithaca, N.Y.: Cornell University Press.

Grant, Michael, trans. 1977. *Tacitus: The Annals of Imperial Rome*. Rev. ed. Harmondsworth: Penguin.

Green, Steven J. 2004. *Ovid, Fasti 1: A Commentary*. Leiden: Brill.

Griffin, Dustin. 1994. *Satire: A Critical Reintroduction*. Lexington: University Press of Kentucky.

Griffith, John G. 1969. "Juvenal, Statius, and the Flavian Establishment." *Greece and Rome*, 2nd ser., 16: 134–50.

————. 1970. "The Ending of Juvenal's First Satire and Lucilius, Book 30." *Hermes* 98: 56–72.

Grimal, Pierre. 1984. *Les Jardins Romains*. Paris: Fayard.

Gruet, Brice. 2006. *La rue a Rome, miroir de la ville, entre l'emotion et la norme*. Paris: Presses de l'université Paris–Sorbonne.

Gummere, Richard M., trans. 1917–25. *Seneca: Epistles*. 3 vols. Loeb Classical Library. Cambridge, Mass.: Harvard University Press.

Gunderson, Erik. 1996. "The Ideology of the Arena." *Classical Antiquity* 15: 113–51.

————. 2005. "The Libidinal Rhetoric of Satire." In *The Cambridge Companion to Roman Satire*, ed. Kirk Freudenburg, 224–42.

Habinek, Thomas. 2005a. "Satire as aristocratic play." In *The Cambridge Companion to Roman Satire*, ed. Kirk Freudenburg, 177–91.

————. 2005b. *The World of Roman Song: From Ritualized Speech to Social Order*. Baltimore: Johns Hopkins University Press.

Hall, Jennifer. 1983. "A Black Note in Juvenal: Satire V 52–55." *Proceedings of the African Classical Association* 17: 108–13.

Handley, Eric W., and John Rea. 1957. *The Telephus of Euripides*. London: Institute of Classical Studies.

Hardie, Alex. 1998. "Juvenal, the *Phaedrus*, and the Truth about Rome." *Classical Quarterly* 48: 234–51.

Harris, William V. 2001. *Restraining Rage: The Ideology of Anger Control in Classical Antiquity*. Cambridge, Mass.: Harvard University Press.

Heller, John L. 1946. "Labyrinth or Troy Town?" *Classical Journal* 42: 123–39.

Henderson, John. 1989. "Satire Writes 'Woman': Gendersong." *Proceedings of the Cambridge Philological Society* 215: 50–80.

————. 1995. "Pump Up the Volume: Juvenal, *Satires* 1.1–21." *Proceedings of the Cambridge Philological Society* 41: 101–37.

————. 1997. *Figuring out Roman Nobility: Juvenal's Eighth Satire*. Exeter: University of Exeter Press.

———. 1998. *Fighting for Rome: Poets and Caesars, History, and Civil War*. Cambridge: Cambridge University Press.

———. 1999. *Writing Down Rome: Satire, Comedy and Other Offences in Latin Poetry*. Oxford: Oxford University Press.

———. 2004. *Morals and Villas in Seneca's Letters*. Cambridge: Cambridge University Press.

Heseltine, Michael, trans. 1913. *Petronius: Satyricon*. Loeb Classical Library. Cambridge, Mass.: Harvard University Press.

Heurgon, Jacques. 1964. *Daily Life of the Etruscans*. Trans. J. Kirkup. London: Phoenix.

Highet, Gilbert. 1954. *Juvenal the Satirist*. Oxford: Oxford University Press.

Hinnant, Charles H. 1995. "Augustan Semiosis." In *Cutting Edges*, ed. James Gill, 256–74.

Hooley, Daniel. 1997. *The Knotted Thong: Structures of Mimesis in Persius*. Ann Arbor: University of Michigan Press.

———. 1999. "Horace's Rud(e)-imentary Muse" *Sat.* 1.2." *Electronic Antiquity* 5.3.

———. 2001. " 'What? Me a poet?' Generic Modeling in Horace *Sat.* 1.2." In *A Festschrift in Honor of Eugene N. Lane*, ed. C. Callaway. http://www.stoa.org/lane.

———. 2007. *Roman Satire*. Malden, Mass.: Wiley-Blackwell.

Hopkins, Keith. 1983. *Death and Renewal*. Cambridge: Cambridge University Press.

Hopkins, Keith, and Mary Beard. 2005. *The Colosseum*. London: Profile.

Hornum, Michael B. 1993. *Nemesis, the Roman State, and the Games*. Leiden: Brill.

Houellebecq, Michel. 2001. *The Elementary Particles*. Trans. Frank Wynne. New York: Vintage.

———. 2007. *The Possibility of an Island*. Trans. Gavin Bawd. New York: Vintage.

Howell, Peter. 1995. *Martial: The Epigrams Book V*. Warminster: Aris and Phillips.

———. 1980. *A Commentary on Book One of the Epigrams of Martial*. London: Athlone.

Hubbard, Thomas K. 1998. *The Pipes of Pan: Intertextuality and Literary Filiation in the Pastoral Tradition from Theocritus to Milton*. Ann Arbor: University of Michigan Press.

Hudson, Nicola. 1989. "Food in Roman Satire." In *Satire and Society in Ancient Rome*, ed. Susanna Morton Braund, 69–88.

Iddeng, Jon W. 2000. "Juvenal, Satire and the Persona Theory: Some Critical Remarks." *Symbolae Osloenses* 75: 107–29.

Janan, Micaela. 2001. *The Politics of Desire: Propertius IV*. Berkeley: University of California Press.

Jenkinson, J. R. 1980. *Persius: The Satires*. Warminster: Aris and Phillips.

Jessen, Julius. 1900. "Zu Juvenal." *Philologus* 13: 505–20.

Johnson, W. R. 1993. *Horace and the Dialectic of Freedom*. Ithaca, N.Y.: Cornell University Press.

Jones, Brian W. 1992. *The Emperor Domitian*. London: Routledge.

Jones, Frederick M. A. 1990. "The Persona and Dramatis Personae in Juvenal Satire Four." *Eranos* 88: 47–59.

———. 2007. *Juvenal and the Satiric Genre*. London: Bristol Classical Press.

Junkelmann, Marcus. 2008. *Gladiatoren: Das Spiel mit dem Tod.* Mainz: von Zabern.

Kaster, Robert A. 2005. *Emotion, Restraint, and Community in Ancient Rome.* Oxford: Oxford University Press.

Kay, Nigel M. 1985. *Martial Book XI. A Commentary.* London: Duckworth.

Keane, Catherine. 2002a. "Juvenal's Cave-Woman and the Programmatics of Satire." *Classical Bulletin* 78: 5–20.

———. 2002b. "Satiric Memories: Autobiography and the Construction of Genre." *Classical Journal* 97: 215–31.

———. 2006. *Figuring Genre in Roman Satire.* Oxford: Oxford University Press.

———. 2007. "Philosophy into Satire: The Program of Juvenal's Fifth Book." *American Journal of Philology* 128: 27–57.

Keitel, Elizabeth. 1992. "*Foedum spectaculum* and related motifs in *Histories* 2–3." *Rheinisches Museum für Philologie* 135: 342–51.

Kenney, Edward J. 1962. "The First Satire of Juvenal." *Proceedings of the Cambridge Philological Society* 8: 29–40.

———. 2012. "Satiric Textures: Style, Meter, and Rhetoric." In *A Companion to Persius and Juvenal,* ed. Susanna Morton Braund and Josiah Osgood, 113–36.

Kernan, Alvin 1959. *The Cankered Muse: Satire of the English Renaissance.* New Haven, Conn.: Yale University Press.

Killeen, J. F. 1969. "Juvenal 7.126ff." *Glotta* 67: 265–66.

Knapp, Bettina L. 1969. *Antonin Artaud. Man of Vision.* New York: David Lewis.

Knoche, Ulrich. 1975. *Roman Satire.* Trans. Edwin Ramage. Bloomington: Indiana University Press.

Köhne, Eckart, and Cornelia Ewigleben. 2000. *Gladiators and Caesars. The Power of Spectacle in Ancient Rome.* Berkeley: University of California Press.

Kondoleon, Christine. 1991. "Signs of Privilege and Pleasure: Roman Domestic Mosaics." In *Roman Art in the Private Sphere: New Perspectives on the Architecture and Décor of the Domus, Villa and Insula,* ed. Elaine K. Gazda, with Anne E. Haeckl, 105–15. Ann Arbor: University of Michigan Press.

Konstan, David. 1993. "Sexuality and Power in Juvenal's Second Satire." *Liverpool Classical Monthly* 18: 12–14.

———. 2008. *"A Life Worthy of the Gods": The Materialist Psychology of Epicurus.* Las Vegas: Parmenides.

Korfmacher, William C. 1935. "Grecizing in Lucilian Satire." *Classical Journal* 30: 453–62.

Krapinger, Gernot, ed. 2007. *[Quintilian] Der Gladiator (Groessere Deklamationen, 9).* Cassino: Università degli Studi di Cassino.

Kristeva, Julia. 1982. *Powers of Horror: An Essay on Abjection.* Trans. Leon S. Roudiez. New York: Columbia University Press.

Kurdi, Maria. 2007. "Gender, Sexuality and Violence in the Work of Martin McDonagh." In *The Theatre of Martin McDonagh,* ed. Lilian Chambers and Eamonn Jordan, 96–113.

Kyle, Donald. 1998. *Spectacles of Death in Ancient Rome.* New York: Routledge.

LaBelle, Maurice M. 1980. *Alfred Jarry: Nihilism and the Theatre of the Absurd*. New York: New York University Press.

LaFleur, Richard A. 1974. "Artorius and Catullus in Juvenal 3." *Rivista di Studi Classici* 22: 5–9.

———. 1976. "Umbricius and Juvenal Three." *Ziva Antika* 26: 383–431.

———. 1979. "*Amicitia* and the Unity of Juvenal's First Book." *Illinois Classical Studies* 4: 158–77.

Lampe, K. 2008. "Seneca's Nausea: 'Existential' Experiences and Julio-Claudian Literature." *Helios* 35: 67–87.

Langlands, R. 2006. *Sexual Morality in Ancient Rome*. Cambridge: Cambridge University Press.

La Penna, Antonio. 1993. "Sarmentus: un picolo avventuriero dell'età Augustea." In *Saggi e Studi su Orazio*, 389–92. Florence: Sansoni.

Larmour, David H. J. 2004. "The Incurable Wound of Telephus: Noise, Speech and Silence in Juvenal's *Satire 1*." *Intertexts* 8: 55–76.

———. 2005a. "Lightening the Load: Castration, Money and Masculinity in Juvenal's *Satire 12*." *Syllecta Classica* 16: 139–72.

———. 2005b. "Statesman and Self in the Parallel Lives." In *The Statesman in Plutarch's Works, Volume II: The Statesman in Plutarch's Greek and Roman Lives*, ed. Lukas de Blois et al., 43–51. Leiden: Brill.

———. 2007. "Holes in the Body: Sites of Abjection in Juvenal's Rome." In *The Sites of Rome*, ed. David H. J. Larmour and Diana Spencer, 168–210.

———. 2010–11. "Tracing Furrows in the Satiric Dust: Echoes of Horace's *Epistles* in Juvenal 1." *Illinois Classical Studies* 35–36, 155–73.

———. 2012. "Nights of Egeria: Juvenal's *De Memoria Deorum*." In *Memory and Urban Religion in the Ancient World*, ed. Martin Bommas et al., 149–76. London: Bloomsbury.

Larmour, David H. J., and Diana Spencer, ed. 2007. *The Sites of Rome: Time, Space, Memory*. New York: Oxford University Press.

Latham, Jacob. 2012. "'Fabulous Clap-Trap': Roman Masculinity, the Cult of Magna Mater, and Literary Constructions of the Galli at Rome from the Late Republic to Late Antiquity." *Journal of Religion* 92: 84–122.

Latham, Ronald. 1951. *Lucretius: On the Nature of the Universe*. Harmondsworth: Penguin.

Lawall, Gilbert. 1958. "Exempla and Theme in Juvenal's Tenth Satire." *Transactions of the American Philological Association* 89: 25–31.

Leigh, Matthew. 1997. *Lucan: Spectacle and Engagement*. Oxford: Clarendon.

Lelièvre, F. J. 1972. "Virgil and Juvenal's Third Satire." *Eurphrosyne* 5: 457–62.

Leo, Friedrich. 1889. "Varro und die Satire." *Hermes* 24: 67–84 [=1960. *Ausgewählte Kleine Schriften*, ed. E. Frankel, vol. 1, 283–300. Rome: Edizioni di storia e letteratura].

Lincoln, Bruce. 1985. "Of Meat and Society, Sacrifice and Creation, Butchers and Philosophy." *L'Uomo* 9: 9–29.

———. 1986. *Myth, Cosmos and Society: Indo-European Themes of Creation and Destruction*. Cambridge, Mass.: Harvard University Press.

Lipovetsky, Mark. 2001. "Russian Literary Postmodernism in the 1990s." *Slavic and East European Review* 79: 30–50.

Littlewood, R. J. 2002. "*Imperii Pignora Certa:* The Role of Numa in Ovid's *Fasti*." In *Ovid's Fasti: Historical Readings at its Bimillennium*, ed. Geraldine Herbert-Brown, 175–98. Oxford: Oxford University Press.

Livers, Keith. 2002. "Bugs in the Body Politic: The Search for Self in Viktor Pelevin's *The Life of Insects*." *Slavic and East European Journal* 46: 1–28.

Lourie, Richard, trans. 1985. "A Circle of Friends," by Vladimir Voinovich. In *The Portable Twentieth-Century Russian Reader*, ed. Clarence Brown, 558–83. Harmondsworth: Penguin.

Luckhurst, Mary. 2007. "*Lieutenant of Inishmore:* Selling (-Out) to the English." In *The Theatre of Martin McDonagh*, ed. Lilian Chambers and Eamonn Jordan, 116–29.

Manzella, Simona Manuala. 2011. *Satira III*. Naples: Liguori.

Markus, Donka. 2000. "Performing the Book: The Recital of Epic in First-Century C.E. Rome." *Classical Antiquity* 19: 138–79.

Martín Gaite, Carmen. 1981. *El cuarto de atrás*. Barcelona: Destino.

———. 2000. *La búsqueda de interlocutor*. Barcelona: Anagrama.

Martindale, Charles. 2005. "The Horatian and Juvenalesque in English Letters." In *The Cambridge Companion to Roman Satire*, ed. Kirk Freudenburg, 284–98.

Martyn, John R. C. 1970a. "Juvenal 2.79–81 and Vergil's Plague." *Classical Philology* 55: 49–50.

———. 1970b. "A New Approach to Juvenal's First Satire." *Antichthon* 4: 53–61.

Mason, Harold A. 1963. "Is Juvenal a Classic?" In *Critical Essays on Roman Literature: Satire*, ed. J. P. Sullivan, 93–176. London: Routledge and Kegan Paul.

Matz, Aaron. 2006. "Terminal Satire and *Jude the Obscure*." *English Literary History* 73: 519–47.

Maurin, Jean. 1984. "Les barbares aux arenes." *Ktema* 9: 102–11.

Maxwell, Robert L. 1996. "*Quia ister Tusco verbo ludio vocabatur:* The Etruscan Contribution to the Development of Roman Theater." In *Etruscan Italy: Etruscan Influences on the Civilizations of Italy from Antiquity to the Modern Era*, ed. J. F. Hall, 267–85. Provo, Utah: Brigham Young University and Museum of Art.

Mayer, Roland. 1994. *Horace: Epistles Book 1*. Cambridge: Cambridge University Press.

———. 2005. "Sleeping with the Enemy: Satire and Philosophy." In *The Cambridge Companion to Roman Satire*, ed. Kirk Freudenburg, 146–59.

Mayor, John J. 1886. *Thirteen Satires of Juvenal*. 4th ed. London: Macmillan.

McDonagh, Martin. 2003. *The Lieutenant of Inishmore*. New York: Dramatist's Play Service.

McGann, Michael J. 1969. *Studies in Horace's First Book of Epistles*. Brussels: Latomus.

———. 1973. "The Three Worlds of Horace's *Satires*." In *Horace*, ed. Charles D. C. Costa, 59–93. London: Routledge and Kegan Paul.

McNelis, Charles. 2012. "Persius, Juvenal, and Literary History after Horace." In *A Companion to Persius and Juvenal*, ed. Susanna Morton Braund and Josiah Osgood, 239–61.

Meister, Karl. 1924–25. *Die Hausschwelle in Sprache und Religion der Römer*. Heidelberg: Sitzungsberichte der Heidelberger Akademie der Wissenschaften, Philologisch-historische Kl. 15.3.

Merli, Elena. 2006. "Martial between Rome and Biblilis." In *City, Countryside, and the Spatial Organization of Value in Classical Antiquity*, ed. Ralph Rosen and Ineke Sluiter, 327–48. Leiden: Brill.

Millar, Fergus. 1998. *The Crowd in Rome in the Late Republic*. Ann Arbor: University of Michigan Press.

Miller, Paul Allen. 1995. "The Minotaur within: Fire, the Labyrinth, and Strategies of Containment in *Aeneid* 5 and 6." *Classical Philology* 90: 225–40.

———. 1998. "The Bodily Grotesque in Roman Satire: Images of Sterility." In *Vile Bodies*, ed. Susanna Morton Braund and Barbara Gold. *Arethusa* 31: 257–83.

———. 2005. *Latin Verse Satire: An Anthology and Critical Reader*. London: Routledge.

———. 2010. "Persius, Irony, and Truth." *American Journal of Philology* 131: 233–58.

———. 2012. "Imperial Satire as Saturnalia." In *A Companion to Persius and Juvenal*, ed. Susanna Morton Braund and Josiah Osgood, 312–33.

Montiglio, Silva. 2006. "Should the Aspiring Wise Man Travel? A Conflict in Seneca's Thought." *American Journal of Philology* 127: 553–86.

Moore, Clifford H., trans. 1925. *Tacitus: Histories Books 1–3*. Cambridge, Mass.: Harvard University Press.

Morford, Mark. 1973. "Juvenal's Thirteenth Satire." *American Journal of Philology* 94: 26–36.

———. 1977. "Juvenal's Fifth Satire." *American Journal of Philology* 98: 219–45.

Morgan, Peter. 2007. *Frost/Nixon*. London: Faber and Faber.

Motto, Anna Lydia, and John R. Clarke. 1965. "*Per Iter Tenebricosum*. The Mythos of Juvenal 3." *Transactions of the American Philological Association* 96: 267–76.

Moussy, Claude. 1977. "Esquisse de l'histoire de *monstrum*," *Revue des Etudes Latines* 55: 345–69.

Muecke, Frances. 1979. "Horace the Satirist: Form and Method in 1.4." *Prudentia* 11: 55–68.

———. 1990. "The Audience of/in Horace's *Satires*." *Journal of the Australian Universities Language and Literature Association* 74: 34–47.

———. 1993, ed. *Horace Satires II*. Warminster: Aris and Phillips.

Murley, Clyde. 1939. "Lucretius and the History of Satire." *Transactions of the American Philological Association* 70: 380–95.

Nadeau, Yvan. 1983. "Juvenal Traduced (Juvenal 2.149–159)." *Liverpool Classical Monthly* 8: 14–16.

Newbold, R. F. 1975. "Cassius Dio and the Games." *L'Aniquité classique* 44: 589–604.

Newlands, Carole E. 2002. *Statius' Silvae and the Poetics of Empire*. Cambridge: Cambridge University Press.

————, ed. 2011, ed. *Statius Silvae Book II*. Cambridge: Cambridge University Press.

Nisbet, Robin, and Niall Rudd. 2004. *A Commentary on Horace: Odes Book III*. Oxford: Oxford University Press.

Nock, Arthur Darby. 1932. "Cremation and Burial in the Roman Empire." *Harvard Theological Review* 25: 321–59.

Nora, Pierre. 1996. "From lieux de mémoire to Realms of Memory." In *Realms of Memory: Rethinking the French Past. Vol. 1: Conflicts and Divisions*, ed. Pierre Nora and Lawrence D. Kritzman, xv–xxiv. New York: Columbia University Press.

————. 2001. General introduction to *Rethinking the French Past: Les lieux de mémoire, Vol. 1: The State*, ed. David P. Jordan, vii–xxii. New York: Columbia University Press.

Ogilvie, Robert M. 1965. *A Commentary on Livy: Books 1–5*. Oxford: Clarendon.

O'Gorman, Ellen. 2000. *Irony and Misreading in the Annals of Tacitus*. Cambridge: Cambridge University Press.

Oksala, Johanna. 2009. *Foucault on Freedom*. Cambridge: Cambridge University Press.

Oliensis, Ellen. 1991. "Canidia, *Canicula*, and the Decorum of Horace's *Epodes*." *Arethusa* 24: 107–38 [= Oliensis 1998, 68–90].

————. 1998. *Horace and the Rhetoric of Authority*. Cambridge: Cambridge University Press.

Ostenberg, Ida. 2009. *Staging the World: Spoils, Captives and Representations in the Roman Triumphal Procession*. Oxford: Oxford University Press.

O'Sullivan, Timothy M. 2011. *Walking in Roman Culture*. Cambridge: Cambridge University Press.

Pailler, Jean Marie. 1988. *Bacchanalia, La répression de 186 av. J.C. à Rome et en Italie. Vestiges, images, tradition*. Rome: École française de Rome.

————. 1998. "Les Bacchanales: dix ans après." *Pallas* 48: 67–87.

————. 2005. "Les Bacchanales: du scandale domestique à l'affaire d'État et au modèle pour les temps à venir (Rome, 186 av. J.-c.)." *Politix* 71: 39–59.

Palmer, Robert E. A. 1974. "Roman Shrines of Female Chastity from the Struggle of Chastity to the Papacy of Innocent I." *Revista storica dell'Antichità* 4: 113–59.

Parker, Robert. 1983. "A Note on Juvenal, Satire 1.17–18." *Liverpool Classical Monthly* 8:123.

Parker, W. H. 1988. *Priapea: Poems for a Phallic God*. London: Croom Helm.

Patey, Douglas Lane. 1998. *The Life of Evelyn Waugh: A Critical Biography*. Oxford: Blackwell.

Paulson, Ronald. 1967. *The Fictions of Satire*. Baltimore: Johns Hopkins University Press.

Pearce, T. E. V. 1992. "Juvenal 3.10–20." *Mnemosyne* 45: 380–83.

Pelevin, Viktor. 1996. *The Life of Insects. A Novel*. Trans. Andrew Bromfield. New York: Farrar, Straus and Giroux.

————. 2001. *Babylon*. Trans. Andrew Bromfield. London: Faber and Faber. [= *Generation П, Homo Zapiens*].

Plass, Paul. 1995. *The Game of Death in Ancient Rome: Arena Sport and Political Suicide*. Madison: University of Wisconsin Press.

Platner, Samuel B., and Thomas Ashby, 1929. *A Topographical Dictionary of Ancient Rome*. Oxford: Oxford University Press.

Plaza, Maria, ed. 2009. *Oxford Readings in Classical Studies: Persius and Juvenal*. New York: Oxford University Press.

Poe, Edgar Allan. 1980. *The Fall of the House of Usher and Other Tales*. New York: Signet.

Pontrandolfo, Angela, and Agnes Rouveret. 1992. *Le tombe dipinte di Paestum*. Modena: Panini.

Potter, David. 1996. "Performance, Power, and Justice in the High Empire." In *Roman Theater and Society*, ed. William Slater, 129–60.

Powell, Jonathan G. F. 1987. "The *Farrago* of Juvenal, 1.86 Reconsidered." In *Homo Viator: Classical Essays for John Bramble*, ed. Michael Whitby et al., 253–58. London: Bristol Classical Press.

Pryor, A. D. 1962. "Juvenal's False Consolation." *Journal of the Australian Universities Language and Literature Association* 18: 167–180.

Purcell, Nicholas. 1995. "Eating Fish: the Paradoxes of Seafood." In *Food in Antiquity*, ed. John Wilkins et al., 132–49. Exeter: Exeter University Press.

Putnam, Michael C. J. 1987. "Daedalus, Virgil and the End of Art." *American Journal of Philology* 108: 173–98.

Radermacher, Ludwig. 1935. "*Sulcius acer et Caprius*." *Weiner Studien* 53: 80–84.

Radice, Betty, trans. 1969. *Pliny: Letters and Panegyricus*. 2 vols. Loeb Classical Library. Cambridge, Mass.: Harvard University Press.

Ramage, Edwin S. 1973. *Urbanitas: Ancient Sophistication and Refinement*. Norman: University of Oklahoma Press.

———. 1989. "Juvenal and the Establishment: Denigration of Predecessor in the 'Satires.'" *Aufstieg und Niedergang der römischen Welt* 2.33.1: 640–707.

Raschke, Wendy J. 1987. "*Arma pro amico*—Lucilian Satire at the Crisis of the Roman Republic." *Hermes* 115: 299–318.

Rawson, Piers B. 1987. *The Myth of Marsyas in the Roman Visual Art: An Iconographic Study*. Oxford: British Archaeological Reports.

Reader, Keith. 2006. *The Abject Object: Avatars of the Phallus in Contemporary French Theory, Literature and Film*. Amsterdam: Rodopi.

Rees, Catherine. 2007. "The Politics of Morality: *The Lieutenant of Inishmore*." In *The Theatre of Martin McDonagh*, ed. Lilian Chambers and Eamonn Jordan, 130–40.

Reeve, Michael D. 1973. "Gladiators in Juvenal's Sixth Satire." *Classical Review* 23: 124–25.

Relihan, Joel. 1993. *Ancient Menippean Satire*. Baltimore: Johns Hopkins University Press.

Rheinfelder, Hans. 1928. *Das Wort, Persona*. Halle: Niemeyer.

Richardson, Lawrence. 1992. *A New Topographical Dictionary of Ancient Rome*. Baltimore: Johns Hopkins University Press.

Richardson-Hay, Christine. 2006. *First Lessons: Book 1 of Seneca's Epistulae Morales, A Commentary*. New York: Lang.

Richlin, Amy. 1984. "Invective against Women in Roman Satire." *Arethusa* 17: 67–80.

———. 1992. *The Garden of Priapus. Sexuality and Aggression in Roman Humor*, 2nd ed. Oxford: Oxford University Press.

———. 1993. "Not before Homosexuality: The Materiality of the *Cinaedus* and the Roman Law against Love between Men." *Journal of the History of Sexuality* 3: 523–73.

———. 1997. "Gender and Rhetoric: Producing Manhood in the Schools." In *Roman Eloquence: Rhetoric in Society and Literature*, ed. W. J. Dominik, 90–110. London: Routledge.

———. 2009. "Juvenal and Priapus." In *Oxford Readings in Classical Studies*, ed. Maria Plaza, 305–26.

Rimell, Victoria. 2005. "The Poor Man's Feast: Juvenal." In *The Cambridge Companion to Roman Satire*, ed. Kirk Freudenburg, 81–94.

———. 2008. *Martial's Rome. Empire and the Ideology of Epigram*. Cambridge: Cambridge University Press.

Rix, Helmut. 1995. "Il latino e l'etrusco." *Eutopia* 4: 73–88.

Robert, Louis. 1940. *Les gladiateurs dans l'Orient grec*. Paris: Champion.

Roche, Paul. 2011. *Pliny's Praise. The Panegyricus in the Roman World*. Cambridge: Cambridge University Press.

———. 2012. "Self-Representation and Performativity." In *A Companion to Persius and Juvenal*, ed. Susanna Morton Braund and Josiah Osgood, 190–216.

Roller, Matthew B. 2004. "Exemplarity in Roman Culture: The Cases of Horatius Cocles and Cloelia." *Classical Philology* 99: 1–56.

———. 2012. "Politics and Invective in Persius and Juvenal." In *A Companion to Persius and Juvenal*, ed. Susanna Morton Braund and Josiah Osgood, 283–311.

Rosen, Ralph. 2007. *Making Mockery. The Poetics of Ancient Satire*. Oxford: Oxford University Press.

Rudd, Niall. 1956. "Horace and Fannius. A Discussion of Two Passages in Horace, *Serm.* 1.4." *American Journal of Philology* 76: 165–75.

———. 1966. *The Satires of Horace*. Cambridge: Cambridge University Press.

Rutledge, Steven H. 1967. "Virgil's Daedalus." *Classical Journal* 62: 309–11.

———. 1971–72. "The Opening of *Aeneid* 6." *Classical Journal* 67: 110–15.

Sage, Evan T. 1936. *Livy. History of Rome. Books 38–39*. Loeb Classical Library. Cambridge, Mass.: Harvard University Press.

Saylor, Charles. 1987. "Funeral Games: The Significance of Games in the *Cena Trimalchionis*." *Latomus* 46: 593–602.

Scarry, Elaine. 1985. *The Body in Pain. The Making and Unmaking of the World*. Oxford: Oxford University Press.

Schlegel, Catherine. 1999. "Horace *Satires* 1.7: Satire as Conflict Irresolution." *Arethusa* 32: 337–52.

———. 2005. *Satire and the Threat of Speech*. Madison: University of Wisconsin Press.

Schneider, Carl. 1930. *Juvenal und Seneca*. Diss. Wurzburg.

Scobie, Alex. 1986. "Slums, Sanitation and Morality in the Roman World." *Klio* 68: 399–433.

———. 1988. "Spectator Security and Comfort at Gladiatorial Games." *Nikephoros* 1: 191–243.

Scodel, Ruth. 1987. "Horace, Lucilius, and Callimachean Polemic." *Harvard Studies in Classical Philology* 91: 199–215; repr. in *Horace: Satires and Epistles*, ed. Kirk Freudenburg (New York: Oxford University Press, 2009), 212–30.

Seo, Mira. 2013. *Exemplary Traits: Reading Characterization in Roman Poetry*. Oxford: Oxford University Press.

Shackleton Bailey, David R. 1959. "Seven Emendations." *Classical Review* 9: 200–202.

———, trans. 1993. *Martial: Epigrams*. Cambridge, Mass.: Harvard University Press.

———, trans. 2003. *Statius: Silvae*. Cambridge Mass: Harvard University Press.

———, trans. 2009. *Cicero XVa, Philippics 1–6*. Revised by John T. Ramsey and Gesine Manuwald. Loeb Classical Library. Cambridge, Mass.: Harvard University Press.

Shadrake, Susanna. 2005. *The World of the Gladiator*. Stroud: Tempus.

Sharland, Suzanne. 2010. *Horace in Dialogue: Bakhtinian Readings in the Satires*. New York: Lang.

Shero, Lucius R. 1923. "The *Cena* in Roman Satire." *Classical Philology* 18: 126–43.

Slater, William J., ed. 1996. *Roman Theater and Society*. E. Togo Salmon Papers I. Ann Arbor: University of Michigan Press.

Small, Jocelyn P. 1982. *Cacus and Marsyas in Etrusco-Roman Legend*. Princeton, N.J.: Princeton University Press.

Spencer, Diana. 2010. *Roman Landscape: Culture and Identity*. Greece and Rome, New Surveys in the Classics, 39. Cambridge: Cambridge University Press.

Stallybrass, Peter, and Allon White. 1986. *The Politics and Poetics of Transgression*. Ithaca, N.Y.: Cornell University Press.

Stein, J. P. 1970. "The Unity and Scope of Juvenal's Fourteenth Satire." *Classical Philology* 65: 34–36.

Stein, Susan I. 2000. "Humor, Hostility and the Psychodynamics of Satire." *Literature and Psychology* 46: 26–41.

Steingräber, Stephan. 1986. *Etruscan Painting. Catalogue Raisonné of Etruscan Wall Painting*. English-language edition, ed. David and Francesca R. Ridgway. New York: Harcourt Brace Jovanovich.

Sullivan, John P. 1991. *Martial: The Unexpected Classic. A Literary and Historical Study*. Cambridge: Cambridge University Press.

Sweet, David. 1979. "Juvenal's *Satire* 4: Poetic Uses of Indirection." *California Studies in Classical Antiquity* 12: 283–303.

Swift, Jonathan. 1729. *A Modest Proposal for preventing the Children of Poor People from being a Burthen to Their Parents or Country, and for making them Beneficial to the Publick*. Dublin: Harding.

———. 2005. *Gulliver's Travels*. Oxford World's Classics. Oxford: Oxford University Press.

———. 2008. *A Tale of a Tub.* Ed. Angus Ross and David Woolley. Oxford World's Classics. Oxford: Oxford University Press.

Szemerényi, Oswald. 1975. "The Origins of Roman Drama and Greek Tragedy." *Hermes* 103: 300–32.

Szilágy, J. G. 1981. "*Impletae modis saturae.*" *Prospettiva* 24: 2–3.

Szondi, Peter. 1988. "Walter Benjamin's City Portraits." In *On Walter Benjamin,* ed. Gary Smith. Cambridge, Mass.: MIT Press.

Taggart, Ashley. 2007. "An 'Economy of Pity': McDonagh's Monstrous Regiment." In *The Theatre of Martin McDonagh,* ed. Lilian Chambers and Eamonn Jordan, 162–73.

Tannahill, Reay. 1975. *Flesh and Blood: A History of the Cannibal Complex.* New York: Dorset Press.

Taylor, Rabun. 2008. *The Moral Mirror of Roman Art.* Cambridge: Cambridge University Press.

Tennant, P. M. W. 1995. "Biting Off More Than One Can Chew: A Recent Trend in the Interpretation of Juvenal's 15th Satire." *Akroterion* 40: 120–34.

Test, George A. 1991. *Satire: Spirit and Art.* Tampa: University Press of Florida.

Thuillier, Jean Paul. 1985. *Les jeux athlétiques dans la civilisation étrusque.* Rome: École française de Rome.

———. 2013. "Etruscan Spectacles and Sport." In *The Etruscan World,* ed. Jean MacIntosh Turfa, 831–40. London: Routledge.

Toner, Jerry P. 1995. *Leisure and Ancient Rome.* Cambridge: Polity.

Townend, G. B. 1969. "Juvenal's Automedon." In *Hommages à Marcel Renard,* ed. Jacqueline Bibauw, 725–727. Brussels: Latomus.

———. 1980. "Calpurnius Siculus and the *Munus Neronis.*" *Journal of Roman Studies* 70: 166–74.

Tracy, Valeria. 1976. "Roman Dandies and Transvestites." *Echos du Monde Classique* 20: 60–3.

Turfa, Jean MacIntosh, ed. 2013. *The Etruscan World.* London: Routledge.

Uden, James. 2007. "Impersonating Priapus." *American Journal of Philology* 128: 1–26.

———. 2015. *The Invisible Satirist: Juvenal and Second-Century Rome.* Oxford: Oxford University Press.

Ullman, B. L. 1915. "Horace, Catullus, and Tigellius." *Classical Philology* 10: 270–96.

———. 1917. "Horace on the Nature of Satire." *Transactions of the American Philological Association* 48: 111–32.

Van den Berg, Christopher. 2012. "Imperial Satire and Rhetoric." In *A Companion to Persius and Juvenal,* ed. Susanna Morton Braund and Josiah Osgood, 262–282.

Van den Hout, Michel P. J. 1999. *A Commentary on the Letters of M. Cornelius Fronto.* Leiden: Brill.

Vernant, Jean Pierre. 1991. *Mortals and Immortals. Collected Essays.* English ed. F. Zeitlin. Princeton, N.J.: Princeton University Press.

Versnel, Henk S. 1970. *Triumphus: An Inquiry into the Origin, Development, and Meaning of the Roman Triumph.* Leiden: Brill.

———. 1976. "Two Types of Roman *Devotio*." *Mnemosyne* 29: 365–410

Veyne, Paul. 1990. *Bread and Circuses: Historical Sociology and Political Pluralism.* Abridged with introduction by Oswyn Murray, trans. B. Pearce. London: Allen Lane (=1990. *Le pain et le Cirque: Sociologie historique d'un pluralisme politique.* Paris: du Seuil).

Ville, Georges. 1981. *La Gladiature en occident des origines à la mort de Domitien.* Rome: École française de Rome.

Vittinghoff, Friedrich. 1936. *Der Staatsfeind in der römischen Kaiserzeit. Untersuchungen zur damnatio memoriae.* Berlin: Junker and Dünnhaupt.

Von Stackelberg, Katherine T. 2009. "Performative Space and Garden Transgressions in Tacitus' Death of Messalina." *American Journal of Philology* 130: 595–624.

Wallace, Rex E. 2008. *Zike Rasna. A Manual of the Etruscan Language and Inscriptions.* Ann Arbor: Beech Stave Press.

Walters, Jonathan. 1998. "Making a Spectacle: Deviant Men, Invective, and Pleasure." In Vile Bodies, ed. Susanna Morton Braund and Barbara Gold, *Arethusa* 31: 355–67.

Warmington, Eric Herbert. 1979. *The Remains of Old Latin.* 2nd ed. 3 vols. Loeb Classical Library. Cambridge, Mass.: Harvard University Press.

Watmough, Margaret. 1997. *Studies in Etruscan Loanwords in Latin.* Florence: Olschki.

Watson, Lindsay. 2003. *A Commentary on Horace's Epodes.* Oxford: Oxford University Press.

Watson, Lindsay, and Patricia Watson, eds. 2003. *Martial: Select Epigrams.* Cambridge: Cambridge University Press.

———. 2014. *Juvenal: Satire 6.* Cambridge: Cambridge University Press.

Waugh, Evelyn. 2002. *Black Mischief.* New York: Back Bay Books.

———. 1997. *A Handful of Dust.* London: Penguin.

———. 2001. *Decline and Fall.* London: Penguin.

Weinbrot, Howard. 1982. *Alexander Pope and the Traditions of Formal Verse Satire.* Princeton, N.J.: Princeton University Press.

Welch, Katherine E. 2007. *The Roman Amphitheatre from its Origins to the Colosseum.* Cambridge: Cambridge University Press.

Welch, Tara S. 2005. *The Elegiac Cityscape: Propertius and the Meaning of Roman Monuments.* Columbus: Ohio State University Press.

Wiedemann, Thomas. 1992. *Emperors and Gladiators.* London: Routledge.

Wiesen, David S. 1989. "The Verbal Basis of Juvenal's Satiric Vision." *Aufstieg und Niedergang der römischen Welt* 2.33.1: 708–33.

Wilkinson, Lancelot P. 1969. *The Georgics of Virgil.* Cambridge: Cambridge University Press.

Wilson, Frank Percy, ed. 1925. *The Plague Pamphlets of Thomas Dekker.* Oxford: Clarendon.

Winkler, Martin M. 1983. *The Persona in Three Satires of Juvenal.* Hildesheim: Olms.

———. 1990. "A Virgilian Echo in Juvenal's Eleventh Satire." *Rheinisches Museum für Philologie* 133: 375–78.

———. 1995. "Alogia and Emphasis in Juvenal's Fourth Satire." In *Roman Literature and Ideology: Ramus Essays for J. P. Sullivan*, ed. Anthony J. Boyle, 227–49. Bendigo, Australia: Aureal.

———. 2009. "Juvenal: Zealous Vindicator of Roman Liberty." In *Writing Politics in Imperial Rome*, ed. William J. Dominik et al., 463–82. Leiden: Brill.

Winterbottom, Michael. 1974. *The Elder Seneca: Declamations*. 2 vols. Loeb Classical Library. Cambrdige, Mass.: Harvard University Press.

Wirszubski, Chaim. 1950. *Libertas as a Political Idea at Rome during the Late Republic and Early Principate*. Cambridge: Cambridge University Press.

Wiseman, T. P. 1988. "Satyrs in Rome? The Background to Horace's *Ars Poetica*." *Journal of Roman Studies* 78: 1–13.

———. 2004. *The Myths of Rome*. Exeter: University of Exeter Press.

Wistrand, Magnus. 1990. "Violence and Entertainment in Seneca the Younger." *Eranos* 88: 31–46.

———. 1992. *Entertainment and Violence in Ancient Rome: The Attitudes of Roman Writers of the First Century A.D.* Goteborg: Acta Universitatis Gothoburgensis.

Witke, Charles. 1970. *Latin Satire: the Structure of Persuasion*. Leiden: Brill.

Woodman, A. J. 1983. "Juvenal 1 and Horace." *Greek and Rome*, 2nd ser., 30: 81–84.

Worman, Nancy. 2009. "Bodies and Topographies in Ancient Stylistic Theory." In *Bodies and Boundaries in Graeco-Roman Antiquity*, ed. Thorsten Fögen and Mireille M. Lee, 46–62.

Yonge, Charles D., trans. 1903. *Cicero, Philippics*. London: Bell and Sons.

Zetzel, James E. 1980. "Horace's *Liber Sermonum*: the Structure of Ambiguity." *Arethusa* 13: 59–77

———. 2002. "Dreaming about Quirinus: Horace's *Satires* and the Development of Augustan Poetry." In *Traditions and Contexts in the Poetry of Horace*, ed. Dennis Feeney and A. J. Woodman, 38–52. Cambridge: Cambridge University Press.

Zimbardo, Rose. 1998. *At Zero Point: Discourse, Culture, and Satire in Restoration England*. Lexington: University Press of Kentucky.

Zomchick, John. 1995. "Satire and the Bourgeois Subject in Frances Burney's *Evelina*." In *Cutting Edges*, ed. James E. Gill, 347–66.

Index

Page numbers in *italics* indicate illustrations.